William A. Stirling

Register of Royal Letters

Relative to the Affairs of Scotland & Nova Scotia from 1615 to 1635 - Vol. 2

William A. Stirling

Register of Royal Letters
Relative to the Affairs of Scotland & Nova Scotia from 1615 to 1635 - Vol. 2

ISBN/EAN: 9783337169251

Printed in Europe, USA, Canada, Australia, Japan

Cover: Foto ©Andreas Hilbeck / pixelio.de

More available books at **www.hansebooks.com**

THE EARL OF STIRLING'S

REGISTER OF ROYAL
LETTERS

RELATIVE TO THE AFFAIRS OF SCOTLAND AND NOVA
SCOTIA FROM 1615 TO 1635

Vol. II.

The Small Paper Impression is limited to One hundred and fifty copies, of which this is No.

EDINBURGH : PRINTED BY BURNESS & COMPANY, PRINTERS TO HER MAJESTY.

REGISTER OF ROYAL LETTERS.

To the Exchequer.

Right, &c.—Whareas, for the mantenance of a secound minister at our churche of Halieroodhous, and for the use of the poor of the Channogaet, wee have been pleased to signe ane signatour of the upsettis of tradis of the small impost of wynes, and of the benefeitt of alterages and hospitallis dotit by some religeous persones of old for pious uses within that paroche, And efter the reformatione of religeone gifted by our dearest grandmother Queen Marie, of blissed memorie, to the churche of the Channongaet, for the interteinment of a minister and ther poore whareof (as wee are informed), wee nor our predecessouris have never receaved any benefeitt, which wee wer the rather moved to doe becaus the course is much agreable to our intentione in our decree, and may save us from a further charge for the mantenance of ane secound minister at that churche, which necessarlie requirethe a helper in regard of the eminencie of the place and greatnes of the charge : Oure plesoure tharefore is, that you consider of the premissis, and if you find it not materiallie prejudicious unto us, nor any of our subjectis, that furthwithe you caus exped the said signatour in due and competent forme, according to the tennour thareof : And for your soe doing, &c.—Whitehall, the fourth of Januare 1630.

To the Chancellare.

Right, &c.—Whareas, at the time of our agreement with the Marques of Huntlie for his shirrefships of Aberdeen and Innernes, wee wer pleased that he should be relaxed from all horningis whareunto he was denunsit for not apprehending of those persones whome he hade charge to tak, the doing whareof (as wee are now informed) is delayed till he should apprehend such of them as he is bound to exhibit, as landeslord of the boundis whare they dwell ; sieing wee have granted a commissione to the Lord Gordoune, whose may best performe that which his father should have done tharein, Wee doubt not bot he will assist his sone to give us contentment in anything that concernis our service : And sieing wee desire not theis shirref-shipps being dimitted that the expressing of our favour towardis him be soe strictlie interpreted, wee have thought it more fitt to acquent you, then otherwayis to doe it in a more publict maner, that it is our plesour, and wee doe heirby require you, to caus relax the said Marqueis fra all horningis used aganis him as Shirreiff or landslord for not apprehending of papistis before repairing to our court : And to the effect he may the better shaw his affection to our service in causing apprehend those persones, that you grant him licience to repair northward : And whareas his dochters are to be removed from him, according to the course intended to be taken with such noblemen's childring by the generall ordour, sieing they are mariage-able, wee hold it not expedient that they at this time should be taken from thare mother, but will that point in thare behalff to be dispensed with till our forther plesure be knowen : And as wee have signified our plesour what we wold have done heirin, soe, being confident of your affectione to our service, wee remitt the conditiones and maner how it may be most convenientlie done unto you, that the same may be per-formed, or that you will adverteis what forther is requisite from us to be done in that purpose : Which specialie recommending to your care, Wee bid you farewell.—The 4 of Januar 1630.

II.   A

To the Counsell.

Right, &c.— As we wer pleased to wreat to you before in favours of . . . Maistir James Hannay, minister at our churche of Halierudhous, requiring you to considder of the reasones which wer exhibited unto us in his behalff, and inclosed in our former lettres, concerning the provision of that churche with ane honest and competent mantenance to the minister, according to the eminencie of the place and greatnes of his charge : And wee being informed that the same could not convenientlie be performed before the pronunceing of our decreitt : Oure plesour tharefore is, and we doe heirby authorise, will, and require you, that now, after the publicatione of our said decree, you tak the said reassones in your serious consideratiounes, and with all convenient diligence you setle and appoint to the said Maister James and his successouris, ministers at our said Kirk, ane honest and sufficient mantenance as you shall think fitting for the said place and charge.—Whitehall, the seavint of Januar 1630.

To the Erle of Seafort.

Letter to repair to Court, in the usual form.—Whitehall, the 7 of January 1630.

To the Sessione.

Right, &c.—Whareas thare are actiones of law intendit and dependand before you betuix the burgh of Edinburgh and some inhabitantis of Leithe concerning the rightis and priveledges of our said burgh : These are to will and require you with all convenient expeditione to administer justice to both parties in thare actiones, according to thare rightis and the lawes of that our kingdome : Soe we, &c. Whitehall, the 7 of Januar 1630.

To the Counsell.

Right, &c.— Whareas wee have understood by your lettre of the inconveniences that are like to come to that our kingdome by strangers, whome, planting thameselves in the Ile of the Lewis by means of a patent granted to the Erle of Seafort not as yet exped, wold usurp the benefitt of the fishing in theis seas adjacent tharevnto, to the great prejudice of our subjectis wishing that the samen may be prevented : We doe approve your opinione, and have taken another course to our consideratione, whiche, as wee doe conceave, may verie much import the good of that our kingdome : Wharevpone we have required the said Erle and a commissioner for the borrowes to repaire vnto us at the first of Marche nixt to come, that after due deliberatione wee may think fitt what is to be done tharein : And in the meantime it is our plesour that you give ordour for stopping the said Erle his patent in Exchecquer, or otherwayis, till after the said time you shall heir farther from us, as likewayis that the strangers whoe are alreadie planted thare be made liable to the lawes of the cuntre, and find catione for thare compirance when they shalbe cited to auster for transgressing our actis of parliament, and that noe others be suffered to plant thare till wee have resolved what shalbe fittest for the publict good of that kingdome.—Whitehall, the 7 Januar 1630.

To the Advocat.

Trustie, &c. Whareas thare hath been ane signatour of some landis belonging to . . . Sir James Oliphant, Knight Baronett, presented to be signed by us, as wee are willing to doe him any laufull favour, soe wee are loath that any thing which might be prejudiciall unto us should pas, and tharefore wold give noe ordour for expeding of the same till first your opinion warr maide thaireament : Tharefore our plesour is, that iff you find noething thairunto which is prejudiciall unto us, or contrarie to our late decree or ony other reservatione send home to our Exchequer, that you ether caus pas the same or returne it docated for our hand for that effect.—Whitehall, the 7 Januar 1630.

To the King of France.

Treshaut tresexcellent et trespuissant nostre tres cher et tresame bon frere beau frere cousin et ancien allie Le seiur de Suinton porteur de la presente qui a este cy devant Archer de vos gardes de corps, nous ayant faict entendre le desire et entention qu'il auoit de sen retourner en France avec sa femme et ses enfans pour y passer le reste de ses jours, et nous ayant supplie de le favoriser de nos lettres de recommendation vers vous, nous l'avons bien voulu accompaigner de celle cy, pour vous prier, comme nous faisons effectueusement, qu'en consideration des bons et longs services qu'il a rendu au sou roy de hereuse memoire vostre pere et a vous en la dicte place de l'archer des gardes du corps, en laquelle il y a tesmoignage de vous avoir bien et fidelement servie le space de vingt et huict ans, comme aussi en des autres occasions ou il y a este employe pendant ce temps la. Il vous plaise le laisser jouer de mesmes franchises et priviledges dont il a jouy par cy devant au vostre royaume et luy departir aus occasions le benefite de vos favours pour luy donner moyen de vivre et subsister en sa viellesse, et de vous rendre les services ou il vous plaira encores de l'employer selon l'affection entiere, quil tesmoigne tousiours y avoir. A quoy vous le obligeres d'autant plus estroitement, et encourageres les autres de sa nation pour ceste faveur laquelle aussy deferre a nostre recommendation nous recognoisserons en pareille occasion enverz les vostres Et sur ce nous prierons Dieu, Treshaut, tresexcellent et tres puissant prince, nostre tres cher et tresame bon frere, beau frere, cousin, et ancien allie, quil vous ait tousiours en sainete et digne garde.—A nostre pallace de Westminster, 7 Januarii 1630.

To the Admiralitie.

Right, &c.—Whareas wee wer informed that our burgh of Edinburgh hath of late encroached much upon the priviledges and liberties of . . . the Duke of Lennox in his office of Admiralitie : And tbareupon wee, haveing considered with the Commissioner of the said burgh, find that our said burgh is verie willing to cleer themselves from any usurpationes of whatsomever libertie or priveledge properlie belonging to our said cousen in his said office : Oure will and pleasour tharefore is, that you conven with such commissioners as our said burgh shall nominat and trye what priveledges and liberties by the lawes of that our realme doe properlie belong to our said cousen in his said office of Admiralitie, that our said cousen may enjoy the same ; Or els that you may in some peaceabill way soe compose the differences as all occasione of contraversie or debate may be taken away heirefter, and that you certifie us of your proceedingis and of the trew estate of the said bussienes : Soe, wee bid you farewell.—Whitehall, the 7 Januar 1630.

To the Counsell.

Right, &c.—Whareas wee have been peticoned by Johnne Innes of Crombie, showing the great losse and charges susteened by him in the leaviceing and keeping together a companye of footmen for our uncle the King of Denmark his service, and wee, commiserating his distres, have thought fitt to refer the triall thareof to your consideratione : Oure pleasoure tharefore is, that you tak speciall notice of the peticcons heir inclosed, and after triall thareof that you certifie us bak again what you find requisit for us to doe thareanent, wharcby his losses (if any be by that service) may be repared, and he in tyme coming enabled when occasione shall offer to doe us service.—Whitehall, the 7 of Januar 1630.

To the Counsell.

Right, &c.—Whareas thare hathe been some articles exhibited unto us aganis our burgh of Edinburgh in name of the toune of Leithe, whareof such particulars as are submitted to us by Mr Johne Hay, in name of our said burgh, conteined in thare chartour in anno 1603, to be surrendered to us, conforme to the noat inclosed in the lettre writen by us to our advocat, willing him to secure us of the same, and after sight of thare evidentis, to acquent us what forther is necessarie for us to advert heirto, assuring ourselves of the discharge of his duetie heirin : Likewayis wee have given commission for composing the differences betwene that our burgh and the noblemen and gentlemen of Wast Louthian, anent thare chartour in anno 1603, in soe farr as concerneth thare interest, that they may either setle the same or certifie us what they find fitt for us to doe tharein : And for those thingis in contraversie betuix them and Leithe, Wee desire you to tak theis articles which we have sent you heirwithe to your consideratione, and haveing hard both parties and thare laufull defences, what is fitt in law for you to judge of, or refer to others judicatories to whome the judging thareof dothe properlie belong, that you tak such ordour as wee did lathe wreat touching that purpos, as is most agreeable to law and equitie ; and if you think it necessary, that you certifie us of your proceedingis and opiniones tharein : Soe, not doubting but you will have such care heirof as is requisit, &c.—Whitehall, the 7 of Januar 1630.

To the Exchequer.

Right, &c.—Whareas wee have been humblie peticeoned by . . . Doctor James Chambers, one of our ordinarie Phisicians, making mention that he haveing payed four hunderthe poundis sterling unto Alexander and Robert Irewingis towardis thare transportatione and subsistance abroad, in consideratione and for a lease of certane landis lent unto him by the saidis persones during thare lifetimes, which he allodgeth he cannot legallie enjoy without our confirmatione or grant of thare escheat and liferent, as fallen and become in our handis by thare excommunicatione or denunciatione to our horne : And forasmuch the said Alexander and Robert Irewingis have given band to leave that our kingdome for shunning all occasione of scandell unto the discipline of our churche thare, and for that our said servand Doctor James Chambers humblie intreatethe for the guiftis of thare escheatt and lifrent, for his better securitie of his said lease : Therefore, and in regard of the long and faithfull service done unto our late dear father and us by the said Doctor James Chambers, wee have been graciouslie pleased to signe unto him a signatour of thare said escheat and lifrent, and doe heirby will and require you to pas the same accordinglie, and to ratifie and confirme unto him his said lease or tak of the saidis landis in such legall forme and maner as you in your discretiones shall think most fitting for his securitie : And for your soe doing, &c.—Whitehall, the 8 day of Januar 1630.

To the Counsell.

Right, &c.—Whareas wee did formerlie write our lettres unto you concerning the place of our coronatione in that our kingdome : Oure pleasoure tharefore is, that you consider what place is most convenient, and that you adverteis us of your opiniones concerning the same, and whither you think St Geillis church in Edinburgh or the Abbey churche of Halyerudehous to be more convenient place for such a publict actione, that upon notice of your opiniones wee may tak such forther course and give such forther directiones as may seem most fitting for setling the preparationes fitt for that actione, and with als litell charge as may be convenientlie.—Whitehall, the 8 of Januar 1630.

To the Advocat.

Trustie, &c.—Whareas our Commissione of surrenders and tithes hath not as yet determined anything concerning the landis of our propertie and principalitie, nor concerning the changed tennouris in that our kingdome : And forasmuch as the time of prescriptione now approchethe, wharebly our title unto the saidis landis and tennouris may perhappes tharefter ether be doubted of or contraverted under collour of the said prescription, except some summondis and proces be timelie intended and execute at our instance for interrupting the said prescriptiones : Oure pleasure tharefore is, and wee doe heirby authorise, will, and require you, with all convenient diligence, duely to weighe and considder of the said prescriptiones, and speedelie to advise and execute some legall course by summondis of improbatione, reductione, warning, and removeing, or some such other faire and laufull way, against our vassellis of the premissis as in your judgment and opinione may seem most meet for interrupting the said prescriptiones, and for avoiding all such prejudice as the same may inter against oure croune and titill unto the saidis landis and tennouris ; and speciallie oure pleasour is, that you have a care of our propertie of Ettrick Forrest : All which we recommend unto your speciall care and diligence, &c.—Whitehall, the 8 of Januar 1630.

To Sir Thomas Edmond, his Majesties' Ambassidour in France.

Right, &c.—Whareas the bearer heiroff, James Swentoune, laveing certificatts from France of his long and faithfull services done thare theis twentie-eight yeers past as one of the Archers of the Guard of the bodie of our brother the most Christiane King, hath humblie intreated our recommendatione unto our said brother, that he may enjoy his royall favour, and the priveleges formerlie enjoyed by him as a Scottisman within the kingdome of France : And haveing been graceouslie pleased to grant his said desire, wee have writen unto our said brother for that purpose, and doe heirby will and require you to assist the said James Swentoune by all the faire wayis and means you can towardis his said Christian Majestie that he enjoy his royall favour, may subsist in the full fruitione of his wounted promises, and may be the better used heirefter as one specialie recommended from us, whoe have taken particulare notice of his worthe and partis, and of his long and faithfull services, and of his birthe and descent testiefied unto us under the Great Seall of the kingdome of Scotland where he was borne ; and soe wee bid you hartlie fareweell.—Whitehall, the 8 of Januare 1630.

To the Advocat.

Trustie, &c.—Whareas wee did formerlie write unto you that wee haue agreed with the Lord Lowdoune for the heretable office of Shirrefship with the superiorities of Kyllesmoor and Barmoor, with his heretabill office of Baillierie and regalitie thareof, and to wedset unto him the saidis superiorities, few-deuties, and casualities of the same for the somme of eighteen thousand merkis, till be retayned by him till wee should be pleased to redeem the same from him by payment unto him thareof : And wee being humblie peticeoned by George Read of Dandilling, in behalff of himselff and the tennentis of

Killesmoore and Barmoore, to accept of them as our imediat tennentis to the same, they paying unto us the soume of twelff thousand merkis scottis as the greatest parte of the price of the few-deuties wee are to give to the said Lord Lowdane, making resignatione thareof in our handis : Though wee doe like of that intention heirin, yet wee will tak noe course heirin till first we have considered of thare petitione which wee have sent you heirwith inclosed : Tharefor our pleasour is, that you consider of the demandis of thare peticeone, and that you certifie unto us what course yee think fitt to be taken heirin, that tharefter we may signifie our further pleasour unto you thareanent.—Whitehall, the 10 of Januar 1630.

To the Advocat.

Trustie, &c.—Whareas wee are informed that by the confessione of one Alexander Hamiltoune, questioned for witchcraft, thare are divers persones dilated as complices with him in some divellische practises against the life and estate of Sir George Home, Knight, whom the persones accused, with thare favorers, traduce as ane subornour of Hamiltoune to accuse them falslie, and doe all they can to hinder the triall, wharebly the innocencie or giltienes of the said Sir George or the persones of the accused might be made apparent : Wee being moved to tak the bussienes into our serious consideratione as a thing concerning the glorie of God and good of that our kingdome, that such hynous crimes shonld not pas without severe punishement : And haveing tharefor expreslie recommendit the exact triall of it to . . . the Erle of Monteith, our Justice-Generall of that our kingdome ; Wee are likwayis pleased heirby to will and require you to give your best concurrance in the prosecutione and triall thareof, that noething may be omitted which may tend to the impartiall clering of everie circumstans in the bussienes, that soe the innocent may be acquited, and the guiltie may receave such due punishment as by the lawes of that our kingdome is to be inflicted upon them : Soe earnestlie recommending this unto your speciall care, &c.—Whitehall, the 13 of Januar 1630.

To the Erle of Anguse.

Letter to repair to Court, in the usual terms.—Whitehall, 14 January 1630.

To the Prince of Orange.

Mon cousen nous a este presentee par le commissiaire des villes royalles de nostre auncien royaume d'Escosse au nome des magistrats eschevecus burgeois et conseilleirs de dictes villes avec remonstrance de plusieurs enfraints des articles leur accordes par contract faict entre eux et les magistrats de la dicte ville de Camphire en Zelande estant l'estaple et seule port et havre assignee pour recevoir les commodities et marchandises exportees hors de nostre dict royaume de Escosse aux provinces unies du pays bas Et combien que le dit commissaire nous a prie au nome de dictes villes royalles de les permettre changer leur dict estaple port et havre pour estre restablie en quelque autre endroict ou leur traffique pourra estre mieux accommodee, et nos marchands mieux traictes. Neantmoins nous avons trouve bon vous adventir de leur desyre et remonstrance afin que vous ayant donne ordre pour la preservation du dict contract avec mandament aux Magistrats de la dicte ville de Camphire de mieus traicter nos dicts marchants qu'auparavant, et de leur octroyer telles autres favours lesquells les pourroent encourage de continuer leur dict estaple dans la ville de Camphire.—Whythall, le dixisesme de Januier 1630.

To the Exchecquer.

Right, &c. Whareas . . . James Carmichell, one of our   was mony years since appointed by us to be chamberlen of our principalitie for receaving all the rentis and casualities thareof, and of all annueties ishueing out of the same, and of all compositiones arising for or out of any parte thareof, alsweel superioritie as tennendrie : Oure pleasoure tharefore is, that you tak a speciall care to saile him in the said office according to the contentis of his guift or guiftis thareof, and that noe other persones may be by you authorised or permitted ony wayis to intermeddle with any point of the said office, or with the rentis, casualities, compositiones, or annueties due out of any parte of the landis and teithes off or within our said principalitie, but that the saidis James Carmichell and his deputies may have the sole and full intromissione tharewithe in all time coming, as one whome wee have specialie trusted with the receipt thareof, he alwayis accompting for the same in our Exchecquer as in his said gift or giftis is mentioned : And for your, &c.—Whitehall, the third of Februar 1630.

To the Counsell.

Right, &c.—Being credibillie informed of the prejudice arising unto that our kingdome by the abundance of forrain coyne currant thare and great scarcetie of our owne, Wee wonder verie much that you should have suffered a thing soe hurtfull to our subjectis and aganis the custume of all weell governed estattes to have soe farr prevailed : Theis are tharefore to require you, that, haveing thought of the premissis, you tak such speedie course for redressing of the said abuse and for bringing in the wonted bulzeon as you shall think fitt for the good of our said kingdome, wharby noe such absurditie may heirefter be seen at the time of our coming to that our kingdome, and that you acquent us with your proceedingis heirin.—Whitehall, the 3 of Februar 1630.

To the Advocat.

Trustie, &c.—Whareas wee have been pleased to present our trustie and weelbeloved servitour and chaplen Mr Johne Patersone to the personage of Oldhampstockis ; and understanding that the Erle of Balcleuch pretendit right to the said patronage, wherby our royall intentione in planting the churche may not be impedit, and our right of patronage thareof not prejudged, Wee will that you concurr with the said Mr Johne, and doe your endevore for persueing or defending our right of the said patronage, alsweell be way of actione as be way of exceptione ; and alsoe that you intend reduction in our name, with your concurrance for our interest, or at the instance of the said Mr Johne, for reduceing or annulling of the said Erle his pretended right of patronage of the said churche, iff need be, and persue all other actione necessare and competent for establlishing our right foirsaid in the persone of our said servitour, according to the lawes of that our kingdome, as you will doe us acceptabill service.—Whitehall, the 1 of Februar 1630.

To the Counsell.

Right, &c.—Whareas wee did latelie in August last wreitt lettres unto you for a dispatche of the caus concerning the twoe privateer French schippis called the St Peter and St Michaell, alledged taken since the pacieficatione made with France : And forasmuch, as wee are informed by the parties interested, that the said caus is not as yet determined, nether any answer come from you concerning the same : Therefore, at the humble peticeone of the said parties, wee doe heirby again will and require you with all expeditione to caus decide the said controversie according to justice and equitie, least the tediousnes of the suite should seem to be a delay of justice, and a greevance to the parties whome wee wold glaidlie have freed from any just caus of clamour : Soe houping you will not suffer any more to be trubled or importuned with this bussienes, wee bid, &c.—Whitehall, the 4 February 1630.

To the Counsell.

Right, &c.—Whareas peticeone is exhibited unto us by Luba of Caleis, alledging that his schip, called the Amitie of Caleis, loadned with salt, was in September last bipast taken from him and his company neir unto the citie of Bergin, in Norway, by ane Capitane Andersone, upon pretence that the same did belong to Dunkirk, as by the within peticeone may appeir, wharein speedie justice is humbly prayed : Oure plesour therefor is, and wee doe heirby authorise, will, and require you upon sight heiroff, to minister justice with all such summary proceedingis as may be best agreeabill to justice and equitie and the lawes of that our kingdome, the peticeoners being strangers and not able to attend any long suite without extream prejudice and loss : And for your soe doing, &c.—Whitehall, the 4 Februare 1630.

To the Sessione.

Right, &c.—Whareas peticeone hath been exhibited unto us by one Walter Rombottome, citizen of Lubeck, complaning of ane alledged undue sentence pronunced in the Court of Admiralitie of that our kingdome, wharreby the schip called the St Laurence, taken from Marteen Muller in Lubeck in Anno 1627 by Sir William Alexander, Knight, loadned with salt, was judged to be good and laufull prise, as by the said peticeone within may appeir : And wee conceaving that our supream judicatorie of our sessione to be the onlie competent court of justice for reversing [or] reduceing of all undue sentences pronunced in any other judicatorie within that our kingdome : Oure plesure therefore is, and wee doe heirby will and require you, to admitt the parties interested unto thare laufull summonds and proces of reductione before you, and if you shall find any errour into the proceedingis in our said Court of Admiralitie, or any inquirie in the sentence or any other just or laufull caus or ground of reductione, that you doe speedelie releive the peticeoners from the same, and with als summarie proces as the lawes of that our kingdome can permitt, wharreby the parteis may be restored to thare said schip and goodis, or value thareof, if the same be sold or put away, and if you find not any laufull ground of reductione of the said decreet pronunced in our said Court of Admiralitie, then you are to justifie the proceedingis thareof by granting absolvitour from the said reductione as use is in such cases : Soe committing this particulare unto your care, wee bid you, &c.—Whitehall, the 4 Februar 1630.

To Sir Williame Alexander.

Right, &c.—Whareas wee have by our Infeftment under the Great Seall of our kingdome of Scotland granted unto you and your heirs authoritie to be our Lewetennent of New Scotland and Cannada, with power to confer titles of honour thare upon such inhabitantis as shalbe aidding and assisting unto the plantaceon thareof ; and wharras alsoe, for the better encouragement of our subjectis of our said kingdome to plant and contribute towardis the plantatione of the said cuntrey, we have erected the ordour and dignitie of Knight Baronet in our said kingdome of Scotland, and by our lettres have appointed and licensed the Knight Baronettis of our said kingdome, to carie and weare a cognissance and orange tanney ribbane about thare neckis : Therefore wee doe alsoe heirby authorise and require you and your heirs and successouris to authorise, licience, and appoint the Baronettis of New Scotland and Cannada, appointed or heirefter to be appointed by you or them in the said territorie and dominione of New Scotland and Cannada, to wear and carie the like cognissance and ribbane for thare better distinctione from the others freeholders and inhabitantis thareof, and that you caus registrat this our warrand in the bookis of counsell, sessione, and exchequer of our said kingdome, and in the registers of our said territorie and dominione of New Scotland, and for your soe doing theis our lettres under our Privie Signet shalbe unto you and your heirs and successouris a sufficient warrand in that behalff.—Whitehall, the fourt day of Februar 1630.

To the Exchequer.

Right, &c.—Whareas our Right trustie, &c. [the Earl of Mortoune] hath done unto us good and acceptable services, whareof we have taken speciall notice ; Tharefore, and for divers others important causes concerning us, Oure plesure is, that with all possible diligence, against the terme of Witsonday nixtocum, you readilie pay unto the said Erle the somme of 5000lib sterling, out of any of our custumes, great or small, of that kingdome, and out of the first and reddiest of our rentis, duetics, and casualities, or other benefitt whatsoever now dew unto us, or which heirefter shal happin to be due and accres to us in our said kingdome, or out of any of the first taxationes that shalbe granted unto us thare : And incais the said somme be not payed unto him or his foirsaidis betuix this and the terme foirsaid, that he have the ordinarie annuelrent till he be fullielie satisfiet of the wholl somme : And that this precept be registrat in the bookis of exchequer, and that one act of Exchequer be made tharcupon for the said Erle his better securitie ; and for your soe doing, &c.—Whitehall, the eight day of February 1630.

To the Exchequer.

Right, &c.—Whareas wee are resolved to be served in our Chappell Royall in that our kingdome with such musitians borne within the same as are continoualie or placed of new by the Deane of that Chappell, and by Edward Kellie, our servand, to the effect they may be the more able to discharge our service tharein : Oure pleasoure is, and wee doe heirby will and require you, that with all convenient and possible diligence you caus pay out of the reddiest of our rentis or casualities whatsoever in that our kingdome, unto the said Edward into the behalff of the said musitians, all such arrears of thare feeis as shalbe found justlie due unto them, or any of them, conforme to any guift or guiftis granted by us thareupon, least our said service at our comming thither be ether neglected or they not litt to be in such a place and charge : And for your soe doing, &c.—Whitehall, the 8 of February 1630.

To the Advocat.

Trustie, &c.—Whareas heving accepted of a surrender from my Lord Naper of the somme of Seaven thousand merkis scottis, which was payed to him yeerlie by Williame Dick, merchand, out of our revenues of Orknay, by and attour the former rent which wee hade thare : And being pleased of late to dispose of the same to . . . the Erle of Annandale, by a sufficient right under our hand, with poware to him to uplift not onlie the said seaven thousand merkis, bot likewayis whatsoever was restand due by the said Lord before his surrender : Therefore our plesour is, and we require you, that

ii   ii

incaice the said Erle receve not satisfactione according to the grant given by us to him, you complier in our name for obtining of whatsoever shalbe found due by the said Lord at any time unto us or him by reasone of the said superplus proceeding the dait heirof.—Whitehall, the 8 of Februar 1630.

To the Toune of Jedburgh.

Trustie, &c.—Whareas . . . the Lord Drumlanrig hath receaved some prissoners latlie by a warrand from us taken into the borders by . . . Sir Richard Grahame, Knight, to deliver unto you : It is oure pleasour that, imediatlie after he shall arryve at our toune of Jedburgh, you receave from him the saidis prisoners, and keep them in safe ward till they receave thare triall upon such maters as they are to be charged withall.—Whitehall, the 8 of Februar 1630.

To the Advocatt.

Trustie, &c.—It is our will and plesour that after the sight heiroff you call unto you the Advocattis of Franceis Steuart, and that, consulting with them, you find out and demonstrat unto us some of ane sure course in law how the forfaltour off Frances, Erle Bothuell, and this disabilitie of the said Frances, his sone, may still be reserved in our absolute pouare, and he fred from all dangers of the act of prescriptione ; and likwayis, if noe such course can be found in law as accordis with our foirsaid resolutione, that with all possible diligence, without forder delay, you adverteis us, that tharefter we may tak such a speedlie and safe course tharein as wee shall think fitt, the exact performance whareof wee recommend to your speciall care and trust, as yee wilbe answerable to us, and to haste bak the answer heirof with all diligence.— Whitehall, the 8 day of February 1630. Also another Letter to the said Advocate on the same subject on the following day.

To the Erle of Monteathe.

Right, &c.—Whareas . . . the Vicount of Drumlanerck, his sone, heving by a commissioune from us apprehendit in the border these thrie theeflis, fugitives, and rebellis, Williame Weigin, in Whisgillis, and James Weigin, his sone, and Johne Armestrang, alias Tueden, was most contempteouslie opposed in the executione of the said commissione by a number of lewd persones named in the roll heir inclosed, whoe did rescue in a most insolent maner, and assisted the said rebellis for thare better avoiding without respect of our said commissione, and sedetiouslie convocat others for that purpos to our heigh contempt, authoritie, and lawes, the like whareof was never committed in our late deir father's nor our time ; ffor the better preventing the like untollerabill and dangerous courses heirefter, Wee are heirby pleased to require you that you call before you all those that are named in the said roll, and others whoe shall be dileited by the said Vicount, or his sone, to have opposed our commissione ; and efter triall of thare outrageous misdamanour, that you tak such a speedlie course for thare conding punishement that others, by thare example, may be terrified from all such detestable insurrectiones and convocationes : And likwayis that you give ordour for apprehending the saidis rebellis, and being taken, that you caus committ them in some of our save wardis, thare to be keept till such punishement be inflectit upon them as is agreabill with our lawes provided in the like cases.—Whitehall, the nynth of Frebruar 1630.

To the Advocat.

Letter upon the same subject and of the same date.

To the Advocat.

Trustie, &c.—Being resolved to bring bak againe to oure croune all the heretabill offices, Regalitics, and superiorities, and being informed how necessare it is for us to have all and haill the landis, milnes, ducties, and privelieges contined in a note direct heirwith in oure handis, alseweell in regard of the value of the thingis themselves as of the neirnesse of thare lying to our cheeff cittie and palace, Wee have agriett with . . . Robert, Erle of Roxburgh (whoe as wee are informed), hath undoubted right unto them: Therefore our plesour is, that you draw upp a sufficient lettre of dispositione, contining a procuratorie of resignatioun be our said trustie cousen and counsellare (with consent of Sir Williame Ballanden) to us of the premisses, as likwayis that you draw upp a sufficient right and securitie of the samen landis and others as is abone writtin, to our said trustie cousen and counsellare, and his heirs, that they may be fully secured thareof, aey and whill they be secured of the soume of   to be given to him as ane parte of the price thareof; and siclik that thare be a speciall provisione sett doune and insert in his said securitie that it shalbe nowayis lesome to us to redeme the saidis landis and others abone nominat from them, untill such time wee mak thankfull payment of the soume of   to be specified and contined in ane particulare band to be made be us to him to that effect, and that by and attour the other soume abone writtin, which will compleit in the haill the soume of   ; The which band we likewayis desire you to draw upp: Ffor doing thareof thir presentis shalbe, &c.—Whitehall, the 9 day of Februaro 1630.

To the Lord of Lorne.

Right, &c.—Haveing understood by your father of ane great extremitie whareunto he is likelie reduced by reasone of ane debt due by him unto a merchand of Londone, which he expected should have been payed by a voluntarie contributione granted by his procurement from his freendis in Argill, ffor which he was desirous to have repared thither for some time: But becaus wee cannot convenientlie give way to his desire, wee are verie confident that he will use his best endevouris; These are to recommend unto your care the providing of his releeff according to the agreement for that purpose, &c.—Whitehall the Sexteinth day of Februar 1630.

Whareas warrantis hath been issued from the Lordis of our privie counseil of Scotland for apprehending of Johnne Neall, whoe hathe been thir many yeers bypast reputed a notorious witche and delaitted guiltie of a most bussie practiser of that cryme within our said kingdome of Scotland; and we being informed that the said Johnne Neill, being presentlie in Tuedmouth or Clusher, within the bordour of this our kingdome of England, doth by that means avoid apprehensione and punishment: Theis are therefore to will and require yow and everie one of you to caus tak and apprehend the bodie of the said Johnne Neill, wharesoevir he may be found within our said kingdome of England; and him soe apprehendit, that you send him from constable to constable untill he be brought into Scotland, thare to be delivered unto . . . Sir Williame Cokburn of Longtoune, Knight, Barronet, our Shirreiff of the shirrefdome of Berwik, and his deputie, to be by him convoyed and delivered unto the Lordis of our privie counsell of our said kingdome of Scotland, thare to be dealt withall according to the lawes of that our kingdome: And for your soe doing, &c.—Whitehall, the 19 of Februar 1630.

> To our trustie and weelbeloved Heigh Shirreff and Justice of the
> Peace of our cuntrie of Northumberland, and to all others
> our Shirreitlis, Maiouris, Justices, Coroners, Baillies, Con-
> stables, and all others oure officiars and loving subjectis,
> whome theis presentis doethe or may concern.

To the Exchequer.

Right, &c.—Whareas wee are informed by . . . the Duke of Lennox that divers of our subjectis doe wrong and encroach upon the offices of Admiralitie and chamberleenrie of that oure native and ancient kingdome, and that they acquire divers grantis and rightis in prejudice of our oure cousen and the saidis offices : In consideratione whareof, and that wee are most willing to restore the said offices to the full integreetie and for the good of our said consen, Oure expres pleasour and will tharefore is, that you stop heireftor the passing of all grantis and rightis which shalbe presented to you in hurt and prejudice of our said consen, concerning the said offices, or what belongis tharto : And wharein our said consen is prejudged by the passing of the late tak of Orknay to Williame Dick, including the admiralitie tharcoff, that preservyve speedie remedie heirament ; and for redres tharcof wee ordane you to grant to the said Williame Dick a new tak of Orknay, conforme to that which is past to him of late, leaving out what concernis the saidis offices and prejudice tharof, and bearing noe prejudice or hurt to our said cousen ; and that you mak speciall actis heirament into our buikis of Exchecquer ; ffor which theis presentis shalbe unto you a sufficient warrand.—Whitehall, the secund of Marche 1630.

To the Chancellare.

Right, &c.—Whareas wee are informed that about tuoo yeirs agoe or thareabout the Commissioners of our Exchecquer did pas unto Sir Lodovick Houstoune, of that Ilk, Knight (as it hath been usuall with them to doe to others in cases of like nature), a signatour of certane landis belonging to him, which imediatly tharefter being by you exped under our great seall, is as yet undelivered unto him : Oure pleasure is, that without forder delay you either eans rander the same unto him, or to any of his name, or otherwayis, if you have upon any occasione forther conccaved anything wharby the same may prejudge us, we require you to exhibit the same undone before our said commissioners to be againe perused by them ; and if you and they doe not condiscend as at first touching the deliverie thareof unto him, that with all convenient diligence you certiefie us the reassones thareof, that we may give such forder ordour tharein as wee shall find just caus ; Wee bid you farewell, &c.—Whitehall, the eight day of March 1630.

To the Erle of Monteathe.

Right, &c.—Whareas wee are informed that thare is a nomber committed to Jeyell in Drumfrees for theift, receipt of theiffs, and fugitives, which abuse, by neglect of punishment this some time past, is become soe frequent that unles strict ordour be taken with the committers thareof, thare is small hope to bridle such disordouris : We desire tharefore that after you have been at the Justice Court in Jedburgh, and have used justice aganis such as are to be punished in that place, you faill not to goe to the toune of Drumfrees and use justice aganis suche as are in Jeyll, or such others as are fitt to be called in questione thare, ffor we think it most convenient, both in the case of our subjectis and for the good of that service, that the male-factouris abyde thare triall in partes whare thare willes are best knowen : We doe likewayis recommend to your speciall care that the resaittouris of the theeffis themselves and fugitives be noe les punished than the theeffis themselves, since the lawes of that our kingdome doeth strictlie appoint the same : And it is impossible to frie that cuntrie from such villanie iff the resoutters and fosterers of theeffis be not exemplarlie punished : And becaus we have trusted our servand, Sir Richard Cockburn, Knight, and hath alreadie receaved good prooff of his affectione to the quiet of our late borders, it is oure speciall pleasour, and by theis presentis wee command and authorise you, to call the said Sir Richard to be present, and to assist with you and the rest of the commissioners at all times heirefter, considering how requisit it is to have his opinione at all occasiones in that border service: Wee desire you likewayis, for the forther encouragement of our said servant, that you acquent our Counsell with that trust wee have imposed upon him, and will them, if occasione shall offer, to give thare best assistance for ease of his panis: Which commandement we likewayis will you to mak knowen to our wholl commissioners of that our kingdome, wharby mutuall correspondence may be interteyned amongis them to the joynt commissione which wee are about to exped: Soe recommending thir particulars to your speciall care, as our trust is in you, We, &c.—Whitehall, the eight day of March 1630.

To the Exchequer.

Right, &c.—Whareas we wer pleased to write to you of befor that thare was 300ᵘ sterling rased at our Citie of Londone, for which . . . the Lord Traquhair standeth engadged, from one Williame Morehead, factour thare, and that towardis the furnessing of armes to those soldiouris whoe under the conduct of the Erle of Mortonne war to repair unto France for our service thare, Theis are therefore to require you againe, for the saidis Lordis releeff, that you pay with all convenient diligence to Williame Dick, merchand at our burgh of Edinburgh, the said somme of 300ᵘ sterling, togither withe the ordinarie interest for the time of the forebearing, and that out of the first and reddiest of our rentis, casualicties, and ducties of that our kingdome.—Whitehall, the Tent of Marche 1630.

To the Exchequer.

Right, &c.—Whareas wee are informed that the Infeftment of the Lord Douglas and his Ladie is not as yet past for the implement of thare Contract of Mariage, be reasone that Sir James Douglas his signatour is stopped by you, which should be passed for the securing him of the moneyis due unto him by the Erle of Anguise, his brother: Therefore, we being verie desirous that the said Lord Douglas and his Ladie be weell and speedelie secured, the said Erle and his creditouris being first secured for the somme of ane hundreth thousand merkis Scottis reserved to him in the said contract, Oure pleasoure is, that with all expeditioun you pas the said Sir James Douglas his signatour, without questione of itt any forther inserting onlie in the said signatour ane claus that it shall not be prejudiciall to our revocatione in any sort: And for your, &c —Whitehall, the tenth of Marche 1630.

To the Exchequer.

Right, &c.—Whareas we have been moved in the behalff of the Lord of Balmirrienoche and James Creichtoune of Fendraucht, and the toune of Selkirk, for granting unto them signatouris of thare landis: Oure pleasour therefore is, that you peruse and reforme the said signatouris by the advise of our advocatt, and that you pas the same accordingly without prejudice unto us, as is usuallie in such caisses, remembering alwayis to insert ane claus tharein that noething tharein mentioned be prejudiciall unto our revocatione, annuctie, ministers' stipendis, and others pious uses, or to the generall submissione and our decree following tharupon: And for, &c.—Whitehall, the 10 of Marche 1630.

To the Archbischopp of St Androis.

Right, &c.—Whareas wee are informed by your lettre of the frequent Simonicall compactes betwene the patrones and the presentatione ministers within that our kingdome, which is ane abuse worthie of our princelie reformatione and your pastorall animadversione, for the good and mantenance of the church from delapidationes and unlawfull admissiones : Oure pleasoure tharefore is, and wee doe heirby strictlie will and require you, to caus the cannons of the church to be orderlie observed for preventione off all kind of Simonie in time coming, and that no persone be admitted, instituted, or inducted in any church heirefter untill he doe first tak his corporall oath before his ordinarie that he hath not anywayis come to his presentatione by any Simonicall compact whatsoever, directlie or indirectlie ; and if you have alreadie found, or shall heirefter find, any Simonicall errour committed by any, wee require you to punish the partie alsweell named in your lettre as all other offenders in that kind, by proces in the heigh commissione, or by deprivatione, suspensione, or otherwayis, as you shall find agreable to the cannons of the church, or lawes and practique of that our kingdome : Requiring you alsoe to intimat this oure pleasure unto all the rest of the Archbischopps and Bischopps within that our Kingdome, whereby they may carefullie look unto such abuses heirefter.—Whitehall, the 10 March 1630.

To the Sessione.

Right, &c.—Whareas wee are informed by our clergie thare that Mr Patrik Hepburne, the sone of the late Minister of Oldhamstockis, haveing confessed the giving of ane soume of money to the Erle Balcleuche for his presentatione to the said churche after his father's deceis, doethe endevore to defend and mantein his said impious act of Simonie under collour of the generalitie of the wordis of ane act of Parliament made in anno 1612, which he and his lawers labour to wraist for thair owne purpose : And forasmuche as the generall wordis of many actis of parliament which hath not been in use nor practise are not fitt to be raschlie put in executione, or wraisted into any impious sence, contrair to the intentione and true meening of the estates of parliament, Oure pleasure is therefore that you seriouslie and consciebillie advert unto the said case of Simonie, and that yee cautiouslie prevent any precedent which may be urged for the defence of soe wicked a cryme as is not only permitious to the estate, but alsoe may prove to be the uter overthrow of the church thare, whose decayed rwines we wold glaidlie to be repared by all the faire and lauchfull means and wayis which can be devised : Soe recommending this particulare unto your serious consideratione, unto our nixt parliament may provide some wholesome remeid, we, &c.—Whitehall, the tenth of March 1630.

To the Exchecquer.

Right, &c.—Whareas wee are pleased to signe a signatour for some yeers to James Philp upon a motione made unto us in his behalff that the transportatione of milnstones and all others kind of stones fitt for building and dressing of houses and divers others uses, from thence into this our kingdome, never heirtoefore (as we are informed) practised, or by any might or means to set many of our poore subjectis thare a wark, and in some sort better our custumes both heir and thare ; which, if you as yet have not caused exped, wee require you to doe it with all convenient diligence, granting unto him and his partiners, for the forthering of his intentione heirin, all such priveleges as you shall find to be requisit and usuall in the like nature : For doing whareoff, &c.—Whitehall, the tenthe of March 1630.

To the Commissioners of the Parliament.

Right, &c.—Whareas wee did latelie caus prorogate our Parliament unto the first day of Junij nixt to come, in houp that wee could have been our self in persone at that time : And now considering that the present estate of our affairis can not permitt us to be thare convenientlie as we desyred, And yet being unwilling to be absent from our said parliament, and desyring to receave our croune in persone, and to setle all bussienes thare for the good and weell of that our ancient and native kingdome, and with the applaus of all our good subjectis thare : Oure pleasoure tharefor is, and wee doe heirby authorise, will, and require you, to caus fense our said court of parliament by vertew of our commissione latelie granted unto you by us, and to prorogat or continow the said parliament again to the first of August nixtocum, with continoua-tione of dayis, that wee may have time to setle our affairs heir before wee begin our jornay towardis that our ancient kingdome : And for doing of the premissis, &c.—Whitehall, the 10 of Marche 1630.

To the Erle of Marr.

Right, &c.—Being resolved, as wee hade formerlie determined, to repair unto that our kingdome, and notwithstanding of the provisiones alreadie made, wee consider that thare wilbe sindrie other thingis requisit, whareof wee desire you as you tender our service to have a speciall care; And becaus it is necessare that some one should come hither whoe doethe understand the estate of thingis thare, as like-wayis what is fitt to be furnesit from hence ; and haveing alreadie hade experience of the sufficiencie of . . . Sir James Baillie of Lochend, Knight, and his affectione to our service, wee think it necessare, and it is oure pleasoure, that you direct him hither, being instructed with all that may concerne our service in this bussienes, and that you satisfie of that which was formerlie allowed unto him for his repairing hither according to the warrand which he formerlie hade when he was send for, as likewayis at this time.—Whitehall, the eleventh day of Marche 1630.

To the Exchecquer.

Right, &c.—Whareas wee have granted unto . . . Maister Williame Haig, one of our sollicitouris under oure royall signatour, a commissione for imbringing to our use in a legall way some soumes restand due unto us of the ordinary taxationes 1621 and 1625 : Wee are now informed that you have as yet delayed the expeeding of the same : Wee doe verie much wonder thareof, since wee hade granted the same upon soe good deliberatione after wee hard divers objectiones proponed unto us against it : Therefore it is oure plesour, and wee doe heirby require you, that you ether give way to the said commissione, or otherwayis that you send unto us a noat of suche reasones against the expedience of itt as our advocatt has not answered unto us, and that without dropping upon any pointis which in this case aucht to be discussed and judged by the Lordis of Sessione.—Whitehall, the eleventh day of Marche 1630.

To Sir Robert Gordoune.

Trustie, &c.—In regard wee approve the laudable custume of that our kingdome in choosing thare commissioners yeerlie in everie shire for attending at Parliamentis, conventiones, and other generall meetingis of the estates of the said kingdome, Wee have thought fitt, out of our princelie care both for church and commonewelth, to require you to proceed to a new electione of twoe such persones as you know to be sufficient and able, weell affected to our service and the publict good of that shire whareof you are ane shirreff against the nixt parliament, which wee intend in persone shortlie to hold thare ; And wee haveing alreadie good prooff of your sufficiencie and affectione to our service and the publict good, wee wishe that yourself might be chosen as one of the said twoe commissioners, if by any faire and laufull means you can procure the same to be done : Soe wee bid, &c.—Whitehall, the 16 of Marche 1630.

To the Bischopp of Dumblaine.

Reverend, &c.—Whareas wee did formerlie write unto you divers lettres concerning the celebratione of the Communione at Easter yeerlie, and thought wee did not doubt bot you will carefullie performe the directione of our said lettres, yet to quicken your endevouris heirin, Oure pleasoure is, that you give warning to the Lordis of our Counsell, and the Judges and members of our College of Justice, and others mentioned in our said former lettres, to performe thare partes prescrived be our said former letters : And that you certiefie unto us the names of the Communicantis, and of those that, being warned, doe not Communicatt, that wee may tak such forther ordour as is most suteable with the government of our church thare : Soe recommending this to your speciall care, wee bid you, &c.—Whitehall, the saxteenth day of Marche 1630.

To the Advocat.

Trustie, &c.—Whareas wee are informed that the Commissioner of Dunkell, haveing some charge of the estate of Atholl in the minoritie of the Erle thareof, did without any warrand from us or our counsell release tuoe notorious theeffis from prisone after they wer laufully convicted and condemned, This abuse, if it be treu as is informed, being committed in contempt of our authoritie and against the due course of justice, and which by the exemple may prove dangerous : Oure pleasoure is, that you informe your selffis of the treu estate thareof, and if you find what is heirin alledged to be true, that in our name yee proceed against the said commissioner, according to justice and the course accustumed in cases of the like nature : And for your soe doing, &c.—Whitehall, the 16 day of Marche 1630.

To the Exchequer.

Right, &c.—Whareas . . . Doctour Johne Yong, Deane of Winchester, being imployed within that our kingdome for the service of our late dear father, and hade moneyis appointed by his speciall directione to be payed unto him thare, whareof (as we are informed) he is like to be disapointed by the deathe of Archibald Prymrose, late clark of the taxationes, whoe hade taken allowance for the same : And wee, being very loath that one whoe hade deserved weell of us should be defrauded of that which was allowed him for his charges, Oure pleasour is, that noe guilt of Exchequer be past of the said Archibald his goodis, unles our said servand be first satisfied of that which is due unto him out of the same, or otherwayis, if it be not alreadie payed or allowed in the saidis Archebaldis comptis, that you tak a course for his satisfactioun : ffor doing whareoff, &c.—Whitehall, the 16 day of March 1630.

To the Counsell.

Right, &c.—Whareas we have writen our princelie directione unto our commissioners of Parliament to prorogat and continow the same unto the first day of August nixtocum, whaireby wee may have some more time and leasour to be thare in persone in the said parliament, and to resave our croune for the peace and tranquilitie of that our native and ancient kingdome ; oure pleasoure therefore is, and wee doe heirby will and authorise and require you, that after the said parliament shalbe prorogated and continowed as said is, you caus intimat the said prorogatione and continowatione to all our good lieges within our said kingdome be oppen proclamatione at the merkatt crose of Edinburgh, and other places needfull ; and warn all prelattis, noblemen, commissioners for borrowis, and all others haveing place, vote, or owing attendance in the said supream court of parliament, to attend and wait upon the same the foirsaid day, withe continouatione of dayis, and to performe all and sindrie such other thingis as to thare places and offices doeth apperteen : And for doing of the premissis theis our lettres, &c.—Whitehall, the 16 day of Marche 1630.

To the Bischopp of Caithnes.

Reverend father, &c.—Whareas wee did formerlie wreitt unto the Archbischopp of St Androis that notwithstanding of ane ordour of our privie counsell, whareby you are appointed to repair unto your dyocie and mak your aboad thare, yet he should suffer you to remain in the pairtes of your ordinarie residence during the winter seasone, in regard wee wer to use you in some thingis touching our service ; and sieing now we intend verie shortlie to doe the same, Wee have thought good heirby to require you to remain still in your ordinarie residence till you heir further from us, and (if need be) you acquent the said Archebischop with theis presentis : And for your soe doing, &c.—Whitehall, the 18 day of Marche 1630.

To the Counsell.

Right, &c.—Whareas it hathe been complaned unto us by . . . the Duke of Lennox that divers of our subjectis, and specialle the burgh of Edinburgh, hath encroached upon the offices of Admiralitie and chamberlaurie of that our native and ancient kingdome of Scotland, usurping honouris, privelieges, and benefeittis belonging thareunto : And in regard that Mr Johne Hay, Commissioner for our said burgh, did affirme in our royall presence that they hade not acquired any thing belonging to the said offices ; and furthermore, that iff our said burgh hade acquired any rightis in prejudice thareof that they wold willingly denude themselffis of the same in favouris of our said cousen : Oure expres will and plesour tharefore is, that you conveen before you the Magistratis of Edinburgh, Leith, and all others requisit in requiring them to give satisfactione to our said cousen, or to them intrusted by him, according to the said assurance made and given us by the said Mr Johne Hay, and our Advocatt concurr with the Advocattis of our said cousen in doing anything that may tend to the recovering of that which is wrongfully deteyned from him, or in securing of him in that which is or shalbe condiscendit upon, as they will answer upon thare trust : And that you caus speedelie advise and raise summondis, righting our said cousen, to be called in the nixt parliament of that our kingdome aganis any persones whatsoever that have wronged or encroached upon the honouris, priveleges, and benefeittis of the saidis offices : And that you provide and use speedelie all others laufull means for preventing any inconveniences and redressing all prejudices that hes or may heirefter ensue and befall to our said cousen heiranent by prescriptione or otherwayis ; the doing and performance whareof we recommend to your speciall care : And soe wee bid you fareweell.—Whitehall, the 18 of Marche 1630.

To the Erle of Marr, Thesaurer.

Right, &c.—Though wee have ever been confident of your affectione to our service, and of the continouance of your endevouris to the place wharein you serve ; yet haveing by your lettre unto us, that in regard of your present infirmitie you are willing if wee be pleased tharewith to demitt the office of Thesaurer in favouris of . . . the Erle of Mortoune, wee approve of your resoluteone tharein, and upon your demissione shall presently grant the said place unto him, not doubting but, as you wrett unto us, you will still be carefull to attend our service as one whome wee specialie respect : And soe, &c.—Whitehall, the 20 day of March 1630.

H   c

To the Advocat.

Trustie, &c.—Haveing perused the answer that yee sent untô us for preventing any inconvenient that might arrise unto Frances Steuart, sone to the late Erle of Bothuell, be means of the late act of prescriptione : After divers consideratiounes, the noblemen heir present whoe have interest in that which he doeth clame are willing to renunce all benefitt that they, thare heirs or successouris, or any haveing right from them or to thare behove, can pretend against the said Frances, be vertew of the said act of prescriptione, to the effect that the pouare may still remain in our persone to determine tharein as wee think best, as if the said act hade never been made : Tharefore our plesour is, that you with all diligence imediatlie caus draw upp all such securitie or sureties as you think requisitt in law for the effect foirsaid, that the tuoe noblemen heir present may presentlie renunce all benefitt that they, thare heirs or successouris, or any haveing right from them or to thare behove, may clame against the said Frances, be vertew of the said act of prescriptione : And it is our forther plesour that you mak interruptione in our name to . . . the Erle of Bdelouch, and to all other persones whoe doe not renunce in due time all benefitt that may arrise to him or them, or to any of them, of the saidis landis, tithes, wadsettis, and others by vertew of the foirsaid act of prescriptione, as the noblemen heer present are content to doe, see that the said Frances be put in noe worse case by means thareof, But that the said estate may still remain in our handis to be disposed upon ; and if the said Erle, or any other interested in that state, shall not as they doe renunce all benefeitt that can arise by vertew of the said act, if you find the interruptione made in our name will not be sufficient against the said Erle or others whoe doe not in due time renunce for the effect foirsaid, Wee are likewayis pleased you draw upp a pouare for the said Frances from us in his owne name to mak interruptione to the said Erle or to any whoe doeth not renunce in maner abone specifeit ; Provyding alwayis that he have noe pouare to proceed forther then to mak the said interruptione, unlese he have a farther warrant from us for that purpose : And soe, becaus of the schortnes of the time, recommending earnestlie unto your care that all diligence possible be used for effectuating that our intentione abone expressed, Wee bid you, &c.—Whitehall, the 21 March 1630.

A Precept to the Erle Marr.

It is our plesour that [with] all possible diligence you caus pay to the bearer, James Querriers, one of our falconers, the accustumed yeerlie allowance for bringing of some haulkis unto us from the northern partes of that our kingdome, and that you give unto him your best fortherance for this effect ; ffor doing thareof, &c.—Whitehall, the 24 March 1630.

To the Advocat.

Trustie, &c.—Whareas we have been plesed to present our weelbeloved Maister Johne Guthrie to the churche of Duffus, in Murray, Wee have thought fitt to require you, if any doe pretend rycht to the patronage of the said churche (as heirtofore sindrie have done in the like case), wharebv our royall intentione in planting the churche may be impedit, and our right of patronage thareof prejudged, that you concurr with the said Maister Johne, whome we have been pleased to present, and doe your endevore for persewing or defending our right of the said patronage, alsweell by way of actione as by way of exceptione ; And alsoe that you intend reductione in our name with your concurrence for our interest or at the instance of the said Maister Johne, for reduceing or annulling (if need be) the right of any persone whoe shall pretend to the said patronage, and persew all or other actione necessare and competent for establilishing our right foirsaid in the persone of the said Maister Johne, according to the lawes of that our kingdome.— Whitehall, 24 Marche 1630.

To the Advocat.

Trustie, &c.—Whareas thare hath been a signatour of some landis belonging to . . . the Erle of Buchane presented to be signed by us, as wee are willing to doe him any laufull favour, soe wee are laith that any thing which may be prejudiciall to the generall directiones which you have from us should pas. And tharefore wold give ordour to doe the same till last your opiniones ware made thareanent : Tharefore our plesour is, that iff you find noething thareinto which is prejudiciall unto us or contrarie to our late decree, or any reservationc sent thareon to our Exchecquer, that you other caus pas the same or retorne it docated for our hand for that effect : Soe wee bid, &c.—Whitehall, the 24 Marche 1630,

To Sir Alexander Hay of Fosterseat.

Trustie, &c.—Whareas wee are informed that you have conceaved some informatione to have been made unto us against you : As in our princelie judgment wee ar not accustumed to give ear to any report made unto us against any of our subjectis whatsoever without verie apparent evidence and important respectis, much les will wee hearken to any thing that might derogat from you whoe hath been in soe eminent a charge as one of the Senatouris of our Colledge of Justice, and whoe tharein hath soe long served us and our deir father of worthie memorie, without wee made both seen just caus and reall groundis for the same, and made caused acquent you tharewith for the better justieieing of yourselff : Bot wee are soe farr from any such conceptione as may tend to your disadvantage, that wee will not be annoyndfull to expres our forther respect unto you when ony occasione shall convenientlie be offered unto us for doing the same : Whareoff haveing thought fitt at this time to give you notice, Wee bid you, &c.—Whitehall, the 4 day of Aprill 1630.

To the Exchecquer.

Right, &c.—Whareas upon consideratione that the Marques of Huntly and Lord Gordoune, his sone, did voluntarelie surrender in favouris of us and the croune of that kingdome, ad perpetuam remanentiam, the heretable offices of the shirrefshipps of Aberdeen and Innernes, wee wer pleased to grant unto the said Lordis a precept of fyve thousand pundis sterling out of our custums, great and small, of that our kingdome, and that payment should be made unto him or his assigneeis out of theis custumes before any other payment excepting the yeerlie fees due to our Colledge of Justice : And now for theis consideratiounes being willing that he be payed according to our former royall intentione, And being informed that he hath deputed Williame Dick for receaving the payment thereof, to whome a lease of theis custumes is granted by you, Oure pleasoure is, that in behalff of the said Lord you give way to the said Williame Dick, to be payed of that soume out of these custumes, great and small, according in all respectis to the precept formerlie granted : And for your soe doing, &c.—Whitehall, the 4 day of Aprill 1630,

To the Thesaurer and Deputie Thesaurer.

Right, &c.—We have been willing to have some muttons yeerly from that our kingdome, at such seasones of the yeer and in such number as was formerlie brought in custume for the use of our late dear father, to which purpose wee have been formerlie pleased to give ordour at severall times; and understanding that Johne Geddes, whoe hath taken great panis and been at charges to doe us service tharein, was be our appointment imployed in this earand: Oure pleasoure is, that you authorise him tharein to bring hither for our use such and the like number of sheep as wer in use to be brought of before; And that you pay him the like allowancees and feeis as wer paid by Sir Gedeon Murray, our late Deputie Thesaurer, to any persone whoe at that time hade the like charge: And for that purpos that according to our first intentione furness unto him upon accompt present moneyis at his first begining to serve us in that kind; ffor doing whareof, &c.—Whitehall, the fourth day of Aprill 1630.

To the Erle of Monteath.

Letter to repair to Court, dated Whitehall, 13 April 1630.

To the Exchecquer.

Right, &c.—Whereas we have been informed by our servand James Maxuell of Innerweek that his landis and barony of Innerweek are holden of our principalitie by the tennour of ward and releeff whareby the mariage of his dochters by his death may fall in our handis and at our guift if they should happen not to be matched in his lifetime: And wee being weell pleased at his humble sute to compound with him by your advise for the wardschip and mariages of his saidis dochters, if the same shall fall: Oure pleasour tharefore is, that you secure him and them from the danger of the said wardschip and mariages for such compositione as is usuall for the like barrones, or as you think fitting for a man of his qualitie and place, and in such a legall maner as our advocat shall devise, in a signature to be presented by him to your handis to be passed for that effect.—Whitehall, the 16 day of Aprill 1630.

To the Counsell.

Right, &c.—Haveing intentione upon verie good consideratiounes at this time to aid our brother the King of France with such forces as wee can convenientlie spare, We required . . . the Lord Gordoune to leavie in that our kingdome a companye of Tuoe thousand footmen, ffor doing whareof it is fitt that he be authorised by our commissione under the Great Seall of that our Kingdome of Scotland appointing him to be follo Colonell of the said regement, with pouare to him to elect, nominat, and appoint such commanders and officiars as are usuall to be appointed by a Colonell: These are tharefore to will and require you upon sight heirof to caus exped unto the said Lord a commissione under our Great Seall aforesaid in competent forme, giveing and granting unto him full pouare a licience to leavie and transport the said regiment . . . into France for our said brother's service, out of all such persones within that our kingdome as he shall find willing to goe with him thither, granting him libertie to tuck drummes for that purpose, with as large privileges as any other hath hade heirtofore in the like kind, he alwayis giving such satisfactione to everie one of the said number as shalbe agreed upon betuix him and them according to the like cases: ffor doing whareof, &c.—Whitehall, the 20 of Aprill 1630.

To the Counsell.

Right, &c.—Whareas wee did grant a commissione unto . . . the Lord Gordoune, with consent of the Archebischopp of St Androis in behalf of the clergie, for apprehending of such papistis as wer in rebellione. and excommunicated persones in the Northern partes of that our kingdome : And now conceaving the time agreed upon betuix you and him for imbringing of the saidis excommunicated rebellis to be too schort in regard of his present imployment in the other service concerning our brother the King of France : Our pleasoure is, that the said former time condiscended upon betuix you for executing of the said commissione be prorogated till the first day of July nixtocum, &c.—Whitehall, the 20 of Aprill 1630.

To the Excheequer.

Right, &c.—Seing, as wee are informed, it pleased our late deir father to give ordour by a lettre from him that noe guift of the Erle of Nithesdale his lifrent or eschet should be disponed of untill he wer first acquented tharewith : And wee, being noe les carefull of that which may concern the said Erle or the good of his house, doe require you by theis presentis that you pas noe gift of his liferent or escheat till he, or such as shall have warrand from him, be first hard, that the benefitt thareof may be applyed for his debtis, and payment of the same, and releeffing of his catiouers, whome we recommend unto you in like maner, in soe farr as they stand bound for him, &c.—Whitehall, the 20 of Aprill 1630.

To the Viscount Clanneboyes.

Right, &c.—Being informed by . . . the Erle of Nithesdale of the care and diligence taken by you in all thingis that might tend to the advancement of our service, and how carefull you have been to apprehend and send againe some notorious maliefactouris, whoe, haveing committed hyenous crymes in Scotland, haue fled from thence to Irland, thereby preventing the due course of justice fitt to be execute upon all such maliefactouris, Wee doe rander you hartlie thankis for the same, And doe heirby will and require you that, upon adverteisment from our Counsell, or Commissioners of the Middle shires, called the borders, you caus search and apprehend any such persones aforsaid as shalhappin to be within your boundis, or elswhare, as you shall think fitt, and that you caus send them bak againe, which we will tak as acceptable service, &c.—Whitehall, the 20 of Aprill 1630.

To the Viscount Montgumrie.

Another lettre conforme to the former was directed to the Viscecount Montgomrie, verbatim, of the foresaid dait.

To the Erle of Monteath.

Right, &c.—Being informed of the great abuses which arise in the bordouris by a custume latelie used in the holding of Courtis, whareof noe man, how giltie soever of thift or receipt of thift, is put to triall by the Commissioners except the partie accuser doe suer and persue at the tour, by which abuse many notorious theeflis doe daylie escape punishment, the partie from whom the goodis are stolline not darring openlie so to follow the same for fear of forder harme from the maister or freendis of the theeflis ; as likewayis many haveing committed thiftis from Englishemen which are notoriouslie knowen are libered from punishement in regard the parties from whome the goodis are stollen doe not compeir to follow, whoe, ether upon collusione or many other reassones, may pretend cause to be absent from the Justice Courtis : Tharefore our pleasure is, that you, or the rest of the Commissioners of the borders, a dittay being sufficientlie suorne to any one of the Commissioners, or to the clark of the commissione, or the dittay being knowen by pregnant probabilities, conforme to the custume which hath been used befor times, caus the partie accuser byd his triall, and withall that you give ordour that noe cautione be admitted before the generall Justice of such as are inhabitantis in the shires of late called the borders, whoe are accused of thift, receat of thift, or recent slauchter, but that they be appointed to byd thair triall at the Justice Courtis upon the borders : And whareas likewayis thare are divers theeflis and malefactouris whoe, haveing for thare superiouris the Lordis of the regalitie, are protected by them, soe eschewing due punishement which should be executed against them, Wee will that you desire the saidis Lordis, ether by themselves or thare baillieflis, to assist and concurr with you for thare triall, wharcby justice may be ministred ; and for the benefitt that shall arrise thereby it is noe wayis our meening that they be prejudged thereof : And for your soe doing, &c.— Whitehall, the 20 of Aprill 1630.

To the Heighe Commissione.

Right, &c.—Whareas, at the humble sute of the Bischoppe and ministeris of Gallowa, and upon certificat from them of the great necessitie of builbling and providing a churche at Portt Montgumrie, alias Portt Patrik, not onlie for the good of the inhabitantis at the said port, and others neir unto itt, bot also of all our subjectis of our kingdome of Scotland, England, and Irland that doe travell to and from Irland, Wee wer graciouslie pleased to give ordour to our advocat to caus a signatour be drawen upp for our hand, that the church which was then abuilding by . . . Viscecount Montgumrie might be thareby erected into a paroch church, and provided with means competent for the interteinment of a preacher to serve the cure thare : And now, understanding that the said Churche is weell builded and finished by our said . . . . Viscount Montgomrie at his charges, and that by our lettres under our Great Seall of that our kingdome of Scotland the said churche is erected into a paroch churche, and certane landis disguised [devised ?] and alloted thareunto for a paroschine, but as yet thare is noe provisione for a minister, Oure pleasure tharefor is, that you tak a speciall care to sie the said churche weell provided out of the first and reddiest of such tithes, great or small, or other casualties, kirk-rent, which ether are or shalhappin in our handis, and that the samen be annexit to the said churche for ever heirefter for interteinment of the minister thare : Which recommending seriouslie to your care, we bid you fareweell, &c.—Whitehall, the 20 of Aprill 1630.

To the Counsell.

Right, &c.—Whareas wee are informed that divers parties, goldsmithes, gravers, cutters, and others artificers, take upon them to grave, paint, cutt, and give coatis of armes to such persones as are not priviledged by the law of armes nor any way warranted by us to wear coatt armour or cognisance of gentrie : which disordour wee will not suffer any longer to be continued, sieing that both wee, our ancient nobilitie, and gentrie of that our kingdome are heirby wranged, and in particular our King of Armes, whose cheefl mantenance hath heretofore depended (as wee are informed) upon the like services : Therefore our plesure is, and wee doe heirby require you, to call before you all such persones as shalbe alledged by our said King of Armes to transgres in that kind, ordayning to deliver upp to him all bookis of armes, genologies, papers, and all other draughtis touching that purpose which can be found by you to be in thare handis or custodie : Likewayis our plesour is that you fyne and imprissone all offenders in this kind according as the nature of the offence shall require. Ordaning them to find suretie and cautione, under such panis as you shall think expedient, that they doe not in any time heirefter transgres in this maner.— Whitehall, the 20 of Aprill 1630.

To the Chancellare.

Right, &c.—Haveing preferred . . . Sir James Balfour of Kinnard, Knight, to be our King of Armes in that our kingdome of Scotland, And being willing that nee honour belonging to that place and office should be diminished or impared, It is our royall pleasure and will that you with all convenient diligence inaugurat him with all ceremoney due and requisit in als goodlie maner and forme, and als solemnlie in all respectis as ever any Lione King at Armes hath bene crouned in that our kingdome; ffor doing whareof, &c.—Whitehall, the 20 day of Aprill 1630.

To the Counsell.

Right, &c.—Whareas (wee are informed) that divers insufficient persones of noe worth nor reputatione hath latelie, by the neglegences of our late King of Armes, bene promitted, contrare to the law of armes, the honour of us, and of that our ancient kingdome, to be herauldis and pursevantis, whoe for the most pairt being ignorantis, without learning or letters, keepers of tavernes and victualling houses, does soe blemishe and defile that honorable office of armes, contrarie to the oathe given by them at thare admissione: Wee, thinking ourselves heirby verie much interested, doe will and require you that you call oure King of Armes before you, ordouring him to cite the wholl herauldis and pursevantis of that our kingdome, and in our presence, according to the accustume used in the like causes, trie and examine them; requiring you likewayis to discharge from any further exercise of that office all such as shall not be judged worthie by you of soe honorable an office and calling: ffor doing whareof, &c.—Whitehall, the 20 of Aprill 1630.

To the Erle of Linlythquho.

Right, &c.—Whareas wee are informed that you of late, by advise of our Privie Counsell, have not for some causes proceedit against some persones (whoe haue tortered some of the subjectis of our brother the French King) according to the sentence of deathe given against them by your court of Admiralitie, till oure plesour should be first knouen thairein; as wee doe approve of your moderat maner of proceeding in this in seeking the approbatione of us and our counsell, whare you might have caused execute justice of yourself, according to the privelege of your office: Soe now (sieing yee desire to know our plesure heirin), wee will the rather trust your oune judgment and discretione: And tharefore wee remitt unto yourself to tak suche a course touching them as you shall think most fitt and equitable: Soe we, &c.—Whitehall, the 20 of Aprill 1630.

To the Counsell.

Right, &c.—Whareas we have been petitioned by William Ramsay of Pettenweem, in the cuntrie of Fyff, for some duetie to be imposed upon everie tune of goodis which shalbe imported or exported into or out of that our kingdome, in any stranger's bodden, accordinglie as is done with our subjectis in other forraine partis; Though wee think it ressonable that thare should be a difference betuix our native subjectis and strangers in such causes, yet we wold not doe anything heirin till first your advise wer hard of; and tharefor, haveing thought fitt to send you the petitione heir enclosed to be considered of, that haveing certified us bak of your opiniono thairein, we may tak such courses tharefter as we shall think most fitt: Soe we bid, &c.—Whitehall, the 20 of Aprill 1630.

To the Sessione.

Right, &c.—Wee are informed by petitione from James Hereot, our jewaller, that his brother George in his laufull legacie bequethed a legacie of 1000ʰ sterling to Thomas Hereot, ane other brother, with speciall appointment that iff any of the said sounne, or any part of itt, should be unpayed after the decease of the said Thomas, it should descend upon the said petitioner, and that at least tuoe thirdis remain still in the said George his executouris handis, or our toune of Edinburgh, upon ane heretable band, whareby the petitioner, as being his nixt heir, besidis the will of the testatour, hathe the undouted right to at the least the said tuoe-thirdis; Bot that notwithstanding thareof the executouris of the last deceased Thomas his brother acclame the wholl, and by reasone of the peticoner's absence, and that thare clamouris, importonis, or povertie may possibillie prejudge him in his right, These are tharefore to recommend unto you our said servand his right, and to will and require you to look carefullie thareunto, that hee be not prejudged by his absence, it being for our speciall and daylie service but that he may find as a just and equitable, soe a speedie and quick dispatche : Wharein not doubting of your care and diligence, wee bid you fareweell.—Whitehall, the 24 of Aprill 1630.

To the Exchecquer.

Right, &c.—Wee are informed by peticeone from Andro Dicksone that he haveing taken great panis and layed out great soumes of money in reparing and setting furth of those shippes which have ordour for theanse of the estate thare, hath not onlie been prejudged in his healthe, but lyen out of his money all this whill, to his great domage and almost utter undoing : Wee tharefore, in justice and out of our princelie commiseratione, have thought fitt to will and require you forthwith to examine the accomptis of his debursementis, and give ordour for speedie payment of such moneyis as you shall find to be due unto him thareupon, &c.—Whitehall, the 24 of Aprill 1630.

To the Exchecquer.

Right, &c.—Wee are informed by peticeone from Peter Hay that his childring haveing been made executouris to thare grandmother for apprehending certane legacies bequethed from hir unto them, have notwithstanding been keept from the benefitt thareof by the adversouris of hir husband George Bonyman during his liffe, and since his death by the pouare of his freendis, soe as now he hath noe other remedie of thare losse but by our grant of all the chattellis, reall and personall, pertining to the said George during his liftime, and being escheated unto us by vertew of his rebellione : These are tharefore, out of our princelie commiseratione, to will and require you, if the information be trew, to expel in name of the petitioner a grant of the said George his escheat : Yet soe as you tak him bound to mak noe forther use thareof than for the recoverie of the saidis legacies to the behove of his childring ; wharein not doubting of your care, We, &c.—Whitehall, 24 Aprill 1630.

To the Advocat.

Trustie, &c.—Wee are informed by peticeone from Archebald Wood, keeper of our moore of Moore Eamonth, that it is mightie incroached upon by some of the nobilitie and gentrie haveing landis neir adjacent thareto, wharcby not onlie the peticeoner is endomaged, but wee alsoe divers wayis, and especiallie in our right prejudged : These are alsoe to will and require you, if the information be trew, to tak a legall and speedie course for vindicating our right, and the peticeoner's prejudice from any forther intrusione or present encroachment, but honsoever to certictie us of your diligence, and enquire heiranent : Wharein not doubting of your care, Wee bidd you fareweell.—Whitehall, the 24 day of Aprill 1630.

To the Counsell.

Right, &c.—Wee wer heirtofore pleased to recommend unto your cares and endevouris Twoe petitiones of Margaret Ballandyne's, which wer sent unto you inclosed within our lettre daited the thrid of Aprill 1628, willing you to trye the groundis thereof, and tak speedie course to give such satisfactione to hir as in equitie should be by you found fitt, or otherwayis to certictie us what you should think fitt to be done heirin : Nevertheles noething, as wee are informed, beeing done, and wee taking notice againe of the peticeoner's demandis and hir povertie, and alsoe of the losse of hir brother's liffe in our service at the He of Rhea, doe heirby will and require you forthwith to tak the same into your consideratione, and, according to our former lettre that you tak some speedie course for hir releeff, or els certictie us what you think fitt to be done tharein, that tharenpon wee may tak some forther course and ordour for hir releeff.—Whitehall, the 24 of Aprill 1630.

To the Advocat.

Trustie, &c.—Whareas wee are informed that one Keir hath of long time opprest our subjectis in the charge which he hade under Mr Johne Skeen, clark of the Billis in our College of Justice : Oure pleasoure is, that if you find that what is heerin informed unto us to be trew, that you in our name proceed against the said Keer according to the lawes of that kingdome, and to the course accustumed in the like causes.— Whitehall, the 28 of Aprill 1630.

To the Exchequer.

Right, &c.—Whareas wee are informed that one Keir, whoe hade a charge under Mr Johne Skeen, clark of the Billis in our College of Justice, hath both wronged the trust reposed unto him, and oppressed our subjectis, contrarie to our lawes, wharely his landis and moveables fall as escheat at our guilt : And being willing, for consideratione knowen unto us, to grant any benefitt that tharely arrise unto us to Sir Thomas Dischingtoun, our servand : Oure pleasoure is, iff the said Keer be alreadlie found, or shall heirefter be found culpable in that kind, and that wee may laufullie caus evict the said escheat, that our said servand be preferred thareto before any other persone : And to that effect that you pas noe other guift thareof till any other till our forther plesour be signiefied unto you tharein.—Whitehall, the 28 day of Aprill 1630.

To the Cittie of Bristoll.

Trustie, &c.—Whareas wee are informed by testimonie of our College of Phisitians of the integretie of liffe and conversatione, of the learning, care, conscience, and diligence, of . . . Robert Ramsay, practisioner in phisick, and of his habilities in the studie and groundis of that science : Wee tharefore being carefull of you and everie one of your heltthes, doe heirby specialie recommend the said Robert unto you, requiring you to resave, accept, and intertein him as one whoe of himselff desires to leive and bestow his talent amongis you : Which trusting you will doe, we bid you hartlie fareweel. — Whytehall, the 30 of Aprill 1630.

11   c

To the Erle of Home.

Right, &c.—Whereas upon consideratione that our late royall father hade taken soe much panis in seiling some differences betwcen your father and Johne Steuart touching Coldinghame, Wee wer the rather pleased to write heirtofore unto you in that purpose, wharein wee have hitherto found a reddie performance in you obeying our desire tharein, ffor which wee give you thankis: And now being peticoned by divers creditouris of the said Johne, that in respect they have alreadie in his behalff payed thrie thousand of the foure thousand poundis decreed for your satisfactione, thare estates being as yet engadged for the same, and that if compleet payment of the moneyis due unto you be not whollie payed before the tenthe of Junij nixt, you are to enter to the full possessione of all that estate, by schortnes of which time, and, as wee are informed, of thare hard estate to raise those moneyis occasioned by thare brethens soe contracted for paying of you, they are likelie to lose what they have debursed in his behalff (the estate of Couldinghame being the means by which they can expect releeff), oure desire now is, that iff your moneyis, both principall and annuellis, be not payed unto you at that time, you will ether tak such a pairt of that estate as is proportionable to what is justlie due unto him, or otherwayis, that upon sufficient suretie to be given you by them, you will give them the terme of Mertimes nixt for doing thareoff, which wee will take as a favour done unto us; and if they doe not at that time give you compleit satisfactione of what you can justlie demand, wee will never heerefter meddle further in that purpose: Soe desyring your resoluceone heirin to be imparted to the said creditouris, wee bid you, &c.— Whitehall, the fourt day of May 1630.

To the Chancellar and Precedent.

Letter upon the same subject and of the same date.

To the Counsell.

Right, &c.—The inclosed peticeon being presented unto us, Our pleasour is, that you give such ordour for the peticeoner's satisfactione tharein as may best tend to the exact triall of those offences according to the lawes of that our kingdome, and as may best stand with the case of our good subjectis; and to that effect that the peticeoner may have such freedome as is requisit for prosecutione of the triall till it be finallie determined according to justice.—Whitehall, the 4 of May 1630.

To the Erle of Lynlituquho.

Right, &c.—Whereas wee have been informed, in behalff of Captains Andersone and Daw, and thare owners, that since ordour was given for release of the tuoe schippis, alledged to be of Calias, taken by them, it is found by certificat of divers honest men that they did belong to Dunkirk and Ostend: howso-ever, wee are confident that your decreit was pronunced according as at the giving thareof you found just evidence; yet becaus thare demand (seeming to proceed upon forther knowledge of the treuth of theis proceedingis) is only that the same may be tryed according to justice before theis shippis be put from thence, without any long stay or charge of the owners, Wee are heirby pleased (if any ground shall appeir of what is alledged) that, according to the demand of the peticeone which wee have sent you heirwith enclosed, a time requisit for the tryeing of what is alledged be granted, and that a course be taken accordingly for that effect: Which purpose seriou-lie recommending unto your care, Wee bid you, &c.— Whitehall, the seventh of May 1630.

To the Advocat.

Trustie, &c.—We greet you weel, and do thank you hartefullie for the care you have haue, according to oure directione, to prevent any prejudice that might have come unto us by means of the act of prescriptione, and wee are verie confident that the act made in Sessione wilbe sufficient for that purpos; yet in regard of the doubt thareof made by some, apprehending what objectiones are in possibilitie to be made heireftter touching the same, after you have advised with our Chancellare (if he be thare, whare in due time you may meet with him), and that you find it necessarie to proceed in some legall maner as shalbe thought most fitt by you for our better assurance, ether to strengthen oure title (iff need be) or to prevent any inconvenience that in liklichead may arise tharein : Oure pleasoure is, that with diligence you raise summondis, or tak any other course thought necessarie by you for this purpose, against all persones interested in such thingis, whareunto wee have just clame, and from which we have not alreadie secludit ourselves be our declaratione concerning our revocatione, excepting such persones who have submitted themselves unto us for such thingis as by vertew of thare submissiones are comprehendit within our decree : Soe not doubting bot you will vse your best endevouris heiriu, wee bid you fareweel.—Whitehall, the 13 day of May 1630.

To Sir Williame Alexander.

Trustie, &c.—Haveing understood by your lettre, and more ample by report of others of the good success of your voyage, and of the carefull and provident proceeding for planting of a colonie at Port Royall, which may be a means to settle all that cuntrie in obedience, wee give you hartlie thankis for the same, and doe wish you (as wee are confident you will) to continow as you have begune, that the wark may be brought to the intendit perfectione, which wee will esteem as one of the most singulare services done unto us and of you accordinglie, and of everie one of your company that have been good instrumentis in the same, as wee shall have a testimonie of them from you : Soe recommending unto you that you have a speciall care before you return to tak a good course for government of the Colonie during your absence, Wee bid you fareweell.—Whitehall, the 13 day of May 1630.

To the Sessione.

Right, &c.—Being informed that . . . the Erle of Annandale haveing purchased from umquhill Sir Robert Gordoune of Lochinevarr some landis in Irland, whareunto . . . Sir Archebald Achesone, secretarie for that our kingdome, pretendit right; and that it is necessarie that the differences depending thareupoue between them be decided according to the course of justice of the kingdome whare the landis dois lye : Oure pleasoure is, if any actione touching that purpos bee which hath relatioune thareunto shall happen to come before you, that the same be suspendit unto such time as you be certified of the proceedingis thareof in Irland, and then (if need be) that you proceed tharin as you shall find just caus, according to justice.—Whitehall, the 13 day of May 1630.

To the Exchecquer.

Right, &c.—Whareas . . . Sir Johne Scot hath shewen us a way how the Landis of the erectiones may be payed without any money to be given by our thesaurer unto them, by giving of new rightis by us vpon the saidis Lordis and thare vasselis owne resignationes to all such as have clauses irritant in thare out writtes without the saidis clauses ; ffor the which favour we are informed that they wilbe willing everie one to pay for the proportione of thare owne landis to the saidis Lordis, that heirefter they may get from us new writtes, and wee may thareby have our rent of our croune incressed by thare dueties : And as for the rest of the vassellis whoe have not clauses irritant in their ould writtis, it is thought fitt that for some few yeers' discharge of thare few dueties in time coming thay wilbe content to pay thare partis of the saidis fewes to the said Lordis of erectiones, the particulars whareof he is willing to use his best endevouris to cleir unto you : Tharefore we will you to tak theis things into your consideratiounes, and if you find the same profitable for us and our estate, Wee desire you to informe yourssellis of the same by the said Sir Johne, which being cleer, that you goe on in prosecuting of the same for the weell of our service, advertcising us what expectatione you have of the succes of this bussienes, and of what other overtour the said Sir Johne shall propone for the advancement and incres of our estate thare, and certicfieing us of your opinion tharein, that we may caus them be prosecuted, and may reward the said Sir Johne as the succes of the service being perfited may merit and deserve at our hand : Soe, &c.—Whitehall, the 21 May 1630.

[No Address.]

Trustie, &c.—Haveing commandit Frances Steuart to give notice to the noblemen whoe are in contraversie with him, whom wee have taken bound that he shall noewayis be prejudged in anything that is in questione betuix them by means of the act of prescriptiones what he can justlie challenge, by schewing of evidentis or by giving of them knowledge otherwayis : And heering that you have divers wreittis and evidentis belonging to the said Frances in your handis : Tharefore we have thought fitt to desire you that he may have of you what fortherance you can afford him, by delivering unto him all evidentis, wreittis, or otherwayis extractis thareof that are in your custodie, if you have noe just reasone for not doing of the same, as you wold not have us to think that you are accessorie to any prejudice or hurt which may arrise to him by want thareof : Soe we bid you fareweell.—Whitehall, 21 May 1630.

To the Chancellare.

Letter upon the same subject and of the same date.

To the Counsell.

Right, &c.—Whareas wee are informed that one Archebald Tod, in Edinburgh, hath been censured by you for some misdemeanoris used by him against . . . the Erle of Linlithquho, and that some persones wold have been censured againe before you for the same : Being confident that you have proceedit tharein as you at first found just caus, and holding it not fitt that he should be any forther trubled for what by you hath been alreadie considered, without thare be new groundis of a forther complaint aganis him for some other offence or misdemeanour committed by him : Oure plesoure is, that from henceforthe he be not forther pursued nor called in questione for that purpos, and to that effect that you give ordour to our advocat not to insist tharein : Which recommending unto your care, Wee bid you, &c.—Sanct James, the 21 May 1630.

To the Thesaurer and Deputie.

Right, &c.—The widow of one Peter Sandersone, whoe (as wee are informed) hade long and faithfullie served oure late royall mother, of worthie memorie, haveing peticoned us to have those moneyis payed unto hir which by him wer debursed for our said mother's service, the accomptis whareof appearing under hand, and the Lord Nepare, our deputie thesaurer, haveing certifieid under his hand that no allowance hath been taken in Exchecquer for thrie thousand ᶫⁱᵇ· Scotis moneyis of those accomptis : Oure pleasour is, that you pay unto hir or hir assignees the said soume of 3000ᶫⁱᵇ· Scotis out of the first and reddiest of our rentis and casualities whatsoever in that our kingdome, and that with as much diligence as convenientlie may be ; and for your warrand, &c.—Whitehall, the 21 May 1630.

To THE COUNSELL.

Right, &c.—Whareas wee have writen our princelie directione unto our commissioners of parliament to prorogat and continow the same unto the first day of Aprill nixtocum, whareby wee may have some more time and leasour to be thare in persone at the said parliament, and to receave our croune for the peace and securitie of that our native and ancient kingdome : Oure pleasoure tharefor is, and wee doe heirby authorise, will, and require you, that after the said parliament shalbe prorogated and continoued as said is, you caus intimat at the said prorogatione and continuatione to all our good lieges within our said kingdome, by oppen proclamatione at the merkat crose of Edinburgh, and all other places needfull, and warne all prelattes, noblemen, commissioners for barrones and burrowis, and all others haveing place to voit or owing attendance in the said supream court of parliament, to attend and waite upon the same the foirsaid day, with continouatione of dayis ; and to performe all and sindrie other thingis as to thare places and offices doth apperteen : And for doing the premissis theis our lettres shalbe unto you and everie of you from time to time a sufficient warrand and discharge in that behalf.—Whitehall, the 26 May 1630.

To THE COMMISSIONERS OF PARLIAMENT.

Letter upon the Meeting of parliament as above, and of the same date.

To THE COUNSELL.

Letter upon the same subject and of the same date.

To THE CHANCELLARE.

Right, &c.—We are pleased for certane good respectis to discharge the rycht reverend father in God . . . the Archbischopp of St Androis of the taxatione due to us for his parte of the Archbischoprik of St Androis and the benefices annexit ; and tharefter willis you, our collectour of the said taxatione, to grant unto him your discharge and acquittance thareof for the termes bypast, which shalbe allowed unto you in your accomptis, likeas thir presentis shalbe unto you a sufficient discharge and exoneratione in that part.—Whitehall, the 26 May 1630.

To THE COUNSELL.

Right, &c.—Understanding what contentment it will give to you and to all our loving subjectis to know that it hath pleased God to bliss us with ane sone, Wee have thought good with all diligence to adverteis you heirof to the effect, that publict notice being given heirof, they may expres thare joy in such soleme maner as is requisit, or at any time heirtofore have been used : In doing whareof wee are verie confident of your hartie affectione, and doe bid you hartly fareweell.—Whitehall, the 29 May 1630.

These conteyne your Maᵗⁱˢ gift to Archibald Stewart of Hassilside, his heyres and assigneyis, of the baronie of Symonton, Right of Patronage of the Kirks and Chaplaunreis of the same, which by recognition fell at your Maᵗⁱˢ disposition by alienationis made without consent of the superiour of these landis ; the greatest part thairof ar of the rents of the same by Johne Symonton, last possessour thairof, from whom the said Archibald hath of late acquyred the heretabill right.—Whythall, the 2 of Junij.

To the Exchequer.

Right, &c.—Whareas upon considerationes knowen unto us wee did grant unto . . . the Erle of Nithesdale the gift of his lifrent and escheat, and have pleased of late to signe unto Sir Johne Maxwell of Nether Pollocke a guift of his, in respect the samen did fall at the disposing of the said Erle, as superiour of his landis, by his rebellione, as suretie for him to the effect that now forther use be made by the said Sir Johne of any benefitt that may arrise to the said Erle by the falling of Sir Johne his lifrent and escheat in his handlis : Then, in soe farr as he hath suffered by being suretie for the said Erle, Our pleasoure is, if he or any in his name shall mak it appear that this guift may be forther extendit, then, to secure the said Sir Johne from all danger of horningis as cessioner for the said Erle, that the same be remied according as heirby truelie intended, and tharefter to be passed and exped the seallis thare ; But if noething shalbe made appear contrarie to what is alledged by the said Sir Johne, that you caus exped this guift with all convenient diligence.—Whitehall, the 2 of Junij 1630.

To the Sessione.

Right, &c.—Whareas . . . Sir Thomas Dischingtoune, Knight, being imployed in our service abroad, and thare imprissoned and detayned by the space of thrie yeers or thareabout, was likewayis at home (as wee are informed) persewed by his creditouris, and others whoe intendit actiones and causes against him, taken occasione of his absence from the cuntrie and imprisonment to prejudge him in his rightis, by obtining decreettis and sentences aganis him for his not compirance at thare instance before you : Yet (as wee are likewayis informed) in regard of his absence abroad in our service, and upon other good considerations, notwithstanding of the decreittis pronunced against him, you did assigne the first day of August 1630 to him for reduceing of the saidis decreittis by course and ordour of law : Seing that the prefixed time limited by you for his compirance is soe shortlie to expire, and his present attendance heir upon our service cannot convenientlie for a yeer more permitt him to be thare, Wee are pleased to desire you that you prorogat and continow the former limited time by you for his compirance unto that space or for such a time as you in your judgment shall think fitt, that he may reap the benefitt of the favour first intendit by you for him : The doing whareof, in regard of his good and faithfull service done to us, both at home and abroad, wee would not bot earnestlie recommend to you care : Soo we, &c.—Whitehall, the 2 Junij 1630.

To the Counsell.

Right, &c.—Whareas complaint hethe bein made unto us by Sir James Lockard, gentleman of our privie chamber in ordinare, that one Porteous of Hakshaw, and his eldest sone, being outlawes, and ordinerlie sheltering themselves from justice in the bordouris of this oure kingdome, did, in contempt of oure authoritie and lawes, abuse his tennentis of the landis of Fingland and Carterhope, beat and spoill thare cattell and goodis, and thrust them from thare possessiones : 'Oure pleasoure is, iff you find any just caus wharupon this complaint is grounded, that you caus those persones come before you, and if you find that they have offendit in this kind, that you caus inflict such exemplare punishment upon them as may terrifie others to attempt the like heirefter; and if they will not compeir, that you give such speedie ordour for the inbringing of them as you shall think fitt, taking the most expedient course, as our lawes will permitt for his repossessione of theis landis : Which recommending unto your care, wee bid, &c.— Whitehall, the secund day of Junij 1630.

To the Sessione.

Letter upon the same subject and of the same date.

A Precept to the Exchecquer.

Whareas the Reverend father in God, Johne, Bischopp of the Iles, hathe done unto us many good and acceptable services, both at home and abroad, whareof wee have taken speciall notice : Tharefor, and for divers others good and considerable causes knowen unto us, Oure pleasoure is, that with all possible diligence you pay or caus be payed unto the said Johne, Bischopp of the Iles, or his assigney, the somme of sex hunderith poundis sterling, and that out of the first and readiest of our rentis, dueties, and casualities, or other benefitt whatsoever now dew unto us, or which heirefter shallhappin to be due and accres to us in our kingdome of Scotland, or out of any of the first taxationes that shalbe granted unto us thare : ffor your doing whareof, &c.—Whitehall, the 2 Junij 1630.

To James Carmichell.

Trustie, &c.—Whareas we wer pleased heirtofore to mak use of your service for improveing of our rentis and casualities of our principalitie in our kingdome of Scotland, wharein you have done us good and acceptable service : And now seing wee, with the advise of the Lordis of our Exchecquer of that our kingdome, have been pleased to grant a commissione to Sir Alexander Straquhen of Thornetoune, Knight, to receave and call for all our rentis and casualities due unto us by whatsoever maner of way, ether within the regalitie or principalitie of that our kingdome, before the penult day of March in anno 1628, not duelie brought in and accompted to our use in our Exchecquer before that day, reserving unto us such a proportione of the free benefitt thought fitting, and as expressed in the said commissione : And our intentione being to give him all the lauchfull fortherance wee can for prosecutione of our said commissione, Oure plesour is, that you contribute your best endevouris, knowledge, and experience to assist him tharein, as you will answer unto us, which wee will esteeme as acceptable service, whareof wee will not be unmyndfull. —Whitehall, the second of Junij 1630.

To the Thesaurer and Deputie Thesaurer.

Right, &c.—In regard of the trew and faithfull service done unto our late deir father and us by . . . . Thomas, Erle of Kellie, and for divers others respectis, wee are willing to gratiefie Elizabeth Moubray, his grandchild, for forthering of her mariage by bestoweing on her the benefitt of a ward of mariage within that our kingdome : Tharefore our plesour is, and wee will and require you, whensoever the first ward of mariage such as you shall think fitt for hir shalhappin to fall in our handis, that you let her have the benefitt, soe paying unto us the ordinarie compositione due unto us for the same : And for your soe doing these presentis shalbe unto you a sufficient warrand.—Whitehall, 2 Junij 1630.

To the Commissioners of Surrenders.

Right, &c.—Whareas the Erle of Abercorne hath been humble suter unto us that, in regard of his present affairs, he might have libertie to sell his tithes to the heretouris, he alwayis performing and being liable in particulare touching them according to what in the generall is preseryved by our decree, or as others in the like kind shall happen for our interest to performe touching thare tithes : But being carefull least anything be done that ether directly or by the consequence might hinder the generall work that is intended for the good of that our kingdome, wee will not proceed tharein without due advise : Tharefore our plesour is, that you tak his demand into your consideratione, and haveing advised with oure Advocat, or others whome you shall think fitt, that you give way to any purpose that most convenientlie may be taken by him for his satisfactione heirin, without prejudice for our interest, as is above said, and the decree givine by us for appointing the price and quantitie of tithes in the valuatione, wharof wee are confident that you will cause proceed according to the course alreadie preseryved or to be preseryved by you, in caice you shall find just caus to prevent any thing that may hinder a faire and equitable proceeding tharein.—Whitehall, 4 Junij 1630.

To the Erle of Rothes.

Right, &c.—Right, &c.—Wee have receaved your lettre, with ane informatione from Sir Thomas Dischingtoune, Knight, concerning the erection of the Abbacie of Lendoris ; and, conforme to your desire, wee have writen to our Advocat for heering and considering of your groundis, which, if they be found valide, Wee are heirby pleased to give you assurance that you shalbe rewarded as the success of the service doth deserve at our hand.—Whitehall, the 4 of Junij 1630.

To the Advocat.

Letter upon the same subject and of the same date.

Our soveraigne Lord ordeanes a Letter to be made vnder the Great Seall of Scotland, making mention that his Matie vnder-tanding that a number of persones in the said kingdome have transgressed the acts of Parliament made in Anno 1621 aganst the concealers of lent moneyis vngevin vp in Inventaris in the sheriff bookis and bookis of other Judges within that kingdome, and aganst the wrongous vpgivers in these bookis of moneys alledged owing by them to ther creditours for not payment of ther part of the saids taxatiounis granted in the said yeir, and in the yeir 1625, wherof his Maties Right, &c. the Viscount of Dupline, Lord Chancellour, and the Earle of Mar were Collectours : And his Majestie being gratiouslie pleased to cause proceede with the delinquents, as his highnes commissioners eftermentionat shall think fitt to be moderated by them, and componed with the saidis delinquents, and as best may terrifie all others heirefter to committ the lyk great and dangerous abuses in contempt of his Maties authoritie and Lawis, without causeing putt to the full executioun aganst them what be the said act is provyded in the cases, vnless the saids Commissioners shall find a just reasone in the contrair, ather in the behalff of some number or some particular persones, and for some speciall respects as ther continewing in contempt and neglect to compone and agrie for ther transgressions, or for some other causes thoght fitt be the saids Commissioners for the reformation of such a dangerous abuse : Thereftir his Majestie have thoght fitt to committ the trust and manageing of this bussines to such selected persones as he knowis to be well affected to his service and carefull of the well of his people ; and haveing good prooff and experience of his Right, &c. the Viscount of Daplin, Lord Chancellour, William Erle of Morton, Lord Thesaurer, William Erle of Monteith, President of his Majesteis Privie Counsall, Thomas Erle of Hadinton, Lord Privie Seall, Sir William Alexander, Principall Secretarie for Scotland, Sir Thomas Hope, his Ma^{tcis} Advocat, and the Thesaurer-deputie for the tyme, Giving, granting, and committing, lykas his Matie doeth heirby Give, grant, and committ to them, or any tuo of them, with the said Thesaurer, full power and commission to compone, transact, and agrie, with all persones alreadie tryed and fund guiltie, or that heirefter shalbe tryed and fund guiltie in offending against the said Act, for such sowmes of money as they shall pay vnto his Majestie for the penaltie incurred be them ; which composition to be made with them, and the moneyis componed for being payed for his Ma^{teis} vse to the said Thesaurer or his deputie or deputeis authorized be him, and his or his forsaids acquittaneis and discherges gevin thervpon, His Matie decernes and declairis that the saidis acquittances and discharges so to be gevin shalbe as sufficient exoneration to the persones offending in this kynd as if everie one of them had a particular pardon vnder his Majesteis great seall : And lykwyse with full power and authoritie to the saidis Commissioners to call for and intromet with all such part or ports of the saidis taxatiouns as have bene intromitted with be the saids Collectours, ther deputts or vnder receavers, or any vther persone or persones whatsumever, whairof they or any of them have not made accompt of in Exchcker, or which have not bene imployed be them be particular warrandis from his Matie, which moneyis being lykwyse delyvered to his Ma^{teis} said Thesaurer, his acquittance or acquittances vpon receipt thairof shalbe a sufficient exoneratioun and discharge to the said Lord Chancellour and Erle of Mar, ther deputeis, vnder receavers, and vthers as aforsaid for the delyverie thairof in maner above writtin, and generallie with full power and commission to the saidis Commissioners to doe and exercise, &c., firme and stable, &c., and that the said Letter be extendit in the best forme, with all claussis neidful ; and his Matie ordanes this present signature to be a sufficient warrant to the directour of his Majestie's Chancerie for wryting of the said Commission, and to his Ma^{teis} Chancellour for appending his highnes great seall therto without any precept to be passed for that effect vnder his Ma^{teis} signet or privie seall —Gevin at Whythall, the ellevint of Junij 1630.

Our Soveraigne Lord ordeanes a Letter to be made vnder his highnes great seall of Scotland, Makand mention that wheras his Ma^{teis} trustie and weilbeloved Mr David Fullerton, one of the receavers of his Ma^{teis} rents of the said kingdome, did by speciall direction from his Matie receave for his Ma^{teis} vse, for provisions and other things fitt to be in readines at his Ma^{teis} intended goeing at that tyme to the said kingdome, from some persones in his Ma^{teis} kingdome speciallie entrusted in some of his Ma^{teis} affaires, the sowme of eight thowsand pundis sterling money ; and his Matie haveing now vpoun good consideratiouns, and for the well of his service in the said kingdome of Scotland, made speciall choyse of his Ma^{teis} right, &c. the Erle of Morton to be his Ma^{teis} Thesaurer thairof (who by reasone of the great want of moneyis at this tyme in his Ma^{teis} Exchequer occasioned vpon many and important causes) is to seik all the lawfull wayes and meanes wherby moneyis may be had for dischargeing such necessar affaires as his Matie at this tyme hath speciallie entrusted vnto him, and as speciallie doe concerne the good of his Ma^{teis} present and vrgent affaires to be performed ther : Therfore his Matie, and for diverse other good consideratiouns moveing his highnes, have gevin, granted, and committed, lykas his Matie be thir presentis Gives, grants, and committs vnto him his Ma^{teis} full power and commission to call for ane accompt of the said sowme of Eight thowsand pundis, and everie part thairof, at the handis of the said Mr David Fullerton, and at the handis of any other officers whatsoever, persone or persones to whome the saidis moneyis, or any part thairof, had bene delyvered by the said Mr David, wherof accompt hath not bene made be him and them, or any of them, in Exchecker, to be made appear vnto the said Thesaurer, and which he the said Mr David or any of the saidis persones hath not bene alreadie imployed by his Ma^{teis} speciall warrand appearing vnder his highnes' hand, and for the speciall vse of his Ma^{teis} service, with full power and commission to the said Thesaurer to receave and vplift from the said Mr David, or from other persones as aforesaid, the said sowme of eight thowsand pundis, or such part or parts thairof as hath not bene made accompt of in Exchequer as aforsaid, and particularlie imployed by speciall warrand from his Matie, and for the vse of his Ma^{teis} service, as said is, And with power to his Matie said Thesaurer to dispose thairof for the good of his Matie said service : And his Matie doeth heirby declare that the said Thesaurer his acquittance or acquittances granted vpoun the receipt thairof, or any part thairof, pro tanto, shalbe as sufficient exoneration and discherge to the said Mr David, and others officers and persones aforesaid, as if he and everie of them wer particularlie discherged be his Matie efter what maner they could best devyse, and with power to the said Thesaurer all and sindrie vther thingis to doe, vse, and exerce, &c., firme and stable, &c. : And that the said Letter be extendit in the best forme, with all clausses neidfull : And his Matie ordeanes this present signature to be a sufficient warrant to the directour of his Ma^{teis} Chancerie for wryting of the said commission, and to his Ma^{teis} Chancellour for appending the great seall thairto, without any precept to be past for that effect vnder his Ma^{teis} signet or privie seall.—Gevin at Whythall, the 11 of Junij 1630

To the Advocat.

Trustie, &c.—Wee haveing at some lenth writen to our Exchecquer touching some causes of the resignatione to be made in our favouris by the Reverend father in God the Bischopp of the Iles, which you, as one of that number, will perceave, Oure pleasoure is, that you draw upp in sure maner a resignatione of the superiorities, temporall landis, and benefices whatsoever of the Bischoprik of the Iles, the Abbacie and Nunrie of Icolmekill, and Priories of Ardchatan and Orensey, or of any other landis, superioritie, and benefices belonging and annexit to that Bischoprik, reserving specialie the spiritualitie thairof, whereby he may provide the ministerie in that diocie, that wee be not heirefter burdened with thare mantenance : And thareffter that you in our name intend proces and insist by law for drawing bak of that temporall estate for our use, in soe far as justly and laufullie can bee done by you ; at the full recoverie whareof wee will (according to our royall promies made unto the said Bischopp) that the same be restored unto him or his successouris Bischoppis of the Iles, oure yeerlie allowance of thrie hunderith pundis sterling granted unto him being at that time drawen bak to our Exchecquer : Soe, not doubting but that you will prosecute this purpose without exceptione of persones or occasions, haveing legall and convenient groundis for doing thareof, wee, &c.—Whitehall, the eleventh day of Junij 1630.

To the Exchecquer.

Letter similar to the above and of the same date.

To the Exchecquer.

Right, &c.—Whareas upon divers good and important consideratiounes, and for advancement of our service, wee wer pleased in August last to grant vnto .   .   the Earle of Monteathe, precedent of our privie counsell, and our Justice Generall of that our kingdome, a warrant for fyve thousand poundis sterling, knowing how much his abilities, care, and affectione hath advanced the same, and may heirefter contribute therunto : Our speciall pleasure is, that you pay unto him the said somme, or his assignais, according to our said warrand ; But if the same cannot possebillie be payed at this time, in respect of the present wantis in our Exchecquer, that after the ensueing terme of Mertimes, you pay unto him or them, out of the first and reddiest of our rentis, casualities, and taxationes, present and to come, belonging unto us, ordinarie interest for the time of the forbearance thereof (as he might pay unto others); and for his further suretie, that you mak ane act of Exchekquer heirupon : And for your soe doing, these shalbe unto you and averie of you a sufficient warrand and discharge.—Whitehall, the eleventh of Junij 1630.

INSTRUCTIONES TO THE EXCHECQUER.

Right, &c.—Whareas, upon good and important respectis we have at this time given some instruc-tiones to . . . the Erle of Mortoune, our thesaurer, to be by him put in execution, in soe farr as they or any of them shalbe found titt, for the good of our service and the publict good of that our kingdome : Oure pleasoure is, that you grant unto him actis of counsell and Exchecquer upon the said instructiones, or any of them, and what assistance he shall demand, touching the more speedie prosecutione of the same. —Whitehall, the eleventhe of Junij 1630.

TO THE TWOE RECEAVERS.

Trustie, &c.—Whareas the present wantis in our Exchecquer are weell knowen unto you, and the great burtheans undergone by . . . the Erle of Mortoune, our Thesaurer, hathe made us conclude with him, bothe for the urgent dispatche of our present affairs thare, requiring the greatest diligence that can be used, and for his oune releeff of the saidis burdeans, to tak the most exact and speediest way (whareby he may be the more able to be answerable unto us in his charge) ffor leavieing of our rentis and casualities whatsoever belong'ng unto us in that our kingdome : Oure pleasoure tharefor is, that you pay not any moneyis whatsoever belonging unto us, upon any warrant or occasione whatsoever, without speciall directione of our said Thesaurer.—Whitehall, the eleventh of Junij 1630.

TO THE CHANCELLARE.

Right, &c.—Whareas the Erle of Mortoune, our thesaurer of that our kingdome, hathe been stayed heir upon some speciall occasiones concerning our service, and upon hope to have receaved that supplie intendit for him by us, soe that he could not soe quicklie repair thither for dispatch of such thingis as doe concerne his charge from us as was requisit, nether yet tak that course with his creditouris at this time as by them may be expected, in regard he is with all convenient diligence to repair thither : Oure plesoure is, that you (if need be) acquent them with the estate thareof : and in the meantime, if you shall find the estate of his affairs soe to require, to deall with his creditouris in a freendlie maner, to forbear any insisting against him till his homecumming, and wee doubt not but he will shortlie be enabled to give them satisfactione : Wee bid, &c.—Whitehall, the eleventh day of Junij 1630.

TO MR DAVID FULLERTONE.

Trustie, &c.—Though wee doubt not of your care and affection in the charge you have from us, yet, haveing at this time speciallie entrusted the dispatche of divers our most waightie and urgent affairs in that our kingdome unto the Erle of Mortoune, our thesaurer, whoe (by reasone of the present wantis in our Excheckquer, not unknowen unto you) can hardlie rease readie moneyis for that purpose, Wee, for his more timelie doing thareof, have caused considder of all the laufull wayis and means that can be devised for his better releeff and fortherance therein : Wharupon, considering howe wee wer pleased to deliver unto you heir, for our use thare, Eight thousand poundis sterling, we have been the rather pleased, in respect that divers of theis moneyis are (as wee are informed) out of your handis, to grant unto him a commissione for taking a compt of that soume : Tharefore oure plesour is, that you give him such light heirin as can be given by you, and that you forthwith deliver upp to him such parte of the same as you have in our charge, and which you have not as yet payed out of your handis by speciall warrand appeiring under our hand : Soe wee, &c.—Whitehall, the eleventh day of Junij 1630.

To the Erle of Marr.

Right, &c.—Whareas wee were formerlie pleased to grant commission for componing with such persones whoe, contrarie to the act of parliament made in anno 1621, wald defraud us of our taxationes, wherin you wer cheeflie entrusted in making the compositiones, which being agreed upon, wer onlie to have been delivered unto you : Though wee have found by good effectis the great care and affectione you have to our service, both in time of our late deir father and in our owne, and are still confident that you wold discharge yourselff weell therein ; yet, haveing at this time speciallie entrusted the dispatch of divers our most weyghtie and urgent affairs unto our thesaurer, whoe, by reasone of the present wantis in our Exchecquer, weell knowen unto you, can hardlie rais moneyis for that purpos, haveing undergone soe great burtheans for your releeff in our service, Wee, for the better and more timelie supplieing of these wantis, have caused considder of all lawfull wayis and means for that purpose, and doe find non more lawfull and fitt than to grant a commissione of new for compounding with such transgressouris of our lawes with whome no compositione hath been alreadie made : Oure pleasoure is, that you accompt with our said Thesaurer touching the compositiones given to you by reasone of any commissiones granted by us concerning the reformeing of that abuse ; and that yee deliver upp unto him, for the use of our speciall service, such moneyis thareof as have been resaved in your name, and not imployed alreadie for our service, leaving (for the speciall causes aforisaid) to proceed heirefter by vertew of any former commissione granted to you for this purpose ; and in all other thingis concerning the prosecutione of our service heirin, that you give him your best advice and assistance, which wee will tak as a most acceptable service done unto us.—Whitehall, the eleventh day of Junij 1630.

To the Exchecquer Thesaurer.—Securitie concerning Marr.

Right, &c.—Whareas out of our princelie respect to . . . the Erle of Marr, and royall intentione that non of our subjectis suffer for thare affectione to our service, Wee have moved our Thesaurer to engage himselff and freendis for paying of Ten thousand poundis sterling to the said Erle of Marr (which wee wer pleased to bestow upon him as a mark of our princelie favour for his bypast services), and for releeffing of him of all soumes of money levied and expendit by him for oure use, and of the super expensis of his accomptis in the charge he hade from us, wharcby, finding our selffis in honour [bound] to provide for our said Thesaurer's releeff since he and his freendis have undergone theis burdingis for the good of our service, being besidis to leavie great soumes of money for our necessare charges during our abroad in that our kingdome : Oure pleasoure is (for his and thare more frie and readie payment of theis moneyis), that thare be granted unto him and them, and such of them as shalhappen to be bound with him heirefter for the purpos abonesaid, what securitie he shall require upon any of our rentis, casualities, taxationes, present and to cum, in generall or particulare assignementis, and that he and they be secured in maner foirsaid upon any benefitt present, or which heirefter shallhappen to be payed unto our Exchecquer for whatsoever caus, by whatsoever persones or maner of way, and that to be instantlie secured unto him and them by actis of counsell, Exchecquer, or otherwayis as they shall devise, and that all impedimentis in thare uptaking of the saidis moneyis by all or any of the wayis foirsaid be by you removed till they be compleitlie satisfiet of all the said particular soumes for which they are alreadie engadged, or shallhappin heirefter to be engadged for the saidis causes, with ordinarie interest for the same (as it is payed by them to thare creditouris) during the time of the forbearance thareof : And whareas wee have given preceptis and warrantis for payment of great soumes of money to many of our servantis and subjectis, which wee intend by all readie wayis and means to caus pay unto them after the payment of the moneyis abonesaid to our Thesaurer, the doing whareof doeth soe neerlie concern the gud of our service, Wee will you to restrain theis preceptis and pensiones till hee and they be first releiffed ; and that you suffer no precept nor pensione whatsoever to pas in Exchecquer heirefter till you provide that the passing thairoff doe not prejudge our said Thesaurer and his foirsaidis payment and releeff, and that furthwith you caus registrat thir presentis in the bookis of Exchecquer.—[No date.]

To the Exchecquer.

Right, &c.—Wheras we ar formerlie pleased to grant to . . . Robert Buchan a precept receaved and allowed lykwyse in our Exchecker, for moneyis dew by ws vnto him for the pearle hussines ; in regard (as we ar informed by him) the greatest part of the said moneyis restand yet vnpayed to him, As also at this tyme for certane quantitie of his most choyse pearle receaved by ws, wherwith we ar weil pleased : Our expres will and pleasur therfor is, that with all speed yow mak present payment to the said Robert Buchan or his assigneis, as weill for the said pearles now receaved, according to a precept vnder our royall signature to him gevin for the same, as also for such moneyis as are vnpayed to him of his former precept, in regard he hath long wanted the same, contrarie to our royall intention and warrand : And for your soe doeing these presents shalbe vnto yow, and everie of yow, a sufficient warrand and discherge.—Gevin at St James', the 14 Junij, in the sixt yeir of our Regne.

To the Generall Convention.

Right, &c.—Wheras we have bene humblie moved, in behalff of . . . Robt Buchan, that ather some moneyis might be levyed from all such persones ther as would willinglie contribute to the repairing and vpholding of the way, called the King's Calsey, in Courmont, being the ordinarie road from the north to the south parts of that our kingdome ; or, if any landis can be fund formerlie appropriated for vpholding therof, that the rents of the same may be converted to ther vse. The intention seameing to intend to a publict good, many persones being much troubled (as we ar informed) in ther passage by decay of the way, we have bene the rather pleased to tak notice of this purpois, and to recommend it to yow, that if you find the passage fit to be helped, yow consider of the expedience of the demands ; and if any of them (thoght most litt by yow) can be lawfullie and convenientlie granted in such maner as by yow shall be thoght most litt and requisite to be preservyed for the repairing and vpholding of that way heirefter, And if any motion or expedient shalbe proposed vnto yow by the said Robert tuitching this purpois, we ar willing (if you think the same litt to be granted) that yow give way thervnto, In regard of his earnestnes to sie that work effected, wherof (in respect, as we ar informed, of the nearnes of his duelling to that passage) we think fitt that he have the charge; which recommending to your care.—Whythall, 14 Junij 1630.

To the Commissioners for Surrenders.

Right, &c.—Whareas wee have given our determinatione upon that which was submitted to us concerning tithes, appointing price and the maner of the payment that the heretouris should performe for the same, which accordinglie wee desire to tak effect: But being informed that thare is ane great hinderance heirin by the slow progres of the valuationes, occasioned by some indirect means used in the same, and that divers heretouris and titulars are earnest to conclude for thare tithes according to our decree: Oure pleasure is, that you use all reasonable means in hastening the valuationes, and in the meantime that you tak a course with diligence for preventing any inconvenient that may come by leading of tithes, by appointing the titulars who have poware to caus value the tithes which they wer accustomed to lead to doe it before the time of the nixt leading, that the heretouris may lead the tithes of his owne landis, paying or securing thare tithemaisters for the same according to the valuationes made or to be made, ffor wee sie noe reasone why the heretour should not posses his owne tithes if he ether satisfie according to our decree, or till the valuationes be perfeetit (whare the delay is not his fault), pay or secure by your appointment the titular, conforme to the said valuatione made or to be made, at least noe lettres of spoliatione should be granted in that caice, the expeditione whareof we will you to tak in your consideratione and signifie the same to our Colledge of Justice; and wee doe not esteem any partie, ether titular or heretour, of the benefitt of our decree, in whose default the perfectione of that work is hindered, the speedie perfecting whareof we specialie recommend unto your care, leaving the means whare they are not cleir to your owne judgment: Soe we, &c.—Whitehall, the 14 Junij 1630.

To the Exchecquer.

Right, &c.—Whareas wee have been pleased at this time to grant thrie thousand poundis sterling unto . . . the Erle of Monteith, president of our Privie Counsell, upon verie good and weightie consideratiounes specialie importing us, mentioned in our guift granted tharevpone, becaus both the caus and maner of his proceeding with us touching that purpose deserve a speciall consideratione: Oure pleasoure is, that with all diligence you signe and caus exped the said gift, and (if need be) that noe possible or lawfull means be wanting upon your partis for causing answer, and pay the same unto him or his assignes accordinglie, which wee will accept as verie good service done unto us: Soe wee, &c.—Whitehall, 14 Junij 1630.

To the Exchecquer.

Letter similar to the above, with grant of £2000 sterling made to Sir Thomas Hope, of the same date.

To the Counsell.

Right, &c.—Whareas wee have been pleased to signe a remissione unto one Robert Millare, upon informatione made unto us that it cannot be proved against him that the death of one Patrik Craw (suspected to have been procured by him) did anywayis happen by his meanis: But he, fearing least his enemyes should have taken his life before he should be hard to answer for himself, was forced for many yeirs to abandone his house and leave his poore wiff and childring in extreme miserie : Oure pleasoure is, that you, after triall heirof, if noe thing can reallie appear wharebye the death of the said Craw can justlie be layed unto his charge, that with all convenient diligence you pas and exped the said remissione : Soe we, &c.—Whitehall, the 14 Junij 1630.

TO THE THESAURER AND DEPUTIE THESAURER.

Right, &c.—Whareas wee have receaved of . . . Robert Buchan a certain quantitie of his most choice pearle, wharebye wee are weell pleased, which, after true valuatione by our Jewellars, are found to be worthie of the soume of four scoir fyve pundis sterling, Oure express will and plesour is, that you mak present payment unto the said Robert Buchane, or his assiguais, of the said soume : And for your soe doing these, &c.—Given at St James, the 14 Junij 1630.

TO THE MARQUES OF HUNTLIE.

Right, &c.—Being credibillie informed that James and Alaster Grantis, being accompanied with a nomber of other rebellis to the number of fyve or sex scoir, have, in great contempt of our auctoritie and lawes, banded themselves, and in oppen and braving manner oppressed some of our good subjectis in these partes, especiallie such as dwell upon the landis of the Laird of Freu bright ; and having heard that they are assisted by some of your tennentis and followers, whareat wee did verie much wonder, seing wee expected that noe thing concerning our service in using your best endevoiris to settle peace in these partis should have been neglected by you, though not warranted from us or our counsell thare : Oure pleasour is, you haveing particularlie informed yourself of these rebellis, and of thare hantis and residentis, that you [take] the first opportunitie of comming or being within your boundis, whare ye are knowen to have any command or freendship, and that you apprehend and send them to our counsell or Justice Generall for undergoing such punishment as thare offenses shalbe found justlie to meritt : And as wee will not think weel of any neglect or delay heirin upon your part, soe if you doe proceed (as wee doubt not) according to our royall plesour heirin, wee will accompt it is a verie acceptable service done to us, whareof wee will not be unmyndfull when any occasione shall offer wharebye wee may laufully and conveniently expres our respect unto you.—Whitehall, the 15 day of Junij 1630.

TO THE LAIRD OF GRANT.

Letter to the same effect and in similar terms of the same date.

TO THE CLERK REGISTER.

Trustie, &c.—Whareas . . . the Earle of Angus hath at this tyme (as we ar crediblie informed) speciall occasion to sie some writts and records, wherof yow have the charge from ws : Our pleasur is, that with diligence, and at seasonable times, yow mak the same patent vnto him, or to any persone or persones in his name ; and that yow ather sie the search made yourself, or else suffer him or them to mak it, and to tak the Extracts of such things as may any wayes concerne him : And for your soe doing, &c.—Whythall, 22 Junij 1630.

To the Counsell.

Right, &c.—Wheras we ar importuned by diverse petitions from Alexander Hay, Indueller in Leith, compleyning upon a wrong done by letters directed from ws ; considering how much this did concerne ws in honour and justice, if any such just cause had bene gevin, and not onlie ws and our ministers heir, bot likewayes yow of our Counsell and session, to whom our letters wer directed, if yow or they had fund any such thing and not acquainted ws therin, we wer pleased to give ordour to such of our Counsell as wer heir for the tyme to call him before them, and to peruse the extracts of these letters, from whom it was reported to ws that his complaint did proceid from a mere calumnie, without any just caus : And as if we had fund it otherwyse we would have takin ordour therwith accordinglie, so, having understude that such seditious persones deserve to be punished, we gave ordour and caused declair our pleasur tuitching the sending of him to that our kingdome, which, since he has neglected and doeth absent him self heir, therby adding contempt of our royall direction to his former fault, Our pleasur is, that yow caus apprehend him at his comeing ther, and committ him to prissone till you have conferred tuitching this purpois with some of our privie counsell who were heir, and therefter that yow censure and caus inflict such punischment vpon him as yow shall find his offence shall deserve, taking assurance of him that vpon no occasion whatsoever he shall repair to our Court.—Whythall, 22 Junij 1630,

To the Chancellour.

Right, &c.—Our repairing to that our kingdome at the tyme appoynted not standing with the conveniencie of our present affaires, and being desyreous that these bussines that ar of most moment may be prepared, as we may have the less trouble when we come, vpon good considerations we have resolved to have a convention of our Estats at the time which the letter directit for that effect bears : And therefter these ar now to requyre you to consult togidder, that yow may adverteise ws of such things as yow conceive necessarie to be treated of ther, for our service and the good of that kingdome : And if yow find it neidfull, that yow call vnto yow any other whom yow think fitt for that purpois, and that yow acquant ws with that wherupon yow deliberat with as much diligence as possiblie can be vsed, to the effect yow may hear our last resolution, according whervnto yow ar to proceid in due tyme, ffor we desyre that nothing be proponed at that assemblie save that onlie which is warranted vnder our hand, or vnder the hand of the Clerk Register, as he shall hear from ws, ar to be allowed by yow : And so, not doubting bot that yow will have a speciall care of a matter that doeth so neirly import ws, we bid you, &c.—Whythall, the 22 Junij 1630.

To the Advocat.

Trustie, &c.—Hearing of ane Iuseftment takin by the late Lord Boyd of the halff landis of Tealing, which, by act of forfalture by one of his predicessours, wer annexed to our Cronn, as we are informed, and being vnwilling, in respect of the interest of Sir Colin Campbell, our servand, hath in these lands, for which he payeth vnto ws a great few dewtie, wher the same wer hold in ward befoir, that aither ther infeftment should be ane hinderance to our said servand in making the best vse of his right, or ane introduction to any to call in question our right to other landis belonging to ws be that forfalture, without some evident and just caus : Our pleasour is, that with all convenient diligence, efter yow have considered the grounds of our right, you intend action of reduction of that infeftment, and that yow proceid by all lawfull wayes and means for annulling the same.—Whythall, 22 Junij 1630.

To the Lord Lorne.

Right, &c.—Wheras we have sene diverse letters from our royall father tuitching the imploying and satisfieing of the Lord of Lundie for his panes and losses in that service against the Clangregour and Clandonald, cheiflie performed by him, for which your father, haveing bene acknowledged for the same, was long since to have gevin him satisfaction, as by our royall father was first appointed, to which purpois we wer lykwyse pleased to wryt at severall tymes, sieing the consideration for his some our servant's satisfaction heirin is such as doeth in honour to induce ws to repair the same, and should in equitie move your father to tak that course which convenientlie can not be taken but out of his estate which yow pay vnto him yeirlie : And sieing our servand hath bene long without satisfaction (his Lands, as we ar crediblie informed, being these many yeires burdened for the debt vndergone by his said father for that service), we have agane thoght titt to requyre yow to pay vnto him these moneyis, and annuells thairof, out of the first and readiest of that rent and moneyis payable vnto him by yow at the nixt terme, for which we will give yow thanks, and approve of your proceidings, if anything should be moved vnto ws to your disadvantage therin.—Whythall, 22 Junij 1630.

To the Exchequer.

Right, &c.—Wheras by expres letter we have formerlie requyred yow ather to expeid the Commission granted by ws to our lovit Mr William Haig, one of our solicitours, for inbringing to our vse in a legall way some sowmes resting due vnto ws of the ordinarie taxatioun in anno 1621 and 1625, or wryt bak to ws a note of such reasones against the expediencie of it as our Advocat hath not answered vnto ther, and that without tuitching vpon the caus in so far as it oght to be judged by the Lords of the Session : Notwithstanding whareof yow have not returned vnto ws any reasone against the expediencie of the same : And sieing all the power gevin by the said Commission (being onlie to bring vnto our Excheker such sowmes as in a legall way can be discovered to be due vnto ws) shall expyre, vnles in a proces against ten persones onlie, it appears that more sowmes ar due vnto ws then made compt of for the saids taxatiouns : These ar therefor to will and requyre yow that with all diligence you expeid the same, or vther wayes vryt bak vnto ws with all diligens your reasones against the expediencie : So we bid yow farewell from our Court at Whythall, 22 Junij 1630.

To the Chancellour, President, and Others of the Exchequer.

Right, &c.—Wheras humble complaynt hath bene made vnto ws by James Law, one of our heraulds, that he hath not receaved the reward due to him, provydit by Act of parliament made in anno 1621 for such persones who discover conceillers and wrongous vpgivers of ther lent money to deceave ws of our taxatiouns, and that besyds the service alreadie done by him and charges expended therin, for which he hath not receaved any satisfactione, he is able to doe ws greater service in that kynd, wherin for his better encouragment Our pleasur is, that yow hear his accompts, and if yow shall find any thing dew vnto him for his reward and disbursments, that proportionablie as he shall mak appear that any of these moneyis have bene levyed and imployed for our vse by his meanes, that he be satisfied for the same out of the readiest moneyis belonging vnto ws, togidder with his charges which shall lykwyse appear vnto yow that he hath justlie and necessarlie disbursed therin, or if yow find such moneyis levyed by his meanes, and no accompt made thairof as yet for our vse, that yow requyre our Collectour haveing charge therof to tak that course for his satisfaction, and if you find it requisite for the good of our service in that kynd, that yow continew him in that imployment efter such maner, tyme, and condition as yow shall think fitt, and is provydit by the said Act.—[No date.]

To the Advocat.

Trustie, &c.—Wheras our right trustie and right, &c., the Earle of Eglinton is desyreous to treat with us for some heretable offices and other royalteis and Juresdictioues he hath, and that he hath formerlie delt with ws concerneing the Landis which he holdeth within the principalitie of that our kingdome, we ar gratiouslie pleased that yow should nowayes proceid against the said Erle tuitching the premisses till our pleasur herin be furder knowen, and that yow receave particular ordour from ws concerneing him, notwithstanding any former directions, ffor doeing [whereof] the presents shalbe vnto yow a sufficient warrand.—Whythall, 22 Junij 1630.

To the Thesaurer and Deputie Thesaurer.

Right, &c.—Wheras we have received of our trustie and weilbelovit Robert Buchan a certane quantitie of his most choyse pearle, wherwith we ar weill pleased, which, efter trew valuatioun by our Jewellers, ar fund worth the sowme of four scoir and fyve pundis sterling : Our express will and pleasur is, that yow mak present payment vnto the said Robt Buchan or his assigneyis of the said sowme ; and for your soe doeing these presents shalbe vnto yow, and everie of yow, a sufficient warrand and discherge.—Gevin at St James', the 24 Junij 1630.

These grant to Sir George Abercrombie and Sir Coline Campbell, ther administratours, ane sole Licence within Scotland for tuentie-one yeres, to dy and fix all maner of cullours in grayne vpon cloth, yarne stuff, and silks, without help or compositioun of Cucheneill, and to mak the best vse of that invention both at home and abroad : These ar to be as sufficient warrand for some strangers to reside ther for advanceing that invention, as if they had Letters of denization : All persones (others then the patentees and ther forsaidis) vseing ther said Invention dureing the said space ar to be censured as your Maties Counsell shall think fitt, and the halff of the benefite aryseing by things heirby prohibited, to be vsed or made therin to your Matie, and the vther halff to the patentees ; if this be not reallie putt in practeis within 3 yeres these presents ar void.—Whythall, 28 Junij 1630.

These ordeane a protection to be made to James Law for one yeir, provyded he satisfie his creditours of ther annuelrents, otherwyse the protection to be voyd.—Whythall, 28 Junij 1630.

These Grant to William Tennent, his heyres and assigneyis, the escheit of the goodis, possessionis, &c. of Patrik Dicksone, which hath fallin at your Ma{tie's} gift by his being denunced rebell for not subseryveing of the professed religion in Scotland.—Whythall, 28 Junij 1630.

These exoner Dowgall Campbell of Auchinbreck, and Duncan Campbell, his sone, of all criminall actions (the crymes of treasone against your Ma{tie's} sacred persone and dominions, or ather of them, Witch-craft or false coyne being excepted) committed by them by vertew of tuo Commissions granted to the Erle of Argyll for repression of the rebellions of the Clangregour and Sir James M{c}Donald, or recommitted by them in any service wherin he was warranted by the Counsell.—Whythall, 28 Junij 1630.

Presentation to Mr Johne Merser to the kirk of Glenholme.—Whythall, 28 Junij.

The names of the Commissioners, The Chancellour, Thesaurer, President, Privie seill, Secretarie. Thesaurer depute, Clerk Register, Advocat, Justice Clerk, and Mr of Requeists. The quorum consist of any four of them, with the Thesaurer or Thesaurer depute in ther absens.

To the Exchequer.

Right, &c.—Wheras Edward Kellie, our servand, hath bene a humble sutter vnto ws that his accompts tuitching the selling of the Chapell royall by our directione and furnisching of thingis thervnto belonging might be heard, and that he hath formerlie delt with ws concerneing the same, and vpon satisfaction made vnto him of such moneyis as should be fund justlie dew vnto him, a precept of sex thowsand merkis procured by him from ws might be takin bak by yow to be cancelled; wherin finding his demands reasonable and his former paynes to merite some encouragment from ws to continow in our service in that kynd, Our pleasur is, that what moneyis shall appear due vpoun his accompts, that with all convenient diligence yow caus pay the same vnto him, remitting the consideratione of his panes till we shall be pleased to sie the effect thairof.—Whythall, 28 Junij 1630.

To the Counsell.

Right, &c.—Being informed by Edward Kellie of the insufficiencie, non-residence, and dissobedience of some haveing charge in our chappell royall to the ordours preservyed by the deane thairof, and his assistance, for settling of the same in a fitt and decent maner, assumeing vnto themselllis by former guifts of ther offices what friedome and immunitie they think fitt, wherby the service to be performed by them is neglected : Our pleasur is, efter dew examinatioun and finding what is alledged to be done heirin, that yow discharge such insufficient and refractorie persones, if they shall not be fund (efter such tryell as yow shall think requisit) able to discharge a dustie in thair services, and most willing heirefter both to better ther judgments in ther professiones, and to obtemper to all the good ordours alreadie and heirefter to be preservyed by the deane and his assistants; and soe we bid, &c.—Whythall, 28 Junij 1630.

To the Marqueis of Huntlie.

Right, &c.—Vnderstanding that our right, &c., the Erle of Tullibardyne hath some speciall occasions for the good of our service (wherwith he is particularlie to acquent yow) to repair vnto Lochaber and some adjacent places, wher (as we ar informed) yow by diverse wayes and meanes, without trouble or change to yow, may caus assist him therin : We are heirby pleased to desyre yow to doe the same in such convenient and lawfull maner as yow shall think most fitt for that purpois, causing him his partiners and companie (of whom as persones sufficient and able to doe ws service heirin we have made choyse to repair thither from this our kingdome) to be civilie and weill vsed in so far as convenientlie can be done by yow, which we will tak as good service done vnto ws : So we, &c.—Whythall, 28 Junij 1630.

To the Exchequer.

Right, &c.—Whereas we wer formerlie pleased to signe in favours of our right, &c. the Erle of Tullibardyn a signatur of the landis of Atholl, who hath now informed ws that the passing thairof till this tyme was for noe vther caus deferred then for that he could not (becaus of his affaires heir) attend the following therof ther, and that now in respect of the changes of our Thesaurer, the same cannot be done without a new warrand from ws, sieing (as we ar informed) that these ar the onlie causses of the stay therof : Our pleasur is, that yow pass and cause expeid the same with all diligence according to the tenor therof, or vtherwayes, if yow have any reasone why it should not be done, that yow acquant ws therwith.—Whythall, 28 Junij 1630.

To the Erle of Man.

Right, &c.—As your affection and endeavours to doe good service have reaped the due respect from our late dear father, and of late from ws, we ar now verie confident that yow will omitt no meanes wherby yow may be serviceable vnto ws : And therfor these ar to recommend vnto yow that yow have a speciall care for furthering these things that ar to be proponed for the good of our service at this convention of our estats, wherof yow shalbe informed by . . . ; and as yow carie your self in this yow may expect respect from ws accordinglie.—Whythall, 28 Junij 1630.

Ane vther letter conforme to the precedent was writtin to the Erle of Hadinton.—Whythall, 28 Junij 1630.

To the Erle Hadinton.

The long experience of your abilitie and affection to our service, acknowledged by the favour yow have had from our late dear father and from ws, doeth mak ws with confidence to repois vpon your judgment and endeavours : And therfore these ar to desyre yow to express the uttermost effects of both by your self and freinds for the furthering such things as ar to be proponed at this Convention of our Estats for the good of our service, wherby yow shalbe informed by . . . ; and as yow carie your self in this yow may expect respect from ws accordinglie.—Whythall, 28 Junij 1630.

A Warrant to James Rattray.

In regard of the great contempt vsed by ane Alex' Hay in dissobeying our princelie pleasur, from his abandoneing our Court to be sent into Scotland, and that he still remaneth within the precinct therof, or within or about our citie of London, Our speciall pleasur is, that furthwith in our name yow by vertew of your power from ws charge all our officers whom it may concerne, for ayding and causing ayd yow to search and apprehend him and committ him to close prissone till the first opportunitie of a schip goeing from hence thither, at which tyme we desyre yow to send him to our Counsall of that our kingdome, wherof doe not faill, as yow wilbe answerable to ws at your perrell.—Whythall, 28 Junij 1630.

To the Advocat.

Trustie, &c.—Wheras we ar informed that diverse noblemen and others haveing lands of our principalitie and propertie in that our kingdome, whois rights and evidents thairof ar fitt to be renewed, paying such reasonable composition to ws for the same as we should be pleased to caus modifie, wherin respecting the good of our subjects, and our owin benefite : Our pleasur is, that yow to this purpois draw up a Commission in a legall and sure maner, leaveing a blank for the names of such commissioners to be insert therin as we shalbe pleased to appoynt by our thesaurer, and therfor that yow delyver the same to him, docated by yow to be exped according to the tenour therof.—Whythall, 28 Junij 1630.

To the Exchequer.

Right, &c.—We receaved your letter tuitching the Commission granted by ws to Sir Alex.^r Strauchan, kny.^t and baronet, and hath heard these things that ar questioned concerneing the same at leuth debated be ws, howsoever we did grant that Commission upoun good consideratiouns, yet sieing we think it expedient that some things therin be so moderated and cleired as might be most felt for the publict good whervnto we will alwayes have a speciall respect, we have bene pleased to condescend vpon some articles of restrictions which we have send yow signed by ws, Our pleasur is, that the saids Commissions and all our former warrandis and Acts of Exchequer made thervpon stand in full force, except in so far as they ar limited and restricted by the saids Articles which we lykwyse desyre may be dewlie observed in the prosecution of that our service, for the tymelie advanceing whairof we will yow to be verie carefull and diligent, and to that effect that yow appoynt a certane tyme everie week for hearing and dispatching of such things as may concerne our service in that kynd, that he have no just caus to compleane vpon delayis: And we will yow to cause these articles be insert in the books of Exchequer, and publisched efter what maner yow shall think fitt.

To the Advocat.

Trustie—We have heard these things at leuth debated befor ws that wer questioned concerneing the Commission gevin by ws to Sir Alex.^r Strauchan, kny.^t and baronet, howsoever we did grant the same vpon verie good considerations, yit sieing we think it expedient that some things therin be so moderated and cleared, as might be most fitt for the publict good, whervnto we will alwayes have a speciall respect : We have bene pleased to condescend vpon some articles of restrictions which we will yow to be carefull and consider and pervse efter the same have bene publictlie sene and considred at our Exchequer table, and seing we have signifeid to our Exchequer that the saids Commissions, and all former warrands and acts therof made thervpoun, shall stand in full force, as they ar limited and restricted by the saids Articles, Our pleasur is, that yow in our name assist and concurr with the said Sir Alex.^r for the prosecution of our service in that kynd, and that at all tymes and occasions requisite ; And if ther be any things in the saids Commissions vnformall which ar fitt and necessar to be mendit, we requyre yow to doe it, or (if neid be) to certifie ws therof, togidder with your opinion concerneing the same : So requyreing yow to proceid in that service according to your former warrandis vnto yow, haveing respect alwayes to the saids restrictions, we bid yow farewell.—Whythall, 28 Junij 1630.

Articles from his most Excellent Matie concerning the Commission granted to Sir Alex.^r Strauchan.

Sir Alex.^r Strauchan be vertew of his Commission shall cite no pairtie without advyse of his Ma.^{tis} Advocat :

He shall mak no composition bot by advyse of the Lords Chancellour, Thesaurer, President of the privie counsall, Thesaurer depute, his Ma.^{tis} Secretarie, the Clerk Register, Advocat, and Justice Clerk, or any of them :

He shall putt no pennall statute in Executioun till his Maᵗⁱˢ pleasur be heirefter particularlie signifeid heirin :

That he shall not question any man's right, bot onlie call for what was due or may be fund to have bene due vnto his Maᵗⁱᵉ, and not restraynit to be called for by warrants . . . formerlie, and shall have no grant nor power in any composition for a new right by vertew of his Commission, he being first satisfeit befor the right be renewed of his half of the compositions that shalbe takin from the pairteis for that which was due or may be fund vnto his Maᵗⁱˢ as is above specifeit.

If ther be any clause irritant in any infeftment wher thrie termes hath run in ane forfaulting the land and that nather these landis have bene challenged as forfaulted, nor yit the few-dewteis payed, in that caice he shall call for them as omitted by vertew of his Commission :

This Maᵗⁱˢ Thesaurer shall intromet with the half of the compositions belonging to him and the said Sir Alexʳ with the other half, he being sufficientlie dischergit of his Maᵗⁱˢ part.

To the Chancellour, Thesaurer, President.

Right, &c.—Wheras humble complant hath bene vnto ws in behalf of diverse of our frie burrowis who have not schirreffis within themselffis, that they vndergoe great and vnnecessarie charges by travelling to parts far distant from ther duellings, for giveing vp of ther Inventars of ther annual rents to the schirreff of the schyre, wher the same might much more convenientlie and as surelie be done befor ther provest and bailleis, wherin we inclyneing that some ordour be establisched for ther good and ease : Our pleasur is (if yow find that we be not therby prejudged, and that no inconvenient vtherwyse may aryse by the same), that yow signifie our pleasur to our nixt convention of our Estats ther, that they give way thervnto by making such ane act of Convention as yow and they shall best condescend vpon to this purpois to be ratifeid the nixt parliament, wherby both the saids Magistrats and other subjects may from hencefurth be authorized to proceid accordinglie : And wheras we ar informed that our late royall father of his princelie favour pardoned diverse pennall statuts as by Commissions for tryeing of what of them wer fit to be executed, what to be pardoned may appear, we being alwyse willing for diverse good and weightie causses moveing ws at this tyme to give them some such taste of our bountie and favour as may the better induce them not to transgress our lawis heirefter, or expecting further impunitie in caice they should abuse our princelie clemencie heirin, wherof we ar willing that speciall notice be gevin them efter what maner yow shall think fitt : Our pleasur is, that by ane Act of the said Convention to be ratifeid in the ensueing parliament, yow cause discharge all our subjects of all pennall statuts whatsoever preceiding the dait heirof, which wer formerlie remitted in any parliament, and of the fynes of all pennall statuts made in anno 1621 : And for your soe doeing these presents, &c.—Whythall, 28 Junij 1630.

To the Advocat.

Trustie, &c.—Wheras we ar informed that diverse noblemen and others haveing landis of our principalitie and propertie in that our kingdome, whois rights and evidents therof ar fitt to be renewed, paying such reasonable Composition to ws for the same as we should be pleased to caus modifie, wherin respecting the good of our subjects and our owin benefite, Our pleasur is, that yow to this purpois draw vp a Commission in a legall and sure maner, leaving a blank for such names of our Commissioners to be insert therin as we shall be pleased to appoynt by our thesaurer, and therefter that yow delyver the same to him, &c.—Whythall, 28 Junij 1630.

To the Counsell.

Right, &c.—Being informed of the sufficiencie of our right trustie, &c. the Erle of Tullibardyne, and of his affection to our service, we ar moved in regard therof, and for his better encouragment and enabling for our said service to advance and promove him to be ane of our privie Counsall of that our kingdome : Therfor our pleasur is, and we doe heirby requyre yow, that haveing administred vnto him the oath accustomed in the lyk causes, yow admitt him to be one of our privie Counsell. receaveing him in that place as one of your number, for doeing quherof these presents shalbe vnto yow a sufficient warrand.--Gevin at our Court of Whythall, 28 Junij 1630.

To the Exchequer.

Right, &c.—Wheras a signature of the Lordship of Scone, proceiding vpon a resignatioun by the Viscount of Stormont in favours of Sir Mungo Murray, hath bene presented to have bene signed by ws, wherin we ar willing to schaw any lawfull favour for our servand's furtherance without prejudging our selff in the late course intendit by ws for our owin and the publict good ; yit we ar pleased to returne the same vnsigned to be considered by yow, Requyreing yow, if yow fand the same fit and lawfull to be granted by ws, and that ther is nothing therin directlie by the consequence may hurt that course, that the said signature, or any vther to that purpois thoght fair and just by yow be past, and exped our sealls with all convenient diligence ; and so we, &c.—Whythall, 28 Junij 1630.

To Allan Cameron.

Trustie, &c.—Wheras our right, &c. the Erle of Tullibardyn is to repair to Lochaber and some nightbouring partis by our direction, and for our speciall service for the better and more speciall furtherance therof we ar informed that yow can be verie steadable : Our pleasur is, that wherin he shalbe willing that yow give way and assist him in that service, that yow readelie obey the same in so far as it is in your power lawfullie and possiblie to doe, and that yow vse your best meanes for causing him and his companie to be as civilie and weill vsed as the estates of these parts can convenientlie alfurd, that they have no just caus to compleane, and vpon the said Erle his report vnto ws at his returne of your care and diligence to obey ws heirin, we will accompt it as verie acceptable done vnto ws, wherof we will no wayes be vnmyndfull.—Whythall, 28 Junij 1630.

To M'Cleane.

Trustie—being informed that near to some part of your Yland of Mull a Spanish schip was long since cast away, wherin ther wer some ordinance and other things which may be recovered and be steadable for our service : Our pleasur is, for the better and more specilie doeing therof, that yow both assist and caus civilie vse, in so far as lawfullie and possiblie yow can, our right, &c. the Erle of Tullibardyne, his partiners and companie, of whom as persones sufficient and able to doe ws service therin we have made choyse, to repair thither from this our kingdome ; So not doubting of your caire and diligence to obey ws heirin, as we will not be vnmyndfull of yow when any fitt and convenient occasion shalbe offerit vnto ws concerneing yow, we bid yow fairweill.—Whythall, 28 Junij 1630.

To the Counsell.

Right, &c.—Wheras our right, &c. the Erle of Tullibardyne intendeth vpon some speciall occasionis for the good of our service, wherwith he will particularlie acquant yow, to repair to Lochaber, Mule, and other adjacent places, sieing for the better and more speedie advancement in that service we ar pleased to imploy him and his associats, of whois judgments and habiliteis to bring such purposes to some perfection we have bene informed: Our pleasur is, that yow serionslie wryt in ther behalff to any of our officers in these bounds, and to such noblmen and others of qualitie remaneing or haveing power therin (whois help they may have occasion to vse) for assisting the said Erle and his partiners in any thing that may advance our said service in so far as yow think they may lawfullie and convenientlie doe: And in respect that none (as we ar informed) haveing former Commissions for any of these purposes have broght the same to any perfection, bot have long since left the prosecution therof, we further requyre that what shall therby be pretendit by them for any respect or occasion whatsoever be no hinderance to our present service heirin: So we bid, &c.—Whythall, 28 Junij 1630.

To the Convention Generall.

Right, &c.—Wheras we ar informed that our trustie and weilbeloved Robert Buchan hath vpon his owin charge and ground built a Church, and appropriat a sufficient gleib thervnto, which, being distant fyve myles of marich, rockie, and vnpassable way at many tymes in the winter seasone from any vther church in these bounds, will prove verie commodious for the good and ease of many poore people ther, who for the most part hath bene heirtofor destitute of the benefite of hearing God's word: In regard, as we ar lykwyse informed, that Church hath bene consecrated by the bischops of Aberdene and Murray, and that work is lykwyse approved by diverse others of the clergie, we ar heirby pleased to recommend the purpois vnto yow, that if yow find it necessarie, and that compitent meanes out of any tythes therabout may be had for a minister's stipend, without being a meanes to hinder the provision of other churches alreadie establisched neir that part, that yow proceid, in soe far as yow can lawfullie and convenientlie doe, to give such ordour for the setling therof in a distinct parochin, and of a constant stipend for the same, as yow shall think most fitt and necessarie, and as shalbe most agreable to any ordour observed in cases of the lyk nature.—Whythall, 28 Julij 1630.

To the Counsell.

Right, &c.—Wheras wee signified vnto yow our pleasur tuitching the action perswed by our Advocat against Archibald Tod, dischergeing him to proceid further therin in respect of our late interest, wherin sieing vpon good considerationns we wer pleased to give that ordour, and leist we should be troubled heirefter with any new motion concerneing the same, we ar heirby pleased to signifie vnto yow that we friclie remitt vnto the said Archibald Tod, and our burgh of Edinburgh for ther interesse, all actions whatsoever, civill or criminall, compitent to ws against them tuitching that action, requyreing yow to command our Advocat in our name not to insist further therin, and that by Act of Counsall yow discherge the same and all that may follow thervpon; ffor which these presents, &c.—Whythall, last of Junij 1630.

To the Chancellour, Thesaurer, President of the Counsell, and Privie Seall Advocat.

Right, &c.—Wheras Mr Johne Hay, Commissioner of our burgh of Edinburgh for removeing all questions betuixt the noblemen and gentlmen of West Lothian and that burgh concerneing the extention of ther schirrefschip and crownerschip, and halding the gild Courts and Custome of the load of aill, conteynit in the Chartour granted to them in anno 1603, made certane offers vnto ws, which we formerlie sent vnto yow, our Chancellour, wherby all occasion of contraversie may be takin away : We therfor give and grant vnto yow our full power and commission to call befor yow the Commissioners of both the sauds pairteis and hear ther differences, and so compose the same as is most fitt for the good of both and ther severall interests for avoydeing all question in tyme comeing, and that yow sie the same done in a legall forme : And if any difficultie shall aryse which cannot of consent of both pairteis, or be by yow composed, that yow certifie ws of your opinions therin, that we may tak such course for setling therof as in our princelie judgment we shall think fitt.—Whythall, last of Junij 1630.   Which recommending vnto your care, &c.

To the Counsell.

Right, &c.—Haveing bene formerlie pleased vpon some good considerationns then moveing ws to requyre our Right, &c. the E. of Murray to surrander his Commission, bot being informed that the Insolenceis and oppressions daylie committed within these northerne parts in great contempt of our authoritie and lawis requyre a speedie course to be takin for repressing therof : And being still confident of the said Erle, his affection to our service, and that he will vse the executioun of that Commission, which we intend not to renew at the expyreing of the dait therof, in such moderat and fair maner, as non of our subjects can have just caus to compleane : Our pleasur is, that the said Commission be continewed according to the tyme and tenour therof, and be as effectuall vnto him in all respects whatsoever as if we had never requyred him to surrander the same ; And if it be by yow fund requisit, that yow approve the same, ather by Act of Counsell or by causing intimat our pleasur herin in such parts and efter such maner as yow think fitt, or otherwyse efter what other forme yow for that purpois shall think most requisit.— Last of Junij 1630.

To the Advocat and Henrison.

Trustie, &c.—Wheras we have bene petitioned by Edward Maxwell schowing the great losses susteaned by him in our service : And being vnwilling that he or any of our gude subjects should suffer in that kynd as he pretendis : Our pleasur is, that haveing called vnto yow such persones as can best give yow light in the said Edward his debursments, panes, and losses, yow tak speciall notice of the petition heirin enclosed, and haveing informed your self of his cariage in that service, that therefter with all diligence yow acquant ws what he hath deserved, that accordinglie we may tak a course for his satisfaction.—Whythall, last of Junij 1630.

A precept to Sir Andro Gray, of the date of the preceding letter.

To the Exchequer.

Right, &c.—Wheras we have bene pleased to signe ane gift of ane yeirlie pension to Sir George Elphingstoun of Blythswood, knyt, of two thowsand merks Scotts, for many good and faythfull services done by him vnto our late dear father and ws : Our pleasur therfor is, for the better encourageing the said George to continew in the lyk good services heirefter, that yow caus exped the same vnder our sealls with all possible diligence according to the forme accustomed ; for doeing wherof these presents shall be vnto yow, and everie of yow, a sufficient warrant.—Gevin at Whythall, the last of Junij 1630.

II   G

Articles to be proponed from ws vnto the Convention of Estats, now warned, That they may returne to ws their opinions thervpon.

To consider of the best course how the Valuatiouns of Tythes may be most speedelie and exactlie perfected, that these things conteyned in our decrie may tak effect.

To consider how Manufactours for making the best benefite of the wooll, and for employment of our people, may be most convenientlie setled as hath bene formerlie intendit.

To give ordour for proceiding according to our commission granted for reveweing the Lawes and practique of that our kingdome, that all things necessarie to be treated of in the nixt parliament may be the better prepared against that tyme.

In regard of the great charges requisit for our Intertenement dureing the tyme of that our being in that our kingdome, and for payment of the debts contracted for buying of heretable offices, that a Taxatioun may be had such as our loveing subjects for so great a cause shall willinglie grant.

To the Arch Bishop of St Andrewis.

Right, &c.—Haveing caused pervse the translatioun of the psalmes, wherof our late dear father was authored by learned divynes, who fund it exactlie and trewlie done and intending to be allowed to be sung in all the churches of this our kingdome, befor we proceid therin in that our kingdome, we have send yow a copie therof to be pervsed by yow or by such as shall have direction from yow to that effect : It is our pleasur, if yow find the said work to be well done and worthie to be sung in churches, that yow with advyse of your brethren, haveing duelie considered of the same, give ordour how it may be most convenicutlie ; which recommending vnto your care as a purpois speciallie concerneing ws, &c.

To Earles .

Right, &c.—Being informed of your affection and liabilitie to doe ws service, and desyreing to have a prooff of the same at this tyme wherin sindrie things ar to be proponed from ws for the good of that kingdome as will appear by the Articles which we have sent for that effect : And that yow may be the better informed, we have desyred our trustie and weillbeloved Counsellours, Sir William Alexander, our Secretarie, principall Secretarie for our kingdome of Scotland, to acquant yow more particularlie therwith, whom yow shall trust in any thing that he doeth deliver vnto yow in our name concerneing our service at this tyme, and as we find your endeavours to prove, we will acknowledge the same accordinglie.— Whythall, 3 July 1630.

Ane Letter to ane Erle and tuo Lordis and tuo gentlmen, of the tenour and date of the precedent, and ane to Lochinvar, of the tenour and date of the precedent, with this clause more,—As lykwayes in the treatie with yow concerneing your bailliarie and regalitie.

Earle Carnagie.

Right, &c.— Haveing bene informed of your affection and abilitie to doe ws service as hath appeared both in tyme of our late dear father and since, These ar to recommend vnto your care the doeing of that which may tend to the furthering thairof at this tyme, and as yow had a mark of honour from our late dear father, as we find yow to deserve, we will be no less willing to acknowledge your merite : As for the particulars wherin we desyre to vse your diligence, we have imparted them vnto our trustie and weilbelovit Counsellour Sir William Alexander, knyght, our principall Secretarie of our kingdome of Scotland, whome yow shall trust from ws for the advancement whairof, being confident that yow will vse your best endeavours.—[No date.]

To the Burrowis.

Trustie, &c.—Haveing gevin Mr Johne Hay, your Commissioner, all reasonable satisfaction in that he did demand in your name, and haveing now vse of your service at this Convention, wher Articles ar to be proponed from ws by our Chancellour for the good of that our kingdome : These ar to will yow to vse your best endeavours for advanceing our service therin : As for the particulars besyds what we have spokin to your Commissioner, we have requyred Sir William Alexander, our Secretarie, to impart the same vnto yow, whom you shall trust from ws ; which recommending to your care.—Whythall, 3 July 1630.

To the Counsall.

Right, &c.—Ther being at this tyme some controversie betuixt us and the French concerneing the title of Landis in America, and particularlie of New Scotland, it being alledgeit that Port Royall, wher the Scottish Colonie is planted, should be restored, as takin since the making of the peace, by reasone of the Articles made concerneing the same, as we ar bund in dewtie and justice to discharge what we ow to everie nyghbour prince, so we most have a care that none of our subjects doe suffer in that which they have vndertakin vpon just grounds to doe ws service : Nather will we determyne in a matter of so great moment till we vnderstude the trew esteat thairof : Therefore our pleasur is, that yow tak this bussines into your consideratiouns ; And becaus we desyre to be certifeid how far we and our subjects ar interessed therin, and what arguments ar fitt to be vsed when any question shall occure concerneing the same, for the defence thairof, that efter dew information we may be furnished with reasone how we ar bund to manteine the patents that our late dear father and we have gevin : So, expecting that haveing informed your selffis sufficientlie of this bussines, ye will returne ws ane answer with diligence.—Whythall, 3 July 1630.

To the Bischop of Ross.

Right, &c.—As we have ever fund your earnest endeavours and affectioun in all things wher your panes might contribuit to any good for furthering our service : These ar to recommend to your speciall care at this tyme of the Convention of Estats, according as yow shalbe informed by our trustie, &c. Sir William Alexander, our Secretarie, whome we know yow will trust from ws : So, remitting the particulars therof to his report, being verie confident that yow will not frustrat our expectatioun, we bid yow, &c.—Whythall, 3 July 1630.

Generall Convention of Estats.

Right, &c.- Haveing, vpon verie weghtie consideratiouns, been moved to deferre our repairing to that our kingdome till the nixt Spring, and desyreing that all things necessarie, both for our intertenement and for setling of affaires, may be so prepared in the meane tyme that they may with the less trouble to ws and yow be then concludit for the good and honour of that kingdome which we exceidinglie affect, we have sent vnto our right, &c. the Viscount of Dupline, our Chancellour, such Articles for that purpois as we thoght most fitt to be considered of, wherin we requyre your advyse and supplie, being verie confident that yow will vse your best endeavours for our satisfaction heirin, who shall ever be cairfull of that which may concerne your good, and bid yow farewell.—Whythall, 3 July 1630.

To the Counsell.

Right, &c.—We being no less favourablie enclyned toward our burgh of Edinburgh, and such other our burghes as will joyne with them tuitching the componeing with them for ther extraordinarie taxatiouns then our late royall father was, and as we vpoun good consideratiouns have bene heirtofoir, Our pleasur is, that yow compone with such of them as ar willing to goe on in that course, according to the forme accustomed, if ye think the same best for the good of our service : For doeing whairof these presents shalbe your warrand, so, &c.—Whythall, 3 July 1630.

To the Counsell.

Right, &c.—Wheras we ar informed that ane Mr Wm Kellie vseth meanes to stop the depute of our servand Sir Robert Dowglas, our baillie of the Lordschip of Dumbar, from holding Courts ther in our name, intrudeing himsellf by indirect meanes in the superioritie thairof, wherby to oppress the vassalls of the same, and to wrest from our Croun a priviledge so ancientlie belonging thervnto : Our pleasur is, that yow informe your sellis of the trew estate heirof, and that yow vse your best endeavours for causing him leave that course, otherwayes that ye in our name requyre our Advocat to insist by Law for reduceing of any right he pretendeth in that kynd over these vassalls.—3 July 1630.

To the Exchequer.

Right, &c.—Wheras vpon good consideratiouns we have bene pleased to signe a remission to Sir Dowgall Campbell of Auchinbreck, and Duncan Campbell, his sone, for anything that can be criminallie objected against them for helping to performe that service in repressing the rebellion of Clangregour, and of Sir James McDonald, as by the Commission may appear : Our pleasur is, that with all convenient diligence yow pas and caus exped the same according to the tyme therof.—Whythall, 3 July 1630.

To the Session.

Right, &c.—Being informed that Mr Robert Broun, minister at the paroche kirk of Kirkdene, hath not receavod the last yeir the stipend due and payable vnto him out of the rentall bolls of the parsonage and viccarage therof ; And that William Maxwell, our servand, is lykwyse dissapoynted of what is justlie due to him out of the same ; by want wherof the said minister is much dissabled in the Church of his cure, and our said servand much prejudged contrarie to our royall intention ; Our pleasur is, that yow administrat Justice vnto them with all convenient diligence in any action intended by them to this purpois, these tythis being lyable to our annuitie, and subject to any good ordour alreadie preservyed or to be preservyed by our Commissioners of surrenders, as shalbe takin in causses of sic nature : And for the more speedie executeing of Justice heirin and ease of our subjects, we leave it to your owin choyse to remitt the decyding heirof to the ordinarie Judge in the bounds from whence the said paroche is not far distant or otherwayes befor your selflis ; which recommending, we bid, &c. —Whythall, 3 July 1630.

To the Erle of Hadinton.

Right, &c.—The long experience of your abilitie and affection to our service, acknawledged by the favour yow have had from our late dear father and from ws, doeth mak ws with confidence to repose vpon your judgment and endeavours : And therfor these ar to desyre yow to express the ottermost effects of both by your self and freinds for furthering such things as ar to be proponed at this convention of our estats for the good of our service, wherin yow shalbe informed by our trustie, &c., Sir Wm Alexander, kny^t : As yow carie your self in this yow may expect respect from ws accordinglie.—Whythall, 3 July 1630.

To the E. Mar.

Right, &c.—As your affection and endeavours to doe good service have reaped the due respect from our late dear father, and of late from ws, we ar now verie confident that yow will omitt no meanes wherby yow may be serviceable vnto ws, and therfor these ar to recommend vnto yow that yow have a speciall care for furthring these things that ar to be proponed for the good of our service at this convention of our estats, wherof yow shalbe informed by our trustie Sir Wm Alexander, and as yow carie your self in this, yow may expect respect from ws accordinglie ; and we bid yow, &c.—Whythall, 3 July 1630.

Your Matie, for your self as Royall King, and as lawfull administratour to the Prince his Highnes, doe grant to Alex^r Balmanno, the gift of nonentrie of the landis and baronie of Truyner and Myrton Kennedie and others particularlie thairin mentionat, and of all yeres and termes bypast since the samyne hath bene in nonentrie, and of thrie termes to come.—Whythall, 5 July 1630.

Your Matie, for your self, and as lawfull administratour to the Prince his highnes, doeth heirby dispone to your Ma^{tis} lovit Sir George Auchinlek, kny^t, of Balmanno, the fyftie merk land of the baronie of Auchinleck, comprehending the landis of Keitlastoun, Cruikstoun, and Rogertoun, with ther pertinents lyand within the principalitie and stewartrie of Scotland, schirrefdome of Air, and bailliarie of Kylstewart, vacand in the handis of the prince, his highnes superiour thairof, be reasone of recognition to be holden ward of his highnes and successours princes and stewarts of Scotland.—Gevin at Whythall, 5 July 1630.

These grant Commission to the above-nameit persones to trye the honouris [and] priviledges belonging or which did belong to the Office of high Constable of Scotland, with power (if neid be, to search the Registers and Rolls for clearing thairof) to try, in so far as they can convenientlie, what ar the honours, priviledges belonging to the lyk office in forrayne kingdomes, and how far any of them ar fitt to be added to the said office, haveing respect how the same may be agreable to the Lawis and customes of Scotland ; And generallie with power to them to try what other things in ther judgment ar fitt to be added to the said office, with command, efter they have considered the premisses, to certifie bak ther opinions therin betuixt and the .—Whythall, 5 of July 1630.

To the Chancellour.

Right, &c.—Haveing bene informed that our Privie Counsell hath caused suspend the decreit gevin be our Colledge of Justice in favours of our burgh of Edinburgh against some of the inhabitants of Leith; and perceaving, by a lettre delyvered vnto ws by our Right, &c. the Erle of Murray, that sindrie noblemen and gentlmen doe alledge that they may suffer great harme if the said decreit be put to executioun: Becaus we would be loath that any contraversie should aryse heirvpon betuixt the Lords of our Counsall and Colledge of Justice, and as we desyre our said burgh to enjoy what is ther right, according to the ordinarie course of Law, So we wold willinglie have any great inconvenience prevented which the saids compleaners may justlie fear; Therfor it is our pleasur that yow, taking the advyse of such of our cheiff officers as yow shall pleas to assume vnto yow, efter dew consideratioun of that which is aboue specifeit, tak such a course with diligence as in your judgment may seme most just and fair for setling these differences, in such sort that none of the saids pairteis have just caus to compleane; or otherwyse, that yow certifie ws what, in your opinion, is best to be done heirin: The doeing heirof we commend seriouslie vnto yow, and so bid yow fairwell.—Whythall, 5 July 1630.

A Warrant to the Erle of Mar.

Our will and pleasur is, that immediatlie efter sight heirof yow kill or cause to be killed a brace of fatt bucks of this seasone for the vse of our trustie, &c. Sir William Alexander; for doeing wherof these presents shalbe your warrant.—Whythall, 5 July 1630.

To Sir Archibald Achesone.

Trustie, &c.—Haveing for weightie affaires caused convene the Estats of that our kingdome at this tyme: These ar to will yow to vse your best endeavours in all things that may cum within the compas of your power for furthering our service, for the particulars wherof we remitt yow to the report of our trustie Sir Wm Alexander, whom we will yow trust from ws: And so being verie confident of your best meanes heirin, We bid yow farewell.—5 July 1630.

To the Chancellour.

Right, &c.—We have sent heirwith such Articles as we think fitt to be treated of at Convention of our estats now warned, whilks we will yow heirby to propone vnto them from ws, and efter dew deliberation that yow certifie ws bak with our Secretarie, whom we have send expreslie for that purpois what is determined or thoght fitt to be done in everie ane of them, wherin we ar confident of your best endeavours as ane whome we cheiflie trust: And doe bid yow farewell.—Whythall, 5 July 1630.

To the Advocat.

Trustie, &c.—Wheras we have bene moved in behalff of the Lords of Balmerino and Torphechin, and James Creichtoun of Frendraught, and the toun of Selkirk, for granting vnto them signaturs of ther landis: Our pleasur therfor is, that yow peruse ther severall signaturs, and docquett the same to be sent vnto ws, and passed our hand, remembring alwyse to insert a clause therin, that nothing therin mentione] be prejudiciall to our annuitie, ministers' stipends, and other pious vsses, or to the generall submission and our decree following theron: And for your soe doeing these our letters shalbe vnto yow a sufficient warrand.—Gevin at our Court of Whythall, 5 July 1630.

To the Chancellour, Thesaurer, President.

Right, &c.—We have sent yow heirwith such articles as we have thoght fitt to be proponed to our estats at this Convention now warned, and thogh in our owin judgment we think them fair and fitt to be done, Yit with all vnderstanding what emergent consideratiouns may aryse out of present occasions occurring to your judgments wherwith we ar not acquanted, which in regard of the tyme at leist for conveniencie may requyre, that some of them be not now proponed or be proponed efter some other maner, we heirby authorize yow to present, had bak, or alter any of the saids Articles, or to ad others of new, as efter due advyse yow thrie, with our Secretar, the bearer heirof, shall think most requisite and necessarie for the good of our service; wherwith trusting your judgments, and being confident of your affections, we bid yow farewell.—Whythall, 5 July 1630.

To the Arch Bischop of Sᵗ Androis.

Right. &c.—In regard of your long experience in publict affaires, the tyme of our late dear father and of ws: These ar therfor to recommend to your care that which may concerne the good of our service at that tyme in the Convention of the estates, the particulars wherof shalbe imparted vnto yow by our trustie Sir Wᵐ Alexander, whom yow shall trust from ws: And we expect not onlie your owin endevours heirin, bot that yow wilbe carefull to dispose the rest of your brethren, the Clergie, for furthering the same; by doeing wherof ye shall obleidg ws to continew as we ar confident of your affection thervnto, and to acknowledge the same accordinglie.—Whythall, 5 July 1630.

To the Exchequer.

Haveing considered of the submissione offered vnto ws by Wᵐ Forbes of Cragievar of that part of the abacie of the Lundors therin mentionat, with such reservatiouns as by the same may appear, we sie no reasone why we should give him any satisfaction for the same, vnles he had made ane absolute submission therof to ws, that by concludeing with him we might have cum to a present possession of the superioriteis and few-dewteis, and setled the estate of the vassalls, but desyreing to have nothing that belongeth vnto him, vnless we satisfie him for the same in ane equitable maner: Our pleasur is, that yow call him befor yow, and considering the nature of his right to these things by yow thoght fitt and necessarie to be gevin vnto ws, and of the value [of] what may therby aryse for our benefite, and haveing heard and considered all which is proponed by any persone whatsoever for clearing our title, as lykwayes the vassalls what they can demand lawfullie or will offer for supplieing the defects of ther rights: That therefter yow vse your best meanes for setling all thingis concerneing our and ther severall interests vpon such reasonable termes as yow shall think most fitt for the good of our service and ther satisfaction, and lykwyse to compose the differences between him and these other persones: And if yow cannot condescend vpon the premisses, that yow certifie ws of the reasones therof, with your opinions tuitching the same.—Whythall, 5 July 1630.

To the Advocat.

Trustie, &c.—Wheras we ar informed that diverse noblemen and others in that our kingdome whois rights and evidents thereof ar fitt to be renewed, paying such reasonable composition to ws for the same as we should be pleased to caus modifie, wherin respecting the good of our subjects and our owin benefite : Our pleasur is, that yow to this purpois draw vp a Commission in a legall and sure maner, leaving a blank for the names of such Commissioners to be inserted therin, as we shalbe pleased to appoynt by our thesaurer, And therefter that yow delyver the same vnto him, docated by yow to be exped according to the tenour thairof.—Whythall, 3 July 1630.

Our Soveraigne Lord, vnderstanding the long, good, and faythfull affection of vmquhill Sir William Boyes, knyt, late Captan of the Tour and Guarisone of Berwick-vpoun-Tueed, to the service of his Maties royall and dear father, of blessed memorie ; and his Matie, in tender commiseration of the now distressed estate of his Widow, Dame Kellse Powell, being willing that schoo dureing hir lyftyme have the pension of ane hundreth poundis sterline money be yeir, for hir better releiff now in hir aige : Therfor his Matie, with speciall advyse and consent of his Maties Right, &c. William, Erle of Morton, Lord Dalkeith and Aberdour, of his Maties right trustie and weilbeloved Counsellour, Archibald, Lord Naper of Merchingetoun, his Maties principall Thesaurer and deputy-thesaurer, in the offices of thesaurie, comptrollerie, collectorie, and thesaurarie of the new augmentatiounes of the kingdome of Scotland, or of the high thesaurer or thesaurie deputie for the time being, and of the commissioners of his Maties Exchequer of that kingdome, who ar or shall be, Ordeanes a letter of pension to be made and exped vnder the privie seall therof in dew forme, giveing, granting, and disponeing, lykas his Matie, with speciall advyse and consent forsaid, gives, grants, and dispones to the said Dame Kellse Powell, relict of the said Sir William Boyes, dureing all the dayes of hir lyftyme, ane yeirlie pension of ane hundreth pundis sterlin money to be vplifted and receaved be hir, hir assigneyis, factours, servandis, or other haveing hir power to that effect, out of the first and readiest of his Maties rents, dewteis, and casualiteis whatsoever of the said kingdome, at tua termes in the yeir Witsonday and Mertimes, by equall portiones, whairof the first termes payment to be and begin at the terme of Mertimes of this instant yeir of God jm vjc threttie yeres, and so furth yeirlie and termelie dureing hir lyftyme, with full power to hir, the said Dame Kelse Powell, or hir forsaidis, to vplift and receave yeirlie at the saidis termes of Witsonday and Mertimes, dureing hir said lyftyme the said yeirlie pension of 100lib sterling from his Maties said principall thesaurer and deputie thesaurer for the tyme being, or which shal happin to be heirefter : And with speciall command and direction to the said Thesaurer and deputy-Thesaurer, and others officers as aforesaid, to mak good and thankfull payment yeirlie at the saidis termes, at Witsonday and Mertimes, dureing the lyftyme of the said Ellse wherof the first terme to begin at the said terme of Mertimes nixtocum, of the said yeirlie pension of 100lib sterling money forsaid, to the said Dame Ellse or hir forsaidis, and with speciall command lykwyse to the Auditours of his Maties Exchecker for the tyme, or who shalhappin to be heireiter, to defease and allow in ther yeirlie accompts the said yeirlie pension, these presents be once schawen in Exchequer, and registrat as efferis : And his Matie ordanes that the said letter be extendit in the best forme, with all clauses neidfull.—Whythall, 6 July 1630.

These grant to the Widow of Sir Wm Boyes a pension of 100lib st. yeirlie, to be vplifted out of your Maties rents, and casualiteis of Scotland, at tuo termes of the yeir, Witsonday and Mertimes, wherof the first to begin at Mertimes nixt.

To the Exchequer.

Right, &c.—Wheras humble sute hath bene made vnto ws in behalff of Thomas Burnet, that we might be pleased to grant vnto him the arrears of the feyis and livereys belonging to his office as Mr of the Larder in that our kingdome, with a new gift therof, in respect that he at the tyme of the comeing of our late dear father to the Croun of this our kingdome, was to have succeided, as we ar informed, to be Mr of that office as being first ayd of the samyne by a gift vnder the privie seall, bot being vnwilling ather to grant him these arrears, or any new office importing a further charge to our Exchequer, yit out of our royall clemencie comiserating the hard esteat of ane old servand who hath these many yeires suffered by want of a charge from our said late dear father or ws, Our pleasur is, that yow try what feyis and arrears ar due vnto him by his office of the first ayde of the Larder ther; and if yow find any thing belonging to him be vertew of his gift, that yow cause pay the same vnto him for the tyme past, and to cum conforme thervnto, wherin we desyre that a speedie course may be taken, to the effect he may be enabled to give his attendance in any charge in our service which shalbe thoght fitt for him at our comeing to that our kingdome.—Nonsuch, 14 July 1630.

To the .

Right, &c.—We being often humblie moved vpon this inclosed petition of reference, and that the petitioner's case should be by yow considered, and that ordour should be takin for his satisfaction thairof, so be it wer fund by yow that his demand was just and reasonable, have agane thoght good according to the will of our late dear father to refer the consideratioun thairof vnto yow, willing yow, efter dew examinatioun of the petitioner's requeist, to tak such a speedie course for his releiff as the equitie of his cause shall in justice requyre, which we desyre the rather to be takin in regard as we ar informed that both in the tyme of our late dear father and our owin, he hath bene so many yeres putt of from haveing of that which he demandeth heirin, and from the office he had in our father's service as gentlman of the Larder in this our kingdome, that we may be no further troubled with his complaynts: So we, &c.—Nonsuch, 14 July 1630.

To the Archbischop of St Androis.

Right, &c.—Haveing bene credibilie informed of the abiliteis of our trustie and weilbeloved Mr John Scharp, doctour and professour in Divinitie, we wer pleased to recommend him vnto our trustie and weilbeloved Consen the Duik of Lennox (at whois gift the presenting to the place of a principall of St Leonardis Colledge doeth belong), for preferring him to that charge, whervnto sieing we have had a speciall care to caus mak choyse of him out of a respect of his sufficiencie, and being hopefull that his cariage therin will second our good opinion of him, We will expect at your handis that in any thing concerneing his setling, benefite, and priviledge whatsumever belonging to that charge, yow will vse your best endeavours that he posses and enjoy the same; So we bid yow fareweill.—Nonsuch, 14 July 1630.

To the Counsell.

Right, &c.—Wheras complant hath bene made vnto ws that some schips and goods alledged to belong to some persones duelling in France have bene vnjustlie takin by some of our subjects ther, and at still deteyned without tryell or due course of Lawis provyded in these caices, wherin haveing formerlie signifeid our pleasur vnto yow in ane particular concerneing some of them, we are heirby pleased agane to requyre yow to give speciall onlour vnto our Admirall and his assessours to administer Justice with all diligence vnto the pairties justlie interessed in these schips and goods, that the strangers have not just cause to compleane of any further delay : So we bid, &c.—Nonsuch, 14 July 1630.

To the Counsell.

Right, &c.—Haveing gevin furth our decree vpon things that ar submitted vnto ws in such sort as efter due information (haveing heard all pairteis) we conceived it to be best for the publict good, and haveing gevin ordour for making interruptiou that we oght no way be prejudged by the Act of prescription, which we can never think was at first intended for any prejudice of the Croun, We made choyse rather to obviat any inconvenient that may come therby by publict acts in Counsell and Session then to trouble our leidges by particular citatiouns : Therfor we have thoght litt to recommend the same vnto yow, that they may be confirmed by yow our Estats convened by ws at this tyme : And lykwyse wher our late dear father and we have erected the dignitie of Barronetts for advanceing the plantation of New Scotland, granting Lands therwith for that effect, we recommend lykwyse the same in so far as shalbe lawfullie demanded to be confirmed by yow : And so, not doubting bot that yow wilbe carefull both of these and other thingis that may import the honour of that kingdome or the good of our service, We bid, &c.—Nonsuch, 14 July 1630.

[No Address.]

Right, &c.—Being informed of your affection and abilitie to doe ws service, and desyreing to have a prooff of the same at this tyme, wherin sundrie things ar to be propounded from ws for the good of that kingdome, as will appear by the Articles which we have sent for that effect, and that yow may be better informed, we have requyred our trustie, &c. Sir William Alexander, our principall Secretarie of that our kingdome, to acquant yow more particularlie therwith, whome yow shall trust in any thing he doeth delyver vnto yow in our name concerneing our service at this tyme : And as we find your endeavours to prove, we will acknowledge the same accordinglie.—Nonsuch, 14 July 1630.

Ther ar tuo letters more verbatim vt supra.

Ther ar four letters more verbatim.

Thrie Ratifications signed the same tyme. One of the Act of Interruption ; One therof the determinations and Act of Annuitie ; And the thrid in favours of the barronetts of the title of barronett.

To the Generall Convention.

Right, &c.—Wheras we ar informed that our Right, &c. the Erle of Nithisdale did send vnto Carlile diverse malefactours borne in that our kingdome vpon evidence gevin him by Sir Ritchard Grhame, knyt and barronet, and that they had committed diverse thifts and other crymes vpon the bounds of the Midleschyrs of this our kingdome, and that some of them efter tryell and by due course of Justice did suffer death for the same : Becaus the said Sir Ritchard was vpon ane extraordinarie vocation, and great complaynt made aganst these crymes imployed by ws for sieing the offenders punished according to our Lawis, we have the rather thoght litt at this tyme to signifie vnto yow that we ar pleased with that service, and doe dispensse with any thing that can be objected aganst the said Erle for the same, being willing that such a course may be takin heirefter, that nather of our kingdomes might shelter such malefactours, bot that justice may have the due course in the bounds wher the crymes ar committed ; And to that effect that a reciprocall ordour be observed by both nations till the setling thairof : This shalbe no president for sending such malefactours to this kingdome, vnless it be by our speciall warrand, or that the lyk ordour be enacted and observed therin.—Nonsuch, 14 July 1630.

To the Counsell.

Right, &c.—Wheras we wer long since pleased to signifie our pleasur that Robert Creichtoun and Alex^r Alexander should be preferred to the first vacing offices of Masserie, wherof notwithstanding they have bene dissapoynted (as we ar crediblie informed), contrair to our royall intention : Now, least others should ather vnreasonablie importune ws to have these tuo offices, or least the said Robert and Alexander be further dissapoynted of what we intended for them, Our pleasur is, that yow tak notice of our royall intention heirin ; and if any such office doe vaik at our gift by death, demission, deprivation, or othervyse, that yow hearken to none bot shall have leave or shalbe sutters vnto ws or yow for the same, sicing according to our first intention we have resolved to grant the first place so vaiking vnto the said Robert and the nixt vnto the said Alex^r, and to this effect that yow cause mak ane Act of Counsell and sederunt, and for your so doeing these presents shalbe a sufficient warrand.—Nonsuch, 14 July 1630.

To the Justice Generall.

Right, &c.—Wheras humble complant hath bene made vnto ws in behalff of Margaret, Jeane, Elizabeth, and Barbara Barnes, of the slaughter of Johne Barnes, ther brother, committed by ane Blair of Pettindreich, his sone, and ther accomplices, wherin, being willing that Justice be administred without delay, according to our Lawis provyded in the cases, Our pleasur is, that yow cause cite them befor yow, and if, efter due tryell they are fund guiltie of that slaughter, that yow give ordour for executeing of Justice vpon them, according to our said Lawis, that by the exemple of ther punishment others therefter may be terrifeid from such barbarous crymes.—Nonsuch, 20 July 1630.

To the Convention of Estats.

Right, &c.—Wheras we ar informed that the Cathedrall Kirk of Dunkeld is so ruynous that, without a speedie course be takin for repairing therof, scarce any monument of so good a work will remaine, whervpon haveing heard a proposition made in behalff of our trustie and weilbeloved James Creichtoun, Clerk of the Commissariot ther, that the best meanes for helping therof wer by a voluntar contribution of our subjects, Our pleasur is, that yow consider of this purpois, and if yow find it expedient to be granted that yow give such ordour for collecting that contribution, and tuitching the maner, tyme, and limitations therof, and for the expeiding of the same for the vse of that work as yow shall think most fitt and necessarie, wherin, in respect of the said James his care and affection to sie that work be effected, we think fitt that he be imployed : So we bid, &c.—Nonsuch, 1630.

To the Chancellour.

Right, &c.- Haveing granted a Commission to your self and some others for tryeing the great abuses which (as we ar informed), wer committed by ane Keir against our subjects ther : And sieing it is agrieable to Justice that such persones be tryed and punisched if fund guiltie, wherby others may be terrifeid from practizeing the lyk heirefter, Our pleasur is, that with diligence yow expeed that Commission vnder our great seall, otherwayes that your returne reasone vnto ws why yow delay the same : We bid yow farewell.—Bagschot, 6 August 1630.

To the Erle of Monteith.

We have agane writtin to the Lord Naper that we have gevin full power vnto yow to deall with him for surrendrie to ws of his office of deputie thesaurer, and that we expect that he will the more willinglie condescend therin with yow, in regard we have delt with him efter so fare a maner : Therfor our pleasur is, that yow agane deall with him to this purpois, and if he will not yeild to any fair or reasonable proposition made by yow therin, we requyre yow to caus putt him to a tryell tuitching anything that justlie can be objected aganst him in the executioun of that office, which course we will further authorize (if neid be), efter what maner shalbe fund most requisit : We bid, &c.—Titchburne, 12 August 1630.

To the Lord Naper.

Wheras we gave power to our Right, &c. the Erle of Monteith, to deall with yow for surrendring to ws your office of deputie Thesaurer, whervnto (as we ar informed) yow ar vnwilling till yow hear our pleasur from our owin mouth : These ar therfor to signifie vnto yow that we have for causses just knowen vnto ws, commanded him to deall with yow therament, which we expect yow give him a willing ear to this our pleasur, by which we doe not intend yow should ather be disgraced or a loser : We bid, &c.— Titchburne, 12th August 1630.

Our Soverane Lord ordeanes a Remission to be made and exped vnder the great Seall of the king- dome of Scotland, makand mentioun that wher some 35 yeires agoe Duncan Campbell of Glenlyon, in his minoritie of 13 yeires of aige, hapned casuallie, he being in companie with some of his father's men when in rescue of his father's cattell stollen be ane Johne McMurthie McO'neill, and his complices, common theives and broken ylmen, the said John McMurthie O'neill, and some of his Companie wer killed in this conflict as common theivis, haveing ther prey with them : And in regard it doeth appear vnto his Matie that the said Duncan Campbell was then but a young boy, and not able to doe any harme ; and that the said Johne McMurthie McO'neill and some of his companie wer killed in the cryme be the said Duncan's father servandis, and that he can hardlie be troubled for that fact, or perswed befor any Judge, efter so many yeires silence : And his Matie, considering that if any of these old done deids should be now rypt vp and called in question, the exemple by consequence might prove dangerous and terrible to his Maties good subjects, who hath long lived in quyetnes since the begining of his Maties late royall father's happie entrance into the governement of his Maties kingdome of England : Therfor his Matie, of his speciall grace, mercie, and favour, hath accepted, and be thir presents accepts, the said Duncan Campbell vnder his royall protection and saveguard, frieing and exonering. lykas his Matie doeth heirby frie and fullie exoner him, the said Duncan Campbell, for now and ever, of all action and cryme that can in aney maner of way be imput vnto him through his being art or part or through his being in company at the slaughter of the Johne McMurthie McNeill and his complices, which was committed in the yeir of God, &c., and of all said question, challenge, and persute that may follow thervpoun aganst the persone of the said Duncan, his landis, goodis, or geir : Dischargeing. lykas his Matie doeth heirby speciallie discherge, his Maties Justice- Generall, Clerk, and Justice-Depute, his Maties thesaurer, deput thesaurer, Advocat, and all his Maties officers,

Judges, and ministers of his Lawis whatsumever, spirituall and temporall, for the tyme being, and who shal-happin to be heirefter, and ther deputts, or any of them, for seiking, apprehending, calling in question, imprissoneing, or any wayes troubling or molesting at any time heirefter of the said Duncan Campbell for being art or part of the slaughter of the said John M'Murthie M'Neill and his complices, or any of them: Ordeaneing the said Letter of Remission to be exped in the best and most ample forme, with all clauses neidfull.—Windsore 4 Sept' 1630.

To the Exchequer.

Right, &c.—Wheras the enclosed signature of some tythis of the Lordschip of Aberbrothok, con-tencing a reservatioun of our annuitie and of the constant locall stipend to the minister of the parochin wher the tythis ar, hath bene presented to be signed by ws, bot we being willing to proceid by due advyse in any purpois of that nature, have remitted the consideratioun thairof vnto yow, requyreing yow forthwith to pass the same if yow find nothing therin that can prejudge our late decrie: And if ther be anything therin thoght fitt by yow to be amended that efter the same shalbe accordinglie reformed, yow pass it with all diligence; and for your soe doeing these shalbe sufficient warrant: We bid, &c.—Hampton Court, 24 Sept. 1630.

To the Counsell.

Right, &c.—Wheras our Right, &c. the Marqueis of Hamilton is to levy sex thowsand men in that our kingdome, and to transport them into Germanie for assistance of our brother, the King of Sueden, in his warres, vndertakin for releiff of our distressed freindis ther, which generous interpryse of our loveing Consen we have not onlie approved, bot have lykwyse caused provyd him with competence of moneyis for performance of the same, and sieing this interpryse so much concerneth the libertie of our freindis and the common good of Christendome: Our will and pleasur is, that vpon sight heirof yow cause expede vnto him a commission vnder our great seall for levyeing and transporting of the said sex thowsand men according to the best and most speedie maner that hath bene at any tyme heirtofoir accustomed, or as can lawfullie and possiblie be granted: And that he and all persones imployed vnder him have your best furtherance, alsweill in the levyeing as for the transportatioun of his men, wherin we will not doubt bot your endeavours wilbe answerable to our expectation.—Hampton Court, 24 Sept. 1630.

To the Erle of Antrym.

Right, &c.—Wheras we ar crediblie informed that yow have agried with the Erle of Abercorne for payment of a sowme of money in consideration of the contract made betweene his father and yow for matching your sone, the Lord Dunluce, and his daughter, the Lady Lucie Hamilton, who being as yit within aige, can not so well acquyt by a lawfull discharge as the said now Erle can doe, who in honour is bund to be carefull of his said sister, and to match hir wher he best can with that sowme agried vpon by yow: And becaus we wish weill vnto the said Lady, and that schoe may be speedelie provyded for and preferred to some good match: Our pleasur therfor is, and we doe heirby pray and requeist yow to pay over the said money vnto the said now Erle to the vse of his said sister vpon his acquittance and securitie to frie yow for the same at the hands of the said Lady, and all others whatsoever, and for performeing vnto yow the substance of your last agriement wherevnto we wilbe ayding and assisting with all the lawfull favour we can: So recommending this particular vnto your speedie care and performance, as our trust and confidence is in yow, We bid, &c.—Hampton Court, 24 Sept. 1630.

These conteyne a Remission to Robert Dumbar of Bourgie and his Complices for the alledged slaughter of vmquhile Johne Dow. and for all other crymes alledgit to be committed by the said Robert (the crymes of treasone against your Maties persone, false coyne, and witchcraft excepted).—Hampton Court, 2 Octo^r 1630.

Vpon your Maties former grant concerneing the erection of ane kirk at Portpatrik (builded by the Viscount of Montgomry be his owin charges). and your Maties promeis to provyde the samyne with compitent meanes, and vpon his purchassing from the Commendatour of Salset the whole fruits and rents of the samyne, alreadie dimitted by him for the vse of that kirk : These contenethe a Chartour of Mortification for dissolveing the Abbacie thairof, wherby the spiritualitie and temporalitie of the samyne ar vnited to the said Kirk : Reserving to your Matie and successours the presenting of Ministers at Salset and Kirkmayden, the onlie tuo kirks which formerlie belonged to that abbacie, with the locall stipends to the ministers serveing the cure, and with provision that, at what tyme your Matie or successours shall mortifie and assigne to the minister at Portpatrik, as much other good rent, with the few-maills and few-dewteis of that temporalitie then this mortification therof to be payed, that ar to be ratifeid in the nixt parliament.—Hampton Court, 2 Octo^r 1630.

These conteyne a Licence for 19 yeires to James Jaksone, phisitan, his heyres, associats, &c., to vse within Scotland a new Invention for dryving all sorts of watter works, provyded he doe it with consent of the owners. All others, save he and his forsaids, ar prohibited to putt it in practeis dureing that tyme, vnder pane of Confiscation of ther engynes to the patentees. They ar to putt it in practeis within 3 yeires, otherwyse these to be voyd.—Hampton Court, 2 Octo^r 1630.

These conteyne a Lease to the Viscount Air, his heyres and, &c., for   yeires, of the ore of gold and silver within his owin landis, and ane heretabill disposition of all other mettalls therin, with power to export the best mettalls to ane forrayne part, being in league with your Matie, paying the customes vsed in the lyk cases, or as shalbe modifeid by the thesaurer or Excheker. They have libertie to bring in strangers for working of these mettells, who ar to have the benefite of naturalization. They are to pay to your Matie the   part of the ore, or the   part of the refyned mettall, with a yeirlie dewtie of dureing the said Lease for the said ore of gold and silver, and   for all other sorts of oris, in name of blencshe ferme. The part of the Master of the Mynes is reserved. These ar to be ratified in the nixt parliament.—Hampton Court, Octo^r 1630.

A PRECEPT TO THE THESAURER.

In regard of the faythfull service done vnto ws be Johne Sandilands, gentlman of our privie Chalmer in ordinarie, and of his continuall abyd about our persone, and for diverse others consideratiouns moveing ws : Our pleasur is, and we doe heirby will and require yow to caus pay vnto him or his assigneyis, with all diligence, the sowme of 600^{lib} sterling. and that out of the first and readiest of our rents and casualiteis whatsoever of that our kingdome, or out of such moneyis growing due or which shall accress vnto ws within the same by whatsoever maner of way : And for your so doeing these presents shalbe vnto yow a sufficient warrant and discherge.—Hampton Court, 2 Octo^r 1630.

To the Exchequer.

Right, &c.—Wheras a gift of the ward nonentrie and releiff (when it doeth happin) of certane Landis which did belong to one David Symsone, deceissed, and of the mariage of his aires, hath bene presented vnto ws, though we ar willing therby to gratifie Mr David Ayton, younger, for the panes takin by him in discoverie therof; yet not knowing how much the granting of the same vnto him may concerne ws, we ar pleised heirby to remitt the consideratioun therof vnto yow, that if the said ward, &c. be at our dispositioun, the gift therof may be exped in his favouris for some reasonable composition to be payed by him for the same, and giveing suirtie for his performance of such things as in caces of the lyk nature is vsuallie gevin by others.—Hampton Court, 2 Octor 1630.

To the Session.

Right, &c.—Haveing vpon good consideratiouns allowed our late Thesaurer to sitt in our Colledge of Justice, and the lyk consideratiouns, induceing ws at this tyme to have his place supplied by our Thesaurer now being, of whois sufficiencie and qualificatioun we ar verie confident: Our plesur is, that yow receive and admitt him in our said late Thesaurer's place in the Session, taking his oath as is accustomed iu such caces, and that he have and enjoy all the priviledges and other things of that place as his predicessouris therin did hold the same.—Hampton Court, 2 Octor 1630.

To the Counsell.

Right, &c.—Wheras by the within petition we ar informed of the many abuses committed in that kingdome by the common sort of practisers in phisick, and we being most willing the same may be amended by the Corporation mentioned in the petition, or by some other lawfull way as yow shall think fitting for the credit of that our kingdome and the good of our subjects ther: Our plesur therfor is, that yow tak the said petition into your serions consideratioun, and proceid therin, as yow in your judgments shall think fitting for encourageing of learneing and restrayneing of abuses in the said profession and practeis of physik, and when your opinion therin shalbe certifeid vnto ws, we will be the more readie to authorize and establishe what yow shall authorize in that kynd; And for that effect we desyre yow to requyre our advocat to draw and doquet a signatur fitt for our hand, and for recommending this bussines to your speciall care, we bid, &c.—Hampton Court, 2 Octor 1630.

To the Erle of Morton, Thesaurer.

Right, &c.—Wheras petition hath bene made vnto ws by Lady Agnes Maxwell, the daughter of the late Lord Maxwell, humblie praying our princelie letters vnto our Exchequer for geving ordour for payment of the arreirs of hir pension, and yeirlie in tyme comeing for hir mantenance, the same being bot 41lib. sterling per annum, or therabout: Though, by reasone of the present wants of our Exchequer, we have reserved to give ane ordour for the payment of any arreirs of pensions, yit, haveing commiseratioun of hir pure and distressed estate, and of hir want of all other meanes wherby now to live in hir old aige, we could wish that yow tak some course for hir present supplie, for which yow shall have what warrand yow shall cause draw vp for our hand: and therefter that yow mak payment to hir of hir pension, according to hir gift therof.—Hampton Court, 2 Octor 1630.

To the Excheqter.

Right, &c.—Wheras we ar informed that ane annual-rent out of the Landis of Murkhill and Trapren was bought and mortifeid by our late dear father for the vse of our Chappell Royall, which therefter was ratifeid in parliament ; And that now it is feared that if any disposition or deid should be made by ws or our successours, of or concerneing these landis, our Chappell right to that annual-rent wilbe endangered : Though we sie not just caus to suspect any such thing, yit to avoyd any fear that may be concerned in that kynd, Our pleasur is, that yow consider if ther be any such necessitie for taking a course to prevent what is heirin feared, and if yow find it necessarie, that yow mak ane Act of Exchequer thervpon, or otherwayes that yow doe therin as yow shall think most fitt for that purpois, which we, if neid be) will further authorize as yow to this effect shall best devyse : So we bid, &c.—Hampton Court, 2 Octo' 1630.

To the Exchequer.

Right, &c.—Wheras we are pleased to ratifie in favours of our Right, &c. the Viscount of Air, a Chartour of Confirmatioun granted by King James 3, confirmeing a Chartour of Alienatioun of certane landis mentionat in the ratificatioun which wer govin by one Sir Robert Creighton of Sanquhar, kny[t], to one Lawrence Creichton : Sieing what we have done heirin appeareth to be granted vpon a deed of one of our royall predicessours, Our pleasur is, that yow pass and cause expeed the said ratificatioun, according to the tenour therof, otherwayes that yow returne reasone to ws why the same cannot be done.—Hampton Court, 7 Octo' 1630.

To the Bischop of Brichan.

Reverend Father—Being informed that the Church of Munckie is not provydit of a preacher, and that Patrik Maull, our servand, is the cheif man of that parochine ; And being confident that he will present a sufficient and qualifeid persone for dischergeing of that function, our pleasur is, that whomsoever he shall name vnto yow, ye admitt him vnto the said Churche, as you will doe ws acceptable service.—Hampton Court, 7 Octo' 1630.

To the Counsellours Comeing vp.

Right, &c.—Haveing occasion at this tyme to confer with yow tuitching some things concerneing our service, We requyre yow with all diligence to repair vnto our Court, wher our farther pleasur shalbe made knowen vnto yow.

Ane other, conforme to the former, of that same dat lykwyse.

To the Thesaurer.

Right, &c.—Wheras our right trustie the Erle of Monteith hath, by express command from ws, for the vse of our Chappell royall, agried with the Lard of Syneton for the tythis of the landis of Markhill and Trapren, for payment vnto him of 500[lib] sterling, being willing (if convenientlie it can be done this yeir) that the tythes of these Landis for this crop may be had for the vse of our said Chappell ; Our pleasur is, that with all convenient diligence yow pay vnto the said Lard of Sincton the saidsowme of 500ᵇⁱˢ, and that out of the first and readiest of our rents, casualiteis, and others dewteis whatsoever due vnto ws, within our said kingdome ; and for the soo doeing these presents shalbe vnto yow a sufficient warrand and discherge.—Gevin at Hampton Court, 10 Octoᵣ 1630.

To the Counsell.

Right, &c.—Wheras we ar informed of some trouble that is lyklie to aryse betuixt our right trustie, &c. The Erle of Galloway and Johne Gordon of Lochinvar, tuitching one William Gordoun of Muryfade, and one who was a servand of the said William, for preventing whairof, being willing to have all differences between them composed on a freindlie maner, Our pleasur is (haveing takin these differences into your consideratioun) that yow vse your best meanes to remove them, according as yow shall find just caus ; but if yow find any of the pairteis (whome we will yow to call befor yow) refractorie to what yow shall think fitt to be concluded betweene them that yow returne your opinion what is fitt to be done by ws therin.— Hampton Court, 10 Octoᵣ 1630.

To the Advocat.

Trustie, &c.—Wheras we ar informed that nothwithstanding of the agriement made betweene . . . Gordon of Rothemay and James Creichton of Frandraught, tuitching the late accident betwene them, he, the said James Creichtoun, is as yit exceedinglie oppressed by such as wer of the pairtie of Rothemay, and by such rebells who, vnder cullour of that enmitie, doe wast and spoyll his landis and goods, to the great contempt of our Authoritie and lawis : Therfor our speciall pleasur is, that with all possible diligence yow insist in our name against them in a legall maner, according to any cause formerlie vsed against such malefactours and oppressours, and that yow grant vnto the said James Creichtoun your best ayd and concurrance, ather by intending and raising of letters and processes and prosecuteing Justice aganst them, in so far as can by your place in our or in his name, or both, as yow shall think most necessarie for that purpois.—Hampton Court, 10 Octoᵣ 1630.

To the Counsell.

Right, &c.—Wheras we ar informed that vntill our late dear father's taxt being in that our kingdome, all sowmes formerlie granted vnto him or any of his predicessours by the Estats of that our said kingdome in name of taxatioun wer so dewlie appearand amongest them from tym to tyme past memorie of man by the mutuall Consent of all the Estats, and by such way of assotiation as the Ecclesiasticall lands and benefices payed the one halff of the said taxatioun, and the noblemen, barrones, and frieholders of the Croun, tuo thrid parts of the other halff, and the regall burrows the other thrid part of the said halff (being the just part of the whole taxatioun) Conforme to the Act of parliament, lawis, and practique of that our kingdome, inviolablie observed vntill the last tuo taxatioun wherin the taxt rolls then suddenlie made did minister some colour to the benefices and burghes to compt for less then ther due proportion, and less then was then taxed and collected from the seuerall vassalls and burgesses of the saids benefices and burroughs ; And in regaird the said disproportion was compleyned vpon by our Solicitour, Mr Wm Haig, vnto quhom we did latelie grant a Commission for discoverie therof in the said last tuo Taxatiouns ; And we being verie desyrous to have that errour (if any be) amended and prevented for the tyme to cum, and in such convenient maner as none of our particular subjects may have any just occasion to think that ather we ar frustrated of ther benevolence granted, or they disproportioned in the

II I

division therof contrarie to the former lawis and practique of the said kingdome : Our pleasur therfor is, and we doe heirby authorize, will, and requyr yow to advert seriouslie vnto the making of the tax roll of this present taxatioun, and so in equitie to proportion the same as (respect being had to the pound landis) the burrowis may be taxed to no more than the sixt part of the wholl, as the continuall custume was in payment of all former taxatiouns of definit sowmes : As also, that yow have a care that the particular beneficos and vassalls therof, and the particular burgesses and inhabitants of burrowis be taxed to noe more then according to the quantitie of ther frie rent and irie geir respectivelie, conforme to the tenour of the Act of parliament : And that the saids sowmes so to be levyed or payed in name of taxatioun may be duelie accompted for to our vse : Which recommending, &c.—Hampton Court, 10 Octo⁺ 1630.

A signature was signed for M⁺ Andro Bruce, principall of S⁺ Leonard's Colledge of S⁺ Andrewis, wherby he was to be nominated and presented to the deanrie, Chaptour of S⁺ Androis, and kirk of S⁺ Leonard's, and to the constant stipend therof, modifeit by the Lordis Commissioners of parliament, &c.— Hampton Court, 12 Octo⁺ 1630.

M⁺ Johne Fyff, present minister of Findogask, by this presentatioun was to be nominated and presented to the Archdeanrie of Dumblane, and benefice thairof, and to the haill teynd sheavis and others teyndis, as well personage as viccarage, of the kirk and parochin of Findogask, being ane part of the patrimonie of the said Archdeanrie, except the teynd scheavis of the landis of Keirprone allanerlie, lyand within the said parochin.—Hampton Court 12 Octo⁺ 1630.

Sub⁺   A. B. DUMBLANE.

TO THE ARCHBISCHOP OF S⁺ ANDROIS.

Right, &c.—Being informed that by displaceing M⁺ Joseph Lawrie, late Minister at Stirling, and the not restablisching ather of him, or placeing some other able and qualifeid persone ther, the Inhabitants of that burgh ar diverse tymes dissapoynted of the benefite of God's word, and ther Infants delayed in receaveing tymelie baptisme : Our pleasur is, and we doe herby will and desyre yow, if yow find that by the ordour of the Churche the said M⁺ Joseph cannot be re-established, yow sie him speedelie provyded with such a sufficient preacher as they shall present vnto yow.—Hampton Court, 12 Octo⁺ 1630.

TO THE BURROWIS.

Trustie, &c.—We caused the Commissioners sent hither of late concerneing the fisching to meitt and confer with such as wer appoynted by ws heir to treat in that purpois, haveing our selfis heard at lenth the reasones and grounds of that bussines, the tymelie and provident prosequution wherof may tend peculiarlie to your good, and increase of trade and schipping ther, and to the good of all our kingdomes in generall : And becaus it is nowayes intented that yow should therby be wronged in your ancient priviledges or benefite, we are confident that yow will vpon your part goe on in the most effectuall maner for advanceing of that purpois, the particulars wherof, as they have bene debated heir, we remitt to the relation of your Commissioner, who will at lenth impart the same vnto yow from ws ; and as hitherto in all things con-cerneing our service recommended vnto yow by ws, and particularlie in this last assemblie of our estats, we have fund your affection to our service, for which we give yow hartlie thanks, so we ar confident that in all other things concerneing the good therof yow will continew as we have ever fund yow.—Hampton Court, 12 Octor 1630.

To the Arch-B. of St Androis.

Right, &c.—Haveing vnderstude how affectionatlie yow and the rest of the Clergie wer readie to further these things which wer propounded concerneing the good of our service at the last convention, we give yow hartie thanks for the samyne, willing yow to signifie the rest of your brethren how weill we ar satisfeit therwith, which we shall ever be willing to acknowledge when any occasion is offered that may fairlie tend to your good : And as yow was cairfull of our service at that tyme, we expect the lyk of yow at the nixt meitting for the erecting of a generall fisching, which is a great, a glorious, and beneficiall work, cheiflie for the good of that our ancient kingdome : And therfor being verie confident that yow will apply your best Counsells for the advancement therof, We bid, &c.—Hampton Court, 12 Octor 1630.

To the Counsell.

Right, &c.—We have fund your affection to our service at this last Convention of the Estats, for which we give yow hartie thanks. As tuitching the propositions sent by ws vnto yow concerneing the improveing of the Fischings ther, we have caused the Commissioners (sent hither to treat in that purpois) to meeit and confer with such as wer appoynted by ws heir to that effect, haveing our selfis heard the reasones and grounds for prosecuteing that bussines, wherin, efter that they have delyvered vnto yow what hath bene debated heir at this tyme. We will yow to insist, as yow have begun, to give your best advyse and furtherance for bringing a work of so great consequence to the intended perfection, which, amongst other good services done by yow for the publict good of that our ancient kingdome, will accompt this one of the greatest ; and efter yow have heard the opinion of such of the Estats as ar to convene for that purpois, we desyre yow to returne Commissioners, with instructions to treat heirin, with ane absolute power to conclude for avoyding all delayes, becaus the work, for diverse considerations, requyreth haist.— Hampton Court, 12 Octor 1630.

To the Assemblie of Estats.

Right, &c.—We have fund by report such as wer present at your last meeitting, and by effects your affection vnto our service, wherwith we rest weill satisfeit, and doe give yow most hartlie thanks for the same, assureing yow that we will not be wanting in any thing that we can contribute to the good of that our ancient kingdome ; for which effect some propositions wer sent by ws to be considered of by yow concerneing the improveing of the fischings ther, whervpon yow sent as we requyred Commissioners hither to treat of that purpois, we have caused them, and such as wer appoynted by ws heir for that effect, to meeit and confer togidder therin, haveing our selfis heard the reasones and grounds for prosecuteing that bussines, which, as we conceave (if it be providentlie followed), may prove a work of great consequence for the generall good of our whole kingdomes, and more particularlie for the benefite of that our ancient kingdome, by the daylie improveing of trade and schipping therin : And sieing it is not heirby intendit that any of your ancient priviledges nor benefits formerlie enjoyed be anywyse hindered, bot, on the contrarie, that your trade, schipping, and consequentlie the strenth and glorie of the kingdome be encreased, These wil therfor seriouslie recommend vnto yow the said purpois, as it shalbe delyvered vnto yow by them who wer Commissioners vnto ws, that you may consider how this work may be best and speedili done, what toimes and plantations ar to erected for this purpois: And to the intent yow on your part should give that contribution, help, and furtherance which is requisite for so good and glorious a work, that yow condescend among your selffis what help and supplie may be expected from thence, and haveing weill considered what is fitt to be done vpon your parts for advancement of this great work, that Commissioners may be sent bak with absolute power to conclud therin, without any restriction, bot of our approbation.—Hampton Court, 12 Octo^r 1630.

Postscript with his Maties owin hand.

This is a work of so great good to both my kingdomes, that I have thoght good by these few lynes of my owin hand seriouslie to recommend vnto yow, the furthering or hindring of which will ather oblidge or dissoblidge me more than any one bussines that hath happened in my tyme.

Subscribitur   C. R.

To the Sessione.

Right, &c.—Haveing resolved to change some persones who had extraordinarie places in session, according as we vpon good Considerationns had formerlie intendit, and being confident of the sufficiencie and qualificationn of our Right, &c. The Lord Traquair, we ar heirby pleased to will and requyre yow to admitt and receave him in the session in the place of the Lord Erskene, and that yow tak, as is accustomed in such cases, the oath of the said Lord Traquair, whome we will to have and enjoy all the priviledges and other things belonging to that place; and for your so doeing, &c.—Hampton Court, 12 Octo^r 1630.

Sir William Alexander to be admitted in place of Sir Archibald Achiesone.

To the Session.

Right, &c.—Haveing resolved to change some persones who had extraordinarie places in Session, and so furth, conforme to the precedent letter, his Matie willing that Sir John Hamilton, Clerk Register, be admitted in the Session in the place of Sir John Scott, directour of the Chancerie.

And ane other of the same date, and conforme to the precedent, admitting in the Session in the place of

To Four Noblemen.

Right, &c.—Considering how inconvenient it is that such a great number of Commissioners should be vpon our Exchequer as ar for the present, it would seme more expedient that none should be admitted thervpon save our Officers of Estate: And yit being desyreous to have it done without any just caus of discontent to these noblemen and others who have bene in it the tymes bypast, and have deserved well of ws, we have lykwyse takin to our consideratioun that these officers, or a certane number of them, might be the quorum, Our thesaurer or deputie thesaurer being alwyse one, without removeing any of the rest for the present: Bot in regard this is a matter of speciall moment, we would not determyne in any thing without your advyse: Therfoir we desyre yow that yow consider of both these tuo wayes, or of any other that in your judgment may seme better, and at yow resolve lett a Commission be drawin vp accordinglie and sent vnto ws: So recommending that speciallie vnto your care as vnto those whome we speciallie trust, We bid, &c.—Hampton Court, 12 Octo^r 1630.

To the Lord Erskene.

Right, &c.—Though to prosecute that caus which vponn good consideratiouns was intented and delayed by ws at our last placeing yow vpon the Session, We have removed yow from that Judicatorie for a tyme, we ar so far from doeing it out of any dislyk of your cariage therin, or in any vther thing concerneing our service, that these ar to give yow most hartie thanks for the same, assureing yow that we shall not be vnmyndfull therof whensoever any convenient occasion is offered wherby we may express our respect vnto yow: We bid, &c.—Hampton Court, 12 Octo^r 1630.

Ane other of this style verbatim done to Sir John Scott.

Instructions from the King his Matie to the Right Hon^{le} the Erle of Monteith, Lo; President of his Ma^{teis} privie Counsall of Scotland.

It is his Ma^{teis} pleasur that the said Erle gave ordour to his Ma^{teis} Advocat carefullie to advert to his Ma^{teis} interruption of the prescription, and that he vse his best meanes that nothing be omitted that may save his Ma^{teis} Actions from prescription.

That the said Erle seik and requyre ane accompt of such letters and directions as his Matie hath formerlie gevin concerneing the rectifieing the abuse of Coyne.

That the said Erle give ordour to his Ma^{teis} Advocat to try the right of Sir Mungo Murray to the Lands of Hountingtour, and to report the estate thairof to his Matie.

That the said Erle desert out of his Court of Justice-Generall any dittay concerneing Wm Gordoun of Murefade, and of one who was a servant of his, becaus his Matie hath requyred his Counsell to vse ther best meanes to compose these differences in a friendlie maner.

That the said Erle confer and advyse with his Ma^{teis} Chancellour Thesaurer concerneing the fisching bussines, and that they enjoy togidder in what and in everie thing that may concerne the advancement of his Ma^{teis} service.

That the said Erle confer and advyse with the Lord Chancellour the Archbischop of St Androis, Thesaurer Privie Seall, and his Ma^{teis} Advocat, or any thrie of them, whither it be feit for the good of his Ma^{teis} service to mak vse of the Commission signed for the Exchequer wherin the officers ar onlie joyned with the Thesaurer and deputie Thesaurer, or if the saidis officers, or some of them, shall onlie be putt vpon the quorum, or otherwayes what Commission they shall think best to be vsed therin, that one may be drawin vp accordinglie for his Ma^{teis} hand.—Hampton Court, 12 Octo^r 1630.

To the Chancellour.

Right, &c.—Wheras we wer pleased vpon good consideratiouns to commend vnto yow for vseing the fairest and best way in making that act vneffectuall which was made aganst the decrie gevin by our Colledge of Justice in favours of our burght of Edinburgh tuitching some of the Inhabitants of Leith, and therefter in composing in a freindlie maner the differences betuixt them which at the tyme yow could not convenientlie effectuat becaus of our service entrusted vnto yow in the ensueing Convention, and the vacancie following thervpon: Though we have heirin at lenth signifeid our pleasur to our Counsell, these ar agane seriouslie to recommend vnto yow that purpois, that we be not further troubled with any question that may aryse therin.—Hampton Court, 12 Octo^r 1630.

To the Toun of Edinburgh.

Trustie, &c.—Vnderstanding how that immediatlie efter Mr Johne Scharp did find himselff dissappoynted of that place of principall of St Leonard's Colledge (whervnto of our owin motion and knowledge of his sufficiencie we had recommended him), yow had by the advyse of the Archbischop of St Androis made choyse of him to serve in your Church or Colledge, we give yow hartie thanks for the same, and the rather for that yow did efter so readie and frie maner : And as we doubt not bot he will discharge a dewtie in that charge, so we wilbe confident that yow will contribute (as occasion shall requyre) to any thing that may tend to his further advancement and furthering of his good.

To the Counsell.

Right, &c.—Wheras we have bene informed that yow have caused suspend the decrie gevin by the Session in favours of our burgh of Edinburgh aganst some of the Inhabitants of Leith : Though we doubt not yow have had some speciall Considerationns moveing yow thervnto, yit desyreing that everie Judicatorie may be preserved in the owin integritie, and sieing as we conceave that decrie was pronunced by our Colledge of Justice as a civill matter properlie belonging vnto them, we sie no reasone why it should not tak effect as was intendit without any hinderance by any meanes whatsoever : Therfor our pleasur is, that yow tak a course for making the Act made aganst the decrie vneffectuall, that our Lawis may have ther frie course amongst all our subjects whatsoever, and our said burght may enjoy ther liberteis conforme thervnto : As for removeing of that difference which is amongst them concerneing garnelling of victuall in Leith, we have signifeid our pleasur to our Chancellour, Thesaurer, and President of our Counsell, that such a course may be amicablie takin therin, as if our said burgh shall dispense with ther libertie in that poynt the saids inhabitants may [make] such retribution vnto them in other things as in reasone and equitie in such causes is allowable.—Hampton Court, 12 Octo^r 1630.

To the Exchequer.

Right, &c.—Wheras we have signed a signature of Confirmatioun of the contract past betweene the Lord Lyndsay and the Lard of Barnes, concerneing his tythis of West Barnes, within the paroch of Craill, as a paterne for the rest of that paroch : Our pleasur therfor is, that yow expect the same, and the lyk signature vnto the rest of the parochiners of the said paroch, with reservatioun of our annuitie and others mentionat and reserved in the said signature : And for your so doeing, &c.

Drawin by Sir Archibald Achiesone, and procured to be signed by the Marqueis of Hamilton.

To the Chancellour.

Right, &c.—Wheras we have writtin our princelie letters to the Lords of our privie Counsall concerneing the approportioning of this present taxatioun and setling of the tax rolls therof : And considering that yow ar our Collectour-generall of the said taxatioun, and absolutelie trusted by ws in anything which may concerne the same or the dewteis of your place, wherin we ar confident that yow will endevour to satisfie our just desyres in so duelie proportioning the beneficis and burroughs vnto the taxatioun of the pound Landis of the nobilitie and gentrie, and other frie holders of our Croun, as the sowmes to be levyed by vertew of the taxt rolls so to be made may be dewlie collected and accompted for to our vse: Our pleasur therfor is, that yow seriouslie advert vnto the making vp of the taxt rolls of this present taxatioun, wherby such due proportion may be observed therin, as had wont to be in all former taxatiouns of definite sowmes, wherof (as we ar informed) the burrows did ever pay halff as much as the nobilitie and gentrie frieholders of the Croun, and the benefices as much as both, viz. :—the benefices one-halff, the burrows one-sixth part, and the pound lands the rest, being two sixth parts, conforme to the act of parliament, lawis, and custome of that our kingdome, inviolablie observed past memorie of man : So recommending this particular vnto your speciall care of our service and proffeit, against which, if any objection shal happin to be made, we desyre yow to caus our Advocat and sollicitour Mr Wm Haig mak answer therto in writting, that the same may be consdered of by ws : So we bid, &c.—Hampton Court, 12 Octor 1631.

By Sir Ard Achiesone.

To the Advocat.

Right, &c.—Wheras we have writtin our princelie letters vnto the Lords of our privie Counsall of that our kingdome concerneing the due setling of the taxt rolls of this present taxatioun in such ane equitable maner as the benefices and burrowis may be justlie apportioned vnto the pund lands of the nobilitie and gentrie, conforme to the ancient laudable custome observed in all former taxatouns of definite sowmes, wherin the borroughs ever payed halff as much as the Nobilitie and gentrie, and the benefices as much as both : Our pleasur therfor is, and we doe heirby will and requyre yow to have a speciall care of our interest in the said taxatioun, and to sie the taxt rolls therof so duelie made as the said due proportion may be observed by the saids benefices and brughs relative to the pound Landis of the nobilitie and gentrie holdin of our Croun : And also that yow doe vrge, for our interest, that all sowmes to be taxed vpon the particular benefices and vassalls of benefices, and particular burgesses and inhabitants of brughs, may be so dewlie accompted for to our vse, as we be not frustrat of ther benevolence, nor they disproportioned fra the sowme payable out of the pund landis : So recommending this vnto your speciall care and wounted dextruous proceiding in our service, we bid you fairwell.—Hampton Court, 12 Octor 1630.

By Sir Ard Achiesone.

To the Viscont of Air.

Right, &c.—Wheras ane Assemblie of our Estats ar to meit vpon the second of Nor nixt to treat vpon some things concerneing the good of our whole kingdomes in general, and in particular to the honour and benefite of that our ancient kingdome : Though we know that the matters to be treated therin ar such as may induce a desyre in all our subjects to advance the same, yit to the end our royall intention therin for ther good may be rightlie vnderstude from such who know the Estate therof, and from such of whois affection to our service we ar confident : These ar to requyre yow to be present at that assemblie, and as in all things concerneing the good of our service we have hitherto fund your hartie affection, so we will expect that in these things to be treited now (the concludeing wherof we most earnestlie affect), yow will vse your best meanes both by your self and otherwayes to further the same, which we will accompt a speciall service done vnto ws, and will not be vnmyndfull of what we last promised vnto yow, And that with the first in that kynd : We bid, &c.—Hampton Court, 19 Octor 1630.

These conteyne a grant vnto Johne Halyburton, his heyres and assigneyis, of the nonentresse, maills, fermes, and dewteis of the landis and baronie of Borthuik, which pertened vnto vmquhill

Johne Lord Borthuik, vmquhill William Lord Borthuik, his sone, vmquhill William Mr of Borthuik, his eldest sone, vmquhill James Lord Borthuik, his brother, vmquhill James Lord Borthuik, his brother, vmquhill James Lord Borthuik, his sone, and last deceissed, or any of them holdin immediatlie of his Matie vaiking, by reasone of nonentrie or reduction of ther rights or otherwyse for all termes bygane and to cum dureing the nonentrie.—Hampton Court, 25 Octor 1630.

These conteyne a ratification of ane alienation of the teynd scheanes and others, Tithes, personage and viccarage, of the baronie of the Westbarnes, in Fyff, and of ane assignatioun to the taks thairof made by the Lord Lyndsay, as patrone of the Church of Craill, and generall taksman of the tythes of the paroche to Alexr Cunynghame of Westerbarnes, and Johne Cunynghame, his sone, and his heyres and successours, heretours of the said baronie, in performance of his Maties decree and determination made thereanent : Reserveing to his Matie and successours the annuitie due furth of the saidis tythis, conforme to his highnes for said decreit, and decree of valuatioun of the saidis tithes gevin or to be gevin theranent, and all exactions and impositions made or to be made for pious vses concerneing the same, and they releiveing the said Lord Lyndsay and his heyres of all the saidis annuiteis, ministers' stipends, taxatiouns, fabrick of the church and churchyard dyks, elements to the Communioun and others, burdens, impositions, and dewteis whatsoever imposed or to be imposed vpon the saidis tythes of this cropt 1630, and in all tyme coming : His Matie promises to ratifie the same in the nixt parliament, and to mak vnto them such further securitie thairof as he doeth to any other heretours of ther owin tythes.—Hampton Court, 25 Octor 1630.

A PROTECTION TO Mr WILLIAM LEVINGSTOUN OF SALTON FOR ONE ZEIR EFTER THE DATE HEIROF, 25 Octor 1630.

TO THE EXCHEQUER.

Right, &c.—Wheras we ar informed that ther is no peculiar place as yit appoynted for the recept of our revenewis and casualiteis in that our kingdome, or for issueing of payments, according to the severall warrants, rather yit any particular registratioun of the saids recepts and payments, wherby our leidges may be eased and secured, and we certifeid what is payed in or payed out, or what may be remaneing in our Exchequer from tyme to tyme : Our pleasur therfor is, and we doe herby will and requyre yow to appoynt a particular place for the saids recepts and payments, and for registring the warrands and acquittances therof by our Clerk Register and Remembrancer, and ther deputeis, for ther ease and securitie of our subjects ; and that the same may the better be charged for in the accompts, and certifeid vnto ws from tyme to tyme, according to our former instructions gevin vnto our said Remembrancer : And for your so doeing, these presents, &c.—Hampton Court, 25 Octor 1630.

By Sir Ard Achiesone.

TO THE CHANCELLOUR.

Right, &c.—Wheras we have writtin a former letter vnto yow concerneing the proportioning of the ordinarie taxatioun, and being now informed that the compounding of the extraordinarie taxatiouns may not onlie prove prejudiciall to our profitte, bot also may oppin a way to others to defer ws of ther due taxatiouns, by putting out ther sowmes in the names of some of the compounders: Our pleasur therfor is, and we doe heirby will and requyre to have a preventious care of both the saids dangers. And in such a sure way as both we and our leidges may enjoy the benefite of the act of parliament conceaved concerneing the extraordinarie taxatiouns and concealed annual-rents: So we, &c.—Hampton Court, 25 Octo^r 1630.

By Sir Ar^d Achiesone.

To the Counsell.

Right, &c.—Wheras our trustie . . . . ane humble sutter vnto ws for the lyk licence to export out of that our kingdome Ten thowsand stane weght of wooll as yow granted to Williame Dick, and other merchands, vnto which his humble desyre we ar gratiouslie pleased to hearken, for causses knowen vnto ws: Our pleasur therfor is, and we heirby will and requyre yow to grant vnto him the lyk licence for the same as yow did venallie grant, and latelie have granted, vnto the said Williame Dick and vther merchands the last yeir; and that the said licence be made ather in his owin name or the name of any other whom he shall nominat and appoynt, he and they alwayes paying our due custome for the same; And that yow grant noe other licence till any persone whatsoever till all the saids 10,000 stane weght be exported, provyded the same be exported within the space of ane yeir after the dait of the said licence.—Hampton Court, 25 Octo^r 1630.

By Sir Ar^d Achiesone.

To the Counsell.

Right, &c.—Wheras we have bene moved, vpon the inclosed petition for giveing way to erect lights in the Yland of May, in the firth of Forth, as a purpois expedient for preventing of shipwrakis therabout, wherin, expecting the good and saiftie of our subjects, we ar heirby pleased to remitt the consideratioun of the petition vnto yow, that haveing pervsed the same, and hearkned to what can be further propounded to yow tuitching that purpois, yow may resolve if ther be any expedientie for erecting of these Lights, and of the meanes and wayes to keip the same; and if yow find it necessarie, and a willingnes of such of our subjects as ar most interest therin to pay such a dewtie to the same, as yow and they can best condescend vpon, that a patent be drawin vp for our signature heir, or to pass our Cosnet ther as yow shall think fitt for the petitioners, and that for such number of yeirs for such a dewtie to be imposed according to the schipp's burden, and such other limitatiouns and provisions as yow shall think fitt to preseryve for the good of our kingdome and saftie of our subjects.—Hamptone Court, 25 day of October 1630.

To the Advocat.

Trustie, &c.—Haveing granted a Commission to our trustie and weilbeloved Mr Wm Haig, as solister, vpon apparent reasones proponed by him for our benefite and the publict benefite of that our kingdome in discoverie of more moneyis due vnto ws then ar accompted for our vse of the tua preceiding taxatiouns, And being willing to advance (in so far as we can lawfullie doe) any proposition tending to that purpois, we have heirby thoght fitt to requyre yow to assist him in the prosecution of that Commission, and seriouslie to consider such thingis as he shall propone vnto yow concerneing the taxt rolls, wherin expecting such effects of your panes as is answerable to your charge, and the prooff we have had of your former affection to our service, we bid, &c.—Hampton Court, 28 Octo^r 1630.

ii   K

To the Session.

Right, &c.—Wheras we ar informed that our late dear father did in behalff of our late servand James Pringle recommend vnto that our Colledge of Justice ane Action depending befor them concerneing the Landis of Lees in regard of the interest of that action of Lancelot Pringle, his brother, who (as we ar informed) can not mak any long residence ther, and of the aige and inabilitie of his father to prosecute that action, We ar heirby pleased to recommend vnto yow the speedie dispatch therof in so far as may be agrieable vnto Justice, and the equitie of the cause.—Hampton Court, 28 Octo' 1630.

To Four Counsellours.

Right, &c.—Wheras we ar informed that Symeon Ersken was by our late Thesaurer assigned to paye rests of the bygane taxatiouns which he hath not receaved in regard of the persones inhabiliteis who wer to pay the same, in seiking wherof he hath both lost his tyme and meanes ; We being most willing (according to our late father's royall intention) that he be payed of the 5000 M. scotts designed by ws for his satisfaction for haveing so frielie adventured his lyff abroad in killing of one in single combat who had vnjustlie caluminat our said late father, of worthie memorie : Our pleasur is, that yow consider and examyne the warrant gevin vnto him by our said late thesaurer, and what he receaved of the 5000 Merks, and therefter that yow tak such a course for his payment for what shal happin to be due vnto him out of these concealed taxatiouns as yow shall think fit, and as may be most agrieable to your Commission from ws.

To the Erle of Buccleuch.

Right, &c.—Finding the tyme appoynted for your repairing to Court at Michaelmes last for the setling of all differences betuixt yow and Francis Stewart to be expyred, We ar pleased to requyre yow to repair vnto ws for that purpois betuixt this and the last day of No' nixt, that we may determyne therin as we have resolved, for immediatlie therefter we intend to proceid, and will delay no longer : Thus haveing signifeid our pleasur heirin vnto yow, we bid yow farewell.—Hampton Court, 29 Octo' 1630.

Ane other conforme to the precedent of that same date to the Erle of Roxburgh.

These concerneing ane Ratificatioun of the two Chartours granted by your Ma'tie for erecting of one burgh royall, called the burgh of Galloway, with ane new gift of the samyne of the tenour of the former, onlie changeing the boundis to ane more commodious place, with power to the provest, baillies, and ther successours to infeft and sease the Inhabitants in ther tenements and portions to be holdin of your Ma'tie in frie burgage, according to the custome of burgh, and secluding all others from the liberteis of ane frie burgh in burgh of baronie, mercatts, and fayrs within the bounds alone designed, to be holdin of your Ma'tie in frie burgh royall for payment of ten merks of barronie maill.— Whythall, 5 No'.

Our Soveraigne Lord, in regard of the abilteis of his Ma'tis Right, &c. Johne, Lord Traquair, being willing, for the good and furtherance of his Ma'tis service, to joyne him with the Lord Naper as his Ma'tis deputie-thesaurer of the kingdome of Scotland, Ordeanes a Letter to be exped under the great seall therof in due forme, making and constituteing the said Lord Traquair to be joyned with the Lord Naper in all the offices of Thesaurarie, Comptrollerie, Collectorie, and thesaurerie of the New augmentatiouns; And with power to the said Lord Traquair to exerce the said office of deputie Thesaurer in all things whatsoever, which did or may apperteane to any deputie thesaurer of that kingdome, And to enjoy all priviledges, honours, digniteis, and immuniteis thervnto belonging, with power lykwyse to the said Lord Traquair, as his Ma^{tis} deputie-Thesaurer to receave all and sindrie his Ma^{tis} rents, customes, casualiteis, as well of his Ma^{tis} ancient patrimonie and propertie of the Croun and principalitie, as of all ecclesiasticall rents and dewteis whatsumevir, and all and sindrie, his Ma^{tis} rents which have of late accreassed, or shall happin heirefter to accrease to his Matie within the said kingdome: To exerce and enjoy the saids offices, priviledges, honours, &c., as the said Lord Traquair shalbe particularlie warranted by his Matie, and authorized heirefter, excepting the said Lord Naper his feyis and proffeits belonging to that place of deputie thesaurer: Ordaineing these presents, &c.—Whythall, 6 No^r 1630.

To the Chancelloer.

Right, &c.—Wheras our trustie and weilbeloved Mr William Haig, our solister, hath made a proposition vnto ws semeing expedient for ordouring the rolls to be gevin out for collecting the borrowis and beneficos parts of this taxatioun, wherby yow may find a clearer way to doe ws service in that kynd for our benefite and the good of our subjects then hath been practized in Collection of the last two taxatiouns, wherin being willing to further any thing tending to such a purpois; Our pleasur is, that yow consider of the proposition which we have commanded him to give yow in writt, And (vnless ther be some speciall reasons in writt to the contrarie, against which our Advocat and our said solister can give no reasone), that yow proceid accordinglie, and if any course be alreadie takin for the Collecting of these taxatiouns contrarie to this expedient (being approved), that the same be reduced and ordered according to the said proposition, vnless it be made appear that this same may not be done without charge or trouble vnto ws, hurt to our subjects, or prejudice to the ordour preservyed by acts of parliament in the collection of taxatiouns; wherin expecting the care and diligence for the good of our service, we bid, &c,—Whythall, 5 No^r 1630.

To the Counsell.

Right, &c.—Wheras we ar informed of the lamentable accident falling out by burneing the Tour of Frendraucht, with the Viscount of Aboyne and some others therin: As we ar soriefull for the same, so we desyre, for removeing of all suspition that may seme to aryse of any foirthegh fellonie, that yow caus vse all lawfull and possible meanes for tryeing the maner therof, and if yow find the same to have proceidit out of any malicious intention. Our express will and pleasur is, that according to the Lawis of that our kingdome justice be execute vpon the offenders in the most exampliarie maner, to the terrour of all others who shall attempt the lyk heirefter, and that yow have a speciall care that no trouble aryse therby in these boundis.—Whythall, 5 No^r 1630.

To the Exchequer.

Right, &c.—Wheras we ar informed that yow have carefullie cause surveigh the estate of some of our houssis within that our kingdome, and find many things therin fitt to be helped befor our Masters of Works do medle therin for keiping therof in such good ordour therefter as by Contract between ws and them they ar bund to doe, becaus that condition was made vpon verie good consideratiouns for our benefite, we think it expedient that yow conduce with Artificers and others persones thoght fitt by yow for putting them in such good ordour as is requisit : Or otherwyse, that yow condescend with the Masters of Work themselffis for doeing therof in the best maner yow can for our behaiff, that thairefter they vpon ther parts may proceid according to the said Contract ; And for advanceing of moneyis to that purpois, which we desyre may be done with as much diligence as may be, these presents shalbe vnto yow, our Thesaurer, and others whom it may concerne, a sufficient warrant and discharge.—Gevin at our Court of Whythall, 5 Nor 1630.

To the Commissioners for Surranders.

Right, &c.—Wheras complaynt hath bene made vnto ws that the tythis of Dysert, wherof the Lord Sinclair is patron, have bene much vndervalued, wherby both we in our annuitie, the patron and persone of Dysert, ar prejudged, whairof, and of the whole bussines of the valuations in generall (recommended by ws vnto yow befor), we desyre yow seriouslie to consider that if the Sub-Commissioners have not takin a right course in ther valuations, yow sie the same rectifeid, as shalbe most expedient for the publict good, and the bussines itsellf hastned with as much diligence as can be ; which earnestlie recommending to your care, We bid, &c.—Whythall, 5 Nor 1630.

To the Advocat.

Trustie and weilbeloved Counsellour, We greet yow well.—Wheras our trustie and weilbeloved Johne Gordon of Lochinvar hath of himsellf friclie and without any condition agried to surrender vnto ws his regalitie of Corsmichaell and bailliareis of Kilpatrik and Tungland : These ar to desyre yow to draw vp such a surrender, ane or mae, of the same as yow shall think fitt to be made in our favours, and haveing sene him signe the same, that with all diligence yow send them to Sir William Alexander, our Secretarie, And for his proceiding so fair with ws as he shall find by effects we will acknowledge the same : So we bid yow farewell from our Court at Whythall, 6 Nor 1630.

To the Thesaurer.

Right, &c.—Haveing caused deall with the Lord Naper for a surrender of his Office of Deputie Thesaurer in our hands, and finding him altogidder vnreasonable in his demandis, we have for the good of our service appoynted the Right, &c. Lord Traquair to be lykwyse our deputie Thesaurer, of whois care and abilitie to doe ws service we ar confident, and therfor our pleasur is, that in all things concerneing our service yow mak speciall vse of him : And befor your repairing to our Court yow mak knowen to our Exchecker that it is our speciall pleasur that in your absence he supplie your place in the said service, and in all things whatsoever concerneing the same : Which recommending to your care, we bid yow farewell.—Whythall, 5 Nor 1630.

To the Erle of Morton, Thesaurer.

Our pleasur is, and we doe heirby will and requyre yow, for speciall and good considerationns moveing ws, that yow caus pay with all diligence vnto our right the Lo. Naper, our deputie thesaurer, or to such as have his power, his whole feyis, pensions, or other things due from ws vnto him, by whatsoever maner of way resting vnpayed vnto him at any tyme preceiding this terme of Mertimes, and that out of the first and readiest of our rents, dewteis, and casualiteis whatsoever in that our kingdome; and for your soe doeing these presents, togidder with his or his forsaids acquittances thervpoun, shalbe a sufficient warrand and discherge vnto yow.—Whythall, 16 No^r 1630.

To the Erle of Morton, Thesaurer.

Right, &c.—Being informed that Mr Wm Kellie insisteth to trouble the Vassalls of our Lordship of Dunbar, notwithstanding we had formerlie writtin in ther favours, and that he challengeth priviledges over them which doe not belong vnto him, Our pleasur is, haveing first heard Alex^r Narne of Sandfurd tuitching the bargane he made betweene the late Erle of Holdernesse and the said M^r W^m concerneing the sale of his Lands within that Lordship, that in our name yow deall with him to sell the same vnto ws at the rate he bought them from the said Erle, or otherwayes, that yow condescend with him as yow shall think fit; but if he will not hearken thervnto, sicing these lands did belong vnto our Croun of that kingdome, we will yow to requyre our Advocat to insist in our name and for our intrest, in so far as he can lawfullie doe, for reduceing the right of the said Mr William thervnto; And in the meanetyme that yow vse your best endeavours for defence of these vassalls, in so far as lawfullie and convenienthe can be done by yow.—Whythall, 16 No^r 1630.

To the Excherquer.

Right, &c.—Wheras vpon good consideratiouns of the loss sustened by Williame French of Frenchland, formerlie made to ws, we granted a warrant for payment to him of 200^{lib} sterling for the space of sex yeires till the sowme of 1200^{lib} wer payed vnto him out of our customes, rents, and other dewteis of the Midleschyris of that our kingdome, bot in regard we had for causes speciallie importing the good of our service gevin ordour vnto yow, our Thesaurer, that vpon no consideratioun whatsoever none of our rents, casualteis, or other dewteis should be particularlie assigned for the payment of any persone : Yit being willing he be payed out of our Exchequer at the tymes mentioned in the said warrant according to the maner accustomed, Our pleasur is, that out of the first and readiest of our rents, dewteis, and casualiteis whatsoever of that our kingdome, due, or which heirefter shall accress vnto ws by whatsoever maner of way within the same, yow mak payment vnto him or his assigneyis of the said sowme of 1200^{lib} at the tymes mentioned in the said warrant; and if any termes be alreadie past at which some part of these moneys should have bene payed vnto him by vertew of our said former warrant, Our further pleasur is, that he or his assigneyis be payed therof in this instant yeir of God 1630 : And for your soe doeing these presents shalbe vnto yow a sufficient warrant and discherge.—Whythall, 18 No^r 1630.

A presentatioun was signed for Mr Archibald Monerciff to the kirk of Abernethie, which was vacund in his Maties handis, gift, and disposition, be the dimission therof made be Mr Archibald Monerciff, elder, last minister of the said kirk.—Whythall, 23 No^r 1630.   Sub^t A. B. Sanctand.

The humble Petition of Johne Cunyngham of Barnes.

Humblie scheweth— That diverse schipwraks have fallin and doe daylie fall out by want of Lights in the Iland of May, in the entrie of the firth of Forth, the cheiff place of trade within that your Maties ancient kingdome.

Sicing that Iland doeth belong vnto your petitioner, who can more easelie and in a cheap maner manteane these lights then any other persone whatsoever, and that this is a purpois tending to the publict good : May it therfoir pleas your most excellent Matie to remitt the consideratioun thairof vnto your Ma^{teis} most honorabill Counsall ther, and that they hear what further proposition shalbe made by the petitioner or others interessed tuitcheing this purpois that if they find it expedient for the good of such as trade and adventure by sea ther, A patent for manteaneing of these Lights vpon his own charges may be granted vnto him for such a number of yeires and for such a ductie to be payed of everie schip or bark haveing hir course to be from that way according to hir burden, as in cases of the lyk nature is vsuall, or as they in ther judgments shall think fitt, haveing a respect allwyse (if so be they shall think it expedient) that a difference be made betwene natives and strangers in payment of the said ductie.

To the Clerk of Register.

Trustie and weilbeloved, &c.—Wheras ther hath bene petition sent vnto ws from our Counsall of that our kingdome, in name of our Right, &c. the Erle of Annandale, concerneing some differences betuixt him and Sir Ritchert Grham, kny^t and barronet, for pasturage vpon the Lands of Rollands Merse ; sieing we can determine in nothing therin till we have heard both pairteis or sene these records or treateis which hath bene betweene the tuo kingdomes concerneing ther merches, wherby the grounds whervpon the saids differences doe aryse may be cleared, Our pleasur is, that yow carfullie search and consider all such treateis and records tending to the clearing of the saids differences as ar in our Castele of Edinburgh, or can be fund by yow elsewher, wherof (if any be) we requyre yow to send bak vnto ws, with all diligence vnder your hands, the extracts, togidder with such informatioun and advyse as yow can give tuitcheing the removeing of the saids differences ; which recommending, &c.—Whythall, 25 No^r 1630.

To the Exchequer.

Right, &c.— Wheras we latlie did grant vnto our servand Walter Stewart, gentlman of our privie Chalmer, a gift of the wardschip and mariage of the Lord Salton and others his predicessour's lands and nonentrie therof, without any intention that he should pay any composition at all vnto ws for the same : Our pleasur therfor is, and we doe heirby authorize, will, and requyre yow to pas the same vnto our said servant gratis, without any composition and with all possible diligence, that he may the more speedelie enjoy the benefite of the same, according to our royall intention therin expressed, or else with all diligence schew caus to the contrarie : And for your so doeing these our letters shalbe ane sufficient warrand and discharge in that behalff.—Whythall, 2 De^r 1630.

To the Exchequer.

Right, &c.—We ar informed by petition from Patrik Lyndsay that in recompence of long service ther was 1000^{lib} granted to him by our late dear father, wherof he never received but 300 merks : We therfor, commiserating his aige and povertie, have thoght fitt to will and requyre yow to examyne and try the treuth of the premisses, and if any thing be fund dew vnto him, ather to give ordour for his satisfaction therin, or otherwyse to certifie ws, that we may give further warrant theranent : So, not doubting of your care heirin, We bid, &c.—Whythall, 2 De^r 1630.

By his Ma^{teis} command. Subscribe JA. GALLOWAY.

To the Exchequer.

Right, &c.—Being petitioned by John Kennedie, sometyme of Blairquhan, and Margaret Stewart, his spous, that about ellevin yeires since, he being then near the aige of 21 yeires, was circumvened and induced by Josias Stewart, then styled of Bonyton, to sell vnto him the landis and liveing of Blairquhan for twentie-fyve thowsand merks scotts, they being worth one hundreth thowsand and vpward, which Josias and James Kennedye, thar styled of Culzeane, his sone-in-law, and William Stewart of Dundaff, gave band to pay vnto them at a certane terme bypast, with the ordinarie interest thairof, but never performed the same; And lykwyse that the said Josias and Williame Stewarts and James Kennedie ar our rebells, lying at horne vnrelaxed, wherby the said Johne and Marie, his spous, ar frustrat of the benefite of ther estats, except our gratious favour be vnto them extendit; Our pleasur therfor is, that yow try the estate of the premisses, and finding it trew that the said Johne and Mary have heir alledged, that yow pass vnto them a signature of the escheit and lyfrent of the said Josias and William Stewarts and James Kennedie, but so as they doe not extend farther then to the satisfaction of what is justlie due vnto them: They alwyse giveing such reasonable compositioun to ws for the same as to yow shalbe thoght fitting, and for your soe doeing these shalbe your sufficient warrant.—Whythall, 2 Dec 1630.

By Sir JAMES GALLOWAY.

To the ADVOCAT.

Trustie, &c.—Wheras we ar informed by William Tyrie of Drumkilbo that some persones haveing intendit ane Action questioneing some of his landis hold ward of ws, wherby, if the same should happin to be evicted from him, we will lose our superioritie therof, and wilbe a dangerous president for taking diverse superioriteis of that nature from our Croun, a course far contrarie to what we had intended for drawing in of all superiorites justlie belonging to ws within that our kingdome: Our pleasur is, that yow consider of the trew estate of that action, and if yow find that we ar lyklie to suffer in our interest therin, that yow carefullie advert thervnto, that (in so far as lawfullie may be) nothing be done therin to our prejudice; And (if neid be) that yow advertise ws of the estate therof, and of your advyse tuitching the same; So we, &c.—Whythall, 3 Dec 1630.

To the EARLE of SEAFORT.

Right, &c.—Haveing occasion to confer with yow at this tyme in some things concerneing our service, Our pleasur is, that with as much diligence as convenientlie can be vsed, yow repair to our Court, wher further pleasur shalbe imparted vnto yow; We bid, &c.—Whythall, 3 Dec 1630.

To the COUNSELL.

Right, &c.—Wheras we ar informed that our service committed to the Charge of our Right, &c. the Erle of Tullibardyne and his associats for performeing that part of a Contract betweene ws and them concerneing such things as might be vsefull for our Navie, cannot be performed vnless Johne Grant of Glenmoristoun, with whome, as we are lykwyse informed ther is a necessitie to agrie for furnishing tymber to that purpois, have libertie to provyde and delyver the same, which he is not able to performe, becaus of some hornings vsed against him by our Right, &c. the Erle of Murray for Criminall causes, but offereth, if he wer permitted by yow to goe on in that service, to give vnto yow sufficient securitie for his appearance befor yow at all tymes efter a lawfull summonolis; wherin his demand seameing to ws to be verie reasonable, and the consideration of what he vndertaketh to be of great consequence for the good of our service: Our pleasur is, that yow ather caus frie him of the saids hornings or suspend the execution therof to the effect he may frielie and speedelie proceid in our said service, taking such sufficient suretis of him for his appearance at such tymes as yow shall think fitt to appoynt for answering befoir our Justice-Generall anything that can be justlie objected aganst him; And the better advanceing our said service, that yow grant him all such lawfull favour and furtherance as convenientlie yow can, he alwyse caryeing himselff in a civill and lawfull maner.—Whythall, 9 Der 1630.

To the Commissioners of Surrenders.

Right, &c.—Wheras we wer pleased of late to requyre our Right, &c. the Erle of Roxbrugh, to repair to Court for setling of all bussines betweene him and Francis Stewart, in regard he cannot be able for the present till the first day of Junij nixtocum, to attend vpon what may concerne him in that Commission of the Tythis, by reasone of his necessarie attendance heir, for hearing our determination anent the saids differences, wherin we ar now to proceid without any further delay: Our pleasur is, according to our former letter vnto yow tuitching this purpois, that now lykwyse whatsoever shall cum befor yow concerneing the said Erle his Tythis be continewed till that day: We bid, &c.—Whythall, 7 Der 1630.

To the Counsall.

Right, &c.—We wer pleased heirtofoir, out of just and reasonable consideratiouns, to grant a yeires protection to the Mr of Herreis, and being now agane informed by petition from him that certane actions of his towards the payment of his creditours ar yit vndetermined and depending still befor our Judges, which, without the continuance of our protection will be vnysefull to his said intention, as lykwyse that the rigour of his creditours is such as no reasone will satisfie them without the restraynt of his persone, wherby they would enforce him to tak such course as they please, but vnnaturall . . . a sone to the prejudice of his father; we therfor, out of our princelie consideratioun, have signed him a protection for ane whole yeir, willing and requyreing yow to expeed the same, efter yow have taken him band for performeing of such equitable conditions as are expressed in the said grant; wherin, not doubting of your Conformitie to this our pleasur, we bid, &c.—Whythall, 13 Der 1630.

By Sir Ja. Galloway.

To the Lord Gordoun.

Right, &c.—We ar informed from the Lord Archbischop of St Androis, and other bischops of his dyocie, of your carefull and diligent proceidings vpoun that Commission latelie gevin vnto yow aganst the papists in the North, and the good effects which hath followed thervpon, of quyeting the cuntrey and repressing ther insolenceis, wherin, as yow have ws and to the cuntrey good and acceptable service, so we have thoght it our part, towards the encouragement of your self or others in services of that nature heirefter, to give to yow our particular thanks; and wheras we ar further informed by them that by this your forwardnes yow have incurred the displeasur and indignation of many great persones, both at home and abroad, Our desyre is that yow doe not putt them in a balance with our good opinion, but beleive that as yow have bene carefull and diligent in the performance of our service, we lykwyse shall not be wanting by our good countenance to contervale the loss of any such malicious and evill disposed persones; wherof, desyreing yow to rest assured, we bid, &c.—Whythall, 17 Der 1630.

By Sir Ja. Galloway.

To the Thesaurer.

Right, &c.—Humble sute hath bene made vnto ws in behalff of the reverend father in God, the bischop of Brechin, to cans pay vnto him his pension of 500M. Scotts, the meanness wherof and the persones qualitie requyreing some favour heirin, we have thoght fitt seriouslie to recommend the payment heirof vnto yow, togidder with the arrears (if any be due) and that with as much diligence as can, for doeing wherof, these presents shalbe your warrant.—Whythall, 20 Der 1630.

To the Chancellour.

Right, &c.—Wheras our right, &c. the Lowl Lowdoun hath surrendered vnto ws his heretable office of the schirrefdome of Air, wherby the placeing of a schirreff ther is at our disposeing, being informed of the sufficiencie of David Dumbar of Enterkine to serve ws in that charge, and least our service in that kynd should be neglected, Our pleasur is, that yow in our name Authorize him to be schirreff of Air till a new Election be made : And for your so doeing these presents shalbe vnto yow a sufficient warrant.—Whythall, 20 Der 1630.

To the Exchequer.

Right, &c.—As we wer pleased of late to wryt to yow for preventing of what might be feared by any deid to have bene made by ws concerneing the lands of Markle and Trapren, least it might endanger the right alledged to belong to our Chappell royall of ane annuel-rent out of the same ; So being willing that the lands and other things which formerlie belonged to the late Erle of Bothwell remane vnquestioned or changed from the estate wherin they now ar till we have gevin our decreit vpon the submission made vnto ws by the persones cheiflie interested, wherin we intend to proceid with all diligence : Our pleasur is, that till that tyme nothing be exped which may anwyse concerne that estate ; which recommending vnto your care, &c.—Whythall, 20 Der 1630.

To the Arch Bischop of St Androis.

Right, &c.—Wheras we have bene petitioned in behalff of the poore Ministers of that our kingdome that they may be exempted from our taxationis, we ar no less willing then any of our predicessours have bene to favour them heirin : Yit being informed that sindrie abuses have bene committed vnder that pretext, Our pleasur is, that yow confer with our Chancellour, Collectour of our taxationis, that efter due consideratioun a course may be sett doun how the poore may enjoy the benefite of our favour heirin, and yit that our intention be not abused in being extendit further then what shalbe fund requisit for the effect forsaid ; ffor doeing wherof let such a warrant as yow agrie vpon be sent vnto ws for our hand : And so remitting the forme therof vnto yow, we bid yow farewell.—from our Court at Whythall, 21 Der 1630.

To the Advocat.

Trustie and weillbeloved Counsellour—Wheras we ar informed that Sir George Home of North Berwick hath not subseryved the generall submission, intending besydis as titular of the Tythis of certane landis belonging to our right trustie and right weillbeloved cousen the Erle of Angus, to tak a more strict course with him tuitching the same then hath bene formerlie accustomed, the said Erle and his predecessours (as we ar lykwyse informed), haveing bene these many yeires kyndlie taksmen therof for paying of a certane reasonable dewtie, wherin we dislyk of the said Sir George, his intention, as altogidder disagreeable to the course intended by ws for the publict good, both in avoyding to signe the said submission contrarie to what the most part of our good subjects have done, and by endeavouring the contrarie at this tyme in

II.   I.

his owin particular, while a purpois of such consequence is bot as yit in the setling : Our pleasur is, that ye in our name requyre him to submitt as others have done, otherwyse if he refuise that yow tak all such information from the said erle, or otherwyse as may conduce to the evicting of his right, and therefter that yow intend action aganst him in so far as yow can in a lawfull maner : And for your, &c,— Whythall, 24 Der 1630.

Names of Commissioners for Concealed Moneyis.

Chancellour President Privie Seall Lord Traquair, Thesaurer depute, Sir William Alexander, Secretar, Sir James Skene, president of the Session, Clerk Register Sir Thomas Hope, Advocat Sir George Elphingstoun, Justice-Clerk Sir James Baillie, Sir Johne Scott, Sir Andrew Fletcher of Innerpeffrey, Sir James Bannatyne of Newhall, Sir George Auchinleck of Balmano, Sir John Spottiswood of Newabay, Mr Alexr Seton of Kilcreith, . . . McGill of Cranstoun, Mr George Haliburtoun of Foderonne. —28 Der 1630.

The Last Words of a Presentation.

Commanding also the Lords of Session vpoun the sight of the said presentatioun, and the said Right reverend father his testimoniall of admission following thervpon, to grant and direct letters vpoun ane simple charge of Ten dayes allanerlie at the instance of the said A. B. against all and sindrie the heretours, fewers, fermoreris, tennents, taksmen, occupyeris, and possessours of the lands lyeing within the said paroch, others intromettours with the teynds thairof, and adebtit and in vse of payment of the said stipend, for causing of the said A. B., his factours, tennents, and others in his name, to be readelie answered, obeyed, and payed of the stipend abone-writtin of the cropt and yeir of God, and sielyk yeirlie and ternelie in tyme cuming during all the dayes of his lyftyme, and that the said Letter be extendit with all clausses neidfull.—Gevin, &c.

A List of such as ar most fittest and have most interest to do his Mateis Service for Commissioners in the Middle Schyres : To be authorized by themselflis and ther Deputeis for the apprehending of Fellowis and Fugitives.

On the Scottish Syd.	*On the English Syd.*
Williame Lord Marqueis Dowglas.	Thomas, Earle of Arundell and Surrey.
Robert, Erle of Nithisdale.	Aulgernoun, Earle of Northumberland.
Robert, Erle of Roxberwgh.	Francis, Earle of Cumberland.
Johne, Erle of Annandale.	Theophilus, Earle of Suffolk.
William, Erle of Drumfreis.	The Lord William Howard.
William, Erle of Queinsberrie.	Henrie, Lord Maltravers.
Johne, Erle of Traquair.	Henrie, Lord Clifford.
James, Lord Johnestoun.	Sir Francis Howard.
Robert, Lord Kirkcudbrygh.	Sir Johne Fenwick, knyght and barronett.
Sir William Scott, dureing Erle Buccleuch's minoritie.	Sir Ritchard Grahame, knyght and barronett.
Sir Robert Greirsone.	Sir George Daltoun, knyght.
Sir Johne Charteris.	Sir William Carnby, knyght.
Sir Johne Maxwell of Conlath.	Sir William Witherington, knyght.
Sir William Dowglas, Shirreff of Teviotdale.	Sir Johne Lowther, knyght.
	Rodger Witherington, knyght.

To the Counsell.

Right, &c.—Whems we ar informed that in regard of the death of the late Lord Oliphant without leaveing any aires-male lawfullie procreat of his bodie to succeid vnto his title of honour, ther is a question fallin out betnixt Lady Anna Oliphant, his daughter, his heyre of blood, and ane Patrik Oliphant, pretending right to the said title, by tailzie and disposition flowing from the said late Lord, by which he assumes title and place; and being lykwyes informed that the proces is alreadie intented befor the Judges Ordinarie, for decydeing of the saidis parteis' rights: It is our expres will and pleasur, to the effect we be nather wronged in our princelie prerogative, nor ather pairtie in ther right that yow, vpon sight heirof, in our name discharge both the saidis pairteis from presumeing to vsurp to tak vpon them the said title or place vntill such tyme as by the Judge Ordinarie it be legallie decydit to whom the said place doeth lawfullie pertene.—Whythall, 5 Jar 1631.

To the Erle of Murray

Right, &c.—We vnderstand by a letter from our Counsell how good a service you have done vnto ws by apprehending of James Grant, the rebell, by your successfull endeavours therin approveing our judgment in granting that Commission vnto yow; and as we know that this was not done without great charges and paynes, soe we will accordinglie esteame tharof, as we have writtin vnto our Counsell, willing that nothing be done to the prejudice of your Commission, bot that it have the full power allowed therin to the expyreing of the same, dureing the which tyme we wish yow to proceid as yow have done hitherto, according to the tenour therof: And so, expecting your best endeavours, and wishing your good successe, &c.—Whythall, 7 Jar 1631.

To the Counsell.

Right, &c.—We vnderstand by your letter how good a service is done vnto ws by our Right, &c. the Erle of Murray in apprehending James Grant, the rebell, and his complices, which we acknowledge and will esteame therof as it doeth deserve: Bot sieing we conceave that a persone of his qualitie could not have soe subsisted or proceidit therin without the ayd or encouragment of others, as this service hath made ane end of his treacherous and malicious course, so to prevent, by the punishment of this, the attempting of any the lyk heirefter, Our pleasur is, that yow caus examinat the said James (if he be alyve) or any others that adheared vnto him, of the meanes how he hath bene supported, that ordour may be takin with all that have contributed any voluntarie help for assisting of him, in so far as the lawis of that kingdome will allow: And in the meanetyme, sieing our said cousen's Commission hath produced so good effects, our further pleasur is that nothing be done to the prejudice therof, bot that it stand in the full force and effect till the expyreing of the same: Any so, not doubting of your care heirein.—Whythall, 7 Jar 1631.

To the Chancellour.

Right, &c.—Wheras we have writtin vnto our Counsell for causeing examyne James Grant (if he be alyve) or any others who adhaered vnto him, of the meanes how he hath bene supported dureing the tyme of his rebellion, and that ordour may be takin with all such as shalbe fund to have contributed any voluntarie help towards his mantenance: and being verie desyreous that all meanes should be vsed for finding out such persones (if ther be any), we conceave that it may be better tryed by a privat number than befoir the haill table ; and in such a cause we doe heirby will and authorize yow that, ather by your selff, or if yow shall find it neidfull that yow assume vnto yow such of our privie Counsell or others as shall seme best vnto yow, and that yow vse your best endeavours for tryell of the same, as yow will doe acceptable service vnto ws : And our further pleasur is, that the said James, or any others who have had hand in that cryme, being in close prissone, yow give speciall ordour that none have access to speik with them without your particular warrant.—Whythall, 7 Jaʳ 1631.

To the Advocat.

Trustie, &c.—Haveing vnderstude that, nochtwithstanding of the presentatioun granted by ws of the Church of Duffus, the assisting wherof we recommended vnto your care, yit the same persone whom we wer pleased to gratiefie therwith hath takin another right, neglecting that which he had from ws, whervnto yow have opposed your selff for manteyneing our title, We approve your cariage heirin, and the care yow have schawin therby of our service : And it is our pleasur that yow proceid for defending that presentatioun which was granted by ws, in so far as the Lawis of that our kingdome will allow ; and that yow tak the lyk course in all other caices of the lyk nature, that we may recover any patronages that ar vnjustlie deteynied from ws, wheranent these presents shalbe vnto yow a sufficient warrant.—From our Court at Newmerkit, 23 Jaʳ 1631.

To the Counsell.

Right, &c.—Being informed of a contraversie betuix Thomas Kirkpatrik of Lisburne and ane Bryce Semple, wherby the said Thomas was lyklie to be vtterlie ruinated in his whole estate by the said Bryce, Our pleasur is, that, haveing cited the pairteis befor yow, yow tak such ane equitable course by ther submission vnto yow, or otherwyse, if yow shall think requisit, for preventing any wrong that the said Thomas may suffer by that meanes ; and in caice that ather of the pairteis will not hearken vnto reasone, that yow acquant ws therwith, that therefter we may proceid therin as yow shall think most convenient : Which recommending vnto your care, &c.—Newmarkit, 29 Jaʳ 1631.

To the Session.

Right, &c.—Being informed that in tyme of our late dear father the differences betweene our right trustie, &c. the Erle of Annandale and Sir Archibald Achiesone, knyᵗ, our Secretarie for that our kingdome, tuitching some landis in Irland, wer be them referred vnto Sir William Alexander, our principall Secretarie ther, and Sir James Fullertone, late of our bed chalmer, to have bene composed by them in a freindlie maner : And now we being willing becaus of the said Sir James his deceis, and that they cannot mutuallie agrie betweene themselffis for setling these differences between them, that they be takin away in ane arbitrarie course, We think it fitt that ather yow or they themselffis may choyse to this purpois of such persones who best vnderstand the Lawis of Irland and the estate of these lands in question : and if the said Erle and Sir Arᵈ Achiesone will not condescend to this course, or if it doe not tak that effect, that yow certifie ws therof, that we may give such farder speedie ordour therin as in justice we shall think fitt and reasonable.—Whythall, 13 Febʳ 1631.

To the Viscont Duplin, Chancellor.

Right, &c.—In regard of the prejudice that diverse of our loveing servandis and subjects doe suffer by want of these moneyis which we vpon good consideratiouns and for the good of our service laud condescended to give unto them. Our pleasur is, that whatsoever moneys yow shall receave of any taxatioun wherof yow ar Collectour, that, with the concealments thairof, yow delyver the same to the E. of Morton.—[No date.]

To the Exchequer.

Right, &c.—In regard we have agried with Sir Alex^r Strauchan of Thornetoun, kny^t baronet, for surrendring his Commissions granted by ws vnto him for the sowme of 3000^{lib} st^g, for payment wherof vnto him, or vnto others of whois estates he hath made vse, our thesaurer principall, and the Lord Traquair, our deputie thesaurer, have gevin ther bandis : And sieing it is nowayes our intentioun that they should any wyse suffer in the same, it being done by our direction, Our pleasur is, that the said sowme of 3000^{lib} st. be allowed vnto them in ther owin handis out of the first moneyis arysing be the said Commission, or out of any other our rents and casualiteis whatsoever, till they be compleitlie releived : And in regard we have lykwyse [agreed] with the Lo. Naper for surrendring vnto ws his place of deputie thesaurer, as lykwyse in contentatioun of his pensioun, which he bought from Walter Stewart for the sowme of 3500^{lib} st., to be gevin to him, it is our further pleasur that the said sowme be lykwyse allowed to them in ther owin handis out of the first and readiest of any of our rents and casualiteis whatsoever, and that, for ther further securitie, yow mak ane act of Exchequer heirvpon : And for your soe doeing, &c.—Whythall, 13 Feb^r 1631.

These conteyne your Ma^{teis} gift of recognition of Ten merk land of Headrig, and the fyve merk land lyand within the Lordschip of Brigham, which did apperteane to ane Robert Dicksone in favours of Johne Clevie, apothecarie, his aires and assigneyis, with power to them in ther owin name, or by the assistance of your Advocat, to persew declaratouns of recognition thervpon till the finall decisioun therof, and to quarrell and improve all infeftments and writts granted in prejudice of his gift : To be holdin of your Matie and successour for the rights and services vsed and woont.—Whythall, 13 Feb^r 1631.

Our Soveraigne Lord, with advyse and consent of his Ma^{teis} right trustie and weilbeloved Cousen and Counsellour, William, Erle of Mortoun, Lord Dalkeith and Aberdour, high Thesaurer, Comptroller, and Collectour generall of his Ma^{teis} new augmentatiouns within the kingdome of Scotland, and of his highnes' trustie Cousen and Counsellour, Johne, Lord Stewart of Traquair, and Archibald, Lord Naper of Merchistoun, his highnes' deputeis in the saidis offices, and supplying the thesaurer principall his place in his absens, and also of the remanent Lordis of his highnes' Exchequer of the said kingdome of Scotland, his highnes' Commissioners, Ordeanes a Letter to be made vnder his highnes' privie seall in dew forme to and in favours of his highnes' lovit Doctour Walter Whytfoord, one of his Ma^{teis} Chaplanes, making mentioun that forsameikle as the said Doctour Whytfoord being president of the subdeanrie of Glasgow, with the whole fruits and pertinents belonging thairto, he his Matie as vndoubted patrone of the said benefice, the patronage whairof being bought in question by Sir James Cleland of Monkland pretending right to the samyne, the said Doctour Whytfoord, efter long and troublesome dispute in Law intendit and prosecute vpon his owin propper charges, obteining sentence and decreit befoir the Lordis in foro contradictorio, establisching the right of the said patronage in his Ma^{teis} persone as apperteneing to his royall Croun, which his Matie accepting as good and thankfull service done by his said service : And thairfor being informed that ther ar certane arrearages of the fruits and rents of the said benefice restand awanl vnpayed of certane yeires preceiding the said Doctour Whytfoord his entrie to the samyne, hes gevin, granted, and disponed, and be thir presents, Gevis, grants, and dispones to his servitour foresaid, all and sindrie fruits, teynds, few-dewteis, and others dewteis whatsumever restand vnpayed of the patrimonie of the said benefice or oney part therof of aney terme or eropt preceiding his provision and entrie thairto, except such a part thairof as is alreadie decreet and adjudged by the Lords decreit to others: With power to him to ask, crave, receave, and vplift the samyne, call, follow, and persew thairfoir be whatsumever action necessarie and compitent, compone, transact, and agrie theraucnt acquittances and discharges: And siclyk for the said Doctour Whytfoord his better securitie and right of the said benefice, and frie enjoyeing thairof in tyme comeing, Gevis and grantes to him full right and power to intent, follow, and prosecute actionis of Inprobationis, reduceinis, and others necessars for improveing, reduceing, and annulling all and whatsumever pretendit rights and securiteis of tho fruits of the said benefice or aney part thairof, alledged, made, and granted be his Maᵗⁱᵉ or aney of his royall predicessours, titulars of the said subdeanrie, and that ather in his highnes' name, and at the instance of his Maᵗʳⁱˢ Advocat, or in the said Doctour Whytfurd his owin name, with concurse of his Maᵗʳⁱˢ Advocat present and to cum, whom by thir presents his Maᵗⁱᵉ wills and commands to assist and concurre with the said Doctour Whytfurd to the effect forsaid, and that the said Letter be extendit in the best forme, with all clausses neidfull.— Gevin at Whythall, the 13 Febʳ 1631.

May it pleas your Sacred Maᵗⁱᵉ—
These conteyneth a gift to Doctour Walter Whytfurd, one of your
Maᵗʳⁱˢ Chaplanes, of the Arrearages of the subdeanrie of Glasgow,
latelie evicted by him aganes Sir James Cleland, Togidder with
ane libertie and power to persew whatsumever action of reduction and improbation for improveing of the rights of the said
subdeanrie and rents thairof, with ane command to your Maᵗʳⁱˢ
Advocat to concur with him therin.   Sir Tho. Hope.

May it pleas your Sacred Maᵗⁱᵉ,
These conteyneth ane Ratification of the toun of Kinroche, in ane burgh of baronie, with ane new
erection thairof in ane burgh of baronie in favours of your Maᵗʳⁱˢ trustie cousen and counsellour William,
Erle of Morton, your Maᵗʳⁱˢ Thesaurer, with the whole priviledges and liberteis belonging to ane burgh of
baronie, and speciallie with the libertie of tuo yeirlie frie fayres within the samyne burgh, and also of ane
weiklie mercat to be holdin vpon Setterday, and of all customes and casualiteis belonging thairto.—
Whythall, 13 Febʳ 1631.
                                                                       Sir Tho. Hope.

Charles, be the grace of God, king of Great Britane, France, and Irland, defender of the fayth, &c.—
To all Admiralls, Vice-Admiralls, and Captanes of aney of our schips serveing ws on the seas, and to all
Justices of peace, Mayors, Schirreffis, Bailleis, Constablis, Customers, and Searcheris, and to all others, our
officers, ministeris, and loveing subjects to whome it may apperteane, Greeting: Wheras of our speciall
grace we have licenced, and by these presents doe licence our right trustie and weilbeloved cousen
Archibald, Erle of Argyll, And our trustie and weilbeloved Henrie Campbell, Esqʳ, his sone, to pass out of
this realme vnto the parts beyond the seas, ther to remane the space of sex yeres nixt efter ther departure
out of this our realme: We will and command yow and everie of yow to suffer them quyetlie to pass by
yow out of this our realme, with sex servandis and ane hundreth punds in money, with the necessar
carages and vtensills as yow tender our pleasur: And these our Letters or the duplicat of them shalbe als
well vnto yow as vnto our said cousen, and to the said Henrie Campbell, sufficient warrant and discherge in
that behalff, provyded also that our said Cousen and the said Henrie Campbell nor ather of them doe not
haunt nor resort into the territoreis or dominions of any forreyne prince or potentate, not being with ws in

league or amitie, nor yit wittinglie bear companie with aney persone or persones departed out of this our realme without our licence, or that Contrarie to the same doe yit remane on the other syd of the seas, and that they nor ather of them vse not the Company of any Jesuit, seminarie prevists, or otherwayes evill effected persone to our state, provyded also that notwithstanding any thing in this our Licence whensoever it shall seme good vnto ws to call our said consen and the said Henrie Campbell home befor the end of the terme befoir limited, and shall signifie the same vnto them or ather of them by our owin letters, or by the letters of any four of our privie counsall, or by meanes of any our ambassadours, That then it shalbe lawfull for our said consen or the said Henrie Campbell, or ather of them, to abyd on the other syd the seas any longer tyme then the distance of ther abode shall requyre and our Lawis doe permitt, and if they doe not without vrgent and verie necessarie cause to the contrarie returne in the maner above said, then we will this our Licence to be takin as voyd and of non effect from the begining, and to be interpreted and adjudged to all intents and purposes as thogh no such licences had bene gevin, bot they departed without the same.—Given vnder our signet at Whythall, 19 Feb' 1631.

This conteyneth your Maties Licence to the Erle of Argyll and Henrie Campbell, Esqr, his Lo, sone, to travell in parts beyond the seas. Ther ar severall blanks left to be filled vp by your Matie for the tyme they ar to stay abroad, for the number of his servandis, and for the sowme of money which he is to have for his transportation.

Your Ma^teis pleasur signifeid by Sir Wm Alexander, kny^t barronett.

To the Erle of Morton, Thesaurer.

Right, &c.—Wheras we have gevin ordour for payment of severall sowmes of money to your self and diverse others as by your and ther warrants may appear, And as we have more particularlie expressed our mynd, sieing our Exchequer, out of which the same was cheiflie payable, cannot at this tyme affoord them: Our pleasur is, that as moneys of our taxatioun and concealments therof shalbe delyvered vnto yow by our Chancellour, Collectour therof (to whome we have gevin ordour to that effect), yow pay vnto them and deteyne for your self the sowmes particularlie mentioned in these warrants, and that at such tymes as the same can be most convenientlie done, and as may be most agriable with the proportion of the sowmes to be delyvered—Whythall, 19 Feb' 1631.

To the Counsell.

Right, &c.—We ar informed from our beloved Sir James Balfour, kny^t, our Lyon King at Armes, that he by our letters patentes of that service vnder our great seall is exempted from payment of any taxatiouns, and that for many aiges his predicessours in that service hath enjoyed the same and such lyk priviledges from our royall progenitours: We therfoir, out of our princelie consideratioun and regard to the preservatioun of the ancient esteame of that office, have thoght fitt to will and requyre yow to tak notice and tryell of the said grant and presidents of former aiges, and according to them expeid vnto the said Sir James ane immunitie and exemptioun from payment of taxt, stent, or impositione granted vnto ws in that our kingdome; wherin not doubting your conformitie to this our pleasur, we bid yow farewell.—Whythall, 22 Feb' 1630. stylo Angl.

To the Exchequer.

Right, &c.—Wheras vpon good consideratiouns knowen vnto ws we ar pleased to grant for the space of sexteine yeires the customes and imposts of the wynes in that our kingdom vnto our right, &c. the

Marqueis of Hamilton : Our pleasur is, that furthwith yow pass and cause expeed vnder our great seall the signature granted by ws thervpoun : And for so doeing these presents shalbe vnto yow and everie of yow a sufficient warrand and discherge.—Gevin at our Court of Whythall, 26 Feb^r 1631.

To Sir Thos Hope, Advocat.

Trustie, &c.—Being informed by our trustie servand James Chalmer, one of our phisitianes in Ordinarie, that Sir Wm Forbes, sone of William Forbes, late of Cragievar, intendeth to pas a new grant of the landis, tythis, superioriteis, and patronages purchassed by him from the Lord of Lundoris to the prejudice of ws and diverse of our subjects interest therin : Our pleasur is, that ye in our name compeir befor our Exchequer, and give your reasones for staying therof, vnless he mak such ane absolute surrander of the premisses as yow shall find to be agrieable to our former letters writtin to that purpois, and to the course preservved by ws in caces of the lyk nature, vnto which purpois we have writtin vnto the bodie of our Exchequer.—Whythall, 2 March 1631.

To the Exchequer.

Right, &c.—Wheras we ar informed by our trustie servand James Chalmer, one of our phisitianes in Ordinarie, that Sir William Forbes of Cragivar intendeth to pas a new grant of such things as his father had purchassed from the Lo. Lundoris, wherby we and our diverse of our subjects interessed therin wilbe prejudged, to whois purpois we have writtin to our Advocat to compeir befoir yow for our interest : Our pleasur is, if any such writt be presented vnto yow, that yow mak stay therof, and that nothing be granted of new to prejudge ws or our saids subjects, according to our pleasur formerlie signifeid to that purpois.— Whythall, 2 March 1631.

Archbischop of St Androis and Glasgow.

Right reverend, &c.—Wheras we ar informed that it hath bene the custome not to charge any ministers whois names ar gevin vpon roll by yow, and the remanent of our bischops as persones whois meanes wer so small that they could not possiblie pay ther parts of the taxatiouns : And we being willing to caus observe the lyk pious and charitable customes, Our pleasur is, that yow consider of the Estate of such ministers as ar within your dyocris who have no releiff, and whois meanes ar so small that they cannot pay ther part of the said taxatiouns, And that yow cause the lyk course be kept by the other bischops within ther dyocris ; And if yow find any of them vnable, that yow give vp ther names vnder your hands to our Collectour generall of these our present taxatiouns, or to his deputeis and collectours, that they be not troubled for the same, provydeing alwyse that these who ar to receave this favour from ws be fund by yow obedient to the ordouris establisched in the church : Which recommending vnto your care, We, &c.—Whythall, 2 March 1631.

Vponn resignation vnto your Matie of the mylne landis office of bailliarie above-writtin, belonging to Sir William Anstruther, in the Lordschip of Pittinweyme, your Matie doeth dispone the same of new vnto him, his heyres and assigneyis, heretablie, with power to call for and receave all casualiteis and feyis belonging to that office, with the servitude and services adebtit by the tennents, to hold Courts according to the jurisdiction of that Lordship, and as other bailleis therof did or might lawfullie doe, with priviledge of the common mure of Pittinweyme, answerable according to his lands ther, the proffeits and dewteis therof for the yeires and termes bypast, fallin by whatsoever maner of way, ar remitted vnto him to be holdin of your Matie and successours in few ferme for payment of the accustomed dewteis, deduceing fyftie shillings Scotts yeirlie for the fie of the office, as vse is. His heyres are to double the few ferme the first yeir of ther entrie.—Whythall, 4 March 1631.

These concernes ane disposition to Mr Alex^r Guthrie, common Clerk of Edinburgh, and his heyres, of the four pund land of Freireass, with the fisching and mylne thairof, and the astrictit multures of the threttie-sex pund land, pertoneing of old to the Abbay of Melros, within the parochin of Dunscoir, with the office of bailliarie of the samyne threttie-sex pund land which pertened heretablie befor to Johne Maxwell of Tempilland, and wer holdin of him immediatlie of befoir of the Lord of erection of Melros, and now of your Matie and ar fallin in your Ma^{tie}s landis be recognition, throw not payment of the few-dewtie, be reason of the clause irritant conteynit in the old chartours of the saids lands, with ane gift de novo damus, and a power to tak a seasine vpoun the ground of aney part of the landis forsaidis for the haill : To be holdin the saids lands of your Matie in few ferme for payment of ther few dewteis abone specifeit, with ane clause irritant in caice of not payment of the few dewtie for the space of thrie termes and four dayes, the infeftment to be null, and tripleund the few ferme the first yeir of the entrie of the heyre, and the office of bailliarie to be holdin bleusch for payment of ane peney.—Whitehall, 4 March.

To the Chancellour and Clerk Register.

Right, &c.—Wheras we ar informed of the hard esteat of our right trustie and weilbeloved Counsellour, the Bischop of Dumblane, deane of our Chappell royall, and how he is willing to give all reasonable satisfaction vnto our trustie and weilbeloved Sir David Lyndsay of Balcarras, kny^t, concerneing ane action of Tythes depending betweene them befor our Colledge of Justice, to which purpois we have writtin to them of befor : And being willing that some ordinarie meanes be vsed for composeing all differences betweene them in ane equitable and friendlie maner, least the said bischop, who now is aged and vnable to attend any long proces in law, be dissabled to attend our service committed to his charge, Our pleasur is, that yow tak these differences vnto your consideratioun, and therefter that yow deall with them both for removeing therof in a freindlie and amicable maner, and to that effect that yow vse your best endeavours which we will tak as acceptable service done vnto ws, becaus the said bischop is a persone of good qualitie and parts, and hath bene a long faythfull servand to our late dear father and ws, which recommending vnto your care, &c.—Whythall, 4 March 1631.

To the Counsell.

Right, &c.—We ar informed by petition from the Masters of work, deacons, and friemen of the Maissons and hammermen of that our kingdome that the Lairds of Rosling for many ages have bene by sindrie grants from our royall progenitours constitute Judges and overseiris of that trade, and that by the late intermission therof, many abuses have been caused both to the prejudice of ther trade and the common good of the subject, for remedie qulerof they have requeisted ws to confer the said power and judicatorie vpone Sir Williame Sinclair, now Lard of Rosling, and his aires, with confirmatioun of any such grant made heirtofoir to his predicessours : We therfor, out of our princelie care to obviat any disordour in tymes comeing, and considering the petitioners to be christlie interessed therin, have signed the said grant at ther

II   M

request, willing and requyreing yow to give way, and furthwith to expeid the same, if it may not other-wayes prove prejudiciall to the ordour or governement ther establisched alreadie; wherin not doubting of your conformetie to this our pleasur, we bid, &c.—Whythall, 4 March 1631.

To the Exchequer.

Right, &c.—We ar informed by petition from George Foulis, Master of our Cunzie hous, that he haveing devolved vpon him a great burden of debts from his kinsman Thomas Foulis, late taksman of the Lead Mynes, who contracted the same by the great charg and loss that he had in finding out and prose-cuteing of these works; for which burden the petitioner haveing no vther releiff bot the hope of benefite that might aryse thence, and haveing at the instance of our Counsell made some tryell thairof, that he findis the benefite (if any may be raised) can not counterpoyse the panes, bot that he must now be enforced to desist from prosecuteing the said work, except we be pleased, out of our princelie consideratioun, to dispense with the tak dewtie payable to ws for our tenth, to the behuiff of him and his eldest sone: We therfor, not otherwyse knowing the treuth of the premisses, and out of our princelie care, being desyreous the said works, so beneficiall to the cuntrie and any poore, may be continewed, though without benefite to ws, for a tyme, if otherwyse may not be, have thoght fitt to will and requyre yow to tak the premisses to your consideratioun, and to doe and settle therin with the petitioner according as yow in your wisdomes shall think fitt and expedient for the common good, or interest and encouragment of the petitioner; wherin not doubting of your care, We, &c.—Whythall, 4 March 1631.

To the Commissioners for Surrenders.

Right, &c.—Wheras by our former warrand direct to yow we gave Ordour for expeiding the valuation of led tythis, wherin, as we understand, yow have proceidit soo wyslie that within schort tyme the valuatioun of led Tythis shalbe concluded: Bot as to the Tythis which ar bruiked by the heretours joyntlie with the Lands wherin the probation is common both to titular and heretour, we ar informed that the samyne proceidis verie slowlie, and that partlie by reasone of the negligence of the titulars and heretours in persewing of ther valuations, or be the contestation betwixt them efter report, wherin so much tyme is spent vpon everie particular, that the work is mightelie hindred, and lyk to be frustrat, except some remedie be provydit thereto: And we considering that the difficultie and contestation aryses for the most part vpon the constant rent of stok and tyth, whereas no difficultie can be in the present rent, we think it nowayes reasonable, wher the present rent is certane, that vpon the contestation anent the constant, ather the titular should be frustrat of the payment of the just tyth or we of our annuitie: And therfor we think it necessar, for the good of the great work and our service, that ane act be made ordeaneing all titulars and heretours to expeid and conclude ther valuations betwixt and the first of August nixtoeunn, and if any contestation shalhappin to fall out betwixt them efter that day, in that caice that it be enacted and ordeaned that the heretour shall pay his just tyth according to the fyveth of the present rent, togidder with our annuitie furth of the samyne according therto, and of all yeires bygane and in tyme cuming, ay and whill the constant rent of the said stok and tyth shalbe fullie agried vpon betuixt them by your sight, and if it shalhappin any led tythis to be vnvalued efter the said first day of August nixt, ather in default of the titular or heretour, in that caice, as we allow the ordour taking by yow for leiding of the tythis be ather of them who shall not be fund in default of the not valuation, so we think it just and reasonable that the intromettour with the tyth should be obleidged in payment of our annuitie according to the just worth of the tythis led dureing the yeires of his leading, deduceing oulie therof the fyveth part for the ease and that which is payed to the ministers for ther stipends, and that ay and whill the valuatiouns be concludit: And to the effect that ther be no delay on your part in considering of the reports, and discussing of the difficulteis anent the valuatiouns, we think it fitt that yow grant committeis to some of your number, ane or mae, for hearing of the difficulteis betwixt the titulars and heretours, and decyding the same, except in such difficult cases which shall deserve the hearing of the whole table.—Whythall, 6 March 1631.

To the Counsell.

Right, &c.—Wheras we ar informed that certane informatiouns gevin vnto ws against the Lord Naper were by ordour from yow putt vpon record, wherin, sieing he hath gevin ws satisfaction, and that non of onr subjects ar therin interessed, we will not that anything tuitching the saids informations be left as a ground to wrong him or his posteritie in the reputation due vnto them : Therfor our pleasur is, that yow mak the said informations and articles of accusation vneffectuall, by cancelling or rasing of the same : And for your so doeing these presents shalbe vnto yow a sufficient warrand.—6 March 1631.

To the Exchequer.

Right, &c.—We ar informed from James Bonele, by petition instructed by diverse certificats vnder the hands of our Secretarie of state, that he of late yeires haveing with great charge, panes, and danger performed many good services to our state and freinds, is now for want of health and strenth becum vnable to purches the meanes of lyveliehood and mantenance to himsellf, requeisting ws therfoir, and for the interest of our dearest freinds his recommenders, to bestow vpon him some meanes of sustenance in that his native cuntrie indureing his naturall lyff: We therfor have thoght to refer and recommend him vnto yow to have such proportion of meanes allowed him ther as yow in your wisdomes efter pervsall of his saids certificatts and recommendatiouns shall think fitt ; wherin not doubting of your care, &c.—Whythall, 7 March 1631.

By Sir James Galloway.

To the Exchecquer.

Right, &c.—Wheras we did formerlie wryt vnto yow that yow should expeid vnto our weilbeloved Walter Stewart, gentleman of our privie chalmer, a gift of the wardschip and mariage of the Lord Salton and vthers his predicessonris landis, and of the non-entrie thirof, or else to wryt bak to ws your reasones aganst the expedioncie of the same : And sieing yow have not returned vnto ws any, it is our express will and pleasur, without any further delay, yow pass the samyne vnto our said servand gratis, without any composition, and with all possible diligence, that he may the more speedelie enjoy the benefite of the same, according to our royall intention therin exprest : And for your, &c.—Whythall, 14 March 1631.

To the Counsell.

Right, &c.—Wheras we ar informed that James Creichton of Frendraucht is to onderly the Law for the death of the late Viscont of Melgun and Rothmay, the maner wherof was so barbarous and odious, as we desyre that all meanes may be vsed wherby the treuth therof may be broght to light, bot becaus the matter is of so great importance and so much difficultie in the tryell, in regard the Erle Monteith, president of our privie Counsell, who is our Justice Generall, is to remane heir some tyme as called by ws to attend our service heir; And that we would be loath to have that bussines putt to a tryell by a deputie dureing the tyme of his absens: Our pleasur is, that yow taking sufficient assurance continew his tryell till sic a day in Juny nixt to cum as yow shall think most fitt, that our said Justice Generall may be present that the samyne may be exactlie tryed, which we exceedinglie desyre that punischment vpon the offenders may be accordinglie inflicted: And our further pleasur is, that in the meane tyme such persones as ar alreadie in prissone for suspition of the said fact may be still safelie deteyned in firmance vnto the said tyme.— Whythall, 14 March 1631.

To the Commissioners for Surrenders.

Right, &c.—Wheras we ar pleased of late to requyre our right, &c. the Erle of Buccleugh to repair to Court for setling of all bussines betuix Francis Stewart and him; in regard he cannot be able for the present till the first day of Junij nixtocum vpon what may concerne him in that Commission of the Tythis, by reasone of his necessarie attendance heir for hearing our determinatioun anent the saids differences, wherin we ar now to proceid without and furder delay, Our pleasur is, that whatsoever shall cum befoir yow concerneing the said Erle his Tythis be continewed till that day: And for, &c.—Whythall, 16 March 1631.

To the Session.

Right, &c.—Wheras we wer pleased of late to requyre our right, &c. the Earle of Buccleugh to repair to our court for setling of all bussines betwixt Francis Stewart and him: In regard, he hath some actions depending befor yow, vpon which he cannot be able befor the beginning of the nixt session to attend, in regard of his necessarie attendance heir, for heiring our determinatioun anent the saids differences, wherin we ar now to proceid without any further delay, our pleasur is, that yow continew all actions that cum befor yow, concerneing the said Erle till that tyme, that he may convenientlie attend them.—Whythall, 16 March 1631.

To the Erle Nithisdale.

Right, &c.—Haveing bene informed of the good service yow have done vnto ws in apprehending, putting to tryell, and executioun of diverse malefactours and Outlawis in the borders of our kingdome of Scotland, we doe heirby render yow hartie thanks for the same, and we assure yow that we will not be vnmyndfull therof when any further occasion shall offer wherby we may express our favour vnto yow.— Whythall, 18 March 1631.

To the Counsell.

Right, &c.—Wheras we ar informed that notwithstanding Henric Ramsay of Ardownie was denunced to the horne as suretie to James Beaton of Westhall, who haveing left the kingdome is now returned, and may satisfie his creditours, and releive his cautioner, yit delayeth to doe the same, wherby the Estate of the said Henric is lyklie altogither to perishe, speciallie by being disabled by reasone of the said horning to tak any course for his owin releiff, whervpon, we being humblie petitioned that he may be licenced to stand in judgment to plead in that behalff, and for recoverie of such debts as ar justlie dew vnto him, wherby to satisfie all his creditours, we ar heirby pleased (if yow find what is affirmed to be trew, and the consideratioun of his demand to be reasonable, as we conceave it to be), that yow grant vnto him a protection for ane yeir, with licence to stand in judgment for recoverie of his releiff, and all other actions concerneing him, taking alwyse such ordour as yow shall find to be most requisit, that the creditours be not defrauded of what is justlie dew vnto them.—Whythall, 18 March 1631.

To the Counsell.

Right, &c.—Wheras we ar informed that Sir Johne Ogilvie of Craig, kny^t, since he was apprehendit by the Erle of Monteith, president of our Privie Counsall, who is our Justice Generall, and since his imprisonment in our Castell of Edinburgh, hath caryed himself moderatlie, nather govin nor offered any scandell to the professed religion : And being humblie petitioned in his behalff that he may be confyned within his owin boundis, in regard his estate is lyklie altogidder to perishe by his absence, and that his aige and great seiknes, whervnto he is much subject, requyred our princelie consideratioun towards him, we ar heirby pleased to remitt the consideratioun of his demand vnto yow, that if yow find not some speciall reasone to the contrarie, yow give ordour for his enlargeing and confinement in his owin boundis vpon such conditions as yow shall think fitt to preseryve, for mantenance of religion and quyet of these parts.—Whythall, 18 March 1631.

To the Commissioners of Parliament.

Right, &c.—Wheras we did latelie caus prorogat our parliament vntill the first day of Aprill nixtocum, in hope that we could have bene ther our self in persone : And now, considering that we cannot be ther at that tyme, and yit being vnwilling to be absent from our said parliament, and desyreous to receave our Croun in persone, and to setle all bussines ther, if our affaires can convenientlie permitt ws to repair thither, as we earnestlie desyre, Our pleasur is, and we doe heirby authorise, will, and requyre yow to cause fense our said Court of parliament, by vertew of our Commission latelie granted vnto yow by ws, and to prorogat and continew the said parliament agane to the fourt of August nixtocum, with continuatioun of dayes, that we may have time to setle our affaires heir befoir we begin our jorney towards that our ancient kingdome : And for your soe doeing, &c.—Whythall, 18 March 1631.

To the Counsell.

Right, &c.—Wheras we have writtin our princelie direction vnto our Commissioners of parliament to prorogat and continew the same vnto the fourt day of August nixtocum, wherby we may have some more tyme and leasure to be ther in persone at the said parliament, and to receave our croun, for the peace and and securitie of that our native and ancient kingdome, if our affaires can convenientlie permitt : Our pleasur therfor is, and we doe heirby authorise, will, and requyre yow that efter the said parliament shalbe prorogated and continewed as said is, yow caus intimat the said prorogation and continuatioun to all our good leidges within our said kingdome by oppin proclamatioun at the mercat croce of Edinburgh, and other places neidfull, and warne all prelatis, noblemen, Commissioners for barrones and burghs, and all others haveing place, voit, or owing attendance in the said supreame Court of parliament, to attend and wait vpon the same, the forsaid day, with continuatioun of dayes, and to performe all and sindrie such other things as to ther places and offices doe apperteane : And for doeing the premisses, these our letters shalbe vnto yow and everie of yow from tyme to tyme a sufficient warrand and discharge in that behalff. So we bid yow farewell from our Court at Whythall.—18 March 1631.

To the Counsell.

Right, &c.—Haveing gevin Commission vnto our right, &c. the Marqueis of Hamilton for the levy of 6000 men within that our kingdome, and sieing that the speidie doeing therof doeth highlie concerne ws and our freinds abroad, and that the seasone doeth now approache for ther transportatioun : Our pleasur is, that yow vnanimouslie concure by all possible and lawfull meanes to vse your best endeavours to that purpois; wherin as yow shall doe vnto ws most acceptable service, soe we will not be vnmyndfull of your affection and panes takin therin.—Whythall, 21 March 1931.

A presentation was signed this day in favours of Mr Henrie Wilkie to the kirk of Portsnook, vacand in his Maties handis by the dimission of Mr John Wilkie, minister of the said kirk.—Whythall, 24 March 1631.

These give a Licence to Andro Haig, his heyres, assigneyes, and partiners, for the space of 21 yeires, to mak prinnes, Needles, and to draw wyre within Scotland, without restrayneing the Merchands to bring in the lyk commoditeis, prohibiteing all others to mak them without ther licence, vnder the pane of confiscation, the ane half to your Matie, and the other to the patentees. They ar to sell them at the rates now accustomed. They ar to putt ther works in practeis for the publict good in 3 yeires, otherwyse these to be null.—Whythall,   March 1631.

These ratifie the Letters, Act, decreit, and ratification therin conteynit, gevin by the present provest, bailleis, deane of guild, thesaurer, and remanent counsellours and deacons of Crafts of Edinburgh, in favours of the deacon brethren, burges, and friemen of the skynners within that burgh, for keeping good ordour amongst them of that trade.—[No date.]

To the Counsell.

Right, &c.—Being informed of the sufficiencie of our right, &c. Johne, bischop of the Yles, and of his affectioun to our service we ar moved in regard therof, and for the better encouragment and enabling for our said service to advance and promove him to be one of our privie Counsall of that our kingdome : Therfoir our pleasur is, and wee doe heirby requyre yow that haveing administred vnto him the oath accustomed in the lyk caces yow admitt him to be one of your number; for doeing wherof, &c.—Whythall, 24 March 1631.

To the Chancellour.

Right, &c.—Being informed by the reverend father in God, the Bischop of the Ylls, of your forwardnes in our service tuitching the restoreing of the decayed estate of that bischoprik, for which we give yow hartie thanks, we ar now pleased that yow continue as yow have begun by vseing your best endeavours to that purpois, in so far as the disposition of your bodie and conveniencie of your charge from ws will permitt, and to that effect that yow deall with the persones possessing the temporale estat therof to submitt vnto ws as others have done in the lyk caces, otherwyse if they will not condescend thervnto we remitt vnto your consideratioun if we may not proceid aganst them by any legall course whatsoever, or by withholding from them heirefter the ordinarie favour granted by ws to others, our subjects, in passing the rights and confirmatiouns, or any other benefite concerneing them that may flow from our gift, wherin efter yow have advysed what is fitt for ws to doe, and conferred with our Advocat in poynt of Law (to whom we have writtin to that purpois), returne your opinion to ws vnder both your handis that therefter we may give such specific ordour for restoreing of that estate as we shall find just caus : And further, our pleasur is, that ye represent vnto our Counsall the necessitie of reparatioun of Churches and planting of Scools in the said Yles, and that yow consider of the best expedient how that course may be best effectuated, and therefter caus putt in practeis what by yow can be most convenientlie done to that purpois.—Whythall, 24 March 1631.

PRECEPT.

Wheras the Reverend father in God, Johne, bischope of the Yles, hath done vnto ws many good and acceptable services, both at home and abroad, wherof we have takin speciall notice therfor, and for diverse vther good and considerable causses moveing ws : Our pleasur is, that yow pay vnto him or his assigneyis the sowme of 300ᵇᵇ· stg. money yeirlie and termelie at Witsonday and mertimes ; And that out of the first and readiest of our rents, dewteis, casualiteis, and other benefits whatsoever now due vnto ws, and which heirefter shal happin to be due and accress to ws in that our kingdome, the first payment of which sowme of 300ᵇᵇ· money forsaid, begining at the terme of Witsonday last, anno 1630, is to be made to him or them at Witsonday nixt now ensueing, and so furth to be continewed yeirlie and termelie till the temporall estate of the bischoprik of the Iles be fullie restored, or the said bischop otherwayes competentlie provydit : And for his better securitie, Our further pleasur is, that yow caus registrat this precept in the bookis of Excheker to be a sufficient warrand, not onlie to yow and everie of yow whom from tyme to tyme it may concerne, bot lykwyse a warrant to the Auditours of Exchecker for the tyme to defease, and allow to yow and everie of yow the said yeirlie sowme in your yeirlie accompts : And for your so doeing, &c.—Whythall, 24 March 1631.

TO THE SESSION.

Right, &c.—Haveing writtin to our Chancellour to deall with the persones possessing the temporall estate of the bischoprik of the Yles to submitt vnto ws therin, as others have done in the lyk caces, vtherwyse to certifie ws of his opinion how far it is fitt to proceid aganst them ather in a legall course or by any other lawfull meanes whatsoever : And becaus the restoreing of that bischoprik doeth much import the good of our service and the mantinance of religion in these barbarous and remot pairts, Our pleasur is, till we be further resolved that in all actions intendit or to be intendit aganst the saids persones, yow be cairfull that Justice be administered with all expedition according to the lawes of that our kingdome, and that in all other actions concerneing him that shall cum befoir yow, yow tak the lyk diligence, least he should be distracted from his charge.—Whythall, 24 March 1631.

TO THE ADVOCAT.

Trustie, &c.—Haveing writtin to our trustie, &c. the Viscont of Dupliu, our Chancellour, to deall with the persones possessing the temporall esteat of the bischoprik of Yles, to submitt vnto ws as vthers hath done in the lyk caces, otherwyse to certifie ws his opinion how far it is fitt to proceid aganst them ather in a legall course or by any vther lawfull meanes whatsoever : Our pleasur is, in regard of your charge from ws, and that the restoreing of that esteat doeth much concerne the good of our service, that (haveing heard at leuth what can be informed to that purpois by the reverend father in God, the bischop of the Yles) yow concure with our Chancellour by giveing him your best advyse in poynt of law for reduction of ther rights, that therefter, haveing your opinions therin vnder both your handis, we may give such further ordour tuitching the same as we shall find just caus: And in the mean tyme, till we be further resolved, Our farder pleasur is, that yow, without exceptioun of any of the saids persons, insist to persew all actions alreadie intendit or to be intendit aganst them tuitching that purpois, and that ather in our name or in name of the said bischop, as may best subsist in law for the good of that cause, which we will tak as a speciall service done vnto ws.—Whythall, 24 March 1631.

To the Session.

Right, &c.—Wheras we ar informed that yow have pronunced your decrie tuitching that action depending befor yow concerneing the patronage of Duffus, but as yit doe delay to enroll it till our pleasur be knowen for our interesse, wherin we approve of your proceidings, that with administration of Justice yow have had so great a care of our right : Our pleasur is, that vnless yow think that we may therby be prejudged further then his submission can satisfie, and that it be necessarie that our title be first cleared with all convenient diligence, yow caus extract the same, that the reverend father in God, the bischop Murray, may have the full benefite therof : And in the meane tyme to whosoever the right of that patronage shalbe adjudged that his sone have the benefite of our presentatioun.—Whythall, 24 March 1631.

To the Advocat.

Trustie, &c.—Being informed in the behalff of the reverend father in God the bischop of Ross that certane patronages belonging to that bischoprik ar by the Lord Balmeino vnjustlie challenged befoir our Colledge of Justice to belong vnto him ; wherby sieing that both we and the said bischop may be prejudged, Our pleasur is, that in all actions intentit or to be intented aganst him tuitching that purpois, yow compeir for our interest, and give your best assistance in so far as yow can lawfullie doe.—Whythall, 24 March 1631.

To the Session.

Right, &c.—Wheras we ar informed that ther dependis befor yow ane action of Law betwixt the Laird of Hintsfeild and ane Margaret Kilpatrik, who in regard of hir distressed Estate, sex, and of hir being vnmaried, doeth in the caice of Orphanes beg for our princelie favour towards hir, in so far as the equitie of hir caus and extremitie of hir estate doe requyre, the consideration wherof have moved ws to recommend hir action vnto yow that schee may have justice with all expedition.—Whythall, 24 March 1631.

To the Advocat.

Trustie, &c.—Being informed in name and behalff of the reverend father in God the bischop of Dunkeld that certane charges belonging to that bischoprik ar by some persones vnjustlie challenged befoir our Colledge of Justice to belong vnto them ; wherby sieing that both we and the bischop may be prejudged, Our pleasur is, that in all actions intendit or to be intendit aganst him tuitching that purpois yow compeir for our interest, and give him your best assistance in so far as yow can lawfullie doe.—Whythall, 24 March 1631.

To the Counsell.

Right, &c.—Wheras we wer pleased, at the desyre of the Colledge of Justice, to give way to the tyme of ther sitting, bot being of late informed of some objections made against the same, and considering that this purpois is of that weght and consequence which requyre due advyse: Our pleasur is, that yow give ordour that they mak nothing in ther sitting bot continew the accustomed course therof, and in the meane tyme that yow informes your selfis of the objections made against it; and efter yow have dewlie considered therof, that with all convenient diligence yow returne ws your opinion tuitching the same, that we may give such further ordour therin as we shall find just caus.—Whythall, 25 March 1631.

These conteyne ane Commission of Counsell of Scotland, whairof 7 is the quorum, the Chancellour or President of Scotland being one of the sevin, and in ther absence the eldest Counsellour, to whome your Matie committis the whole administration and governement of your Maties said kingdome in as ample power and authoritie as hath bene heirtofoir in any tyme bygane; with this provision alwise, that the samyne shall not be prejudiciall to the Commission of Excheker; and that in matters of great importance the Chancellour sie that the Counsell be more frequent, and if any being advertised absents themselfis, they ar to be censured by the table; and thir presents to be ane sufficient warrand for the great seall.—Whythall, 25 March 1631.

Counsellour's Names.

Archbischop St Androis, Chancellour; Thesaurer, E. Monteith; President, E. Hadinton. B. Glasgow, Marques of Hamilton, E. Marschell, E. Mar, E. Winton, E. Linlythgow, E. Perth, E. Wigtoun, E. Tullibardyn, E. Roxburgh, E. Kellie, E. Buccleuch, E. Annandale, E. Galloway, E. Seafort, E. Lauderdaill, E. Carlile, Viscount Stormont, Viscont Air, B. Dunkeld, B. Aberdene, B. Ross, B. Dumblane, L. Gordon, L. Lorne, L. Erskene, Lo Melvill, L. Carnagy, L. Jedburgh, L. Naper; L. Traquair, M^r of Elphingstoun, Two Secretareis; Sir Johne Hamilton, Sir Thomas Hope, Sir George Elphingstoun, Sir Johne Scott, Sir James Baillie, Sir James Galloway.

Was Mr Robert Bruce present by his Matie to the Church of Culros, being at his Ma^teis gift by the death of Mr Robert Colvill, last minister at the said kirk?—Whithall, 25 March 1631.

To the Chancellor.

Right, &c.—Wheras vpon information made vnto ws in behalff of the bischops in that our kingdome of diverse grevances sustened by them, we have bene pleased to mak choyse of yow to hear and compose the same in so far as yow can lawfullie and convenientlie doe: Our pleasur is, that to this purpois yow meit with the Commissioners, to be choysen by them out of ther owin number, and that yow vse your best endeavours for setling such matters, wherin they find themselfis justlie greived, otherwyse that if vpon any poynt whervpon yow and they cannot condescend, yow certifie ws of the true estate therof, that we may give such further ordour therin as we by your advyse shall find just caus.—Whythall, 25 March 1631.

To the Counsell.

Right, &c.—Haveing intention vpon verie good considerationis at this tyme to ayd our brother, the king of Sueden, with such forces as we can convenientlie spare: Our pleasur is, that yow grant vnto

II   N

George Dowglas, Lewetenent-Colonell vnto Sir James Ramsay, kny', a sufficient warrant to levy and transport 300 men over seas for the assistance of our said brother out of all such persones within that our kingdome of Scotland as he shall find willing to goe with him thither, granting him libertie to tuck drumes for that purpois, with as large priviledges as any other hath had heirtofoir in the lyk kynd, he alwyse giveing such satisfaction to everie one of the said number as he shall agrie vpon betwixt him and them, according to the former customes in the lyk caces.—Whythall, 29 March 1631.

To the Chancellour.

Right, &c.—In regard that our right trustie, &c. the Duik of Lennox, being ane of whome we have a speciall care, haveing licence from ws, is gone abroad to travell for some tyme that he may be the better enabled for our service heirefter, being loath that dureing the tyme of his absence he should anywyse suffer in his affaires within that our kingdome, ather in the valuation of tythis or otherwyse, and being loath with all to command anything in his particular wherof the preparative in matters of greater moment may be prejudiciall vnto ws : Our pleasur is, that haveing conferred with such as ar intrusted with the Charge of his affaires ther, and taking notice of the particulars that ar demanded for his advantage, haveing heard the opinion of our Advocat therin, that yow adverteis ws what we can lawfullie or conuenientlie doe for his good, and that yow caus him draw vp any writt for our hand which he shall think requisit for that effect to be sent vnto ws—Whythall, 29 March 1631.

To the Exchequer.

Right, &c.—Being informed that ther ar diverse fynes of the Circuit Courts raised of late from persones fyned within the boundis of the baronie and regalitie of Glasgow, belonging to the house of Lennox, which being now sequestred, vntill such tymes as it be decydit befor yow, whither the samyne doe appertene to ws or to our right, &c. the Duik of Lennox, in whois estate, being vnwilling that anything be changed dureing his absence, to which purpois we have bene formerlie pleased to wryt vnto our right, &c. the Erle of Monteith, who is our Justice-generall in that our kingdome : Our pleasur is, and heirby we doe requyre yow to cause foorthwith the fynes aforsaid to be delyvered vnto our said cusen, his Commissioners or agents, and that in all things that shall cum befor yow concerneing him yow give your best assistance, which we will tak as speciall good service done vnto ws.—Whythall, 29 March 1631.

To the Erle Monteith.

Right, &c.—Being informed that ther be diverse fynes of the Circuit Courts raised of late from persones fyned within the boundis of the baronie and regalitie of Glasgow, belonging to our Right, &c., the Duik of Lennox, which being now sequestred vntill such tyme as it be decydit befor the Commissioners of our Exchequer, whither the samyne doe appertene vnto ws or to our said Cousen, in whois estate being vnwilling that any thing be changed dureing his absence, Our pleasur is, and heirby doe requyre yow to have a care to sie that the fynes aforsaid be delyvered vnto our said Cousen, his Commissioners or agents, and that in all things concerneing him yow give your best assistance as yow can laufullie doe, which we will tak as a speciall service done vnto ws.—Whythall, 29 March 1631.

Warrant.

Our pleasur is, that for good and considerable causses knowen vnto ws, yow licence and permitt our trustie and weilbeloved Alex' Erskene of Dune, his Chalmerlane and Others, haveing his power to transport from that our kingdome to any port or part within our dominions the quantitie of so much victuall of wheat, barley, and oatts belonging vnto him as shall amount to four scoir Chalders or therabout, he paying vnto ws such custome for the same as hath bene accustomed to be payed in caces of the lyk nature, and that none of yow attempt nor tak in hand directlie or indirectlie to hinder to stay him or them from doeing therof, bot that this our licence may be effectuall vnto them vntill the first day of October nixt ensneing; and for your soe doeing these presents shalbe your sufficient warrant and discherge. —Gevin at our Court at Whythall, 30 March 1631.

To our Right, &c. the Erle of Morton, our Thesaurer, and Lord
Traquair. our deputie-Thesaurer, and to all our customers,
fermers, searchers, and all other our officers whatsoever or
wheresoever in our kingdome of Scotland.

To the Counsell.

Right, &c.—Wheras our right trustie, &c. the Erle of Annandale hath informed ws that certane leadner mart kyne belonging vnto him have bene vnjustlie and violentlie takin away from his servandis, wherby (as we ar lykwyse informed) both we in our right of superioritie of some landis in Annandale, and he as our tennent therof hath bene wronged, and by the exemple wherof we may be lykwyse prejudged in matters of the lyk nature: Our pleasur is, that yow call befor yow such persones as in the name of the said Erle shalbe delated vnto yow to have had ane hand in that bussines, and efter due tryell if yow shall find the said kyne ather vnordourlie or vnjustlie takin away, that vpon due consideration and merite of the offence yow fyne and cause punisch them accordinglie that others may be terrifeid from attempting the lyk heirefter: Which recommending, &c.—Whythall 30 March 1631.

To the Advocat.

Trustie, &c.—Haveing writtin vnto our Counsall to examyne a ryot alledged to be committed aganst our servand our Right, &c. the Erle of Annandale, wherin and by the consequence (as we ar informed) we ar. and he may be prejudged, our pleasur is, that yow informe yourselff of the true estate therof, and our interest from the said Erle or others in his name, or otherwayes as yow shall think fitt; and if yow find that both we and he will be prejudged if a tymelie course be not takin, according to justice. to punish the said ryot; and to prevent the lyk heirefter, that yow cause raise summondis, ather in our name or in his, as yow shall think fitt for that purpois against the committers therof, or in ther absens against ther landslords or masters, by vertew of the generall band, to compeir befor our Counsell to answer for the said ryot, and that yow insist aganst them according to law and justice in so far as by your charge from ws is compitent for yow to doe; And lykwyse if neid be that yow compeir befor our session and Exchequer to defend our right in things of the lyk nature if any objection shalbe made aganst the same; which recommending vnto your speciall, we bid, &c.—Whythall, 30 March 1631.

To the Exchequer.

Right, &c.—Wheras by your letter vnto ws yow have acknowledged that our trustie and weilbeloved George Abercrombie hath deserved benefite at our handis, at leist recompense in some measur for the loss and expensses vndergone by him in the bussines tuitching James Gordoun of Latterfurie, And that thogh our right, &c., the Lord Gordon hath performed in that particular what in the generall was vndertakin by him for suppressing poperie in the north parts of that our kingdome, yit the said James hath gevin no testimonie of his obedience: Becaus of the necessitie of our Cofferis at this tyme wherby we cannot convenientlie satisfie the said George, and that your opinions vnto ws tuitching to that purpois seame to inclyne that he have the benefite of our gift of the escheit and lyfrent of the said James, Our pleasur is, that yow delyver the same vnto him, and if neid be that yow strenthen him in any thing which he shall lawfullie desyre for his peaceable enjoying therof.—Whythall, 14 Aprill 1631.

PRECEPT.

Wheras vpoun good consideratiouns we wer pleased to allow vnto our right, &c., the Lord of Lorne, the sowme of 4000 lib. st., the halff wherof he was to receave and detene in his owin handis of the dueteis of Ila and Kintyre belonging to ws, and the other halff of the fynes which should happin to be due vnto ws by the course of our Justice Courts and Justiciareis within the said kingdome, which being otherwayes disposed of, and the said Lord dissapoynted, Our pleasur is, that yow pay vnto him or his assigneyis, the sowme of 2500lib st., and that out of the first and readiest of our rents, dewteis, annuiteis, and casualiteis whatsumever now dew vnto ws, and which heirefter shalhappin to accresce and be dew in the moneth of July last anno 1630: And for your soe doing, and everie of yow, from tyme to tyme, it may concerne a sufficient warrant and discherge.—Whythall, 16 Aprill 1631.

TO THE SESSION.

Right, &c.—Wheras we ar informed that the Lord of Luss hath intented ane action of reduction aganst our right trustie, &c., the duik of Lennox, concerneing certane landis which of a long tyme hath bene vnquestioned and peaciablie possesst by the house of Lennox, in regard of his absence, and that we have takin vpon ws in his minoritie to have a care that nothing be decernit aganst him in that action or in any other till his returne into our dominions, or till yow first certifie ws in respect of our interest of the estate therof, that we may give such furder ordour therin as the cause shall be fund to requyre.—Whythall, 16 Aprill 1631.

TO THE ARCHBISCHOP OF St ANDROIS.

Right, &c.—Wheras vpon information made vnto ws by the reverend father in God, Johne bischope of the Yles, in behalff of the bischopes in that our kingdome, of diverse greevances sustened by them, we have bene pleased to have gevin ordour vnto our right, &c., the Viscont of Dupline, our Chancellour, Erle of Morton, our Thesaurer, and E. of Montcith, president of our Privie Counsall, and to our trustie and weilbeloved Counsellour, Sir William Alexander, our Secretarie, or oney tuo of them, to meitt and hear the same, Our pleasur is, that yow advertise your said brethren that the Commissioners to be choysen out of your number may meitt and treit with these our Commissioners for setling such matters wherin yow find your selfis justlie greeved, and in any poynts wherevpon yow and they can not condescend, and wherin yow cannot proceid without a further warrand from ws, we requyre both yow and them to certifie ws of the trew estate therof, that we may give such further ordour therin as we shall find just caus.—Whythall, 16 Aprill 1631.

Precept.

Wheras the Erle of Tullibardyne, one of the Lords of our Privie Counsall of our kingdome of Scotland, was by our speciall warrant and direction appoynted in July last to imploy for our service in the Yle of Mule some able men for dyveing and recovering certane sunck ordinance and other wraked goodis whervnto the said Earle and his servandis haveing repaired wher onlie then a tryell was made, bott nowayes fullie putt in executioun : These ar therfor to chairge and command all our loveing subjects, and everie of them whom these presents may in anywayes concerne, to have a speciall care that the said Erle his partiners and servandis imployed in the said work, be weill and kyndlie vsed and assisted as weill in the said Yle of Mule as elswher therabouts vpon ther reasonable expenssis in recovering and transporting the said ordinance and other wraked goodis to our citie of London, and that none presume to hinder or stop ther proceidings vpon pane of our indignatioun and high displeasur as they will answer the contrarie at ther perrells.—Whythall, 16 Aprill 1631.

Trustie and weilbeloved, Wheras our Thesaurer, by our direction, have gevin warrant vnto yow for a lease to be made vnto the Lord Vchiltrie, one of the leaseis, for tuenticone yeres, of the benefite which may happin to ws by the year day and wast of all fellones landis and houses, rendring 500lb st. per annum : Bot be reasone the said Lord Vchiltrie is not a frie denizone, he cannot reallie enjoy the said grant in his owin name, which he desyreth : These ar therfor to will and requyre yow to prepair a bill readie for our signatur wherby to mak the said Lord Vchiltrie a frie denizen of this our kingdome of England and dominions therof ; with this speciall caution, that it be nowayes prejudiciall to ws in our customes : And for your soe doeing these shalbe your warrand.—Whythall, 19 Aprill 1631.

To the Counsell.

Right, &c.—Wheras, for the better cleiring of the treuth tuitching the burneing of the tour of Frendraucht, yow have, according to ane act of Counsall made by yow for tryeing of Johne Meldrum and John Toscheoch, caused the said Toscheoch to be tortured, bot have for some tyme and vpon some consideratiouns to tak the lyk course with the other ; being of late informed that ther ar more apparent presumptions of the guiltines of the said Meldrum, at least of his more certane knowledge concerneing that purpois then of the said Toscheoch, We ar pleased that all lawfull meanes be speedelie vsed for tryeing the treuth therin : Therfor our pleasur is, if yow find grounds for what is heirby alledged, that yow putt Meldrum lykwyse to his tryell according to the course takin with the said Toscheoch : And wheras humble complaynt hath bene made vnto ws, in behalff of James Crechton of Frendraucht, that diverse oppressiouns hath bene committed vpon his landis, we ar the rather pleased, in regard of his absence from his estate, and of his being lyable to abyd the tryell of our lawis tuitching the said Accident or fact, to recommend vnto yow that, vpon trew information of the estate of that Complaint, yow caus try and punish the offenders according to Justice.—Whythall, 19 Aprill 1631.

To the Justices of Irland.

Right, &c.—Wheras our right trustie and weilbeloved the Lord Vchiltrie, Our trustie and weilbeloved Counsellours Sir Peirce Corsbie and Sir Archibald Achiesone, knyts and baronets, and our trustie and weilbeloved Sir Walter Corsbie, knyt and baronet, intent to plant a Colonie near vnto the river of

Canada, in America : Becaus the purpois is honorabill, and may conduce to the good of our service, Our speciall pleasur is, that from tyme to tyme, as they or any of them shall have occasion, yow grant them Commissions and warrants requisit for transporting thither such persones as shalbe willing to be imployed in that plantation ; And that yow licence and caus licence them, and such as shall have ther or any of ther warrants, to transport provisions of Victuall, Ordinance, munition, and all other necessareis whatsoever fitt for ther vse ; ffor doeing wherof, as these presents shalbe vnto yow a sufficient warrant, so we will accompt your care in forthring of them as good and acceptable service done vnto ws : We bid yow farewell.—Whythall, 19 Aprill 1631.

TO THE ADVOCAT.

Trustie, &c.—Wheras our right, &c. the Lord of Lorne hath informed ws that we have vndoubted right to the Isle of Gigay ; and becaus the tryell therof in Law will prove chargeable, and that vpon recoverie therof he offers to augment our rent payable therin, he humblie desyreth to becum teunent therof ; wherin, for these and other good respects of his services done vnto ws, being willing that in our right he be preferred to any other persone, Our pleasur is, that, in so far as may lawfullie flow from ws, yow draw vp vnto him such rights and securiteis of that Islet as yow can best devyse, which we will yow to docat and send vnto ws, or to pass vnder our signet and sealls ther, as shalbe most fitt for his and his aires better securitie ; And therefter that in his persute therof in a legall maner yow Compeir and Concure with him for our interest.—Whythall, 19 Aprill 1631.

TO THE SESSION.

Right, &c.—Wheras we ar informed that ther is ane action in law to be decydit befor yow betwen James Maxwell, one of our bedchalmer, and Sir Alexr Moresoun of Prestoungrange, one of your number : Becaus the said James cannot convenientlie nor long attend the following nor issue thairof, as in such cnces is requisite, in regard of his charge in our service, We ar heirby pleased to recommend vnto your serious consideratioun the Estate of his cause, and of his proceidingis therin ; and therefter that yow determyne in the said action as the equitie therof in justice requyre, and that with as much diligence as convenientlie can be.—Whythall, 25 Aprill 1631.

TO THE ARCH. BISHOP OF ST ANDROIS.

Right, &c.—Wheras humble sute hath bene made vnto ws in behalff of Wm Dureham of Grange, and of the remanent gentlmen of the paroch of Monyfeith that none be admitted to be preacheour efter the death of Mr John Rutherfurd (who by reasone of his aige and seiknes incident thervnto cannot long attend that charge), bot such a persone whois sufficiencie by your approbation may merit ther consent, sieing we ar crediblie informed that ther intention heirin is onlie to have ane liable and sufficient preacher : Our pleasur is, that taking the advyse of the said William yow mak choyse of such a persone as yow and he shall best condescend vpon, he being by yow fund qualifeid for the same, and conforme to the canons and ordours of the Churche.—Whythall, 25 Aprill 1631.

TO THE EXCHEQUER.

Right, &c.—Being crediblie informed of the great expensses and trouble vndergone by our right, &c. the Erle of Merschell in haveing the Charge of our schip called the Lyon, wherof by our entrusting of hir to him we have bene freed this long tyme bypast, and that hir repairing and outreiking (which at this tyme ar necessarlie requisit) wilbe verie chargeable vnto him, he haveing so small a tyme of any assurance from ws wherby to adventure for recoverie of his former losses, Our pleasur is, that he have the grant of hir for the space of fyve yeres efter the expiration of the tyme limited in the former signature, he alwyse performeing the conditiones mentionat therin : And that yow mak ane Act of Exchequer heirvpon if yow think it may secure him to this purpois, otherwyse that yow cause our Advocat draw vp a grant of new, ather immediatlie to pass our cachet and sealls ther, or to be first signed by ws heir as yow shall think most requisit : And for your soe doing, &c.—Whythall, 25 Aprill 1631.

To Sir Wm Muschamp.

Trustie, &c.—Wheras we ar informed that certane persones have bene questioned befor yow for alledged murther of a chyld borne in a place belonging to the Count Palatyne of Durchame by a Scotts woman namet Margaret Moresone, which chyld hath bene abstracted and (as is supposed) made away within ane of our tuo kingdomes ather by the mother or some other in whois hands it is proved to have bene : Our pleasur is, that yow insist with all possible care in the tryell of that matter to find out whither the chyld be murthred or not, to the effect that if any persone of this our kingdome of England be fund guilty of that cryme they may be punished according to Justice : And in regard (as we ar lykwyse informed) that the mother is to be questioned tuitching that supposed murther within our kingdome of Scotland wher schoe is now resident : Our further pleasur is, that yow transmitt vnto the Judges of our said kingdome of Scotland a true authentik copie vnder your hand and seall of the whole examinations by yow made or to be made heirin, as also that yow cause any persone or persones that can give evidence in or concerneing this matter to goe vnto Scotland at what tyme they shalbe requyred (ther reasonable charges being borne by the pairtie persewing) ther to depone befor the Judges what they know tuitching the hearing, abstract, or supposed murther of the chyld, to the effect that Justice may be administred as cause shall appear : We bid, &c.—Whythall, 25 Aprill 1631.

Charles, by the Grace of God, &c.—To the Thesaurer and vnder Thesaurer of our Exchecker for the tyme being, Greeting : Wheras we ar gratiouslie pleased to bestow a portion vpon our right dear and weillbeloved cousen the Lady Ann Stewart, sister to our right trustie, &c. the duik of Lennox vpon hir mariage with Lord Dowglas, sone to our right, &c. the Erle of Angus : Our will and pleasur therfor is, and we doe heirby will and command yow of our Treasure remayneing in the recept of our Exchecker furthwith to pay or cause to be payed vnto the said Erle of Angus or his assigneyis the sowme of Tuo thousand pundis of lawfull money of England, the same to be takin to him in part of satisfaction of the said portion which we ar gratiouslie pleased to bestow vpon our said cousen the Lady Ann Stewart as aforsaid, and without accompt imprest or other charge to be sett vpon him or his assigneyis for the same or any part thairof : And these our letters, &c.—Gevin at Whyhall, 25 Aprill.

> This conteyneth your Maties warrant to the Exchequer to pay vnto
> the E. of Angus the sowme of 2000lib stg as part of portion
> which your Matie is pleased to bestow vpon your Consen the
> Lady Ann Stewart, sister to the Duik of Lennox, vpon hir
> Mariage with the Lo. Dowglas, the said Erle's sone.
>
> Signiefeid to be your Maties pleasur vnder your signe manuall.

To the Counsell.

Right, &c.—Wheras yow have recommended to our princelie care the advancement and manteneing of the work of Plantation of New Scotland; being lykwyse petitioned by our whole estats convened for taking some course which might best tend for effectuating that Interpryse, And being of ourselffes daylie more and more sensible how much the prosecution of it concerneth ws in honour, and the estate of that our antient kingdome many wayes in benefite; Considering lykwyse the course which we had layd down for it in conferring a title of honour vpon some deserveing persones who should engadge themsellfis for the advancement therof hath made bot slow progress, and that diverse noblemen and others generouslie affect have contracted with our trustie and weilbelovit Sir Wm Alexander, Our Secretarie, who is speciallie intrusted by ws to prosecute that work, for the more speedie effectuating of our designe in it, the doeing wherof is verie acceptable vnto ws: Our pleasur is, that yow mak choyse of a certane number amonges yourselffis of such as have alreadie testifeid ther ernest affection to the work by contracting in that kynd with our said servand, that they may tak seriouslie vnto ther consideratiouns by what meanes our desyres in this may be best accomplished, that being acquanted therwith we may, by your advyse, tak such further course as shalbe requisit; ffor ther shalbe nothing wanting in ws that may second so just desyres and honourabill designes: Which earnestlie recommending vnto your cares, we bid yow farewell.—Whythall, 29 Aprill 1631.

These conteyne a gift of pension to Sir Peter Raggamor, kny^t, and Dame Marie Bruce, and to the longest leiver of them tuo of Four thowsand merks scotts yeirlie, to be payed vnto them or any haveing ther power out of his Ma^{teis} Exchequer, the first termes payment thairof to be and begin at the feist and terme of Mertimes last past, and so furth, yeirlie and termelie, dureing ther lyftyme, and the longest leiver of them tua dureing his Ma^{teis} pleasur.—Grenwitch, first of May 1631.

Our Soveraigne Lord being crediblie informed that Johne Livingston, younger of Donypace, becam suretie for his father Sir David Livingstoun of Donypace, knyght and barronett, in his minoritie, and nather the said Johne Livingstoun was infeft in the Landis which ar lyable to the payment of the debt for the which his said sone becam surtie, nather hath he benefite nor can expect any by these Lands, besyds that his said father may tak a course himsellf for defraying of that debt. In which respect (the said Johne, who by that occasion is both dissabled to attend his other affaires and what may concerne his releiff heirin) hath becum ane humble sutter vnto ws that he may have some compitent tyme allowed vnto him for vseing his best endeavours to deall with the Creditours to tak the readiest course in equitie for ther owin satisfaction and his disengadgment: Therfor his Matie, out of his royall authoritie kinglie power, grace, mercie, and clemencie, onleanes a protection to be made vnder his highnes great seall of Scotland, accepting the said Johne Livingstoun, vnder his speciall power and safeguard, Giveing and granting vnto him, dureing the space of tuo yeres begining from the passing of thir presents vnder the said seall, licence, power and libertie to peaceablie and safelie dwell, stay, and remane within any part of the said kingdome as best pleaseth him, without any molestatioun, trouble, challenge, persute, or danger of apprehending or warding of his persone, Dischargeing expreslie by thir presents all his Ma^{teis} schirreffis, stewarts, captanes, provests, baillcis, constables of burghs, Justices of peace, and all other judges, officers, and ministers of his highnes Lawis, both by burgh and land, ther deputeis, servands, and all others whome it efferes within the said kingdome, that they in nowayes presum, attempt, nor tak in hand, directlie nor indirectlie, be day nor night, to seik, tak, or apprehend the said Johne Livingstoun, his persone, or to mak any disturbance, interruption, or violatioun of this, his Ma⟨tie⟩ protection, vnder pane of incurring his highnes' vtter wrath and high displeasur, notwithstanding of any letters of horning, caption, warrants, commissions, charges, or commands alreadie gevin or to be gevin by his Ma⟨tie⟩ himself, the Lords of Session, or any other persone whatsoever within the said kingdome in favours of whatsumever persone or persones, for apprehending warding of the said Johne, his persone, for any debts or sownes of money adebtit be him as suretie for his said father in maner forsaid, wheranent his Ma⟨tie⟩, out of his highnes' royall princelie power and prerogative, be thir presents dispensses in that part dureing the space of two yeires ; And to the effect the said Johne may in the meanetyme recover payment from his debtours of just and lawfull debts owing vnto him, his Ma⟨tie⟩, of his authoritie, royall princelie power and prerogative, gives vnto him personam standi in judicio in all causses and actions intended, or to be intended aganst him, or at his instance, notwithstanding of whatsoever proces of horning vsed against him for whatsoever civill causses, wheranent his Ma⟨tie⟩, of his authoritie royall and princelie power, dispensses in that part dureing the said space of two yeires, Ordeaneing thir presents to be a sufficient warrant to the writter to the great seall, and for appending of the same thervnto, but passing any other sealls or registers wheranent thir presentis shalbe vnto them a sufficient warrant.—Gevin at Grenwitch, 5 of May 1631.

Our Soveringe Lord considering the good and faythfull service done vnto his Ma⟨tie⟩ by his right, &c. Johne, Lord Stewart of Traquair, his Ma⟨teis⟩ Thesaurer-depute of the kingdome of Scotland ; Therfor, with speciall advyse and consent of his Ma⟨teis⟩ right, &c. William, Erle of Morton, Lord Dalkeith and Aberdour, his Ma⟨teis⟩ principall Thesaurer of the said kingdome, and of the remanent noblemen and others of his Ma⟨teis⟩ Commissioners of Exchequer, Ordeanes a Letter to be past and exped vnder the privie seall thairof in dew forme, Giveing, granting, and disponeing Lykas his Ma⟨tie⟩ be the tennour heirof, and with advyse and consent forsaid, Gives, grants, and dispones vnto the said Johne, Lord Stewart of Traquair, dureing all the dayes of his lyftyme, all and haill a yeirlie pension of 200⟨lib⟩ sterling, to be vplifted and receaved by him, his assigneyis, factours, servandis, or others in his name, haveing his power for that effect at two termes in the yeir, witsonday and mertimes, be equall portions, and that out of the first and readiest of his Ma⟨teis⟩ rents, dewteis, and casualiteis of whatsoever kynd, as well of the ancient and accustomed rents, dewteis, and casualiteis belonging to his Ma⟨tie⟩ within the said kingdome, as of the few-dewteis of kirk lands and others, dewteis and casualiteis whatsoever of late establisched and fallin, or which heir-after shall happin to be establisched and fall vnto his Ma⟨tie⟩ or successours within the same, the first terme's payment to be and begin at the terme of Mertimes last, and so furth yeirlie and termelie at the saids termes of Witsonday and Mertimes dureing all the dayes of his said lyftyme, With full power to the said Johne, Lord Stewart, to keip and deteyne yeirlie and termelie in his owin handis, and for his owin vse so much of his Ma⟨teis⟩ saids rents, dewteis, and casualiteis in maner abone said, as shall extend to the said yeirlie pension of 200⟨lib⟩ sterling ; or otherwyse, if the said Johne Stewart shall think it rather fitt to receave the said pension from the Thesaurer-principall or vnder receavers, who at for the present or who shall happin to be for the tyme from any of them his Ma⟨tie⟩ in that caice doeth heirby expeslie command and authorize them the officers abone-writtin, or any of them from tyme to tyme dureing the lyftyme of the said Johne, Lord Stewart, to readelie answer and pay vnto him or his forsaids, at the saids termes of Witsonday and Mertimes, the said pension of 200⟨lib⟩ sterling, the first terme's payment therof to be and begin at the said terme of Mertimes last, and that out of the first and readiest of his Ma⟨teis⟩ saidis rents, dewteis, and casualiteis whatsoever in maner particularlie abone expressed, and lykwyse with speciall command and direction to his Ma⟨teis⟩ Auditours of Exchequer for the tyme being to defease and allow the said yeirlie pension, yeirlie in the accompts of the said Lord Stewart or in the accompts of the saids ather officers or any of them, these presents being once schawin in the Excheker and registrat as effeires, and that the said Letter be extendit in the best forme with all clauses neidfull.—Grenewitch, 5 May 1631.

II   U

These conteyneth a gift by your Matie for your self and as administratour to your Ma^teis darest sone, to Johne Birsbane, elder of Bischoptoun, in lyfrent, and Johne Birsbane, younger, his sone, his heyres and assigneyis, of the sextene merk land of the baronie of Gogosyd, contening the particular lands, commonteis, and others abone-writtin, with the burgh of baronie of the forsaids lands called the Newtoun of Gogo, with the priviledges belonging thairto ; and sielyk, all and whole that portion of land called the Larges and Larges Mure, with the toun and village of Larges port and heavin thairof, murs, coalls, muntanes, mosses, and commoditeis belonging thairto, and that in so far as the samyne may effect and correspond to the proportion of the propertie of the sextene merk land of the said baronie of Gogo abone-specifeit, and that vpon the resignation of the said Johne Birsbane, elder, and of Sir William Alexander, your Majesteis Secretarie, with ane Confirmatioun of all former Chartours granted to the said Johne Birsbane and his authors of the saids lands and others forsaids, with a new gift of the samyne, with supplement of all defects, with ane new vnion of the whole in ane baronie to be called the baronie of Gogosyd, all to be holdin of your Matie and your Ma^teis said darest sone for payment of services vsed and wont befor the said Resignatioun.— Grenewitch, 5 May 1631.

These conteyne ane ratification of the two former Commissions of Barronetts and all patents and Infeftments granted conforme thairto preceiding the date heirof, with ane new Commission geving power to certane Commissioners abone nominat, or any fyve of them, to receave resignation of Lands lyand within the cuntrie of New Scotland vpoun the resignation of your Ma^teis Secretarie, Sir William Alexander, Livetennent of Nova Scotia, and to grant infeftments thairvpon of the saids lands to the persones in whois favours the samyne is made : Togidder with the title and dignitie of baronett : And also contenes ane Ratificatioun of the Seall and Armes of New Scotland, with power to the saids commissioners, with advyse of the said Sir William Alexander, to change the samyne : And last conteynes ane ratificatioun of ane warrand gevin by your Matie to the saids Barronetts for bearing and wearing of ane badge and cognoscence, with a new warrand for bearing and weiring of the samyne in maner abone-specifeit, discheargeing the vse of the saids former Commissions efter the date heirof, and this to indure without revocatioun, ay and whill the full number of ane hundreth and fyftie barronetts be made and compleit.— Grenewitch, 5 May 1631.

Our Soveraigne Lord Ordeanes ane Letter to be made vnder his Ma^teis privie seall in dew forme to his highnes' lovit Johne Veitch, eldest lawfull sone to William Veitch of Dawich, his aires or assigneyis, ane or mae, of the ward, nonentress, maills, fermes, proffeits, and dewteis of all and whole the twentie pund land and baronie of Dawich, with the tour, fortalice, maner place, housses, biggings, orchards, yards, tennents, tennendreis, service of frie tennents, advocations, donations, rights of patronages of kirks and Chaplanreis, pairts, pendicles, and pertinents thairof whatsumever, lyand within the Schirefdome of Peeblis of all yeres and termes bygane, that the same hes bene in the handis of his highnes or his Ma^teis predecessours superiours thairof be reasone of ward or nonentrie or ather of them since or throw the deceise of vmquhill . . . Veitch of Dawich, grandsir to the said Johne Veitch of Dawich, donatour forsaid, or any other of his predecessours or successours last lawfull immediat heretable tennents to his highnes or his predicessours of the samyne, lawfullie entred therto, or thrugh reduction of whatsumever retour or retours, infeftments, seasines, or others writts and evidentis of the saids lands and baronie abone-writtin, with the pertinents made to the said vmquhill . . . Veitch and his predicessours thervpon or otherwayes ; And sielyke, for all the whole termes and yeires of fyve yeires immediatlie following the date heirof, with full power to the said Johne Veitch, his heyres and assigneyis forsaids, to intromett with, receave, and vplift all and sindrie his Ma^{tcis} maills, fermes, proffeits, and dewteis of the saids lands, baronie, and others abone-writtin, with the pertinents of all the saids yeirs bygane and in tyme cuming dureing the tyme of the said ward nonentress, and ather of them, and thervpon to vse and dispone at ther pleasur, and to occupy and posses the said lands, baronie, and others forsaids, with ther owin propper goodis, or set the samyne to tennents as he shall think most expedient, with court plant, herezeld, bludwyt, vulawes, amerciaments, and escheits of the saids courts, and with all and sindrie others, friedomes, commoditeis, &c., frielie, quyetlie bot revocatioun, and that the said letter be farder extendit in the best forme, with all clausses neidfull.—Grenwitch, 5 May 1631.

Our Soveraigne Lord Ordanes ane Letter to be made vnder his highnes' privie seall, To his Ma^{tcis} dearest Cousen, James, Duik of Lennox, Erle Darnelie, Lord Torboltoun, Methven, St Andrewis, and Abiegne, &c., his heyres and assigneyis, ane or mae, of the Gift af the Escheit of all goodis, moveable and vnmoveable, cornes, cattell, insicht, plenisching, jewells, gold, siluer, cunzeit, and vncunzeit, acts, contracts, lands, obligatiouns, sentences, decreits, debts, sowmes of money, taks, steidlings, rowmes, possessions, reversions, actions, canssis, writts, goods, and geir whatsumever perteneing to Sir James Cleland of Monkland, kny^{t}, and now perteneing to our said Soveraigne Lord, fallin and becum in his Ma^{tcis} handis and at his highnes' gift and disposition by reasone of escheit throw being of the said Sir James Cleland ordourlie denunced his Ma^{tcis} rebell, and putt to his highnes' horne be vertew of the Letters of horning, raised and execute aganst him at the instance of the said James, Duik of Lennox, and his curatours, for ther interests for not payment to them of the sowme of eight thowsand nyne hundreth fyftie-fyve pundis sex schillingis eight pennyis money of this realme, and certane liquidat expensses and sentence silver contenit in ane decreit obtenit befoir the Lordis of Counsell and Sessioun vpoun the eightene day of December the yeir of God j^{m}vj^{c} threttie yeires, at the instance of the said James, Duik of Lennox, and his saids curatours theranent ; And sielyk throw being of the said Sir James Cleland denunced our Soveraigne Lords rebell and putt to his highnes' horne be vertew of Letters and charges of horning raisit and execute aganst him at the instance of Johne Cunyngham, laird of Drumwhassill, for not removeing himselff, his wyff, bairnes, familie, servandis, goods, and geir furth and from the maner place and house of Dormansyd, with yairds, orchards, pairtis, and pendicles of the samyne, lyand within the parochin of Paisley and Schirrefdome of Renfrew, conforme to ane decreit of removeing obtenit at the instance of the said Johne Cunynghame against the said Sir James to the effect forsaid befoir the Lordis of Counsall and Session vpoun the sevint day of Feb^{r} 1630 as the Letters of horning respective abone-writtin dewlie execute, indorsat, and registrat, at lenth bears : With full power to the said James, Duik of Lennox, his aires or assigneyis, ane or mae, to search, seik, intromett with, and vptak all and sindrie the said Sir James Clelands' cornes, cattell, insicht plenisching, debts, sowmes of money, goods, and geir perteneing to him wherever the samyne can be apprehendit, and if neid beis, to call, follow, and persew thairfoir, compone, transact, agrie, and discherge theranent, vse and dispone thervpoun at ther pleasur, and also to occupy the saids taks, steidlings, rowmes, and possessions, with ther owin propper goodis, or to sett the samyne to tennents as they shall think most expedient dureing all the tyme thairof, frielie, quyetlie, bot revocatioun, &c., and that the said Letter be farder extendit in the best forme, with all clausses neidfull.—Grenewitch, 5 May 1631.

To the Session.

Right, &c.—We ar informed that some persones, and speciallie one Francis Fraser, receaved moneyis from our Right, &c. the Lord Rae for levying a Companie of men to have bene by him imployed in the service of our vncle the King of Denmark, bot nather did levy the men for that purpois, nor pay bak the moneyis, wherin besyds the breach of trust and paction vpon ther part, the course by the consequence is dangerous if persones of the lyk disposition should tak the lyk course, speciallie when ather our imployment at home or abroad might requyr a speedie levy of our subjects; Therfor our speciall pleasur is, that in all matters comeing befor yow which may any wayes concerne the said Lord, his satisfaction heirin, or any action intendit in his name, yow grant vnto him all such speedie justice as the lawis of that our kingdome can affoord; which seriouslie recommending vnto your care, We bid yow farewell.—Whythall, 5 May 1631.

To the Counsell.

Right, &c.—Haveing bene moved by our right, &c. the Lord Rae in the name of the King of Suaden for transporting some forces from that our kingdome for his better supplie in the warres, wherin he at this tyme is engadged : Our pleasur is, that yow grant vnto the said Lord, or to any other whom he shall appoynt, a Commission with a sufficient warrant to levy and transport 2000 men for the purpois aboue-said, with as large priviledges as any generall, Colonell, or Commander hath had heirtofoir in the lyk kynd, he alwyse geving satisfaction to everie ane of the said number as shalbe agried vpon betwixt him and them according to the custome in the lyk cases ; ffor doeing wherof, &c.—Grenwitch, 5 May 1631.

To the Exchequer.

Right, &c.—Being informed of the prejudice sustened by ws in our rents and casualiteis of that our kingdome by granting of assignements thervnto, wher it wer more expedient that the assigneyis should have recourse to the payments of our Exchequer : Our pleasur is, and we doe heirby will and requyre yow to suffer no such assignements to pass at any tyme heirefter : And that yow endeavour to reduce in a fair and legall maner such as ar alreadie past.—Grenwich, 5 May 1631.

To the Commissioners of the Midlsothyres.

Right, &c.—Being crediblie informed of the sufficiencie of Andro, Lord of Jedwart, and of his affection to our service, and with all that it is fitt for the good therof to adjoyne him to your number as one weill acquanted with the estate of those parts, wherin for the sieing of our peace preserved we have appoynted yow our Commissioners : Our pleasur is, and we doe herby requyre yow to admitt him to be one of your number according to the forme accustomed in the lyk cases : And for your soe doing, &c.—Grenwich, 5 of May 1631.

To the Exchequer.

Right, &c.—Wheras we have bene informed that the Landis of Eister Stanelie and Thornelie wer resigned in our hands by Johne Maxwell, some tyme heretable proprietar therof (who held them of the Prince and Stewart of that our ancient and native kingdome), in favours of Lord and Lady Ross, and that ther was a signature of the samyne past and componed by yow in ther favours befor the birth of our dearest sone the prince, which as yitt is not putt vnder our sealls, wherby it is necessarie that the samyne be renewed and past over agane, and our said dearest sone, the prince's name, insert therin as superiour therof : Therfor we as administratour vnto him authorise yow to renew and expeed the same for the former composition agreid vpon of befor : And for your soe doeing these presents shalbe vnto yow a speciall warrant.—Grenwich, 5 May 1631.

To the Advocat.

Trustie, &c.—Being willing to renew the Commission of our Exchequer in such forme as is fund most requisit for the good of our service : Our pleasur is, that yow draw vp a Commission therof according to the inclosed Articles, and haveing docated the same, that yow delyver it to be sent vnto ws by our right, &c. the Lord Traquair, our deputie thesaurer : And for your so doeing, &c.—Grenwich, 5 May 1631.

To the Thesaurer.

Right, &c.—Wheras we ar informed that ther ar diverse vnnecessarie feyis and pensions wherwith that Exchequer of that our kingdome is burdened, wherby (besydis the inconvenients that may aryse vnto the estate therof) our owin vrgent necessarie affaires can hardlie often tymes be so effectual as is requisit for the good of our service, wherin desyreing that a due consideratioun may be had, our pleasur is, that yow call vnto yow, our Thesaurer deputie, and such of the Commissioners of our Exchequer as yow think fitt, and that yow and they consider of the burden therof and what yow think vnnecessarie, and what payments may be vpon some considerations, and for some tyme be discontinewed ; and therefter that yow report vnto ws your opinions tuitching the same, that we may give such further ordour as we think fitt ; and for your so doeing, &c.—Grenwich, 5 May 1631.

To the Exchequer.

Right, &c.—Wheras we ar informed that the schirrefschip of Murray (being ane heretable office and falling in the hands of a minor) is comprysed for some small sowmes of money : As we doe verie much dislyk of the course intended therin by Robert Dunbar of Burgie, so we doe commend your care in not giveing way to the confirmeing of his assignement thervnto, and least Justice in executioun of that office be frustrated, we requyre yow to caus our thesaurer or deputie-thesaurer to deale with the said Roᵗ Dunbar of Burgie for his right, which being established vpon ws, and the minor secured vpon repayment of what shalbe fund due vnto ws at his perfyte aige in a reasonable satisfaction to be condescended vpon betweene ws and him for his heretabill title, we recommend vnto yow that a sufficient and liable man may discharge that office vntill our further pleasur be knowen : And if the said Robert shall refuis to deale heirin, that yow certifie ws therof that we may give such further ordour tuitching him and that bussines as we shall find just caus.—Grenwich, 5 May 1631.

To the Counsell.

Right, &c.—Wheras ane humble complaint hath bene made vnto ws in behalff of diverse our subjectis within the schirrefdome of Forfar, that notwithstanding of two severall decreits gevin by yow for the Schirreff of Forfar his holding Courts at the burgh of Forfar, and the shirreff-clerk his residing ther, as the most commodious pairt of the schyre for that purpois, it being seated, as we ar informed, about the middle therof, and the place ancientlie accustomed for holding of shirreff Courts ; yit the present shirreff doe hold his Courts at Dundie, which, as we ar lykwyse informed, is seated in a corner of that schyre, wherby our subjects who most attend at these Courts did suffer great hurt, contrair to our royall intention : Sieing yow have proceidit so far as to pronunce your decrie heirin, and that we have not heard from yow, nor other-wayes any persone, why it should not have bene obeyed, We will not that any of our subjects contemne nor neglect that authoritie yow have from ws : Our pleasur is, that yow tak a course that the said shirreff, and all others bearing the lyk charge, heirefter hold ther Courts at the said brugh of Forfar, according to your said decrees and the ancient custome and liberteis granted, as we ar informed, to the head brugh of overie schyre.—Grenwich, 5 May 1631.

To the Advocat.

Trustie, &c.—The publict affaires of that our kingdome requyreing at some tymes that publict Commissiones be gevin by ws for advanceing our service ther, wherin, and speciallie in the Commission of our Exchequer, to be drawn vp by yow at this tyme, least any mistakings should be ather to prejudge, hinder, or alter any thing tuitching the generall course takin by ws concerneing the submission made vnto ws of tythes and other things therin mentionat, and our decrie following thervpon; we have bene pleased to confer therin with our right, &c. the Erle of Monteith, president of our Privie Counsall, to whome we have at lenth imparted our pleasur concerneing the same: Therfor we requyre yow (till by his letter he acquant yow more particularlie with our mynd heirin) that yow be carefull in the meane tyme that nothing be done therin any wayes to prejudge, hinder, or alter the said generall course and Commission of surranders, as yow wilbe answerable vnto ws: So, &c.—Grenwich, 6 May 1631.

To the Counsell.

Right, &c.—We wer pleased of late to wryt vnto yow that nothing be changed tuitching the sitting of our Colledge of Justice till our further pleasur wer signified therin: Bot now, haveing takin into our princelie consideration that though some materiall groundis might be proposeit for altering therof, yit we would doe it so consideratlie and by such advyse as so grave a matter and of such consequence doeth requyre: Therfor our pleasur is, that yow give speciall Ordour that no innovation be made therin till a parliament or generall convention of our Estats be called by ws, wherin, amongst other thingis concerneing the publict good, that purpois may be resolved vpon and ordered as by them shall be fund most expedient. —Grenwitch, 6 May 1631.

To the Session.

Right, &c.—Wheras it is expedient for the good of our service that our Thesaurer or deputie Thesaurer be present at all such processes in Law wherin we ar a pairtie, in regard of ther charge from ws: Our pleasur is, that heirefter nothing be heard nor concluded in any such processes or action without our said Thesaurer, or, in his absence, the deputie-Thesaurer, be present: Which speciallie recommending vnto your care, we bid, &c.—Grenwich, 7 May 1631.

[Not addressed.]

Right, &c.—Wheras we ar informed that our trustie and weillbeloved Thomas Thomesone of Dudingstoun hath signed the submission made vnto ws, and, according to our decrie, hath bought his owin tythes, being lyable to the payment of the annuitie due vnto ws out of the same: And wheras he feareth least, efter so great panes and charges takin by him in setling the estate of his tythes according to the ordour preservyed, the patronage of that kirk belonging vnto ws should be granted to any persone whosoever; wherby to prejudge him in his right, who holdeth his landis immediatlie of ws, Our pleasur is, that no such right of that patronage be granted from ws to any whosoever, and that in anything tending to the secureing of him to the tythes so purchased by him, yow give him all the favour in the speedie passing therof that yow can lawfullie grant vnto him: So we bid, &c.—Grenwich, 7 May 1631.

To the Exchequer.

Right, &c.—Wheras we ar informed that our right, &c. the Lord Traquair and his predicessours ar, and hath bene, heretable patrones of the Churche of Bedroule, and taksmen and possessours of the tythes therof, past memorie of man, as also have bene kyndlie taksmen of the viccarage tythes of Innerleithen, and yit have a great many yeires to run of ther last taks, wherby the benefite arysing of the pryces of these tythes doe justlie belong vnto him : And we being willing to contribute to his good and advantage, so far as is agreeable with the course of our decree, Our pleasur is, that the saids tythes being lyable to the pay-ment of our annuitie, vpon reservation of a competent stipend and mantinance to the ministers serveing the cure at the saids kirks, and ther successours, that ther be ane act made in his favours warranting him to dispose vnto the inheritours the aforsaid whole tythes of the parochin of Bedroule and Viccarage tythes of Innerleithen, and that the whole pryces therof, without diminution, be converted to his owin vse.— Grenwich, 7 May 1631.

Instructions for the Lord Traquair.

That no signature pas gratis heirefter without a speciall warrant from his Matie ;

That no heyre be putt in fee of wardlands without a speciall respect be had to his Ma^teis interest :

That all fynes of Contraventions must be exactlie takin vp :

That all bygane Commissions must be called for to the end that what is due to the king may be payed :

That yow advyse with such of the Exchequer as yow shall think fitting anent the present estate of the Coynehouse, and anent the present course of forrayne moneys, and therefter that yow certifie ws of your opinion therin :

That yow try if any fair and advantagious bargane can be made with John Stewart's Creditours for the lease he hath of our king :

That yow consider what may be done for raising of the present tak dewtie of the great customes :

That no pension cost by any of our servants be past in Exchequer :

That yow try how the Torwood is keiped, and that yow caus a certane ordour be preseryved for preserving therof heirefter.—Grenwich, 7 May 1631.

To the Exchequer.

Right, &c.—Wheras we for causes and considerationis knowen vnto ws, and for our trustie and weillbeloved Counsellour Archibald, Lord Naper, his dimission and surrendring of the office of Deputie-Thesaurer in that our kingdome, and for surrendring of ane yeirlie pension of 200^lib st., latelie acquyred by the said Lord Naper from Walter Stewart, gentlman of our privie Chalmer, we have appoynted our right, &c, William, Erle of Morton, our Thesaurer, and Johne, Lord Stewart, of Traquair, our deputie-Thesaurer, to pay vnto him the sowme of 3500^lib sterling : And sicklyk wheras we have appoynted them for the good of our service to pay vnto Sir Alex^r Strauchan, knyt and baronet, the sowme of 3000^lib sterling for his surrendring of two Commissions granted vnto him for recovering of certane our rents and casualiteis alledged concealed, and for simlrie other good services done and to be done by him, flinding our selfis bund in honour to provyde for our saids Thesaurers ther releiff, sieing they have willinglie vndergone the payment of the same, and most vndergoe and levy other great sownes of money for our necessarie service and charges : Our pleasur is, for the more sure and readie payment of these moneyis, that ther be granted vnto them what securitie they shall requyre vpon any of our rents, casualiteis, or taxationis present and to cum, in generall or particular assignements, and that they be secured in maner forsaid vpon any benefite present or which shallhappin heirefter, to be payed vnto our Exchequer for whatsumever cause, by whatsumever personnes in any maner of way, and to be instantlie secured to them by actis of Counsall and Exchequer, or otherwyse as they shall devyse, and that all impediments in ther vptaking of the saids moneyis by all or any of the saids wayes forsaid be by yow removed till they be compleitlie satisfeid of all the saidis particular sowmes of money for which they ar alreadie engadged or shallhappin heirefter to be engadged for the saids causses, with ordinarie interest for the same, as it is to be payed by them to others creditours dureing the tyme of the forbearance therof : And wheras we have gevin precepts and warrants for payment of great sowmes of money to many of our servands and subjects, which will intend by all readie wayes and meanes to cause pay vnto them efter the payment of the moneys aforsaid to our said Thesaurer, the doeing wherof doeth so neirlie concerne ws and the good of our service : We will yow restrayne the payment of these precepts and pensions till they be first releived, and that yow suffer no precept nor pension whatsoever to pass in Exchequer heirefter, till yow provyde that the passing therof doe not prejudge our saids Thesaurers and ther forsaids payment and releitf, and that for the which yow caus registrat thir presents in the books of Exchequer : And for your, &c.—Grenwich, 8 May 1631.

Our Soveraigne Lord understanding that the buying of the ward and mariage of the aires of Thornydyks fra his highnes' Thresaurer of Scotland, did stand to his Ma^{teis} lovit. William French of Frenchland, in the sowme of foure thowsand merkis vsuall money of the realme of Scotland, which money he did borrow, and hath payed annual-rent and interest therfoir thir twelff yeires bygane which, with the charges debursed be him in his highnes' behalff for persewing of the said ward amounteth far above the sum of twelff hundreth pundis English money, and hithertills hath receaved no satisfaction nor contentation therfor to the vtter vndoeing of the said William French, his widow mother, nyne fatherles children, and others, the said William, his freindis, who stands engadged for these sowmes payit vnto his Ma^{teis} Cofferis, and takin on in following legall persute on his Ma^{teis} behalff, for satisfaction and full contentation to the said William French of the sowmes of money payed and debursed be him in maner abone-writtin : Ordeanes a letter to be made and past vnder his highnes' privie seall of the said kingdome in due forme : Giveand, grantand, and disponeand to the said William French, and to his aires and assigneyis whatsumevir, All and whole the sowme of Two hundreth pundis vsuall money of the realme of England yeirlie, to be vplifted and takin at two termes in the yeir, Witsonday and Mertimes, in winter, be equall portionis furth of the first and readiest of his Ma^{teis} rents, dewteis, and casualiteis whatsumevir within that his Ma^{teis} kingdome, due or which heirefter shall accress vnto his highnes by whatsumever maner of way within the same, beginning the first termes payment therof at the feist and terme of Witsonday j^{m} vi^c twentie-nyne yeires, and sua furth yeirlie and termelie therefter dureing all the dayes, space, yeires, and termes of sex yeires nixt and immediatlie following the said terme and feist of Witsonday, with full power to the said William French dureing the space forsaid, and his forsaidis, he himselff, his factours, and others in his name, To ask, crave, receave, intromet with, and vptak the forsaid sowme of Two hundreth pundis money forsaid fra our Thresaurer, principall deputy-Thresaurers, and receavers of our saids rents, dewteis, and casualiteis whatsumever of the said Kingdome, and thervpon to dispon at ther pleasur, and to call and persew therfoir, if neid be, as accordis of the Law : With command therin to the said Thresaurer, principall deputeis, and others forsaids to readelie answer, intend, and mak readie payment to the said William French and his forsaidis, ther factours, and others in ther names, of the forsaid sowme yeirlie and termelie, dureing the space abone specifeit, with command lykwyse to the Lordis of his highnes' Exchecker within the said kingdome, to defease and allow the forsaid sowme of two hundreth pundis money to the said Thresaurer, principall deputie-Thresaurer, and others forsaids, the forsaid Letter being produced in Exchequer in compt, and registrat in the books thairof as vse is with ane sufficient dischearge be the said Williame French or his forsaidis shalbe ane liberation therof to the receavers yeirlie ay and whill the compleit payment of the said sowme of twelff hundreth pundis money forsaid; and that the saids Letters be farder extendit in ample forme, with all clausses neidfull.—Gevin at Grenewich, 9 May 1631.

May it pleas your Matie,

These conteyne your Ma^{teis} grant to William French, of Frenchland, of Tuo hundreth punds sterling per annum dureing the space of six yeires nixtocum furth of the first and readiest of your Ma^{teis} rents and casualiteis within the kingdome of Scotland the first termes payment at Witsonday nixt.

Our Soveraigne Lord in regard of Archibald, Lord Naper of Merchistoun, his demission of the office of depute thesaurer in his Ma^{teis} handis: Therfor his Matie, knowing the sufficiencie and affection to his highnes' service of his Ma^{teis} right, &c., Johne, Lord Stewart of Traquair, Ordanes a Letter to be made and exped vnder his highnes' great seall of the kingdome of Scotland, making, constituteing, and ordeaneing, lykas his Matie for himsellff, and taking burden on him for Charles, his sone, Prince and Stewart of Scotland, Maks, Constitutes, and Ordanes the said Johne, Lord Stewart of Traquair, dureing all the dayes of his lyftyme, his highnes' deputie thesaurer of the said kingdome, and to that effect gives and grants vnto him full power, authoritie, and command as his Ma^{teis} said deputie thesaurer, to joyne with his Ma^{teis} Right, &c. William, Erle of Morton, his Ma^{teis} principall Thesaurer therof, in all things concerneing his Ma^{teis} service for dischergeing of the offices of Thesaurie, Collectorie, Comptrollerie, and thesaurie of the new augmentatiouns, and of the offices of Collectorie, thesaurie of the Annuitie granted or to be granted vnto his Matie and successours of the tithes of the said kingdome, imposed or to be imposed therypon, and of all other augmentatiouns that have accressed and shallhappin to accress vnto his Matie or successours by the submissioun made vnto his highnes of Tithes and others things therin mentionat, and his Ma^{teis} decreit following therypon, as also in absence of his Ma^{teis} said Thesaurer out of the kingdome, or from Counsall, Session, or Excheker, To doe all and whatsumever things that may concerne his Ma^{teis} service in any of the saids offices, as if the said principall thesaurer wer present himsellff in persone: And his Matie doeth heirby give and grant vnto the said Lord Traquair dureing his lyftyme the whole feyis, priviledges, immuniteis, casualiteis, honour, and place belonging or which at any tyme heirtofoir hath belonged vnto the said office of depute-Thesaurer: Requyreing the Lordis of his Ma^{teis} privie Counsall, Session, and Excheker for granting and directing Letters of horning at his instance for paying of the samyne vnto him, and requyreing them to be ayding and assisting of him in injoyeing of the priviledges and others things dew vnto the said place.—Grenewitch, 9 May 1631.

Our Soveraigne Lord ordanes a Letter to be made vnder his heyres privie scall of the kingdome of Scotland, makand mentioun that his Matie, perfectlie vnderstanding the good and acceptable service done to his Matie be his highnes' trustie and weillbeloved Mr George Fletcher of Restenneth, and lykwyse the fidelitie, care, and sufficiencie of the said Mr George to exerce the office and place of Receaver of his Ma^{teis} rents and casualiteis within the said kingdome, now vacand in his Ma^{teis} handis be the death of Mr David Fullerton, one of his Ma^{teis} receavers of the saids rents: Therfor his Matie, with advyse and consent of his Ma^{teis} right, &c. the Erle of Morton, Lord Dalkeith and Aberdour, high thesaurer, Comptroller, Collectour, and thesaurer of the new augmentatiouns within the said kingdome of Scotland, and of his Ma^{teis} trustie, &c. Johne, Lord Stewart of Traquair, his Ma^{teis} deputie in the saids offices, and of the remanent Lordis and others, Commissioners of his Ma^{teis} rents and Exscheker of the said kingdome, hath made, constitute, and ordaned, lykas his Matie, with advyse, consent, and assent forsaid, be the tenour heirof, maks, constituts, and ordanes, the said Mr George Fletcher, dureing all the dayes of his lyftyme, ane of his Ma^{teis} receavers of all and wholl and sindrie of his Ma^{teis} rents, customes, imposts, and casualiteis, as well of his Ma^{teis} thesaurerie, propertie, comptrollerie, and collectorie and thesaurie of the haill new augmentatiounis of the said kingdome of Scotland, as of all fynes, compositions, and vthers proffeits and dewteis of his Ma^{teis} coynehous, of all sowmes of money, and others, rents, casualiteis, and dewteis whatsoever, presentlie belonging, or which heirefter shall happin to accress and belong to his Matie, ather in propertie, collectorie, or casualitie, or be any other maner of way, within the said kingdome of Scotland : And his Matie, with advyse forsaid, hath gevin and granted, and be thir presents gives and grants to the said Mr George Fletcher the office thairof, to be bruiked and enjoyed be him dureing his lyftyme, with all feyis, casualiteis, priviledges, and liberteis perteneing thairto, alse frielie in all respects as any other receaver doeth enjoy or hath enjoyed the said office at any tyme preceiding, Giveling, granting, and committing to the said Mr George Fletcher full power and Commission dureing his lyftyme to vplift, receave, and intromett with all and sindrie his Ma^{teis} rents, maills, fermes, coynes, customes, and others casualiteis, as weill of his Ma^{teis} Thesaurie, propertie, Comptrollerie, and Collectorie, and receaverie of his Ma^{teis} new augmentatiounis of the said kingdome of Scotland, as of all fynes, compositions, and others proffeits and dewteis of his Ma^{teis} Coynhous, and of all sowmes of money, and others rents, casualiteis, and dewteis whatsumever, presentlie belonging, or which heirefter happin to accress and belong to his Matie, ather in propertie, collectorie, and casualitie, or be any other maner of way, within the said kingdome of Scotland, and that as well of all yeres, cropts, and termes bygane, restand awand vnpayed, as of all yeres and Cropts to com dureing his lyftyme : And vpoun the said Mr George recept, acquittances, and discherges, to mak, give and delyver which his Matie, with advyse forsaid, declares be thir presents to be valide and sufficient to the receaveris, and his Matie, with consent forsaid, Ordanes the said Mr George Fletcher to discharge such sowmes of money in his Ma^{teis} service and affaires as shalbe thoght necessar and expedient, and as he shalbe directed by his Ma^{teis} thesaurer, principal deputie, or Lordis of his Ma^{teis} Exchequer to that effect, to whom the said Mr George shalbe subject, to mak just compt, reckonyng, and payment of his whole intromission, whensoever he shalbe required, in all tyme cuming : Lykas his Matie gives, grants, and allowis to the said Mr George Fletcher, for his paynes and travells to be takin in the said office, the sowme of fyve hundreth merkis Scotts yeirlie, which his Matie be thir presents commandis to be defaised and allowed to him yeirlie in his accompts, and that the said Letter be extendit in most ample forme, with all clausses neidfull.—Grenewitch, 9 of May 1631.

To the Exchequer.

Right, &c.—Wheras we wer pleased to wryt vnto yow signifieing our pleasur that our Thesaurer principall and deputie Thesaurer should be first payed out of our rents and casualiteis of such sowmes of money as they had disbursed for our service, which was intendit without prejudice vnto our Thesaurer principall, And vnto the Erle of Monteith, president of our privie Counsall, in the payment of such moneys as by former precepts and warrants we had granted vnto them, to be payed out of the last taxatiouns granted vnto ws ; Therfor we ar heirby pleased to signifie our further pleasur vnto yow, that notwithstanding of any warrant or precept whatsoever, granted or to be granted heirefter, the saids Erles be first payed out of the saids taxatiouns according to the saids warrants, And to that effect that yow mak ane act of Exchequer heirvpon.—Grenwich, 9 May 1631.

Precept to the Thesaurer and Depute Thesaurer.

Wheras Sir Alex^r Strauchan hath at our command surrendred vnto ws and in our favours, by a procuratorie of resignation signed by him of the dait the last day of Aprill last bypast, our Commissioners granted vnto him mentioned in the said Procuratorie, as the same in itsellf at lenth doeth bear ; And hath bene at great charges, by oft repairing to our Court and attending ther our pleasur concerneing that bussines, we ar now pleased in consideration therof, and of diverse other good services done by him vnto ws, as to bestow vpoun him 3000^{lib} sterling money, which it is our pleasur that vpon sight heirof yow pay vnto him out of the first and readiest of whatsumevir moneyis, rents, casualiteis, and others due or what shall accress or be due vnto ws in that our kingdome, and that the Auditours of our Exchequer allow the same vnto yow in the first end of your accompts, the precept and warrant being satisfeit by yow vnto the said Sir Alex^r ; ffor doeing whairof these presents shall be vnto yow and everie ane of yow a sufficient warrand.—Grenwich, 9 May 1631.

Articles of Exchequer.

That a Commission of Exchequer be drawin of new with power to the persones therin nominat to doe and grant to any of his Maties leidges whatsoever hath bene done or granted befoir by any former Commission of Exchequer.

That they have power to grant De Novo damus for supplement of defective Titles, and that ather of the proprietie or principallie for such compositiouns as the Thesaurer principall, or in his absens the Deputie Thesaurer shall think reasonable.

That the said Commission nor no thing therin conteyned be derogatorie from the Commission of our Counsall.

The Commission is to indure onlie during his Ma^{tes} will and pleasur.—Grenwich, 10 May 1631.

Charles, be the Grace of God king of England, Scotland, France, and Irland, Defender of the fayth.— Wheras our trustie and weilbeloved William Clayborne, one of our Counsall, and Secretarie of State for our Colonie of Virginia, and some other Adventurers with him, have condescendit with our trustie and weilbeloved Counsellour Sir William Alexander, kny^t, principall Secretarie of our kingdome of Scotland, and others of our subjects who have charge of our Coloneis of New Scotland and New England, to keip a course for interchange of trade amongst them as they shall have occasion, as also to mak discovereis for increase of trade in these parts; and because we doe verie much approve of all such worthie intentions, and ar desyreous to give good encouragment to ther proceidingis therin, being for the weill and comfort of these our subjects and enlargement of our dominions : These ar to licence and authorize the said William Clayborne, his associats and companie, frielie, without interruption, from tyme to tyme to trade and traffique for corne furis or any other commoditeis whatsoever, with ther schips, menboatis, and merchandice in all seas, coasts, rivers, creiks, herbereis, landis, territoreis in, neir, or about these parts of America for which ther is not alreadie a patent grantit to others for the whole trade : And for that effect we requyre and command yow, and everie of yow, particularlie our trustie and weilbelovit Sir John Hervie, kny^t, governour, and the rest of our Counsall of and for our Colonie of Virginia, to permitt and suffer him and them, with the saids schips, boats, merchandice, and cattell, mariners, servandis, and such as shall willinglie accompanie or be imployed by them from tyme to tyme, frielie to repair and trade to and agane in all the aforsaids parts and places as they shall think fitt and ther occasions shall requyre, without any stop, arreist, search, hindernace, or molestation whatsoever, as yow and everie of yow will answer the contrarie at your perrells : Giveing and by these presents Granting to the said Williame Clayborne full power to direct and governe, correct and punishe such of our subjects as shalbe vnder his Command in his waye and discovereis : And for your soe doeing these presents shalbe your sufficient warrand.—Gevin at our maner at Grenwich, the 16 of May 1631, the sevint yeir of our regne.

> To our trustie and weil beloved our Governour and Counsall of Virginia : To all our Livetennents of provinces and Cuntreyis in America, governours and others haveing any charge of Coloneis of any of our subjects ther, and to all Captanes and Masters of Schipps, and generallie to all our subjects whatsoever whom these presents doe or may concerne.

These, conteneing your Ma^{teis} Ratification of ane assignement made by Sir James Scott to David Beaton and his wyff of the fermes, few-maills, and others dewteis of Kingsbarnes, assigned to them of new in yeirlie pension dureing ther lyftymes, and the longest leiver of them, in the saids fermes and dewteis, ther first entrie to be this yeir.—Grenwitch, 17 May 1631.

These conteyne a Ratification of the toun of Kinrochen in a burgh of baronie, with ane Erection thairof of new, in favours of the Erle of Morton, your Ma^{teis} Thesaurer, with the priviledges and liberteis belonging to a burgh of baronie, and speciallie with libertie of tuo yeirlie frie fayres within the same, and of a weiklie mercat, to be holdin vpon . . . and of all customes and casualities belonging therto : In the moneth of Junij, the mercat to be holdin.—Grenewitch, 25 of May 1631.

To the Archibischof of St Androis.

Right, &c.—Wheras we did some tuo yeres agoe signe a presentatioun send vp vnto ws vnder your hand for the Church of Pencatland in favours of Mr Ritchard Broun, and since that sieing your hand to ane other presentatioun of Mr Johne Oswaldis, we signed that lykwyse : Bot being informed that this presentatioun was for that church which we formerlie gave to Mr Ritchard Broun, though not then voyd as we conceaved : We have therfor signed a thrid presentatioun in behalff of the said Mr Ritchard, and hearing that ther is lyk to be a sute in Law betuixt the saidis pairteis concerneing a right to the same, wherof we no wyse lyk of, sieing our intention was onlie that the said Mr Ritchard should have it, and the rather becaus we could nowyse doubt bot he is weill qualifeid, his first presentatioun being vnder your hand : Therfor our pleasur is, that yow immediatlie give collation to the said Mr Ritchard, and that yow putt him to present and peaciable possessioun therof without any further trouble at all, and that yow think of some other course for the accommodating of the said Mr Johne, with some other benefice : And with all that yow signifie this our royall pleasur (if neid be) to any others to whome the consideratioun of the premisses may any wayes apperteane : And for your soe doeing, &c.—Grenwich, 25 May 1631.

To the Session.

Right, &c.—Wheras we ar informed that notwithstanding the rentall bolls ar within the full worth of the tythes of these landis wherof we ar titular, that if a tymelie and provident care be not had by adverting to the valuations therof we may be therby prejudged : Our pleasur is, that yow carefullie look vnto the same, that nothing be done therin to prejudge ws : And in the meane tyme that yow vse your best endeavours for furthring the generall course of the valuations.—Grenwich, 25 May 1631.

To the Exchequer.

Right, &c.—Being informed that the signature of our servand James Maxwell, which we have sent yow heirwith doeth differ nothing from the securitie of the persones from whom he doeth purches the lands mentioned therin, save onlie that we doe licence of new to erect the toun of Dirlton, in a brugh of baronie : Our pleasur is, that yow peryse the same, and if yow find what is affirmed to be trew, and that nothing therin doeth prejudge ws, that with all convenient diligence yow pass and cause expeid it according to the tenour therof ; and for your soe doeing, &c.—26 May 1631.

Our Soveraigne Lord haveing taken speciall notice of the good and faythfull services alreadie done to his Matie by his right, &c. The Erle of Monteith, Lord Grhame of Kilpont, President of his Ma^ries most honorabill privie Counsall of his kingdome of Scotland, both in the said place and all other occasions being employed by his Matie, and of his habilities and affection to continew in the same ; Therfor his Matie ordanes a Letter to be made vnder his highnes' great seall of the said kingdome, makand, constituteand, and ordeaneand his said, &c. William, Erle of Monteith, president of his heynes' said counsell, dureing all the dayes of his lyftyme, with full power to him to enjoy and Exerce the samyne, with all honour, liberteis, friedomes, and priviledges and digniteis belonging thervnto : And lykwyse ordanes the said W^m, Erle of Monteith, president of his highnes' privie counsall, to have place and precedencie nixt and immediatlie efter his highnes' Thesaurer principall of the said kingdome, in all places and at all tymes requisit heirefter : Ordaneing thir presents to be a sufficient warrant to the writter of the great seall and keeper thairof for wryting of thir presents to the great seall and appending of the great seall heirvnto, but passing of any other seals or registers whatsoever qnharmanent these presents shalbe vnto them a sufficient warrant, &c.— Grenewitch, 28 of May 1631.

To the Session.

Right, &c.—Being informed of diverse acts and statuts made for preventing all vnnecessarie delayes which our subjects might sustene in ther actions befoir yow, and of the great prejudice they receave thrugh the not putting of the same in execution, and being desyreous for ther good that the same should be putt in practeis : Our pleasur is, that yow renew, and in ane Act of new, all such acts and statuts as wer made to this effect ; for the doeing wherof these shalbe your warrant :

And considering lykwyse how the administratioun of Justice doeth necessarilie requyre your daylie attendance, and that besydis your extraordinarie paynes excessive charges ar requisit for the same, which your feyis being so litle yow ar not able to vndergoe : And being willing to redress the same, Our pleasur is, that yow convene and consult amongst yourselffis of such overtures, wherby your feyis may be augmented with the least burden to ws, and that yow acquant ws with the same that we may give such further ordour as we shall find requisit.—Grenwich, 28 May 1631.

To the Chancellour.

Right, &c.—Wheras for severall good services done vnto our late dear father and ws by the Reverend father in God, Patrick, bischop of Ross, we wer pleased to grant vnto him the sowme of fyve thowsand pundis sterling, wherof as yit he hath receaved no part : And being desyreous, till a course be takin for his satisfaction according to our former warrant granted vnto him, or otherwyse as we shall find occasion, that he might deteyne in his handis such moneyis of our taxatiouns last granted vnto ws as wer payable by him vnto yow as our Collectour generall therof, We ar heirby pleased that yow allow vnto him whatsoever is to be payed by him for his part of the saids taxatiouns in his owin handis taking his acquittance thervpon : And for your, &c.—[No date.]

To the Bischop of Aberdene.

Right, &c.—Wheras, vpon humble sute made vnto ws in behalff of Robert and Alexander Irwings and Thomas Meinzeis, that they may have libertie to trade in merchandice in that our kingdome of Scotland, and to setle some of ther necessar affaires, wherwith they, in humble obedience of our lawis for ther sudden departing from thence, could not have tyme to tak ordour, and in all things else to be restrained in what is not ordinarlie allowed to any stranger repairing thither for trade, We have bene pleased to wryt vnto our Chancellour concerneing that purpois, and to grant them licence to setle the saids affaires and trade as strangers within our said kingdome, with a restriction that they doe nothing therin to hurt or derogat from the estate of the pesent professed religion : Therfor we have thoght it titt to recommend them vnto yow, that if they performe what is heirby provyded by ws tuitching the religion, yow give way vnto them, in so far as may concerne the dispatch of ther lawfull affaires.—Grenwich, 28 May 1631.

To the Chancellour.

Right, &c.—Wheras humble sute hath bene made vnto ws that Robt and Alexr Irwings and Thomas Meinzeis might have libertie to settle some of ther necessarie affaires within that our kingdome, wherwith they, in obedience of our Lawis for ther sudden departing from thence, could not have tyme to tak ordour, And in all things then to be restrained in what is not ordinarlie allowed to any stranger repairing thither for trade, without which, as we ar informed, they can not subsist : These consideratiouns, joyned with that of ther losses sustened, as we ar lykwyse informed, by them in abandoning that kingdome and settling themselflis in Deep, in France, hath moved ws so far to give way vnto ther demandis as may not any wayes wrong and derogat from the estate of the present professed religion : Therfor we have thoght good to impart our pleasur heirin vnto yow, that, if neid be, yow may impart the same to our Counsall, that they may have a licence, without any trouble, to dispatch the said lawfull affaires, vnless just caus of complant be made vnto our said Counsall against them.—Grenwich, 28 May 1631.

Warrant.

Wheras we have bene humblie petitioned in behalff of Robert and Alexr Irwings and Thomas Meinzeis that they may have such libertie to trade in that our kingdome as is granted to any stranger resorting thither ; And the rather becaus that they, out of ane humble and due obedience to our lawis, did abandon our said kingdome, and have setled themselflis, wyffs, and famileis in Deep, in France, wher they, being reduced to great povertie, can hardlie live, as we ar crediblie informed, without they be licenced to repair to and fra that kingdome for dispatch of ther necessarie affaires of trade and merchandice, and in some things concerneing ther owin privat estate, wherwith they, in obedience to our said lawis, could not have tyme to tak ordour at ther departing from thence : These consideratiouns, joyned with that of ther losses sustened, as we ar lykwyse informed, by them, have moved in ws our princelie compassioun so far to give way to ther demand as may not anywyse wrong and derogat from the estate of the present professed religion within the said kingdome, to which purpois we have signifeid our pleasur to our Counsell : These ar therfor to licence the saids Robert and Alexr Irwings and Thomas Meinzeis, dureing the space of sex monethis, to ordour ther affaires within the said kingdome, and to trade within the same from tyme to tyme as occasion shall requyre dureing the said space, they behaveing themselffis as aforsaid: Inhibiteing yow or any of yow from troubleing or molesting the saids persones or any of them at any tyme as aforsaid, or vpon any occasion, in dispatching of the saids affaires, as yow and everie of yow will answer ws in the contrarie at your perrills.—Grenwich, 28 May 1631.

To all and sindrie our Officers, servandis, and others our subjects
whatsoever, as weill ecclesiasticall as civill, of our kingdome of
Scotland, whom these presents doe or may concerne.

PRECEPT.

Our pleasur is, that yow receave the accompts of our trustie and weillbeloved Sir Robert Dowglas, our stewart of our Lordship of Dumbar, concerneing his intromission with our rents thairof; And, for good causses knowen vnto ws, that yow give vnto him, or his factours in his name, a sufficient discharge of the rest of a yeires of Jm vi^c, twentie   yeires, extending to sex scoir threttene pundis sterling money, whilk shalbe allowed vnto yow in the first and readiest of your accompts.—Grenwich, 28 May 1631.

To our right, &c. the Erle of Morton, our Thesaurer and Thesaurer
deputie of our kingdome of Scotland.

TO THE DEPUTIE THESAURER.

Right, &c.—Being desyreous to recover that part of our patrimonie called the King's barones, bestowed by our late dear father vpon the late Erle of Holdernesse in reward of his singular service, in regard it is gone from him and his race to one which hath not deserved anything from ws, wherby the memorie of his merite is takin away; Our pleasur is, that yow deall with Mr Wm Kellie, possessour of the same, to buy them agane; And if he wilbe contented with reasone, lett him have a reasonable condition, with payment of the money agreed vpoun befor he part with the land: And so expecting that yow will vse your best endeavours for effectuating this purpois.—Grenwitch, 28 May 1831.

TO THE CHANCELLOUR.

Right, &c.—Wharas we wer pleased to grant a precept of 5000^{lib} sterling vnto our right, &c. the Marqueis of Hamilton, and in regard of his weghtie imployment at this tyme in our service we ar pleased that yow joyne with the Lord Traquair, our deputie Thesaurer, to pay vnto him or his assigneyis such part therof as remanes vnsatisfeit: And to that effect, our will and pleasur is, that, notwithstanding of any our former commands to yow, yow delyver vnto our said Thesaurer depute, out of the readiest of your intromissions of the taxatioun, such part thairof as remanes vnsatisfeid, which shalbe allowed vnto yow in the first and readiest of your receipts and intromissions whatsoever.—Gevin at Grenwich, the 28 May 1631.

TO THE THESAURER AND DEPUTIE THESAURER.

Right, &c.—We wer pleased to grant a precept of 5000^{lib} st. vnto our right, &c. the Marqueis of Hamilton, and in regard of his weghtie imployment at this tyme in our service, Our pleasur is, that yow pay presentlie vnto him or his assigneyis such part thairof as remanes vnsatisfeit, notwithstanding of any warrand granted vnto any persone for any caus whatsoever, out of the first and readiest of our last taxatiouns granted vnto ws in the moneth of July last, rents, dewteis, and casualiteis, or other benefite whatsumever, now due vnto ws, or which heirefter shallhappin to be due vnto ws or acceress to ws in that our kingdome ; which we will tak as acceptable service done vnto ws.—Grenwitch, 28 May 1631.

To the Commissioners of Surrenders.

Right, &c.—We ar informed, in behalff of our right, &c. the Lord Balmerino, that the personage tythis of Restalrig, wherof he is titular, ar by the sub-commissioners much vndervalued, wherby we in our annuitie and he in the worth therof ar prejudged, and that yow did formerlie allow vnto him a compitent tyme for a new valuatioun befor your sellfs of the greatest part of these tythis, wherin we doubt not bot yow have proceidit therin with good consideratioun ; and ar informed that the same reasones holdis good for taking the lyk course in valueing the rest, and the rather becaus the trew estat therof wilbe more easelie tryed befor yow, in regard the land out of the which they ar led lyeth nar vnto the place of your meitting : Therfoir, sieing he did so frielie submitt vnto ws, and that we ar informed that the heretours by this course wilbe much eased and benefited, our pleasur is, that yow mak ane act of your commission, allowing the said titular a new dyet for a full and finall valuatioun befor your sellfis of the whole personage tythis whatsoever of Restalrig, wherof he and his predicessours hath bene in custome of leading : Which recommending vnto yow, &c.—Grenwitch, 28 May 1631.

Precept.

Wheras for speciall good services done vnto our late dear father and ws by the reverend father in God Patrik, bischop of Ross, we wer pleased to grant vnto him the sowme of 5000^{lib} st., wherof as yit he hath received no part, Our will and pleasur is, that yow pay vnto him, or his assigneyis, the said sowme of 5000^{lib} with all possible diligence, and that out of the first and readiest of our rents, dewteis, annuiteis, last taxatiouns, granted vnto ws in the moneth of July last, and casualiteis whatsumever, now due vnto ws, and which heirefter shallhappin to accress and be due vnto ws in that our kingdome : And for your soe doeing these presents, with his or his forsaidis acquittance or acquittances vpon the receipt therof, shalbe your sufficient warrant.—Grenewitch, 28 May 1631.

To the Advocat.

Trustie, &c.—We have sent yow heirwith a signature presented to ws of some Landis belonging to the Erldome of Dunbar, to be granted in favours of our trustie and weillbeloved Sir Robert Dowglas of Spott, kny^t : And as we desyre to gratifie him, who hath bene our ancient and well deserveing servand, so desyreing lykwyse that none have just caus to compleyne of any wrong done with them, it is our pleasur that, haveing duelie considered of the same, yow draw vp such a signature in his favours of the saidis Landis as we can lawfullie grant without wronging our sellf or any of our subjects, and that yow returne the same vnto ws docated vnder your hand ; for doeing whairof these presents shalbe vnto yow a sufficient warrand.—From our Court at Grenewich, the 29 May 1631.

To the Exchequer.

Right, &c.—Haveing bene moved vpon the inclosed petition that a consideratioun might be takin of the petitioner's charge in our service necessarlie requyreing (as we ar informed) his daylie attendance for the good therof, and for his long and great panes takin therin, both in the tyme of our late dear father and of our owin, without any compitent allowance anywayes till for the same: We ar heirby pleased to remitt the consideratioun of the said petition vnto yow, that such a course may be takin for his interteneement as yow shall find the necessitie of his imployment for the good of our said service to requyre: The maner and doeing therof we remitt to yow, and bid yow farewell.—Grenwich, last of May 1631.

To the Session.

Right, &c.—We ar informed that some persones holding of the Abbacie of Kinloss, vnder cullour of the late course takin by ws tuitching erections and others things mentioned in the generall submissions, doe not pay vnto our right, &c. the Lord Bruce such dewteis as by them ar payable vnto him for some yeres preceiding that tyme, sieing our royall intention was not to question what did preceid that course, bot to setle it heirefter according to our decrie gevin vpon the saids submissions made vnto ws, the said Lord being one who signed the same: We for these respects, and becaus that in regard of his residence within this our kingdome he cannot so convenientlie (as is requisit) attend the prosecuteing of any action in Law ther that doeth concerne him. Ar heirby gratiouslie pleased to recommend vnto yow that in all such processes and actions intented or to be intended befor yow at his instance aganst the saids Vassalls, no advantage may be takin against him be reasone of his submitting vnto ws or of any clame of ours to these bygane dewteis for any tymes preceiding his said submission, bot that such speedie justice may be administred therin as is agrieable to the Lawis of that our kingdome.—Grenwich, last of May 1631.

To the Chancellour.

Right, &c.—We being moved in the behalff of the Widow of Sir Johne Livingstoun (a long and weill deserving servant of our late royall father) that in respect of hir widowhead and residence in this our kingdome, being a stranger to the lawis and customes ther, We would be pleased to recommend vnto our Colledge of Justice such actions of Law concerneing hir as doe or shall happin to cum befoir them; but being rather willing to impart our pleasur heirin to yow then to the bodie of that Juicatorie. Our pleasur is, that yow tak speciall notice of what doeth concerne hir in any purpois, and that therin yow be carefull to sie justice administred with as much diligence as the equitie of the cause and the Lawis of that our kingdome will permitt.—Grenwich, last of May 1631.

To the Counsell.

Right, &c.—We perceave by your letter that yow have rescindit your Act made against the decrie obtenit by our brugh of Edinburgh against some Inhabitants in Leith, except in so far as concerneth the girnalling of victuall, and as yow have desyred by your letter, haveing duelie considered the declaration made to our session insert in the said decreit, That notwithstanding of the said decreit, it should be lawfull to any nobleman, gentlman, or others our subjects, to girnall victuall ther, except the Inhabitants of Leith; And that our said brugh doe not claime any other priviledge then by the lawis of our kingdome is allowed and warranted by former decreits: It is our pleasur that if our said brugh shall ratifie the said declaration conteynit in the said decreit made in favouris of our nobilitie, gentrie, and others expressed in the same befoir yow, that yow, without any further delay, annull the said Act in so far as concerneth the said girnelling of victuall also, and leave the Executioun of the said decreit to our said brugh ay and whill the samyne be lawfullie reduced befoir the Judge ordiner.—Grenwich, 5 of Junij 1631.

H Q

To the Exchequer.

Right, &c.—Wheras our late dear father was pleased to signe a signature of 500 merks Scotts by yeir vnto our right, &c. the Viscount of Stormonth, to be vplifted by him out of the readiest blensh dewteis of Scone, the passing wherof through the sealls being hitherto differed, and earnest sute now being made vnto ws in his behalff that we would signe the same : As we ar vnwilling to retene anything which our father did bestow vpon any deserveing servant, so we desyre to know the caus of the not passing thairof at that tyme : Therfor our pleasur is, that yow'informe yonrsellf, as far as yow can, of the reasones thairof, and adverteise ws of the same, that we may give such farther ordour as we shall find most convenient : So we bid, &c.—Grenwich, 9 Junij 1631.

To the Counsell.

Right, &c.—Wheras we have bene moved vpon the enclosed petition for giveing way to erect Lights vpon the Skairheads as a purpois expedient for the preventing of schipwraks therabout, wherin respecting the saftie and good of our subjects we ar heirby pleased to remitt the consideratioun of the petition vnto yow, that haveing pervsed the same and hearkned to what may be further proponed to yow tuitching that purpois, yow may resolve, if ther be any expedieucie for erecting of these Lights, and of the meanes and wayes to keip the same ; And if yow find it necessarie and a willingnes of such of our subjects as ar most interested therin, to pay such a dewtie to the same as yow and they can best condescend vpon that a patent be drawen vp for our signature heir, or to pass our cachet ther as they shall think fitt for the petitioner, and that for such number of yeres for such a dewtie to be imposed according to the schipp's burden and other limitations and provisions as yow shall think fitt to preservye to the good of our kingdome and saiftie of our subjects.—Grenwitch, 9 Junij 1631.

To the Counsell.

Right, &c.—Vnderstanding perfectlie of the sufficiencie of our trustie and weilbeloved Sir Ro^t Dowglas, kny^t, and of the affection to our service, we ar moved in regard thairof, and for his better encouragment and enabling for our said service to advance and promove him to be ane of our privie Counsall of that our kingdom : Therfor our pleasur is, and we doe heirby requyre yow, that haveing administred vnto him the oath accustomed in the lyk caices, yow admitt him to be one of our privie Counsall, receaving him in that place as one of your number ; for doeing whairof, &c.—Grenwich, 9 Junij 1631.

Ane other Letter of the same nature was signed for Sir Ro^t Ker.—9 Junij 1631.

To the Advocat.

Trustie, &c.—Vnderstanding that ther is a contraversie concerneing the title of the Erledome of Lothian and Lordschip of Newbotle, and we being verie vnwilling that any should usurp the said title till such at it may be made knowen vnto ws how the estate therof standeth in Law, and to whome it doeth justlie belong : Our pleasur is, that yow informe yoursellf thairoff, and that with all convenient diligence yow certitie ws bak as near in your judgment yow [can] to whome the said title doeth justlie belong, and what in justice we ar bund to doe to the right and lawfull heyr therin : Which recommending to your care, We bid, &c.—Grenwich, 9 Junij 1631.

To the Advocat.

Trustie, &c.—Wheras by our gift we did appoynt a certane sowme to be payed furth of our Exchequer ther to the Musitianes of our Chapell royall for ther mantenance yeirlie till such tyme as the rents of the old foundation of our said chappell should be establisched ; And sieing as we ar informed the sowme appoynted by our said gift is not sufficient to manteane such a number in any compitencie as our servandis, Therfor and for ther better mantenance and disburdening of our Exchequer of the said yeirlie sowme, we ar verie willing that our said Chapell royall and musitianes therof be establisched in the old rents and casualiteis alloted therto at or since the foundation therof, according to its owin rights and lawis and practique of our said kingdome : Our pleasur is, that in all actions intented or to be intended at the instance of the deane of our said chappell or of our servand Edward Kellie, tuitching that purpois, yow compeir for our intrest and give them your best assistance aganst any persone whatsoever in so far as yow can lawfullie doe, which we will tak as acceptable service done vnto ws.—Grenwich, 9 Junij 1631.

To the Exchequer.

Right, &c.—Wheras we appoynted our servand Edward Kellie for the Ordouring of our Chapell royall, and being crediblie informed that he hath weill furnisched it with ane expert Organist, singeing men, and boyes, and other thingis therto belonging, wherof we doe heirby approve as good service ; and being lykwyse informed that the said Organist and six boyes hath bene since the 24 Oct' last, and ar as yit, manteaned at the onlie charge of our said servand, We being vnwilling that he should anywyse suffer for his service done vnto ws, Our pleasur is, and we doe heirby will and requyre yow, that with all convenient diligence yow receave his accompts of his disbursments for the mantenance of the said Organist and boyes since the said 24 Octo' last, and accordinglie that yow mak payment vnto him, his heyres or assigneyis therof, and of the arreiris of his former accompts allowed by yow preceiding the said day, and that some course be takin wherby he may be disburdened of the lyk charge in all tyme coming.—Grenwitch, 9 Junij 1631.

To the Session.

Right, &c.—Wheras our right, &c. the Marquis of Hamilton is for our service to goe furth of our dominions, Our will and pleasur is, that in all and everie action comeing befor yow wherin our trustie cousen shalbe anywyse called, that yow delay the same and doe not proceid therinto without first acquainting ws, or vntill the conveniencie of our service suffer his returne and he able to answer for him-self ; ffor the which these presents shalbe your warrant.—Grenwitch, 9 Junij 1631.

To the Exchequer.

Right, &c.—Wheras we ar pleased with the bargane made betwixt our Right, &c. James, Marqueis of Hamilton, Erle of Arran and Cambridge, &c., and William Dick, merchand, burges of Edinburgh, anent the disposition of the Imposts of Wynes, Our will and pleasur is, and we doe heirby will yow, by acts of your table or otherwyse, as Wm Dick shall devyse, to give all further corroboratioun, ratificatioun, and approbation of the said bargane, declaring the forsaid disposition made by our said right trust Cousen to be as good and valide in all respects as if the same had bene made immediatlie by ws to the said William Dick with your consents, and that for the whole space and conditions therin conteyned : And that yow command the said disposition to be registrat in your books of Excheker, and ordeanes allowances yeirlie to be gevin to the said Wm Dick, conforme to the tenour therof: And for the soe doing these presents we will to be registrat, which shalbe vnto yow and everie of yow a sufficient warrand.—Grenwitch, 9 Junij 1631.

To the Viscount of Stormont.

Right, &c.—Being informed of diverse inconveniences often tymes arysing vnto our subjects who have occasion in the winter seasone to cross the watter of Quigh, being the ordinarie passage betweene our burgh of Edinburgh and Perth, and that ther be diverse old and failled wood in our park of Falkland neir adjacent to the saids watters, which might be both convenientlie spared and exceidinglie vsefull for making of small tymber passages over the same: Our pleasur is, that with all convenient diligence yow caus delyver for that vse eight of the most decayed and greatest treis of our said park; And for your, &c.—Grenwitch, 9 Junij 1631.

To the Advocat.

Trustie, &c.—Having writtin vnto our Counsall that they caus justice be execute vpon all such persones as have had hand in the cruell murther of William Grhame, brother of our trustie and weil-beloved servand Sir Ritchert Grhame, kny^t baronet, Our speciall pleasur is, that ye in our name persew the saids malefactours, according to the lawis of that our kingdome, and to that effect that yow informe your selffe from the pairtie interested, or any in ther name, of the estate and circumstances of that fact: which speciallie recommending vnto yow, we bid, &c.—Grenwitch, 14 Junij 1631.

To the Counsell.

Right, &c.—Being informed of the cruell slaughter of Williame Grhame, brother to our trustie, &c. Sir Ritchert Grhame, kny^t and baronet, committed by some of the Irwings in the bordours of that our kingdome, which we seriouslie requyr to be tryed and exemplarlie punisched with all possible diligence according to the Lawis of that our kingdome: Our speciall pleasur is, that yow sie justice execute vpon all such persones as shalbe fund to have ane hand in this murther or anywyse accessorie thervnto, and to that effect, if vpoun citation they doe not appear, that yow grant such Commissiones as the pairteis interests shall lawfullie requyre for the more speedie apprehension of the malefactours; which speciallie recommending vnto your care, we bid, &c.—Grenwitch, 14 Junij 1631.

To the Session.

Right, &c.—Being informed that ane Patrik Crawfurd of Auchnames haveing sued for the benefite of the ward of mariage of John Crawfurd of Kilbirnie, in regaird a small parcell of his estate which was holdin ward of him, though all the rest be holdin ward of the principalitie, and that the Commissioners of our Excheker for preventing such a vigorous course did grant for the vse of the said John the gift of the others lyfrent and escheit, being yeir and day at the horne, and have modifeid vnto him for the said ward a reasonable sowme of money wherof he will not accept, bot will insist by Law to tak the extreamest course against the said Johne, wherin, as we approve of the proceidingis and gift granted by our said Exchequer, so we recommend vnto yow that in all actionis alreadie intended or to cum befor yow by reasone of the said gift, yow administer justice with as good diligence as the course of these our Lawis can affoord; Which commending, &c.—Grenwitch, 14 Junij 1631.

To the Bischop of the Yles.

Reverend father, &c.—Wheras we have sent our Secretarie, the bearer heirof, to that our kingdome to attend that treatie concerneing the Clergie, wherof we wryt formerlie by yow : These ar to desyre yow to have a care in so far as your endeavours can extend, to sie all things in that treatie composed in a freindlie and quyet maner ; and for your furtherance in all other things which he shall impart vnto yow from ws, as yow will have ws to remember that which we promised vnto yow ; And so referring all further to him, We bid yow farewell.—Grenwitch, 14 Junij 1631.

To the Bischop of Rosse.

Reverend, &c.—Wheras we have send our Secretarie, the bearer heirof, to that our kingdome, to attend that treatie concerneing the Clergie, wherof we wryt formerlie by the Bischop of the Yles, haveing the proof of your affection formerlie to our service : These ar to recommend it both in composeing all things in that treatie in a freindlie and quyet maner, And in all other things which he shall impart vnto yow from ws ; And so referring all further vnto him, we bid, &c.—Grenwitch, 14 Junij 1631.

To the Arch Bishop of St Androis.

Right, &c.—According as we wryt vnto yow formerlie, we have sent our Secretarie to sie that treattie putt to a poynt : Bot though we ar verie confident that all your number ar well disposed in any thing that doeth concerne our service, yit we doe rely more particularlie vpon your endeavours, and therfor doe earnestlie desyre yow to have a speciall care to have all the bussines concerneing the Clergie composed in a freindlie and quyet maner ; and lykwyse that yow give your best ayd and advyse in any other thing ther tuitching our service at this tyme, whervpon We have desyred our Secretar, the bearer heirof, to confer with yow as one whome we speciallie trust, and be assured that as we doe speciallie expect your service at this tyme, so we will particularlie acknowledge the same.—Grenwitch, 14 Junij 1631.

To the Commissioners for Valuations.

Right, &c.—As we have sindrie tymes done heirtofoir, so these ar now agane to requyre yow to continew and encrease your care for hastening of that work to ane end which is committed to your charge, and above all things to vse your best meanes that the valuations may be justlie made ; for doeing wherof we ar willing to contribute what yow think can lawfullie proceed from ws for that effect : That this Commission might be the more assiduouslie prosecuted we wer pleased heirtofoir that a sub-committee might be made to sitt daylie when the whole Commission might not attend, bot noway intending therby that the great Commission might intermitt ther ordinarie attendance, bot only that they should still continew to sitt efter ther ordinarie maner, these sub-committies being onlie to supplie them for bringing of the said work the sooner to ane end, which course we doe approve still ; and recommending the prosecuteing therof to your care, We bid yow farewell.—Grenwitch, 14 Junij 1631.

To the Archbischops and Bischops.

Right, &c.—Wheras we have caused revewe and imprint the translatioun of the Psalmes of King David in English meeter, wherof our late dear father was author ; And have allowed them to be sung in all the churches of our dominions, as being, besyd the goodnes of the work itselff, a perpetuall monument to his memorie, it is our pleasur that yow vse your best meanes to have them received in schoolis, and to be sung in all the churches within that our kingdome : And being verie confident that both your love to the work and to the author's memorie will mak yow the more carefull heirof, We bid, &c.—Grenewitch, 14 Junij 1631.

To the Chancellour.

Right, &c.—Wheras we have sent our trustie, &c. Sir Wm Alexander, kny^t, our Secretarie in that our kingdome, for sindrie thingis concerneing our service, chieflie for the fisching and treattie with the bischops, wherin he is to confer with yow at lenth from ws efter yow considered togidder what is best to be done in both for our service, we doubt not bot yow will vse your best endeavours for effectuating of the same : And as we have ever fund the great care yow have had to doe ws service we expect it chieflie at this tyme, which we shall acknowledge as yow shall find by the effects : So we bid, &c.—Grenwich, 14 Junij 1631.

To the Burrowis.

Trustie, &c.—As we have ever fund your affection and best endeavours in all things that wer recommend vnto yow for the furthring of our service, we cannot bot be confident of it at this tyme that yow will vse your best meanes for furthring this association for a generall fisching, whervnto we know ye may contribute more then any of our esteats, and be assured that as ever we have had, so we still will have a care to preserve your liberteis whairvnto this work is nowayes derogatorie, bot may tend much to your advantage and to the honour of that our ancient kingdome : And for your more particular informatioun heirin remitting yow to Mr Johne Hay, we bid yow farewell.—Grenwiche, 14 Junij 1631.

To the Advocat.

Trustie, &c.—The Commissioners for the fisching bussines haveing condescendit vpoun the foundamentall poynts of the Chartours to be drawin for the establisching of that assotiation, according to the severall draughts of our Secretareis for both kingdomes sent yow heirwith : And becaus that purpois is of such consequence that we our self have a speciall care to have it both speedelie and weill effected. Our pleasur is that, haveing considered the draughts, yow draw a chartour thervpon in such legall maner as is most agreeable with the lawis of our kingdome, in your doing wherof let no consideratioun nor poynt of formalitie bred any delay or hinderance ; wherin yow shall doe ws acceptable service.—14 Junij 1631.

To the Counsell.

Right, &c.—Wheras we have gevin ordour to our Thesaurer and Thesaurer depute for causing coyne some farthing tokens, such in weght and quantitie as current in this our kingdome, which we will to cary . . . vpoun the one syd, and . . . vpon the other : It is our pleasur that yow give ordour by proclamation, as is usuall in the lyk cases, for receaveing of them, and for calling in of the copper money called Turnbores, they allwyse who bring them receaving from the Master of our mynt the value of such quantitie as they delyver payed bak in the said new coyne, that they may be no losers therby, and that yow contribute any other help or give any further warrand requisite from yow for furthering heirof.— Grenwich, 14 Junij 1631.

To the Session.

Right, &c.—We ar crediblie informed that ther be some actions of Law depending and may cum befor yow which concerne our right, &c. the Erle of Murray, who, for affaires speciallie importing for the good and quyet of that our kingdome, hath repaired to our Court, as we ar willing that Justice be not prostrat be any delay, so we think it just and requisit that he receive no prejudice by his absence, bot that he be heard by his owin presens in what may concerne him, since he intendis to mak no advantage be his stay heir, bot to returne with alse much diligence as the estate of our service can convenientlie permitt him; and therfor we ar heirby pleased to recommend vnto yow that for the space of this sommer sessione yow doe not admitt nor give proces in any action befor yow concerneing him: Which recommending to your care, we, &c.—Grenwich, 20 Junij 1631.

To the Counsell.

Right, &c.—We wer pleased some years agoe, vpon a proposition made by Robert Seaton for improveing of our Gold Mynes, and the hope gevin ws of a manifest incresce of our revenewis, therby to will and requyre yow to assigne to him some allowance yeirlie for the enabling him the better towards the performance, yit so as the same should continew dureing our pleasur onlie, and that he should to that purpois and vpon certane conditions transact with him : bot being now informed that he does not delay in the bussines, or otherwayes is vnable to mak good his vndertaking, or make the benefite equivalent to his charge, we therfor have thoght fitt to will and requyre yow to try and consider of the premisses, that if the informatioun be trew, yow stop the said assignatioun, that we be not longer deceaved with such frivolous vndertakings, wherin the charge is greater and more certane than the benefite; wherin not doubting of your care and diligence, &c.—Grenwich, 23 Junij 1631.

By Sir James Galloway.

To the Counsell.

Right, &c.—Wheras we have bene pleased to grant warrants to our right trustie, &c. the Marqueis of Hamilton for levyeing and transporting some regiments for the service of our brother the king of Sueden, And being verie desyreous that yow would vse your best meanes for this effect by any lawfull and convenient furtherence that yow can devyse for ther quick dispatch, or that shalbe propounded to yow by the Colonells of the saidis Regiments for waighting them safelie over from thence, Our pleasur is, that with all diligence yow caus provyd schips at such reasonable rates as yow, or commissioners from yow to this effect, can best agrie vpon, or as the custome hath bene in the lyk caces, for transporting of the saidis forces; which seriouslie recommending vnto your care, as a purpois which we doe cheiflie respect, and wherin nor doubting bot that yow will vse your best and readiest endeavours,—Grenewitch, 25 Junij 1631.

To the Admirall.

Right, &c.—Wheras we have bene pleased to grant warrants to our right trustie, &c. the Marqueis of Hamilton for levyeing and transporting some Regiments for the service of our brother the King of Sueden, and being verie desyreous that yow would vse your best endeavours, as we have writtin to our Counsell, that schipps be provydit with all possible diligence for transporting of the saidis forces from thence, and knowing how much yow, as Admirall, may contribute to the furthring of ther quick dispatch, Our pleasur is, and we heirby requyre yow to concurre with our Counsell, giveing your best ayd and furthrance that such a tymelie course may be takin for provydeing schips and sending away of the saidis forces, as by them and yow may be most convenientlie and lawfullie done, and efter what maner they and yow shall think most expedient that may work the desyred end with most conveniencie, &c.—Grenwich, 25 Junij 1631.

To the Advocat.

Trustie, &c.—Wheras we have bene pleased to signe the Commission of our Exchequer which we requyred yow to send vp vnto ws renewed in such forme as is fund requisit for the good of our service, and to send the samyne heirwith bak agane to be filled vp by yow : Our pleasur is, that yow insert the names of all these who wer in the last Commission (save onlie of these noblemen whom we left out of our Counsell), or addit therto since by our letters.—Grenwitch, 25 Junij 1613.

To the Counsell.

Right, &c.—In regard of our resolution for levyeing and transporting some forces from that our kingdome for the better supplyeing of our brother the king of Sueden in the warris, wherin he at this tyme is engadged ; and of the readines and constant affection of our trustie and weilbelovit servand Sir Frederick Hamilton, knyt. to our service in that kynd ; Considering as well the action it self, so full of honour, as the persone and familie of the vndertaker, which we have in speciall recommendation, Our pleasur is, that yow grant vnto the said Sir Frederik Hamilton, or to any other whom he shall appoynt, a Commission with a sufficient warrant to levye and transport twelff hundreth of our subjects of that our kingdome for the purpois above said, with as large priviledges as any generall, Colonell, or Commander hath had heirtofoir in the lyk kynd, he alwyse giveing such satisfaction to everie ane of that number as shalbe agried vpon betweene him and them, And to that effect that yow authorize him to cause beat drumes : Our further pleasur is, that yow give such speedie ordour for causing provyde schippes for ther transportatioun at such reasonable rates as yow or Commissioners from yow to this effect can best agrie vpon, and lyk conditions as hath bene formerlie gevin to others, which seriouslie recommending vnto your care ; and wherin not doubting bot yow will vse your best and readiest endeavours, we bid yow farewell.—from our maner at Grenwitch, last of Junij 1631.

Precept.

Wheras by a Letter from our Exchecker we vnderstand that according to our direction they have examined all the accompts, debts, and disbursments clymed from ws by Sir James Stewart, knyt, and that they have agried with him that he should be fullie dischergeed of them all for the sowme of fyftene hundreth pundis sterling money to be gevin vnto him as full satisfaction for the same : Our pleasur is, and we heirby will and requyre yow, that vpon his surrender or discharge vnto ws of all these debts, accompts, and disbursments, yow pay or cause be payed vnto him or his assigneyis the said sowme of 1500lib sterling, and that out of our readiest rents and casnaliteis whatsoever, or which shall accress vnto ws heirefter in that our kingdome ; and for your soe doeing these presents shalbe vnto yow and everie one of yow a sufficient warrant and discharge.—Grenwitch, last of Junij 1631.

To the Thesaurer and Deputie.

Right, &c.—Wheras our late dear father did vpon good considerations grant a pensione of 500 merks be yeir vnto his servand Sir Peter Young, knyt, and efter his deceis to any of his children whome he should appoynt ; And being informed that he did nominat our trustie servand Sir Peter Young, kny‘, to succeid to the same, as lykwyse that he hath received no part therof since the deceis of his said father. These ar therfor to will and requyre yow that furthwith yow pay vnto the said Sir Peter the pension aforsaid, with the arrieris due for the tyme bypast ; and for your soe doeing, &c.—Grenwich, last of Junij 1631.

To the Exchequer.

Wheras we ar informed that one Christiana Lyndsay, the widow of one William Murray, by diverse occasions being reduced to great wants, is willing to surrender vnto ws a pension of 200ᵈ, with all the arreages resting due, and ane vther of 4 Chalders of victuall, for a certane sowme to be gevin vnto hir for hir releiff of hir present necessiteis ; and being desyreous as weill, in consideration of the service done by hir husband vnto our late royall father, as for disburdeneing of our Exchequer, that some course may be takin, our pleasur is that yow deale with hir for the same, and that yow agrie with hir for such a competent sowme as yow in your judgment shall think fitt ; which we whollie remitt vnto yow.—Grenwitch, last of Junij 1631.

To the Thesaurer and Deputie.

Wheras we ar pleased to grant vnto the Lord Gordon a precept of 5000ᵗʰ sterling for the schirref schips of Innerness and Aberdene, resigned by his father and him in our handis, wherof as yit he hath received no satisfaction : Our pleasur is, that ye pay vnto him or his assigneyis the said sowme out of the first and readiest of the taxatiouns last granted vnto ws, or out of rents, dewteis, casualiteis, or other benefite whatsoever, now due vnto ws, or which heirefter shallhappin to be due and accresce vnto ws in that our kingdome ; and for your soe doeing these presents, with his or his forsaids acquittance or acquittances, vpoun the recept therof, shalbe your sufficient warrand.—Grenewitch, last of Junij 1631.

Wheras we have gevin onlour for coyneing a certane quantitie of copper into farthing tokens in our kingdome of Scotland, and for performance of which work yow ar made choyse of : These ar therfor to requyre and authorise yow to forge, mak, and grave, or cause to be made and graved, in our citie of London, or elswher within this our kingdome of England, all kinds of instruments, presses, engynes, yrones, stampes, coynes, with all others provisions necessarie for the fabrication of the saids farthings, to be delyvered by such as yow shall be directed by our trustie and weillbeloved counsellour Sir Wᵐ Alexander, knyᵗ, that they may be transported vnto our mynt of our toun of Edinburgh, within our said kingdome of Scotland : For doeing whairof, as also for your owin repairing thither for setting vp and establisching the said work, these presents shalbe vnto yow a sufficient warrand.—From our Court of Grenwitch, the last of Junij 1631.

To our trustie and weillbelovit Nicolas Briot, cheiff graver of our
Mynt within our kingdome of England.

To the Commissioners of Surrenders.

Right, &c.—Vnderstanding perfectlie the sufficiencie of our, &c. Patrik Maule, and of his affection to our service, we ar pleased in regard therof, and for his better encouragment and enabling for our said service, to advance and promove him to be ane of the Commissioners for Surrenders : It is therfor our Will and pleasur, and we doe heirby requyre yow, to admitt him to be one of your number, receive him in that place efter such forme as is fitt to be vsed for doeing, &c.—Grenwitch, 7 July 1631.

To the Thesaurer and Deputie.

It is our pleasur that yow caus pay vnto our, &c. the Erle of Tullibardyne, or to such as shall have power from him, the sowme of 500 merkis Scotts yeirlie at Witsonday and Mertimes, togidder with the ariages therof due vnto him, and that with as much diligence as yow can, the first terme's payment to begin at Mertimes nixt, and so furth yeirlie dureing our pleasur, and that towards the mantenance of ane vnder keiper of our forrest of Glenalmond ; for doing wherof, &c.—Grenwitch, 10 July 1631.

Articles for Sir Wᵐ Alexander.

1. To joyne with my Lord Chancellour in treating with the Clergie, according to our warrants gevin concerneing that purpois, and to adverteis ws or repair hither to report as the occasion for the good of our service shall requyre.

2. To deall with all things that may tend to the advancement of the assotiation for a generall fisching, according to the articles agreed vpon, and to that which is conteynit in our letter to the Counsall concerneing the places to be reserved.

3. To advyse with our Advocat what course is fitt to be takin for trying and punisching the wrong done in demolisching the work or mulzeing the goodis belonging to ws in our silver mylnes neir Lythgow, and to cause prosecute the same immediatlie, in such maner as our lawis doe allow, concurring therin with our Thesaurer depute, who is to give what is due to the Informer in lyk caces, preferring him in the composition, in so far as he shall think fitt, to others.

4. To inquyre of our Advocat what he hath fund best to be done in that which we by our letters referred formerlie vnto him concerneing our servand Patrik Murray in bringing of the Abbay of Inchaffray to our Croun presentlie, or in making of the conditions whervpon he should proceid in the actions depending for recoverie thairof.—Grenwitch, 10 July 1631.

To the Chancellour.

Right, &c.—Wheras complaint hath bene made vnto ws in behalff of the widow of Mʳ David Lyndsay, late bischope of Ross, that our late royall father haveing granted vnto Sir Jeromie Lyndsay, knyᵗ, 1000 aiker of land in Irland for the vse of hir and hir heyres, and ane other 1000 aiker vnto Sir Johne Dunbar, knyᵗ, for passing vnto hir by letters patents of the first 1000 aiker, and for planting therof, The said Sir John, contrarie to the trust reposed in him, hath, without hir knowledge or geving hir any satisfaction, sold the said first 1000 aiker vnto Sir William Cole, knyᵗ, wherby our said royall father's bountie intended towards hir is frustrated, and schee in hir widowheid hath now of a long tyme bene heavelie distressed : Sieing that both the Lords of our privie Counsall of this our kingdome and our Commissioners for the Irish affaires (to whom the tryell heirof was by ws remitted) have certifeid that it is fitt for the better clearing of what heirin is alledged that the said Sir Jeromie be examined vpon his proceidingis and knowledge therin : Our pleasur is, that yow call him befor yow, and efter examinatioun of him vpon oath tuitching the same, to certifie ws with diligence what yow doe find theirin, that therefter we may give such further ordour as we shall sie just cause, and as may be most agrieable to our said royall father's intentioun concerneing this purpois.—[No date.]

To the Archbischop and Bischops.

Right, &c.—Wheras the reverend father in God, the Bischop of Ylis, hath informed ws of some greevances sustened by yow, which being desyrous to remove, in so far as lawfullie and convenientlie can be done, we have bene pleased to appoynt our right, &c. our Chancellour, Thesaurer, President of our Counsell, and our principall Secretorie, or any two of them, to meitt and hear the same : Therfor we think fitt that Commissioners be choysen by yow out of your owin number to treit with them for removing therof, otherwyse we requyre them and yow that vpon any poynt whervpon they and yow cannot condescend to certifie ws therof, that we may give such further ordour therin as we shall find just caus.— Grenwitch, 10 July 1631.

To the Advocat.

Trustie, &c.—Wheras we did formerlie wryt vnto our Counsell that in that contraversie betuixt Lady Anna and Patrik Oliphants, that they should discharge in our name ather pairteis from taking vpon them the title or place of the Lord Oliphant, till such tyme as the same wer decydit befor the Judge Ordiner, to which of them it did belong : And being verie desyrous to vnderstand how the estate therof standeth in Law, it is our pleasur that yow informe your self therof, and that with all convenient diligence yow certifie ws as neir as yow can to whom the said title doe justlie belong, and what in justice we ar bund to doe to the right and lawfull heyre therin : Which we recommend, &c.—Grenwitch, 10 July 1631.

[No Address.]

In regard of the great paynes occasioned by extraordinarie cause, Our right, &c. the Viscount of Dupline, our Chancellour, hath takin for imbringing of our taxatiouns granted to ws in anno 1625, which now he hath brought to ane finall poynt, and for doeing wherof he hath had heirtofoir no allowance, it is our pleasur that at the hearing of his accompts yow allow vnto him in his owin handis the sowme of 500^{lib} sterling for his further encouragement to doe ws service heirefter ; And for your soe doeing these presents shalbe your warrant.—Grenwitch, 10 July 1631.

Precept to the Thesaurer and Deputie.

In regard of the good and faythfull service done vnto ws by Sir William Alexander, our Secretarie, it is our pleasur that yow delyver vnto him for his vse all and whole the moneyis that doe or shall belong vnto ws (as feyis justlie due being defrayed) for our share by the Coyneing of the farthing tokens, or of any such Copper coyne as yow shall think fitt to be coyned by vertew of our warrant sent vnto yow for that effect, and that ye send vnto ws any further warrant that yow think neccessarie heirin ; ffor doeing wherof, in delyverie the same to him by vertew of this warrant, or for drawing vp of another, these ar to secure yow as a sufficient discherge and warrant.—Grenwitch, 10 July 1631.

To the Thesaurer and Deputie.

Right, &c.—Wheras ther hath bene a proposition made vnto ws for coyneing a quantitie of farthingis tokins within that our kingdome such as ar current heir, and considering in regard of the scarcitie of money for the present ther, that some such kynd of coyne wer the more necessarie at this tyme for the vse of the meaner sort, and for the smallest sowmes ; Yit becaus we desyre to proceid heirin as circumspectlie as can be, both for the good of our owin subjects and that such correspondencie may be keipit heirin with our other kingdomes as in such caice is requisit, Our pleasur is, that haveing conferred with them who have the Charge of our Mynt, as lykwyse with the propounders of this course, that yow mak the fayrest and best bargane yow can for our advantage, and that yow sequester the moneyis arysing therby to be bestowed as yow shall have a particular warrant from ws for that effect.—Grenwitch, 10 July 1631.

To the Session.

Right, &c.—Haveing resolved to change some persones who had extraordinarie places in our Colledge of Justice, according as we vpon good considerations had formerlie intended, and being confident of the sufficiencie and qualification of Sir William Alexander, our Principall Secretarie of Scotland, we ar heirby pleased to will and requyre yow to admitt and receave him in the Session in the place of Sir Archibald Achiesone, our secretarie therof, and that yow tak (as is accustomed in the lyk caices) the oath of the said Sir Wm Alexander, whom we will to have and enjoy all the priviledges and others things belonging to that place : And so, &c.—Grenwitch, 10 July 1631.

To the Counsell.

Right, &c.—Haveing considered that the Letter which yow wryt vnto ws concerneing the places for fisching in these seas which yow think necessarie to be reserved for the sole vse of the natives of that our kingdome, we cannot conceave what necessitie can be for reserveing of so many severall places, and lykwyse of fyftene myles within the sea, distant from everie schoar, wher it would seame expedient that these of the assotiation for this generall fisching, as they have libertie to land in any place, paying the ordinarie dewteis, should lykwyse be frie to fisch wher ever they ar to pass : And as we ar willing to reserve for the natives all such fischings without which they cannot weill subsist, and which they of themselflis have and doe fullie fisch, so we will not reserve any thing to them which may be a hinderance to this generall work, which may so much import the good of all our kingdomes : And therfor we requyre yow, as yow affect our service, to contribute your best helpes, all and everie one of yow, in everie thing that may conduce to the accomplishment of this work, and that yow certifie ws bak by our trustie Sir William Alexander, knyt, our Secretarie, the bearer heirof, of your opinion heirin, and what yow think fitt for ws to doe as in a matter which we highlie value.—Grenwitch, 10 July 1631.

Warrant.

Right, &c.—Wheras ther is a finall agreement made betuixt ws and our good brother the French king, and that, amongst other particulariteis for perfecting heirof, we have condescendend that Port Royall shall be putt in the estate it was befor the begining of the warre, that no pairtie may have any advantage ther dureing the continuance of the same, and without derogation to any preceiding right or title be vertew of any thing done ather then or to be done by the doeing of that which we command at this tyme : It is our will and pleasur, and we command yow heirby, that with all possible diligence yow give ordour to Sir George Home, knyt, or any other haveing charge from yow ther, to dimolisch the Fort which was builded by your some ther, and to remove all the peoplis, goods, Ordinance, munition, cattell, and other things things belonging vnto that Colonie, leaveing the boundis altogidder waist and vnpeopled, as it was at the tyme when your said some landed first to plant ther by vertew of our Commission ; and this yow faill not to doe, as yow wilbe answerable vnto ws.—Grenwitch, 10 July 1631.

Prorogation of Parliament from the 4th August in Anno 1631 to the 12 Aprill 1632.

Cum fide certa et indubitata nobis constet presentium latorem Johannem Kynnardum subditum nostrum gente Scotum et antiquae familiae principem bonorum Omnium que Barbara Kynnebarda Cockburni chiliarchae vidua non ita pridem defuncta ejus soror possiderat heredem ex asse tabulis testamentariis ob ipsa constitum eumque negotia ejus varia neque exigui momenti quae hic peragenda habet presentiam ipsius et maturum in haec loca reditum postulent nec moram in regno vestro diuturniorem aut tardam et lentam causa comperendinationem patiantur Rogamus obnixe serenissimam Magestatem vestram vt que solet subditos omnes nostros favore et benevolentia humilem hunc et devotum clientem amplectatur ipsumque (si in ne certa et manifesta controversia vlla movebitur) quantum dictionum vestrarum jura et consuetudines permittent saluta et expedita decisione causae fortunet ne litis contestatio diutius prorogata rebus suis quae hic in periculo versantur damnum non leve et prejudicium afferat Quum pro vero affecta Serenissima Magestas Vestra Justiciam intemerat ancelat et Arma ipsa sacrosanctae Themediparene decear subditosque nostros alios peculiaris favoris sui patrocinio dignetur non ignari sumus quare vt suppliae hinc Serenissima Magestas vestra fareat quantum per leges Aequi bonique perpetuam et constantem vitae vestrae regulam licebit extendere preces nostras hoc tempore desinimus subditisque vestris in simili causa vestro hortatu paris benevolentiae compensationem pollicemur et serenissimae Magestati vestrae Omnia fraterni et sinceri amoris officia vltro deferimus.—Datum in palatio nostro Grenovici, 10 July 1631.

Carolus Dei gratia Magnae Brittaniae Franciae et Hyberniae Rex
fideique defensor &c. Serenissimo principi Domino Gustavo
Adolpho Dei gratia Suecorum Gothorum et Vandalorum Regi
principi Finnlandiae duci Escoviae Careliae Lappiae domino
Ingriae fratri Consanguiseo et amico nostro charissimo.

To the Counsell.

Right, &c.—Sieing we have sene by a letter from yow the ordour of Barronets erected by our late dear father and ws for furthering the plantation of New Scotland was appoynted by the whole estate of our kingdome at the last Convention, And that we vnderstand both by ther reports that cam from thence, and by the sensible consideration and notice takin thairof by our nyghbour cuntreyis, how well that work is begun, Our right trustie and weilbeloved Counsellour Sir William Alexander, our Leivtennent ther, haveing fullie performed what was expected from him for the benefite which was intendit for him by these barronets: Being verie desyreous that he should not suffer therin, but that both he and others may be encouraged to prosecute the good begining that is made, as we hartelie thank all such as hath contributo ther ayde by contracting with him for advancing of the said work alreadie: Our pleasur is, that yow seriouslie consider ather amongst yow all or by a Committie of such as ar best affectionat towards that work, how it may be best brought to perfection (whatever controversie be about it) from quyting our title to New Scotland and Canada, that we wilbe verie carefull to manteane all our good subjects who doe plant themsellfis ther, and lett none of the barronets anyway be prejudged in the honour and priviledges conteynit in ther patentes, by punisching of all that dare to presume to wrong them therin, that others may be encouraged to tak the lyk course as the more acceptable vnto ws, and the nearer to a title of Nobilitie, whervnto that of barronets is the nixt degrie: And if the said Sir William, as our Lievtennent of New Scotland, shall convene the barronetts to consult togidder concerneing that plantation, we heirby authorise him and will yow to authorise him as far as is requisit for that effect, willing that proclamation be made of what has been signifeid, or of what yow shall determine for furthering that work, wherof we recomend the care to yow as a matter importing speciallie our honour and the good of that our ancient kingdome.—Grenwitch, 12 July 1631.

To the Thesaurer Depute.

Right, &c.—Being verie desyreous in regard of the good service and daylie attendance of our trustie and weilbeloved Sir Wm Alexander, our Secretarie for that our kingdome, that he should enjoy the whole benefite belonging vnto his place, and that no other have any part therof : And yit being loath to tak from any other that which they justlie posses, without giveing them reasonable satisfaction, Our will is that yow vse your best meanes to mediat agriement with any persone that is interested that way, and that what ever yow shall find by a just value (efter due consideratioun) fitt to be bestowed for the effect wherby our said servand may come to the whole benefite of this place, this shalbe a warrant vnto yow to pay the same.—Grenwitch, 12 July 1631.

To the Erle Nithisdale, Erle Buccleuch, Robert Pringle, Francis Grhame, and to others Commissioners for the Borders of our Kingdome of Scotland.

Our pleasur is, and we doe heirby expreslie command that yow furthwith apprehend Thomas Irwing, Ritcherd Irwing, rebells, and committ them to jayll till ordour be takin for ther tryells according to Justice, for a murther committed by them on a brother of Sir Ritchart Grhame : Faill not to doe vpon your knowledge, or any notice gevin vnto yow by our said servant or any other, ther being or residing in any of our kingdomes heirin, be carefull as yow will answer the contrarie, for which these presents shalbe your sufficient warrant in this behalff.—Oatlands, 24 July 1631.

To the Two Justices of Irland, The Chancellour, Viscount Loftus, and the Erle of Cork.

Right, &c.—We ar informed that one Thomas Irwing and Ritchart Irwing, rebells, have repaired to that our kingdome, to prevent the tryell of our Lawis to be takin against them for the murther of a brother of our servant Sir Richart Graham, wherin sieing it concerneth ws in our royall authoritie not onlie for the present to cause justice be execute on these malefactours according to the Lawis of our kingdome wher the fact was committed, bot lykwyse to have a speciall care that from hence furth none of our kingdomes be a meanes to shelter such persones wherby to delude the course of Justice due to be execute in any of the other : Our pleasur is, that furth with yow give speciall ordour to all the officers of that our kingdome, whom it may concerne for a diligent and far search to be made for the saids Irwings, and all such other rebells as ar fled out of our borders of Scotland to prevent Justice, whois names yow shall receave from tyme to tyme vnder the hand of our Justice-Generall, and that these or any of them by your care apprehendit may be transmitted to the provest and bailleis of Drumfreis in our kingdome of Scotland ; And as for such malefactours as shall flie from Justice out of the borders of Irland, whois names yow shall receave heirwith vnder the hand of Lord Wm Howard, Sir Ritchart Grham, and Sir George Dawsone, yow shall returne all such persones to our jayll at Carlill in our countie of Cumberland. —Oatlands, 24 July 1631.

To the Bischop of Carlile.

Right, &c.—We have thoght fitt to acquant yow of our good acceptance, and how weill we approve of that work proposed to ws by our trustie and weilbeloved servand, Sir Ritchard Grhame, in building of the Church of Kirkandrous, with two Chappells of ease. We conceave it to be verie necessarie, especiallie in that part of our cuntrey wher ther is so mutch want of Education, the want of which draweth many ignorant people to many inconvenients to the great disturbance of that our kingdome, we have heirin dewlie considered and to this effect have passed our grant and intend our gracious furtherance for the finisching therof, by breives or such other wayes as by yow and our said servand shalbe conceaved most convenient, wherof we recommend vnto your best course and assistance this our servand that he may have the best furtherance yow can afford or shalbe requisite in this or any other thing he shall require : With all not doubting of your care in overlooking the ministrie that ther lyttis and conversation may be good : Our pleasur lykwyse is, that yow receave ane information from our said servant, Sir Richart Grhame, against the Minister of Beweastle, who, as we vnderstand doeth vse his parischoners, with all vnjust rigour worthie of reprooff, and if yow find such things as ar alledged against him to be of weight, that then he be removed, that one of better lyff may be placed ther to the comfort of the people.—Heirin expecting your care, we bid, &c.—Oatlands, 24 July 1631.

To the Advocat.

Trustie, &c.—Wheras we are pleased to signe a signature in favours of Mr Walter Neish of the office of Isherie of our Exchequer of that our kingdome, which is not as yit passed, nather any reasone schawin vnto ws for not passing of the same : And sieing (as we did formerlie writt vnto yow) we ar fullie resolved to draw back vnto our Croun all heretable offices, and to intent actions against all such as will not voluntarlie surrander, Our pleasur is, that yow compeir in our name befor our Exchequer and vrge the passing of the said signatur with all convenient diligence, and tharefter if any persone shall pretend title to the said office, then they may be heard befor the Judge competent : And our further pleasur is, that in all actions intented or to be intented aganst him tuitching that purpois, yow lykwyse compeir for our Interest for his best assistance in so far as yow can lawfullie doe; which we will tak as acceptable service done vnto ws.—Grenwitch, 28 July 1631.

Pro Rege Gallorum.

Carolus dei gratia Magnæ Britaniæ Franciæ et Hiberniæ Rex fideique defensor Omnibus hasce visuri salutem Quando quidem omnino justum æquum et bonum judicamus vt jam tandem pax et concordia nuper inter nos et regem Christianissimum fratrem nostrum charissimum conclusa pristinum vigorem et effectum recuperent atque adeo omnes contraversiæ et difficultates quæ hactenus hinc inde interciderunt inter nostra regna et subditos mutuo redintegrata et perfecta reconciliatione vtrinque removeantur et aboleantur in quem finem nos inter alios conditiones ex nostra parte præstandas consensimus desertionem facere fortalicii seu castri et habitationis portus regalis vulgo Port Royall in Nova Scotia qui flagrante adhuc bello vigore diplomatis ceu commissionis sub regio Scotiæ sigillo pro derelicto captus et occupatus fuerat et illud tamen sine vllo prejudicio juris aut tituli nostri aut subditorum nostrorum imposterum Nos promissorium atque verbi nostri regii fidem quibuscunque contrariis rationibus et objectionibus hac super re illatis aut inferendis ante ferentes hisce literis asserimus et verbo regio promittimus nos præcepturos curatores et effecturos vt a nostris in dicto fortalicio sine castro et habitatione portus regalis vulgo Port Royall subsistentibus subditis sive ceu milites præsidiarii sive ceu Coloni et Incolæ ibidem morentur et habitent immediate quam primum nostræ Jussionis literæ a deputatis vel commissariis qui easdem a præfato nostro fratre charissimo rege Christianissimo eo amandandi habebunt efferendas ipsis erunt exhibitæ et perfecte atque redeundi faculties data dictum castrum seu fortalitium et habitatio in portu regali durantur deserentur relinquantur denique arma tormenta commentus armenta bona et vtensilia inde asportentur In cujus rei testimonium has literas nostra manu nostras et magno regni nostri Scotiæ sigillo signari et confirmari volumus. Quæ dabantur ex Palatio nostro Grenovici die, 28 mensis Julij Anno domini 1631 et nostri regni septimo.

To the Thesaurer Deput.

Right, &c.—Wheras we wer pleased in July last to send our right, &c. the Viscount of Stirling, our principall Secretarie for that our kingdome, about bussines speciallie importing the good of our service, for which he had no allowance of ws towards the defraying of his charges, and that now vpon the lyk reasone we have thoght good to send him bak agane : It is our pleasur that vpon sight heirof yow pay vnto him the sowme of   , And the lyk sowme whensoever heirefter he by our speciall direction shalbe imployed by ws thither out of the first of the readiest of our rents and casualiteis whatsumever.—Grenwich, 28 July 1631.

To the Counsell.

Right, &c.—Vpon ane information made vnto ws of some latelie killed in a casuall encounter in the forrest of Glenhartnay, betuixt the forresters thairof and some of the name of Buchanan, for keiping of the said forrest, being desyreous that the trew estate of that bussines may be dewlie tryed and justice accordingly administred, Our pleasur is, that the tryell therof be delayed till our right, &c. the Erle of Monteith, our Justice generall, who is now heir vpon some speciall thingis concerneing our service, may be present to judge thairof, taking in the meanetyme sick suertie of them as yow shall think fitt for preventing of any farder harme which may aryse by the same ; And haveing heard of late that some of them who ar interessed in that quarrell doe carie haglutts and pistolls throw the said forrest, making it a common passage, which not onlie affrights our dear, bot lykwyse as we ar informed was the caus of the forsaid slaughter, which we wonder that any of our subjects whatsumever should be suffered to doe in regard of our lawis made to the contrarie : It is our further pleasur that yow tak this vnto your particular consideration, and give ordour that no man vnder great penalteis be suffered to cary any of the saids prohibited weapiones, and speciallie within our said forrest, wher we tak the wearing of them for the greater contempt. And therfor requyreing yow not to faill in doeing of this with all diligence : We bid yow, &c.—Grenwitch, 28 July 1631.

To the Archbischop of St Androis.

Right, &c.—We ar informed that ther is a proces of Law depending befor our Colledge of Justice betweene the bischope and the Erle of Murray, wherin hearing that the Erle is most willing to doe vpon his part what shalbe thoght fitt by any indifferent persones, and that all differences betweene them be composed in a friendlie maner, We to that purpois ar pleased that yow deale with the bischope to tak the lyk course, and therefter that yow vse your best endeavours for removeing of all questionis amongst them, Which we the rather desyre, and the more speedie course be takin therin, that by the said Erle his attending the following of that proces, some of our affaires committed to his charge may not be neglected.—Oatlands, last July 1631.

To the Chancellour.

Right, &c.—We have at this tyme, vpon some speciall considerationns tuitching the good of our service, directed thither the Erle of Monteith, vnto whom amongst other our instructionis we have at lenth signifeid our pleasur tuitching the tythis and Commission of surrenders which we still resolve to cause bring to a full conclusion according to our first determination, we haveing long prooff of your affection to our service, both in the tyme of our late dear father and our owin, ar still confident that in all things tuitching the advancement of that particular service, or in other things concerneing the same which the said Erle shall import from ws vnto yow, yow will joyne with him in your most hartie affection and readie endeavours, for which as these presents shalbe a sufficient warrant, soe we will accompt it as verie acceptable service done vnto ws.—Oatlandis, last of July 1631.

To the Exchequer.

Right, &c.—We ar informed that one Robert Philp, sometyme schirreff-Clerk of Drumfreis, haveing power to receave some of the taxatiouns granted in the tyme of our royall late father, did befor his death give ane accompt of his whole charge therin, save of a small parcell which therefter in the accompts of the Erle of Mar, ther Collectour, was allowed as moneyis desperat to be recovered, which being (as we ar informed) a matter of small value, we ar willing to remitt vnto Mr Robert Philp, his sone, who, by reasone he cannot convenientlie setle his father's esteat ther, hath caused move ws to that effect : Therfor our pleasur is, that yow discharge him, his heyres and executours, of the said rest, and of all intromissions of his said father, with any preceiding taxatiouns ; and for your soe doeing, &c.—Oatlandis, last July 1631.

To the Commissioner of Surrenders.

Right, &c.—Wheras we formerlie willed yow not to proceid in any thing concerneing the tythis of the Erle of Buccleugh till the first of Junij, that he might be ther present himselff ; And now sicing that day is expyred, and the differences betuixt him and Francis Stewart, for which the said Erle was called hither to attend, ar not as yit determinat, which we intend schortlie to doe without any further delay : Our pleasur therfor is, that yow continew all proceidings concerneing these saidis tythis till the first day of Nor nixt ensueing.—Oatlandis, last July 1631.

To the Archbischop of St Androis.

Right, &c.—Wheras vpon information made vnto ws by yourselff and others of the Clergie, how by the vnjustnes of the valuatioun of the tythis not onlie we in our annuitie, but the Estate of the Church in that our kingdome was lyklie to be prejudged, We, for rectifieing therof in so far as convenientlie could be done without prejudice to the generall course preserryved by ws tuitching the tythis and superioriteis of erectionis, wer pleased to direct the Viscont of Stirling to treat with yow therin : Bot haveing now of late receaved a letter from yow concerneing diverse things tuitching that purpois, which, haveing perysed and considered everie particular therof, we have at lenth imparted our pleasur therin to the Erle of Monteith, whom at this tyme, vpon some speciall considerations for the good of our service, we have directed thither, with speciall command to returne with all diligence ; and we haveing good prooff of his affection and sufficiencie for advanceing our service tuitching the publict good of the Estate of the Church, and of the professed religion, we have directed him to answer everie particular of your said letter, whom we will yow trust therin as delyvered from our owin mouth : Therfor our pleasur is, that yow propois vnto him what may concerne that purpois, both tuitching the prejudgeing of the Church and ws in our annuitie, with the expediencie yow can find for rectifieing thairof, that we may give such farther ordour therin as we shall find just caus, for be confident that we will not be wanting in anything that may tend to the good of the

II   8

Church, provyded it doe not prejudge the said generall course tuitching the said tythis and superiorities which we, haveing by due advyse so deliberatlie digested for the publict good of that our kingdome, we will not have any wayes invented or delayed. [All these words following by the King's owin hand.]— I have choysen this bearer, not onlie to give a speedie dispatch to the bussines of the tythis (wherby to putt yow Churchmen out of your needles fears), but also to bring me a trew report of your greevances in particular, which I have heard so much talk of in generall: Wherfoir I expect that yow deall with him with as much confidence as yow have reasone to beleive, that I shall give yow a quick redress of whatso-ever thing yow have just reasone to compleyne of.—Oatlands, last of July 1631.

To the Advocat.

Trustie, &c.—We have takin occasion at this tyme, vpon speciall considerations for the good of our service of that our kingdome, to send thither our right, &c. the Erle of Monteith, to whom, amongst other instructions speciallie importing the good therof, we have at lenth communicated our pleasur tuitching the bussines of the tythis, and other matters of the greatest consequence which at this tyme we have within the same, becaus we have preservyed vnto him no longer tyme of stay then the first of Sept[r] ensueing, we requyre yow from tyme to tyme, dueing his abode ther, to tak his directions in all things concerneing our service as delyvered from our owin mouth, for which, as these presents shalbe vnto yow a sufficient warrant, so we shall accompt your travells to be takin therin as acceptable service done vnto ws.— Oatlands, last July 1631.

To the Counsell.

Right, &c.—We receaved your letter desyreing that no restraynt might be agenst the importatioun or exportatioun of Salt from that our kingdome, bot that it might be in that same case as it was heir-tofoir: Though ther has bene made ane overture vnto ws, which as we conceave may tend to our benefite, and nowyse to the trouble or hurt of any of our leidges, yitt, out of the care we have of that our ancient and native kingdome, we have resolved that ther shalbe no restraynt at any tyme comeing agenst the importing or selling of any Scotts salt in this our kingdome; provydeing alwyse that as much be imposed to the vse of our Exchequer ther vpon everie weght of salt which is imported vnto this our kingdome, as the natives are content to pay in the lyk caces heir.—Oatlands, last of July 1631.

To the Erle of Monteith.

The whole Letter was writtin with his Ma[ties] owin hand.

Monteith—I have gevin yow diverse instructions, wherof I expect a particular accompt of, and to which I most add this one word, that is, yow must deall about the reservations for the fisching bussines to keip these places from being reserved that I have told you of, becaus I forsee that otherwyse that great business, wherof I have had so great a care of, will run a hazard. So God speed your endeavours.

         Subscribitur,   C. R., Oatlands, 31 July.

To the Counsell

Right, &c.—We have heard yow have made the Laird of Grant to produce ane Allaster Grant, a rebell, to be subject to the tryell of our lawis, wherin, as we doe approve of the maner of your proceiding, so we doe of your care and diligence in the speedie executioun, for which we give yow hartie thanks, and ar willing (if yow find it convenient) that yow insist not onlie to tak the lyk course with the said Lard of Grant, bot lykwyse with our right, &c. the Marqueis of Huntlie, for produceing all such rebells who as yit stand out, and whom by the generall band they ar bound to exhibite, and with all such noblemen and others who, by vertew therof, ar subject in the lyk kynd when the lyk occasions shalhappin to occur, which we will accept as acceptable service done vnto ws.—Oatlands, last July 1631.

To the Counsell.

Right, &c.—We vnderstand that according to our pleasur signifeid vnto yow for tryeing the maner of the burneing of Frendrauchts Tower, yow have omitted nothing that convenientlie could have bene done for tryeing therof, for which we give yow hartie thanks, yit the presumptious (as we ar informed) being great that it was done out of a malicious intent, have made ws to think that a continewed tryell to be takin therin may happelie produce some good effects for clearing of the truth : Therfor our pleasur is, that yow insist by all lawfull and possible meanes for a speedie and sure tryeing therof : And if yow think it fitt, we ar willing that yow select a committee out of your number, who more convenientlie, without interposition of other affaires (which the bodie of our Counsall can hardlie avoyd), may proceid in the tryell with all convenient and possible diligence till it be broght to a full conclusion ; which seriouslie recommending vnto your care, &c.—Oatlands, last July 1631.

To the Viscount of Sterlinge.

Right, &c.—We receaved a letter of late from the right reverend father in God, &c. the Archbischop of St Androis, tuitching the purpois wherin the Clergie of that our kingdome thought themsellis greived, for knowing the trew groundis wherof we, at your last departure from our Court, had gevin yow direction, haveing occasion at this tyme to send thither our right, &c. the Erle of Monteith, president of our privie Counsall, tuitching some of our speciall affaires, which he will impart vnto yow, we have bene pleased to remitt the answer of the said Letter by him, with whome, as in that particular so and in all other things tuitching the advancement of our service, we doubt not bot yow will concurre and give your best advyse and assistance : We bid, &c.—Oatlands, last of July 1631.

To Mr Johne Hay, Toun Clerk of Edinburgh.

Trustie, &c.—Haveing at this tyme, vpon speciall occasions tuitching the good of our service in that our kingdome, directed thither our right, &c. the Erle of Monteith, whom we have commanded to returne with all possible diligence ; And knowing by former prooff your sufficiencie and affection to our service, both in the tyme of our late dear father and our owin, We will expect at your hands that what directions shalbe imparted vnto yow at this tyme by the said Erle concerneing the advancement of any particular tuitching our said service, yow wilbe carefull to receave and obey them, as directed from our owin mouth ; and as we had formerlie resolved to be myndfull of your care and paynes in our service, we have now signifeid our pleasur tuitching the same vnto him, whom yow shall trust therin as from ws, And expect our favour accordinglie.—Oatlands, the last of July 1631.

Privat Instructions from his Matie To the Erle Monteith.

To deall with the Clergie for setling of the said greevances in the matter of Valuation of Tythis, and to answer to everie poynt of the letter writtin by the Archbischop of St Androis to his Matie.

To have a care that the bussines of the fisching may be weell and tymelie concluded, and the Commission returne befoir the middle of Sepr ensueing.

To advert to the bussines of the Salt and Coall.

To deall with the burgh of Edinburgh, that they may buy so much of that bargane which his Matie hath agreid for with the Erle of Roxburgh as is fitting for them to have.

That the said Erle returne vnto our Court with the rest of the Commissioners befor the tent of September ensueing.—Oatlands, last Julij 1631.

To the Commissioners for the Tythes.

Right, &c.—Wheras we ar informed that our right, &c. the Erle of Home and the Countess his mother ar now in proces for the valuation of the stok and tythis of the parochin of Innerweik, and that the vassells of the parochin of Gulane intend the lyk : And being credibile informed that in these valuations our servant James Maxwell hath speciall interest, who being to give his attendance in our service heir, is lyklie in his absence to be prejudged if he doe not in persone attend the proceidings to be made in these valuations ; Our pleasur is, that vntill he can ather convenientlie repair thither him self, or that we be pleased to signifie our further pleasur for your proceiding therin, that no course be takin in the samyne, and that yow give ordour accordinglie.—Oatlands, last Julij 1631.

To the Exchequer.

Right, &c.—We ar informed that at Sir James Sinclar, kny^t and Colonell, his first vndertaking of imployment for the late service of our Vncle the King of Denmark, he and his freinds did enter in band to Wm Dick for levyeing of moneyis for that purpois, haveing besydis engadged vnto him diverse evidents for the same : And vnderstanding by your letter vnto ws that the said Colonell hath both vsed his best endeavours in that service, and hath therin trowlie bestowed the whole moneyis bestowed vpon him, We think it vnreasonable, sieing (as we ar informed) these moneyis ar otherwyse allowed vnto the said William Dick, that the said Colonell and his freindis should now suffer therin : Therfoir our pleasur is, that yow call Wm Dick befor yow, and if yow doe not find a sufficient reasone to the contrarie, that yow caus him discharge the said Colonell and his suirteis of all moneyis for which they stand band for that imployment, and to delyver bak vnto him what papers wer delyvered tuitching that purpois ; for which these presents &c.—Oatlands, 7 August 1631.

To the Counsell.

Right, &c.—Wheras we have declared our pleasur that the trew worth aryseing by the forfaltour of the late Erle Bothwell's estate being fund by yow vpon strict examinatioun, we have, out of a due consideration, allotted vnto Francis Stewart, his sone, a considerable part therof, to be takin out of these Lords' possessionis who have all the benefit of the said foirfaltour ; declaring that everie one of them shall doe whatever shall be thoght fitt in Law and is in ther power to performe for secureing of the other of that which we have appoynted to be done, a care being alwyse to be had, as we will tak ordour for that effect, that the division which we have declared shalbe justlie and equitablie made, giveing to everie one his proportion for avoyding of future stryff in the parts wher it may ly most convenientlie for ther vse ; sieing that heirin we have takin so great paynes, and have brought all things to that perfection that nothing resteth but to know the trew worth of that estate, which convenientlie can not be done heir. And we being vnwilling to entrust the tryell therof to any saveing to such in whom we absolutelie repoise a cheiff trust, Our pleasur is, that not onlie yow cause exhibit vnto yow the trew rentalls of the said estate efter what maner yow shall think fitt, bot lykwyse that yow give ordour to our Advocat to draw vp the securiteis for that purpois, leaveing the blanks of the quota to be filled vp by ws: In all which we desyreing yow proceid with all convenient diligence till it be broght to perfection, according to our royall intention, We bid, &c.— Oatlands, 8 August 1631.

His Maties Decree.

Francis Stewart haveing petitioned ws to have compassion on his deplorable estate, and that his father's fault, of which we find him nowyse guiltie, may not vtterlie ruyn him, of which petition we haveing duelie considered, doe find it fitt so far to satisfie him, that he may have a competent mantenance to live vpon, to which end we, haveing spokin with these Lords who have all the benefite of the late Erle of Bothwell's forfaltour, and they, as reasone is, haveing submitted to what we shall determyne heirin, doe herby declare our pleasur that the trew worth of the said forfaltour being fund out vpon strict examinatioun by our Counsell of Scotland, and that being divydit into . . . parts, we allot . . . parts to Francis Stewart, to be takin respectivelie out of each of the foirsaids Lordis possessions, and that everie ane of them shall doe whatever shalbe thoght fitt in Law, and is in ther power to performe for secureing of the other of that which we appoynt to be done, a care being had, as we shall give ordour for that effect, that this division which we have declared shalbe justlie and equallie made, giveing to everie one his proportion for avoyding of future stryff in the parts wher it may ly most convenientlie for his vse : And these presents shalbe a sufficient warrant for our Advocat to draw vp securiteis heirvpon.— Oatlands, 8 August 1631.

These words following ar writtin with his Ma^{tes} owin hand.

I have not filled vp these blanks, though I have done these of the Decree, Becaus the rentalls true value may be found out with the less partialitie.

To the Laird of Lawers.

Trustie, &c.—We ar informed it is fitt our forrest of Glenalmond be enlarged by taking in some grounds adjacent thervnto belonging vnto yow, and being willing to caus deall with yow for a reasonable satisfaction to be gevin vnto yow for the same, we have to that purpois imparted our pleasur to our right, &c. the Erle of Monteith, whom we have directed to surveigh the ground, and with whom we desyre that yow condescend concerneing the pryce for payment, whairof vpon your agreement we will by him give ordour for your satisfaction : So expecting that in a purpos wherin no sene prejudice can be sustenit by yow, yow will conforme your self to this our pleasur.—Oatlands, 8 August 1631.

To the Counsell.

Right, &c.- -Wheras we habene pleased to grant vnto our trustie and weilbelovit servand Sir Alex^r Home, knyt, the favour of our royall protection, that he may frielie repair vnto Scotland for setling of his affaires, which he cannot convenientlie doe without the concurrance of his father, Sir George Home of Manderstoun, in whois behalff we have lykwyse signifeid our pleasur vnto yow, that he might have libertie to cum in publict for prosecution of the tryells of certane persones dilated as guiltie of divilish practeizes against his lyff and estate (which we ar informed) ar not broght as yit to a finall period ; Therfor, as weell for our said servandis better furtherance in the setling of his affaires, as also that the said Sir George may be liable to bring the saidis tryells to a full conclusion, we ar heirby pleased to recommend him vnto yow that he may have such farther libertie to cum in publict as yow shall find requisit for the one and the other.— Oatlands, 8 August 1631.

To the Erle of Morton.

Right, &c.—Having considered that it is requisit for avoyding of partialitie in valueing the rentalls to be made of the late E. Bothwell's estate to keip vp for some tyme the proportions designed by ws in our decree tuitching the division therof, haveing to that effect keipt cloise in our owin custodie the decree itselff : Our pleasur is, that what yow know therin, or hath bene by ws imparted vnto yow tuitching that purpois, yow keip the same secreit ; wherin, not doubting bot yow will obey our pleasur.—Oken, the 10 August 1631.

To the Erle of Monteith.

Right, &c.—As tuitching that part of your letter concerneing the Erle of Murrayes interest in the thrid of Duffus, and in the patronage therof, we find no reasone for ws to tak any course therin to onr owin disadvantage, Sieing the Erle of Murray hath submitted vnto ws his interest therin, and that we conceave that if ther be any farther right then our owin, it is in the persone of the bischop of Murray : Therfor we still hold it expedient, as formerlie we have done, to remitt the tryell therof betwixt the said E. Murray and bischop . . . to due course of our Lawis, requyreing yow to caus our Advocat carefullie to advert therin for our interest, wherin have thoght fitt to signifie our pleasur vnto yow : We bid, &c.—Wodstok, 22 August 1631.

To the Deputie Thesaurer, Lord Traquair.

Right, &c.—Haveing at this tyme gevin instructions vnto our right, &c. the Erle of Monteith for dispatch of affaires speciallie importing ws and the good of that our kingdome, with speciall direction to returne vnto our Court with all possible diligence, and being confident of your affection to our service, we are heirby pleased to requyre yow that what directions shalbe imparted vnto yow at this tyme by the said Erle yow wilbe cairefull to receave them as directed from our owin mouth : So not doubting bot in all things tuitching the advancement of our service yow will joyne with him in your most hartie affection and readiest : We bid, &c.—Wodstok, 23 August 1631.

To the Counsell.

Right, &c.—Haveing intention vpon verie good considerations at this tyme to ayd our brother the King of Sweden with such forces as we can convenientlie spare from all our kingdomes, our pleasur is, that yow grant vnto our trustie, &c. Lodovick Leslie, Livetenent-Colonell to Sir John Hamiltoun of Skirling, knyt, a Commission with a sufficient warrant to levy and transport thither 200 men, and that towards the recrue of the said Sir Johne his Regiment out of all such persones within that our kindome as he shall find willing to goe with him thither : Granting him libertie to tonk drumes to that purpois, with as great priviledges as any other hath had heirtofoir in the lyk kynd, he alwyse giveing such satisfaction to everie one of the said number as shalbe agried vpon betuixt him and them.—Wodstok, 28 August 1631.

To the Counsell.

Right, &c.—Whens heirtofoir we have sufficientlie signifeid vnto yow our pleasur for exhibiteing vnto ws the trew rentalls of the lands of the Erledome of Bothwell, possessed by the Erle of Buccleuch, and intending the selff same course with the Abacie of Kelso, which we did not mention in our former letter, We have therfor thoght fitt heirby to will and requyr yow (notwithstanding of any preceiding warrant) presentlie to goe on in the lyk course with the Abacie of Kelso, by exhibiteing vnto ws a trew and perfect rentall of all the temporall landis of that whole Abacie, togidder with a perfect valuation of the spiritualitie therof: And fearing your ordinarie way of valuatioun prove long and tedious, we heirby lykwyse will yow to embrace whatever speedier course yow in your judgment shall find most fitt; and in respect of your not frequent meittings in vacation tyme, we lyk it well that a Committie be choysen out of your number of such as reside narrest our brugh of Edinburgh, who for the speedie dispatch of these rentalls and valuations may with the greater convenience meitt so often as the necessitie of this service shall requyre.—Nonsuch, 28 August 1631.

To the Counsell and Session.

Right, &c.—Wheras we did formerlie recommend to yow ane action persewed by our trustie servand and chaplane Doctour Walter Whytfurd concerneing the subdeanrie of Glasgow, wherin, as we acknowledge your good service done vnto ws in reduceing by your sentence the patronage of that benefice to our Croun, Soe we ar willing to provyd for refounding our said servant in his great charges in persewing that action, by his enjoying the fruitts of that benefice, for which caus we have gevin command to our Advocat to assist and concurre with him in all actions tending or that may tend to that purpois, and ar pleased heirby to signifie vnto yow that it is our express will and pleasur that yow proceid to minister justice in these actions, according to the Lawis of that our kingdome, with all lawfull expedition, wherby our said servand may have possession of the rents of that benefice and others encouraged to doe ws the lyk service; which recommending to your speciall care, &c.—Nonsuch, 28 August 1631.

Was signed a presentation of Robert Hamilton to the Church of Stanehous, 15 Sept[r] 1631.

To the Archbischop of S[r] Androis.

Right, &c.—Haveing occasion to declair our pleasur vnto yow touching some thingis concerneing our service, We requyre, at the repairing hither of our Court of the Lord President of our Privie Counsell, and of our Principall Secretarie, yow lykwyse repair hither, wher our further pleasur shall be imparted vnto yow: We bid yow farewell.—Theobald's, 15 Sept. 1631.

To the Erle Strathern, Erle Menteith, Lord President.

Right, &c.—Haveing at your last departure from our Court granted vnto yow no longer tyme to stay ther then the fyftene of this moneth, bot knowing that it is requisit for the good of our service that yow be present at that meitting of our Counsell which is appoynted to be schortlie at our brught of Perth, Our pleasur is, that yow be present therat, and immediatlie therefter repair to our Court: We bid, &c.—Theobald's, 15 Sept[r] 1631.

To the Counsell.

Right, &c.—The Lord Vchiltrie haveing bene examined befoir our Counsell heir tuitching some informations gevin by him reflecting vpon some nobilitie of that our kingdome, we have bene pleased to remitt him thither to be tryed according to the lawis therof, haveing to that purpois sent yow heirwith enclosed some depositions vnder his owin hand, and the authentik copeis of others, wherof the principalls we cause reserve heir becaus they lykwyse concerne other persones : Our pleasur is, that haveing gevin ordour for receaveing and committing him to safe custodie, yow caus try and censure him according to our saids lawis befoir what Judicatorie and judges yow shall think fitt and compitent for that purpois; and for your soe doeing these presents shalbe your sufficient warrand.—Hampton Court, 24 Sept. 1631.

To the Archbishop of Sᵗ Androis.

Right, &c.—Being informed of the sufficiencie and qualification of one Mʳ Andro Eliot, and that he is a persone fitt to succeid to the Minister at the Church of Innerkeillour, wherof the parochiners, be vertew of the ministeris great aige and seiknes, stand in neid of ane liable persone for helping him in the charge of the ministrie : We ar heirby pleased to recomend the said Mʳ Andro to yow, that if he be fund qualified, as is affirmed, he be preferred to any other in that charge when it shall happin to vaik, and that then yow send ws a presentatioun to that purpois.—Hampton Court, 24 Sept 1631.

Regi Swecorum.

Carolus Dei gratia Magnæ Britanniæ Franciæ et Heiberniæ Rex Fideique defensor, &c. Serenissimo ac Potentissimo Principi Domino Gustavo Adolpho eadem gratia Suecorum Gothorum Vandalorumque regi Magno Principi Finlandiæ Eschoviæ Careliæque duci ac domino Ingriæ, &c. fratri consanguineo nostro Salutem. Serenissime frater ac consanguine charissime quem non ita pridem Majestati commendavimus vestræ Johannem Kinairdum domino Jacobo Oliphanto senatoribus vni nostris non leviter oberatum nunc demum accepimus pro in commune nec in patriam vedeundi nec solvendi prorsus Kinnardo sit annus a nobis hasce impetravit supplex Oliphantus literas vt in quo tenetur .Ere Kinnardus liberare si se minus conetur legibus mandatisue vestris secundum jus et æquum facere satis cogatur quod vt nobis pergratum erit sic paribus officiorum vicibus clemereri studebimus. Datum in palatio nostro Hampton, 12 Mensis Octoʳⁱˢ 1631.

To the Chancellour.

Right, &c.—We ar informed by petition from Patrik Cor that he haveing in obedience to our Lawis, and late ordour of our Counsell, retired him self and his familie furth of the cuntrie befoir any proces intended aganst him for not conformitie, was, notwithstanding, by the presbyterie of Aberdene excommunicat efter his departure, and by the consequent thairof that these to whom he entrusted his estate hath hitherto and may still, though vnjustlie, detenit fra him, except we, out of our princelie consideration, dispense with the rigour of the Law, and grant him our licence to abyd and follow his bussines within the cuntrie for ane whole yeir : We thairfor, considering that the petitioner being from his cradle bred in poperie, and haveing yeilded humblie and tymelie obedience to our lawis and governement, ought not in equitie or reasone to incur the punischments that ar due to dissobedients onlie, have thoght fitt, if the information be trew, to grant vnto him licence to abyd within the cuntrie and follow his bussines for the space of ane whole yeir, and to dispense with the consequences of his excommunication for the said space, in so far as they may concerne or prejudge the libertie of his persone or the recoverie and enjoying of his estate : Willing, therfoir, and requyreing yow to give notice heirof to any whom it may concerne, especiallie to the tuo supreame twines of Judicatoreis, our Counsell and Colledge of Justice, and by your authoritie from ws give ordour for the petitioner's securitie and saftie as shalbe neidfull: Provydeing alwyse that enduring the said space he give no scandall nor just offence to the Churche or governement: Wherin, not doubting of your care and conformitie to this our pleasur, we bid yow, &c.—Whythall, 28 Octor 1631.

To the Counsell.

We have duelie examined and considered the caus wherin the Erldome of Lothian and Lordschip of Newbotle doeth presentlie stand, both by sieing the patent therof granted by our royall father, of happie memorie, to Robert, the late Erle therof, vpon his resignation of the former made to Erle Mark, and the Act of Parliament Confirmeing the same: And haveing takin advyse of these with whome we have thoght fitt to consult about it, being persones of honour and vnderstanding, and well acquanted with the bussines, we doe planelie perceave that his purpois was that, if failzeing of heyris-male of his bodie, his eldest daughter without division should be his heyre, both to his whole estate and honour, in so far as in him lay, to establish it vpon condition that schoe should marie a well borne gentilman of the surname of Ker, who should be bund to bear the said Erle's Armes: and sieing that according to his intention his eldest daughter, the Lady Anne Ker, hath maried Sir William Ker, sone to Sir Robert Ker of Ancrum, knyt, gentilman of our bedchalmer, and so on hir part hath fulfilled the condition sett on hir by hir father: and hir husband as also willing to bear these armes and leave his owin, and that Sir Robert Ker, his father, hath vpon the mariage redeamed the Lordschip of Newbotle out of ther handis who had comprysed the same for the late Erle's debts, and by adding his owin estate to it, and other Compitent meanes, wherby of a perplexed and almost ruinated estate, by God's assistance, he hath made it capable of the former dignitie; haveing also provydit a portion to the Lady Jeane, the late Erle's younger daughter: All which considered, out of our grace and favour to the saids persones, and, if God will, to keip vp the house to them and ther posteritie, who have done soe much for it, we have thoght fitt to creat the said Sir William Ker of Ancrum, and his aires-male, erles of Lothian and Lords of Newbotle; and becaus that we hear that Sir William Ker of Blaikhope, brother to the late Erle of Lothian, hath takin on him (as pretending to be air-male of the house) to style himselff by that title without our licence and authoritie: Therfoir it is our express will, and we command yow, that yow call befoir yow the said Sir William Ker of Blaikhope, and freindlie reprove him in our name for so great presumption, letting him know what we have bene pleased to doe, and stratlie chargeing him that he nor nane of his successours, ather gottin of his bodie or brethren, who might perhaps pretend the same heirefter, if he should die without aires, presume to vse that title heirefter; and if he have anything to alledge why this should not be done, lett him seik his releiff by the Lawis of that our kingdome, and shall have such just hearing as we doe willinglie grant to all our subjects; but if the said Sir William Ker of Blaikhop keip himselff out of the way to avoyd this just reprooff, or that he cum not readelie to hear this our declaration, then it is our will that yow so mak knowen this our pleasur, that by his freinds he may be adverteised of it, and that none give that styll but to these vpon whom by letters patents we have conferred it.—The last of Octor 1631.

To the Chancellour.

Right, &c.—Wheras we did formerlie wryt vnto our Counsell for proceiding in the lyk course tuitching the rentall of the Abbacie of Kelso, as we wer pleased to requyre to be takin of such of the estates of the late Erle of Bothwell as was possest by the Erle of Buccleuch, but considering that convenientlie nothing can be done without the presence of our right, &c. the Erle of Roxbrugh, and that we ar to deteyne him for some short tyme for causes concerneing the good of our service; Our pleasur is, that yow proceid not in anything concernenig him or that Abbacie till the fyftene day of Januar ensueing, which we have appoynted him preciselie to keip ; And that yow signifie our pleasur heirin to our Counsell and Commissioners for the surrenders : So we bid yow hartie farewell.—Whythall, 9 No^r 1631.

To the Counsell.

Right, &c.—Wheras we have gevin ordour to some of our cheiff officers in that our kingdome, who ar heir for composeing of such feuds and differences as ar amongst the name of Grant, not intending therby that such malefactours of that name who have transgressed our Lawis and broken our peace in these parts be lett goe vnpunisched, if anywayes fund guiltie or accessorie thervnto ; And vnderstanding that Allaster Grant (who for a long tyme hath bene a prissoner for crymes alledged aganst him of this kynd) is schortlie to be putt to his tryell, and that it is requisite for the better cleiring of the treuth heirin that some longer tyme be preseryved for that purpois, our pleasur is, that the said tryell be continewed till the tent day of Aprill ensueing, befoir which tyme we will expect that further light wilbe gevin therin : We bid yow, &c. —Whythall, 10 No^r 1631.

To the Threasurer Depute.

Wheras our right, &c. the Erle of Stratherne, Lord President of our privie Counsell of that our king-dome, did not long since, by our speciall direction, levy a pension of 500^{lib} st. from the Erle of Carrik, who be him is secured in his landis for payment of these moneyis yeirlie which ar condescended vpon between them, wherby we have gayned vnto our Exchequer the arreirs of that pension, extending to 2000^{lib} st.. which wer due to have bene payed to the said Erle of Carrik : These considerations, being more then Ordinarie, have justlie moved ws that the said Lord President be made no loser by our meanes ; Therfoir we will and requyre yow that, according to our grant of that pension, yow mak good and readie payment therof vnto our weilbelovet Cousen the Countess of Stratherne, or hir assigneyis, whois names is insert in the said grant : And for your soo doeing these presents shalbe vnto yow a sufficient warrant and discherge, notwithstanding of any former restraynt or direction to the contrarie.—Whythall, 16 No^r 1631.

To the Counsell

Wheras we have fullie resolved to repair at the ensueing spring of the yeir to that our ancient king-dome for receaving our Croun and holding a Parliament ther ; And being cairfull (according to our former pleasur signifeid to that purpois) that at that tyme all things may be in good ordour and decent as most convenientlie can be done, and as shalbe fund most requisite, Our speciall pleasur is, that yow speciallie consider of what is fitt to be looked vnto and provydit at our comeing dureing the tyme of our abode ther ; And that yow signifie this our pleasur, and give ordour accordinglie, to all our officers and subjects whom it may concerne ; and, amongst other things, that yow have a speciall care for causeing preserve our game in our Parks, forrests, and other places of sport accustomed by our late royall father, and to that effect that yow give ordour for doeing of such things, and preseryveing such cautions and penalteis to be inflicted vpon the transgressours, as yow shall think fitt and most necessarie to that purpois : All which we doe in a speciall maner recommend vnto your care.—Whythall, 16 No^r 1631.

To the Counsell.

Right, &c.—Wheras we ar informed by petition from Johne McDonald, Captane of Clanronald, that he being summonded to give his appeirance befoir yow in this present moneth, is not able to performe the same without great tryell and danger of the vnseasonablenes of the tyme of the yeir and the great distance and perrells of the way, by both sea and land; bot that he hath gevin sufficient surteis for answering whatsoever can be lodged to his charge at the next generall apparence of the Ylanders, vnder paine of great sowmes of money; As lykwyse that, in regard of the anticipating of that dyet this yeir, he should be forced in schort tyme to mak that so dangerous a journey tuyse: We therfor, considering the premisses, have thoght fitt to will and requyre yow to dispense with the petitioner's particular apparence vnto the nixt generall dyet of the Islanders, which we have requyred yow for some speciall occasions to appoynt in the spring of the yeir; wherin not doubting of your conformitie of this our pleasur, we bid, &c.—Whythall, 16 No^r 1631.

Was a presentatioun signed in favours of Mr George Young to the Viccarage of Calder and Monkland, with all sindrie things perteneing thairto.—Whythall, 17 No^r [1631].

TO THE LORD LOWDEN.

Right, &c.—Haveing gevin ordour for delyverie of these moneyis which ar payable by ws for the redemeing the wodsetts of these superioriteis mentioned in the transaction betuixt ws and yow, we have returned that signatur signed by ws concerneing yow for your proceidings, wherin in so frie and voluntar a maner we give yow hartie thanks, and will acknowledge the samyne as good service done vnto ws: And be confident that as [we] will not that any superiour be interposed therin between ws and yow, so if we shal-happin at any tyme heirefter to schaw any favour to any of the lyk kynd, be assured yow shall find the same in also great a measur as any vther: And in that particular which we promised yow at your being heir, be lykwys confident that we will performe the same vnto yow at our home cuming amongst the first of that kynd, and will sie yow satisfeid of what is further due vnto yow: We bid, &c.—Whythall, 17 No^r 1631.

TO THE ADVOCAT.

Trustie, &c.—Wheras we have writtin vnto our right, &c. the Erle of Winton to deall with Mr William Kellie, Advocat, and his tuo sones in Law, for surrendring vnto our Croun ther title to the Eistbarnes, which is a part of our propertie of the Lordschip of Dunbar: And being willing so to proceid with them therin as both our ancient patrimonie may be restored and they satisfeid in so fair and reasonable maner for ther interest, Our pleasur is, that yow learne of the said Erle if they will be content to accept of a reasonable satisfaction for ther right thervnto; and if not, that yow proceid by a due and legall course for bringing bak of these lands vnto our Croun: And becaus locall assignements to our propertie doe no less prejudge ws, and ar of no less dangerous consequence in prejudgeing thairof, Our further pleasur is, that yow tak the lyk course with such of the assigneyis who will not accept of ther payments out of our Exchequer according to the ordinarie and approved manner.—Whythall, 17 No^r 1631.

TO THE ERLE OF WINTON.

Right, &c.—Haveing resolved, for restoreing of the Lordschip of Dunbar, which is a part of the antient patrimonie of our Croun, to cause vse all such fair wayes and meanes as both our royall intention therin may tak effect and as may best tend to the advantage of our subjects interessed therin, We to this purpois, haveing considered the long and reall prooffes of your affection to our service, both in the tyme of our late dear father and our owin, and being informed of some interest that Mr Wm Kellie, advocat, hath in yow, and that his two sones in Law and himsellf have possession of Eastbarnes, a parcell of that Lordship, have thoght it expedient to vse yow as a fitt instrument to deall with them to this purpois, and to vse your best and most readest endevours therin ; whervnto if they condescend, acquant our thesaurer or deputie thesaurer therwith, that they may farther agrie for ther satisfaction for their title vnto the said lands efter some reasonable maner : bot if they will not be content to goe on therin, we have directed our Advocat to proceid against them by due course of Law for bringing bak of the saids lands vnto our Croun.—Whythall, 17 Nor 1631.

To the Thesaurer.

Right, &c.—Haveing fullie resolved to repair vnto that our ancient kingdome in the ensueing spring of the yeir, and knowing that ther is nothing more necessarie at our comeing then to have our housse wher we intend to be dureing the tyme of our abod ther in that good ordour and decencie as is requisit : And that this purpois, amongst these others, which ar the caus why at this tyme we have gevin ordour that a restraynt of the issueing of moneyis is none of the leist : Our speciall pleasur is, that yow furth with pay vnto our masters of work such moneyis as by advyse of our privie Counsell wer condescended vpon by contract betwein ws and them, and that from the dat therof to the tyme limited therin : And for your soe doeing these shalbe a sufficient warrant, notwithstanding of any former direction to the contrarie.—Whythall, 17 Nor 1631.

To the Commissioners of Surrenders.

Right, &c.—Wheras the bussines of the Commission for Surrenders and Tythes hath takin long tyme, and not schortlie be effected vnless ther be a daylie sitting of Commissioners for dispatch therof, and we being most desyreous to have these affaires putt to ane end befoir our comeing to that our kingdome, We have thoght it meitt that of your owin number some be selected and putt apart for the work such as may be best spared from other our services in Counsell, session, and Exchequer : It is our speciall pleasur, and we doe heirby requyre yow, to mak a Committie vnto the persones nominat by ws and sent in a roll to our Chancellour, to which number we have ordaned our right, &c. the Viscont of Dupline, our Chancellour, The Erle of Morton, our thesaurer, The Erle of Stratherne, Lord President of our privie Counsall, The Erle Hadington, Lord Privie Seall, the Viscont of Stirling, our principall Secretarie, and Sir Thomas Hope of Craighall, knyt and baronet, our Advocat, shalbe added and shalbe present when shall please them and our other weghtie affaires shall permitt, which committie we have ordeaned to convene at our palace of Halyrudhous vpon the first day of Febr ensueing, and daylie therefter to sitt in such places and at such hours as they shall think most fitt for prosecuteing that work, and bringing the same to some good conclusioun : And that the said Committie shall proceid in all such poyuts and heads as ar warranted by our generall commission, and according to the severall decries pronunced by ws and published in print, making report allwayes of ther proceidingis to the generall Commission, that the same, being by them allowed and approved by ws, may receave a finall determination ; and if any differences shall aryse betuixt the Committie and yow tnitching things by them appoynted, we will that the same be remitted to our selfis, that we may determine therin as we shall find just cause ; ffor the more speedie effecting of all which we have requyred our Chancellour to caus a proclamation be made for publisching our intention heirin, warneing all our subjects whom this bussines doe concerne to give attendance vpon the said Committie at the dyetts to be assigned vnto them, and dischergeing all warrants and licence ather procured or to be procured in favours of whatsumever persones for continuatioun or delay in thir particulars, certifieing them and everie of them that shalbe lawfullie warned to appear at the dyets to be assigned, that if they faill in attending the same by themsellfis or ther procuratours, the said Committie shall proceid as if they wer personallie present, for soe we have appoynted and such is our pleasur: Wherin nowayes doubting of your readie furtherance, we bid yow farewell.—Whythall, 21 No' 1631.

To the Thesaurer Depute.

Right, &c.—Being informed that the silver mylne neir our burgh of Linlythgow, tools and works therto belonging, which to the great charge and care of our late royall father ther wer erected for making and fyneing of silver ore ther, ar broken doun, stollen, and takin away, wherby, besydes the great loss we have sustened, we exceidinglie mislyk that any durst attempt any such course: Our pleasur is, that yow and our Advocat informe your selffis of the estate and committers therof, and that yow persue them by due course of Law befoir whatsumever judge or judges compitent, to the effect that Justice may be putt to dew and speedie executioun vpon the offenders, and in regard we compt it verie good and acceptable service done vnto ws that we have bene informed in a course tending to the punischeing of such ane abuse done against ws, we ar pleased that with the haliff of the benefite which shallhappin to aryse by the persute of these persones which is due to the pairtie informer, the haliff lykwyse belonging to ws be gevin to him vpon such reasonable composition as yow shall think fitt to modifie.—Whythall, 28 No' 1631.

To the Chancellour.

Right, &c.—For as much as the Commission of Surrenders hath made a slow proceiding be reasone of the imployments of diverse of the Commissioners in our other necessarie services, and that we ar most desyreous to have the same at a poynt befor our comeing to that our kingdome, and have thoght meitt that a Committie be made of a fewer number that may be best spared from attending our other services in Counsell, session, and Exchequer for sitting daylie vpon the dispatch of that bussines, the list of whois names we have sent enclosed vnto yow, that yow may acquant the Commissioners of our will and pleasur therin: Therfor we desyre yow with all convenient diligence to convene and call the Commission togidder for establisching the said Committie according the roll and quorum therin sett doun, and therefter cause publicatioun to be made of this our pleasur, and Charge by oppin proclamation the persones nominated for the said Committie, as lykwyse all our subjects whom that bussines doe concerne, to attend the dayes and dyetts that shalbe assigned vnto them, according as we in our letter to the Commission have declared: Which recommending to your speciall care and the trust we repose in yow, we bid yow hartie fairwell.—Whythall, 29 No' 1631.

To the Advocat.

Trustie, &c.—Being informed that the Silver Mylne neir to our brugh of Linlythgow, tools and works therto belonging, which to the great charge and care of our late royall father ther wer erected for making and fyneing of silver vre ther ar broken doun, stollen, and takin away, wherby, besyds the loss we have sustened, we exceidinglie mislyk that any durst attempt such lyk course: Our pleasur is, that haveing takin the advyse of our thesaurer deputie, to whome we have writtin to be ayding and assisting vnto yow heirin, yow informe your self of the estate and committers therof, and that yow persew them by dew course of Law befoir whatsoever judge or judges compitent, to the effect justice may be putt to dew and speedie executioun vpon the offenders.—Whythall, 29 No' 1631.

To the Erle of Annandale.

We being informed that yow have both layed arreistments vpon hay of this yeir, which yow have fund to have bene vnjustlie takin away out of our Park and Medowis of Falkland (wherof yow ar the keeper), and vpon some Cattell fund therin other then our owin : Our pleasur is, that yow proceid according to the arreistment and aganst the transgressours in so far as yow ar warranted to doe as our stewart ther, causeing deteyne the Cattell within the parks and groundis belonging thairto till yow receave our further direction therin, and if any persone shall presume to breck your arreistment, we requyre yow to committ them to prissone till our farther pleasur be made knowen vnto yow tuitching them, whairof doe not faill, as yow wilbe answerable vnto ws.—Whythall, 29 No.r 1631.

To the Advocat.

Trustie, &c.—Wheras we ar informed that our royall father did entrust the late Viscount of Stormont with severall charges and intromissions in his service, wherof he hath not in his tyme made accompt, We ar willing that our right, &c. the Erle of Annandale vse his best endeavours to find them out, and for his paines and charges to be takin therin Our pleasur is, that vpon information made vnto yow by the said Erle, or otherwyse, if any thing omitted by the said Viscount in that kynd, yow draw vp a signature or gift therof to pas our hand for the vse of the said Erle : And for your soe doeing these presents shalbe your warrand.—Whythall, 29 No.r 1631.

The Names of these whom his Ma.tie appoynts for a Committie.

The Archbischop of St Androis, The Bischop of Murray, Rosse, Brechin, Dumblane, and Iles.

The Erle of Angus, The Erle of Winton, The Lo. Gordon, The Lo. Lorne, Lo.d Burley, Lo. Weymes.

Sir George Elphingstoun, Sir Robert Gordon, Sir Alex.r Gordon, Johne Leslie of Newtoun, Sir John Charters of Amisfeild.

Mr Johne Hay, The Provost of St Androis, or Commissar Clerk ther, John Cowing, burges of Stirling, Rot Alexander, burges of Anstruther, Mr Rot Tinynghame, burges of Kinghorne, or any tuelff of them with the Archbischop of St Androis, and in his absence the bischop of Murray.

These conteyne a pension of fyve hundreth pundis sterling to the Erle of Morton dureing his lyff, to be vplifted out of your Ma.teis rents and casualiteis of Scotland, at Witsonday and Mertimes yeirlie, wherof the first termes payment to begin at   .—Whythall, 7 De.r 1631.

To the Session.

Right, &c.—Wheras we did formerlie recommend vnto yow in behalff of the reverend father in God, and our right trustie and weilbeloved Counsellour, Johne, bischop of Iles, all actions of Law depending or which should happin to cum befoir yow tuitching the restoreing of the bischoprik of Yles to that integritie which was intendit by our late dear royall father, wherin, thogh hitherto he hath not prevailed, he hath at lenth informed ws of the great care and paines alreadie takin by yow in the same, for which we give yow hartie thanks : And in regard the purpois is of that consequence which may much conduce to the advancement of religion and civilitie in these parts, we ernestlie recommend vnto yow to insist as yow have begun in all actions of that kynd, till the said bischoprik be restored, and speciallie in all such actions which concerne taks whervnto the said bischope hath or doe pretend a lawfull right, which we will accompt as verie acceptable service done vnto ws.—Whythall, 8 De.r 1631.

To the Advocat.

Trustie, &c.—Wheras the restoreing of the bischoprik of Yles to that integritie intended by our late father is a purpois much conduceing to advancement of religion and civilitie in these parts, and being informed that much consisteth in your care and diligence for bringing the same to ane good perfection, Our pleasur is, that ather in our name, or in the name of the said bischop of Ylis, or in both, as it shall seme most expedient vnto him, ye compeir and give your best concurrance in all actions of Law depending or which shallhappin to cum befoir our Colledge of Justice of that kynd, and spetiallie in all such concerning any taks whervnto the said bischop hath or doeth pretend a lawfull right, wherin as yow shall doe vnto ws acceptable service, so we will tak particular notice therof; And being informed of a right which we have to the Yles, as being the antient propertie of our Croun, Our further pleasur is, that at the nixt meitting of the Ilanders befor our Counsall, yow deall with them for restoreing our right in a fair and eqnitable maner; but if yow doe find that they ar not content to goe on therin, that yow informe yourcelff particularlie of our title and right thervnto, and acqnant ws therwith and with your proceidings with them tuitching that purpois, that at our comeing thither we may give such farder ordour therin as we shall find just caus.—Whythall, 8 De' 1631.

To the Counsell.

Right, &c.—Wheras we ar informed that one David Foulls hath against our lawis and contempt of our authoritie committed a ryot in entring violentlie and keiping a house belonging to ane other persone, dispossessing his wyff and children, and manteneing the fact by fortifying the house with muskets and pistolls, for which yow have caused committ him to prissone, becaus the fact is of a dangerous consequence and fitt to be tryed in the most strict and highest degrie according to our Lawis, it being lyklie that the said David hath bene ayded and encouraged thervnto by others : Our spetiall pleasur is, that yow caus try if any persones hath bene anywayes accessorie vnto the same ; and if they be tryed and fund guiltie, that both the said David and they be punisched and censured according to our Lawis, that all others may be terrifeid from attempting the lyk heirefter.—Whythall, 8 De' 1631.

[No Address.]

Wheras we have made choyse of our trustie and weilbeloved Nicolas Briott, our cheiff graver of our Mynt of England, for the coyneing of a certane quantitie of copper coyne presentlie ordeaned by ws and our Counsall to be coyned in the mynt of that our kingdome, for which vse we have expreslie directed him thither : Our pleasur is, yow permitt him to sett vp and establish, in the most convenient place of our said mynt, all engynes and tooles necessarie for that work, and to give vnto him or his deputeis all concurrance and assistance till the said quantitie of copper be fullie coyned.—Whythall, 8 De' 1631.

To the Exchequer.

Right, &c.—Being informed that the escheit and lyfrent of the goods, lands, and others mentioned in a signature which we have signed and sent vnto yow heirwith, which did belong to George Gordoun of Gight, ar now fallin in our handis, and at our gift and disposition, by his being denunced our rebell and remaneing at the horne above yeir and day vnrelaxed ; and being willing, for good considerations knowen vnto ws, to bestow the same vpon Patrik Maule, our servand, Our pleasur is, that yow pas and caus expeid the said signature vnder our privie seill according to the tenour therof and maner accustomed.—Whythall, 9 De' 1631.

To the Counsell.

Right, &c.—Wheras the reverend father in God, and our right trustie and weilbeloved Counsellour, Johne, bishchop of Iles, hath represented vnto ws the great barbaritie vsed amongst the Ilanders of his diocie, and how ther is no ordour amongst them for encreasing ather of religion or civill policie ; And notwithstanding that ther ar Articles condescended vpon tuitching that purpois (none of them, as we ar informed, being observed), yit ther is no punischment inflicted vpon the delinquents : Our pleasur is, that haveing appoynted a day in Aprill or May ensueing, yow call the cheif men amongst them befor yow, and by the advyse of the said bischop that yow vse your best meanes for establisching of religion and governement according to the effect above specifeit ; And if yow find that by that meanes yow cannot effectuat the same, that then yow deteyne them with yow, vntill that we ourselff shall cum to that our kingdome, that we may caus proceid therin as we shall find most requisit : And wheras we wer formerlie pleased to wryt vnto yow for dispensing with the appearance of the Captane of Clauronald vntill the nixt dyet of the Ilanders appoynted to be in the spring of the yeir, intending that the lyk generall course might have bene takin be him as with the rest of the Ilanders, haveing bene since informed by the said reverend father the bischop of Ylis, that aganst our lawis and in contempt of our authoritie a preist was violentlie takin out of his custodie by some persones who did depend vpon the said Captane, for whom he should be answeralde, and besyds that violence was offered to the persone of the said bischop : Our pleasur is, thar be no dispensing with the said Captane's compeirance, bot that yow proceid aganst him as yow find the nature of the offence to requyre.—Whythall, 10 De^r 1631.

To the Lord Chancellour.

Right, &c.—We have bene often importuned by petitions from James Kennedie for taking notice of certane rigorous and vnjust delayingis vsed by sindrie ther aganst him, wherof we, not knowing otherwyse the treuth, have thoght fitt to send this his petition enclosed vnto yow, willing and requyreing yow to call the parteis interessed, and if yow find the informatioun aganst them to be trew, that yow endeavour ane agriement betwixt them ; or otherwyse, to certifie ws how the caice standis, that accordinglie we may know how heirefter to putt off such importuniteis both from our self and yow ; wherin not doubting of your care, &c.—Whythall, 13 De^r 1631.

To the Counsell.

Right, &c.—Wheras vpon our pleasur formerlie signifeid vnto yow tuitching the copper coyne, yow gave ordour for coyneing of fyftene hundreth stone weight of copper vnto farthing tokens of the lyk weight and value as they ar current in this kingdome : Being now informed by our Right, &c. the Viscount of Stirling, our principall Secretarie ther, that diverse of our loveing subjects conceave the division of the penney sterling formerlie vsed to be more convenient for exchange and reckonyng then the new division into four farthings, and that (for avoyding the danger of counterfitting, and for the more exactnesse of the impression) it is thoght fitt to mak the copper money of a greater proportion of weght : Our pleasur is, that the said quantitie of copper be coyned in several spaces of penny, tuo penny, and four penny peices, and that a fyftene part therof be coyned into penneyis weying eight granes the piece (being the weght formerlie allowed by yow to the farthings), and the remanent quantitie be equall division into tuo and four penny pieces of proportionable weght to the penny, causing distinguish them be ther bearing on the one syd the figure or number of ther value vnder ane imperiall Croun with our Inscription, and on the other the Thistle with the vsuall Motto, and that ther be made of the said thrie peices the said quantitie of Copper so ordeaned by yow to have bene coyned in farthings, with what addition yow shall now or heirefter think fitt in regard of the alteration of the weght of the peices, and as the necessitie of the cuntrie shall requyre: Which Coyne we will to have course amongst our subjects for the vse of the poore and change of small commoditeis without any other imposition in the payment of great sowmes ther hath bene formerlie accustomed in the Copper Coyne of that our kingdome, or shall from tyme to tyme seme expedient vnto yow: And in regard of the necessitie of a speedie returne hither for occasion concerneing our service of Nicolas Bryat, our cheiff graver of our Mynt heir, whom we directit thither for Coyneing these moneyis. We speciallie recommend vnto yow that no farder delay be made in putting that work to perfection.—Whythall, 13 Der 1631.

To THE COUNSELL.

Right, &c.—We have sene the Lo; Vchiltrie his petition which yow sent vnto ws, and considering how requisite the conference with the divynes is for him at this tyme, and how necessarie for his affaires the meitting with his wyff or these his freindis on the imployment of that his servant at all occasions may be to him: Our pleasur is, that yow give warrant for these particulars, or for his further ease within the prisone as yow shall think fitt during the dependance of his tryell, according to the tenour of his petition, which we returne yow heirwith: For doeing wherof these presents salbe to yow a sufficient warrant.—Whythall, 28 Der 1631.

To THE THESAURER AND DEPUTIE.

Right, &c.—Wheras diverse good considerations move ws to have a speciall care of what may concerne the estate of our Right, &c. the Duik of Lennox, espetiallie now in his absence, Our pleasur is, and we doe heirby will and Command yow, that yow furthwith mak good and readie payment to his curators, or others for his behaiff, of the pension which we have granted vnto him, yeirlie and termelie, according to the grant gevin therrpon, togidder with the arriers therof (if any be), and that notwithstanding of any warrant or ordour to the Contrarie: And for your soe doeing, &c.—Whythall, 29 Der 1631.

To THE COUNSELL.

Right, &c.—Wheras vpon our pleasur formerlie signifeid vnto yow tuitching the Copper Coyne yow gave ordour for Coyneing fyftene hundreth stane weght of Copper into farthing tokens of the lyk weght and value as they ar current in this our kingdome, being now informed by our right, &c. the Viscount of Stirling, our principall Secretarie ther, that diverse of our loveing subjects conceave the division of the penny sterling, &c. (as is forsaid in the other letter).—[Not dated.]

To THE SESSION.

Right, &c.—We ar informed by our right, &c. the Erle of Annandale that he hath some actions of Law depending befor yow, tuitching one whairof he was to have appeared vpon the eight day of this moneth of Januar for giveing his oath befor yow, bot being deteyned heir by appoyntment of our Privie Counsall of this our kingdome for appearing befor them vpon the twentie-thrid of this moneth, so that he can hardlie keip the said eight day ther, we recommend vnto yow to dispense with his appearance befoir yow till the last day of Februar ensueing, and till that tyme that no further proceiding be in that action concerneing Johne Murray of Brochton, or any other action concerneing the said Erle, becaus (as we ar informed) he hath particular interest therin as necessarlie requyre his owin presence ; bot if at the said last of Februar he shall not appear and caus insist in these actions, We will that yow without further delay proceid therin according to the Lawis of that our kingdome : We bid yow hardlie farwell.—Whythall, 3 Jar 1632.

To the Counsell.

Right, &c.—We wer well pleased to wryt vnto yow of late that our right, &c. the Erle of Roxburgh could not (in regard of occasions concerneing our service) repair to that our kingdome befor the fyftene day of this moneth of Januar, so the verie same occasions being a reasone vnto ws for his further stay, Our pleasur is, that these bussines concerneing him signifeid by our former letter be continewed till the fyftene day of Februar nixt ensueing; And to that effect that yow caus intimat this our pleasur to our Commissioners of Surrenders, and to the Committie appoynted by yow for giveing vp a trew rentall of the Abbacie of Kelso : Which recommending vnto your care, &c.—Whythall, 3 Janr 1632.

To the Counsell.

Right, &c.—We wer pleased some monethis agoe seriouslie to recommend vnto yow the speedie and exact tryell of the burning of the house of Frendraucht, and the death of the Viscount of Melgun, and other gentlmen that wer with him : But being now informed by the Lord Gordoun that, in regard of the publict bussines which continuallie occure vnto yow, yow cannot have convenience so speedelie to goe thrugh that tryell as the haynousnes of this cryme (if any shall be fund) doeth requyre, We therfor have thoght fitt to propone to yow the desyre of the Lord Gordon, which is that a Committie furth of your number should attend without delay to performe that tryell, willing therfor and requyreing yow ather to give present way and ordour for expeiding of a Commission thervpon vnder the great seall of that our kingdome, or otherwayes, that by your owin authoritie yow establisch the lyk Committie in all poynts according to the tenour of the Commission sent yow heirwith ; wherin not doubting of your conformitie to this our pleasur, we bid yow farewell.—Whythall, 9 Jar 1832.

To the Chancellour.

Right, &c.—Being informed of the good and acceptable services done vnto our royall father in the Midle Merchis of these our kingdomes by Harbert Maxwell, whose great aige and absence from thence (his ordinarie residence being within our realme of Irland) requyre our princelie commiseration in what in justice and equitie may concerne him ; we to that prooff being lykwyse informed that he hath a lyfrent right of the Lands of Caverse and Mylne of Prestoun, have, vpon his humble suto for recommending his cause to the Colledge of Justice, thoght it more expedient to wryt vnto yow for dealing with the pairtie interested, for setling of him without trouble in his right, otherwayes, if he be forced to seik it by course of Law, we, for the respects of his said service, aige, and ordinarie absens from that kingdome, doe recommend vnto yow to have a care that justice may be duelie and readelie administred vnto him, according vnto our lawis, in any action belonging vnto him which shallhappin to cum befor that Judicatorie ; which we will tak as acceptable service done vnto ws.—Whythall, 9 Jar 1632.

To the Exchequer.

Right, &c.—Wheras vpon spetiall considerations known vnto ws we have bene pleased to signe a signature in favours of our, &c. the Erle of Morton, our principall thesaurer of that our kingdome, which we have sent yow heirwith : Our pleasur is, that with diligence yow expeid the same, according to the tenour therof : And for your soe doeing, &c.—Whythall, 13 Jar 1632.

To the Commissioners for Surrenders.

Right, &c.—Haveing sene the Overtures which yow sent hither to ws for expeiding the valuations, wherby we perceave your care and affection for the speedie effectuating of our desyres in bringing that great work to ane end, we approve your judgments in the course yow have takin, and in the severall propositions which in these overtures yow have recommended to our consideratioun for the prosecution of the work heirefter, wherfor it is our pleasur that yow goe on to the establisching of the work according to these your propositions in everie severall poynt, and that yow appoynt of such as be of the Committie as hath bene alreadie made choyse of, and to supplie any of ther absences by others as yow shall think expedient, without secludeing any of the Commissioners who can be able to attend, and we doubt not bot the continuance of your care heirin will produce effects answerable to your intentions and our expectation, which we will tak as acceptable service done vnto ws.—Whythall, 13 Jar 1632.

To the Counsell and Eschequer.

Right, &c.—Wheras some Overtures hath bene propounded to ws by Sir Wm Seton, knyt (as we ar informed), to our benefite and the good of our subjects in that our kingdome : Our pleasur is, that yow call him befor yow, and efter consideratioun of his propositions, if yow find them to be such as he affirmeth, that yow give ordour he proceid therin, and to that effect that yow give vnto him all assistance that he can lawfullie demand, or the bussines shall necessarlie requyre ; And becaus he hath bene ane ancient and well deserving servand to our late dear father and ws, that yow pay vnto him, out of the first and readiest of the benefite that shall happin to aryse therby, the arrears of his pension ; ffor doeing of all which these presents shalbe vnto yow and everie of yow a sufficient warrant : We bid, &c.—Whythall, 13 Jar 1632.

To Mr James Hannay.

Trustie, &c.—We have bene informed of the great paines yow have takin, and of the great charges yow have bene at in repairing the Abbay Church of Halyrudhous : And these ar to encourage yow to proceed as yow have begun, assureing yow with all that we will not suffer yow to be a loser any way therby, but will have yow payed for your charge of that work according to the warrant that was formerlie gevin by ws vnto our Exchequer for that purpois, not doubting bot ordour wilbe takin for your payment accordinglie ; and so we bid yow farewell.—From our Court at Whythall, 13 Jar 1632.

To the Counsell.

Right, &c.—Being informed that it would much conduce to the setling of our peace in the Midlchyris that our Commission therof for that our kingdome be executed according to the intent of the same without advocation of any particular proper to be judged by vertew therof to any other our Judicatoreis, vnless yow shall find a necessitie to the contrarie, or a neglect in the Commissioners in putting anything in dew and tymelie execution committed to ther charge : Our pleasur is, that no replegiation be made of any particular incident to that Commission, vnless it be vpon the exceptions aforsaid, and wher any hath bene made, that the particular whervpon it did proceid be remitted bak to that Commission : We bid, &c.— Whythall, 16 Jar 1632.

To the Counsell.

Right, &c.—Wheras vpon your representing to ws the great loss sustened by Captan Robertsome, latelie deceissed, and the contempt offered vnto ws by some Hamburgers, we wer pleased to grant to him and his partiners letters of Reprysall, being now informed of his modest cariage befor his death, in his patiente suffering of his losses, without any violent course takin against any of the Hamburgers, dureing such tyme as yow (out of a respect to that state) had preservyed, and that now both the tyme limited is expyred, and no satisfaction gevin to him befor his death, nor since to his partiners, we ar gratiouslie pleased, vpon humble suto made vnto ws in behalff of Andrew Hensky, Johne Cowan, George Arnot, and other his partiners, and of his widow and children, that yow grant vnto any persone whom they shall mutuallie appoynt for that purpois letters of reprysall of new, according to the trew intent and provisions mentionat in the former, and to that effect that yow give ordour for expeding therof vnder our great seall ; and for your soe doeing these presents shall be vnto yow and our Chancellour, and all others quhom it may concerne, a sufficient warrant and discherge.—Gevin at Whythall, 16 Jar 1632.

To the Counsell.

Right, &c.—Haveing considered of your letter concerneing the Lo' Vehiltrie, and of the process sent therwith, we doe conceive no necessitie of any further direction then was formerlie gevin ; And that it is our pleasur that yow proceid according thervnto in the ordinarie way of Justice for his tryell ; and as for the doubt arysing about the confronting of the said Lord with the Lord of Rea, they wer confronted befor the Committie appoynted by ws for that purpois in all such things as wer thoght fitt to be cleared between them at that tyme ; and if any difference doe aryse in that kynd, wherof ye desyre to be resolved, acquant ws therwith, and ane answer shalbe returned with diligence ; So expecting your diligence for a fair and legall tryell, we bid yow farewell.—Whythall, 16 Jar 1632.

To the Session.

Right, &c.—Haveing, vpoun speciall considerations for the good of our service, directed our Advocat to insist in our name by Law for reduction in a grant procured from ws to Mr William Forbes, late of Cragievar, of certane lands, tythis, and superioriteis holdin of the Abacie of Lundoris, wherin we have at some lenth writtin to our Advocat, to be more particularlie imparted by him vnto yow ; We ar heirby pleased effectuallie to recommend vnto yow the action of reduction of that grante intendit befor yow, that Justice may be speedelie administred therin according to our lawis ; which we will tak as verie acceptable service done vnto ws.—Whythall, 17 Jar 1632.

To the Counsell.

Right, &c.—We have heard of the perplexed Estate wherin the children of Johne Grant, late of Carron, ar left by debts, wherwith ther lands ar burdened, in seiking our lawes against the committers of his slaughter, and by the contraversie in Law betwcen some of ther kinsmen in pretending to be ther tutours, wherby the governement of ther estate hath bene hitherto neglected, so that if ther creditours should at this tyme tak a strict course for sueing for ther whol moneyis, it would altogidder ruinat the estate of the minors, and leave them in a miserable condition : And wheras we ar informed that ther narrest kinsmen doeth offer to pay yeirlie to ther creditours ther annualrents, and to give sufficient securitie to pay vnto them, within a few number of yeires, ther principall sownes ; which offers seameing vnto ws to be reasonable, and the consideration of the vutymelie death of the father and the present estate of the children, being, as we ar informed, infants of four yeres or therabout of aige, moveing in ws a princelie compassion towards them in so far as it is agreeable to Law and equitie, we ar heirby pleased to recommend ther cans vnto yow ; and to that effect to call the creditours befor yow and propound vnto them the saids offers, wherof if they will not accept, we requyre yow to certifie ws thairof, togidder with your opinions how far we may cause proceid according to equitie and the lawis of that our kingdome, for the good of the saids minors, without prejudice to the creditours.—Whythall, 17 Ja' 1632.

To the Advocat.

Right, &c.—Wheras, vpon severall informations made vnto ws by some of our subjects haveing lands and tythis of the Abbacie of Lundoris, and vpon your opinion in Law, certifeid (as we ar informed) to the Commissioners of Exchequer, of the vnlawfulnes of a grant of the heretable offices, superioriteis, and others mentionat therin, procured by William Forbes, late of Cragievar, wherof not onlie we in our right, but these vassalls, wer lyklie to have bene exceedinglie prejudged, we wer pleased to requyre yow to reduce the said grant in our name ; wherupon a submission being offered vnto ws by Sir William Forbes, his sone, whairof we would not accept beaus of the reservations and provisions therin, We did wryt vnto some of that Commission and your self for composeing the differences betuixt him and the vassalls tuitching things to be performed by each pairtie to other, and the benefite that might therby aryse vnto ws ; otherwyse to certifie vnto ws the reasones and your opinions therin : Notwithstanding (without answer returned) we are now informed by James Chalmers, phisician in Ordinarie to ws, and our dearest sone the Prince, that vpon the said Sir William his preferring of a new signature to our Exchequer, wherby, to wrong ws and the saids vassalls, some of them have bene moved to compone and agrie onlie with the said Sir William for new grants, and that such of them as would not bot stand our right have bene forced at severall tymes to cum from ther duellings to Edinburgh, wher, never being called vpon by the said Sir William, they have returned, to ther great prejudice : Our speciall pleasur is, and we doe heirby command yow, that without further delay yow proceid and prosecute the reduction of the grant procured by his said father, and that according to our lawis, as yow will tender the good of our service ; and that in all other things concerneing that purpois yow carefullie advert that nothing be done therin that may anywayes prejudge ws in our right, and to that effect that yow acquant the Lords of our session and Exchequer with our pleasur heirin. —Whythall, 17 Ja' 1632.

To the Counsell.

Right, &c.—Wheras we ar informed that yow have of late appoynted the 19 of this moneth for the compeirance of all those that ar interested in the estate of the Erldome of Bothwell, to hear your proceidings concerneing the rentalls of the said Erldome ; Sieing our right, &c. the Erle of Buccleuch cannot repair to that our kingdome, for considerations knowen to ws, at the day preseryved by yow, Our pleasur is, that what may concerne the said Erle in the tryell in the rentalls of the said Erldome of Bothwell yow contenew the same vntill the 15 of Februar ensueing, and to that effect that yow caus intimat this our pleasur to such persones as yow shall find it may concerne : Which recommending vnto your care, we bid, &c.—Whythall, the 17 Ja' 1632.

To the Thesaurer Depute.

Right, &c.—Wheras, for the recoverie of the losses, both of tyme and meanes, susteaned by the Reverend father in God the Bischop of the Yles in prosecuting that charge conferred vpon him by ws, We were pleased to grant vnto him a precept of 600^{lib} sterling, togidder with a pension of 300^{lib} sterling, till the temporall estate of that bischoprik wer fullie restored, wherof (as we ar informed) he hath not as yit receaved any payment, wherby he is lyklie to be troubled by his Creditours, to whom he standeth engadged for moneyis borrowed by him for that service; least the charges in that function (it being of all others of that kynd in that our kingdome the most troublesome, and most necessarie to be executed) should be deserted for want of meanes, espetiallie sicing our late royall father and ourself hath takin so great paines for establisching therof, as a purpois so much conduceing to the good and quyet of these parts, and setling of religion ther, and that it concerneth ws in honour not to sie him suffer, by relyeing vpon what we had vpon so good considerations intended for him: Our pleasur is, and we doe heirby will and command yow, that furth with yow pay vnto him, or such of his creditours as he shall assigne vnto yow, the said pension, with the arreirs of the same, Togidder with the moneyis of the said precept, according to the intent thairof, and that notwithstanding of any former warrant or restraynt, for whatsoever caus or occasion gevin, to the contrair: And for your soe doing these presents shalbe vnto yow and everie of yow a sufficient [warrant] and discharge.—20 of Ja^r 1632.

C. Rex., subscripsit Fiat.

Our Soveraigne Lord, considering That King James the Fourt, of worthie memorie, did by advyse of Parliament speciallie discharg, vnder the pane of punishment as reatf, that no persones should presume to exact or tak, vnder the name of Caulps, the best aucht, whither it war ox, cow, horse, or mare, from any of his subjects of the kingdome of Scotland, which was ratifeid by his Ma^{teis} late royall father and estats of Parliament in his tyme; And his Matie considering that the abuse is most barbarous and not to be suffered in any civill kingdome, and without putting these laudable acts in executioun the abuse can hardlie be rectifeid, And how it is necessar that a sufficient and able persone be made choyse of for prosecuting of that his Ma^{teis} service; Therfor his Matie, with speciall advyse and consent of his Ma^{teis} Right, &c. the Erle of Morton, and of his Ma^{teis} weilbeloved Counsellour Johne, Lord Stewart of Traquair, his Ma^{teis} deputie thesaurer in that kingdom, and of the remanent of the Commissioners of the Exchequer thairof, Ordeanes a Commission to be made and exped vnder his highnes' great seall ther, Giveing full power and commission to his Ma^{teis} trustie and weilbeloved Captan William Campbell and his deputts, for whome he is to be answerable, To search and try out, dureing the space of fyve yeires, all such persones who have in ther tymes (allanerlie) transgressed the said Act of Parliament in exacting or taking vnder the name of Caulps the best aucht, whither it wer ox or horse, mare or cow, from any of his Ma^{teis} subjects; And doe herely grant vnto the said Captan William and his forsaids, dureing the saids yeires, full power and authoritie to call and cite the saidis transgressours befoir whatsumever judges or judicatorie competent, and therby the speciall assistance and concurrance of his Majestie's Advocat for the tyme to question and accuse them or any of them according to the decrees and sentences which shall happin to be pronounced by the saids judges, with speciall command to his Ma^{teis} said Advocat to compeir and concure to that effect; with power to the said Captan Williame and his forsaids to compone, transact, and agrie with such of the transgressours as shalhappin to acknowledge ther faults therin, and be willing to give composition for the same to his Ma^{teis} vse, wherof the one half to be receaved by the said Captan William and his forsaids, and made accompt of by them to his Ma^{teis} principall thesaurer, and the other half to be deteyned by the said Captan and his forsaids to ther owin vse as ther propper goods for the paynes and charges vndergone and expended be them in that service, and that the acquittances and discherges to be gevin by him to them shalbe a sufficient discharge and exoneratioun to the saids transgressours or any of them in all tyme enueing for the saids abuses formerlie committed be them, or otherwyse, that a certificat vnder the said Captane or his forsaids hands shalbe as sufficient to the keeper of the great seall and writter thervnto for making and expeeding to all the saids transgressours, or any of them, generall or particular pardones or remissiones, as they shall best condescend vpon for ther being discherged of the saids facts and abusses so committed by them or any of them at any tyme preceiding; With speciall command and direction lykwyse to the Lords of his Maᵗⁱˢ Privie Counsall to give out from tyme to tyme, during the saids yeires, letters and charges for strenthning of the said Captane and his forsaidis to putt the said service and acts of parliament in Execution in maner as is above exprest; And to that effect to command (if neid beis) the schirreffis of the pairts, wher the saidis transgressours doe remane, or shall for the tyme, to apprehend and present them to Justice in caice of ther dissobedience to transact in a fayr maner with the said Captane or his forsaids; And his Maᵗⁱᵉ ordeanes thir presents to be a sufficient warrant to the keeper of the great seall and wryter thervnto for wryting heirof for the said seall, and appending the great seall therto.—Whythall, 23 Jaʳ 1632.

May it pleas your most sacred Maᵗⁱᵉ—

Your Maᵗⁱᵉ doeth heirby constitute Mʳ Robert Lyndsay, sone of Bernard Lyndsay, deceised, during his lyff, your Maᵗⁱˢ searcher and taker of schipps and goods to be imported or exported at the portes of Leith and Newhaven and Mylheaven, with all feyis and priviledges belonging to that office, as his said father or as his brother Bernard Lyndsay, younger, had the same, which office the said Bernard, younger, in regards of his service in the warres with the Marqueis of Hamilton, hath disponed to his said brother Mʳ Robert.—Whythall,   1632.

To the Counsell.

Right, &c.—Wheras we have bene petitioned by Andrew Fethie to have libertie to goe to that our kingdome, that by him self and Lawers he may be heard in judgment for causes in Law conccrneing his aged parents, becaus ther estate requyreth ane princelie compassion, his father (as we ar informed) being blind, and his mother a criple, haveing litle or no meanes, we have thoght fitt to remitt the consideratioun of the enclosed petition vnto yow, if at the sight of the right reverend father in God, and our trustie and weilbelovit Counsellour, the Archbischop of Sᵗ Androis, the petitioner shall cum himself modestlie, without giveing scandale to the professed religion, we requyre yow to grant vnto him what tyme and libertie shalbe requisit for following his saids parents' actions and his owin, and to that effect that yow signifie our pleasur heirin to our Colledge of Justice: We bid yow hartlie farewell.—Whythall, 28 Jaʳ 1632.

To the Archbischop of Glasgow.

Right, &c.—Wheras Doctour Whytfurd, our Chaplane, who hath deserved verie well of ws, is to remove from his Church at Moffat: And we being desyreous to sie that place well provydit againe, have made speciall choyse of ane for that purpois, wherin we have signifeid our pleasur to the right reverend the Archbischop of Sᵗ Androis: These ar to desyre yow to admit of the man whom he from ws shall nominat to succeid in place of the said Doctour, and we will esteme the same as verie acceptable service done vnto ws.—Whythall, 28 Jaʳ 1632.

To the Clergie.

Right, &c.—Your greevances being represented vnto ws by the right, &c. Archbischop of St Androis, and by the right, &c. bischop of Murray, efter diverse conferences haveing fullie considered therof, we have accordinglie gevin ordour for provyding of the remedie, and for preventing inconveniences heirefter, wherof we doubt not bot the Committie made choyse out of the Commissioners for surrenders for the more speedie dispatch of such affaires will have a speciall care; and we doe heirby earnestlie requyre yow to give your best assistance heirin that no delay be in your fault, And be assured that we will no way lett the Church suffer therby, bot will have a care of that which is hir due, being ever willing, wher ther is reasone and meanes to doe the same, rather to augment nor diminisch your benefite: And soe, as yow would have ws to doe for yow expecting your best endeavours for the speedie accomplisching of that good work, We bid, &c.—Whythall, 28 Ja^r 1632.

To the Counsell.

Right, &c.—Being informed that vpon some consideratiounes we wer pleased not long since to grant a protection to Sir Johne Leslie of Wardess, and a certane number of his cautioners, from being troubled by ther creditours for some schort tyme, and hearing that a number of the said Sir Johne Leslie his cautioners wer omitted in the said protection, wherby ther estats ar lyklie to be seized vpon, We have thoght fitt for ther better ease to recommend speciallie vnto yow that these cautioners omitted, whois names shall be gevin vp to yow, performeing to the creditours such things as ar mentioned in the said protection, the lyk in all respects be granted vnto them, and that the same be immediatlie exped (without further trouble to ws) vnder our great seall for which these presents shalbe vnto yow, our Chancellour, and others whom it may concerne, a sufficient warrant.—Whythall, 28 Ja^r 1632.

To the Bischop of Carlile.

Reverend father in God, &c.—We wer formerlie pleased to wryt vnto yow in a particular tuitching our servant Sir Ritchart Grhame, kny^t and baronet, and the persone of Bewcastle, wherin we ar informed that yow have vsed your best endeavours to obey our directions, for which we give yow hartie thanks: But hearing since that some lett hath bene in the prosecution therof, contrairie to our royall intention, by wanting of our further warranting of yow to that purpois, Our speciall pleasur is, and we will heirby command yow, furthwith to proceid in that particular according to our former direction signifeid by our letter; and for your more absolute warrant for what yow doe in that particular, and what is fitt to be done in caices of the lyk kynd, yow shall schortlie receave our further warrant for authorising of yow, wherin be confident that we shall not be anywayes wanting as occasion shall fitlie requyre to encourage your proceidings.—Whythall, 2 Feb^r 1632.

To the Exchequer.

Right, &c.—Wheras we ar informed by a certificat from our Counsell that, according to the vndertaking of our servant Edward Kellie, he hath performed all thingis necessarie for the vse of our Chappell royall, against our comeing to that our kingdome, and doeth vndertak to continew that service therin in lyk due and ordourlie maner in all tyme heirefter, and to have alwyse in readines sufficient Musick for our Coronation, and all other Church musick necessarie: To the effect the musitianes and others belonging to that Chapell be manteaned, with the rents belonging thervnto, and our Exchequer disburdened of the present allowance of 3000 merkis scotts yeirlie, payable to them for ther mantenance till they be provyded. We ar pleased to send vnto yow the signature heirwith enclosed conceaved in favours of the said Edward for the vse of our Chappell ; and haveing called vpon yow the reverend father in God, and our trustie and weilbeloved Counsellour, the bischop of Dumblane, the deane thairof, and haveing pervsed the said signature, if yow find no thing therin that doeth prejudge ws, Our pleasure is, that yow furth with exped the same vnder our Cachet and great seall ; and for your soe doeing these presents shalbe vnto our Chancellour and other whom it may concerne a sufficient warrant and discherge : And that yow assist our said servant in all things for the furtherance of that service, which we will tak as acceptable service done vnto ws.— Whythall, 2 Febr 1632.

To the Commissioners of Parliament.

Right, &c.—Wheras of late our Parliament was prorogated by yow according to our royall direction till such a day as we thoght fitt we could have been ther ourself in persone : And now considering we can not be ther at that tyme, and yit being vnwilling to be absent from our said parliament, and desyreous to receave our Croun in persone, and to setle all bussines ther if our affaires convenientlie permitt ws to repair thither as we earnestlie desyre : Our pleasur is, and we doe heirby authorize, will, and requyre yow to cause fense our said Court of parliament by vertew of our Commission granted vnto yow to be to prorogat or continew the said parliament agane to the 13 of August nixtocum, with continuatioun of dayes, that we may have tyme to setle our affaires heir, befor we begin our journey towardis that our ancient kingdome : And for your soe doeing these presents shalbe your sufficient warrant.—Whythall, 9 Febr 1632.

To the Counsell.

A Letter conforme to the preceilling letter that was writtin vnto the Counsell concerneing the prorogating of the parliament was writtin the 9 Febr 1632, at Whythall, that it may be continewed to the 13 of August nixt ensueing.—9 Febr 1632.

To the Session.

Right, &c.—Wheras we wer informed that ther ar some actions in Law betwixt our Toun of Edinburgh and the Inhabitants of Leith, presentlie depending befor yow, in regard our said burgh is to give speciall attendance in our service at our home comeing, God willing, this yeir to that our kingdome : We ar pleased to recommend vnto yow in a serious maner that speedie justice be administred in all such actions in soe far as yow shall find agreeable to justice and the Lawis of that our kingdome, without delay therin : So not doubting of your care in that, we bid, &c.—Whythall, 9 Febr 1632.

To the Session.

Right, &c.—Wheras we ar informed that ther ar several actions in Law to cum in befor yow for preservatioun of the rights and priviledges of our frie royall burgh of that our kingdome, and for rectifieing, according to Justice and the lawis therof, such abuses wherof we ar informed diverse burghes of baronie have vsed against them, by encroaching vpon ther ancient priviledges and liberteis : Sieing that they of all other the burghes of that kingdome ar onlie lyable to the payment of our taxatiouns and have voit in parliament : And that they have gevin reall prooff, both in the tyme of our late royall father and our owin,

H   X

of ther affection to our service : And to the effect they may the more readelie and convenientlie attend vpon the same now at our comeing to that our kingdome which we intend this yeir, We ar heirby pleased in a particular maner to recommend vnto your serious care that speedie justice be administred in all such actiones that may tend to the reformatioun of these abuses committed by the saidis brughs of baronie, or which otherwayes may concerne our said frie burgh, in so far as yow sall find agrieable to justice and lawis of that our kingdome, And that they be not frustrat or delayed heirin; which lykwyse we recommend to your care, and bid yow fairwell.—Whythall, 9 Febr 1632.

To the Counsall.

Right, &c.—Wheras we formerlie wryt vnto yow tuiching Our burgh of Edinburgh, that thay might enjoy ther priviledges and liberteis according to the Chartour granted to and confirmed by diverse of our royall progenitours, and conforme to the severall acts of parliament made thervpon, and being willing in our tyme to approve what vpon so warrantable grounds hath bene granted vnto them : And haveing therwith considered the reall prooffs they have gevin, both in tyme of our late royall father and our owin, for advanceing our service recommended vnto them : We doe heirby speciallie recommend vnto yow that in all such causes concerneing ther rights and priviledges as cum befoir yow, they may have ordour gevin for setling therof as our Lawes doe allow, with all convenient expedition, and in all things of that nature that ar judged befoir our Colledge of Justice, or any other Judge compitent, that yow vse your authoritie in so far as the nature of the caus shall requyre for putting of the same in execution, that they may frielie enjoy the saidis rights in the accustomed maner according to our pleasur formerlie signifeid to that purpois.—Whythall, 9 Febr 1632.

To the Counsell.

Right, &c.—Being informed of the great abuses committed in the Torwood, by cutting of trees and killing of the deir and otherwayes, and being verie desyreous that a strict course may be takin for the better preservation therof thereafter : It is our pleasur that yow grant a Commission, with full power to the keeper thairof to persew according to the lawes of that our kingdome all such delinquents, as weill for our part as for his owin : And that yow be readie to give him your best assistance in the said persute, wheresoever it shalbe desyred of yow, as lykwyse that yow tak him strictlie bund for the keeping therof in tyme comeing; and in consideratioun of the Charges he is to be at, that yow delyver vnto him all fynes to be takin for the tyme bygone for his owin vse : And for your soe, &c.—Whythall, 9 Feb. 1632.

To the Counsell.

Right, &c.—Wheras we had determined to repair to that our ancient kingdome this nixt somer, which, as we had of a long tyme extreamelie desyred, soe we had at the said tyme most certanelie resolved so to doe : Bot now in regard of some late consideratiouns speciallie concerneing forrayne affaires, the estate wherof is sufficientlie knowen to be verie considerable at this tyme ; And we ar induced to continew our comeing till the nixt yeir, at which tyme, God willing, we shall not faill to cum ; And for that effect we have presentlie to goe : And as for our parliament ther, We have sent yow warrant heirwith to prorogat the same till the 13 of August nixt, that it may be prorogat from that tyme till the certane tyme that we ar to repair thither, vnless yow shall think it more fitt to prorogat it presentlie at the first till the said tyme : And in that caice we will and doe authorize our Commissioners for the parliament heirby to prorogat the same to the eightene day of Junij the nixt yeir, bot remitting the doeing of the one and the other as yow shall think most fitt.—[Not dated.]

To the Chancellour.

Right, &c.—We ar informed from Mr Nathaniell Edward that he is confident of a way for improveing the bussines of Salt, both to the generall good of our kingdomes and our particular benefite, without any greevance to the subjects, which way he is desyreous to approve first ther, and to your hearing; We therfore have thoght fitt to will and requyre yow to tak the joynt assistance of the Lord Privie Seall and Thesaurer deputie, and call the said informer and some of the cheif Salt makers befor yow, to hear and consider of such propositions as he shall mak to them and ther answers, and to returne to ws your opinion of both that we may therefter resolve how far it may be fitt for ws to proceid therin : So not doubting of your carefull diligence heirin : We bid, &c.—Whythall, 18 Febr 1632.

To the Counsell.

Right, &c.—We doe send yow heirin enclosed two crosse petitions, the one conteyning a charge of so barbarous oppression of the poore, and the other so fair a profession of Innocencie, as doe justlie deserve ane exact tryell and exemplarie punischment of the delinquent : And becaus we can hardlie believe that any gentlman would so far wrong himself ather to committ such a ryot or haveing done it so confidentlie to plead innocencie ; Nor on the other part that so meane ane accuser durst without great ground of treuth appeall to our justice, and knowinglie incurreth punischment due to so bold and malicious detractions : We therfor have thoght fitt to recommend to yow the tryell of both, and the repairing or punischment of ather as yow in justice shall find caus, willing and requyreing yow to give vnto the complener your protection against the horning as he alledgeth vnjustlie led against him, and that for such competent tyme as yow in your wisdomes shall think fitt; wherin not doubting of your carefullnes and conformitie to this our pleasur. —Whythall, 18 Febr 1632.

Charles, by the grace of God, &c.—To our right trustie and weilbeloved Cousen and Counsellour the Erle of Morton, Thesaurer of our kingdome of Scotland, the Erle of Stratherne, President of our privie Counsall, the Viscount of Stirling, our principall Secretarie of our said kingdome, greeting : Wheras we have bene pleased by our letter of gift vnder our privie seall of our said kingdome, bearing the date the 9 of Decr 1630, To constitute Mr Walter Neish our Isher of our Excheker ther : Our pleasur therfor is, and we doe heirby will, requyre, and desyre yow and everie of yow, joyntlie and severallie, to tak the said Mr Walter, sworne by his oath de fideli administratione officii in our said service, and admitt him to be our actuall servand in the said office, and for that effect that yow choyse a Clerk or notter, whome we doe heirby authorise and ordeane to Extract and delyver to the said Mr Walter authentik acts and instruments in the premisses, and for your soe doeing here in England we dispense with the place : And these presents shallbe vnto yow and everie of yow, as vnto the said Clerk or notter and the said Mr Walter, a sufficient warrant and Commission.—Whythall, 19 Febr 1632.

To the Exchequer

Right, &c.—Wheras we send heirwith inclosed vnto yow a signature of Ten thowsand pund sterling in favours of our Right, &c. the Lord Viscount of Stirling, to be past and expedd by yow vnder our great Seall, least any mistaking should ensue thervpon, we have thoght it good to declare vnto yow that (as it may appear by itself) it is nowayes for quyting the title, ryght, or possession of New Scotland, or of any part therof, bot onlie for satisfaction of the losses that the said Viscount hath, by giveing ordour for removeing of his Colony at our express command, for performeing of ane Article of the Treatie betuixt the French and ws, and we ar so far from abandoneing of that bussines as we doe heirby requyre yow and everie ane of yow to affoord your best help and encouragement for furthering of the same, cheiflie in perswading such to be baronets as ar in qualitie fitt for that dignitie, and come befor yow to seik for favour from ws, bot remitting the maner to your owin judgment, and expecting your best endeavours heirin, willing thir presents to be insert in your books of Excheker and ane Act made thervpon : We bid, &c.—Whythall, 19 Feb^r 1632.

To the Counsell.

Right, &c.—Being informed that Sir William Ker of Blaikhop, kny^t, brother to the late Erle of Lothian, taketh vpon him the title of the Erle of Lowthiane without our licence or authoritie, or without proceiding [by] course of Law to defate the right of his said brother's eldest daughter and hir husband, who have proceidit more ordourlie in the right of the said Erle by the letters patent grantit vnto him by our late royall father, which we have sene and considered, and have proceidit therin as we thoght just and fitt : Our pleasur is, that yow call the said Sir William befoir yow, and haveing reprehended him for taking vpon him the said title without warrant from ws, that yow charge him in our name that he presume not heirefter to tak vpon him any title of nobilitie which did belong to his said brother, or to tak any place or prerogative therby without our licence, requyreing yow to mak this knowen in such sort at the Counsell boord, that if he absent himselff it may come to his knowledge, and that yow cause mak ane Act of Counsell for discharging him, his sone and successours, and his brethren and ther Children, to vse any of the titles belonging to the said late Erle, without the said Sir William doe insist by due course of law evict the same as justlie belonging to him, that our subjects may be warnit not to give to him or any of them such title heirefter, bot vnto such vpon whom by our letters patents we have conferred the same.—Whythall, 19 Feb^r 1632.

To Doctour Whytfoord.

Trust, &c.—Wheras we and our father, of blissed memorie, wer gratiouslie pleased to wryt to our Chancellour and the Archbischop of Glasgow that in the action depending befoir our Colledge of Justice betuixt the Lord Boyd and Sir James Cleland, kny^t, nothing should be determined to the prejudice of our right, &c. the Lord Blantyre, till his taks of Monkland and Calder wer ratifeid : And though of late we wer lykwyse pleased to wryt in your favours to the said Colledge that justice might be administred vnto yow with all convenient diligence, for your interest in that bussines, yit we wer so far from thinking that your ends wer then to question the said Lord his taks, that we beleived yow had gevin him satisfaction befor that tyme theranent : Our pleasur is, that as yow tender our service, yow proceid no longer in such rigorous course with him as yow have done heirtofoir, bot that yow tak such a course for his satisfaction heirin, that we may not be farther troubled heirwith : And so much the rather becaus we ar informed he did contribute his best endeavours for your setling ther : And with all (he reasone that yow have engadged yourselff by promeis vnto him for ratifieing of the saidis taks) not doubting of his conformitie to this our pleasur, &c.—Quhythall, 19 Feb^r 1632.

To the Advocat.

Trustie, &c.—Wheras our right, &c. the Lord of Lowden hath, according to the generall course intended by our Commission for surrenders, and by a particular Contract between ws and him, surrendred in our favours his heretable offices of his schirrefship of Air, regalitie and Justiciarie of Kylsmure and

Barmure, with the superioriteis and few-dewteis thairof, we, for performance of a part of that contract, ar pleased to secure him of all such lands whairof he or his predicessours have, according to the lawis of that our kingdome, acquyred the right of propertie : Our pleasur is, that yow pervse the Contract and what is to be performed on our part for secureing these lands to him, his aires-maile, and assigneyis, that furth with, by advyse of our theasurer and deputie, draw vp from ws in his and ther favours a signature of the same, to be exped vnder our Cachet and great seall ther, and that yow express therin these landis by ther severall and accustomed names : ffor doeing of all which these presents shalbe vnto yow, and other officers whom it doeth concerne, a sufficient warrant : We bid yow farewell.—Whythall, 19 Febr 1632.

To the Exchequer.

Right, &c.—Wheras we ar informed that the tennents of Kylsmure and Barmure ar lyk to suffer by the reasone of the not performeing of our part of that contract betweene ws and the Lord Lowden, they haveing payed, as we ar informed, these moneyis to our Exchequer which, for our advantage in that bargane, was condescendit vpon between them and the Viscount of Stirling, our Secretarie, and that ther estates, vpon dependence of performeing that contract, rests vnsecured, wherwith being willing that a course be takin for ther satisfaction and disburdening of ws of any obligation in that kynd : Our pleasur is, vpon performance of such things agreid vpon to be done vnto ws by the Lord Lowden, that at your and our Advocat's sight yow tak some present and convenient course for his satisfaction of the moneys, principall and annual-rent, due vnto him by the said contract, otherwyse that yow secure him for the same in such maner as yow and he can best condescend : And in the meane tyme that no signature of any of these landis be exped in Exchequer in favours of any persone, be resignatioun, confirmatioun, or other-wayes, till these moneyis be fullie payed vnto him : And for your soe doeing, &c.—Whythall, 19 Febr 1632.

To the Advocat.

Trustie, &c.—Wheras our right, &c. the Lord Colvill, out of the affection he caryeth to our service, hath made offer frielie to resigne in our favours his right and title to the Abbacie of Culrois, and all things belonging thervnto, referring himselff to our Royall discretion for his satisfaction, wherof we will not be vnmyndfull when any fitt occasion shall offer, wher we may convenientlie gratifie him for the samyne : Therfor our pleasur is, that yow draw vp such writts as may fullie secure ws of the said Abbacie, and all other things belonging thervnto ; And that thervpon yow immediatlie signifie vnto the Commissioners of our Exchequer that it is our express pleasur that it be discharged of the blensch dewteis due vnto ws of the said Abbacie for the tyme bygane ; and for your soe doeing, &c.—Whythall, 19 Febr 1632.

To the Counsell.

Right, &c.—Being informed of the skill of our trustie and weillbeloved John Balmer in the tryell of Mineralls, and of his desyre to mak some experiment thairof in finding of gold mettall in Crawfurdmure, according as his father had done formerlie in the same place ; and we being willing to encourage him, Our pleasur is, that yow grant vnto him such a licence to that effect as yow shall find to be fitt, otherwyse (if he shall think expedient) that yow licence him or aney in his name to transport from thence such quantitie of the earth or gravell wherin the said goldin mettall is vsuallie to be fund as he for making of experi-ments shall demand of yow.—Whythall, 19 Febr 1632.

To the Counsell.

Right, &c.— The enclosed petition haveing bene exhibited vnto ws in behalff of the petitioner, wherby, conceaveing his demand to be verie reasonable, and in respect of his aige and intirmitie of bodie to repayre our princelie commiseratioun, Our pleasur is, that furthwith yow grant vnto him licence to repair vnto his sone, or otherwayes, if yow think the indisposition of his bodie will not permitt him to travell to the part wher his sone is, that vpon conditions accustomed to be takin in the lyk caces yow confyne him, by the advyse of the reverend, &c. the Archbischop of St Androis, to such a place within that our kingdome wher he may most convenientlie enjoy the meanes alloted vnto him : Which recommending, &c.— Whythall, 19 Feb^r 1632.

These conteyne ane Ratificatioun of certane Chartours granted by your Maties predicessours, of worthie memorie, of the burgh of Lanark, and common landis perteueing thairto, And of the office of heretable schirreffschip of the said burgh ; Togidder with ane new gift of the said burgh, and of the common landis thairof, within certane boundis, meithis, and merchis expressit in the signatur, and of the said heretable office of schirrefschip ; And of the altarages and chaplanreis situat within the said burgh, with the right of patronage of the samyne, with certane frie landis, whairof they ar in possession : To be holden of your Matie, and of your highnes' successours, for payment of the sowme of sex merks sterling as for the old burrow maile, with the sowme of tuo merks vsuall money of Scotland for the saids frelands and alterages in name of few-ferme.—Whythall, 20 Feb^{rie} 1632.

These conteyneth a Ratificatioun to the brugh of Bruntyland of the liberteis and priviledges of ther brugh, with a new gift therof, Port and heaven of the same, within the bounds above designed ; with power of Watter Courts, fayris, and mercatts, and other priviledges perteneing to a frie burgh ; to be holdin of your Matie in frie burgage for payment of the old common maill.—Whythall, 20 Feb^{ry} 1632.

These ratifie vnto Mr Alex^r Hay, one of the ordiner Clerks of Session, during his lyftyme, all former warrandis granted by your Matie for his imployment in your Ma^{tris} affaires of session insident to the office of a clerk, and for registring all your Ma^{tris} writts necessarie to be registrat in the books of counsall and session or sederunt. His fie is flourtie pund sterling, according to a former right vnder the privie seall. These conteyneing your Maties grant vnto him of new of the said Office, and so dischergeing all other persones to medle in that imployment dureing his said tyme.—Whythall, 20 Feb^{ry} 1632.

To the Session.

Right, &c.—Wheras our right trustie, &c. the Erle of Annandale hath informed ws that in respect of his affaires heir he cannot convenientlie repair this moneth to that our kingdome, therfor humblie desyreth that ather a commission may be sent hither by yow (as is ordinarie in the lyk caces) for tak[ing] of his oath heir in ane action of law concerneing him, or to allow vnto him the last day of the nixt moneth for his appeirance befor yow, for which tyme he vndertaketh ather to mak his said appeirance, or be content to lose his action : We recommend to your consideratioun to mak choyse of the best expedient of these his propositions, and as yow desyre to proceed accordinglie therin with as much conveniencie as may be.— Whythall, 20 Feb^r 1632.

To the Exchequer.

Right, &c.—Wheras we have bene pleased to signe the enclosed signature conteyning ane ratificatioun of certane chartours granted by our predecessours of worthie memorie of the Burgh of Lanark and Common Landis perteneing therto, and other thingis mentioned in the said signature: Our will and pleasur is, if yow find the same fitt and laufull to be granted, and that ther is nothing therin that directlie or by the consequence can be prejudiciall vnto ws in the late course intended by ws for our owin and publict good, that with all diligence yow pass and exped it according to the tenour therof : And for your soe doeing.— Whythall, 20 Feb^r 1632.

Direction.

To the most mightie and right noble Prince, The Great Lord Emperour, and great Duik Michaell Theodor, M^rch of all Russia, sole commander of Volodemour, Muskoe, and Novogarod king of Cazan, king of Astroan, king of Sibra, Lord of Wolskey, great duik of Somalskey, Tueskley, Vgurskey, Parmiskey, Watskey, Bolgaskey, and of other countreyis, Lord and Great Duik of Honogored, in the Lower Countreyis of Cheringo, Rozan, Polotzkey, Rostone, Yaras, Lanskey, Belozeiskey, Leuslandskey, Yondeskey, Obdloiskey, Condinskey, and of all the northerne parts Lord and Commander, Lord of the Cuntrie of Hyverskey, Cartalinskey, and Gruzinskey, king of the cuntrie of Cabeydlinskey and Cherehaskey, and of the Daikdomes of Igviskey, with many other kingdomes, Lord and Commander.

Charles, be the Grace of God, King, &c., To the Most high, mightie, and right noble Prince, The Great Lord Emperour and Great Duik Michaell Pheodor, M^rch of All Russia, sole Commander of Volodomer, Moskoe, Novogarod, King of Cazan, king of Astroan, King of Siberia, Lord of Volskey, and great Duik of Smoleskey, Tueskey, Vgorskey, Parmskey, Vatskey, Bolgaskey, and of the other cuntreyis ; Lord and Great Duik of Novogored in the Lower Cuntreyis, of Cheringo, Rezan, Polotzkey, Rostone, Yares, Lanskey, Belozeiskey, Leuslandskey, Yondeskey, Obdloiskey, Condinskey, And of all the northerne parts Lord and Commander ; Lord of the Cuntrey of Hyverskey, Cartalinskey, and Gruzinskey ; king of the cuntrey of Cabeydinskey and Cherehaskey, and of the Duikdomes of Igviskey, with many other kingdomes, Lord and Commander, Greeting.—Most Excellent Prince, and dear brother and freind, We have sene and pervsed your imperiall Letters of Commission and credance that your Matie, our dear brother, hath gevin to your Ma^teis Generall Major Sir Alex^r Leslie, one of our faythfull subjects of our kingdome of Scotland, of noble and illustrous descent ; Which letteris thrughout all our dominions, according to our imperiall requeist, shalbe in all brotherlie requeist observed and performed : And that so much the more becaus your Emperiall affection hath bene most enclyned to have our faythfull subjects' armes and valoris imployed in your Ma^teis warres, And in consideration thairof hath made our said subject Sir Alexander Leslie Major Generall of your Ma^teis warlyk forces, which preferment is by ws most kyndlie accepted and greatlie esteamed, in preferring one of our Scotts subjects to such high dignitie, assureing your Matie (our dear brother) from ws that ther is no subject in our dominions, who ar willing to serve your Matie in the qualitie of commander or souldier, bot we will give them our frie leave, consent, and libertie to serve your Matie, which we have [thought] good to certifie vnto your highnes by these our letteris, not doubting bot your Matie will at our requeist continew towarts your Ma^teis servants our subjects all perfection and promotion ; Whom we desyre your Matie will continew as yow have begun to advance him, as lykwyse to performe vnto him, and all others our subjects vnder your Ma^teis Command, as ar mentionat in your Ma^teis imperiall Commission and letteris of Credence gevin vnto him : Moreover, we have, in regard of your Emperiall Commission gevin to your Ma^teis Generall,

Sir Alexander Leslie, granted libertie vnto our faythfull subject Captan David Leslie for to returne him selff vnto your Matie emperiall court ther, to attend your Matie service, of whois wisdome, valour, and faythfulnes we have thoght good to certifie your Matie, as descendit from noble, illustrious, and marschall parentage, and quho in his owin persone hath gained to him self great honour, and hath gevin sufficient prooff thairof for many yeires that he hath caryed charge in the qualitie of a Commander in the Warres of France, Germanie, Sweden, and the Low Countreyes : Therfor [having] thoght good to recommend him with these our saids letteris of recommendation vnto your Matie, that he may be employed according to his qualitie, worth, and merite. Our part shalbe to doe the lyk, And to answer your Matie, our dear brother, gratious inclination and disposition by all princelie offices of love and respects, to manteane and preserve the amitie and mutuall correspondencie [of] long and happie continuance betweene our Crounes and Kingdomes : And so we leave your Matie to the protection of Almightie God.—From our Palace of Westminster, the 26 of Feb., in the 7 yeir of our regne of Great Britane, France, and Irland.

                                      Subscribitur,   CHARLES R.

To the Viscount of Stirling.

Right, &c.—Wheras we did formerlie give warrant vnto our Counsall of Scotland for passing Letters of Reprysall vnder our great seall ther, in favours of the partiners of vmquhill Captane Robertsone, and that they accordinglie have passed the same and sent them to yow, that vpon our pleasur signifeid they might be delyvered to the partiners ; and knowing sufficientlie the great losses susteaned by our subjects, and the neglecting the Hamburggers in delaying of justice or restitution, Therfor we heirby requyre yow to delyver vp vnto the saidis partiners the saids letters efter sight heirof.—Newmarket, 3 March 1632.

To the Session.

Right, &c.—Wheras we ar informed that ther is ane action in Law betweene Sir William Alexander, knyt, and some citizens of Lubec, depending befor yow concerneing ane schip which they alledge to be wrongouslie takin from them, and vnjustlie declared pryse by ane Court of Admiraltie ther, wheranent we directed our warrant to yow tuo yeres agoe at ther desyre ; notwithstanding wherof, as we ar lykwyse informed, they have delayed till now to prosecute the same befor yow, thoght the said Sir William hath bene severall tymes present ther since that tyme : Therfor, in regard that his presence for his particular knowledge in the estate of the bussines may conduce to the cleiring of it, and that he can not as yit repair thither for occasions speciallie concerneing our service, Our pleasur is, that all farther proceiding therein be delayed till the first day of Junij next ensueing, that he may convenientlie attend the determination of the same ; for doeing wherof these presents salbe, &c.—Newmerket, 3 March 1632.

To the Commissioners Surrenders.

Right, &c.—Wheras our right, &c. the Erle of Roxburgh is to repair to that our kingdome vpon some affaires tuitching ws, which we have formerlie writtin to our Counsall, and that some speciall occasions heir doe requyre his speedie returne hither ; and being vnwilling, in regard of the schortnes of the tyme of his stay ther, that any advantage be takin of him in any bussines concerneing our Commission : Our pleasur is, that all things which ar befor yow concerneing the said Erle remane in the estate they ar into at this present vnto the first day of Junij nixt ensueing : And for your soe doeing these presents, &c.—Newmerket, 4 March 1632.

To the Counsell.

Right, &c.—Being informed that out of the moneyis made of a certane Lubec schip, the sowme of 2000lib st., being for the tyme in Williame Dickis handis, was applyd for the payment of Marineris, and ane act of Counsall lykwyse made for the repayment therof, to whome it should be fund justlie due, and vnderstanding that our right, &c. the Erle of Lythgow hath right to all, or a great part thairof, as Admirall, being nowyse willing to defraud him of his right, it is our pleasur that, according to the said act, a course be takin for making payment of what shalbe fund due to the said Erle, or otherwyse that yow certifie ws of the true estate thairof and what yow think fitt to be done for his satisfaction ; which recommending, &c.—Newmerket, the 7 March 1632.

To the Archbischop of Canterberrie.

Right reverend. &c.—Wheras by our direction yow perysed the Translationn of the Psalmes of King David wherof our late dear father was author, and that they have lykwyse bene sene since by the two primatts of our other two kingdomes, sieing the work is fund to be well done and far above the former translation, it being so good a work for our Church and so much concerneing the memorie of our said late dear father, which we know will ever be dearlie esteamed of by yow of our Clergie ; We desyre that the saidis Psalmes may be receaved and sung in all the churches of our dominions, bot with all that it may be begun in such forme as may be thoght by yow most expedient ; And therfoir it is our pleasur that, haveing called vnto yow the bischop of London, and such other bischops neir London as yow may most convenientlie have, that yow resolve vpon some course how this our purpois may tak effect, by causeing them ather be receaved by a generall ordour, or to beginn in some Churches by the particular recommendatioun of everie bischop within his owin dyocie, which we will esteame as singular service done vnto ws, wherof we expect ane Compt of your best endeavours, seriouslie recommending the matter, bot remitting the maner how it should be done vnto yow ; We bid, &c.—Newmerket, 13 March 1632.

To the Session.

Right, &c.—Being informed that ther ar diverse actions in Law lyklie to aryse betuixt our right, &c. the Lord Salton and those that ar interested in his Estate, who, in regard of the distresse therof, doeth some to deserve our princelie favour and comiseration in so far as the equitie of his cause and extremitie of such ane ancient familie doeth requyre : The consideration whairof hath moved ws to recommend vnto your care, that in all actions concerneing him, justice may be ministred therin with the most convenient diligence that the lawis of that our kingdome can permitt : Which recommending vnto your speciall care, we bid yow farewell.—From our Court at Newmerket, of March 1632.

To the Erle of Stratherne.

Right, &c.—Thogh we excuse your sudden goeing away, in regard of the occasion that moved yow thervnto, yit haveing brought the bussines concerneing the fisching neir to ane end, we desyre befor it be fullie concludit to have yow present, that we may confer with yow thervpon, as lykwyse vpon other affaires concerneing our service : And therfor expecting yow heir so sonne as yow can convenientlie cum, we bid yow fairwell.—From our Court at Newmerket, the 15 March 1632.

To the Advocat.

Trustie, &c., We greet yow well.—Wheras the Enclosed signatur. tuiching the case of our subjects of all our dominions in being freed from paying other or greater customes in aney of our severall kingdomes then what the naturall subjects therof doe or ought to pay, hath bene pervsed by our attourney-generall heir, and fund to accord in the whole substance with the proclamationns to be made to the lyk purpois for the good of our subjects in that our kingdome : Though we have bene pleased to signe the signatur, yit we thoght fitt to send it first vnto yow to be pervsed ; and if yow find that it is not conceavit as to work the lyk effects ther as is intended by our proclamationns in this our kingdome, that yow draw vp a signatur of new to that purpois, to be past with all diligence vnder our cachet and great seall ther, according to the forme accustomed, for which these presents shalbe vnto our Chancellour, and our other officers whom it may concerne, a sufficient warrand ; otherwyse, if yow find this signatur so conceaved it may work the intendit effect, that furthwith it be exped in Exchequer vnder our said seall according to the tenour thairof, without passing of aney other sealls, with the which by these presents we dispense, and that yow cause publication be made by the said patent thrugh all our burrowis and seaports, that none pretend ignorance thairin ; And that yow returne the same, patent vnder our great seall, with one of the same proclamationns as the same is publisched at our mercat croce of Edinburgh, and indorsat to our Principall Secretarie ; for the which these presents shalbe vnto yow a sufficient warrant.—Newmerket, 15 March 1632.

To Sir James Balfour, Lyon King at Armes.

Trustie, &c.—We have bene latelie pleased to confer vpon our right, &c. Sir William Alexander, knyt, our Principall Secretarie for Scotland, the title of Viscont Stirling, as ane degrie of honour which we have estemed due to his merite : And to the effect ther be nothing wanting which is vsual in this kynd, that this our favour, and the remembrance of his good and faythfull services done vnto ws, may be in record, Our pleasur is, and we doe heirby requyre yow, according to the dewtie of your place, to marshall his Coat's Armour, allowing it to him quartered with the Armes of Clan Allaster, who hath acknowledged him for cheiff of ther familie, in whois armes, according to the draught we send yow heirwith quartered with his coat, we ar willing to confirme them, Repuyreing yow to Register them accordinglie : And we doe further allow to the said Viscount Stirling the Armes of the Cuntrie of New Scotland in ane Inscutchione, as in a badge of his endeavours in the interprysing of the work of that plantation, which doe tend so much to our honour and the benefite of our subjects of that our kingdome : And with all to fitt his said Coat with a convenient crest and supporters such as may be acceptable vnto him ; ffor doeing whairof, and for registring of this warrand and his Coat in your registers for that purpois, or for drawing such further warrant as shalbe requisit, these presents shalbe your warrant.—Newmerket, 15 March 1632.

To all Mayors, Schirreffis, Justices of Peace, Vice-admiralls, Bailleis, Constables, Customers, Comptrollers, Searcheris, and all others our officers whome it may concerne, and everie of them, Greeting.—Wheras William Ker, lawfull sone to the late Mark, Erle of Lothian, is to travell into some parts beyond the seas vpon his necessarie occasions : These ar to will and command yow to suffer him to embark himsellf, with his servants, two or thrie, and necessarie provisions, at any of our ports which he shall think most convenient for his passage ; for which these presents shalbe your warrand.—Newmerket, 15 March 1632.

To the Counsell.

Right, &c.—Being informed of the great abuses committed in the Torwood by diverse persones, by cutting of tries and killing of our deir their, and otherwyse, haveing takin occasion to doe the samyne in regard of the absence of Sir James Forrester, knyt, who should oversie the samyne; And being verie desyreous that a strict course may be takin for the better preservationn therof heirefter, it is our pleasur that yow grant a Commission with full power to Margaret and Marie Forresters, with concurse of our Advocat for ther better assistance, and our interest to persew, according to the lawis of that our kingdome, the delinquents befor whatsumever Judge or Judicatorie compitent, and that yow be readie to give them your best assistance in the said persute, when it shalbe desyred: And in consideratioun of the great charges the said Margaret and Marie ar to be at, Our pleasur lykwyse is, that yow delyver vnto them all fynes, amerciaments to be takin from the saids delinquentis for the tyme bygone for ther owin vse.—Newmerkit, 15 March 1632.

To Thomas Riddell, Esquire, or any other of the Justices of the Countie Palatine of Durham.

Trustie, &c.—Wheras by our former letter direct to Sir William Muschamp, knyt, late deceissed, we wer pleased to requyre him to insist in the examination of certane persones that wer (as we ar informed) questioned befor him for the alledged murther of a chyld borne in a place belonging to the Countie of Durehame by a Scotts woman named Margaret Moresone, which chyld hath bene abstrackit, and, as is supposed, made away within ane of our two kindomes aither by the mother or some athers in whois lands it is proved to have bene, and seing, by reasone of the said Sir Williames deceis interveneing, our former letteris hath not takin effect: Our pleasur is, that yow proceid with all possible care in the tryell of that matter to find out whither the chyld be murthered or not, to the effect if any persone of this our kingdome be fund guiltie of that cryme they may be punished according to Justice: And in regard (as we ar lykwyse informed) that the mother is to be questioned tuitching that supposed murther within the kingdome of Scotland wher schoo is now resident; Our further pleasur is, that yow transmitt to the Judges of our kingdome of Scotland a trew and authentik copie vnder your hand and seall of the whole examinations made or to be made heirin, aither by the said Sir William or by yourself, as also that yow cause any persone or persones within our jurisdiction that can give evidence in or conserneing this matter, to goe into Scotland at what tyme they shalbe requyred (ther reasonable charges being borne by the pairtie persweing), ther to depone befor these Judges what they know tuitching the bearing, abstracting, or supposed murther of the chyld, that Justice may be administred as cause shall appear.—Newmerket, 15 March 1632.

To the Counsell.

Right, &c.—Haveing formerlie writtin vnto yow at diverse tymes how desyreous we wer that yow should cause vse all lawfull and possible meines for better clearing of the treuth tuitching the burning of the tour of Frendraught, and that Justice may be execute vpon whosoever should be fund guiltie of so odious and barbarous a fact in the most exemplarie maner to the terrour of all others who should attempt the lyk heirefter: Our pleasur therfor is, that for the more haistie tryell of that bussines yow employ one day in everie woik vpon the exact tryell of the samyne (which we exceidinglie desyre), and that yow never intermitt the prosecution therof in a maner forsaid till a full conclusion be putt thervnto, and that lykwyse in your procedure all acts of parliament conduceing to that purpois be dewlie putt in executioun as they shalbe produced by the pairties insisteris in the said persute: And for your so doeing, &c.—Newmerket, 15 March 1632.

To the Counsell.

Right, &c.—Wheras for the better claring of the treuth tuitching the burneing of the Tour of Frendraught, yow have by Act of Counsall ordeaned Johne Meldrum to be putt to the tortur of the bootts, bot have for some tyme delayed to tak that course with him, being of late informed that ther ar verie apparent presumptiouns of the guiltines of the said Meldrum, and of his certane knowledge concerneing that purpois : Therfor our express pleasur is, that without farder delay yow putt him to his tryell by tortureing him according to the said act vnless yow have reasone of new so the contrair.—Whythall, 15 March 1632.

A pacquett went to Lo Colvill wherin ther wer letteris of his Ma[tie] : To Stratherne, 2 ; to the Counsell with the fisching signature enclosed, 3 ; To the Counsell concerneing the Torwood, 4 ; To Sir James Balfour concerneing the Viscont of Sterlingis armes.—Royston, 20 March 1632.

To the Counsell.

Right, &c.—Wheras vpon good considerations mentioned in our letters vnto yow tuitching Master Grant, we wer pleased that his tryell should be continewed till the 10 of Aprill ensueing, the lyk reasones now moveing ws a longer tyme be granted : Our pleasur is, that his tryell be continewed till the first of August ensueing, before which tyme we will expect that further light shalbe gevin in that bussines, And that in the meane tyme yow give ordour for composing of the differences amongst the name of Grant, taking such suirtie as is requisit of any persone of whom yow shall think may disturbe our peace in these parts.—Whythall, 29 March 1632.

To the Counsell.

Right, &c.—Being informed of the care of our late royall father in causeing preserve the game of hunting within some distance of boundis of our palace of Linlythgow, haveing to that effect gevin charge to our trustie and weilbeloved Sir Johne Hamilton of Grange to sie these bounds reserved for that vse : And we being the rather willing that the lyk course be takin in regard (as we ar informed) that the bounds so reserved ar verie propper for hunting, and commodious for that purpois, in respect of the neirnes thairof to our cheiff housses wher we intend most ordinarlie to reside dureing our aboade in that our kingdome : Our pleasur is, that yow informe yourselfis of the warrant granted to that effect by our said Royall Father vnto the said Sir Johne, and that in our name yow give vnto him the lyk in all respects, for which these presents shalbe your warrand.—Whythall, 5 Aprill 1632.

To the Chancellour.

Right, &c.—Being willing that a frequent and constant course be kept in giveing ws intelligence of all affaires worthie to be imparted vnto ws, which ar treated of amongst yow of our privie Counsall according to the course accustomed : Our pleasur is, that yow give speciall ordour to the Clerk of our Counsell for sending to our Court weiklie to our principall secretarie the just information and extracts of all such things treated and resolved vpon in Counsall as yow shall think worthie to be made knowen vnto ws that the same may be imparted vnto ws at our best convenience : We bid, &c.—Whythall, 5 Aprill 1632.

To the Advocat.

Trustie, &c.—Hearing that the office of professour of phisick in the Vniversitie of Aberdene is voyd, and at our gift we being informed of the sufficiencie of Mr William Gordon, Doctour of Phisick, to discharge that place: Our pleasur is, that yow informe yourselff of the Estate therof, and if yow find that the right of presenting thervnto be in ws that furth with yow draw vp a presentatioun to that effect in behalff of the said Mr William, that he may discharge the same and enjoy the priviledges belonging thervnto, willing that the presentation pass immediatlie vnder our cachet and prive seall without further warrant; ffor doeing whairof these presentis shalbe vnto yow and other our officeris to whom it may concerne a sufficient warrant.—Whythall, 5 Aprill 1632.

To the Chancellour.

Right, &c.—Wheras we ar informed that such noblemen and others who ar entrusted with the affaires of our right, &c. the Marqueis of Hamilton can not so weill and absolutelie tak vpon them to treat and ordour things concernceing the Valuatioun of Tythes and others incident to our Commission of Surrenders belonging to him as if he wer present himselff, as we ar loath that any stay be made in the setling proceeding of that Commission, soe we will be sorie that the said Marqueis should be prejudged in his absens: Therfor we have thoght to signifie our pleasur apart vnto yow for vseing your best and fairest meanes to stay all proceedingis in the said Commission tuitching the said Marqueis, till his returne if such as ar cheiflie entrusted with his estate doe not condescend thervnto, otherwyse if ther be a necessitie to the contrarie, that yow first acquant ws therwith with your opinion therin befoir aney thing be done in the same, that we may give such further ordour therin as we shall find to be fitt and just.—Whythall, 5 Aprill 1632.

To these that ar entrusted with the Marques of Hamilton's Estate.

Right, &c.—Wheras we vnderstand that yow ar entrusted with the affaires of our Right, &c. the Marqueis of Hamilton, and that yow have bene verie carefull in vseing your best endevours for his good for which we give yow verie hartie thanks, bot with all haveing heard that yow intend to sell some of his Landis for paying of his debts, Conceaveing that ther is no great necessitie for doeing of the same, and that, God willing, at his returne he may be able to defray them otherwayis, and being bath that his ancient estate should be disposed of dureing his absence, that he may not be able to recover it heirefter when his fortunes and our favour may enable him for doeing therof: It is our desyre that yow sall sell rather the remander of the Impost of the Wynes wherof he hath right from ws, and that yow vse all other meanes that convenientlie can be vsed for the saiftie of his estate: The doeing whairof shalbe acceptable service done vnto ws.—Whythall, 5 Aprill 1632.

To the Counsell.

Right, &c.—Wheras our trustie and weilbeloved Colonell Lumisden hath caused move ws in behalff of our brother the King of Sweden, for our licence to levy a Regiment of men of that our kingdome for his service in the warres: To the effect all expedition be vsed for furthring of him therin, our pleasur is, that with diligence yow grant vnto him a sufficient warrant, with as ample Commission for levyeing and transporting of that regiment as heirtofoir hath bene granted to any; And to that effect that yow grant licence to tuk drumes, he alwayes giveing such satisfaction to everie ane of that number as he and they shall condescend vpon, according to the forme accustomed; for doeing wherof, these presents shalbe your warrand.—Whythall, 7 Aprill 1632.

To the Counsell.

Right, &c.—Wheras our right, &c. the Erle of Tullibardyne being to repair to that our kingdome, and to these parts wher the name of Grant doe reside, We, for the better setling of our peace ther by causing remove in a fare and quyet maner, without further danger of trouble or law to our subjects, all such differences as ar amongst these of that name, hath to that effect required him to informe himself of the grounds therof, and the best way how they may be composed, and therin to vse his best endeavours, or at least, to certifie ws of the estate wherin they now stand : Therfor we thoght fit to recommend vnto yow to give vnto the said Erle all such furtherance which yow shall find that he shall lawfullie and necessarlie requyre to that purpois ; wherof not doubting of your performance, we bid yow, &c.—Whythall, ellevinth of Aprill 1632.

To Balthaser Gerbilis, esquyr, our agent resideing with Infanta Archi Dutches at Brussells.

Trustie, &c.—Wheras, vpon complaint made vnto ws by some of our subjects of Scotland, that a schip called The Charitie of Leith was injustlie takin from them by some persones of Ostend, as schoe was arryving at Campheir, the staple part of that our kingdome, we wer pleased to wryt vnto our sister the Archdutchesse desyreing that restitution might be made to the lawfull owners of that schipe and goods, knowing how much your care and paynes to be takin therin may prove stedable vnto them, we ar heirby pleased to recommend ther cause vnto yow ; and to that effect have caused send vnto yow ane information of the proceidingis therin, and Inventarie of the goodis, that haveing therby heir by the owneris owin declaratioun informed yourself of what may best conduce to that purpois, yow may the better and more readelie vse your best endeavours for causing speedie restitution be made vnto them of the said schip, goods, and loss sustened therby, and for causing the takers be punished, as the nature of the offence shalbe fund to requyre by the lawes ther, that a reciprocall course of Justice may be dewlie observed betuixt our subjects as these of our freindis ther, as occasion shalhappin to requyre.—Whythall, ellevinth of Aprill 1632.

To the Counsell.

Right, &c.—Being informed of a barbarous custome vsed by some persones in fisching of salmond and other fisches upon the Sonday, and in tyme of divyne service and administration of the sacraments, contrair to ane ancient and lawdable custome, That none did fisch from the setting of the sun vpon the Setterday at night till the nixt Monday Morning at the rysing thairof, we have thoght fitt to recomend vnto yow the rectifieing of that abuse ; and to that effect that yow give warrant vnto shirreffis wher the abuse is committed, and others our officers and subjects whom yow shall think most fitt to sie your ordour putt be the same to executioun, according to the maner to be preservved by yow : We bid, &c.—Whythall, the 13 Aprill 1632.

To the Counsell.

Right, &c.—The Companie of Gen d'Armes in that our kingdome, appoynted for the service of our brother of the French king, being at this tyme to be levyed and transported vnto France by our right, &c. the Lord Gordon, to whom the charge therof is committed by our said brother, we spetiallie recommend vnto yow to assist the said Lord as occasion shall requyre, in what may anywayes conduce to his speedie furtherance in that purpois ; which we will tak as acceptable service done vnto ws.—Whythall, 18 Aprill 1632.

Our Soveraigne Lord vnderstanding the late lamentable death of the Viscount of Melgm, vpon whome and his Aires-maill, bearing the surname and Armes of Gordoun, his Matie was gratiouslie pleased to conferre that title of honour; And his Matie vnderstanding perfectlie the good service done to his Matie by his eldest brother, his Ma^{teis} right trustie and weilbelovit Counsellour the Lord Gordoun, on whois birth, fortun, and merite in his Matie said service doeth justlie deserve some further merk of his Ma^{teis} favour and respect then he now hath dureing the lyftyme of his father, his right, &c. the Marqueis of Huntlie; And his Matie vnderstanding lykwyse how the said late Viscont of Melgan dyed without aires-maill gottin of his owin bodie vpon whome the said title of Viscount was by his Ma^{teis} letter of patent to have descended : And with all his Matie being willing that the former Viscount shall revive and continew in the persone of such of the sones of the said Lord Gordoun, bearing the name and Armes of Gordon, as he shall mak choyse : Therfoir his Matie, of his princelie power and prerogative royall, Ordeanes letters patentes to be made vnder his highnes' great seall of the kingdom of Scotland, creating, making, and constituteing ; Lykwyse his Matie, by the tenour heirof, creats, maks, and constituts the said Lord Gordoun, dureing the lyftyme of his said father, and James Gordoun, his sone, efter his father's succeiding to the title of Marqueis, or otherwyse, efter his said father's death, and his aires-male bearing the surname and Armes of Gordon, Viscont of Aboyne, Giveing and granting to the said Lord Gordoun dureing the lyftyme of the said Marqueis, his father, and to the said James Gordoun, his sone, in maner forsaid, and to his aires-male bearing the surname and armes of Gordoun, the title, honour, rank, and dignitie of Viscount of the said kingdome ; And his Matie be these presents investeth the said Lord Gordoun in the said title of a Viscount, to be called dureing the lyftyme of his said father Viscount of Aboyne, and the said James Gordoun, his sone, efter his said father his succeiding to the said title of Marqueis, or other-wayes, efter his said father's death, and his saids aires-male as aforsaid in the said title of Viscount, to be called in all tyme heirefter Viscounts of Aboyne : To be haldin and to be had the said title and rank of dignitie of the said Viscount, with vote and voyce in parliament, and all other prerogatives, preheminences, dignities, and honours whatsoever apperteneing to the said dignitie of Viscount to the said Lord Gordoun dureing the lyftyme of his said father, and to the said James Gordoun, his sone, and his aires-male bearing the surname and Armes of Gordoun in maner forsaid, in all his Ma^{teis} and successours parliaments and publict conventioun of Esteats of his Ma^{teis} kingdome forsaid ; And that they enjoy the power, place, and right of votting therin, with all prerogatives and digniteis in all and everie thing which any other Viscount hath heirtofoir bruiked and enjoyed, or at this present doeth bruik and enjoy, within the said kingdome ; And that the said Lord Gordoun, dureing the lyftyme of his said father, shalbe styled and named Viscount of Aboyne, and the said James Gordoun, his sone, efter his father's succeiding to the said title of Marqueis, or efter his said father's death and his aires forsaids, and everie one of them successivelie, shall in all tyme heirefter be styled Viscounts of Aboyne, and they and ther forsaids to be all honoured with all the dignitie and respect which is compitent to the said title of honour : Commanding the Lyon king at Armes, and his brethren heraulds, to give and preseryve addition of bąg and cognisance to the present Armes of the said Lord Gordon and his said sone, as is vsuall and compitent in such cases ; And that the said letter be extendit in the best and most ample forme, with all clauses neidfull : Ordeaneing these presents to be a sufficient warrant to the Keeper of the great seall and writter therto for wryting heirof to the said seall, and appending the said great seall thervnto, without passing any other sealls or register, and without any farther warrant to be directed in that behalff.—Gevin at Whythall, the 20 of Aprill 1632.

These ar for creating the Lord Gordon dureing the lyftyme of his
father, the Marqueis of Huntlie, Viscount of Aboyne, and
James Gordoun, his sone, efter his father succeiding to the
title of Marqueis, or efter his father's death, and his aires-male
bearing the surname and Armes of Gordoun, Viscount of Aboyne.

To the Bischop of Cathnes.

Reverend Father in God—Being willing that such progres be made in the course of the Commission of Surrenders as at our comeing thither, God willing, the nixt yeir All things tuitching that bussines be so prepared as we may fallie putt ane end to the same : And to that effect being willing that our Commissioners (wherof yow ar one of the number) give such attendance as may best conduce to that purpois, our pleasur is, that yow carefullie attend the said Commission all this somer seasone, and that no other occasion divert yow otherwayes if your health and disposition of bodie will permitt.—Whythall, 20 Aprill 1632.

To the Counsell.

Right, &c.—Wheras Johne Grant of Glenmorestoun hath long attendit at our Court, humblie craveing of ws that we would be pleased to give ordour that a course might be takin for his tryell tuitching some imputations wherwith we wer informed agaist him, who being willing to vnderly the law, and to that effect to be tryed ather befor the Justice Generall or any other Judicatorie yow shall think compitent : Our pleasur is, that yow tak sufficient surtie for him, and for his sones, brothers, and servandis appearances befor yow or any Judicatorie thoght compitent by yow, at such a day as yow shall think titt to preseryve, that he may enjoy the benefite of our lawis as is ordinarie in the lyk caices : We bid, &c.—Whythall, 21 Aprill 1632.

To the Chancellour.

Right, &c.—Wheras we have writtin severall tymes that payment might be made vnto our right, &c. the Lord Gordon of his part of 5000ᵇᵇ, becaus the granting therof was for so good a consideration as the surrendring of thes his heretabill offices of Schirrefschip in favours of our Croun : We ar lykwyse pleased at this tyme, becaus of the said Lord his urgent occasions, and levyeing and transporting vnto France of the Gendsarmes for the service of our brother the French king, spetiallie to recommend vnto yow to vse your best endeavours that speedie payment be made to him or his assigneyis of these moneyis and annuall rent thairof ; and least he or his surteis should at this tyme be vnseasonablie troubled or be diverted from a purpois of such consequence as the tymelie transporting of these men, that if neid be yow deall with William Dick to desist till Mertimes ensueing fra troubling of the said Lord Gordon or his surteis : Which recommending, &c.—The 21 Aprill 1632.

To the Mair and Eldermen of London.

Right, &c.—How commodious the River of Thames is to this our Realme of England, and speciallie to our Citie of London, and what great care our late dear father had of the Conservation heirof yow cannot be ignorant : To which end he granted letteris to his servant Johne Gilbert to vse and exercise certane engynes (the invention whairof he brought into this kingdome) to remove the shelfis and keip the river navigable : And the said Gilbert being hitherto depryved of the benefite thairof, wherby the service intended hath bene neglected, We have thoght good for a work so generallie good, and in redresse of the said patente, to renew and revive his letteris patents ; and vnderstanding that he cannot proceid with effect vnless the gravell and sand may be takin off his handis, and that by a provident Act of parliament the same is to be disposed for the ballasting of schippis, We lett yow know that it is our express will and pleasur that yow, to whom the conservation of the river stand committed, tak present ordour for that imployment of the said Johne Gilbert and James Freeze, his fellow patente, whome we commend vnto yow, to cleanze the said river, and that yow caus the gravell and sand to be takin vp by them to be disposed and takin from them at moderat pryces according to the Statute, not permitting any other to tak the benefit of Gilbert's labours and inventions, that so the service may be effected, our expectation satisfied, and the generall good advanced, of which we shall expect ane accompt of yow, being the conservatours of the said river and for our further satisfaction : Our will and pleasur is, that yow mak enquyrie by what meanes the sand and gravell may be disposed that is takin vp by the Engynes, and certifie ws that such further ordour and course may be takin that the service be not longer hindred.—Whythall, 30 Aprill 1632.

To the Advocat.

Trustie, &c.—Haveing bene informed that some Isles of that our kingdome, with others particulars mentionat in the inclosed information, doe justlie belong vnto our Croun, as being the ancient propertie thairof, and which, vpon good and weghtie considerations, have bene by act of parliament annexed thairvnto, and vnjustlie deteyned by some of our subjects, to the great prejudice thairof : Our speciall pleasur is, and we doe herby will and command yow, that haveing informed your self of the estate of our right thervnto, yow furthwith intent summondis in our name, and insist by a legall course for reduction of all such grants and infeftmentis mentionat in the particular information, speciallie of the Isle of the Lewis, and for such other things of that nature as shall cum to your knowledge, which hath bene granted in prejudice of our Croun.—Whythall, first of May 1632.

To Sir Henrie Martine.

Trustie, &c.—Wheras ther is ane Action in Law depending befoir yow betweene tuo of our Subjects of Scotland, Johne Gordon, Esqr, and one William Weir, mariner, concerneing a cause presentlie persewed in Scotland, from whence we have notice thairof gevin vnto ws by our privie Counsell of that our kingdome : These presents ar to requyre yow that yow proceid no further therin till yow hear agane from ws tuitching that purpois : We bid yow farewell.—Whythall, first of May 1632.

Carolus Dei gratia Britanniarum Franciae et Hyberniae Rex Fideique defensor Omnibus regibus principibus tam ecclesiasticis quam secularibus Archiepiscopis Episcopis ducibus Marchionibus comitibus baronibus equitibus aliisque nobilibus necnon omnibus Admirallis sive Thallasiarchis Vice Admirallis Classium Navium sinuum portuum provinciarum vrbium Arcium pontium castrorum prefectis sive gubernatoribus Omnibus denique per vniversam Europam magistratibus imperium qualecunque terra marine habentibus sive excercentibus fratribus patribus consanguineis amicis Confederatisque suis Salutem plurimam benevolentiam fraternam gratiam favoremque suum regium pro cujuscunque status conditionisque ratione dicit. Quandoquidem serenissimi illustrissimi reverendissimi illustres magnifici et generosi domini fratres patres consanguinei affines amici confederati nostra nobis sincere dilecti Generosus hic subditus noster Captaneus Walterus Stewartus laudabili peregrina castra sequendi artem militarem ex actinis addiscendi et mores hominum cognoscendi studio ductus et sibi (pace nostra) aliquandiu peregrine profisci supplex et enixe petiit ejusque tam equis postulatis nequaquam remendum censuimus quin potius Serenitates Reuer^{tias} Celsitudines Magu^{tias} Amplitudinesque vestras amice rogatus cupimus vt si ditiones alicujus vestro maria sinus portus vrbes opida locare alia vestre cure aut prefecture commissa memoratus generosus noster

II z

subditus appulerit intraritue non solum nulla injuria affectum libere manere aut abire sinatis rerum ea humanitate tractetis quam vestras a nobis expectare velitis si ditiones quoque nostras similiter commendati intraverint in eisue negotiabuntur. Valete. Dabantur ex palatio nostro regio . . . primo die mensis Maii Anno salutis humanæ millesimo sexcentesimo trigesimo secundo.

To the Emperour of Russia.

Great and Mightie Lord, our dearest brother and freind—Still gevin to vnderstand of your great preparations for your intended warres, And taking vnto your royall consideration that the service of these gentlmen our subjects whois approved valour and experience in martiall affaires may be verie convenient and vsefull for the advancement of your Maties service, We have heirvpon takin this particular occasion by these our speciall letters, both in regard of the great respect we have to your Matie, and to the prosperitie of your great affaires, and in contemplation of the favour we bear to men of worth and merite, to recommend vnto your Imperiall Matie this bearer, our weilbeloved subject James Ramanten, a Livetennent-Colonell in the Warres, for one that hath gevin verie ample testimonie to the worth of his imployments, valour, and worth throughout Germanie, Sueden, Polland, and Low Countreyis; And for as much as he most earnestlie desyreth to serve your Matie, Therfoir at his humble requeist we have bene pleased to licence him to repair vnto your imperiall dominions, desyreing that your royall Matie our dear brother would for our saik be gratiouslie pleased to grant him such imployment in your service as yow shall find him capable of, and we doubt not bot his cariage shall merit your high favours by his vigilent care and faythfulnes therin answerable to this Our royall recommendation; And so, our most dear brother, alley, and good freind, we pray to God that your Soverintie may long and gloriouslie reigne over your great and famous kingdomes, and that your royall Matie may happelie prosper in all the royall affaires yow tak in hand.—Gevin at our royall palace at Whythall, the 4 of May the yeir of our most blissed Soverane Jesus Chryst 1632, and of our regno of Great Britane, France, and Irland, &c.—Subscribitur,

CHARLES R.

Direction.

To the Most high, mightie, and right noble Prince The Great Lord Emperour and Great Duik Michaell Pheodor monarch of All Russia, sole Commander of Volidomer, Muskoe, Novogorod, King of Cazan, king of Astroean, king of Siberia, Lord of Vobskey, and great Duik Smolenskey, Tuerskey, Vgoiskey, Permskey, Vatetskey, Bolgarskey, and others, also Lord and Great Duik of Novogorod, of the Lower Cuntreyis, Chernigonskey, Reizanskey, Polotskey, Rostroneskey, Yarlanskey, Belosurskey, Condiskey, and of all the northern Parts, Lord and Commander; Also Lord of the Cuntrie of Eynerskey, Cartaleinskey, and King of Granz.

To the Counsell.

Right, &c.—We ar informed of the hard estat of Robert Levingstoun by being suirtie for Johne Levingstoun of Donypace, younger, to whome for some good Considerations we had for some tyme granted a protection, Though the distress of the said Robert in that kynd, occasioned, as we ar informed, by the others necessiteis, doeth seame to requyre the lyk pitie and proportion of our favour; yit vpon his humble suite made vnto ws for the same, we would not absolutelie grant it till yow had first considered his cace heirin, and how far it war fitt to proceid in his behalff without defrauding his Creditours, To which purpois we have sent yow heirwith a protection, that if yow find his estate heirin, to requyre the lyk favour as was granted vnto the said Johne, and that though the Creditours ly out of ther moneyis for some schort tyme, that they will not be defrauded of what shalbe funé dew by the said Robert as suretie for him, Yow caus expeid the said protection vnder our great seall, for which these shalbe sufficient warrant.—Whythall, 4 May 1632.

To the Archbischop of St Androis.

Right, &c.—Wheras we did formerlie wryt vnto yow and to the Clergie of that our kingdome concerneing the receaveing of the Psalmes that wer translated by our late dear father to be sung in the Churches ther, which we particularlie recommended vnto yow at your last being heir, and haveing a great desyre that the same may be establisched with all possible convenience, sieing the sufficiencie therof hath bene approvin by all our kingdomes: It is our pleasur that yow call vnto yow such of the bischops of that our kingdome as yow can convenientlie have, and that yow resolve vpon the maner and tyme when they shalbe receaved, that ordour may be gevin for provydeing of bookis to that effect; and so not doubting bot, as yow tender that work and the memorie of our father, yow will have a care therof; We bid, &c.— Whythall, 5 of May 1632.

To the Primat of Ardmaugh,

Right reverend father in God, and right, &c.—We have bene informed of your approbatioun of the Psalmes translated by our late dear father and of your affection to his memorie therin, which is verie acceptable vnto ws; And in regard that we ar desyreous that these Psalmes be receaved in all the Churches of our dominions, and that ther is a cours taking for that effect: These ar lykwyse to requyre yow, with advyse of such of the bischops or others of the Clergie of that our kingdome as may convenientlie soonest meitt with yow, to consider of some course wherby our desyre heirin may be best effectuated, and acquant ws with the same, which we will esteme as verie acceptable vnto ws; and expecting your best and speediest endeavours heirin, we bid yow farewell.—Whythall, 5 May 1632.

To the Ministerie of Edinburgh.

Trustie, &c.—Wheras we have bene pleised at this tyme to signifie our pleasur vnto the right, &c. the Archbischop of St Androis, for calling vnto him such of the bischops of that our kingdome as convenientlie he could for resolveing vpon the maner and tyme when the Psalmes translated by our late royall father might be receaved and sung in the Churches therof; wherin knowing how much your care and paynes may contribute to that purpois, and being confident of your affection to our service and love of a work of that kynd, which is approved in those our other kingdomes, we have thoght fitt speciallie to recommend the same vnto yow for vseing your best endeavours that these Psalmes be receaved and sung in our Churches of our burgh of Edinburgh, haveing for your better assistance therin writtin to the Magistrats of that burgh; and wherin not doubting bot the effects of your endeavours will answer our expectation, We bid, &c.—Whythall, 5 May 1632.

To the Burgh of Edinburgh.

Trustie, &c.—Wheras we have caused pervse the Psalmes that wer translated by our late dear father, the sufficiencie whairof hath bene approved in all our dominions, we ar desyreous that the samyne may be generallie receaved and sung in all the Churches of our kingdomes, and have gevin severall ordour to the Clergie therof to that effect : And as we ar confident of your affection to any thing may concerne our service, and cheiflie what may concerne the memorie of our said father, we have thought good to requyre yow that yow would concurre with your ministrie for the furtherance of our desyre in this particular, according to the ordours shalbe preservyved be the Clergie for that effect, not doubting bot as yow ar the cheif of our brughs in that our kingdome, and have bene the first in other things concerneing our service ther, so yow will give exemple to others for effectuating of what we so earnestlie desyre in this : Which recommending vnto your care, &c.—Whythall, 5 May 1632.

To the Chancellour.

Right, &c.—Wheras, vpoun good Consideratiouns schawin vnto ws, We did grant a Commission of late for reviseing the Acts of Parliament, that such of them as wer considered and collected by our Commissioners appoynted for that purpois might be in readines to be rectifeid and ordoured in the nixt parliament, according to the intent of that Commission : Bot heiring that litle or no progress was made in that bussines, and we still intending to have all things tuitching that purpois in readines at our comeing thither, God willing, the nixt yeir, ar heirby pleased that in our name yow requyre the saids Commissioners to proceid according to the meaneing of the said Commission, which (if neid be) we ar willing to be renewed ; otherwayes, if at the holding of our first parliament anything shalbe defective in that kynd, we cannot bot be discontent, and imput the faill vnto them.—Whythall, 5 May 1632.

To the Chancellour Hadinton, Winton, Carnagie, Advocat.

Right, &c.—Being informed of some differences betuixt Sir Robert McClellane of Bombie, knyt, gentlman of our privie Chalmer in ordinarie, and Johne Gordoun of Lochinvar, which hapned dureing our said servant his charge of a horse Companie in Irland, from whence he could hardlie repair thither without speciall licence from our generall of our Armie ther : And being willing that these differences be removed in a fair and quyet maner, that our said servand be not distracted from his charge, Our pleasur is, that yow call them befor yow, and haveing informed yourselffis of the estate of these differences, that yow vse your best endeavours to compose the same, or certifie ws of the reasones of the pairtie fund refractorie by yow to this course, that yow may give such farder ordour therin as we shall find just caus.—Whythall, 5 May 1632.

To the Exchequer.

Right, &c.—Hearing that for the farthering of our service Johne Stewart of Coldinghame did subscryve the generall submission, haveing therby denudit him self in our favours of his right to that abbacie, and such persones to whome for payment of his debts he hath made conveighances therof and disposeing of that estate to his hurt : To which purpois he hath humblie petitioned ws that we might not sie him suffer for his affection to our service, speciallie by these who hath not submitted for ther interest in that estate as he hath done, whervnto, and for our owin interest, haveing a respect that we nor ye be not prejudged, Our pleasur is, that hencefurth no signature concerneing that abbacie be exped in exchequer till we be first acquanted therwith, that we may give such farther ordour therin as we shall find to accord with justice and equitie.—Whythall, 8 May 1632.

To the Session.

Trustie, &c.—Whoms we ar informed that vpon the signification of our plesur vnto yow for admission of Robert Crachton and Alex' Alexander to the first vacand places of Maisserie, yow have alreadie admitted the said Robert to the place of ane Chalmers, who did bear that Charge, and being lykwyse willing that the said Alex' Alexander, who hitherto hath bene, and heirefter may be, as occasion presents, imployed abroad in our service, may lykwyse enjoy the benefite of our royall intention, and that by his absence at any tyme he be not therof frustrat, Our spetiall pleasur is that, attending to our former letter to that purpois, he be preferred to the first vaiking place of Maiserie thats halhappin to vaik by death, dimission, or deprivation, or aney way else howsoever, and that at his comeing he may be receaved thervnto, and the former Act of Counsell and Sederunt be renewed in favours of the said Alexander Alexander to that effect; and for your soo doing these presents shalbe your sufficient warrant.—Greenwitch, 18 May 1632.

To the Exchequer.

Right, &c.—We ar informed by the Lord Naper that our late royall father did give vnto him a benefite out of the Tallow transported furth of that our kingdome, and that thervpon ther ar Acts of Exchequer, of which gift ther is yit a remainder vnpayed to him: It is our pleasur that he enjoy the said benefite, as the foirfaltours shall occure, till he be fullie payed of that which yow shall find to be justlie dew vnto him, And if neid be, to tak acts of new to that purpois, Causing registrat these presents, which shalbe a sufficient warrant.—Grenwich, 18 May 1632.

To the Counsell.

Right, &c.—Wheras we ar informed that be vertew of our letters of reprysell granted to Captan Robertsone, deceissed, some schippis and goodis of the Hamburgers have bene takin of late by his partiners, who being to receave satisfaction of them, we ar vnwilling that these Hamburgeris be troubled for any other cause or occasion whatsoever, to the effect that that State finding our just intention in what may concerne ther good, correspondence may be keipt betweene them and our subjects : Therfoir our pleasure is, that satisfaction being made to these partiners of what shalbe fund due vnto them, ather in behalff of our interest pretendit in our name, or in the name of any of our officers or subjects whatsoever : Which recommending, &c.—Grenewitch, 18 May 1632.

To the Masters of Work.

Trustie, &c.—Being willing that no materialls and things necessarie, whairof yow shall find that vse wilbe necessarlie requyred for building and repairing our housses ther, be takin away or any way wanting, spetiallie when the same can be had in the boundis properlie belonging vnto ws, Our pleasur is, that yow suffer no sort of coall or friestone to be takin for the vse of any persone whatsoever, other than our owin, out of the precinct of our Castells, housses, and parks thervnto belonging, without warrant from ws.—Grenewitch, 18 May 1632.

To the Counsell.

Right, &c.—Wheras we have often bene importuned by diverse persones vnjustlie compleyneing and informeing ws of wrongs done to them, wherby both we ar vnseasonablie troubled and sindrie of our good subjects wronged by false calumneis : To the effect remedie be provydit against such abuses, our pleasur is, that yow consider how the same may be best prevented heirefter by causing publische or otherwayes putt in executioun what yow shall think fitt to that purpois, as of late yow have ordered tuitching ane Lnnisdeu, wherin we approve your course, and ar willing that yow putt it to executioun, to give exemple to others not to committ the lyk heirefter: Which recommending, &c.—Grenewich, 18 May 1632.

To the Thesaurer Depute.

Right, &c.—We have bene pleased to wryt vnto our Exchequer for causeing exped of Robert Maxwell of Portrak, for the vse of the Erle of Nithisdale, a new gift of what may be demanded in our name, by reasone that the Lands and others belonging to the said Erle have fallin in nonentrie, wherof we ar pleased that yow tak particular notice for sieing our pleasur therin obeyed accordinglie, and that as occasion shall occure in our Exchequer, which may concerne him or his freinds, yow give all lawfull and readie assistance for ther good and furtherance therin: Which we will tak as good service done vnto ws. —Grenewich, 18 May 1632.

To the Advocat.

Trustie, &c.—We ar informed that ther ar severall actions in Law persewed aganst the E. of Nithisdale at the instance of diverse persones, wherin a collour of our interest is onlie vsed without any benefite to ws, wherby yow, being requyred to compeir therin in our name, the said Erle is and wilbe much prejudged: Our pleasur is, that yow doe not compeir heirefter in any action aganst the said Erle or his freindis, if yow doe not find that we ar particularlie interested therin tuitching our benefite: ffor the which these shalbe your warrant.—Grenewich, 18 May 1632.

To the Exchequer.

Right, &c.—Wheras we ar informed that some nonentrie dewteis of the Lands and others belonging to the E. of Nithisdale ar to be called for in Exchequer for our vse, sieing we wer formerlie pleased to grant a gift of some thairof to Robert Maxwell of Portrak in behalff of the said Erle, and being vnwilling that any course be takin for exacting of the same, or what doeth since fall vnto ws in that kynd: Our pleasur is, that without composition yow pass and cause exped vnder our privie seall in dew forme vnto the said Robert, his aires and assigneyis, a new gift of what may be demandit in our name by reasone of non-entrie, ather proceiding or since the said gift, and to that effect that yow give present ordour that no proceidingis be vsit aganst the said Erle or aney others in that behalff; for which these presents shalbe vnto yow a sufficient warrant.—Grenewich, 18 May 1632.

To the Archbischop of Glasgow.

Right, &c.—We ar informed that certane taks of Tythes belonging to our right, &c. the Duik of Lennox ar expyred, and that the power of renewing thairof is in your handis, we haveing a particular care of our cousens Estate speciallie now in his absence: And sieing what is demanded in his behalff is conforme to our intention in our Commission for surrenders, Our pleasur is, and we doe heirby will and requyre yow, that he and his vassalls be preferred to any persones whatsoever in haveing new leases of all such tythes as ar in your power, wherin, though we had not speciall interest in our said cousen, we will expect a Conformitie in yow as a course which in the generall is agrieable to our royall intention, and establisched for the publict good.—[Not dated.]

To the Counsell.

Right, &c.—Haveing bene pleased to consider of the differences betuixt the Noblemen interested in the forfaltour of the late Erle Bothwell and Francis Stewart, his eldest sone, as may appear by the directions that we have gevin concerneing the same, We doe heirby agane requyre yow to proceid in the tryeing of the trew rent of the Estate that they injoy by his forfaltour, which hath at any tyme heirtofoir bene payed to the late Erle Bothwell, or to any other who had the saidis landis or beneficces befor him, or vnto them who had them of late, and whatever is claymed by the said Francis, whilk they or any of them have of that nature wherof they ar ther authors, wer not in possession by a good right preceiding the forfaltour and the said Francis inhabilitie : It is our pleasur that ather they quyt the benefite of the forfaltour pro tanto of that which is in contraversie, taking theirto ther other rights, or otherwayes that it be valued and cum vnder our consideratioun with the rest : And as we desyre that all rents, tythis, and other commoditeis belonging to the premisses be dewlie valued, so lykwyse, wher ther is any laick of patronages or churches ather of the erldome or Abbacie, We will that the ministers stipendis being dewlie deduced, the remainder of the saidis Churches and patronages be dewlie estimated as the reall rents therof, and the samyne to be trewlie reported vnto ws, that we may finallie determine thervpon : Which recommending vnto your care, &c.—Grenwitch, 28 May 1632.

To the Session.

Right, &c.—Being informed that the action intended befor yow in our name for reduction of the Infeftments of the heretable Isherie of our Exchequer hath of a long tyme depended befor yow, and as yit doeth remane vndecydit, to the prejudice of the persone whome of late we have appoynted to discharge that office, and the generall course establisched for bringing bak of heretabill offices to our Croun : Therfoir our pleasur is, that yow tak the said caus vnto your serious consideratioun, that justice may be ministred therin with convenient expedition : Which recommending, &c.—Grenwitch, 29 May 1632.

To Sir Henrie Marten.

Trustie, &c.—Wheras we have bene petitioned concerneing a schip of Lubec, that some yeres agoe was declared pryse in our Court of Admiralitie in Scotland, we ar desyreous befoir we give any ordour therin to have your opinion according to the cace which we send yow heirwith : Therfor our pleasur is, that yow pervse it and delyver vnto ws your opinion concerneing the same, that we may be the better informed to give such ordour as shalbe further requisite.—Grenwitch, 29 May 1632.

To the Thesaurer and Deputie Thesaurer.

Our pleasur is, that out of the readiest of our present rents or casualiteis whatsoever of that our kingdome, or which shall accresce vnto ws heirefter by whatsoever maner of way, yow pay with all diligence vnto Sir Robert Gordon, knyt, gentlman of our privie Chalmer in Ordinarie, the sowme of 2000lib sterling : And for your soe doeing these presents shalbe vnto yow and all others whom it may concerne a sufficient warrant and discharge.—Grenwitch, 7 Junij 1632.

To the Exchequer.

Right, &c.—Wheras we have bene pleased, vpon good considerations knowen to ws, to let the Commission expyre which was granted to our, &c. the E. of Murray, and vnderstanding that he hath bene at great charges in citeing of sindrie persones to appear befoir him for Crymes whervpon they wer accused, whois processes as yit he hath not had tyme to finish, to the effect that he may noway be defrauded of the escheits or fynes of them that ar fund guiltie, as was granted vnto him by his Commission, Our pleasur is, and we doe heirby grant vnto him, the escheits, fynes, or benefite arysing otherwyse from any persones that hath bene cited by him by vertew of his Commission that shalhappin to be decerned befoir any Judge whatsumever; for allowing wherof vnto him these presentis shalbe vnto yow a sufficient warrant.— Grenwitch,   Junij 1632.

To the Session.

Right, &c.—Wheras diverse persones wer denunced rebells at the instance of our right, &c. the E. of Murray, according to the power granted vnto him by a Commission from ws, wherby he hath intended or is to inteud some action befoir yow concerneing causes determined befor the expyreing of his said Commission to have declaratiouns thervpon : These ar to requyre yow that in any such case he may have all the Expedition that the due course of Justice can allow to the effect that he may enjoy the benefite granted vnto him by the said Commission : Which recommending to your care, &c.—Grenwitch, 7 Junij 1632.

To the Counsell.

Right, &c.—Wheras we wer pleased, vpon good considerations knowen to ws, to give ordour for continewing the tryell of Allaster Grant for a certane tyme, as our letters writtin for that effect doe bear ; Though we did delay it for that space, it was noway our intention to defraud Justice : And therefor it is our pleasur that efter the expyreing of the said tyme yow give ordour for the tryell of him, and all others who wer accused or to be accused as engadged in the said rebellion, and that all persones who band themselflis for produceing of the broken men who ar complices with James Grant or the said Alaster, that they exhibite them according to the ordour preseryved by yow in that case : Which recommending to your care, we bid, &c.—Grenwitch, 7 Junij 1632.

To the Chancellour.

Right, &c.—Being informed that in regard the Lo Vchiltrie is now vnder a criminall processe, yow have stoppit the passing of a patent granted vnto him and Sir Pieris Crosbie and other ther partineris who had long since contracted with our right, &c. the Viscont of Stirling for some landis in New Scotland, and being willing to secure all such vndertakers in that plantation, and to encourage them to prosecute ther vndertakings for the good of our service and increase of our dominions, We, for these respects, and particularlie calling to mynd the good service done vnto ws by the said Sir Pieris, and conceaveing hopes of his future service in New Scotland, we [are] pleased that the said patent be exped vnder our great Seall, causeing raze out the Lo Vchiltreis' name, otherwayes (iff yow find a necessitie), that yow caus draw a patent of new to that purpois to be exped vnder our Cachet and Great Seall, without passing other sealls or registers ; ffor which these shalbe a sufficient warrant.—Grenwitch, 7 Junij 1632.

To the Thesaurer and Thesaurer Deputie.

Our pleasur is, according to our former warrant to the E. of Mar, then our Thesaurer, that yow pay vnto James Bowie, serjant of our wyne seller, or his assigneyis, the feyis dew vnto him as master of our wyne seller of that our kingdome, according as is mentionat in the gift grantit thervpon by our late royall father, togidder with the arrieris therof, and that out of the first and readiest of our rents or casualiteis whatsoever remaneing in your handis, or which heirefter shall accrese vnto ws : And for your soe doeing these presents shalbe vnto yow a sufficient warrant and discharge.—Grenwitch, 7 of Junij 1632.

To the Counsell.

Right, &c.—Wheras we ar informed that some learned Gramarians of these our kingdomes have approved of a Gramer perfected and dedicated vnto ws by ane Mr Robert Williamsone, as a work in that kynd verie exact and fitt speedelie to advance students to the knowledge of the Latine tongue, wherin sieing he hath bene at the charge of the printing and other wayes, and that he is onlie desyreous at this tyme to mak vse therof in so far as it shalbe fund heirefter fitt for the publict good ; Our pleasur is, that yow cause pervse the said Gramer, and if yow find it such as is pretendit, and that no inconvenience can aryse vnto our subjects by granting vnto the said Mr Robert the benefite of his owin wark, that yow give vnto him and his partiners dureing the space of 21 yeires licence to print and sell the said Gramer : And to that effect that yow give way for expeiding a patent thervpon vnder our Cachet and Sealls in the vsuall maner, with such Conditions and restrictions as yow shall find to be necessar in the lyk cases ; for which these presents shalbe your warrand.—Grenwich, 7 Junij 1632.

To the Session.

Right, &c.—Haveing heard that ther ar some actions depending befoir yow for reduceing of decreits that wer gevin by our Admirall vpon pryse schippes dureing the tyme of the late warris, we ar confident that he hath not proceidit in any such processe bot vpon verie just grounds, and no decreit gevin by our Admirall of this our kingdome can be reduced befoir any other Judge, save by such as ar especiallie appoynted by ws for that purpois, and though we doe not intend to derogate from our Judicatorie in aney thing that is [the] propper object thairof, yit in regard that our right, &c. the Duik of Lennox, our Admirall, is absent for the present, and a minor of whome we have takin charge, and that we would not have aney just caus gevin to discourage others heirefter to vndertake in our service in the lyk kynd when they shall sie these to suffer who, efter sentence gevin in the ordinarie Court, have disposed of the goodis according thervnto : We have thoght fitt to recommend vnto yow that yow proceid the more warelie in any action persewed befor yow of this nature, that these our subjects who ar or shalbe interested in that kynd may find all the just favour and encouragment which the practeis of other nationes and the Lawis of that our kingdome may allow : Which especiallie recommending vnto your care, we bid, &c.—Grenewitch, 14 Junij 1632.

To the Advocat.

Trustie, &c.—Wheras we have bene humblie moved in behalff of Johne Dundas of Newlistoun that a signature of the Mylne called Brestmylne (whairof he is proprietar) might be exped vnto him, his wyff, and Patrik Dundas, ther sone, his aires-maill and assigneyis, vnder our great seall, wherby they might becum our immediat vassalls for payment vnto ws of the few-dewteis accustomed to be payed by him vnto the Lord of Torphechin, who (as we ar informed), contrarie to the generall course of our Commission for Surrenders, hath sold his superioritie of that mylne (which is a part of his erection) to ane James Inglis, both to defeat ws of our right thervnto, and of the whole erection tuitching the reduction wherof ther is ane action in Law depending at our instance ; Our pleasur therfor is, that yow consider of the inclosed petition, and informe yourselff of our right to the said Mylne, and if yow find the same to be good, and the course intended by the petitioner to be conforme to the course of our Commission, that yow sie a signatur of that mylne exped in Exchequer in the petitioner and his forsaids behalff, representing (if neid be) vnto our Commissioners therof our just title, and if yow find a necessitie and just groundis in Law whervpon to proceid, that yow in our name intend processe of retraction of what hath bene done by the said Lord and the said Inglis to our prejudice heirin : Which recommending, &c.—Grenwitch, 14 Junij 1632.

To the Exchequer.

Right, &c.—Wheras, vpon information made to ws of our right to the superioritie of Brestmylne, and that we ar lyklie to be prejudged therin by a disposition of the superioritie therof made be the Lord of Torphrchin to ane James Inglis, contrarie to the course of our Commission for surrenders, we have requyred our Advocat to represent vnto yow, if neid be, our just title thervnto ; which, if he shall mak appear vnto yow to be good in Law, and conforme to the course of our said commission, Our pleasur is, that yow pass and cause be exped vnder our Cachet and great seall a signatur of the said mylne in favours of Johne Dundas of Newlistoun, proprietar therof, his wyff, and Patrik Dundas, ther sone, his aires-male and assigneyis, according to the ancient holdings and accustomed few dewteis.—Grenewitch, 14 Junij 1632.

To the Counsell.

Right, &c.—Being informed that James Law of Snanden, herauld, did mak vse of some of our taxations (with the Collection whairof he was entrusted), for not delyverie of which vnto our vse he is now a prissoner, and that by his panes and charges in discoverie of sindrie concealed moneyis which wer broght in for our vse, and for other good services done by him vnto ws, we ow him some sowmes of money ; Our pleasur is, that yow consider his paynes and examyne his accompts, and that yow remitt and discharge him of what shalbe fund dew vnto ws by him ; And that thervpon ane act of Exchequer be made for his exoneratioun at the handis of our Collectour-Generall of our taxations, now or who was for that tyme, and of all other whom it may concerne, giveing ordour that he be not any longer deteyned in prisson for that cause.—Grenwich, 14 Junij 1632.

To the Bischop of Aberden.

Reverend father in God, &c.—Humble sute being made vnto ws in behalff of Walter Robertsone, burges of Aberdone, and his eldest sone, that they might have libertie to trade in Merchandice in that our kingdome, and to setle some of ther necessarie affaires, wherwith they (in humble obedience of our lawes by ther sudden departur from thence) could not have tyme to tak ordour ; In all things else to be restrayned in what is not ordinarlie allowed to any stranger repairing thither for trade ; We ar heirby pleased to recommend them vnto yow, that if they doe nothing to hurt or derogat from the estate of the present professed religion, yow give way vnto them, in so far as may concerne the dispatch of ther lawfull affaires.—Grenwitch, 14 Junij 1632.

To the Exchequer.

Right, &c.—Being informed that our trustie and weilbeloved James Dowglas hath not received payment of his pension these diverse termes bypast, contrar to our royall intention, sieing, vpon the consideratioun of the long and painefull service done by him to our late dear father, of worthie memorie, the same was granted vnto him : Our pleasur therfoir is, efter due tryell how much he is behynd of the said pension, that with all convenient and speedie diligence yow caus pay vnto him the arrieris therof, togidder with the samyne yeirlie and termelie, according to his gift granted to him thervpon : And for your so doeing, &c.—Grenewich, 14 Junij 1632.

To the Advocat.

Trustie, &c.—Wheras, vpon the late treatie betuixt ws and the French King, we wer pleased to condescend that the Colonie which was latelie planted at Port Royall, in New Scotland, should befor the present removed from thence, and have accordinglie gevin ordour to our right, &c. The Viscount of Stirling, our Principall Secretarie for Scotland ; also by all our severall ordours and directions concerneing that bussines we have ever expressed that we have no intention to quyt our right title to anie of these boundis ; yit in regard our meaneing perchance will not be sufficientlie vnderstude by these our loveing subjects who heirefter shall intend the advancement of that work, ffor ther further satisfaction heirin, we doe heirby will and requyre yow to draw vp a sufficient warrant for our hand to pas vnder our great seall to our said right, &c. the Viscount of Stirling to goe on in the said work, whensoever he shall think fitting, wherby, for the encouragment of such as shall interest themsellfis with him in it, he may have full assurance from ws in verbo principis that as we have never meaned to relinquish our title to any pairt of these cuntreyis which he hath by patents from ws, so we shall ever heirefter be readie by our gracious favour to protect him, and all such as have or shall heirefter at aney tyme concurre with him for the advanceement of the plantations in these boundis forsaidis ; And if at aney tyme heirefter by ordour from ws they shalbe forced to remove from the saidis boundis, or aney part therof, wher they shall happin to be planted, We shall fullie satisfie them for all loss they shall susteane by aney such act or ordour from ws : And for your so doeing, &c.—Grenewich, 14 Junij 1632.

To the Viscount of Aboyne.

Right, &c.—We are informed by your willingnes and the watchfull care of your religious Lady towards the education of your children to learneing, and in especiall in the true Catholique religion publicklie professed in our dominions, And to that purpois that yow have bene, not onlie at extraordinarie charges in transporting your whole familie to the Vniversitie of Aberdene, and liveing ther these tuo yeres bypast, bot hath lykwayes for that cause susteaned sum loss and incurred the displeasur of some powerfull freindis ; We therfor have thoght fitt to tak favourable notice therof vnto yow, onlie to requyre yow not to be deterred by any privat discouragment, bot constantlie to continew in these and such lyke your religious endeavours which so neirlie concerne the futur quyet of these parts in that our kingdome ; wherin as yow shall doe ws acceptable service, so we lykwayes, when occasion shall offer, will be willing by our Countenance and favour to acknowledge the same, and weigh down any loss that yow shall susteyne therby ; wherin not doubting of your loyall care, we bid yow fairwell.—Gevin at our Manour of Grenwitch, 14 Junij 1632.

To the Counsell.

Right, &c.—Haveing considered the great prejudice that We receave in our dominions by the abuse of Coyne, the best of our gold and silver being exported to Forraeyne nations, and a base sort of money imported in place therof, We have the more willinglie hearkned to such propositions as wer made for remedie of the same, that we may therefter, with your advyse and with advyse of our Counsell heir, resolve what course is best to be takin for reformeing the present abuses and preventing the lyk heirefter : Our pleasur is, that yow tak the proposition which we send yow heirwith into your consideratioun, as lykwayes any other that shalbe made by Johne Achiesone, general of our Mynt, or any other of our Mynt heir, haveing called for them for that effect; And efter yow have seriouslie considered of them, that so soon as convenientlie yow can, yow certifie ws of your opinion what yow think best to be done therin, that we may therefter tak such a course theranent for the well of our kingdomes.—[Not dated.]

To the Exchequer.

Right, &c.—We have bene petitioned of late by Alexr Peeres concerneing a water pound for the vse of our Court of Halyrudhous, wherof he vndertuik the building vpon a former warrant vnder our hand, and vnderstanding his informatioun that the said work is exactlie performed, bot that the charge of it amounts higher then as was at first expected or warranted by our former ordour: It is our pleasur that yow direct some of your number, with the assistance of the Masters of work, for pervseing of his accompts; And in regard of his paines and lyeing out of his moneyis since the perfecting of the work, that yow give such further ordour as he may receave speedie satisfaction in what salbe fund justlie dew to him according to his accompts; and for, &c.—Grenewich, 18 Junij 1632.

These 20 of Junij a packet went to Scotland direct to Sir Ard Achiesone, wherin ther was 5 letteris of his Matie: 1o To the Advocat, New Scotland, Session Lubec schip, Exchequer James Dowglas, Chancellour Sir Piers Corsbie, Counsell Mr Rot Williamsone.

[Not addressed.]

Trustie, &c.—Wheras complant hath bene made vnto ws by James Hay, one of our subjects in Scotland, that the whole moneyis, goodis and merchandice which wer in a schip of Kirkcaldie, belonging to him, by one Michaell Rambot of Ostend, vnjustlie and most violent maner takin from him of late, schoe being in hir voyadge from London to Newcastle, these wronges being accompaneyed with diverse others complaynts of our good subjects whois goods have bene by some persones ther vnjustlie takin from them since Our late treatie with Spayne, wherof we wer loath at first to tak notice of everie particular circumstance, have moved ws at this tyme to requyr yow to vse your best and most speedie endevours with our dear sister the Infanta, that not onlie these Hay his goodis and losses may be speedelie refounded according to justice, and the Correspondence fitt to be keiped betweene our and hir subjects, bot that a generall course may be takin heirefter that no such just complants be made vnto ws by any of our subjects to the effect that we have not a just caus heirefter to give way vnto them to seik repetition of ther losses according to justice and equitie: Which recommending, &c.—Grenewitch, 20 Junij 1632.

To the Session.

Right, &c.—We have bene informed by our right trustie Counsellour the Lord Jedburgh, that by a process in law he is now lyk to suffer in a great part of his estate, and that onlie through not produceing of some of his evidents, which being in the handis of ane other, seames to be maliciouslie kept vp from him: And being vnwilling that ane ancient and deserveing familie, and whois late air was so faythfull a servant to ws, should vnjustlie suffer aney such occasion; Our pleasur is, that yow tak such ordour that all such evidents, if any such ther be in aney hand, may be produced befor yow, and that if yow find them true and valide, the said Lo. Jedburgh may enjoy the full benefite of them in everie kynd in so far as the lawes and practique of that our kingdome can allow; and for your, &c.—Greenwich, 25 Junij 1632.

To the Advocat.

Trustie, &c.—We ar informed that the Lo/ Jedburgh hath good rights as well of the bailliarie and of diverse landis holdin of the Abbay of Jedburgh, and that some of the saidis rights hath bene granted vnto him by our father, of blissed memorie, and that ther is processes intended against him for the annulling thairof: Our pleasur is, that in so far as may not be derogatorie to any right belonging vnto ws, yow assist the said Lord Jedburgh and such as have right from him in defence of all trew right granted vnto him, espetiallie such as ar vnder the great seall of that our kingdome of the saidis landis or bailliarie against whatsumever persones pressed to impugne the same: Which recommending, &c.—Grenewich, 25 Junij 1632.

Protection to Captain Wallace.

Our Soveraigne Lord, vnderstanding how that Colonell Lunnisden, haveing charge vnder the King of Sweden for levyeing of some men in Scotland be his Ma^{tis} permission for the said King of Sweden his service in the warres of Germanie, and how to that effect his Matie have gevin a Commission to the said Colonell, who haveing made choyse of Captan David Wallace to be his serjant Major, for the sufficiencie and knowledge of the said Capitane David Wallace hath in militarie discipline, did for that purpois send for the said Capitane Wallace out of Irland, wher he hath the Charge of Livetenment in the Regiment of the Erle of Buccleugh: But the said Captan Wallace hearing that in his absence from thence he was putt to the horne, or lyklie to be troubled in that kynd for some debt or other civill cause, wherof as yit he doeth not trulie know the estate, wherby he dar handlie repair to that kingdome for dischargeing that place conferred vponn him be the said Colonell, so that that service committed to his charge is lyk to be neglected, to the great hinder of the said levy: And his Matie being informed that if the said Capitane Wallace had some competent tyme allowed vnto him for taking ordour with his creditours or other persones with whome he hath to doe, he would quicklie tak a course for ther satisfaction, wher if he at his first approach to that kingdome they should vnseasonablie trouble him, it would both dissapoynt the saids Creditours or other persones, and disable him lykwayes from the said imployment: Therfor his Matie, both haveing a speciall regarde heirin to the advancement of these levyis, and that a course may be takin be the said Capitan Wallace for satisfieing the saids persones within a schort tyme, according to justice and equitie, of his princelie power and royall authoritie, Ordeanes a protection to be made vnder his highnes' great seall of Scotland accepting the said Capitane Wallace vnder his speciall power and safeguard, giving and granting to him dureing the space of thrie moneths, begining from passing of the presents vnto the said seall, Licence, power, and libertie to peaceablie and safelie duell, stay, and remane within any part of the said kingdome, without molestatioun, trouble, challenge, persute, or danger of apprehending or warding of his persone: dischargeing expreslie by thir presents all his Ma^{teis} schireffis, stewarts, provests, baillies, constablis of barrons, Justices of peace, and all other Justices, Judges, Officers, and Ministers of his highnes' lawis, both by burgh and land, ther deputeis, servands, and all others whom it effeires within the said kingdome, That they on nawayes presume, attempt, nor tak in hand, directlie or indirectlie, by day or night, to seik, tak, or apprehend the said Captan Wallace, his persone, or mak any disturbance, interruption, or violation of this his Ma^{teis} protection, vnder pane of incurreing his highnes' vtter wraith and high displeasur, notwithstanding of any Letters of horning, Captions, warrandis, Commissioners, charges, or commandis alreadie gevin or to be gevin by his Matie himsellf, the Lordis of Session, or any of his Ma^{teis} Judges, officers, or other persones whatsoever within the said kingdome, in favours of whatsoever persone or persones for apprehending and warding of the said Captan his persone, for any debts or sownnes adebtit by him as suretie or principall, Wheranent his Matie, of his highnes' royall and princelie power, be thir presents dispensses in that part dureing the space of thrie monthis, Ordaneing thir presents to be a sufficient warrant to the writter to the great seall and keeper tharof for wryting of thir presents to the said seall, and appending the said seall thervnto, without passing of any others sealls or registers; wherunent thir presents shalbe vnto them a sufficient warrant.—Gevin at our Manour of Grenwitche, the 26 of Junij 1632.

Our Soverane Lord ordeanes ane Letter to be made vnder his highnes' privie seall in dew forme to his lovit Peter Andersone, indueller in the Cannogate, nominatand and presentand him dureing all the dayes of his lyftyme to the office and keeping of his Maties Chapell Royall of Halyrudhous, whole keyis, locks, and dores thairof, with the keyis of his highnes' loft, and all other rowmes and places within the samyne, revestreis, and whole pertinents whatsumever perteneing thairto, or within the samyne, And to all feyis, casualiteis, proffitis, digniteis, emoluments, and dewteis whatsumever righteouslie perteneing and belonging to the samyne, or to be mortifeid or dottet thereto, now vacand in his Maties handis, and at his highnes' gift and disposition be dimission made of the samyne office by Robert Weir, last keiper of the said Chappell royall, in his Ma^{teis} or his highnes' Commissioner's handis, or by the seiknes and inhabilitie of the said Robert not being able to keip and exerce the said office, or by his deceis, when it shalhappin to vaik and becum in his Ma^{teis} handis, Requyreing and desyreing heirby Our Reverend father in God, Adam, bischop of Dumblane, deane of the said Chappell royall, to admitt and receave the said Peter Andersone in and to the said office vpon his oath of obedience, And that the said letter be extendit in the best forme with all clausses neidfull, And with command therin to the Lordis of Counsall and session vpon the sight of his admission and presentation to grant and direct Letters at his instance vpon ane simple charge against all and whatsumever persones within this realme subject in payment of the feyis, casualiteis, and dewteis belonging to the said office at any tyme bygane, or that shall happin to be subject therto in tyme comeing ffor causeing the said Peter Andersone, his factours, servitours, and others in his name, to [be] readelie answer it and obey it of the saids whole feyis, casualities, proffits, emoluments, and dewteis perteneing and belonging to the said office of the said Chappell royall at any time bygane, or shall happin to pertene and belong therto, And that of the Cropt and yeir of God 1632. And sicklyk yeirlie and termelie thairefter and in tyme cuming dureing all the dayes of his lyftyme.—Greenewitch, 26 Junij 1632.

To the Counsell.

Right, &c.—Wheras vpon good considerations we wer pleased a yeir agoe to grant our weilbeloved servand Sir Alex^r Home a protection for ane yeir, wherby to frie him of some encombrances broght vpon him in his younger yeres, and to the end that he might have the concurrance of his father, Sir George Home (necessarlie requisit vnto him), yow did vpon our letter grant a protection to the said Sir George, in regard that at that tyme our servand, for occasions speciallie concerneing our service, was forced to repair from thence to our Court, wherby he did lose the opportunitie of that tyme granted to him: Our pleasur therfor is, that according to your first intention yow grant of new to our said servand and his father libertie to cum in publict for the lawfull setling of ther affaires till the ending of the ensueing winter session.—Grenewitch, 27 Junij 1632.

To the Exchequer.

Right, &c.—Wheras we have bene pleased to grant vnto our right trustie and right weilbeloved Cousen and Counsellour the Viscount of Stirling, our principall Secretarie for Scotland, the benefite arysing to the Copper money to be coyned in that our kingdome according to his patent thervpon for his satisfaction dew vnto him by ws efter deduction whairof, with the charges of the werk, he is to be accomptable to ws for the superplus, and we being pleased vpon good considerations, and with consent of the said Viscount for his interest, that our servant Sir Robert Gordoun have the fourt part of the frie benefite of these Copper moneyis till he be payed of 2000ᵐᵇ sterling latelie granted to him by our precept, Our pleasur is, that yow give your best assistance heirin to the said Sir Robert Gordon, and tak some course as may be sufficient to enable him by himself or assigneyis to receive the said fourt part till he be payed of the said sowme, allowing to the said Viscount in his accompts the deduction of that same for that vse.—Grenwitch, 27 Junij 1632.

To the Counsall.

Right, &c.—Wheras our right, &c. the Erle of Tullibardyne, being to repair to that our kingdome, to these partes wher these of the name of Grant doe reside, we for the better setling of our peace ther, by canseing remove in a fair and quyet maner, without farder danger of law or trouble to our subjects, all such differences as ar amongst these of that name, have to that effect requyred him to informe himself of the groundis therof, and the best way how they may be composed, and that to vse his best endeavours, or at least to certifie ws of the Estate wherin they now stand: Thairfor we have thoght litt to recommend vnto yow to give vnto the said Erle all such furtherance which yow shall find that he shall lawfullie and necessarlie requyre to that purpois.—Grenewich, 27 Junij 1632.

To the Session.

Right, &c.—The inclosed petition sent by ws to be considered vpon by yow being presented vnto ws by our weilbeloved servand, Sir Alexᵣ Home, who though he be (as he affirmeth) deiplie interested in that caus, yit in regard of his service about our persone he cannot long attend the issue thairof, we ar pleased seriouslie to recommend vnto yow that, efter strict examination of such persones as can give evidence in the matter, and exact tryell of everie circumstance that may tent to the clearing of the treuth, Justice be administred with expedition according to the Lawes of that our kingdome, wherin not doubting of your care, &c.—Grenwitch, 28 Junij 1632.

To the Thesacrer and Deputie Thesacrer.

Our pleasur is, that out of the readiest of our present rents or casualiteis whatsumever of that our kingdome, or which shall accresce vnto ws heirefter by whatsumever maner of way, yow pay with all diligence vnto Sir Robert Gordon, knyᵗ, gentlman of our privie Chalmer in ordinarie, the sowme of 2000ᵐᵇ sterling; and for your sua doeing these presents shalbe vnto yow and all others whom it may concerne a sufficient warrant and discherge.—Grenwitch, 28 Junij 1632.

To the Counsell.

Right, &c.—Wheras we ar informed of a practeis in appearance so pernicious and neerlie concerneing ws, as we could not bot tak some tryell thairof both by ourself and some of our Counsell appoynted by ws for that purpois: Bot in the meane tyme, becaus of some sinistrous rumours maliciouslie raisit thervpon to the prejudice of our right trustie and weilbeloved Cousen and Counsellour the Marqueis of Hamiltoun, and the Earles of Hadinton, Buccleugh, and Roxburgh, and some others, least the lyk reports be broght into our earis, we have thoght good heirwith to declair that not onlie we have fund by the tryell we ourselffis takin, that they ar altogidder innocent and cleir thairof, bot lykwyse that the pryme informer thairof hath now cleared them vpon oath, testifieing them (as we know them to be) as good and faythfull subjects as aney we have in aney of our kingdomes : And for the lassines itselff whensoever it shalbe fullie tryed, we will therefter express our further pleasur concerneing others interested therin, according as we shall find just caus ather in punisching aney persone who shalbe fund guiltie, or in punisching aney persone that shalbe fund to have gevin false information : And wheras we have formerlie by our letters recommendit vnto yow our right, &c. the Marqueis of Hamilton for furthering the speedie levy and transportation of men with all possible diligence, these ar agane to requyre yow to contribute your best help that your authoritie or endeavours can afturd to that effect, wherof both out of the regard we have to him and to that imployment, being verie confident of your best care : We bid, &c.—Grenwich, 29 Junij 1632.

Wheras our servand Sir Ritchart Grhame is to attend vpon ws with his horse and houndis at these tymes in the yeir when our hunting is in seasone, for which cause we doe heirby acquyt and discherge him of all dewteis and cuntrie services belonging vnto ws from him within our counteis of Yorkschyre and Cumberland : To which purpois we will and requyre yow, our officers vnder writtin, that at your generall musteris and assembleis yow doe not charge him to schow light horses, nor impose vpon him any other services or dewteis whatsoever ; for which the sight of these presents shalbe vnto yow and everie of yow a sufficient warrand.—Oatland, 3 July 1632.

Wheras our servand Sir Ritchart Grhame hath keipt and bred houndis for our vse, which for the better furnishing of ws he doeth dispense to severall others of our subjects within our counteis of Yorkschyre and Cumberland : These ar therfoir to will and requyre our said servand, and such as ar vnder writtin, to tak and dispose of all Greyhoundis, Whippets, and Mangrells yow shall find in these parts wher yow shall vse to hunt within our saidis counteis, and to tak and dispose vpon aney vnlawfull engyne vsed contrarie to our Lawis and statuts provyded for preserving of our game ; wherin if yow or aney of yow shall find aney persone refractorie, returne ther names to our Counsell table : All which we requyre to be strictlie performed with care and diligence, as yow wilbe answerable to ws.—Oatlandis, 3 July 1632.

To our trustie and weilbeloved Sir Thomas Mideaff and Sir Hugh
　　Bechell, knyts, George Best of Meltoun, and Marmaduk
　　Wilsone of Torfeild.

Ane other of the same tenour was directed in favours of Sir Ritchart Grhame to Johne Oglenbie, Thomas Lother, William Lother, and Tobie Eden.

Wheras our servand Sir Ritchart Grhame doeth keip and breid houndis for our vse, for the better perfecting wherof, to be readie for our sport, we doe authorize him to hunt and kill out of everie Park, forrest, or chace two brace of staggs and bucks of this seasone, Two brace of hyndis and does in the winter seasone : That is to say, out of Pomfort Park, the forrest or Park of Blarsky, the forrest of Winsidale, and chace of Bischopdale, and Coverdale, and chace and Park of Pakering, within our countie of York ; Twisdale Chace and Marwood and Ramshwoorth Park, within our bischoprik of Durisme ; our forrest of Inerdale, within our Countie of Comberland : Our will and pleasur is, that yow permitt and suffer our said servand as aforsaid, and this shalbe your warrand.—Oatlands, 3 July 1632.

To our Rangers and Keipers ther.

To the Commissioners of Surrenders.

Right, &c.—We ar informed that the Tythes of the kirk of Dunbar, wherin we have some particular interest, are to be valued ; whairof desyreing that some further consideration be had befoir any proceiding be vsed in the said Valuation, that therefter it may goe on according to the generall course of our Commission, Our pleasur is, that yow continew the valuation of these tythes to the first day of No^r nixt ensueing, and that no further warrant be granted concerneing them then what is alreadie gevin : And for soe, &c.—Grenewitch, 6 July 1632.

To the Clergie.

Right, &c.—Though we have formerlie recommended vnto your care that a course might be takin for the receaveing of the translation of the Psalmes of King David, whairof our late dear father was author, to be sung in all the churches of that our kingdome, and ar lykwyse confident of your best affectionat endeavours in it ; Yit vnderstanding that yow ar schortlie to be assembled togidder, our earnest desyre of the work, with the fitnes of the occasion of your joynt assistances for the doeing thairof, have moved ws at this tyme agane to requyre yow at last to effectuat that which we so much desyre, not onlie for the memorie of the author, and the approved sufficiencie of the work, bot for the good which we hope shalbe reaped by the vse of it in the Church : Wherin expecting your care and diligence, we bid yow farewell.—From our Court at Grenwitch, the 6 of July 1632.

Our pleasur is, that furthwith, vpon offer made vnto yow of ane authentik extract of the service wherby the now Lord Ogilvie did enter himself heir to the late Lord Ogilvie, his father, yow accept therof, and exped the same in our Chancerie without further delay, as yow will answer vnto ws, that such as be interested therin may have the benefite of our lawis ; ffor doeing wherof these presents shalbe vnto yow a sufficient warrand.—From our manour at Grenwitch, the [not dated].

To . . . Sir Johne Scott of Scottarvet, kny^t, directour of our
Chancerie in our kingdome of Scotland.

To the Chancellour.

Right, &c.—Wheras the first of August is appoynted by our former warrant in our letters to our Counsell ther for the tryell of Allaster Grant : These ar to requyre yow to continew the Executioun of the sentence, if any shalbe gevin against him, till our further pleasur shalbe made knowen ; and that yow signifie this our pleasur to the Lordis of our Counsell, or whome it may concerne for this effect, efter the tryell, bot not befor : And for your soe doeing, &c.—Grenwitch, 6 July 1632.

To Sir David Wood of Bonytoun, Sir Alex^r Erskine of Dun, and Sir Coline Campbell of Lundie, Shirreff of Forfar.

Trustie, &c.—Wheras we ar informed by petition of James Ogilvie, sone of the Late Lord Ogilvie, that he alledgeth himself as his air by Contract of mariage betuixt him and his late lady, the petitioner's

11   2 II

mother, to provyde certane sowmes of money for the aires to be procreat between them, and that efter his fatheris death, the now Lord Ogilvie his brother, efter many yeres desyreing to enter himsellf as air to his father, hath now in end served himsellf air to his father, bot hath not retoured the service to our Chancerie, according to the custome, therby laboreing to suppress the same in the Clerkis handis, to the petitioner's great prejudice : Our pleasur is, therfoir, and we doe heirby requyre yow, and any of yow being shirreffs at the tyme of the said service, and who now is, that with all diligence, as yow will answer to the contrarie, yow caus your Clerk for the tyme, or that now is, in whois hands the roll of that service doeth remane, to delyver ane authentik extract therof, as the custome is, to such as shalbe appoynted by our trustie and weilbelovit servand Alexr Auchmowtie, the petitioner's father-in-law, for receaveing therof : And for doeing, &c. we bid, &c.—At our Court at St James, 12 July 1632.

To the Counsell.

Right, &c.—Efter long tyme and many meittings betuixt the Commissioners of both our kingdomes, for a generall association for the fisching, wherat we oursellf for the most part was present, the bussines being now to our great contentment, being concludit with mutuall consent of both, as may appear by the Chartours which we send yow heirwith, drawen vp according to the heads that wer agried vpoun, wherin we have had a speciall care to preserve the dignitie of that our antient kingdome, both in the placeing therof and in appending the seallis : And our pleasur is that yow pass the Chartour which we have gevin as King of Scotland (wherin yow have first place immediatlie vnder our great seall), as also when the Chartour of this our kingdome of England, with the great seall therof, cum vnto yow, wherin it hath first place, that yow lykwayes append the seall of that our kingdome thervnto in the secund place ; or if yow shall find by the custome of that our kingdome the ordinarie course is of necessitie to be followed, and that the seall cannot be immediatlie appendit vnto the Chartour which we have sent yow heirwith, or to the other which is to cum heirefter, yow shall mak vse of these two signaturs, which we have lykwyse sent to yow in the vulgar tongue for that purpoise, or of one of them, as yow shall find expedient to be passed in the ordinarie way, a speciall care being had for conformitie with the Chartour heir, that the translation of them in Latine be verbatim the same which we have now sent yow heirwith : And this yow faill not to doe with all diligence ; ffor doeing whairof, &c.—Oatlands, 15 July 1632.

To the Counsell.

Right, &c.—Being informed of the great wrongs done by strangers inhabiting the Lewis, and repairing therto in tradeing and fisching, agianst the lawis of that our kingdome ; and how that vpon a former complaynt made vnto yow thervpon by our frie burghs a decreit was gevin by yow aganst the Earle of Seafort, wherby he was ordored to bring in these strangers before yow that a course might be takin for causing them observe our acts of parliament provydit in these caices : Our pleasur is, that yow cause our said decreit be put in execution, and the strangers censured for ther transgression, both in tradeing or fisching aganst the lawis, or for transporting of forbidden goodis for not payment of our Customes, or from saylling from thence without conpeit, causeing them find sufficient securitie for absteneing of the lyk in all tyme cuming : And that yow give ordour to the Inheritours of the Yles not to suffer any stranger to trade or fisch within the same, vseing your best and readiest endeavours that the whole fisching be reserved for the vse of the natives and subjects who ar frie of the societie of new erected by ws, wherby they may be encouraged to sett forward in so great and hopefull a work, wherof we ar pleased to tak vpon ws the protection : Which speciallie recommending vnto your care, We bid yow farewell.—Oatlands, 15 July 1632.

To the Counsell.

Right, &c.—Wheras vpon humble complaynt exhibited to ws by Captan David Robertsone of the great injureis and losses he had susteaned of the Hamburgers in his goods and losses of sindrie of our subjects lyffes, we wer pleased to direct our letteris to that state craveing redress thairof, and efter returne of ther answer haveing sent it vnto yow, and receaveing your opinion concerneing it, finding that justice was ather denyed or delayed, we wer pleased to grant letteris of reprysall thervpon wherby some schippis and goodis wer takin which ar now in that our kingdome ; And now that the State of Hamburgh haveing sent hither commissioners to ws, who pretend that justice was nather denyed nor protracted, bot that they ar willing still to administer justice for repairing the losses sustened according to the custome of nations in that kynd, desyreing that the Letteris of Reprysell may be recalled, and the schippis and goods restored, we have thoght good to send yow heirwith the substance of that which they have propounded in ther papers, requyreing yow to consider thairof and informe yourselfis of particular proceidingis formerlie in that bussines, whervpoun the letteris of reprysell wer granted, and to certifie ws thairof with your further opinion what may be most fitting, that we may returne such answer to that state as may be most agricable to reasone and justice.—Oatlands, 15 July 1632.

To the Advocat.

Trustie, &c.—Being willing, according to our Commission for Surrenders and decrees following thervpon, that a speedie way be vsed for bringing to our Croun the few-dewteis of the Abbacies, Pryoreis, and others beneficies of that our kingdome, wherby our rent may be encreased, and diverse of our subjects holding of the Erectours may becum our immediat tennents : Our pleasur is, that from tyme to tyme that by advyse of our Thesaurer or deputie Thesaurer and remanent Commissioners of Exchequer yow vse all convenient expedition in advanceing that bussines, and in particular that yow deall with the Lord Palmerino for satisfieing him according to our decree, to which purpois we have at this tyme gevin ordour to our Thesaurer, otherwyse if vpon these termes he will not surrender that yow insist by a legall course for effectuating thairof ; for whilk these presents shalbe your warrand.—Oatlands, 19 July 1632.

To the Exchequer.

Right, &c.- Wheras we ar pleased to remitt to yow the consideration of the losses sustened by Alex^r Peeres, keiper of our Tynneiss Court in that our kingdome, in building a Tynneiss Court for our service adjoyneing to our palace of Halyrudhous, whervpon yow selected of your owin number the President of our privie Counsell and our Thesaurer deputie to consider thairof, and moderat a composition to him for the same, for which ane act of Exchequer was made, sieing (as we ar informed) the tynneiss court is weill done and commodiouslie seated for the vse and decoreing of that our palace, we ar the rather pleased that the more speedie course be takin for helping to repair his losses a long tyme vndergone by him : Therfor our pleasur is, that vpon report of the saidis officeris (which we requyre to be made with all convenient diligence) yow furthwith give ordour therefter that payment be made to him or his assigneyis accordinglie, and that thervpon yow caus mak act of Exchequer ; ffor doeing of all which these presents salbe vnto yow and our Thesaurer and deputie Thesaurer a sufficient warrant : So, &c.— From our Court at Oatlands, 19 July 1632.

To the Archbischop of Glasgow.

Right reverend father in God, &c.—We have bene petitioned by the L^o Sempill humblie schewing vnto ws that yow intended to proceid against him with the censures of the Church ; and though we approve your Zeall in these courses recommended formerlie by ws to your care for the peace of the trew religion professed amongst ws ; Yit being loath to lose aney of his qualitie so long as ther is aney hope to reclayme them by fair meanes, Our pleasur is, that yow grant him yit some further delay vntill the tyme we may be particularlie informed by yow of his cariage, and the reasones of your proceidingis so against him ; And that in the meane tyme yow suspend your further censure till our pleasur shalbe knowen efter your report vnto ws thervpon ; ffor doeing, &c.—Oatlands, 19 July 1632.

WARRANT.

Our pleasur is, that yow prepare a bill for our signatur to the governour and other officers of the East India Companie, wherby our right trustie and weilbeloved the Viscont of Stirling, our Principall Secretarie of our kingdome of Scotland, conforme to a former warrant granted to him by our late dear father, may have power by his deputie haveing his letteris of deputation to Enroll in a book the names of such persones borne in Scotland, ather haveing ther ordinarie residence ther or in this our kingdome of England, as ar employed from hence in any voyadge from East India, and that no wages or adventures of any such persones deceissed befor ther returne hither be payed vnto aney heir without the knowledge and consent of his deputie for the tyme, to the end that the goodis of the persone deceissed be made knowen and cum to the vse of the trew air or others haveing good right thervnto, wherof the deputie is to mak tryell and to give such evidence therin as he can find in Scotland or elsewher. He is to have dureing his deputation twelff pense of everie pund money to be payed to the air of the persone deceissed ar any other justlie interested : For doeing, &c.—Oatlands, 19 July 1632.

To our trustie and Weilbeloved William Noy, our Attornay generall.

TO THE SESSION.

Sir Johne Hope, Sessioner, by dimission of Sir James Oliphant : Sir Johne Scott, Sessioner, by death of Prestoungrange.—Oatlands, 28 July 1632.

TO THE COUNSELL.

The State of the Low Cuntreyis did procure a warrant from his Matie for the levie of 1500 men for the saids States the 28 July 1632.

TO THE DEPUTIE OF IRLAND.

Right, &c.—We ar informed that certane rebells called Williame Irwing, John and Wm Charltons, who ar indicted for murther and severall heynous feloneis both in this our kingdome and Scotland, have for preventing of Justice fled to that our kingdome, wherin it concerneth ws in our royall authoritie not onlie to cause justice be speedielie executed according to our lawis aganst these malefactours wher the facts wer committed, but lykwyse to have a care that heirefter none of our kingdomes be a meanes to schelter such persones to delude the cours of Justice due to be executed in aney of the other, Our pleasur is, that yow give speciall ordour to our officers ther whom yow shall find that this purpois doeth concerne, for causing a diligent and sure search be made for these thrie rebellis, and for transporting them to Carlile in England, or Drumfreis in Scotland, to be receaved by the Mayor, provest, and bailleis thairof to be lyable to Justice, as the sute of our subjects interest and as bussines of the lyk nature shall happin to fall out heirefter ther, vpon notice gevin yow thairof by our Counsell heir or of Scotland, the Justice Generall thairof, or such as ar or shalbe interested by ws for keiping our peace in the Midleschyres, yow be cairfull to doe accordinglie which shalbe &c.—Oatlands, 30 July 1632.

These conteyne a Ratification to your Maᵗⁱˢ royall burrowis of all gifts, patents, and acts of parliament made to and in favours of the said royall burrughs by your Maᵗⁱˢ predecessours, of happie memorie, generallie and particularlie exprest in the signatur anent the frie and onlie traffick of merchandice within and without the kingdome, and of the arryveing of all schips at the said frie burrowis for making of ther entrie and paying of your Maᵗⁱˢ customes, and of the frie exercise of Crafts with the samyne, with prohibition thairof in the suburbs by and contigue to the saids frie burrowis, and of the liberteis and priviledges of the generall Conventions granted to the saids royall burrowis by the Lawis and Acts of parliament: Togidder with ane new gift of the premisses in favours of the saids royall burrowis, and with power and commission to them, ather in the said generall convention, or to everie burgh apart, To appoynt Judges and bailleis to sie and cognosce against all vnfriemen and transgressours of the saids acts of parliament, making them sole judges therin in prima instantia, but prejudice to the Lords of Session who ar severall judges vnder your Maᵗⁱᵉ in all causses civill to proceid therin by way of reduction in secunda instantia, and that thir presents shalbe ane sufficient warrant for appending of your Maᵗⁱˢ great seall.—Oatlands, the last of July 1632.

May it pleas your Maᵗⁱᵉ—

These conteyne ane disposition by your Maᵗⁱᵉ to Johne, Erle of Rothes, his heyres-male and assigneyis, of the particular landis above writtin, all erected in one baronie called the baronie of Inchgall, patronage of the personage and viccarage of the kirk of Ballingrie vpon the resignation of Andro Wardlaw of Torrie and Mʳ David Aytoun, with ane new gift of the whole lands and others forsaids, and ane vnion of the samyne in ane frie barronie, to be called the baronie of Inchgall, and that ane seasine to be takin at the place of Inchgall salbe good and valide for the whole, to be holdin of your Maᵗⁱᵉ and highnes successours in frie heretage and frie baronie for ever, for payment of the dewteis and performeing the services and conditions conteynit in the old Infeftments payed to .your Maᵗⁱᵉ befor the Resignation.—Oatlands, last July 1632.   Subᵗ,   Sⁱᴿ Tʜ. Hope.

Hereby your Maᵗⁱᵉ appoynteth Mʳ William Hay, Commissar Clerk of Edinburgh, dureing his lyftyme to the high Commission, with power to tak and vse the prollites belonging to that office, and to collect and pay to your Maᵗⁱˢ vse the halff of the feyis due to your Maᵗⁱᵉ by that Commission which shallhappin to be imposed by the Commissioners vpon delinquents, whairof for his service done and to be done in that Charge your Maᵗⁱᵉ bestowis vpon him a yeirlie pension of 500ᵗⁱᵇ Scotts.

May it pleas your most sacred Maᵗⁱᵉ.—

These conteyne a grant to Johne Hamiltoun, burges of Edinburgh, his partiners and ther airis, &c., dureing the space of 21 yeirs, for winding, thraveing, and trusting of silk, dyeing and fixing of all maner of cullours thervpoun within Scotland, with power to them to conduce with strangers and other persones whatsoever to vse and practeise these tradis, to which strangers your Maᵗⁱᵉ grant all such priviledges and immuniteis as ar or hath bene granted to any strangers denized or naturalised persone of the said kingdome, provyded that they reside ordourlie within the same and be subject to the lawis thairof, the patentes and ther forsaids furnisching the kingdome at cheaper and easier rates then merchandis doe, have power to sell the commoditeis abroad, paying custome and other dewteis for what they shall import or export : All others, saveing the saids patentees, are dischargel to vse the saids trades vpon pane of forfaltour of the commoditeis, the one-halff to your Ma^{tis} vse, and the other to the patentees : The merchandis may import the lyk commoditeis without aney restraynt : This grant to be voyd if within thrie yeires the saids tradis or aney of them be not practized for the good of the commonwealth.—Oatlands, last July 1632.

To the Counsell.

Right, &c.—Wheras we ar informed that it was carefullie provydit by diverse acts of Parliament into the tyme of our late royall progenitours that the Maltmen in these tymes wer restrayned to a certane quantitie of victuall or pryces in selling ther malt, which they wer not to transgresse, as may by the Acts appear : but by reasone of the long tyme since these statuts wer made, the pryces of all thingis ar much changed, so that it is thoght necessarie for the reformation of the present abuse, committed by Maltmen to the great prejudice of the Commongood, that new ordours and pryces according to the tymes be establisched and new penalteis preseryved to be inflicted vpon the delinquents : Our pleasur is, that haveing considered of the saidis Acts, yow give ordour for the pryces in tyme cuming to be takin by the Maltmen betweene the boll of barley and the boll of bear, preseryveing penalteis in caice of dissobedience in such maner as yow shall think fitt, and as may be most agriceable to the pryces of the present tymes : Whervpoun we will yow to caus mak ane act of Counsall till further ordour be takin (if yow shall find it expedient) in our nixt Parliament, And in the meantyme that the executioun of the former acts, in so far as doeth concerne the saidis pryces, shall ceise in all tyme cuming, without prejudice alwayes of the bygane Escapes of the saidis acts, when we shalbe pleased to call for them : We bid yow hartlie farewell.—From our Court at Oatlands, last July 1632.

To the Counsell.

Right, &c.—Wheras we ar informed that diverse priviledges and liberteis have bene granted to our frie burghes of that our ancient kingdome by diverse of our royall progenitours, which therefter we confirmed vnto them by severall acts of Parliaments, for which they are subject to the payment of our taxations and diverse services tending to the publict good, whervnto no other brugh being tyed ar discharged by speciall acts of Parliament to enjoy the lyk priviledge, which being willing to confirme from tyme to tyme for the vse of the said frie burghes in so far as is agrieable to our saidis lawes : Our pleasur is, that in the erection of all brughes of baronie heirefter ther be no further libertie granted to them in any patent than by the Lawes of that our kingdome is competent to a brugh of baronie, and that nane of them heirefter be erected with any priviledges which by the lawis and statuts of that kingdome ar onlie propper to our brughs royall ; which recommending to your care, We bid, &c.—Oatlands, last July 1632.

To the Counsell.

Right, &c.—Wheras we ar informed that our ancient kingdome doe verie much suffer by want of Manufactoreis, wherby the native Commoditeis might be made more vsefull and beneficiall for the publict good, and a number of our poore subjects ther be putt to work, speciallie by making of cloath and of all kynd of stuffes, wherin haveing a speciall care, by causeing putt in practeis what is heirby intendit conduceing to the good estate thairof, Our pleasur is, that yow Call befoir yow the Counsall of our brugh of

Edinburgh, or such others of our brughes and subjects whom yow sall find willing to vndertak the inbringing of tradesmen for fitting vp works to that effect, granting vnto them such privileges and liberteis as may encourage them to works of that kynd, restrayneing all others dureing the tyme yow shall limitt vnto them by ther patentes or licences, which we will approve and confirme as yow shall find requisit for the publict good.—Oatlands, last July 1632.

To the Counsell.

Right, &c.—Wheras our burgh of Edinburgh hath made offer vnto ws to build vpon ther owin charges fair and convenient housses and rowmes for the vse of our Counsell, Exchequer, and Colledge of Justice, and for receaveing the Estates of that our kingdome in the tyme of Parliament and generall assembleis therof ; And we being willing to encourage them to prosecute what they have for the honour of that our ancient kingdome so willinglie offered and vndertakin, Our pleasur is, that yow caus surveigh the saidis buildingis, and if yow find them for the purpois above specifeit, and be assured that they will accomplish the same, certifie ws therof accordinglie, for we think that the work doeth deserve encouragment, and we will mak vse of it as we find caus : So recommending this vnto yow, We, &c.—Oatlands, last July 1632.

To the Chancellour.

Right, &c.—Being informed of the qualitie and sufficiencie of our trustie and weilbelouit James Murray of Kilbabertoun, and of his affection to doe ws good service ther, Our pleasur is, that with all ceremonie requisit yow dub him knyght, according to the vse and custome of that antient kingdome observed in the lyk caices ; and for your soe doeing these presents shalbe your warrand : So we bid yow farwell.—From our Court of Oatlandis, last July 1632.

To the Chancellour.

Right, &c.—Being informed that ane Mr James Cokburne, shirreff-deputie of Eist Lothiane, hath exercised that office this many yeires bypast, both for the good of our service of that kynd and to the good lykeing of such of our subjectis whom it did concerne ; and that in regard of his long practeis therin and sufficiencie otherwayes, great prejudice would aryse to our service and to our subjectis if he wer removed : Our pleasur is, that at the yeirlie election of our shirreffiis yow give ordour that he be elected and continewed in that charge ; and for your, &c.—Oatlandis, last July 1632.

To the Viscount of Dauplin, our Chancellour of Scotland, and our Collectour Generall of Taxatiouns granted ws in that our Kingdome.

In regard of the good and acceptable service done vnto ws by our servand David Firynghame, who is to attend heir in the charge he hath from ws, Our pleasur is, that yow discharge him and his factours of his part of all such taxatiouns for his moneyis in that our kingdome as wer granted in the tyme of our late dear father and our owin, and of all penalteis and forfaltours incurred, or which heirefter can be exacted for concealment thairof, or otherwayes, and that vnder your owin hand as collectour generall, or as hath bene accustomed in the lyk caices, and wher your owin discharge will not serve to this purpois, that yow caus mak ane act of Counsell or Exchequer, or what discharge shalbe sufficient fund for his exoneratioun of his part of these taxatiouns ; for which these presents shalbe vnto yow and all others whom it may concerne a sufficient warrand and discharge.—Oatlandis, last July 1632.

To the Agent Bruxells.

Trustie, &c.—We ar informed that a schip called the St Peter of Kinghorne, in Scotland, hath bene of late vnjustlie takin by one Nicolas Maschler in Ostend, in hir voyadge from that our kingdome to Caleis, in France, whither or in some part of this kingdome shee was to vnload, as by the inclosed information and other papers for giveing light to this purpois yow may informe your selff, if our subjects can mak appear by themselllis or otherwayes, that ther schip and goodis hath bene vnjustlie takin be the said Captane his forceing of them to fill vp a blank left in the indentours between them and ther partiners for the place of the vnloading of ther goodis: Our pleasur is, that yow vse your best and most readie endeavours with our sister and the Archdutchess hir officers, and others whom it may concerne ther, that speedie restitution be made vnto them of the said schip and goodis, with ther losses, causeing punisch the takers according to the lawes ther, wherin we will yow to vse such panes and diligence as possible may be for ther satisfaction, which we will tak as good service done vnto ws.—From Oatlandis, last of July 1632.

To the Counsell.

Right, &c.—We have bene humblie moved in behalff of our frie brughs in that our kingdome that we might be pleased to cause preserve ther liberteis and priviledges as our late dear father did, and as we have hitherto done; To which purpois ther humble sute is that they suffer no prejudice therin by a Commission granted by ws for tryeing the priviledges of the office of high Constabularie of that kingdome, if any new patent be granted thairvpon concerneing additions derogatorie to ther former rights and customes, as our intention is to caus try what doeth justlie belong to that office, that according as shalbe fund our high Constable may enjoy the same in such maner as any of his predicessours hath formerlie done: So we doubt not therby that our saidis brughes be prejudged in their rights and priviledges which they have ancientlie enjoyed, by grants of our royall predicessours; Therfoir our pleasur is, that no new gift be exped tuitching the said office of constabularie, if any heirefter shalbe presented vnto yow, till the Commissioners of our saidis brughtis be first lawfullie cited and heard to object against the same; and if any question shall aryse anent ther liberteis and priviledges, that yow stay the passing of the said gift, in so far as concerneth the differences betuixt our high constable and them conteynit in the said gift, vntill they be legallie tryed and decydit befoir the judge competent to whome we will that the tryell thairof be remitted.—Oatlandis, last of July 1632.

To the Counsell.

Right, &c.—Wheras in the Chartour granted by ws to the Companie of the generall fisching of Great Britane and Irland we have gevin libertie to fisch in the seas of all our dominions, saveing such places as for the necessarie vse of the natives we should particularie reserve and declair by our proclamationn, as by the said Chartour may appear: Vnderstanding that many of our subjects dwelling vpoun the bounds adjacent vnto the rivers and firthis of Forth and Clyd hath bene at all tymes heirtofoir, and still ar, at all tymes of the yeir cheiflie mantened by the fisching thairof, as serveing for ther necessarie vse, so that they can hardlie subsist, It is our will and pleasur, and we doe heirby expreslie declair, that non, be vertew of that generall Association for the said fisching, fisch betweene St Abbes Head and Readhead, or in any place within that firth; And, for the Clyde, that non fische between the mylves of Galloway and Kintyre, or in any place within the same, except the natives, according to the ancient customes; and this yow can publisch by proclamationn at all places thoght necessarie by yow for that purpois, which we will that yow caus putt vpon record, that all our subjects both now and heirefter may tak notice of our pleasur heirin.—Oatlandis, last July 1632.

To the Counsell.

Right, &c.—Efter long tyme, and many meetingis betweene the Commissioners of both our kingdomes for a generall assotiation for the fisching, wherunto we ourself for the most part was present, the bussines being now, to our great contentment, concluded with mutuall consent of both, as may appear by the Chartours which we send yow heirwith, drawin vp according to the heads that wer agreed vpoun, wherin we have had a speciall care to preserve the dignitie of that our ancient kingdome, both in the placeing thairof and in appending the sealls: And Our pleasur is, that yow pass the Charter which we have gevin as king of Scotland, England, and Irland immediatlie vnder our great seall of Scotland in the first place, that thairefter the same may be returned, and the great seall of Ingland appendit thervnto in the second place; to the other Chartour gevin by ws as king of Ingland, Scotland, and Yrland, wherunto the seall of Ingland is alreadie appendit in the first place: And for your farther warrant heiranent (besyds these presents) we sent vnto yow tuo signaturis, conforme to the custome of that our kingdome, as warrants for both the Chartours, togidder with the Latine Chartour signed by ws as king of Scotland, Ingland, and Irland, of which Chartours and signaturis yow shall mak vse as yow shall think fitt, or as neid shall requyre: And becaus it is thought expedient that both the Chartours be of one date, it is our farther pleasur that yow mak yours of the date with the other for this our kingdome, which is dated at Westminster, the Nyntene of July 1632, that a greater conformitie be in such records as concerne a work of that consequence. —Oatlands, last July 1632.

To the Counsell.

Right, &c.—Wheras we ar crediblie informed that it was compleyned vpoun of the last conventioun of the Estats of that our kingdome that, contrarie to the lawis and custome thairof, ane Robert Buchan, vnder cullour of preserveing our watters from vnseasonable fisching of Pearle, and encreasching our yeirlie revenewes, had procured a patent, wherby he appropriats the whole benefite thairof vnto himself; wherin we respecting the ancient custome and lawis of that our kingdome, and preferring the generall good of the publict to our owin particular pretendit interest, or the ends of any privat persone, Our pleasur is, that yow call the said Buchan befoir yow, and discharge his patent, and all farther prosecution therby, causeing publish by proclamatioun that all our subjects hath libertie frielie to fisch and tak pearle in all the rivers and watters in that our kingdome in all tyme cuming, And that no other patent be exped heirvpon heir-efter; ffor which, &c.— Oatlands, last of July 1632.

To the Chancellour.

Right, &c.—Haveing directed a warrant to the Senatour of our Colledge of Justice for receaveing of Sir Johne Scott to ane Ordinarie place of session: Therefter, in regard of the course we have formerlie established for distinguisching of our Judicatoreis ther, it is our pleasur that yow require the said Sir Johne to absteane from sitting any more at our Counsell table or Exchequer ther, conforme to our said course formerlie established; for doeing, &c.—Oatlands, last July 1632.

To the Counsell.

Right, &c.—Haveing at this tyme, amongst other things concerning our service in that our kingdome, imparted our mynd at lenth tuitching the Lo. Vchiltrie vnto our right, &c. the Erle of Stratherne, We have to that purpois gevin direction vnto him to signifie our pleasur vnto yow, willing that such a course be takin with the said Lord Vchiltrie as the said Erle shall acquant yow from ws; ffor doeing, &c. Oatlands, last of July 1632.

To the Counsell.

Right, &c.—Wheras we ar informed that the fisching of Ballintrae dooth verie much hinder the plentie of herring fisching in the West Coastis of that our kingdome and Yles thairof, and these pairtis of Irland opposit thairto, by destroyeing of the fry of herrings at vnseasonable tymes, which (as we ar informed) if they wer spared might produce such plentie in all these coastis as might verie much advance the intendit work for fisching now establisched by ws for the generall good of all our dominions, and speciallie of these parts : Therfoir our pleasur is, that yow caus proclamatioun to be made dischargeing the vnseasonable fisching thairof in all tyme cuming, causeing sufficient surtie to be takin for that effect of these who wer accustomed to fisch ther : and that yow give ordour to the schirreffis Justices of Peace and others persones of qualitie therabouts, whom yow shall think fitt for that purpois, to sie the said proclamatioun putt in due executioun, signifieing vnto them our great care that nothing be done which any wayes may hinder the said intendit work of fisching for the generall good of all our subjects : Which speciallie recommending, &c.—Oatlands, last of July 1632.

To the Counsell.

Right, &c.—Wheras the office of Justiciarie, in the boundis of the Ilis and other parts mentionat in our grant therof vnto our right, &c. the Lord Lorne, is establisched, and all questionis removed which wer objected against that office to the effect that justice may be dewlie and tymelie executed in these parts according to the lawis of that our kingdome : Our pleasur is, that from tyme to tyme as the said Lord or his deputeis shall have occasion to vse your ayd in any thing that may concerne his furtherance in the lawfull executioun of that office, yow grant the same vnto him.—Oatlands, last of July 1632.

To the Deputie of Irland.

Right, &c.—Wheras we ar informed that the patent of honour of the late Lord Castelstewart hath bene long deteyned from the seall by the occasion of the death of Francis Edgworth, late Clerk of the Hamper of that our kingdome, the same patent haveing fallin into the handis of his executors who, efter many delayes, have now of late delyvered the same vnto the late Erle Castelstewart's eldest sone and air, wherby the seall may be appendit therto, according to the intention of our late royall father ; and we being vnwilling that his said sone and air should be any wayes frustrated of that honour or place of precedencie intendit for him, or that any lyk later erections should be prejudiciall vnto him, he being ane whom we doe verie much respect, both for his owin abilities and noble descent, and also for his said late father's many publict services performed to our late dear father and ws : These ar therfor to will and requyre yow, with all convenient diligence, to append the seall to it and delyver it vnto him as a mark of our royall favor vnto that familie ; And for your soe doeing these our letteris shalbe your sufficient warrant.—Gevin at our Court of Oatlands, the last of July 1632.

To the Thesaurer and Deputie.

Right, &c.—Wheras we wer formerlie pleased with advyse of the Commissioners of our Exchequer to give a monethlie allowance to the Masteris of Works ther for vpholding our housses and palaces in that our kingdome, secureing the same vnto them by ane assignement vpon the assignements which we have bene pleased of late to dispose of otherwyse, wherby they find thenuselllis dissapoynted of ther payments, and therby disabled to performe ther dewtie to the great hazard of the ryine of our housses. The vpholding whairof doeth much concerne ws and the honour of that our ancient kingdome; and haveing heard thairof from our saidis Commissioneris, We have thoght fitt that tymelie ordour be takin : Our pleasur therfoir is, that haveing considered of the best meanes wherby they may receave satisfaction, yow give ordour to our Advocat for drawing vp such further warrant for our hand, wherby they may be secured in alse ample maner in tyme cuming as they wer formerlie, And in the meanetyme that yow give satisfaction in what is alreadie due vnto them to the effect they may be the better enabled for performeing ther dewteis in vpholding our housses in that kynd which is necessarie, wherin not doubting of your conformtie to this our pleasur, &c.—Oatlands, the last of July 1632.

To the Erle of Linlythgow.

Right, &c.—Wheras we ar informed yow intend to dispose of your heretable right to the keiping of our palace of Linlythgow and Castle of Blakness by your best advantage, we ar desyreous to have the same in our handis, to be disposed of heirefter by ws as we shall at all tymes find expedient, and being willing with all that yow should receave such satisfaction as in reasone is due, we have gevin ordour to our right, &c. the Erle of Stratherne, President our privie Counsall, to treat with yow thereanent, which we recommend to your consideratioun, and expecting the issue that may be answerable to our desyre and your satisfaction, We bid, &c.—Oatlands, last July 1632.

To the Erle of Stratherne.

Right, &c.—Wheras we ar informed that the Erle of Linlythgow is to dispose of his heretable right to the keiping of our palace therof and Castell of Blakness, by selling of the same to some pairtie for his best advantage, And in regard of our generall intentioun to draw vnto our owin handis vpon everie convenient occasion all such rights, we have thoght good in this particular to mak choyse of yow by treating with the said Erle for to obtene his interest for keiping of these two housses at the easiest rates yow can agrie vpon, and whatever pryce yow shall reasonablie Condescend vpon to advance vnto him for that his right, we doe heirby promeis in verbo principis to refound vnto yow whensoever we shall desyr to retire that same bargaine from yow vnto ourselfies, togidder with all the interest and losses yow may in the meanetyme sustene by this advancement of moneyis, which for the present we recommend vnto your care. —Oatlandis, last of July 1632.

To the Counsell.

Right, &c.—We ar informed that our right trustie and weillbeloved Cousen and Counsellour the Marqueis of Huntlie, is charged for presenting befoir yow ane Findlay M'Grimon, rebell, who had secretlie alandoned the kingdome befoir, wherin though we doubt not bot yow have some good consideratiouns, moveing yow to tak that course ; yit vpon humble motion made vnto ws in his behalff, that sieing hardlie the rebell can be brought bak (it being vncertaine what part abroad he is gone), he will obleidg himself to exhibite him, if at any tyme heirefter he shall returne to that our kingdome, which conceaveing to be reasonable, we think fitt (vnless ther be some speciall reasone to the contrair) that yow accept of his offer, and to that effect that yow authorize him (if neid beis), or the Viscount of Aboyne, his sone, with what warrand and commission yow shall think fitt to that purpois, taking of them such surtie as yow shall find expedient, &c.—Oatlands, last of July 1632.

To the Scotts residing in Polland.

Trustie, &c.- We ar informed that ther ar diverse abuses committed amongst yow by some of your owin number, that yow suffer often by others, and that onlie by want of your joynt concurrences wherby some ordours might be establisched for preventing the miscariages of your owin, and for enabling yow the better to remedie any losses yow might sustene from others, and out of our royall care that your cairages may not be derogatorie to the honour of our ancient kingdome whervnto yow belong, nor your negligences be aney more occasion of your owin losses, we have thoght good heirby to recommend vnto your generall cares that, considering the place wher yow ar and the necessitie of your affaires ther, yow would by a joynt and mutuall consent determyne vpon some course that might be answerable to our desyres in the advancement of your commoun good, according as we have gevin particular directions to our agent ther ; and as we shall heirefter hear from him of your diligence heirin, we shalbe readie to contribute what we shalbe informed may be further requisit from ws by our letteris or mediation with our brother, the King of Polland, for your advantage.— Beawlie, 15 August 1632.

To the Commissioners of Surrenders.

Right, &c.— We have heard of the good progresse made by yow in the matter of tythes and valuations therof, approveing both of the ordour takin by yow for drawing of the same befor yourselfis if the heretours and titulars doe not ther diligence at the tymes appoynted by yow, and of your care takin for rectifieing the reports at the instance of our Advocat wher the tythes ar vndervalued to the prejudice of the Churches maintenance and of ws in our annuitie, and being informed of the course lykwyse takin by yow for giveing to all heretours indifferentlie the leading of ther owin tythes, vpoun suretie for payment of the tythes valued to the titulars they haveing submitted or not (it being a course which in all equitie oght to be vniversall), we give yow hartie thanks for your care and diligence therin, and doe will yow to proceid in that work according to these rules alreadie begun till it be finished, and wher the tythes be vndervalued wherin the Church and we must suffer most : Our pleasur is, that though both titular and heretour be silent that yow have a speciall care to rectifie these valuations, and that the persute goe on in our Advocat's name, least ther might be collusion between them to our prejudice : Which recommending, &c.— Beawlie, 15 August 1632.

To the Counsell.

Right, &c.—Wheras we have bene petitioned by the Mr of Maxwell that a ryot hath of late bene committed by some persones depending vpon the Laird of Johnestoun, wherby the tennents of his brother, the Erle of Nithisdall, and others, our subjects, hath bene much wronged contrarie to any ordour of law or justice as by the enclosed petition and roll of the delinquents names, which for your better information we have sent yow heirwith, may appear ; for preventing of the lyk heirefter, and least any new occasion should be gevin for kindling of the old rancor, which (as we ar informed) hath bene betweene the names of Maxwell and Johnestoun, Our pleasur is, that yow call the pairteis interested befoir yow, and efter exact tryell heirin if yow find the persones accused or any of them guiltie, that yow cause punish or censure them as yow shall find the offence to deserve, taking of both pairteis if yow shall find it requisit sufficient cautioun for preserveing our peace heirefter in these boundis.—Beawlie, 15 August 1632.

To the Thesaurar Deputie, Traquair.

Right, &c.— The treatie of the fisching bussines, wherin we our selfis have takin great paines, being now concluded, so that nothing so much resteth as that our good subjects goe on according to the course preseryved, We have to that purpois gevin instructions to our right, &c. the Erle of Stratherne and Mr Johne Hay : Our pleasur is, that yow informe yourselflis from them of what may conduce to this purpois, and that accordinglie yow vse therin your best and your most readie endeavours, wherby at the vpcomeing of our said consen and of the said Mr Johne, the bussines may be the more speedelie pult to a finall conclusion, so remitting this and some other thingis concerneing our service otherwyse to be imparted vnto yow by our said Consen, &c. — Beawlie, 15 August 1632.

To the Counsall.

Right, &c. — Wheras by our others letteris and patents that ar sent vnto yow with the progresse of what doe concerne the work of the generall assotiation for fisching, and have gevin yow our furth directions theranent, whairof we expect a speedie accompt thairof from yow. Ther ar yit severall propositions for the advancement of that work which we have thoght fitt to recommend vnto your considerations by our right, &c. the Erle of Stratherne : And it is our pleasur that according to the propositions, or as yow and the Counsell of that assotiation for that our kingdome shall best resolve vpoun for conduceing to the begining and advancement of this great work yow proceid accordinglie, and with all acquant ws therwith by the said Erle. — Beawlie, 15 August 1632.

To the Bergh of Edinburgh.

Trustie, &c. — Though we have bene pleased by ane other letter to acquant the burrowis in generall with the great regaird we have had to the honour and weilfair of that our ancient kingdome, and to ther interest in it in this last treatie of a generall assotiati** for fisching, which is now happelie concludit recommending earnestlie to them the vseing of ther best endeavours to contribute to the advancement of it, wherin we doubt not bot they wilbe dewtiefull to ws and cairfull of ther owin good, yit we have thoght good in particular to recommend the same to your care, as whom amongst them it doeth first and most concerne, we have formerlie fund your good exemple powerfull and effectuall in that which concerned our service and the good of the cuntrie, and we doubt not bot yow will continew in this particular with your best advyse to others and assistance from yourselflis to secure our desyres in advanceing this great work according as we have gevin particular direction to this bearer, wherwith he will acquant yow. — Beawlie, 15 August 1632.

To the Deputie of Irland.

Right, &c. — Wheras we have bene pleased, for the generall good of all our subjects, to caus proclamationn be made in these our kingdomes of England and Scotland that none of our subjects of any of our dominions shall pay in aney of them ather more or other customes or dewteis mentionat in the proclamatioun than what the natives of the place wher the custome is takin ought to pay : To which purpois, our royall intention being that the lyk course be takin in that our kingdome, we have sent yow the lyk proclamatioun vnder our owin hand : Therfoir our pleasur is, that yow caus exped and publisch the same in such sort that all our subjects ther may tak notice of our pleasur heirin, and that yow sie the same dewlie observed. — Beawlie, 15 August 1632.

Instructions gevin by his Matie to the Erle of Stratherne to be communicated to the Counsell of Scotland anent the advancement of his Maties royall [intention] of the fischingis of Great Britain and Irland.

Yow shall recommend to ther consideratioun the Act of Parliament made by his Maties predicessours, vmquhill King Ja. 1, Part 1, cap. 1, anent the putting out of Busches be the nobilitie, gentrie, barrones, and them of the M. Ma... ... ... the b... ... ...

Y... ... ...

... ...

To the Borrowers.

Trustie, &c.— Where we have bene ever carefull in all things to preserve and conferre your liberties and privileges, wher f we have gevin evident proff not once in this treatie of the generall associ... ...

... ...—Berlin, the 15 August 1632.

To the Baronetts.

Trustie, &c.— Wheras our late deir father, out of his pious Zeall for the advancement of religeon in the remote parts of his dominions, wher it had not bene formerlie knowen, and out of his royall care for the honour and well of that our ancient kingdome, was pleased to annex to the Croun therof the dominion of New Scotland, in America, that the vse of it might aryse to the benefite of that kingdome; we, being desyrous that the wished effects might follow by the continuance of so noble a designe, wer pleased to confer particular marks of our favour vpon such as should voluntarlie contribute to the fartherance of a plantation to be established in these boundis, as appeared by our erecting of that ordour of baronetts wherwith yow ar dignifeid, whervnto we have ever since bene willing to add what further we conceaved to be necessarie for the testifeying our respect to these that ar alreadie interested, and for encourageing of them who shall heirefter interest themsellfis in the advancement of a work which we so reallie tender for the Glorie of God, the honour of that nation, and the benefite that is lyklie to flow from the right prosecution of it : But in regard that notwithstanding the care and diligence of our right, &c. the Viscount of Stirling, whom we have from the begining entrusted with the prosecution of this work, and of the great Charges alreadie bestowed vpon it, hath not takin the root which was expected, partlie, as we conceave, by reason of the Incommoditeis ordinarlie incident to all new and remote beginnings, and partlie, as we ar informed, by want of the tymelie concurrance of a sufficient number to insist in it, bot especiallie the Colonie being forced of late to remove for a tyme by meanes of a treatie we have had with the French : Thairfor, we have takin vnto our royall consideratioun by what meanes agane may this work be established; and conceaveing that ther ar none of our subjects whom it concerneth so much in credit to be affectioned to the progres of it as these of your number for justefieing the groundis of our princelie favours which yow have receaved by a most honorabill and generous way, we have thoght fitt to direct the bearer heirof, Sir William Alexander, kny[t], vnto yow, who hath bene ane actor in the former proceidingis, and hath sene the cuntrie, and knowen the commoditeis therof, will communicat vnto yow such propositions as may best serve for making the right vse heirefter of a plantation trade in these boundis, for encouraging such as shall adventure therin, and we doubt not bot if yow find the groundis reasonable and fair yow will give your concurrance for the further prosecution of them : And as we have alreadie gevin ordour to our Advocat for drawing such warrandis to pass vnder our sealls ther, wherby our loveing subjectis may be fred from misconstruction of our proceidingis with the French anent New Scotland, and secured of our protection in tyme cuming in ther vndertakeris vnto it ; So we shalbe readie to contribute what we shall heirefter find we may justlie doe for the advancement of the work and the encouragement of all that shall joyne with yow to that purpois : Which recommending vnto your care, we bid yow farewell. Beawlie, 15 August 1632.

To the Toun of Edinburgh.

Trustie, &c.— Wheras we ar informed that our late royal father did ordeane that at the election of your deacones and tradis, and counsellours for the same, yow should mak choyse of the most expert handie laborers and tradismen, as persones best experienced and able to give advyse in things concerneing ther trades and improvement of manufactoreis, we being carefull to have that continewed which by our said father was ordeaned for the publict good ; and haveing of late writtin to our privie counsell Initching the erecting of manufactoreis, wherby the native commoditeis of that our ancient kingdome may be putt to the best vse, and poore and ydle people sett a work : Our pleasur is, that in all tyme comeing, at the election of these deacones and counsellours yow mak choyse of none bot of such as ar handie labourers, chope keiperis, vsers of ther tradis, and best skilled therin, That when occasion shall requyre, we may have ther advyse in such thingis as concerne ther trads : Which recommending vnto your care, as yow will tender the good of our service : We bid yow farewell from our Court at Beawlie, the 15 August 1632.

These approve Sir Henric Wardlaw in dischargeing the office of Chalmerlanrie at Dumfermeling, Rosse, Ardmanagh, and Ettrik Forrest, of the office of receaver of your Maties rents, and of the taxatiouns of the said Lop^s of Dunfermeling and Ettrik forrest, dischargeing his aires and executours of all clams and question that may be moved against them in that behalff.—Beawlie 17 August 1632.

A Commission was signed for hearing the E. of Mortone's accompts by the Chancellour St Androis, &c.—Beawlie, 17 August 1632.

Our will and pleasur is, that for our vse yow bring from our kingdome of Scotland about Michaelmes ensueing, the lyk number of muttons, and in such maner as was formerlie accustomed to be brought from thence by Charles Murray for the vse of our late royall father or for our owin by yourselff, according to our former appoyntment for your imployment in that service, and that accordinglie yow continew yeirlie to doe the same till we shalbe pleased ather to approve that service by a further warrant or discharge it ; And in the meane tyme the lyk allowance and feyis shalbe yeirlie payed vnto yow as wer gevin for that purpois in the tyme of our said late royall father, wherof doe not yow faill as yow will answer vnto ws.— Gevin at our Court of Beaulie, 17 August 1632.

To Johne Geddes, burges of our burgh of Drumfreis.

To the Erle Marshell.

Right, &c.—Haveing formerlie fund by experience your affection to our service, and being now informed of the continuance thairof in advanceing (in so far as in yow lyeth) the bussines of the Tythis, and what else doeth at this tyme concerne ws ther we give yow harty thanks for the same, desyreing yow to continew as yow have begun, speciallie vseing at this tyme your best endeavours to advance the generall bussines of the fisching of great Britane and Irland now sett afoot by ws, tuitching which purpois sieing we have gevin particular instructions to our right, &c., the Erle of Stratherne, we ar willing that yow informe yourselff from him of what may concerne your endeavours for furthring therof, and that yow proceid accordinglie as lykwyse in all other things tuitching our service which he shall impart vnto yow from ws.—Beaulie, 17 August 1632.

To the Clergie.

Right, &c.—We have vnderstude by your letter your earnest care to have the psalmes translated by our late royall father receaved in the Churches of that our kingdome according as we did recommend vnto yow by our former letteris to that effect ; And hearing from yow that the delay of that work proceideth from the want of a number of copies fitt to be distributed thrugh the dyoceis of that kingdome, we have gevin ordour that such a number be sent vnto the Archbischop of St Androis as convenientlie can be had as may be most expedient, and have by our letter vnto him particularlie signifeid our mynd heirin to be imparted vnto yow ; Our pleasur is, that yow selle some speedie course how they may be receaved, and sung in the Churches ther, and therypon we will furthwith give ordour for the reforming or adding to the said work what shalbe fund necessarie, that therefter a course for a full Impression from tyme to tyme may be establisched, wherin expecting your care and diligence, we bid, &c.—Wanstead, 13 Sept. 1632.

To the Archbischop of St Androis.

Right, &c.—We have vnderstood from our Clergie the continuance of ther desyres to have the Psalmes translated by our royall father receaved in the Churches of that our kingdome, haveing vndertakin to doe the same, bot that the want of a number of copeis fitt to have bene distributed in the severall dioceis therof, occasioned a delay in putting that work to a speedie poynt : Therfor we have gevin ordour that such a number of copeis be sent vnto yow as convenientlie can be had at this tyme, to be disposed of as yow shall think most expedient : And becaus the Impression of such a number of books as from tyme to tyme wilbe fund necessarie for the publict vse will requyre a present charge, we have requyred them to setle a course how they may be receaved and song in the Churches ther ; And thervpon we will furthwith give ordour to hasten the said Impression, and for reformeing or adding to that work what shalbe fund necessarie : And wher at the last meitting we hard that your seiknes was some hinderance to the progres of that work, we will now expect at your handis some speedie furthrance therin as your charge and affection to our late royall father's memorie will lead yow vnto, that the work may be fund setled at our comeing, God willing, at the nixt spring of the yeir to that our kingdome, which we will tak as verie acceptable service done vnto ws.—Wanstead, the 13 Sept. 1632.

To the Thesaurer.

Right, &c.—Wheras we have gevin ordour to our Advocat to persew the Lard of Lusse for the cryme of Incest alledged to have bene committed by him : Though he can deserve no favour for himself in what the course of our Lawis can inflict vpon him in his persone or estate, yit haveing compassion of the suffering of his wyff and children, and of so antient a familie, Our pleasur is, that if his escheit, lyfrent, or landis sall fall in our hands, in the disposeing therof yow have a speciall care that no creditour of his be defrauded of that what is justlie dew vnto them ; and that the mantenance of his wyff and children and the standing of his house be provydit for, he onlie suffering in his owin persone all that by the course of our Lawis vsuall in the lyk caice may be imposed vpoun him : Which seriouslie recommending vnto your care, we bid, &c.—Wanstead, 13 Sept. 1632.

To the Advocat.

Trustie, &c.—The foulnes of the cryme alledged to have bene of late committed by the Lard of Luss haveing justlie moved ws to have the same tryed according to the Lawis of that our kingdome, and him punished if fund guiltie, that others be terrefied from committing the lyk heirefter ; our pleasur is, that yow cause summoned him to appear befor the Judges compitent for his tryell, and that in our name yow insist therin, according to our saidis lawis and custome in caices of the same or lyk nature : ffor which, &c. —Wanstead, 13 Sept. 1632.

Similar Letter to the Earl of Stratherne, Justice General.

To the Toun of Jedbrugh.

Trustie, &c.—Vnderstanding that it pleased our dear royall father, vpon diverse good considerations mentionat in his letter to that our burgh of Jedbrugh, to desyre them to choyse and elect ther provestes by the advyse of Sir Andro Ker, then Captane of the guard, so vpon the lyk considerations, We (haveing heirtofoir writtin that they should mak choyse of ther provests by advyse of our right, &c. the Lord of Jedbrugh) ar pleased to recommend vnto yow the doeing therof heirefter, which we will acknowledge as good service done vnto ws : We bid, &c.—Wanstead, the 13 Sept' 1632.

To the Counsell.

Right, &c.—Humble sute hath bene made vnto ws in behalff of the Lady of the late erle of Wigtoun, deceissed, that we would be pleased to give ordour for causeing exhibit befoir yow hir daughter by the said erle, that it might be in hir frie choyse ather to reside with hir mother, or the now Erle of Wigtoun, hir brother, in whois hands hir portion is, and to whom the same is to returne in caice he die vnmaryed, the interest therof being, as we ar informed, allowed vnto hir for hir maintenance, wherof the mother offering to be at the charge, wherby the annualrent may be reserved for hir daughter's vse, we thoght litt so far to harken to hir demands heirin as to remitt the same to your consideratioun, requyreing yow to caus the pairteis interested appear befor yow, and haveing heard what can be objected on ather syd, that yow tak such a course therin as yow shall find to be most agrieable to equitie and the good of the young Lord. - Wanstead, 13 Sept. 1632.

To the Bischop of Caithnes.

Reverend father in God, &c.—Being desyreous that the Commissioners for surrenderis, wherof yow are one, should so prepare that bussines against our comeing to that our kingdome that we may the more readilie putt ane end to the same ; and being informed that some of your number, by ther remote duelling from Edinburgh, and others by ther infirmitie of bodie, ar not so able to attend the Commission as yow ar, we think it litt till our comeing thither, or till we shalbe pleased to signifie our further pleasur heirin, that yow mak your ordinarie residence at your church of Jedbrugh, to be the more near and readie for that service, and such as we may have occasion to imploy yow, wherin we will expect your carfull attendance that no bussines draw yow from it, if your health permitt ; and if neid be that yow acquant the Arch-bischop of S' Androis with this our pleasur, or any other whom it doeth concerne.—Wanstead, 13 Sept. 1632.

A pacquet sent to Sir Wm Alexander, wherin ther wer two letters anent the Psalmes, one to the Clergie, one to the B. of S' Androis ; 3 concerneing the L. Lusse to the Thesaurer, Advocat, E. Stratherne ; one to the B. of Caithnes, and to the toun of Jedbrugh, procured by Sir Ro' Ker.

To the Counsell.

Right, &c.- We have bene pleased heir to express our care for tryeing the death of the Viscount of Melgun and others, haveing at that purpois writtin at severall tymes for examyng such persones as wer most suspected to have bene guiltie, or any wyse necessorie to that fact : But now of late a complaint being made vnto ws in behalff of our Right, &c. the Marqueis of Huntlie, that in the late proceedings for tryeing of ane Tosheoch, delay hath bene made to the hindrance of Justice : Our pleasur is, that yow call him befor yow, and haveing considered the complaynt to be gevin in befor yow by the said Marqueis and others interested tuitching that purpois, that yow certifie ws of your opinions therin, that we may give such farder ordour tuitching the same as we shall think expedient ; and in the meanetyme that yow tak a course that no such delay be made heirefter in the trying of that bussines : We bid yow farewell. - Hampton Court, 27 Septr 1632.

To the Erle of Stratherne.

Right, &c.—Wheras we ar informed that as yit ther is bot a small progres made in the tryell of th lamentable death of the Viscount of Melgun and others, we haveing writtin at severall tymes that all lawfull and speedie meanes might be vsed for bringing the tryell of that matter to light, and particularlie for the tortureing of ane John Meldrum, of whois guiltines ther ar some great presumptions, proceiding (as we ar informed) from his owin Confession : And sieing it is enacted by our Privie Counsell that he should be tortured, which if it be done in tyme may much conduce to any subsequent tryell for clearing of that bussines, Our pleasur is, and we doe heirby authorize yow, to caus torture the said Meldrum with all diligence.—Hampton Court, 27 Sept. 1632.

To the Erle of Stratherne.

Right, &c.—Yow will perceave by our letter to our Counsall our intention tuitching a complaynt made vnto ws in behalff of our right, &c. the Marqueis of Huntlie, that in the late proceiding for trying of one Toshecch tuitching the death of the Viscount Melgun, delay was made by the Justice deputs to the hinderance of Justice, wherin, sieing our princelie care still is that all lawfull and speedie wayes may be vsed for bringing the treuth of that bussines to light, we will expect at your handis both in regard of your Charge and trust from ws that yow sie no lawfull meanes omitted for the due and tymelie tryell of that complaynt, and that yow will therin vse your most effectuall and readie endeavours and certifie ws of your opinion tuitching the same.—Hampton Court, 27 Sept. 1632.

To the Archbischop of St Androis.

Right, &c.—The inclosed petition being presented vnto ws, we wer pleased to remitt the consideratioun therof vnto yow that if by good evidences yow shall find the petitioner's losses to be such as he affirmeth, and that his estate and that of his familie requyre some help, yow vse the ordinarie meanes that the Churche's Charitie may be granted vnto him efter what maner yow shall think fitt to preseryve, or as hath bene accustomed in the lyk cacos.—Hampton Court, 27 Sept. 1632.

To the Counsell.

Right, &c.—We have bene humblie petitioned by some of our subjects mentionat in the inclosed petition, schewing that in transporting their lawfull merchandice from this our kingdome vnto Irland (for which, as we ar informed, the custome dew to ws was payed), the same was takin from them at sea by one Nutt, a pirat, who sold these goodis to some of our subjects resideing in that our kingdome, as by the petition will more fullie appear : Becaus it is compleaned vpon by the petitioners that our saidis subjects ther did know that these goods wer vnlawfullie takin, and that the said Nut was a pirat, for which, if it be trew, they deserve to be punisched, and be lyable to restore the goodis to the trew owners : Our pleasur is, that, taking unto your assistance our Admirall for the tyme for his interest, yow call befor yow the first buyeris of these goodis from the said Nutt, and if yow find they knew of the same wer not lawfullie acquyrit by him, or that he was not warranted by coquet or other evidence in that kynd to dispose of the same, That yow tak a speedie course that the goodis, or the value thairof, apprysed by such as yow shall appoynt for that purpois, may be restored to the petitioners, or aney haveing their power, and the delinquents punished as yow shall find the nature of the offence to deserve.—Hampton Court, 27 Sept. 1632.

To the Commissioners for Surrenders.

Right, &c.—Wheras our right, &c. the E. of Roxbrugh is by our appoyntment to repair to our Court and stay thairat this winter, wher we ar to setle these differences that ar betwcen him and Francis Steuart, and ar to imploy him in other affaires concerneing our service, least in his absence he be prejudged in the valuation of the tythis of the kirk of Dumbar, wherin, as we ar informed, we have a speciall interest, our pleasur is, that yow continew the valuation therof till the first day of Aprill nixt ensueing : And for your soe doeing, &c.— Hampton Court, 3 Octo^r 1632.

To the Advocat.

Trustie, &c.—Wheras the E. of Buchan is content to surrender vnto our Croun the Schirreffschip of Banff, wherof being pleased to accept, our pleasur is, that yow draw vp and sie perfected such a surrender as yow shall find necessarie for that purpois ; and hearing that the last Schirreff Clerk of Clakmanan did without any respect to our service sell that office, Our pleasur lykwyse is, that yow informe yourselff if ther be any way by law how the same may be brought bak vnto our Croun ; and if any be fund by yow, that yow insist for reduction of the offices of such Schirreff Clerks as ar onlie at the disposeing of the heretable Shireffis, that yow insist for reduction of them vnto our Croun, begining at the Shirref Clerkschip of Clakmanan : Which recommending vnto your care, &c.—Hampton Court, 3 Octo^r 1632.

To the Thesaurer.

Our pleasur is, and we doe heirby will and requyre yow, that yow furthwith [pay] or caus to be payet vnto Nicolas Briot the sowme of Ten pund sterling for the making of a press and toolis thervnto belonging, for the vse of our great seall of our kingdome of Scotland, which press and toolis wer by him delyvered to our Chancellour ther, and these moneyis, with any thing that shalbe due for your levyeing therof heir, shalbe allowed vnto yow in the readiest of your accomptis of our rents and casualiteis of that our kingdome.—Hamptoun Court, 3 Octo^r 1632.

Wheras we intend this winter to determyne in these differences between the noblemen interested in the late Erle Bothwell's Estate and Francis Stewart, his sone, within which the landis of Robert Ellot (for the which he and the Lady Jeane Stewart have petitioned ws), the Lands of Markill by our late royall father for the vse of our Chapell royall in that our kingdome, the Landis of Groundestoun and some superioriteis belonging (as we ar informed) to Sir Patrik Heburne of Wauchtan, knyt, ar comprehended ; wherin, sieing they pretend to have speciall interest, we have heirby thoght fitt to requyre yow to putt ws in mynd at the tyme of the division to be made by ws of that estate, That nane of these particular landis and superioriteis be mentionat in the said division, bot that they be left to be considered of apart by ws efter we have heard the particular interests and rights of our said Chappell, and of the saidis persones pretending right thervnto, to be therefter remitted or disposed of by ws as we shall find just caus. This faill not to doe as yow will be answerable vnto ws.—Gevin at Hampton Court, 3 Octo' 1632.

To William, Viscount of Stirling, our principall Secretarie for our
    kingdome of Scotland.

To the Counsell.

Right, &c.—Haveing at severall tymes writtin vnto yow that the abuses of formyne Coyne current in that our kingdome might be rectifeid for the publiet good and credit of that our antient kingdome, we have now to that purpois sent expresslie thither our servant Nicolas Briott, cheiff graver of our Mynt heir, of whois knowledge in matters of coyne we have experience : Therfoir our pleasur is, that yow hear and consider of aney proposition made by our said servant or by any other to that purpois, and that heirefter yow tak aney course that yow shall think most fitt for the tymelie rectificing of these abuses, which we will tak as verie good service done vnto ws.—Hampton Court, 3 Octo' 1632.

To the Counsell.

Right, &c.—Wheras humble sute hath bene made vnto ws by Sir Patrik Hepburne of Wauchtan, kny', that in respect of bussines speciallie concerneing the setling of his estate and other his necessarie and lawfull affaires, some such able and sufficient persone be made chuyse of by yow as yow shall think fitt for supplieing of his charge of schirreff of the Constabularie of Hadingtoun for this yeir, becaus some of his bussines have bene imparted vnto ws, wherby we conceave his demand to be reasonable : Our pleasur is, that yow exoner him of that charge for this yeir for setling of some sufficient and able persone in his place ; for which these presents shalbe your warrant.—Hampton Court, 3 Octo' 1632.

To the Session.

Right, &c.—Wheras Sir Alexander Gordon of Cluny, kny' and baronet, is now imployed in our service in this our kingdome, so that he can hardlie for some schort tyme repair thither, wherby, as we ar informed, if aney actions of Law concerneing him shallhappin to be pleaded befoir yow in his absence, he is lyklie to suffer in regard of a necessitie of his owin being ther for production of writts and witnesses requisit for clearing of his causes, we being willing that a schort tyme be allowed vnto him, ar heirby pleased to recomend vnto yow that no processes concerneing him be pleaded till the first of Aprill, vt supra.

To the Bischop of Aberdene.

Right, &c.—Humble sute being made vnto ws in behalff of Johne Leslie, some tyme of New Leslie, that he may have libertie to returne to that our kingdome to setle some of his necessar affaires, wherwith he, in humble obedience of our Lawis, by his sudden departure from thence could not have tyme to tak ordour, and without which, as we ar informed, being redacted to extreame povertie he cannot subsist : These consideratiouns have moved ws heirby to recommend him vnto yow, that if he doe nothing to hurt or derogat from the estate of the present professed religion, yow give way vnto him in so far as may concerne the dispatch of his lawfull affaires.—Hampton Court, 3 Octo' 1632.

To the Chancellour, President, and Thesaurer.

Right, &c.—Being fullie resolved to repair thither, God willing, the nixt sommer, wher we ar desyreous that all things at our comeing and aboad may be at such readines and ordour as may answer our expectatioun and care of the credit of that our ancient kingdome, wherin conceaveing that is requisite that befoir our comeing things be so forsene and provydit in due tyme, as they wer at the tyme of our late royall father his being ther : Our pleasur is, that yow call to mynd or informe yourselfis of the wayes and meanes preseryved and takin for his receaveing and intertenement, and so forsie for things that nothing necessarie and fitt be wanting at our being ther, and that yow consider of such offices as ar necessarie requisit to be established durcing our residence without drawing upon ws aney superfluous or unnecessar place or Charge ; And to that effect that yow mak a roll of them that ar neidfull, and a list of such persones names as yow shall think most fitt to discharge the same, that we may mak choyse of such of them as we shall think fitt to be done and provydit, vpon all which, haveing deliberatlie treated what is fitt to be done and provydit, let ws be certifeid therof with all diligence by yow, our Thesaurer and President of our Privie Counsall, whom we will fullie intrusted to give ws satisfaction heirin ; bot if yow shall find a necessitie that a commission be gevin by ws to this purpois, we requyre yow to caus our advocat draw such one as yow shall think requisit, and send the same to ws with a blank for the names, which we will caus fill vp and returne with diligence.—Hampton Court, 3 Octo^r 1632.

To the Chancellour.

Trustie, &c.—We ar petitioned by Sir Johne Leslie of Wardess and his Lady for the reparation of eminent losses latelie susteaned by them through our default, bot we being vncertaine ather of the treuth or value of ther clayme otherwyse than from ther owin relation, have thoght fitt to will and requyre yow to call togidder with yourselff in our name our beloved counsellours, our Advocat, Balmanno, Clesters, Senatours of our Colledge of Justice, and that yow joyntlie consider of this ther inclosed petition, and furth report vnto ws your opinions anent both the treuth and value of their clame ; That therefter we may out of princelie justice and consideratioun dismiss them with such satisfactioun as ther case requyres ; wherin not doubting of your care and diligence, we bid, &c.—Gevin at our Court of Newmerket, 11 Octo^r 1632.

To the Exchequer.

Right, &c.—We have bene pleased to bestow the gift of the ward, nonentrie, and mariage of one Anne Nasmyth, which (as we ar informed) ar at our gift and disposition, vpoun the Viscount of Stirling : These ar therefore to will and requyre yow to expeid vnto him vnder our privie scall a gift therof, which we have sent vnto yow heirwith, or aney other that shalbe presented vnto yow in his behalf of what is heirby at our gift, he paying alwayes such composition as yow shall think fitt, or as is accustomed in the lyk caces ; for which these shalbe, &c.—Newmerket, 12 Octo^r 1632.

To the Clerk Register.

Trustie, &c.—We ar desyreous vpon some late consideratiouns to look particularlie into the revenewis of that our kingdome, and to compare the same and the Issues of our Exchequer with the estate thairof as it was left by our dearest father at our entrie to our Croun : These ar therfoir to will and requyre yow furthwith to returne vnder your hand to our Master of Requests, to be presented vnto ws, Our particular lists or Inventareis of the revenue of that our Croun, and of the feyis, pensiones, precepts, and others allowances furth of them, with the sindrie natures of ther gifts, ather by simple donations, locall assignations, or bearing interests, the one as they wer left by our dearest father of happie memorie, and the other as they ar now at this present ; that we being therin trewlie and particularlie informed, may therefter setle such constant ordour for the payments as we in our princelie judgment shall think fitt ; wherin not doubting of your care and diligence, we bid, &c.—Newmerkit, 17 Octo.ʳ 1632.

To the Clerk Register.

Trustie, &c.—As we have of late prosecute seriouslie for the generall benefite of this Yland the association of our subjects for fischings in our northerne seas, and haveing now broght the same to ane finall and reall conclusion, we ar lykwyse desyreous that the justice of our proceidings therin, as it is well-knowen to ourself, may also be takin notice of abroad by our nyghbours thrugh some publict wryting to that purpois, we conceaveing that in the recordis of that our kingdome sindrie authentik evidences may be fund, wherby our Right may clearlie and vncontrablie appear, have thoght fitt to will and requyre yow, with all convenient care and diligence, to search the saidis recordis, and to returne vnder your hand to our master of requeists, to be presented to ws, such evidents, treateis, and agriements with forrane princes, and others writts as yow in your judment shall think best conduceing to our intent ; wherin not doubting of your care and diligence, we bid, &c.—Newmerket, 17 Octo.ʳ 1632.

To the Counsell.

Right, &c.—Ther was latelie presented to ws by Mʳ George Nicoll a breif vene, as he called, of the particulars of our estate of that kingdome, with intimation of certane prejudices sustenit therin, and overtures for preventing the lyk in tyme cuming, and improving the benefite arysing by the casualiteis of that Croun, we wer pleased to pervse the generall Mappe, and fund no just caus of distrust : Bot for the particulars, both of prejudice and improvements, we have suspended our beleiff till such tyme as by compareing them with the publict recordis, and present occonomie of our rents, they be by yow ather approved of or refuted, and that so much the rather becaus some of the allegations and prooffis sene seame hardlie to reflect, both vpon the generall and some particulars of that our kingdome : We being therfor vncertane of the prooff of his prepositions, otherwyse than from his owin relation, and not willing to give trust in matters of so great consequence to any ane subjects bare relation, nor on the other part to discouraig any from making trew and legall overturis for our benefite, have thoght fitt to putt the said Mʳ George Nicoll to a fair tryell befor yow, willing and requyreing yow carefullie to examyne both the generall and everie particular of his allegations heirwith sent vnder the hand of our Master of requeists, and what yow find trew therin and convenient for our benefite to certifie ws thereuntil, that we may accordinglie mak vse thairof, and reward the proposer ; bot what ather vntrew or derogatorie to the generall or any particular, to censure and punish according to the custome and the consequence of the calumnie, that as by the one no man may be discouraged, so by the other everie one may hencefurth be deterred from obloquy and detraction to the present government of that state, wherin as we expect your care and diligence, so we requeist yow to returne to our said Master of requeistis to be presented vnto ws the particular accompts, and of your opinions therin ; and not doubting of ather, we bid yow farewell. — Newmerkit, 17 Octo.ʳ 1632.

To the Chancellour.

Right, &c.—The Commission of Livetenuendrie granted vnto our right, &c. the Erle of Murray being expyred, and the cause whervpon it was first granted being taken away, we wer thervpon pleased (efter we had at severall tymes continewed the same efter it dernued) that in end the execntioun of justice within the bondis of the Commission should be left to the ordinarie way accustumed in that our kingdome, to which purpois we bid writ to himselff for surrending therof, which (as we ar informed) dooth still continew in force till we signifie our pleasur to the contrarie: Therfor we requyre yow to acquant him with our intention to have it determined, and therefter that yow tak a course, ather by his surrender, by act of Counsell, or any other way that yow think maist fair and requisit to the effect above specifeit, that no proceiding be at any tyme heirefter of that Commission or our subjects therby further questioned, for which these presents shalbe your warrant; and in all things tuitching the fynes and escheits of such persones who for crymes wer convicted befor we suffered the execntioun of the Commission to expyre, and tuitching such of the Erle's actions of Law as shall cum befor the session, or any other our Indicatoreis, tuitching that purpois, yow grant him your speedie furtherance according to our former pleasur latelie signifeid to our Exchequer and session, which we will tak as good service done vnto ws.—Newmerket, 18 Octo^r 1632.

To the Erle of Morton, Thesaurer.

Right, &c.—Wheras our right, &c. the Viscont of Aboyne is at this tyme imployed by our brother the French King for levyeing the Gendarmes in that our kingdome (as was accustomed) to be transported into France, for the good and tymelie manageing of which bussines that kingdome is interessed, and he in particular bund for the performance, which, seing it will requyre a present and great charge, he hath bene ane humble suter vnto ws that we might be pleased to give ordour that the more speedie payment be made of his precept, for which we have alreadie govin ordour, and ar still willing to doe, though these other inducements wer not offered, the precept haveing bene granted vpon such valuable considerations as ar not vnknowen to our Counsall ther: Therfoir our pleasur is, that yow mak payment vnto him or his assigneyis, with as much diligence as convenientlie yow can, bot if at this tyme our coffers cannot possiblie permitt the same in respect of our journey, God willing, the nixt somer, that yow tak such a course as yow shall think most fitt for satistieing of him (or such of his creditoris as he shall appoynt) for such moneyis as ar due vnto him.—Newmerket, 18 Octo^r 1632.

To the Exchequer.

Right, &c.—Wheras Sir James Pringle of Gallowscheills, kny^t, hath bene ane humble sutter vnto ws for causeing exped vnder our scalls a gift of the nonentrie of the estate of Borthik, which we had long since granted vnto him for recoverie of such moneyis as wer dew vnto him by the late Lord Borthik, and of such as he had payed as suretie for suretie for him, wherin he dooth onlie desyre such benefite as is granted to others our subjects in the lyk cases: Therfor our pleasur is, that, vpoun his giveing of sufficient surtie as is accustomed, yow exped the said gift vnto him with all diligence, and that yow suffer no other to be exped befor it to his prejudice, or that yow certifie bak vnto ws the reasone why it should not be passed: And for, &c.—Newmerkit, 22 Octo^r 1632.

To the Commissioners of Surrenders.

Right, &c.—Wheras it hath bene represented vnto ws that some actuall ministers serving at ther particular Cures have suffered, and ar lyklie to suffer, by the valuations a great diminution of the Tythes allowed for ther mantenance, wherof they wer in possession, for helping whairof according to our decree they may appeale vnto ws or our Parliament : It being far from our intention any wayes to harme them in that kynd, bot rather to help ther provisions, Our pleasur is, that yow have a speciall care to prevent any such course, and to repair, as far as yow can lawfullie doe, aney thing they have suffered in that kynd, that they be not putt in any worse estate then they wer befoir ; and if it cannot be determined in a fair way by advyse of the Clergie, with mutuall consent of the pairteis, sieing we ar schortlie to repair to that our kingdome, lett aney such valuations compleyned vpon be delayed till our cuming thither ; And in all other things concerneing the said Commission that yow proceid with such diligence as may the better facilitate the effectuating of that great work at our comeing ther, God willing, the nixt sommer : All which we speciall recommend vnto your care.—Newmercat, 22 Octo\u02b3 1632.

Our Soverane Lord vnderstanding how much it importeth the good of his Ma\u1d57\u1d49\u02b3 antient kingdome of Scotland that forts and blokhousses be built in the most necessarie places for defending the roads, harbours, and coasts thairof, And, namelie, that the Lords of Secreit Counsall, be ane act dated the 17 Septe\u02b3 1827 yeires, thoght that it was fitting ane port should be builded at Inchgarvie, his Ma\u1d57\u1d49, being acquainted with ther opinion theranent, signed a signature in favours of the Erle of Linlythgow and his aires, that for the building and keiping of that fort everie schip transporting coall or salt out of the firth should pay two shillings of everie tun of coall or salt to the said Erle for the space of 19 yeires ensueing the date heirof.—Newmeket, 23 Octo\u02b3 1632.

To the Counsell.

Right, &c.—Vnderstanding that, according to our directioun for causeing surveigh and fortifie such places vpoun the coasts of that our kingdome as wer necessarie requisit, yow have made choyse of the Yle of Inchgarvie, within Forth, for building and keiping wherof for the intended vse yow have, by ane act of Counsall exhibited vnto ws by our Admirall for the tyme, imposed a dewtie of tuo schillingis Scotts vpon the tune of coall, and as much vpon the salt, transported from that firth out of the kingdome, wherof we doe approve : Therfor we have bene pleased to signe a grant vnto him dureing the space of nyntene yeres for building and keiping therof with the said allowance imposed by yow, requyreing that it be exped vnder our sealls with all convenient diligence, or any other to that purpois keiping the substance heirof, which may be for the good and saftie of our subjects and others lawfullie tradeing withing the said firth.—Newmerket, 23 Octo\u02b3 1632.

To the Counsell.

Right, &c.—Wheras diverse complaints hath bene made vnto ws and our Counsall heir, in behalff of some of our subjects of this our kingdome and Irland, against such persones who have coft such goodis from pirrotts who had robbed them at sea, to which purpois we did wryt to yow of befor, that the goodis might be restored to the just owneris compleneing in due and lawfull tyme ; in regard it concerneth the good and honour of that our ancient kingdome that such abuses be rectifeid, and the transgressors punisched according to the Lawes therof, we ar heirby pleased to recommend that our Admirall for the tyme have from yow all the lawfull and speedie justice yow possiblie can for punisching the delinquents and restoring the goodis to the right owneris ; bot if both pairteis shall happin to condescend amongst themseltis to submitt ther differences to be composed by our said Admirall in these cases, for avoyding delayes by suittis of Law against them, we requyre yow to allow him (if neid be) to modifie the composition, provydeing that the fynes of any shall happin to be takin from any of the delinquents be modifeit by your consent efter the hearing of pairteis, that none have just caus to compleane.—Newmerket, 23 Octo\u02b3 1632.

Similar letter to the Theasurer and Deputie.

To the Thesaurer.

Right, &c.—Wheras we perceave by the letter writtin from our Counsell of late concerneing the goodis of the Lubek schip clamed by our Admirall for the tyme, that they have condescendit vpon the sowme dew to him, bot in regard of some charges layed out for transporting the goodis vnto Leith, wherwith he doeth alledge he should not be burdened, and of the consideratioun acknowledged dew by our Counsall to him for wanting his moneyis so long, becaus of ther being applyed to the payment of that which was due from ws to the mariners much pressed at that tyme, which is remitted by them to our consideratioun with the estate therof, we not being acquanted cannot particularlie determyne therin, bot being loath that ather we or our said Admirall should be further troubled therwith, sicing he hath gevin satisfaction to all other pairteis haveing interest which we doe approve: It is our pleasur that without any respect to the said Erle for arriells due to him for the tymes past, or for charges for transportation, yow tak ordour for his satisfaction of the sowme, which was acknowledged due by act of Counsell, and applyed to our vse, conforme to our former warrants directed for that effect; ffor doeing wherof, &c.—Newmerket, 23 Octo^r 1632.

To the Counsell.

Right, &c.—Haveing of late writtin vnto yow tnitching our resolution to repair to that our kingdome, requyreing that all things necessarie for our comeing and abode ther might be in such readines and decencie as is requisit, whairof we doubt not bot yow will have a speciall care, we have at this tyme thoght fitt particularlie to recommend vnto yow the preservation of our game, both of hunting and hauking, of all sort of wyld foulls in all the places accustomed in the tyne of our late dear father, or wher yow shall think most fitt, and that yow preseryve such ordours as hitherto hath bene accustomed, or as yow shall find requisite for that purpois: Which recomending to your care, &c.—Whythall, first No^r 1632.

Right, &c.—Wheras our trustie and weilbeloved Sir Alex^r Leslie, knyt, Serjant Major generall now imployed vnder the King of Sweden in the Warre of Germanie, hath sent from Hamhrugh, to be transported to our kingdome of Scotland, the sowme of Nyne thowsand rex dollours for his owin vse, which sowme by want of commoditie of schipping directlie from Hamhurgh to Scotland is cum to our citie of London, from whence humble sute hath bene made vnto ws for our licence to transport to our said kingdome of Scotland according to the intention of the owner, we being trewlie informed of the veritie of the premisses, have thought it agrieable to equitie to give way to the requeist: Therfor our pleasur is, that yow suffer and permitt the bearer heirof, Livetenent Colonell Leslie, brother to the said Sir Alexander, peaciablie to transport the said money according to his brother's direction, without aney lett or hinderance of yow or aney of yow, notwithstanding of any act of parliament or other restraynt whatsumever to the contrair.—Gevin at Whythall, 7 No^r 1632.

To the Erle of Morton, Lord Traquair, The Thesaurer and deputie thesaurer, and to all his Ma^teis fermers, customers, searchers, and all others his Ma^teis officers and loveing subjects whome these doe or may concerne.

To the Counsell.

Right, &c.—Haveing of late sufficientlie expressed our full resolution to repair, God willing, the nixt sommer to that our antient kingdome, and to that effect requyres that a speciall care be had that nothing necessarie and decent be wanting for our receaveing and intertenement ther, we have at this tyme thoght fitt particularlie to recommend vnto yow the preserveing of our game of hunting and hauking in these parts wher our late dear father was wont to vse, and wher yow shall think we may tak occasion to repair, and for causeing amend the highwayes wherin we ar to pass, and to that purpois that yow preseryve such speedie ordours as shalbe fund requisite, becaus the tymelie doeing therof will conduce to the vse of our service in that kingdome, and be less troublsome to such of our subjects as shalbe imployed therin, and if aney persones shall transgress these ordours, that yow call them befoir yow, and censure or fyne them as yow shall find just caus: And hearing that the latnes of the harvest ther is lyklie to occasion great scarsitie of Victuall, our further pleasur is (if yow find it lyklie to prove so), that yow grant no licence nor suffer any corne to be transported out of that kingdome till our comeing thither, vnless yow find that it may be safelie spared without fear of aney ensueing want, which as we desyre at all tymes to be prevented, so speciallie at the tyme of our being ther: All which faill not to doe, as a purpois wherof we will expect the performance at your handis.—Whythall, 7 No^r 1632.

To the Counsell.

Right, &c.—Wheras vpon ane Act of Counsall made by yow for building and keiping a fort at Inchgarvie, we wer pleased to grant to that purpois a Lease of nyntene yeres vnto our right, &c, the Erle of Lythgow to be exped vnder our sealls of that our kingdome, bot haveing occasion at this tyme to consider further of that purpois, Our pleasur is, that yow stay the passing of that Lease till we shalbe pleased to give further ordour concerneing the same; And for your so doeing, &c.—Whythall, 17 No^r 1632.

To the Archbischop of St Androis.

Right reverend, &c.—We ar informed by petition from Mr Ritchart Broun, Master of Arts, that he haveing latelie obtened our presentatioun to the Church of Salton with your owin hand thervnto, and being now about to pass it throw our sealls, and discharge such other dewtois and right which ar customarie and requisite in such a cace, is notwithstanding lyk to be crossed therin by presentatioun of ane other from the Lords Commissioners of our Exchequer: We therfor, both in regard of our owin right and of the compassion of the petitioner's missing of a former presentation to Pencaitland, for which he alledges your promise and assistance to the first occasion that should fall therefter, have thoght fitt to will and requyre yow furthwith to give collation and peaciable possessioun of the said benefice of Salton to this petitioner and no other, he first giveing vnto yow such tryell and testimonie of his sufficiencie and conformitie or any other dewtie as ar requisit in such and the lyk caces; Wherin not doubting of your care and diligence, &c.—Gevin at our Court of Whythall, 17 No^r 1632.

To Sir Johne Auchmowtie, Master of his Maties Garderobe of Scotland.

Trustie, &c.—Haveing resolved to repair so schortlie vnto that our kingdome, and being desyreous that all things necessarie for our intertenement ther may be in due ordour befoir our comeing, it is our pleasur that yow call for plate, hangings, and all other things belonging to our garderobe, belonginge vnto your charge, wher ever they be; and haveing gathered them togidder, that yow cause them be surveighed and considered: And therefter that yow ather cum yourself to informe ws, or certifie bak vnto ws, with diligence what is wanting that must be boght of new, or what is decayed or ruynuts that had neid to be repaired, to the effect that a course be takin for remeding therof in dew tyme: So expecting the performance heirof with diligence, as yow wilbe answerable vnto ws, &c.—Whythall, 17 No^r 1632.

To the Session.

Right, &c.—Wheras Anna Nasmyth, onlie chyld now alyve of Johne Nasmyth, some tyme Chyrurgian to our late royall father, hath humblie petitioned ws in regard of the late death of hir brother, and hir owin educatioun and continewed abode in this our kingdome, being ignorant of the estate of hir affaires ther, that we, out of our princelie care of Justice, might assure hir from prejudice dureing hir staying heir, till schoe can be able to repair thither, which schoe intendis with as much diligence as the seasone of the yeir and the indisposition of hir bodie will convenientlie permitt : And being informed that ane James Nasmyth of Posso intends to serve him self air-male to hir late brother, therby to prejudge hir right of inheritance, we, taking hir estate in commiseration, have thoght litt to requyre yow that yow suffer no such service to pass vntill the first day of Junij nixtocum, that schoe may have this competence of tyme to address hirself thither, and be heard for hir entress; and in the meane, becaus we hear that the choysest and greatest part of hir brother's writts ar lockit vp and scalled in a Cabinet, left as yit standing in the house wher he died, and that the key therof is in the hands of ane other persone, we further requyre that yow caus the same furthwith to be delyvered to our Advocat, to be saillie keiped by him locked and scalled as it is, and to be by him delyvered in the same maner to the said Anna, or to aney haveing hir power : So recommending vnto yow the speedie furtherance, according to Justice, of all hir actions of Law that shall cum befoir yow, &c.—Whythall, 18 Nor 1632.

Charles, be the Grace of God king of Great Britane, &c. To the great Lord and Emperour of Russia, and dear Vncle the King of Denmark, and our dear brother the King of Sweden, and to all other kings, princes, potentats, and governours of commonwealths and citeis, vnto whois dominions and jurisdictions our trustie and weilbelovit subject James Wallace, the bearer heirof, shall cum by sea or land. Greeting.— Wheras we ar heirby graciouslie pleased (at the humble requeist of our loveing subjects the Colonells, Capitanes, and souldiours serveing and resident at Russia, vnder the Command of the said great Lord and Emperour of Muscovia) To appoynt and ordeyne the aforsaid James Wallace a messinger for caryeing letters from ws and our loveing subjects in great Britane and these our subjects in Russia and Muscovia, for the better knowing and vnderstanding the estate of ther affaires and health by intercourse of letters : Therfor by these presents we doe requeist the said great Lord and Emperour, our said dear vncle the king of Denmark, and dear brother the king of Sweden, and other kings, princes, and potentats as aforsaid, To permitt the said James Wallace, with his servands, frielie and saillie to pass, with all freindlie assistance and furtherance, thrugh your kingdomes, dominions, territoreis, and citeis, he behaveing himself honestlie and discreitlie : And lykwyse we will and command all our governours, officers, and ministers of Cinque Ports, and of all other ports within any of our dominions, to assist, further, and permitt the said James Wallace, with his servands, frielie to embark, pass, and repasse without your molestatioun or hinderance to and from the parts aforsaid, as often as occasion shalbe offered : Togidder with all such provisions as shalbe necessarie for his said travells, as yow, our saidis officers will answer, the contrarie at your perrells.—Gevin at our palace of Westminster, the 26 Nor, Anno Salutis 1632, and of our Regne the Eight.

                                        Subscribitur,   Carolus R.

[No Address.]

Right, &c.—Ther was delyvered to ws in Februar last by Mr George Nicoll a trew Relation, as he calls it, of the estate of our revenewis in that our kingdome, for justifieing whairof he hath sett doun vnder his hand sindrie particulars, which, becaus they consist in facto, ar onlie tryable by the recordis of that kingdome ; and therfoir we have heirwith send down the said relation, with the particulars cited for prooffis thairof, vnto yow, willing and repuyreing yow carefullie to examyne the said relation and prooffes thairof by the severall recordis of that our kingdome, as they ar therin cited ; or further, as shalbe requisit, that yow, being informed of the treuth thairof or defect, may accordinglie certifie ws what ye find thairin, and with all convenient diligence returne the saids papers, with your certificat, to our master of our requeistis, to be presented vnto ws : Wherin, not doubting of your care and conformitie to this our pleasur, &c.—26 No* 1632, Whythall.

Our Soverane Lord ordeanes a Protection to be made vnder his highnes' great seall of the kingdom of Scotland to his highnes' lovitts Sir Johne Boswall of Balmouto, kny*, David Boswall, his eldest lawfull sone, fiar of Balmuto, Sir George Boswell of Balgonie wester, and George Boswall of the West Mylnes of Kirkcaldie, makand mention that wheras his Ma** is crediblie informed that they ar bund as cautioners for James and David Boswells, vncles to the said David Boswall, fiar of Balmuto, who, being the onlie principall debtours, have good and sufficient estents, wherby (if putt to good vse) ther creditours may receave full satisfaction of what is justlie dew to them ; Notwithstanding, the said principalls, thogh knowing that ther sureteis ar be ther Creditours hardlie distressed for them, will tak no course to give the saids Creditours satisfaction, wherby the saids Cautioners ar lyklie both to be dissableit to deall with the said principalls for paying ther owin debts, or the best vse they can best mak of ther esteats for satisficing the saids Creditours : Wheryvpon his Ma**, taking into his princelie consideration the hard esteat of the Cautioneris, and the vnjust and vnconsionable dealing, and being villing that the Creditours should seik the Execution of the Lawis against the principall debtours (speciallie sieing they ar able to give them satisfaction) befoir the Cautioners should, by ane vntymelie way, have ther persones troubled and cast in prissone, and to that effect that some small tyme should be granted, at least that the saids Cautioners may have some tyme to mak the best vse of ther owin esteats to give the Creditours satisfaction, if the Principalls cannot in the meane tyme be moved or forced by ordour of Law to doe the same : Therfor his Ma**, of his authoritie royall, kinglie power, grace, mercie, and clemencie, hath accepted, and by the tenour heirof accepts, the saids Sir Johne Boswall and David Boswall of Balmowtie, the saids Sir George Boswall of Balgonie Wester and George Boswell of the Westmylnes of Kirkcaldie, cautioners forsaid, vnder his highnes' protection, safeguard, mantenance, and defence from being aney wayes troubled, molested, or persewed by the saids Creditours for aney debt due vnto them by the saids James and David Boswells, vncles to the said David Boswell of Balmuto, for payment whairof the said Cautioners, or any of them, ar bund as suretie : And gives and grantis vnto the saids Cautioners, and everie of them, dureing the space of ane yeir, begining from the passing of thir presents vnder the great seall, Licence, power, and libertie to peaceablie and safelie duell, stay, and remaine within aney part of the said kingdome without molestation, trouble, challenge, persute, or danger of apprehending or warding of ther or aney of ther persones for being Cautioners for the persones aforsaid ; and no otherwyse dischargeing expreslie by thir presents All his Ma*** Schirreffs, Stewarts, Provests, Bailleis, Constables of Burghes, Justices of Peace, and all Justices, Judges, officers and ministers of his highnes' lawis, both in burgh and land, ther deputeis, servandis, and all others whome it effeires within the said kingdome, that they nor nane of them doe any wayes presume, attempt, nor tak in hand, directlie or indirectlie, by day or night, to seik, tak, or apprehend the saids Cautioners aforsaid, or aney of them, for the said Cautionrie, or mak any disturbance, interruption, or violation of this his Ma*** protection, vnder pane of incurring his highnes' vtter wrath and high displeasur, notwithstanding of our Letters of horning, captions, warrands, commissiones, charges, or commands alreadie gevin or to be gevin by his Ma*** himself, the Lordis of Session, or aney of his Ma*** Judges, Officers, or other persones whatsoever within the said kingdome, in favours of the saids Creditours or aney of them, for apprehending or warding of the saids Cautioners or aney of ther persones for aney debts or sowmes of money for which they or aney of them ar suretie in maner forsaid, wheranent his Matie, of his highnes' royall and princelie power, by thir presents dispensses in that part dureing the space of ane yeir: And to the effect the said Cautioners and everie of them may be the more able to satisfie and pay to ther Creditours the debts owing by them, and in the meanetyme recover payment of ther just moneyis owing to them by ther debtours, his Matie, of his authoritie royall, princelie power and prerogative, doth heirby speciallie authorize the saids Cautioners and everie of them to stand in judgment to persew and defend all actions intended or to be intended, as well at ther owin instances aganst ther debtours as at ther creditours' instance aganst them, notwithstanding of whatsoever processes of horning vsed or to be vsed aganst them for the cautionrie abone writtin, wheranent his Matie have dispensed, and by thir presents dispensses, dureing the said space: Ordeaneing publication heirof to be made and intimat to the saids Creditours, or others haveing interest, at ther duelling-housses, or at the mercat croces of the head burgh of the schyre wher they duell, Commanding the Lords of Sessioun heirby to grant and direct Letters of publication heirvpon for that effect: And ordeaneing lykwyse thir presents to be a sufficient warrant to the wryter of the great seall and keiper thairof for wryting of thir presents therto, and appending the said great seall to the same, without passing of aney other seall or register, wheranent thir presents shalbe vnto yow a sufficient warrand.—Gevin at his Ma^teis Court at Whythall, the 4 of De^r 1632.

Our Soverane Lord haveing sufficient tryell, prooff, and long experience of the good, true, and thankfull service done to his Matie and to his highnes' late royall father, of happie memorie, thir many yeres bypast by his Ma^teis trustie and weillbelovit Sir John Hay of Landis, kny^t, not onlie in ther Ma^teis privat and particular affaires, wherin they of ther owin princelie motives wer pleased to entrust him, bot also in the publict affaires of his Ma^teis kingdome of Scotland; And his Ma^teis perfectlie vnderstanding his habilitie, literature, and qualificatioun for the vseing and exerceing of the place and office of his Ma^teis Clerk of Register within the said kingdome, now vacand in his Ma^teis handis, and at highnes' gift and disposition by the death of vmquhill Sir Johne Hamilton of Magdalens, kny^t, his Ma^teis last Clerk of Register: Therfor his Matie ordeanes a Letter to be made vnder his highnes' great seall of the said kingdome, making, constituteing, and ordaneing, lykas his Matie by the tenour heirof maks, constituts, and ordanes the said Sir Johne Hay of Landis, kny^t, dureing all the dayes of his lyftyme, his Ma^teis Clerk of Register and Rolls of the Counsall and Sessioun of the said kingdome, with full and absolute power to him dureing his said lyftyme to choyse and place deputeis, ane or mae, in the said office dureing ther lyftyme, as oft as he shall think fitt, and from tyme to tyme to vse, bruik, posses, and enjoy all and whatsumever feyis, rents, proffits, and pre-eminences, priviledges, immuniteis, casualiteis, and emoluments apperteneing and belonging to the said office by whatsumever maner of way; With power to him, for his more absolute obteneing and enjoying thairof, to call, persew, and recover, by course of Law and everie way, and in all respects also friclie to exerce, vse, bruik the said office, and enjoy the benefits and priviledges thairof, as the said Sir Johne Hamilton, or any others his predicessours in the said office, hath bruiked and enjoyed the same at any tyme preceiding; And ordeanes the said Letter to be writtin and exped vnder the great seall of his Ma^teis said kingdome, without passing any other sealls or registers; for which these presents shall both be a sufficient warrant to the keeper and writter to the great seall.—Gevin at Whythall, the   day of December 1632.

Our Soverane Lord being crediblie informed that ordinarlie, in all the cheifest kingdomes and parts of Europ wher silks ar worne, the Tradis of winding, thraveing, dying, and fixing of all maner of cullours of silk ar vsed and practized by the natives and inhabitants of these parts, and his Matie in his princelie judgment conceiveing that for diverse important respects it would verie much conduce to [the] generall good of [the] commonwealth of that his Ma^{teis} antient kingdome of Scotland that these tradis wer lykwyse putt in practeis ther for the good of his subjects therof, speciallie by putting to work such ydle and poor people who, without imployment, ar but a burden to that kingdome, and that by the putting and setting vp of such manufactoreis, and putting the saids tradis in reall practeis, diverse disadvantages and discommoditeis aryseing to the merchandis and others his Ma^{teis} good subjects may be prevented by reasone of the decay of cullours, loss of weght, and deceat, and dyeing efter the saids wairis ar to ther great charges imported : And with all his Matie in his princelie judgment considering that of, &c. . . . the vndertakers for setting vp of these manufactoreis never heirtofoir sett vp nor the lyk tradis putt in practeis within the said kingdome wilbe at a great charge and trouble, and run a great hazard to lose ther meanes and estats by adventureing vpon such a worthie desyre for the publict good, vnless they be encouraged by all the fayr and lawfull wayes that can be devysed : Therfor, in consideration of the laudable custome observed by his Ma^{teis} late royall father, of worthie memorie, by granting for some competent tyme the benefite of all Inventions tending to the publict good to the first inventars and putters thairof in practeis, To the effect that all persones haveing ane inclination to the verteous designes for the good of the common weill might be the better encouraged to prosecute the same, His Matie, with speciall advyse and consent of his Ma^{teis} privie Counsall and Excheker of the said kingdome, ordeanes Letters Patent to be made and exped vnder the great seall thairof, Giveing and granting, lykas his Matie by the tenour heirof, for him, his airis, and successours, and with advyse and consent forsaid, Gives and grants vnto the saids, &c., ther aires, executours, partiners, and associats, and to none others, dureing the space of 21 yeres nixt and immediatlie ensueing the date of the passing of thir presents vnder the said great seall, full, frie, and sole libertie, licence, priviledge, and power that thay, the saids, &c., thair aires, executours, partiners, and associats, ther deputeis, factours, servandis, and workmen, to buy and import to the said kingdome all maner of Raw and vnmade silks from tyme to tyme dureing the space of 21 yeires, paying alwayes the customes due to his Matie or his successours for the same, and to build, sett vp, mak, and establisch at ther owin propper coasts and charges in all the parts of the said kingdome, fitt and convenient for that purpois, housses, works, engynes, toules, and vessels for manufactoreis of the saids tradis of winding, throwing, and twisting of silk, dying and fixing of all maner of cullours thervpon, and to that effect to buy and purches ground, tenements, and housses fitt for that purpois : With power lykwise to them, the saidis, &c., ther aires, executours, partiners, and associats, to conduce with strangers and furraners, and all others persones whatsoever, ather within or without the said kingdome, being skilfull in the saids tradis, or any of them, for setting of the saids persones within the same, to vse and practeis the saids tradis, or any of them, to which strangers so brought in for the purpois aforsaid his Matie, with speciall advyse and consent forsaid, gives and grants all such liberteis, priviledges, and immuniteis in the said kingdome as is or hath bene heirtofoir granted to any stranger, denized or naturalized persone of the same, Provyded that they reside and mak ther ordinarie aboad therin, and be subject to the Lawis thairof : Which priviledges and friedomes his Matie, with consent forsaid, doth heirby will and declair that thay and every of them shall as friclie bruik and enjoy to all intents and constructions as if they wer denized and naturalized persones within the same, And as thervpon Letters of denization or naturalization war exped vnder his Ma^{teis} great seall, ather to all of them in generall, or to everie ane of them in particular ; provyded alwyse, that if these strangers shall have neid of apprenticeis, that they accept such of the natives as they shall find capable and willing to be bred and serve in that kynd vpon such reasonable conditions as is vsuall in the lyk cases : With full and absolute power to the saids, &c., ther aires, executours, partiners, and associats, and to none others, dureing the said space of 21 yeires efter the expreding of the saids letters patents vnder the said great seall, to mak ther vse and benefite of the saids so winded, throwin, twisted, and dyed by them and ther forsaids as they shall think most fitt, and that ather within the said kingdome or in any forrayne and nyghbouring kingdome, state, or place whatsoever, being in

league and amitie with his Matie and successours, by selling of the saids commoditeis and warris as they shall think most fitt, paying vnto his Matie and his successours Custome and others dewteis for the exporting or importing thairof, as is accustomed in the lyk cases, Provyded alwyse that they furnish the said kingdome of Scotland with the saids Commoditeis at as easie and cheap rates as the merchandis shall happin to sell the lyk imported commoditeis : And to the end his Ma^teis pleasur heirin may tak the better effect, and that the saids, &c., ther aires, executours, partiners, and associats may the more fullie and frielie enjoy the benefite of this his Ma^teis grant, his Matie for himsellf, his aires and successours, does heirby stratlie charge and command that no person or persons whatsoever, native or stranger, denized or naturalized persone, of or within the said kingdome, of whatsoever qualitie or condition they be, shall presume or tak in hand, directlie or indirectlie, dureing the said space of 21 yeres, without the speciall leave and consent of the said, &c., or ther forsaids, first had and obtenit thervnto, practeis, exerce, putt in vse, or anywyse counterlit, by themsellfis, ther servandis, or others in ther names, the said trads of winding, throwing, or twisting of silk, dyeing or fixing of any maner of cullour vpon the samyne, or to erect, mak, or build any workhouse or place, engyne, instrument, or vessell whatsoever for the same within the said kingdome or any part thairof; or the saids silks being winded, throwen, twisted, or dyed in any sort of cullour, to sell, vent, or exchange the same within the said kingdome, or to convey or transport the same to any forrane part whatsoever, vpon pane of forfaltour of the saids commoditeis, tolls, vessells, and engynes, and everie part and parcell therof, the equall hallf of the benefite aryseing therby to cnm to the vse of his Matie and successours, and the other hallf to the vse of the saids, &c., and ther forsaids : With express command to the Lords of his Ma^teis Privie Counsall and Excheker, or ather of them for the tyme being, that vpon notice gevin vnto them by the saids, &c., or ther forsaidis, or any of them of any persone or persones who, without ther speciall licence as aforsaid, shall happin to practeise or sett afoot the saids tradis, or any of them, or to sell, exchange, vent, or export any of the saids commoditeis prohibited to be made by them, To grant letters and charges from tyme to tyme to all his Ma^teis shirreffs, stewarts, bailleis of regaliteis, provests, and bailleis of burghis, Constables, serjands, Masters of schipps, Customers, and all others his Ma^teis officers and ministers and subjects whom it may anywayes concerne for stayeing and arreisting of the saids silks so winded, throwin, twisted, or dyed, with the works, engynes, vessells, and toolis provided for working of the same, the equall hallf thairof to be immediatlie intromitted with by the saids, &c., or ther forsaids, or any of them, for ther owin propper vse, and the other hallf to be made accompt of and delyvered by the saids officers or others intrometters therwith to his highnes' Excheker for his Ma^teis vse as aforsaid : Commanding lykwyse the saids Lords to authorize the saids officers and others aforsaids to apprehend the Contraveners and present them to the Counsell to vndergoe such censure and punishment otherwyse as they shalbe pleased to cause inflict vpon them : Provyded alwyse, lykas it is heirby speciallie provyded, that notwithstanding of this present grant, or of anything that may follow thervpon, the Merchands of the said kingdome may at all tymes and in all parts therof import all sorts of silks, dyed or vndyed, winded, and throwen, or otherwyse whatsoever, at ther pleasur and option, and to sell or Exchange the same for ther owin gayne and advantage, vnless his Matie and Counsell shall happin heirefter, vpon further consideration of the good of the Commonwealth, to give ordour in that behallf for restrayneing of these merchandis to the Contrarie : And provyded alwyse, that if the saids Patentees nor ther forsaids doe not, within the space of thrie yeres nixt ensueing the passing heirof vnder the said scall, putt in practeis the saids trads, nor any of them, so that no reall effects shalbe sene of ther endeavours and travells therin for the publict good, then this present grant to be voyd and of no effect : Commanding the keeper of his Ma^teis great scall and writter therto to writt and append the said scall thervnto, without passing any others scalls and registers, and that precepts be direct thervpon.
[No date.]

To the Counsell.

Right, &c.—Being pleased at this tyme, vpon some speciall considerations of our owin knowledge moveing ws heirvnto, To cause release Allaster Grant from prissone, We requyre yow, notwithstanding we have not at this tyme granted vnto him a remission, to give ordour to our provest and baillies of our burgh of Edinburgh for setting him furthwith at frie libertie, that he may repair to the pairts where he was borne, or else wher for the dispatch of his lawfull affaires, gevin ordour that none presume to trouble him for any caus or occasion bygane proceiding from the grounds of his present imprissonment, till ther be a warrant from ws : For which these presents, &c.—Whythall, 4 Der 1632.

Carolus Dei gratia magnæ Britanniæ Francie et Hiberniæ Rex dilectis nobis in Christo archidecano subdecano et capitulo ecclesiæ Cathedralis de Glasgow salutem Nobis humiliter est supplicatum vt cum ecclesia predicta per mortem naturalem vltimi Archiepiscopi jam vacet et pastoris solatio sic destituta alium vobis archiepiscopum et pastorem elegendi licentiam nostram vobis concedere dignaremur Nos animum ad supplicationem istam favorabiliter inclinantes alium vobis duximus concedendum Rogantes ac in fide et dilectione quibus nobis tendimus præcipientes quod talem vobis eligatis in Archiepiscopum et pastorem qui Deo divotus nobisque et regno vtilis fidei facimus patentes Teste meipso apud Whythall, 4 die deris 1632.

Carolus dei gratia Magnæ Britaniæ et Hiberniæ Rex dilectis nobis in Christo decano et capitulo ecclesiæ Cathedralis Rossensis salutem Nobis humiliter est supplicatum vt cum ecclesia predicta per translationem vltimi ejus Episcopi locum Archiepiscopi Glasguensis defuncti vacet et pastoris solatio sic destituta alium vobis elegendi Episcopum et pastorem licentiam nostram concedere dignaremur Nos animum ad supplicationem istam favorabiliter inclinantes alium vobis duximus concedendum Rogantes ac . in fide et in dilectione quibus nobis tendimus precipientes quod talem vobis eligatis in Episcopum et pastorem qui Deo devotus nobisque et regno vtilis et fidelis existat In cujus rei testimonium has nostras literas fidei facimus patentes.—Apud Whythall, 4 Deris 1632.

Trustie, &c.—Wheras the Archbischoprik of Glasgow is at this present voyd by the death of the late incumbent ther, We latt yow to witt that, calling to our remembrance the vertew, learneing, and other good qualiteis of Patrik Lindsay, Bischop of Ross, we have thoght good by these presents to name and recommend him vnto yow, to be elected and choysen to the said Archbishoprik of Glasgow : Therfoir we will and requyre yow upon sight heirof to proceid vpon your election according to our lawis of that our realme, and our Conge d'elisre sent heirwith vnto yow to that effect; and the same election so made to certifie ws vnder your Common Seall therof.—Whythall, 4 Der 1632.

To The Archdeane, dean, and Chaptour of the
    Archbischop of Glasgow.

[No Address.]

Trustie, &c.—Wheras the bischoprik of Rosse is at this present voyd by removeing of the late Incumbent to the Archbischoprik of Glasgow, We latt yow witt that, calling to remembrance the vertew, learneing, and other good qualiteis of Mr John Maxwell, now one of the Ministers of our toun of Edinburgh, we have thoght good by these our letters to name and recommend him vnto yow, to be elected and choysen to the said bischoprik of Ross: Therfor we will pray and requyre [yow] vpon receipt heirof, to proceid to your election according to the lawis of that our kingdome, and our Conge d'eslire sent heirwith vnto yow to that effect, and the same election so made to certifie ws vnder your common seall thairof.—Whythall, 4 Dᵉʳ 1632.

[No Address.]

Right, &c.—Wheras it is represented by the inclosed petition some hard and vnusuall proceidings have bene vsed by the Constable of Dundie aganst the Petitioners in causing ryd ther cornes vncutt, and therby value ther tythis contrarie to the course of our Commission, by which (as we ar informed) they ar lyklie to be prejudged: Sieing they have bene humble sutters to ws that we would not sie them suffer in ther particular, contrarie to the generall course intendit by ws for the publict good, speciallie by the said Constable, who refused to submitt vnto ws, Our pleasur is, that yow seriouslie consider of the petition, and give way to their demand therin, in so far as yow can lawfullie and warrantablie doe by your Commission, accepting of no report of the valuation of these Tythis which is contrarie to the course thairof, or made in name of any persone not interessed therin; bot that such as have right insist in ther owin names in the causes belonging vnto them, that no occasion of delay be gevin in the setling of these tythis heirefter; and for your, &c.—Whythall, 4 Dᵉʳ 1632.

To the Counsell.

Right, &c.—As by sindrie of our letters we have gevin yow the aduerteisment for causeing prepare and doe such things as wer necessarie for our repairing to that our kingdome and abode ther, and for causeing mend the hie wayes in these places wher we ar to resort; So, haveing occasion to direct thither our right, &c. the Erle of Stratherne, President of our privie counsell, for these and some other things concerneing our service, to whom we have particularlie imparted our mynd, and whom yow shall trust from ws heirin and in some other things for that purpois, It is our pleasur, efter yow have taken them to your consideratioun, that yow give ordour for effectuating therof with as much diligence as may be, that our said ensen may returne bak fullie instructed to satisfie ws heirin, as we have given him ordour to doe with all diligence; which speciallie recommending vnto your care, and wherof we will expect a speciall accompt, we bid, &c.—Whythall, the 12 Dᵉʳ 1632.

To the Commissioners of Surrenders.

Right, &c.—Wheras in the Commission of Surranders and tythes we have still reserved power in our selffis to adjoyne such persones as from tyme to tyme we shall think fitt to nominat for the better attending on that Commission: Being now informed that it is expedient for the good and furthering of that work that some mae burgesses be nominat and appoynted by ws to that effect, Our pleasur is, that yow admitt and receave vpon the said Commission Johne Sinclair, James Cochrane, William Gray, Robert Achiesone, Archibald Tod, Edward Edzer, Johne Trotter, younger, Stephan Boyd, Charles Hamilton, burgesses of Edinburgh; Andro Wilson, Andro Gray, burgesses of Perth; Andro Mylne, Glen, burgesses of Linlythgow; Johne Scherar, Thomas Bruce, burgesses of Stirling; Johne M'Kiesone, burges of Craill; and Robert Meiklejohne, burges of Bruntyland; and that yow tak ther oathes for faythfull dischargeing of the dewtie in the said Commission, wherauent these presents shalbe your warrand.—Whythall, 12 Dᵉʳ 1632.

To the Counsell.

Right, &c.—Wheras we wer pleased by our letters to yow to give ordour for dateing at Westminster of the Letters Patents of the Association of the fischingis exped vnder the great sealls of both our king-domes, which should have be dated at Camburie: These ar therfor to approve what is done by yow, notwithstanding of our former warrants, and to will yow to pass ane act of Counsell theranent for warrant of what is done, or any other evidence to that purpois yow shall think fitt; for dooing whairof theso shalbe a sufficient warrant.—Whythall, 12 Der 1632.

To the Session.

Right, &c.—Wheras ane extraordinarie place in the Session doeth now vaik at our gift and disposition by the death of Sir Johne Hamilton, our Clerk of Register; vnderstanding the qualificatioun and sufficiencie of our trustie Sir Johne Hay of Lands, knyt, we have made choyce of him to succeid in that place: Ther-foir we have thoght good to nominat and present him to that extraordinarie place of Session, requyreing yow effectuallie to receave and admitt him thervnto, tak his oath as is accustomed in the lyk caces, and let him have voit amongst yow as vse is.—Whythall, 12 Der 1632.

Similar Letter for his admission to the Counsell.

Similar Letter to the Commissioners of Exchequer for his admission.

To the Counsell.

Right, &c.—Haveing bene pleased, vpoun the considerations of the sufficient qualificatioun and affection to our service of our trustie Sir Johne Hay, kynt, to admitt him Clerk of Register in place of Sir Johne Hamiltoun of Magdalens, knyt, latelie deceissed, Our pleasur is, that yow give ordour to caus delyver vnto the said Sir Johne Hay the keyis of all such places and rowmes, ather within our Castell of Edinburgh, or exchequer, or elswher, as the said Sir Johne Hamiltoun did keip by vertew of that office, and that yow lykwayes give ordour to caus delyver vnto the said Sir Johne Hay all such evidents, writts, and publict records as wer in the custodie of the said Sir Johne Hamilton, or ought to be keiped by our Clerk of Register, that they may be made vse of, as occasion shall requyre, for our service and publick good; ffor which these presents, &c. &c.—[Not dated.]

To the Erle of Stratherne.

Right, &c.—Wheras we wer long tyme pleased to grant a Commission for reviseing the Acts of Parliament, that such of them as wer considered and collected by our Commissioners appoynted for that purpois might be in readines to be rectifeid and ordoured nixt Parliament, according to the intent of that Commission, haveing at this tyme directed yow vnto our kingdome of Scotland for affaires speciallie importing the good of our service, we ar pleased, amongst other things, speciallie to recommend vnto yow to informe yourselff of all that hath proceidit in that Commission, and to report vnto ws the trew estate thairof, representing in our name to these Commissioners that they speedelie proceid to have all things tuitching that Commission in readiness at our comeing thither the nixt spring of the yeir, And that yow particularlie recommend to our Colledge of Justice for contributeing ther ayde at their best conveniencie in furthring that work, which we will tak as verie acceptable service done vnto ws, and which we will particularlie acnowledge at ther handis whensoever occasion shall convenientlie offer to that effect.—Whythall, 14 Der 1632.

To the Counsell.

Right, &c.—Haveing signed a gift of the office of Clerk Register to our trustie and weilbeloved Sir Johne Hay, knyt, whome we have directed to returne to our Court with all diligence for our service, tuitching the Commission for the fischings wherin he is a Commissioner, Our pleasur is, that yow give speciall ordour heirwith to caus expeid the said gift vnder our great seall, that no occasion of delay be gevin to hinder him from returneing speedelie hither; for doeing wherof these presents shalbe your warrant.—Whythall, 14 Der 1632.

To the Advocat.

Trustie, &c.—Yow can perceave by our letter to our Counsall our pleasur tuitching some false and malitious calumneis suggested vnto ws by one George Nicoll aganst some of our cheiff officers, and tuitching the punisching of him according to justice : Our pleasur is, that haveing fullie informed yourself of these proceidingis, yow persew him befoir our Justice-generall or his deputeis, till a finall sentence be gevin aganst him, according to Justice; ffor which these shalbe your warrant.—Whythall, 21 Der 1632.

To the Provost and Bailies of Edinburgh.

Our pleasur is, that yow receave from the bearer . . . one George Nicoll, whom we have caused send thither to be censured and punisched for such things whairof we have certifeid our Counsell of his guiltienes, and that yow committ him to safe and close custodie within your Tolbuith of Edinburgh, till we or our said Counsell shall give further ordour concerneing him, for which these presents shalbe your warrant.—Whythall, 21 Der 1632.

To James Rattray.

Our pleasur is, that yow furthwith sease vpon all the papers yow possiblie can find belonging or being in the custodie of one George Nicoll, ather within your owin house or elsewher abroad, and spetiallie in the house of one Peter Reid, seated vpon Fleet Ditch; and haveing takin ane Inventarie therof, that yow delyver them scalled to our principall Secretarie for Scotland, to be disposed of as shalbe fund requisit, or as our said Secretar shalbe warranted by ws; for which these presents shalbe your warrant.—Whythall, 21 Der 1632.

To James Rattray.

Our pleasur is, that by vertew of your warrant from ws yow charge in our name any master owner and skipper of any Scott's bark or schip bound for Scotland whom yow shall find within our port of London or river of Thames, and speciallie . . . to tak vnto his custodie and saillie to transport (wind and weather serving) from hence to that our kingdome the persone of one George Nicoll, and we doe heirby strictlie command the said . . . and aney of the persones forsaid to delyver him to the Provost and bailleis of our burgh of Edinburgh according to this warrant from ws for ther receaveing of him.—Whythall, 21 Der 1632.

To the Erle of Stratherne.

Right, &c.—Haveing writtin to our Advocat to persew George Nicoll befoir yow or your deputeis for such false and malitious calumneis which yow did hear in our presens, Our pleasur is, that yow cause his punischment be speedelie sentensed as best shall accord with justice and the foulness of his offence, which we will tak as good service done vnto ws.—Whythall, 21 Der 1632.

To the Counsell.

Right, &c.—Some papers being presented to ws by one George Nicoll, who did therby pretend the incross of our revenue and good of our service, offering with all to qualifie some great neglect and abuses committed by some of our cheiff officers to our prejudice, we wer pleased to call him before ws and hear him at lenth at severall tymes; bot finding that in the one he had most boldlie suggested vnto ws vnjust and malitious calumneis aganst our officers, and in the other had whollie succumbed in what he had vndertakin to mak good for our benefite, wherwith we being justlie offended, ar heirby pleased to acquent yow with the same, becaus of the foolisch and scandalous rumors that hath bene spred by this meanes, and to remitt him thither to be punisched, that all others not warranted with verie just and evident grounds may by his example be terrifeid from attempting the lyk heirefter: To which purpois we have appoynted our Advocat to persew him befoir our Justice-Generall or his deputts till a finall sentence be gevin against him according to justice, and till that tyme we ar willing that he remane as a delinquent in safe and close custodie within the tolbuith of our burgh of Edinburgh.—Whythall, 21 Der 1632.

To the Archbischop of St Androis.

Right, &c.—Wheras humble sute hath bene made vnto ws on behalff of Mr John Ramsay, Professor of Philosophie in St Androis, that in regard of the good prooff he hath gevin in his studie of Theologie, we might be pleased to present him to the kirk of Lathrisk, vacant at our gift by dimissioun or deceis of Mr William Craustoun, late Minister ther, we have thoght good that yow try his qualification, and if yow find him able and qualifeid for that Charge, that yow send him a presentation vnder your hand for admitting him thervnto, he being alwyse subject to acknowledge our authoritie, and give due obedience to his Ordinarie, as is provydit in the lyk caces.—Whythall, 21 Der 1632.

To the Commissioners of our Five Burghes of Scotland.

Trustie, &c.—We have vnderstude your forwardnes to our service in the bussines of the fisching intended by ws for the publict good of all our dominions, in haveing at this tyme vndertakin to have in readines against the nixt seasone of the busch fisching Thrie scoir busches or fisching barks wherin we doe verie much approve your vndertaking, and do heirby spetiallie recommend vnto yow to have them in readines vpon due adverteisment from ws to be made vnto yow by our trustie and weilbeloved Sir Johne Hay, knyt, at his nixt returne to our Court, to whome we have at this tyme signifeid our further pleasur to be imparted vnto yow tuitching that purpois, and who will schew vnto yow the proceidingis of our Commissioners heir for both kingdomes tuitching the advanceing of that bussines by these who have alreadie vndertakin in this our kingdome.—Whythall, 21 Der 1632.

To the Counsell.

Right, &c.—Haveing considered how schort a tyme was appoynted to them of Hambrugh for doeing justice in that cause concerneing late Captane Robertsone and his partiners, and the willingnes of that state to doe the same with diligence, as we have vnderstude by a Commissioner sent by them expreslie for that purpois, we have thoght it reasonable to allow them a longer tyme for doing thairof, and it is our pleasur that yow cause send some vnderstanding persone thither with a procuratorie to persew the painteis thair: And in the meane tyme that yow cause delyver the schips and goodis that wer takin from them for that caus: And wheras the said Commissioner hath gevin ws sufficient suretie and satisfaction for the payment of such sowmes as shalbe fund due whensoever the sentence shalbe pronounced: It is our further pleasur that the letters of reprysall granted for this effect be discharged and suspended vntill we shall find caus for renewing of them, which we meane to doe heirefter if Justice be delayed or refused be them, for as we desyre to deall justlie with our nighbour states, so we will not have our subjects to suffer vnjustlie by them: So recommending this to be done with diligence, We bid, &c.—Whythall, 21 Der 1632.

To the Advocat.

Trustie, &c.—Wheras we ar verie schortlie, God willing, to repair to that our ancient kingdome to receave our Croun and hold a parliament in persone as we have signifeid to our Counsell ther: These ar therfoir to will and requyre yow to prepare all such bills and informationns as yow shall think fitt to be past and performed for our service, and for that effect that yow propone to the Lordis of our Privie Counsell all such overtures as may concerne our service, and the prosecution of that great work of the Tythis and Surrenders, wherin we and our Commissioners have takin so much panes for the good of our subjects ther.—Whythall, 24 Der 1632.

To the Advocat.

Trustie, &c.—Haveing imposed a charge at this tyme vpon our Thesaurer principall and deputie for vseing all lawfull and possible meanes to levie moneyis for such things as ar necessarlie requisit for our reparationn and intertenement in that our kingdome dureing our aboad ther, to which purpois they wilbe forced to mak the best vse they can of any rents, customes, or dewteis whatsoever now or schortlie heirefter payable to our Excheker by any our vnder officers, and particularlie by our customers: Our pleasur is, that yow requyre them in our name to accept of our saidis officer's precepts, which if they onnawayes refuis to doe, we further requyre yow to consider of ther taks, and if therby yow shall find that they ar anywayes bund to answer our saids officers, that yow insist against them by Law befoir our Exchequer for doeing therof, otherwyse that by advyse of our saids officers yow vse your best endeavours to reduce the saids taks by due course of Law, for which these shalbe your warrand.—Whythall, 28 Der 1632.

To Sir Henrie Wardlaw.

Trustie, &c.—Haveing fullie resolved to repair, God willing, the nixt sommer to that our antient kingdome, wherby our Thesaurer principall and deputie most necessarlie vndergoe a great care and burden for provydeing all things necessarie for our reparationn and Intertenement dureing our abode ther, wherin they will stand in neid of the assistance of such of our good and able officers and subjects as has bene knowen best affected to the good of our service, and haveing heard of your forwardnes at other tymes to levy and to becum suretie for moneyis the better to advance our late father's service and ours, we will expect the lyk affection in yow at this tyme, and therefore doe speciallie recommend to yow for assisting our saids officers or any of them in being cautioner with or for them for such moneyis as necessarlie must be levyed for our jurney, taking your part of such releiff as they shall provyd for themselflis, wherin we will expect your performance as yow will respect our favour and the continuance of the good opinion we have long conceaved of yow : So we bid yow farewell.—[Not dated.]

To the Thesaurer and Deputie Thesaurer.

Right, &c.—As we have hitherto sufficientlie expressed to our Counsall our absolute resolution for repairing, God willing, the next somer to that our antient kingdome for receaveing our Croun and holding a parliament ther; So, in regard that in a peculiar maner it concerneth your charge to forsie and mak readie all such provisions and things necessarie as ar requisit and decent for our reception and intertenement dureing our aboad ther : Our speciall pleasur is, that yow carefullie consider what is fitt and requisit to be provydit for that purpois, and that accordinglie yow tak a tymelie course that the same be in readines ; and that particularlie yow forsie that such of our housses wher we ar to be, be putt in good ordour ; and to that effect that yow give speciall ordour to our masters of work that nothing be deficient vpon ther part ; and that yow carefullie surveigh the estate of our wardrop, by causing amend, change, and provyde of new (if neid be) all such wardrop stuff as is requisit, ather for our standing housses or removes : Commanding to this purpois Sir Johne Auchmowtie, Mr of our Wardrop, to whome we have writtin concerneing the same, to give yow a particular accompt of the estate therof, and whom we requyre from tyme to tyme to be directed by yow for performeing our service in this kynd, so that nothing therin be deficient or indecent : And generallie we will expect at your hands such a care and readines to sie everie thing for our journey so provyded as may best give ws content and be to the honour of that our antient kingdome, we bid yow farewell.—Whythall, 28 Der 1632.

To the Counsell.

Right, &c.—We have sufficientlie expressed our resolution to yow for repairing, God willing, the nixt sommer to that our antient kingdome for receaveing our Croun and holding a parliament ther, haveing writtin to yow that a speciall and tymelie care might be had for giveing ordour to provyde in generall for all things necessarie and decent for our reception and Intertenement during our aboad ther, but becaus ther be diverse things in particular concerneing our Intertenement, whairof in a particular maner a speciall care should be had by our Thesaurer principall and deputie, upon whome we have now imposed a charge therof ; and that the tymelie forsieing and provydeing for the same will requyre more then ane ordinarie care and burden, Our pleasur is, that from tyme to tyme, as our saids officers, or any of them, shall have occasion to vse your advyse and requyre your ayde, furth with assist and concure with them in the speedie execution of what we have particularlie imposed vpon them, or any other thing yow shall find requisit for our service in that kynd.—Whythall, 28 Der 1632.

To Sir James Baillie.

Trustie, &c.—Wheras we ar fullie resolved to repair (God willing) the nixt sommer to that our antient kingdome, haveing to that effect requyred our thesaurer and deputie Thesaurer so to provyde for all things necessarie for our reception and intertenement dureing our aboad ther, that nothing necessarie and fitt be wanting, wherby our saids officers will have occasion to mak vse of more money than the estate of our coffers can at this tyme convenientlie affoord, and that therin they will vndergoe some burding in levyeing thairof, we are heirby pleased spetiallie to recommend to yow to concurre with them for advanceing of such moneyis as ar necessarlie requisit to be levyed for our service at this tyme by becomeing suirtie with or for them to that purpois ; and we doe heirby assure yow that yow shall incure no loss by that meanes, and ar pleased further to declair that wherin our saids officers and yow can agrie for your furder suirtie out of any of our rents and casualiteis, we shall mak the same good in what maner they and yow can reasonablie condescend vpon ; besydes we will tak it as a spaciall service done vnto ws, wherof we will not be vnmyndfull when occasion shall convenientlie offer.—Whythall, 28 Der 1632.

Letters of the lyk nature to Williame Dick, and ane vther to Willliame Gray.

To Sir Johne Avchmowtie.

Trustie, &c.—Since the wryting of our last letter vnto yow tuitching the estate of our Wardrop, we have bene pleased to impose a spetiall charge vpon our Thesaurer and deputie for sieing and haveing all things in readines for our reception and Intertenement dureing our abode in that our antient kingdome, amongst which we have requyred them to surveigh the estate therof, and that from tyme to tyme, as occasion shall requyre, yow tak ther or ather of ther directions concerneing all the wardrop stuff being in your custodie or belonging to your charge by causeing provyde of new, change, or mend, if neid be, what they shall find to be wanting or indecent ; wherin, not doubting of your conformitie to this our pleasur, we bid, &c.—Whythall, 28 Der 1632.

To the Advocat.

Trustie, &c.—Haveing imposed a charge at this tyme vpon our Thesaurers for vseing all lawfull and possible meanes to levy moneyis for such things as ar necessarie requisite for our reception and intertenement in that our antient kingdome dureing our abod ther : To which purpois they will be forced to mak the best vse they can of any rents, customes, annuiteis, and dewteis whatsoever, payable to ws : Our pleasur is, that by advyse of our saids officers, or aney of them, yow think vpon the readiest wayes and meanes, and therin vse your best endeavours (in so far as is compitent to your charge) : That all our annuiteis of Tythis, alsweill valued as vnvalued, due to ws for all yeres and termes preceiding be brought in to our vse with the greatest expedition and conveniencie that may be, for which these presents shalbe your warrand, and wherin yow shall doe good service.—Whythall, 28 Der 1632.

To the Advocat.

Trustie, &c.—Wheras we have writtin formerlie to yow that yow should have a speciall care to provyd such things for our parliament as ar fit to be done by yow concerneing your charge, if yow shall find aney particulars wherin yow cannot fullie determyne without conferring first with ws, in that cace we requyre yow to repair hither to our Court as soone as your health and occasion can convenientlie permitt : Soe, ather expecting yourself or to hear from yow, we bid, &c.—Whythall, 29 Der 1632.

To the Counsell.

Right, &c.—Haveing heard of a caus that was debated befoir yow concerneing the Schirreff Courts of the shirrefdome of Lanerk, whither they should be holden at the toun of Hamilton or the toun of Lanerk, the decision wherof yow did delay till our right trustie, &c. The Marqueis of Hamilton, who was then absent, might be heard for his interest at his returne : And we being moved therin vpon the same consideratioun, and haveing heard that it is prejudiciall to the inhabitants of the nather ward of that schyre, Our pleasur is, that yow proceid no further in the said caus, nor that any innovation be made therin, bot continew as hitherto it hath bene till our comeing ther, or till we shall signifie our further pleasur therin, that thairefter, all pairteis being heard for their interest, the best course may be takin heirin, which is most agrieable with the Lawis and practique of that kingdome nd best ease of our subjects : And so we, &c.—Whythall, 8 Jar 1633.

To the Advocat.

Trustie, &c.—We ar informed that the Laird of Drum intendeth to sie executioun vpon ane land of moneyis extorted by his father from Robert Coutts of Auchtertoull, and William, his sone, in his minoritie, not for aney just and onerous cause, bot as a ty to mak them followers of the house of Drum, and to the end he may wrest them from the superioritie of ther Lands holden of ws, therby forceing them to becum his vassalls wher they ar immediatlie now, which course, if trew (as is pretendit), being contrarie to diverse Lawis made against bandis of manrent, and to the late course sett afoot by ws for frieing our vassalls from any oppression or subjection of other subjects, bot in so far as is agrieable to Justice and our Lawis, Our pleasur is, and we doe heirby will and requyre, that yow informe yourself of the trew estate heirof, and if yow find what is heirby alledged to be trew, that yow concurre and assist in our name and for our interest in reduceing the said band in a legall maner; for which these shalbe your warrand.—Whythall, 8 Jar 1633.

To the Session.

Right, &c.—We ar informed that the action in Law for reduceing the erection of William Forbes of Cragievar is now verie schortlie to be heard and disputed befoir yow, wherin seing we have bene pleased to tak speciall notice for our interest, haveing at severall tymes both writtin to yow and our Advocat for sieing that action prosecuted with diligence and putt to a poynt according to justice, we ar now pleased seriouslie to recommend the same vnto yow, that yow will carefullie and speedelie sie it putt to some speedie and good conclusion, according to equitie and the lawis of that our kingdome; which we will tak as verie acceptable service done vnto ws : So we, &c.—Whythall, 8 Jar 1633.

To the Bischop of St Androis.

Right reverend, &c.—Wheras we intend, God willing, this nixt somer to repair to that our antient kingdome, being verie desyreous that all things necessarie for Intertenement ther be prepared and in good ordour befor our Comeing : And knowing that many things ar to be considered of against that tyme by yow, we have thoght good to wryt vnto yow concerneing the same, especiallie that yow will have a care of that which is to be done at our Coronatioun, in so far as is to be discharged by yow or aney ecclesiasticall persone, And that yow prepare yourself to preach at the day of our entrie into Edinburgh, and at the tyme of our Coronatioun, and that some of the most sufficient preachers of that our kingdome be advertised to be in readines whensoever they shalbe requyred to preach dureing the tyme of our being ther; and as we ar confident of your best endeavours heirin, so we accordinglie acknowledge the same, and so bid, &c.—Whythall, 8 Jar 1633.

II   2 G

To the Session.

Right, &c.—Wheras we ar informed that ther is ane action in Law depending befoir yow at the instance of Johne Fullerton of Dreghorne aganst our right trustie, &c. the Lord Bruce and the Lady Kinloss, his mother, tuitching the Estate of vmquhill Sir James Fullerton, our late servand, whois meanes being acquyred and left in this our kingdome, that caus is most propper to be heard and decydit befoir the compitent Judges heir: Whairfor finding it verie fitt and expedient that none of our judicatories of these our severall kingdomes doe trench vpon ane other, Our pleasur is, that all action and proces depending or which shalhappin to cum befor yow tuitching this purpois doe cease, remitting the pairteis interested to have recourse for justice to the lawis of this our kingdome.—Whythall, 12 Jar 1633.

To the Counsell.

Right, &c.—Haveing resolved to give such ane answer as we in our princelie judgment shall think fitt to ane humble sute made to ws in behalff of the Lady Luss, that schoe might have a sufficient mantenance allowed for the Interteinement of hirselff and childrene, becaus as scho affirmeth scho hath none for the present tyme: Our pleasur is, that yow informe yourselff best to such persones to whome the Lard of Luss hath intrusted the management of his esteat, or otherwayes as yow shall think fitt how the said Lady is provydit, and certifie ws thairof, and of the Estate of that house as now it is, with the wholl debtis whairwith it is burdened, and what will fall to ws by his estate, whairin we will expect to hear from yow with such conveniencie as may be; we bid yow farewell.—Whythall, 12 Jar 1633.

To the Counsell.

Right, &c.—Being informed by Johne Aitkinsone, keiper of the prisone in the Poultrey in London, That ane Robert Tough of Dysert, being of late prisoner in the said prisone for certane sowmes of money due by him, did, vnder pretence to vse his meanes to pay his creditours, intreat the said Aitkinsone, his keiper, to goe abroad with him for that effect, as is ordinarlie accustomed heir, bot haveing escaped and ran away from him to that our kingdome to shelter himselff ther from the due course of Justice, wherby he is lyk to vndoe his keiper in being made lyable by his escape to pay the debt, and defraud his creditours heir, of what is justlie due vnto him: This being contrarie to the due course of Justice, which mutuallie ought to be keiped amongst all our loveing subjects, and ane act in him worthie of censure and punischment, Our pleasur is, that with all possible diligence yow give ordour [for] arreisting of his schip and all other goodis known to belong vnto him, that they be made furtheuming for the payment to his Creditours of what is due vnto them, and of all other charges occasioned by his escape; otherwayes, that yow caus apprehend him, if he can be fund ther, and keip him in close prisone till he satisfie his saidis pairteis according to Justice, and to that purpois that yow give ordour in what yow shall think fitt: Which recommending vnto your speciall care, we bid yow farewell.—From our Court at Whythall, 18 Jar 1633.

To the Session.

Right, &c.—Whairas, vpoun significatioun of our pleasur to our Counsell of that our kingdome, they have granted vnto our servand Sir Alexr Home, and Sir George Home, his father, libertie to cum in publict for the lawfull setling of ther affaires till the last of March nixt: Our pleasur is lykwayes, that in aney action ather of them shall have befoir yow, ather as persewer or defender, yow grant them power to stand in judgment, notwithstanding of any proces of horning civilie led aganst them; for which, &c.—Whythall, 18 Jar 1633.

To the Exchequer.

Right, &c.—A Petition hath bene exhibited to ws in behalff of Mr Alex^r Seatone, ane of the Senatours of our Colledge of Justice, against some proceidings of the Erle of Mar, so much to the Petitioner's disadvantage and loss that we could not bot in justice so far to give ear therto as to remitt both pairteis to be heard befoir yow, and if thingis alledged by the Petitioner be fund trew, that he might receave satisfaction according to his demand in the inclosed petition, which we have sent to be examined and considered by yow : Our pleasur is, that haveing called both pairteis befoir yow, and haveing fullie considered of the petition, and of what further can be propounded or objectit by them, yow so setle and compose the differences betweene them as they shall find to be just and reasonable, and as yow can most convenientlie doe, wherin (if neid be) we will further approve of such proceidingis in such maner yow shall think fitt to prescryve ; bot if yow cannot compose them, so that the petitioner cannot receave such satisfaction as yow shall find reasonable without acquanting of ws for giveing such further order therin as we by your advyse shall think fitt, that yow report the esteat therof vnto ws with all diligence, togidder with your opinion what in Justice and equitie is fitt to be done heirin by ws and for his satisfaction for inbringing of the Concealments of the taxations, we will yow to consider his paynes and charges therin, and therefter to report to ws what yow shall find heirin, that we may give a precept or other warrand requisit for satisfieing out of the rediest of these concealed moneyis : All which we recommend vnto your care, &c.—Whythall, 18 Ja^r 1633.

To the Counsell.

Right, &c.—A motion haveing bene made to ws in behalff of our right, &c. the Erle of Mulgrave for being authorized by ws to caus search and discover mynes of mettalls in that our kingdome, we have to that purpois signed a Lease to him and his partiners for 19 yeires, to be exped vnder our great seall, wherin, thogh we ar informed that ther be diverse beneficiall clausses conceaved for the publict good, yit, leist ther be aneything therin that cannot hold good in Law, or prove prejudiciall to the state ther, we have sent it heirwith to be considered of yow : And it is our pleasur that yow pervse and consider of the same, taking the speciall advyse of our Advocat in any legall poynt yow shall think fitt to be takin ; And if yow find what is in the Lease to be fair and lawfull, that yow furthwith caus expeid it vnder our great seall ; bot if ther be aneything therin to the contrairie, that yow caus reforme it with diligence, and expeid it vnder our cachet and sealls without returneing it bak to ws, or without farder trouble to the nobleman whois affection to our service heirin we tak in verie great part, and will not be wanting in aneything wherin we can lawfullie farther him, spetiallie in this purpois, which possiblie may produce some good and great effects for the weill of that our ancient kingdome.—Whythall, 21 Ja^r 1633.

To the Advocat.

Trustie, &c.—Wheras we ar informed that diverse of the Lordis of the Erection, notwithstanding of ther surranders made to ws of the superioriteis of ther erections, doe call and persew the vassalls for improbatioun and reduction of ther Infeftments, wherby we may be prejudged in our right of superioritie, and to be persewit by the saidis Lordis of erections against the saids Vassalls ; and that yow compeir for ws in our particular interest dew to ws by the generall surrander and submission, and plead for defence of our right and for mantneing of the saids Vassalls of Erections, notwithstanding your name be vsed as our Advocat for our comeing entress in the saidis actions and persuts, and that yow intimat this our command and royall pleasur to the Lords of Session ; for doeing quherof, &c.—Whythall, 28 Feb^r 1633.

To the Master of Work.

Trustie, &c.—We have heard of your great care in forsieing and provydeing for all such thingis necessarie as belong to your charge tuitching the repairing of our house in that our kingdome, for which we give yow heartie thanks ; and now at our comeing thither, God willing, verie schortlie, we will expect at your hands that nothing be wanting or deficient that is fitting to be added of new for the further good of our service, for which we will yow to repair to our thesaurer principall and deputie, to whom we have gevin speciall commission to sie all things fitt and necessarie at our being ther tymelie and weill provydit, to acquant them with your opinion theranent, to the effect yow may be supplied with such moneyis as may be requisit for that purpois : And as for what moneyis as are formerlie due vnto yow we will have a care that yow be satisfeid according to such appoyntments and ordours as we have formerlie gevin tuitching the same ; And we doe further requyre yow in all other things concerneing the good of our service, wherin yow or aney of your predicessours in that charge hath bene imployed at the tyme of the Coronatioun of aney of our royall progenitours, yow will lykwyse tymelie consider therof, and performe the lyk service at the tyme of our being ther.—Whythall, 2 Feb^r 1633.

To the Archbischop of St Androis.

Right, &c.—Wheras formerlie we have expressed our pleasur that the B. of Ross be translated to the See of Glasgow and Mr John Maxwell to that of Ross : These ar to requyre yow with all possible diligence to tak such ordour therin that they may be both furthwith established in these severall Sees according to our former pleasur signifeid to that purpois for the more speedie enabling of them for our service in each of thair charges ; wherin expecting your care and diligence, we bid, &c.—Whythall, 2 Feb^r 1633.

To the Advocat.

Right, &c.—Trustie, &c., as we did requyre yow of late that yow should ather give ws notice or writt of such thingis belonging vnto your charge as yow for the good of our service thought necessarie to be propounded and past in the ensueing Parliament, which we intend to hold, God willing, in persone in Junij nixt, or otherwayis to repair vnto ws yourself sufficientlie instructed to that purpois ; so now becaus the tyme of our comeing will schortlie approach, and that we ar desyreous to know these things befoir our comeing thither, Our pleasur is, that yow ather repair with all diligence to our Court to give ws satisfaction heirin, otherwyse that with the lyk diligence yow send them hither to our Secretarie that they may be considered by ws at our fittest occasion, and that we may signifie bak vnto yow our further direction tuitching the same : And wheras the Parliament was to begin vpon the 18 of Junij nixt, which is continewed till the 20 thereftir, we requyre yow to certifie ws if aney further warrand be neidfull, and the maner therof, for prorogating these tuo dayes.—Whythall, 2 Feb^r 1633.

Our Soverane Lord, of his speciall grace, mercie, and favour, Ordeanes a Letter of Respeit to be made and exped vnder the Privie seall of Scotland in dew forme to George Pott of Corrabeg, and George Ker, his sone-in-law, makand mention that wheras in the moneth of   , the yeir of God j^m vi^c yeres, they, the saids George Pott and George Ker, and one vmqhill William Ritchertsone, in Pringlestead, being in companie with other thrie persones, did fall out suddenlie, without any premeditate malice or foirthoght felonie, wherof some stryks being interchangeablie gevin, the said George Pott receaved the first and greatest wound in the arme, and therefter was strok dead to the earth by the vmquhill William Ritchartsone ; bot befor the said George Pott could recover, his said sone-in-law, think[ing] he had bene dead, did stryk the said Ritchartsone, bot so that no danger of his lyff did therby appear, haveing no deadlie wound, and haveing lived for the space of a moneth therefter : To the effect the said George Pott and George Ker, for the slaughter of Wm Ritchartsone, or for aney action or cause that may be imputt vnto them or aney of them therthrow, or that may follow thervpoun in aney wher, aney of ther persones, landis, goods or gear, dischergeing his Ma^{teis} Justice-generall, and his deputts and judges, spirituall and temporall, ther deputeis and clerks, his Ma^{teis} schirreffs, bailleis, provests, and bailleis of burghis, ther servandis and officers, and all and whatsumever his Ma^{teis} officers whom it doeth or may concerne, from calling, persewing, accuseing, arresting, imprissoneing, or aneywayes medling or proceiding with or against the said George Pott and George Ker, or aney of them, for the said slaughter committed by them or aney of them ; and that the said respett indure for the space of ane whole yeir nixt and immediatlie passing the said respett vnder the privie seall, without any revocatioun : Lykwyse that the said respett be furder extendit in the best and most ample forme with all clauses neidfull.—Signed by our said Soverane Lord at Whythall, the 4 Feb^r 1633.

To the Bischop of Aberdene.

Right, &c.—Wheras humble sutte hath bene made vnto ws in behalff of John Gordoun of Craig, that for dispatch of some of his lawfull [aff]aires, he might have licence to repair to that our kingdome, from whence he was banisched for matters of religion, wherby, in obedience to our lawis, he could not have tyme to setle them befor his departure ; So that now, as we ar informed, iff he have not some small tyme allowed vnto him for that purpois, he wilbe vtterlie vndone : These ar to recommend vnto yow that efter the recept heirof he be not troubled for matters of religion to doe nothing to hurt or derogat from the estate of the present professed religion.—Whythall, 4 Feb^r 1633.

To the Advocat.

Trustie, &c.—Wheras we wryt formerlie vnto yow that yow should caus Mr Andro Aytoun, Mr Thomas Nicolsone, and Mr Lues Stewart, Advocats, convene with yow, to the effect yow might consult togidder what course was fittest to be taken for annulling of the late service of our right, &c. the Erle of Monteith to the Erldome of Stratherne, we did expect befoir this tyme to have sene that which yow should have agried vpoun, certifeid to ws vnder your hands : And it is our pleasur that, if yow have not alreadie done accordinglie, yow certifie ws with all diligence what course yow have condescended vpoun for that effect, and that, joyntlie or otherwyse severallie, if yow be of different opinions, as yow and everie of yow will be answerable to ws.—Whythall, 4 Feb^r 1633.

To M^r Th. Nicolsone, Mr And. Aytoun, Mr Lues Stewart.

Trustie, &c.—As we wryt formerlie to our Advocat that he should convene yow togidder, to the effect yow might consult what course was fittest to be taken for annulling the late service of our right, &c. the Erle of Monteith to the Erldome of Stratherne : So now it is our pleasur that if yow have not done accordinglie, yow meitt and consult, togidder with our Advocat, with all diligence when yow shalbe requyred by him to that purpois, otherwayes that yow certifie ws with the lyk diligence your opinion, as yow think may stand best with the Lawis of that our kingdome tuitching the annulling of the said service, and, ather joyntlie or severallie, as yow shall best condescend vpoun : Whiche faill not to doe as yow and everie of yow wilbe answerable to ws.—Whythall, 4 Feb^r 1633.

To the Counsell.

Right, &c.—Wheras we ar informed that diverse questions in Law ar lyklie to aryse concerneing the succession of the late Erle of Home to his Landis and estate, and being willing that all our good subjects have Justice equallie administred, according to our Lawis; and in the meane tyme, to prevent any disordourlie course, and that no person be defrauded of that which heirefter may be adjudged justlie to belong vnto him, It is our pleasur that yow give ordour with all diligence that no innovation or change be made in aney of the Landis, or other things belonging to the said Erle, without consent of pairteis or course of Law, bot that they may continew in the esteat quherin thay ar now : And in the meane tyme, if aney persone have taken vpon them to tak possession of any Landis, housses, or other things belonging to the said Erle, that the same be putt in the estate wherin it was at the tyme of his death : And our further pleasur is, that yow tak such a course that as yow in your judgment shall think fitt, according to the Lawis of our kingdome, that the writts and evidents concerneing his honour and inheritance may be furthcumand to the vse of such persones, as by the Lawis of that kingdome shalbe fund to have just right thervnto : Which recommending, &c.—Whythall, 15 Feb' 1633.

To the Lord Lorne.

Right, &c.—Being informed that your father and predicessours have these many yeres vsed the office of cheif Mr houshold to our royall progenitours of that our kingdome : Our pleasur is, in regard of your father's absence from thence, that yow at our comeing ther, God willing, the nixt somer, supplie his place in aney thing that may concerne that office, as he hath formerlie done ; wherin not doubting bot yow will weill and carefullie discharge yourselff, we bid yow farewell.—Whythall, 15 Feb' 1633.

To the Exchequer.

Right, &c.—Being informed by our right, &c. the Erle of Abercorne, that some of his vassalls of his erection (whois rights ar defective and who have summonded him to receave a composition) intend to expeid new gifts therof in Exchequer, to prejudge both ws and him in our lawfull rights : Our pleasur is, that no such gift or grant be exped whairof yow shall receave informatioun in behalff of the said Erle, till we shalbe better informed of the estate therof, and give further directioun therin now at our comeing thither, God willing, and if yow find it neidfull, that yow signifie our pleasur heirin to our Commissioners for Surrenders and others whom it may concerne ; for which these presents shalbe vnto yow ane warrant. —Whythall, 18 Feb' 1633.

To the Arch Bischop of Glasgow.

Right, &c.—We have bene humblie moved vpon some differences betweene the petitioner and some other of the parochin of Howstoun and ther minister, and that the hearing thairof might be remitted to yow to the end they may be composed in a fair maner, otherwyse, if yow shall think fitt, that yow provyde him to some other churche, and them of ane other preacher, sieing (as the petitioner affirmeth) they have done him no wrong, bot if aney mistaking or neglect wer vpon ther part, they would have bene contented to have submitted themselffis to him in aney fitt and reasonable maner if he could have accepted therof : We ar heirby pleased to remitt the consideratioun of the petition vnto yow, willing yow to call both pairteis befor yow, and vse your best endeavour and authoritie to reconceill them, otherwyse that yow tak such ane other course as yow shall think fit and reasonable to be done in equitie and for the service of God ; which recommending to your care, &c.—Whythall, 18 Feb' 1633.

To the Session.

Right, &c.—Wheras we did formerlie wryt vnto our Counsell to give ordour that nather of the pairteis pretending clame to the title of the late Lord Oliphant should vsurp the said title vntill it wer decydit by law which of them it did justlie belong, now vnderstanding that the cause is presentlie depending befor yow, we doe heirby requyre yow lykwayes to continew it to the saids pairteis, that they doe not presume to tak vpon them that place or title till the contraversie be decydit, and that in the meane tyme yow proceid to administer justice with all possible diligence therin vntill it be brought to ane end, to the effect we may know the sooner to which of the pairteis the said title doe justlie belong; which recommending vnto yow.—Whythall, 22 Feb^r 1633.

To Sir Ja. Balfour, Lyon Herauld.

Trustie, &c.—Wheras we ar now verie schortlie to repair, God willing, to that our ancient kingdome, we will expect at the hands of all our Officers whom it doeth concerne that all things in ther severall charges concerneing ws and the honour of that kingdome be in readines and in good ordour : bearing that ther be some thingis concerneing our service peculiarlie belonging to your charge at the tyme of our Coronatioun, we are heirby pleased to requyre that yow carefullie performe at that tyme what shalbe condescended vpon by ws, and signifeid vnto yow concerneing that purpois ; wherin not doubting of your diligence and affection to our service.—Whythall, 22 Feb^r 1633.

To the Justice Generall.

Right, &c.—Though we ar pleased, vpoun some false and malicious calumneis suggested vnto ws by one George Nicoll against some of our cheiff officers, to give ordour to yow as our Justice generall to caus his punischment be speedelie sentenced, as should best accord with Justice, with diligence, and the foulnes of his offence, yit vpon some considerations now moveing ws we have requyred our Counsall to tak the ordouring of that caus befor them : Thairfor our pleasur is, that yow cause your deputts ceise from all proceiding tuitching that purpois, leaveing our Counsall to tak such ordour therin as they shall think fitt ; for which these presents shalbe vnto yow and your said deputts a sufficient warrand and discharge.— Whythall, 23 Feb^r 1633.

To the Counsell.

Right, &c.—Though we wer pleased vpon some false and malitious, &c. vt supra, We ar heirby pleased that yow withdraw that cause from the judicatorie of the Justice-Generall, and haveing called the said Nicoll befoir yow, that ye cause censure and punische him in such maner as yow shall think fitt, that by his exemple others may be terrifeid from attempting the lyk heirefter; for which these presents shalbe a sufficient warrand.—Whythall, 23 Feb^r 1633.

To the Session.

Right, &c.—Wheras we wer pleased to give ordour to our Advocat to raise summondis at our instance for reduceing of the service and retour of our right trustie the Erle of Monteith, president of our privie Counsell, as air to vmquhill David Erle of Stratherne, and to vmquhil Patrik, alledgit Erle of Stratherne, as descending of the Mariage betwixt the said Patrik and vmquhill Ewphame Stewart, alledgit onlie daughter lawfull to the said vmquhill David Erle of Stratherne, and alledged spous to the said vmquhill Patrik, by the which summondis the noblemen, barrons, and others that wer vpoun the Inqueist of the saidis services ar convenit vpoun wilfull at leist ignorant errour : And for so much as we ar fullie perswaded that the saidis persones of Inqueist proceided therin bona fide vpoun warrants standing then vnreduced, and which wer sufficient grounds to the assysours for serveing of the said Erle affirmative, and namelie that ther was a renunciatioun granted by the said Erle vnto ws of the annex I propertie of Strathern wherin the said Erle is designed as air to vmquhill David Erle of Stratherne and Lady Ewphame, his alledgit daughter, and to the said vmquhill Patrik, alledged Erle of Stratherne, and alledged spous to the said Ewphame, which renunciatioun was than standing registrat in the books of Exchequer and in the publict register of renunciatiouns, and wer produced by our Advocat to the assyse the tyme of the service, who protested that the said services should be led in corroboratioun of the said renunciatioun and no otherwayes, which protestatioun was admitted by the Judge, and lykwayes it was perfytelie knowen to a number of the said Inqueist that ther was a signatur signed by ws which was past in Exchequer and whervpoun Infeftment efter followed, by which we disponed to the said Erle of Monteith as vndoubted air of blood to the said David Erle of Stratherne, the Lands and baroneis of Vrquhart and Bratzwall, in respect of the which warrants standing than vnreduced and of our advocat his compeirance, and not opposeing the said service, the Assysoris in the dewtie of ther office could not otherwayes proceid, bot by serveing affirmative for the tyme : And therfoir it is our pleasur that the said noblemen, barones, and others, assessours, be declared lykas we by these presents doe declair them and everie ane of them frie and quyt of all errour quhatsumever : Dischargeing them thairof, and of all payne, cryme, prejudice, and censure that they can ineure or can follow thervpoun : And for ther further securitie we doe heirby will and requyre yow that the saidis persones of Inqueist proponeing their lawfull defensses foundit vpoun the groundis and rights of our saidis standeing vnreducit for the tyme, that thervpon and be vertew of this warrant yow admitt and susteine the saidis persones as relevant and provin to produce to the Assyse ane perfyte absolvitour from the intentlit persute and from all errour concludit therin, and that accordinglie yow pronunce absolvitour in ther favours, bot prejudice alwayes of our action of reduction of his services and others craved to be reduced ; commanding yow heirby to cause insert these presents in your books of Session and Sederunt for the saidis pairteis ther better warrant and exoneratioun.—Whythall, 23 Feb[r] 1633.

Carolus Dei gratia Britanniarum Franciæ et Hiberniæ Rex fideique defensor, &c.—Omnibus regibus principibus tam ecclesiasticis quam secularibus Archiepiscopis episcopis ducibus marchionibus baronibus equitibus aliisque nobilibus necnon omnibus Admirallis sive thalassiarchis vice Admirallis classium navium sinum portium provinciarum vrbium arcium pontium castrorum præfectis sive gubernatoribus Omnibus denique per vniversam Europam magistratibus imperium qualicunque terra manrie habentibus sive exercentibus fratribus patribus consanguineis affinibus amicis confoederatisque suis Salutem plurimam benevolentiam fraternam gratiam favoremque suum regium pro cujusque status conditionisque ratione dicit et impertit Quandoquidem serenissimi illustrissimi reverendissimi illustres magnifici et generosi domini fratres patres consanguinei affines amici confoederatique nostri Dilectus subditus noster Nobilis et honoratus dominus Gulielmus Hamiltonius frater germanus illustrissimi principis Jacobi Marchionis Hamiltoni ducis Castelloritii Comitis Arraniæ et Cantabrigiæ ex antiquissimo nobilissimoque Ordine periscelidis sodalis laudabili hominum mores cognoscendi studio ductus vt sibi (pace nostra) exteras aliquot nationes adire liceret supplex et enixe petiit cujus tam æquis postulatis haud qua quam renuendum existimerimus qui potius Lenitates reverentias Celsitudines magnificentias amplitudinesque vestras amice rogatas cupimus vt si ditiones alicujus vestrum maria sinus portes vrbes oppida locave alia vestræ curæ aut præfecturæ commissa memoratus nobilis et honoratus dominus Gulielmus Hamiltonius subditus noster appulerit introiens non solum nulla injuria affectum libere manere aut abire sinatis verum ea humanitate tractetis quam vestros a nobis exspectare velitis si ditiones quoque nostras similiter commendati intraverint in eisne negotiabuntur, Valete.—Dabuntur e regia nostra ad Westmonasteriam ultimo Feb^{rii} Anni per Christum partæ salutis Trecesimi secundi supra millesimum sexcentesimumque.

To the Counsell.

Right, &c.—Haveing pervsed and approved this forme intended for our Coronatioun, which we doe send yow heirwith, to the effect that all things may be prepared accordinglie in dew tyme which ar requisit for that purpois, Our pleasur is, that yow call befor yow all such persones to quhom yow shall find aney charge concerneing the same doeth belong, and that yow give speciall ordour to everie ane of them that they be carefull to discharge ther part of the said service wherwith they ar entrusted, and if aney difference be amongst them tuitching ther particular offices, that yow so compose them as ther may be no trouble heirefter, bot that the service may be performed in good ordour to our Conveniencie, and for the credit of that our kingdome : So remitting this to your care as a matter which doeth speciallie concerne our service, we bid yow farewell.—Whythall, first March 1633.

To the Counsell.

Right, &c.—We have vnderstud by your letters that yow have discharged the Letters of reprysell granted to the late Captan Robertsone till we should find caus for renewing therof, bot have not gevin ordour to delyver the schip and goodis according to our letter writtin vnto yow late tuitching that purpois : wherin sieing that course was intended by ws vpon good considerations, we still continew in our former resolution tuitching the same ; And therfoir it is our pleasur that without further delay yow cause these persones who war entrusted by yow to receave and keip the schip and goodis sequestrat by the command of our letters, to delyver the same to the persones of Hamburgh, haveing right or power from that estate to receave them, and receave ther discharges thervpon ; And we wilbe carefull to sie that our subjects interested be repaired by haveing speedie justice and payment of that which shalbe fund justlie dew vnto them, they alwayes requyreing Justice as is signifeid by our said letter ; wherin not doubting of your conformitie to this our pleasur, We bid, &c.—Whythall, 4 March 1633.

To the Counsell.

Right, &c.—Being informed that Edward Kellie, our servand, did, for the vse of such as should be disposed, mak a bowling-Grene in a convenient place neir our palace of Halyrudhous, wherin as we ar lykwayes informed he had your approbatioun : And hearing that some persones had abused the bowling-greene, we ar heirby pleased to recommend vnto yow to tak such ordour that it be not abused heirefter, spetiallie at the tyme of our being in that our kingdome : And wheras we ar lykwayes informed that dureing our abode ther the said Edward wilbe necessarlie imployed in attending the service of our Chappell royall, we have thoght fitt lykwayes to recommend to yow that he be not troubled by his creditours from this till our returne to this our kingdome, which we have the rather desyred, becaus tho satisfaction to be made vnto him for his service is to be payed by our further direction, wherof we wilbe carefull as the conveniencie of the tyme and the discharge of his service shall appear vnto ws.—Whythall, 4 March 1633.

To the Exchequer.

Right, &c.—Wheras Edward Kellie, our servand, hath bene ane humble sutter to ws that payment might be made to him of such money as he hath disbursed tuitching our Chapell royall: These ar to will and requyre yow to call him befoir yow, and to examyne his accompts tutching that purpois, and if therby yow find aney moneys dew vnto him from ws, that yow tak some speedie course for his satisfaction accordinglie, for which these presents shalbe vnto yow, and everie of yow, a sufficient warrant and discharge.—Whythall, 4 March 1633.

Wheras the good schip called the ⸺ of the burthen of ⸺ is to be sent out by Sir Peirce Corsbie, knight and baronet, one of our Privie Counsell of Irland, towardis America, for setling of a Colonie ther according to such particular warrants as he hath from ws to that purpois: These ar therfoir to will and requyre yow, and everie ane of yow, to permitt and suffer the said schip and her whole furniture, goodis, merchandice, schip's companie, and planters, quyetlie and peaciable, in ther goeing thither, returneing from thence, or dureing ther being furth of aney other part whatsoever, till they shalhappin to returne to aney of our dominions, to pas by yow without aney your let, stayes, troubles, imprests of ther men, or aney other hindrance whatsoever, Whairof yow shall not fall.—Whythall, 4 March 1633.

To The Officers of our Admiralitie, the Captanes and
Masters of our schips, &c.

To Sir Peirce Corsbie.

Trustie, &c.—Wheras we ar informed that yow ar goeing on in preparations for setting furth a Colonie to plant in America according to such warrants as yow have alreadie vnder our hand, and which ar past vnder our great seall of our kingdome of Scotland, your endeavours heirin ar verie acceptable vnto ws: And we doe heirby allow yow to proceid, and for your further encouragment and all such as ar therin entrusted with yow, we doe heirby assure yow that we shalbe ever realie to protect yow in this your vndertaking aganst all persones whatsumever, and as occasion shall offer we will give yow such further testimonie of our favour as may stirr vp others to the lyk generous vndertakingis: So recommending the serious prosecution of a work so much concerneing our service, we bid, &c.—Whythall, 4 March 1633.

To the Erle of Mar.

Our pleasur is, that yow caus delyver with all diligence to our right, &c. the Lord Traquair, our deputie Thesaurer, two broken Cannons within our Castell of Edinburgh, as can be most convenientlie spared and thoght most fitt by our said Officer, or such persones as he shall appoynt for chooseing thairof, to be cast into Bells for the vse of the Abbay Church of our palace of Halyrudhous; ffor which these presents shalbe vnto yow, &c.—Whythall, 4 March 1633.

To the Commissioners of Parliament.

Right, &c.—Wheras our Parliament is appoyntit to be fenced vpon the 18 of Junij nixt ensueing, at which we intend, God willing, to be present in persone, but because it may possiblie fall furth in our

Journey thither that by the occasion of the weather we may be hindered one or tuo dayes otherwayes then we intend, therfoir we think it litt that in caice we be not ther present in persone, that our Parliament be fensed vpon the said 18 day of Junij by yow as our Commissioners, and continewed to the 20 day of Junij therefter, and that ather by adjourneing of the same to the said 20 of Junij, or by fenseing of the Parliament daylie efter the said 18 of Junij, or by declaring of the Parliament to be current and to run till we be present in persone, and that as yow shall think most litt by advyse of the Lordis of our Secreit Counsall, to whome we have writtin to that effect, which we recommend to your speciall care; and for doeing therof these presents shalbe vnto yow a sufficient warrand.—Whythall, 4 March 1633.

To the Counsell.

Right, &c.—Wheras we have writtin our princelie direction vnto our Commissioners of Parliament that vpon the 18 of Junij nixt ensueing it be fenced, at which we intend to be present, God willing, in persone, bot becaus it may possiblie fall furth in our journey thither that by occasion of the weather we may be hindred ane or tuo dayes otherwayes then we intend, we have thairfor requyred our saidis Commissioners, in caice we be not ther in persone, that our Parliament be fensed vpoun the said eighteine day of Junij by them, and continewed to the 20 day of Junij therefter, and that by taking your advyse, to whom we have writtin for that effect, ather by adjourneing of the same to the said 20 of Junij, or by fenceing the Parliament daylie efter the said 18 day of Junij, or by declareing of the Parliament to be current and to run till we be present in persone and as formerlie; so we doe lykwayes now will and requyre yow heirby have a speciall care to warne tymelie all prelats, noblemen, commissioners for barrones and brughs, and all others haveing place vnto or owing attendance in the said Court, to wait and attend vpon the same the forsaidis dayes, and to performe all and sindrie such other things as to ther places and offices doe appertene.—Whythall, 4 March 1633.

To the Commissioners of Surrenders.

Right, &c.—Wheras we, by our former letter direct to our Advocat of the date 28 August 1628, and exhibite by him befoir yow, and allowed by yow to be registrat in your books, ther to remane as a warrant of his proceiding, according to the direction therof, we gave express command to our said Advocat to vse the best meanes by all lawfull wayes to get trew knowledge of the names of such persones who have refuised to submitt, or who have alreadie submitted, bot with further limitations and restrictions than ar mentioned in the generall submission; and alse being crediblie informed that, notwithstanding of the surrender made to ws by the titularis of erection, yit ther ar diverse of ther vassalls who apprehended ane certane fear that the erectours intent to quarrell thair propertie, and to evict the same to themselftis, therby defrauding ws of the interest we might have thairto: Therfoir we willed and commanded our said Advocat to sie all doubts cleared heirin, in so far as he might lawfullie and convenientlie, and that whosoever wer vassalls to aney of the erectours at the tyme of ther submission, or since our revocatioun, may becum so vnto ws, without ather bettering or impareing ther rights, and that all title which these erectours had over them may be devolved in our persone, as our letters direct to our said Advocat in the selft mair fullie proports, since the dait whairof yow have, at the instance of our said Advocat, sett diverse acts for tryeing such as wer not submitters, of whois names we desyre to have notice from yow with the first occasion: And becaus now of late some of the titulars of erections have raised summondis of improbation and reduction aganst diverse persones who wer vassalls to them the tyme of ther submission, which we conceave to be contrair to the trew meaneing of the said generall surrander: Therfor, leist any doubt or scruple should aryse concerneing these who ar and should be thought vassalls to ws by the said generall surrander, we have thought good to declair, Lykas by these presents we declair, that all these must be accompted our vassals by the said generall surrander, who and ther predicessours bruikit the landis the tyme of the said generall submission and of befor, be vertew of Infeftments, Chartours, and seasines granted vnto them and ther predicessours and authours by whatsumever Abbot, pryour, or other beneficed persone whatsumever, befoir the generall act of annexatioun of kirklandis to our Croun, or therefter, by vertew of the rights made to them ther predicessours and Authours forsaidis, flowing from ws or our vmquhill dearest father, by vertew of the said act of Annexatioun, or from the saidis Lordis of Erection since the dait of ther erections, or who bruik the same by retouris, to be haldin of the saidis beneficed persones or of our said vmquhill dearest father, by vertew of the Act of Annexatioun, or of aney of the saidis Lordis of erection as Lordis of Erection : And declaires that it shall not be lawfull to the saidis Lordis and titularis of Erections to call, convene, and persew aney of the persones forsaidis for reduction or improbation of ther rights to the saidis kirk landis so bruiked by them, as said is, vnder pretext of whatsumever defect therof, ather in the originall rights and progres thairof, or for not confirmation in dew tyme, sieing the whole benefite that may aryse by defect of the saidis rights doe accresce to ws by the said generall surrander ; and none can quarrell the samyne bot we, who ar becum immediat superiours to all such persones by the said generall surrander : And it is our speciall pleasur that vpon this our declaration, and conforme thereto, yow mak ane act of your table, and insert the samyne in your books.—Whythall, 4 March 1633.

TO THE SESSION.

Right, &c.—Wheras diverse of the Lordis of Erections (as we ar certanelie informed) have raised summondis of reduction and improbation against some of the Vassalls who was vassalls to them the tyme of the generall submission, and ar now becum our vassalls by the generall surrander conteyned in the said generall submission, and therby intendis to draw the saidis vassalls in question of ther propertie, vpon pretext of some defectis ather in the originall rights or in the progress thairof, or for laik of confirmatioun befor the act of Annexatioun, which we conceave to be direct Contrarie to the trew meaneing of the said generall surrander: Lykas we, by our speciall warrant directed to the Commissioners of Surranders, have for removeing of all scruple which may aryse heiranent made our declaratioune to our saidis Commissioners, who ar to be accompted vassalls surrendered to ws by the said generall surrander, and thairfor it is our speciall pleasur, that whensoever aney such action of reduction and improbatioun shall cum to be disputed befoir yow, yow follow and adhere to that declaration made by ws to the saids commissioners and registrat in ther books; and that yow have a speciall care that we be nowayes prejudged by aney of the saidis actions of the benefite of the said generall surrander.—Whythall, 4 March 1633.

TO THE EXCHEQUER.

Right, &c.—Wheras diverse of the Lordis of Erectioun (as we ar informed) has dealt or intendis to dealt with the vassalls of erections surrandered in our laudis by the generall surrander, to move and caus them mak resignatioun of ther tenendreis in our landis in favours of the saidis Lordis of Erections or others to ther behove, wherby they intend to ingross in ther persones the superioriteis of the saidis vassalls surrendered to ws, as said is, which we accompt ane great prejudice to our right, and contrarie to the trew meaneing and intention of the said generall surrender : Therfoir it is our pleasur that yow pas no signature of any of the saidis landis and tenendries perteneing to whatsumever vassall of erection, vpoun resignation or surrander therof made or to be made in favours of the saidis Lordis of Erection, or any other to ther behove, and that yow tak speciale care to sie our right of surranders manteyned, and that no prejudice be done therto, direct or indirect, vnder any colour or pretext heirefter.—Whythall, 4 March 1633.

To the Session.

Right, &c.—Wheras we ar informed that with your approbatioun breives ar raised out of our Chancerie of that our kingdome for serveing of James Home air-male to the late Erle of Home, in proceiding of which service diverse of the said Erle's evidents wilbe requisit to be sene ; Our pleasur is, that yow give all lawfull ordour to caus furthwith search and produce all wrytings concerneing his honour and esteat, alsweill to give light in the said service as to be secured for the vse of such as shalbe fund to have right thairto, and that in all actions that shall cum befoir yow tuitching that succession Justice without delay or respect of persones may be equallie administred.—[Not dated.]

To the Counsell.

Right, &c.—Wheras we ar infoured that Sir Wm Seaton, kny^t, hath receaved some opposition in the exerciseing of his charge as master of the posts and Journey horsses within that our kingdome, according to the power granted to him by patents from our late dear father and our self, for the good of our service and the ease of our subjects ; These ar therfor to requyre yow to call the said Sir W^m befor yow, and such other pairteis as yow shall find necessarie for clearing of these thingis that ar questioned concerneing that his charge, to the effect that efter hearing of the pairteis yow may tak such course as the said Sir W^m may enjoy the benefite of this patent in such sort as may encourage him to doe the service, and strenthen him the more for it ; which recommending to your care, &c.—Whythall, 8 March 1633.

These conteynis a grant by your Matie to Sir James Lockhart and his aires of the personage teyndis of his twentie pund landis of Lie, and fyftie shilling lands of Nemphlar, lyand within the parochin of Lanerk and Schirrefdome thairof, vpon the resignation of Johne Erle of Mar and James Erle of Buchan, his sone, with ane vnion of the saidis teynd scheavis to the stok of the saids landis and seasine to be takin vpon the ground of the saids landis or oney part therof to be sufficient seasone for the saids teynd scheaves to be hoblin blensch of your Matie for payment of ten schillings money of Scotland in name of blensch ferme, with your Ma^teis annuitie, and releiveand the Erle of Mar and his said sone of the remanent dewteis and burdenes conteynit in ane contract past betwixt the said Sir James and them theranent, which is dated 25th March 1631.—Theobaldis, 15 March 1633. Sub^r, Sm Th. Hope.

To the Counsell.

Right, &c.—Wheras we have heard that yow have charged our right, &c. the Marqueis of Huntlie to present befor yow some excommunicat persones vpon the 28 of the last moneth, which as we ar informed he could hardlie doe with that speed that was requyred, and that the Schirefschip of Aberdene and Invernes ar out of his handis, and otherwyse disposed of by ws ; being resolved to be further informed from yow tuitching the esteat of that bussines at our cuneing verie schortlie, God willing, in that our kingdome, Our pleasur is, that all that tyme yow suffer no proces to be prosecuted against him tuitching that purpois, leaveing yow in the meane tyme to tak what other ordour yow shall think fitt for apprehending and presenting the saidis persones befor yow, and leaveing all others whatsoever anywayes interested to proceid tuitching that bussines according to the due and ordinarie course of our Lawis.—Whythall, 15 March 1633.

Charles, by the grace of God king of England, Scotland, France, and Irland, defender of the fayth, To all our Majors, Shirreflis, Justices of Peace, Vice-Admirall, bailleis, Constables, Customers, searchers,

Comptrollers, and all others our officers and loveing subjects whom it may concerne, and to everie of them, Greeting.—Wheras Ro' Dowglas, our servand, is vpon some necessarie occasiones to goe beyond seas : These ar to will and command yow and everie one of yow to suffer him to imbark himselff and his thrie servandis and other provisions, and lykwayes to returne agane hither without molestatioun or disturbance at anoy of our ports or harbours which shalbe most conveuient for his passage, for which these shalbe your warrand.—Whythall,   March 1633.

Ane vther pass lyk vnto the precedent was past for Francis Spens, gentlman, for himselff with ane servand.—Date vt supra.

To the Archbischop of Glasgow.

Right reverend—We wer pleased to signe a presentation subscryved by the late Archbischop of Glasgow for Admission of M' Patrik Scharp to the Church of Carluk, bot as we ar informed the said Archbischop died befor the returne of the presentatioun thither, wherby the parochiners doe ever since want the benefite of ane ordinarie and constant minister : And therfor have bene humble sutters vnto ws that we might be pleased to give ordour that they might not be any longer vnprovydit in regard the Archbischop now nominat by ws for that charge hath not repaired (as we ar lykwayes informed) to these parts of that kingdome, And that we have conceaved the demand of the parochiners to be good and just : Our pleasur is, if the said Archbischop be not alreadie ther, that furthwith yow give vnto the said M' Patrik, Collation and admission according to the presentatioun and ordour observed in the lyk caces.— [Not dated.]

To the Coussell.

Right, &c.—Wheras by our Letter we wer pleased to requyre our Right, &c. the Erle of Tullibardyne to vse his best endeavours for setling the differences amongst the name of Grant, haveing to that effect writtin to yow to give him your best assistance which yow did, bot in regard of the schortnes of the tyme, and the remotnes and distance between the duellings of the pairteis interested could not convenientlie at that tyme be effected, though (as is certified) the said Erle had takin great paynes : To the end these differences may be the better takin away, we intend befoir our returne from that our kingdome to cause examyne them from the begining for certificing ws of the trew estate thairof, that they may be the more easclie composed and ordered as we shall find just caus : In respect whairof, that no just complaynt of that kynd com befoir ws, speciallie at the tyme of our being ther, Our pleasur is, that all criminall causses and actions now depending amongst these of that name be deferred till the tyme befoir our said returne, and to that effect that yow give ordour accordinglie to our officers and others quhom it doeth concerne : We bid yow fairwell.—Whythall, 21 March 1633.

His Matie was pleased to signe a presentation in favours of M' William Abernethie, minister at the Church of Thurso, to the Archdeanrie of Cathnes, vacand in his Ma^teis handis by deceis of M' Ritchart Merchiestoun, last Archdeane of Cathnes, with two Churches belonging thervnto Bowar and Warton.— Whythall, 28 March 1633.   Sub',   Jo. Bishop Cathnes.

His Matie was pleased to signe a presentatioun in favours of M' James Moir to the Church of Tarves, vacand in his Ma^teis handis by dimission of M' Thomas Gardyne, last Minister.—Whythall, 28 March 1633.   Sub',   Pa. Aberdene.

To the Counsell.

Right, &c.—Wheras we wer formerlie pleased to give ordour that no Levy of men whatsoever for ane forrane pairt should be made within that our kingdome, vnless a speciall direction wer given from ws of new for that purpois, we will yow still continew that same course : bot considering that the standing regiment demanded by Sir John Hepburne, kny^t, for the service of our brother the French king, is of ane other nature, the Intertenement whairof being to be continewed may serve to good vse for sindrie of our subjects in that our kingdome : In regard of this and other causes knowen vnto ws, Our pleasur is, that yow grant vnto the said Sir John Hepburne, or to any other whom he shall appoynt, a Commission with a sufficient warrant to levie and transport 1200 men for the purpois aboveshaid, of all such persones within that our kingdome of Scotland as he shall find willing to goe with him thither, granting him libertie to tuck drumes for that purpois, with as large priviledges as any generall, Colonell, or Commander hath had heirtofoir in the lyk kynd, he alwyes geving such satisfaction to everie ane of the said number as shalbe agried vpon betwixt him and them according to the custome in the lyk caices ; for doeing quherof.— Whythall, 28 March 1633.

To the Counsell.

Right, &c.—Haveing bene formerlie pleased for good considerations knowen to ws to grant our Licence to Sir Alex^r Leslie, kny^t, generall of the forrane forces of the Emperour of Russia, for levyeing and transporting a Regiment of men out of our dominions for the said Emperour his service ; bot vnderstanding that ther laiks ane Companie for compleiting of the same, which we will to be levyed and transported from that our kingdome be Captane James Forbes for the same vse, Our pleasur is, that yow grant vnto the said Captane James a commission with a sufficient warrant to levy and transport 200 men, according to his commission, for the purpois aboveshaid, of all such persones within our said kingdome of Scotland as he shall find willing to goe with him thither ; Granting him libertie to touk drumes for that effect, with as large priviledges as any hath had heirtofoir in the lyk kynd, he alwayes giveing such satisfaction to everie ane of the said number as shalbe agreid vpon betwixt him and them, according to the custome in the lyk caices ; for doeing whairof these presents shalbe to yow sufficient warrant.—Whythall, 28 March 1633.

To the Thesaurer and Deputie Thesaurer.

Right, &c.—Wheras our right, &c. the duik of Lennox is to attend ws as our Chalmerlane ther dureing the tyme of our being ther in that our kingdome, being desyreous that he should want nothing that is due to the said Office that hath bene formerlie enjoyed by any of his predicessours, and speciallie by his vncle the late Duik Ritchmont, in the tyme of our dear father at his last being ther : Our pleasur is, that yow caus provyde for him his ludging and dyet and other things perteneing thervnto in lyk maner as his said vncle had at the said tyme, and this we will yow to signifie from ws to any quhom it may concerne ; for doeing whairof, &c.—Whythall, 28 March 1633.

Our Soveraigne Lord being crediblie informed that George Buchanan, fiar of that ilk, standeth addebted as Cautioner in severall sowmes of money vnto diverse persones within the realme of Scotland, which he is most willing to pay, haveing alredie, for his Creditours' better assurance, renewed divers of these securiteis wherin he was onlie bund to them as cautioner, and becam principall himsellf : And his Matie being crediblie informed that for the more firme assurance of his Creditours' satisfactioun he hes made over the whole of his estate, being far above the value of his debts, in trust onlie for defraying of the saids debts, which was done by speciall advyse and consent of diverse right honorable noblemen who doe much desyre the standing of his estate, haveing in tokin of ther consents subscryved the factorie made be the said George to that purpois: And his Matie learning that the said George hath bene in his Ma^{teis} kingdome of England a long tyme vpon speciall and important occasions concerneing him, and now intends to repair to Scotland for setling of his lawfull affaires, wher, if he should be vnseasoneablie troubled by his Creditours, it would vtterlie at this tyme vndoe his estate, which he hath alreadie appoynted to be lyable for the payment of his saids debts, and is willing, as we ar crediblie informed, to secure them further of it, it being fund requisit for the Creditours' better satisfaction: Therfor his Matie, of his authorite royall, kinglie power, grace, mercie, and clemencie, hath accepted, and by the tenour heirof accepts, the said George Buchanan, fiar of that ilk, vnder his protection for one one yeir: Cetera stylo ordinario, &c.—Whythall, 30 March 1633.

It is our pleasur that with all diligence yow caus pay vnto the bearer, George Haliburton, ane of our falconers, the accustomed yeirlie allowance for bringing of some haulk vnto ws from the northerne pairts of that our kingdome, and that yow give him your best furtherance for this effect; ffor doeing, &c.— Whythall, 2 Aprill 1633.

To THE LORD LOANE.

Right, &c.—Whems we ar informed that within your boundis ther ar some Mangrell haulks, whairof we ar desyreous to mak tryell for our sport at our being in that our kingdome, and to mak vse of some of them yeirlie therefter, in caice they shall pleas ws at that tyme: These ar to recommend to yow that the creis therof be carefullie preserved, and that we be provydit with ane or mae of the best that can be fund of that kynd now schortlie at our being ther, and yeirlie therefter, if we shall think it fitt, wherin yow shall doe ws acceptable service: We bid, &c.—Whythall, 2 Aprill 1633.

The 5 of Aprill a warrant was signed by his Matie for licence to the Lord Montgomrie of Scotland to goe beyond seas, with tuo servands and one or tuo footmen, and other provisions.

It is our pleasur that yow tak out the Ermine of the robe called the New robe of our late royall father, and putt it in the robe to be worne by ws at our Coronation, for it is our resolution to wear the robe of our royall predicessour king James the fourt at our Parliament; ffor doeing quherof.—Whythall, 5.

To . . . Sir John Auchmovtie, kny^t, Master of our Wardrop.

To THE COUNSELL.

Right, &c.—Being willing, at our being now verie schortlie, God willing, in that our antient kingdome, that all provisions necessarie be in readines ther in such plentie as is fitt for such of our subjects of that our kingdome as shall happin to be ther dureing our abode within the same; Our pleasur is, that from hencefurth till our returne to this our kingdome yow authorize all such persones for importing of English beer as shall have certificats from our Theasurers principall and deputie, or ather of them, to that purpois, without suffering them to pay aney further imposition or other dewtie whatsoever for the same then our ordinarie customes; for which these presents, &c.—Whythall, 5 Aprill 1633.

To the Counsell.

Right, &c.—We have sent the enclosed Petition to be considered by yow, and if yow find the errour therin mentionat to have fallin out (as is probablie affirmed) by a casuall oversight in the workmen, and not by designe in the Petitioner, Our pleasur is, that without consequence of anoy tolleration in tyme to cum yow tak for the present such course as without prejudice to our good subjects of that our kingdome may best tend to the petitioner's demand : And for your soe doeing, &c.—Whythall, 6 Aprill 1633.

Wheras we ar pleased to mak choyse of yow for the fabricatioun of our Meduills appoynted by ws for our Coronatioun in Scotland : Our pleasur is, that with all diligence yow mak readie toollis and presses, with all other provisions necessarie for that work, to be in tyme by yow transported vnto our toun of Edinburgh in our said kingdome ; and these presents shalbe to yow and all others, whom it doeth concerne, a sufficient warrant.—Gevin at Whythall 6 Aprill 1633.

To Nicolas Bryot, our cheiff graver of our mynt of England.

To the Archbischop of St Androis.

Right reverend father in God, &c.—Haveing sene a certificat of the Deane [and] Chapter of the See of Glasgow of the admission and election of the reverend father in God Patrik, bischop of Ross, to the Archibischoprik of Glasgow, according to our warrant for that purpois : Our pleasur is, that with all convenient diligence yow give ordour for his translation to the said Archbischoprik and for his enstalment therin in such readie and fitt maner as in the lyk caces is accustomed ; for which these presents, &c.—Whythall, 15 Aprill 1633.

To the Archbischop of Glasgow.

Right reverend, &c.—Haveing vnderstude with what great charges and panes yow have augmented the rents of the bischoprik of Ross, from which yow ar to be translated now to the great hurt of your privat esteat, We think that yow ar, or anoy other bischop doeth deserve for some tyme all the benefite that doeth accress by ther endeavours thus, that others may be encouraged to tak the lyk course : And though we will not begin that preparative vpon one whom we have alreadie recommended to be elected for your successour, yit be confident of this, that as we have takin particular notice of your singular cariage in this kynd, so we will tak vnto our particular consideration, being of a long tyme assured of your good affection to our service, and that yow will continew the same : We bid, &c.—Whythall, 15 Aprill 1633.

Our pleasur is, that yow call to Sir John Scott, directour of our Chancerie, and others who have in ther custodie anoy Chartours, writts, or other evidents concerneing ws, or the copeis therof, commanding and requyreing him in our name to delyver the same vnto yow, to whois charge the keiping therof doeth properlie belong, to be furthcuming at all tymes for our vse and service, wherof we will them they would not faill as they will answer the contrarie at ther perrells.—Whythall, 23 Aprill 1633.

To Sir John Hay of Landis, knyt, our Clerk Register.

To the Counsell.

Right, &c.—Wheras the recordis of Parliament, all publict registeris, evidents, and writts concerneing ws, ought to be keipt by our Clerk of Register, to whome the Charge therof doeth onlie properlie belong :

11

2 I

Our pleasur is, that yow call befor yow all such persones as shalbe knowen to have such registers or records in ther custodie, or doe know wher they ar to be fund, and thairefter caus delyverie be made therof to our Clerk of Register, that they may be furth comeing for our vse and service: Which recommending vnto your care.—Whythall, 23 Aprill 1633.

To Mr Thomas Nicolsone, Mr Andro Aytoun, and Mr Lues Stewart.

Trustie, &c.—We have both sene and heard of your diligence and affection to our service by concurring with our Advocat in geving your opinions tuitching the bussines recommended by ws of late vnto our Advocat and yow, approveing of your proceidingis therin, And give yow hartie thanks for the same, assureing yow that we will not be vnmyndfull of your service therin when occasion shall convenientlie offer, wherby we may express our respect vnto yow: We bid, &c.—Whythall, 23 Aprill 1633.

To the Counsell.

Right, &c.—Wheras we vnderstand that it hath bene the accustomed forme that all petitions to be presented in Parliament wer delyvered to the Clerk of Register for the tyme tuentie dayes befor the holding therof, and that proclamations wer accordinglie made to that effect, we being willing to continew any such receaved and approved custome, have heirby thoght fitt to requyre yow to caus the lyk proclamations be made in due tyme befor the ensweing parliament, wherby our good subjects may tak notice of what is fitt to be done in the lyk caces.—Whythall, 23 Aprill 1633.

To the Chancellour, Thesaurer, Privieseill, Secretarie, Clerk Register.

Right, &c.—Wheras it is thoght fitt for our further securitie that these services of Stratherne and others writts reduced by decreit of session vpon the 26 March last, togidder with the warrants therof and registers wherin the same ar inserted, be cancelled and deleit, to which purpois we have writtin to our Advocat, sieing the warrants of these rights ar in your hands or in the handis of your deputeis, and that the registers thairof ar for the most part in the keiping of our Clerks or of such others to whom the keiping therof dooth Appertene: Therfor it is our speciall pleasur that yow exhibite the warrants which ar in your handis or in the hands of your deputes to be cancelled, and that yow caus all havers of the registers wherin the same ar inserted to exhibite the same, and that yow sie them deleit, for which these presents shalbe to yow a sufficient warrant: Willing that these presents be insert in the books of our privie Counsell to have the force of ane Act thairof, Or in the books of Sederunt in Session, or other of them as yow shall think most fitt for our Securitie.—Whythall, 23 Aprill 1633.

To the Agent at Brussells.

Trustie, &c.—Wheras we ar informed that the schip called the Good Fortune of Dundie, in our kingdome of Scotland, being loadned with salt from France for the vse of the societie of the fisching of great Britaine and Irland, and latelie in hir returne from thence to Scotland, and vpon our owin coasts of this our kingdome, vnjustlie taken by tuo Dunkirkers, to the great hurt of our subjects interested, who by loss of both tyme and meanes in seiking repetition ar vnable to vndergoe what further is incident to strangers and sufferers in the lyk caices: In regard as we ar lykwyse informed that the schip's course both from Scotland to France, and from thence bak to Scotland is warranted by sufficient and accustomed testimoneis, and that nothing can reallie appear to the contrarie, we have heirby thoght fitt, in regard of the distressed esteat of our said subjects, and a consideration by apparent presumptions of the contempt and wrong therby done to ws, speciallie to requyre yow to informe your self of the trew esteat of the premisses, and that therefter yow requyre in our name that the delinquents may be punished, causeing speedie restauration and satisfaction be made to the bearer, James Fletcher, in behalff of himselff and of the persones interested in the said schip and goodis, and for ther charges and losses susteaned by this meanes; And that yow be carefull to vse your best endeavours for causeing restrayne heirefter such insolencies and wrongs as too frequentlie ar committed (as we ar credibilie informed) by the Dunkerkers vpon our Coasts and aganst our subjects in ther lawfull trades, that no further occasion be gevin to interrupt that good correspondence and freindschip which reciprocallie ought to be cheresched and keiped amongst these of our freinds ther and our subjects, to whom if they give not dew satisfaction, otherwayes we must grant the ordinarie remedie that Justice doeth allow, wherby they may repair ther losses : Which speciallie recommending vnto your care. &c.—Whythall, 23 Aprill 1633.

To the Advocat.

Trustie, &c.—Wheras we ar informed that vpon the 26 of March last, a decreit was pronunced in our favours, reduceing the service of Stratherne, togidder with the renunciation of the Infeftment of Vrquhart, and patent of the title of Stratherne; and that it was thoght fitt by yow and the thrie advocatts whome yow called vnto yow by our command that these writts so reduced, and warrands therof, should be cancelled : Therfor our pleasur is, ye prosecute the cancelling of these writts, and warrandis therof, by such ordour as yow shall find most fitt for our service, and that yow sie the same to be deleit and rased out of the registers wherin they ar insert : And at the begining of the said lmssines of Stratherne yow did proceid as a faythfull and vigilant servand in giveing ws notice of the apparent danger which might aryse to ws in our annexed propertie, for removeing whairof the said renunciatioun was drawin vp by our speciall warrand, which yow caused register in all the registers necessarie for that effect, and produced the same at the tyme of the services, protesting that the same should be in corroboratioun of the renunciatioun, which we esteame and declair to be good and faythfull service done to ws in your part : So we give yow the lyk approbatioun in the accelerating and expediing of the said reduction according to our warrant, willing yow to goe on to the cancelling of these writts reduced, and warrants and registers thairof, in maner forsaid ; for doeing whairof, &c.—Whythall, the 23 Aprill 1633.

This I most have punctuallie performed. Hoc propria manu regis.

Wheras yow have in your keiping the paper conteyning the opinion and advyse of Sir Th. Hope, our Advocat, Mr Andro Ayton, and Mr Th. Nicolsone, and Mr Lues Stewart, Advocats, concerneing ane cancelling of the services and retours of Wm, Erle of Monteith, which paper is signed with ther handis : It is our pleasur that yow cans cancell the same, and delyver to our said Advocat, and to the other thrie Advocats, ther owin subscriptions, and from them the copeis gevin to them under your hand, which yow shall also cancell ; for doeing whairof, &c.—24 Aprill 1633.

To the Exchequer.

Right, &c.—Wheras we ar credibilie informed of the abilitie and affection to our service of our trustie, &c. Mr Alexr Colvill, our Justice depute, being willing to encourage and enable him to that purpois, we have heirby thoght fitt to promove him to be ane of the Commissioners of our Exchequer of our kingdome of Scotland : Therfoir our pleasur is, and we doe heirby will and requyre yow to admitt him vpon that Commission to be ane of your number, and that yow administer vnto him the oath accustomed in the lyk caice ; for which these presents, &c.—Whythall, the 24 Aprill 1633.

Humblie schawing that hir husband, being bot latelie decessed, hath left with hir tuo daughters, being as yit verie young children, and of a verie weak and tender constitution : And wheras the Lo/ Carnagie and Sir John Carnagie, his brother, ther administratours and onlie aires (failling issue of ther owin bodies), goe about to tak them from hir vnto ther custodie ; and in regard that in conscience and reasone none can be preferred to hir in the care of hir children, health and education, they being seiklie and weak, especiallie sche being ther naturall mother, a widow, and they hir onlie Children ; hir humble suite is that your Matie would be graciouslie pleased to requyre the Counsell to tak the premisses to ther consideration, that sche may have the custodie of hir children, in regard of ther tender aige, sex, and indisposition of bodie, and if the yeirlie esteat left them be of better value than wilbe necessarie, that the Counsell will appoynt such a proportion therof as they shall think fitt to serve for that purpois, and that they give ordour that the superplus may be made furth cuming for the childrenes vse.— [No date.]

To the Commissioners for the Plantation of New Scotland.

Trustie, &c.—Wheras our late dear father, for the honour of that his ancient kingdome, did grant the first Patent of New Scotland to the Viscont of Stirling, and was willing to conferr the title of knyght baronet on such of his weill deserveing subjects as should contribute to the advancement of the work of the plantation in the said cuntrey ; we wer pleased to give ordour for the effectuating of the same, according to our Commission direct to yow for that purpois : And vnderstanding perfectlie (as we doubt not is weill knowen vnto yow all) that the said Viscont did begin and prosecute a Plantation in these parts, with a far greater charge then could be suppleyed by the meanes forsaid ; And the rather in regard of the late discouragement of some by our commanding him to remove his Colonie of Port Royall for fulfilling the Article of ane treatie betuixt our brother the French king and ws, to mak everie thing betuixt ws be in the esteat wherin it was befor the warre, hearing that ther was a rumour gevin out by some that we had totallie left our purpois to plant in that cuntrey, as haveing surrandered our right therof : Least any further mistakings should aryse heirvpon, we thoght good heirby to clear our intention therin ; which is, That our said Viscount, with all such as shall adventure with him, shall prosecute the said work, and be encouraged by all lawfull helps thervnto, alsweill by compleiting of the intendit number of knyght baronetts as otherwayes : And being informed that some of our subjects of good qualitie in this our kingdome and Irland, who have takin Land in New Scotland holdin from ws, did accept of the said dignitie ther, and more obliged to contribute as much towardis the said Plantation as aney other in that kynd, war putt to far greater charges at the passing of ther rights then the natives of the kingdome wer at in the lyk caice ; It is our pleasur that whosoever aney of our subjects of qualitie fitt for that dignitie within this our kingdome or of Irland, haveing takin landis holdin of ws in New Scotland, and haveing agried with our said Viscount for ther part of a supplie towardis the said plantation, and that it is signifeid so by him vnto yow, that, till the number of baronettis formerlie condescendit vpon be compleit, yow accept of them, and give ordour that ther patents be passed at as easie a rate as if they wer naturall subjects of that our kingdome, and this yow mak knowen to such persones and in such maner as yow in your judgments shall think fitt ; for doeing wharof, &c.—Whythall, 24 Aprill 1633.

Our Soveraigne Lord vnderstanding the long practeis and experience of his Maᵗⁱˢ lovit James Ewing in matters of Herauldrie, and of his sufficiencie and habiliteis otherwyse to discharge a place of that nature : Therfor, and for the better advancement of his Maᵗⁱˢ service in that kynd for the honour of his Maᵗⁱˢ antient kingdome of Scotland, the nobilitie and gentrie therof, his Maᵗⁱᵉ, with advyse and consent of his Maᵗⁱˢ right, &c. the Erle of Morton, his Maᵗⁱˢ Principall Theasurer of the said kingdome, and of his Maᵗⁱˢ trustie, &c. Johne, Lord Stewart of Traquair, his Maᵗⁱˢ depute Theasurer therof, and remanent Commissioners of the Exchequer ther, Ordeanes ane Letter to be made and exped vnder his Maᵗⁱˢ privie seall in dew forme, making, constituteing, and ordeaneing, Lykas his Maᵗⁱᵉ be the tenour heirof maks, constituts, and ordeanes, the said James Ewing, dureing all the dayes of his lyftyme, herauld at armes in the said kingdome, to be named and called at all tymes heirefter in the dischargeing of that office by the name and style of Rothsay Herauld, with power and authoritie to him dureing his said lyftyme to vse, bruik, posses, and discharge the said office of Rothsay herauld, and to enjoy all and whatsumever proffeit, priviledge, proheminences, immunities, casualiteis, and emoluments appertaneing and belonging to the said office, by whatsumever maner of way, in as frie, ample, and beneficiall maner as any other Rothesay herauld doeth bruik at this present time, or hath bruiked and enjoyed at any tyme preceiding : Giveing, granting, and disponeing, lykas his Maᵗⁱᵉ, with consent forsaid, gives, grants, and dispones vnto the said James Ewing the ordinarie yeirlie fie of fourtie-tua pundis vsuall money of that kingdome for dischargeing the said Office of Rothesay Herauld, to be vplifted and receaved by him, his assigneyis, factours, servandis, and others haveing his power, out of his Maᵗⁱˢ rents and casualiteis of that kingdome ; with command and directioun to his Maᵗⁱˢ said Thesaurer, deputie thesaurer for the tyme, and be all officers whatsoever haveing charge heirefter of his Maᵗⁱˢ rents and casualiteis, readelie to answer and pay to the said James Ewing or his forsaids the said yeirlie fie of ffourtie-tua pundis money forsaid out of his Maᵗⁱˢ Exchekor, rents, or casualiteis forsaid, at the termes and tymes accustomed to be payed to his brethren heraulds who ar now in office, the first terme's payment thairof to be and begin at the terme of Witsondey, and so forth yeirlie at the saidis termes or tymes dureing his said lyftyme ; And with command to the Auditours of Exchequer, now and for the tyme being, yeirlie to defease and allow the said yeirlie fie in the accompts of the said thesaurer and others officers aforsaid, these presents being once entred in the Exchekor and registrat as effeires : And that the said Letter be farder extendit in the best and most ample forme with all clausses neidfull.—At Whythall, 26 Aprill 1633.

To the Counsell.

Right, &c.—We have bene pleased to tak speciall notice of the enclosed petition, and conceaveing the demand therin to be verie fair and reasonable, we ar heirby pleased to will and requyre yow to tak the same into your consideratioun, being willing that yow schaw vnto the petitioner what lawfull or convenient favour yow can in ordouring and setling of these so reasonablie demanded by hir ; Which speciallie recommending, &c.—Whythall, last Aprill 1633.

To the Chancellour, Thesaurer, President, Privie Seall, Thesaurer Deputie.

Right, &c.—Wheras it hath bene alwyse accustomed that such writts and articles as wer fitt to be exhibited or motioned in Parliament wer some time befor the sitting therof delyvered to the Clerk Register for the tyme, and vnderstanding that besydis the custome it will conduce the good of our service that the lyk course be continewed now at our ensewing Parliament : Our pleasur is, that yow caus delyver all such papers and articles vnto our Clerk Register that now is as may concerne our service at this tyme, communicating vnto him what further yow shall know to be vnnecessarie to be imparted for the good of our service, or what shalbe proponed vnto yow or any of yow to be considered of at that tyme, and that he enjoy the said office as friclie in all respects as aney of his predicessours Clerks of Register have done at any tyme preceiding : Which recommending vnto your care, we bid yow farewell.—Whythall, last Aprill 1633.

To the Archbischop of Sᵗ Androis.

Right, &c.—Haveing sene a certificat of the deane and Chaptour of the See of Rosse, of the admission and election of our trustie and weilbeloved Mᵗ Johne Maxwell to the bischoprik of Ross, according to warrant for that purpois, Our pleasur is, that with all convenient diligence yow give ordour for his translatioun to the said bischoprik, and for his instalement therin in such readie and fitt maner as in the lyk caces as is accustomed, for which these presents shalbe vnto yow a sufficient warrand.—Whythall, last Aprill 1633.

To the Chancellour.

Right, &c.—We have sent yow heirwith a Commission for tryell of that which is alledged aganst our right, &c. the Erle of Airth, President of our Privie Counsell, with the names of some persones scalled vp to be delyvered to yow, and it is our pleasur that haveing conveued with yow the Archbischop of Sᵗ Androis and Glasgow, the Erles of Morton, Hadinton, and Lawderdaill, the Viscont of Air, the Lord Traquair, and Sir John Hay, Clerk Register, or oney six with yow, yow or any ane of the tuo of the Archbischops being one, and they and yow being appoynted by ws Commissioners for the tryell of this bussines, yow open the Commission befor them, and so proceid for examing of such witnesses as shalbe produced vnto yow according vnto the Commission : and if any of the saids Commissioners shalbe vsed by the pairtie informer as witnesses, though ther doe not remane so many as we have sett doun for the quorum, It is our pleasur nevertheles that the rest shall proceid, and if any of the saids Commissioners shalbe vsed as witnesses, we appoynt that his deposition vpon oath be presentlie takin, and incaice he doe not depone that he heard the said Erle speik that which is alledgit in the tuo Articles gevin aganst him, That he be immediatlie reponed in the place of his Commission, as if he had not bene vsed as a witnes : And it is our pleasur lykwyse that the said Erle be allowed to mak vse of Advocats with whome he may consult and defend his cause, as far as he hath bene or can be lawfullie granted in the lyk caice.—First of May 1633.

To the Thesaurer.

Right, &c.—Wheras we did command Sir George Fletcher, Knyᵗ, to bargane for a pealt of Bellis to be hung vpon our Church at Halyrudhous, which, as we ar informed by Mᵗ James Hannay, minister ther, wilbe in readiness befor the 20 day of this moneth of May, to the effect it may be vsefull speciallie at our first comeing, and being ther at this tyme. Our pleasur is, that yow caus furthwith answer, and pay vnto the founder heir at our Citie of London the pryce condescendel vpoun, that they may be transported thither with all possible diligence : Wherof expecting the performance at your handis, we bid yow farewell.—Whythall, 10 May 1633.

To the Erle of Kellie.

Right, &c.—Wheras for diverse important considerations we have thoght fitt to summond a Court of Parliament to be holdin at Edinburgh, in Scotland, the   day of Junij nixt, and vpon that occasion have caused writts of summondis to be addressed to that purpois, vnderstanding that, in regard of your indisposition of bodie and necessarie affaires within this our kingdome of England, yow ar vnable to attend that service in your owin persone, we ar heirby pleased to give yow licence to forbear your comeing to our said Parliament; So as nevertheles yow cause your proxy to be sent in convenient tyme vnto some of your owin qualitie and rank, who may for yow and in your name give his vote and consent vnto such matters as ar to be treated and concluded in the said Parliament, and these our letters shalbe your sufficient warrant and discharge.—Whythall, 10 May 1633.

LICENCES DIRECTED TO NOBLEMEN SELFFS.

Vpoun the 10 of May 1633 Thrie Licences wer signed by his Ma[tie], granting vnto Viscont Falkland, Lord Bruce and Newbrugh, licence to be absent from the Parliament of Scotland to be holdin at this tyme at Edinburgh, so being they cause send ther proxis in dew tyme: The draught of ther licences, conforme to this of the E. Kelleis that followis heirefter, nothing is altered saveing that the clause of the Indisposition of ther bodie is left out in theris.

TO THE SESSION.

Right, &c.—Wheras we have often by severall letters recommended vnto your care that Justice might be dewlie and spedelie administrat according to Law in ane Action of reduction prosecuted at our instance and by our expres command to our Advocat for recoverie of certane Lands, tythis, superioriteis, and other thingis which did appertene to the Abbacie of Lundoris, being procured without our knowledge by M[r] W[m] Forbes of Craigievar, deceissed, to our great prejudice and grevance of many of our loveing subjects, antient fewers inhabiteing these Lands, the prosecutioun whairof hath now of late bene stayed by a reference vpon a petition of Sir W[m] Forbes, now of Craigievar: We at this tyme taking speciall notice of the prejudice done vnto ws by the procureing of the said grant, and of the former obstinacie of the said Sir William in refuising to submitt and resigne vnto ws in such maner as was fitt, and of the great trouble and charges these fewers and taksmen of tythis have sustened by his meanes, ar resolved, by these and others considerations knowen vnto ws, to have the benefite of our lawis by causeing assist in the said reduction in a legall [manner], and therfor have thoght fitt herby to recommend vnto yow of new (that notwithstanding of the said reference) spedie Justice be administred in the said action, with [out] respect of persones or furder delay, according to our pleasur so often signifeit to that purpois: And that heirefter yow accept of no submission from the said Sir William, without ane absolute resignation, alsweill of his action aganst the Vassalls as of the superioriteis cum omni causa; wherof expecting the performance, we bid, &c.—Whythall, 10 May 1633.

TO THE COMMISSIONERS FOR TRYEING OF THE ERLE OF AIRTH, CHANCELLOUR, ARCHBISCHOPS, THESAURER, AND DEPUTIE CARNAGIE, SIR JOHN HAY, V. AIR.

Right, &c.—Wheras we have bene informed by our trustie and weilbeloved Sir James Skene, kny[t], President of our Colledge of Justice, that he would vndertak to prove that it was said to him that our right, &c. the Erle of Airth, president of our Privie Counsell, affirmed that he should have bene King of Scotland, and that it was said to him that he affirmed to have better or as good right to the Croun as wo our selfis: That it may be truelie tryed whether these treasonable speiches wherwith the said Erle is accused, if they be trew, or if they be bot columneis, It is our pleasur that yow to whom these presents ar directed, or any six of yow, the Chancellour, or any of the tuo Archbischops being one, doe convene and call befoir yow the said Sir James, and caus him condescend vpon the names of his reporters; and incaice they should deny, then yow examyne such witnesses as the said Sir James shall produce aganst his said reporters, and to bring them befor yow; and if his authors have it by report of others, that yow proceid till yow have seue who did affirme to have heard it immediatlie from himsellf, and that yow examyne all such witnesses as shalbe produced vnto yow, they being noblemen or men of good qualitie and reputation, or such as aganst whom ther can be no legall exception vpon the said report, tyme, place, and other circumstances requisit; and therefter when yow have done with the tryell, that yow send to ws the severall depositions of the saidis witnesses, everie ane of them haveing signed that which is his owen. [No date.]

To Nicolas Briot.

It is our will and pleasur that with all possible diligence yow Coyne a certane number of Angells for those whome we ar to toutch who have the King's evill, with the lyk Impression and fyness as they ar which we vse for that purpois in our kingdome of England, and for that effect yow prepare all such yrones, engynes, tooles as ar necessarie.—Halyrudhous, 10 May 1633.

To the Counsell.

Right, &c.—Wheras ther ar diverse differences (as we ar informed) concerneing some priviledges at our Coronation and Parliament amongst our right, &c. the duik of Lennox, our right, &c. the Marqueis of Hamiltoun, the Erle of Angus, the Erle of Erroll, and our right, &c. the Erle of Merschell, we ar desyreous that befoir our being ther all differences of this nature may be removed : And thairfoir it is our pleasur that yow call the saidis pairteis befoir yow, or such as they shall appoynt to answer for them in ther absens ; And haveing heard what things in this kynd ar contraverted amongst them, and the reasones and alledgances of each pairtie heirin, that then if yow can compound the differences amongst them, or if yow can not to report the trew estate thairof, with your opinion what is to be done therin at our comeing thither.—Whythall, 10 May 1633.

Carolus Dei gratia, &c.—Omnibus regibus principibus tam ecclesiasticis quam secularibus Archiepiscopis Episcopis ducibus Marchionibus baronibus equitibus aliisque nobilibus necnon omnibus Admirallis Thallashiarchis Vice-Admirallis classium navium forium pontium provinciarum vrbium arcium pontium castrorum praefectis sive gubernatoribus omnibus denique per vniversam Europam magistratibus imperium qualicunque terra marine exercentibus fratribus patribus consanguineis affinibus amicis confederatisque suis Salutem plurimam benevolentiam fraternam gratiam favoremque suam regiam pro cujusque status conditionisque ratione dicit et importit Quandoquidem serenissimi illustrissimi reverendissimi illustres magnifici et generosi domini fratres patres consanguinei affines amici confederatique nostri Dilectus subditus noster et honoratus dominus Archibaldus Dowglas filius primogenitus et haeres illustrissimi Comitis Angusiae et Abernethiae laudabili hominum mores cognoscendi studio ductus vt sibi (pace nostra) exteras aliquot nationes adire liceret supplex et enixe petiit cujus tam equis postulatis haud quaquam renuendum existimavimus quin potius serenitates reverentias celsitudines magnificentias amplitudinesque vestras amice rogatas cupimus vt si ditiones alicujus vestrum maria prius portas vrbes opida locave alia cura vestra aut praefecturae commissa Memoratus nobilis et honoratus dominus Archibaldus Dowglas subditus noster appulerit introitu non solum nulla injuria affecta libere manere aut abire senatis verum de humanitate tractetis quam vestros a nobis exspectare velitis si ditionesque quoque nostras similiter commendari intraverint in eisuo negotiabantur Valete Dabantur e regia nostra Westmonasterum decimo die May anni per Christum partae salutis tricesimi tertii supra millesimum sexcentesimumque.

To the Counsell.

Right, &c.—Wheras according to our Commission of the first of July 1631 directed to certane Commissioners for trying what priviledges and digniteis belong to the office of high Constabularie of that our kingdome, report both being made vnto ws of what is justlie dew vnto the said office we doe approve the same, bot vnderstanding that ther ar other digniteis and charges which doe belong vnto our high Constable at the tyme of our Coronatioun, which the saidis Commissioners have not taken into ther consideration, which he alledgeth doeth lykwyse belong vnto his said office, ye may know be that part of the book of Coronatioun margened, which he will produce vnto yow, wherin yow will find particularlie mentioned what he thinks does belong vnto him : Our pleasur is, that yow tak the premisses to your serious consideratioun, and if yow find his alledgances to be trew, that ye authorize him for dischargeing of the same and whatsoever else yow find to be dew vnto his place, that no hinderance or trouble be in the executioun therof at our being ther.—May ij, Theobald's, 1633.

Right, &c.—According to the ordinarie draught a letter was past his Ma^{tis} hand for admitting the Erle of Erroll vpon the Counsell, 11 May 1633.

To the Counsell.

Right, &c.—Wheras we have bene pleased to wryt vnto yow at severall tymes that the abuse tuitching forrane Coyne current in that our kingdome might be remended, and wheras at this tyme certane overtures heirwith enclosed hath bene presented vnto ws tuitching that purpois, we ar heirby pleased to remitt them vnto your consideratioun, requyreing efter yow have called the Commissioners of the frie burrowis befor yow for acquainting them with the Overtures, and for hearing what proposition they can mak or what they will contribute thervnto, and finding any of these Overtures litt for rectifieing that abuse, or any other proposition to be thoght vpon by yourseilfis or others that yow certifie ws at our comeing quhat course is littest to be taken for the publict good and credit of that our ancient kingdome.—Theobaldis, 13 May 1633.

To the Excheqver.

Right, &c.—Wheras efter humble sute made to ws these diverse yeres bypast by our servand Michaell Elphingstoun to have his pension of 100^{lib} sterling or therabouts, with arreires therof payed vnto him, hath now petitioned ws that in regard of the scarcitie at this tyme of our Thesaurer, and for his better enabling to serve ws now at our being in that our kingdome, God willing, he may have a gift vpon his surrander of the said pension and arreirs of the concealled ward's mariages and nonentreis, of all such our vassalls of that kingdome, regalitie, and principalitie therof, holding ward or few of ws as have not had our lawfull gifts vnder our sealls, or have not made accompt for the same in Excheqer to our vse befor the dait of thir presents in regard we accompt the discoverie therof as good service done to ws, besydis the benefite accrewcing to ws by the said surrander we have thoght litt to grant his demand : Therfoir it is our pleasur that haveing sene the said surrander legallie made in our favours, yow by ane Act of Excheqer, or efter what other maner he shall find most requisit for his better enjoying of what we have heirby granted to him, appoynt and in our name grant vnto him, his aires and assigneyis, the sole benefite of all such concealled wardis' mariages and nonentress which he shall happin to discover and have not bene accompted for as yet in our Excheqer, and give in vnder his hand to our Advocat within yeir and day efter the date of his surrander, appoynting by the said act or by the maner of suretie to be made to him by yow our Advocat to raise summondis intending action befoir the Session at the instance of our Thesaurer Principall and deputie, and to persew such of them as by our said servand or his foirsaids information shalbe made appear to fall within the compas of this our gift, and that the compositions be made in such forme as salbe most fitt for him, for which these presents salbe your warrand : So speciallie recommending to your care that the said act or other surtie be so conceaved in his favour, and so authorised by yow to that purpois, that he enjoy the full benefite of what he have heirby intendit for him without interruption or delay.—Theobald's, 13 of May 1633.

TO THE THESAURER AND DEPUTIE THESAURER.

Right, &c.—Wheras we have written heirtofoir that Mr James Hannay, Minister at our Church of Halyrudhous, might be satisfeid for his disbursements in repairing that Church with the ordinarie allowance for the forbearance, becaus, as we ar crediblie informed, his service therin was verie vsefull, and that the Charges expended wer his owin meanes, We will that such speedie payment be made to him therof as possiblie can, and the rather becaus his service and attendance in his charge now at this tyme at our being ther, God willing, wilbe verie requisite : Therfoir our pleasur is, that with all diligence yow pay vnto him or his assigneyis the said disbursments, with the ordinarie allowance for the forbearing therof as yow shall find by his accompts, and that in such maner as yow shall think most fitt for his satisfaction ; for which these presents, &c.—Theobald's, 14 May 1633.

TO THE COUNSELL.

Right, &c.—Wheras ther ar diverse differences, as we ar informed, concerneing some priviledges at our Coronation and Parliament amongst our right, &c. the Duik of Lennox, our right, &c. the Marqueis of Hamilton, our right, &c. the Marqueis of Huntlie, and our right, &c. Erle Arrell, the Erle of Marschell, we ar desyreous that befoir our being ther all differences of this nature may be removed : And therfor it is our pleasur that yow call the saidis pairteis befoir yow, or such as they shall appoynt to answer for them in ther absence, and haveing heard what things in this kynd ar controverted amongst them, and the reasones and alledgances of each pairtie heirin, that then if yow can compound the differences amongst them, or if yow cannot, to report the trew esteat therof, with your opinions what is to be done therin at our comeing thither : So expecting your care and diligence, we bid yow farewell.—Theobald's, the 14 May 1633.

TO THE COUNSELL.

Right, &c.—Wheras by our letter vnto yow of late, we wer pleased to approve the certificat that was returned vnto ws concerneing the office of our high Constable, remitting to your serious consideration the justnes of the allegations therein conteyned, being since informed by the Commissioners of our frie burroughs that they ar liklie to be verie much wronged therby : As we desyre not to derogat any way from the said office in what is justlie dew thervnto, So it is nowayes our intention to prejudge any of our saids burrowes in the lawfull rights granted be our royall progenitours vnto them : It is our pleasur that yow call ther commissioners befoir yow, and having heard ther objections in the said matter in presence of the other pairtie, yow shall find ther differences aryse vpoun ther rights and possessions, that if yow can compound ther differences betwene, or if ye can not, then to report to ws the trew estate of the bussines, with your opinion what is to be done vpon it at our comeing, in so far as concernes the saidis differences ; and for your soe doeing, &c.—14 May, Theobald's 1633.

To the Counsell.

Rights, &c.—Wheras the enclosed Petition hath been exhibited vnto ws in behalff of Sir Wm Cokburne, kny^t and barronet, wherby he humblie craveth that according to a decrie before the Lordis of Session in his favours against the Erle of Wigtoun, tuitching the office of our Cheiff Vschear of Scotland, he might discharge that service now at our Coronatioun, God willing, and in tyme cuming, according to our Infeftment granted to his predicessour, Sir Alex^r Cokburne of Langtoun, by our royall predicessour King Robert the Secund, wherin, being willing that yow consider of the royall rights to that office, and they accordinglie setled therin, that all difference be so composed and ordered tuitching the same, that the service therein be tymelie and quyitlie discharged at our being ther, we have heirby thoght fitt to refer the consideratioun of the petition to yow to determyne therin according to Justice, by setling that purpois in that office, to whom yow shall find it justlie belong, without further trouble vnto ws.—Theobald, the 14 May 1633.

To the Clerk Register.

Trustie, &c.—Wheras we have bene moved in behalff of our frie burrowis of that our kingdome anent certain statuts to pass into parliament, we have thought good to remitt them vnto yow; And therfor our pleasur is, that yow tak ther desyres to your serious consideratioun, and to acquaint ws therwith, conforme to the directiouns gevin vnto yow.—[No date.]

To the Toun of Edinburgh.

Trustie, &c.—We have considered at lenth with your Commissioner anent our reception into that our toun, wher we hear yow have had a speciall caus, expressing heirby your affection vnto ws, the which we give yow heartie thanks, and do earnestlie desyre yow to continew your endeavours as yow have begun; for that effect we have gevin direction concerneing your signature for expediting thairof; And as for the high Constable, wheranent we have bene moved, yow may be assured yow shall suffer no wrong therin: And for the matter of our Counsell and Session, and anent your ministers, we will tak such a course at our comeing to yow as may give yow all reasonable satisfaction: And as for all other matters propounded by your said Commissioner, which we find to be meere parliamentarie, being vrged by the straitnes of tyme, we have thoght good to remitt them to our Clerk Register, to be considered at our comeing ther, wheranent and anent all other things may tend to your good, may expect that we will not be vnmyndfull, as in reason may be hoped at the handis of a loveing Prince; We bid yow fairwell from our Court at Theobald's, 14 May 1633.

Ye need not fear in the bussiness anent the Constabularie, for though I meane to manteane the Constabularie in his antient priviledges, yit I shall sie that ye shall have no wrong.

C. R.

To the Counsell.

Right, &c.—Being informed of the sufficiencie of our right, &c. the Erle of Arell, and of his affection to our service, we ar moved, in regard therof, and for the better encouragment and enabling for our said service, to advance and promove him to be ane of our privie counsell of that our kingdome: Therfor our pleasur is, and we doe heirby requyre yow that having administred vnto him the oath accustomed in the lyk caices, yow admitt him to be ane of your number: And for your soe doeing, &c.—Theobald's, 14 May 1633.

To the Counsell.

Right, &c.—Vnderstanding the sufficiencie of our right, &c. the Duik of Lennox, and his affection to our service, we ar moved, in regard therof, and other speciall considerations knowen vnto ws, to advance and promove him to be one of our privie Counsall of that our kingdome, but he being resident about our persone, and we being willing that in the meane tyme he be admitted thervpon with as much diligence as may be befor our comeing thither : Our pleasur is, and we doe heirby requyre that with all conveniencie, yow send hither vnto our Court, wher we shalbe for the tyme, a Commission vnto some of our privie Counsell of that our kingdome, who shalbe heir, for administring vnto him the oath accustomed in the lyk caices, or such as yow shall think fitt to that purpois, wherby he may be admitted to be one of our privie Counsell, and receaved in that place as one of your number; for doeing whairof these shalbe your warrand : We bid, &c.—From our Court, Worsope, 21 May 1633.

To the Clerk Register.

Trustie, &c.—Being willing to informe ourselffis from yow of the Estate of such thingis belonging to your charge as ar fitt to be treated of in the Parliament to be holdin by ws now verie schortlie within that our kingdome, Our pleasur is, that yow repair to our Court at Berwick, vpon the eight day of this moneth, wher yow shall vnderstand our further pleasur and directions, whairof faill not, as yow respect the good of our service : We bid yow, &c.—2 Junij 1633.

To the Lady Dowglas.

Cousen, &c.—Haveing for many causes reasone to carie a particular respect to yow and that familie from which yow ar descendit, we thoght fitt to certifie yow that since the Courtesois of England gives the daughter of a Duik place before all Countesses, we hope that this our antient kingdome wilbe no less courteous then they : And though we desyre not to command anything contrair to the customes of this kingdome of which we ar not as yet weill informed, yit we thoght fitt to intimat this by way of opinion, assureing yow that we for our part shall carie yow the said respect and have yow in the same estimation heir as in any other kingdome whatsumever.—Halyrudhous, 24 Junij 1633.

To the Session.

Right, &c.—Wheras our servand Sir Robert Gordoun is to attend vpon ws in his charge as gentlman of our Privie Chalmer in Ordinarie, hearing that he hath ane action in Law depending befor yow aganst ane John Gordon of Innermarkie, we thought fitt in regard he cannot be long present ther, speciallie to recommend him vnto yow that he may have Justice administred therin with all expedition, that the Lawis and custome of the kingdome in the lyk caices can afford, and that the said Johne Gordon get no advantage by delay in so far as lawfullie can be avoyded, wherin not doubting of your care, &c.—Seaton, the 3 July 1633.

Wheras yow as great Chalmerlane of our kingdome of Scotland and of our houshold heire should have a care of our Wardrop heir : Our will and pleasur is, that yow visite or caus visite our Wardrop heir and mak the Master thairof give ane accompt and Inventarie of such thingis as ar within the same to yow, that yow may acquant ws heirwith.—Halyrudhouse, 10 July 1633.

To the Duik of Lennox, Lord high Admirall and Chalmerlane of Scotland.

To the Advocat.

Trustie and weilbeloved—Being willing that all such our Officers of this our kingdome who necessarlie ar to attend our service now at our Coronation may dewlie performe what belongeth vnto ther charge, and speciallie that our right, &c. the Duik of Lennox, our Chalmerlane of Scotland, and of our houshold therof, may have what is due vnto his place, ather by the custome of our dominions or of other forrane kingdomes : Our pleasur is, that haveing informed yourself in the readiest and best maner yow can of what is due vnto his charge, yow draw vp ane authentik oxlour thairof vnder your hand, and seall and delvyer vnto him the extract therof, with all possible expedition efter yow have caused enroll the same (if what belongs vnto that charge be not sufficientlie enrolled alreadie) in your books, that it may remane the more cleirlie to the posteritie, for which these presents shalbe your warrand.—Halyrudhous, 10 July 1633.

To the Clerk Register.

Trustie, &c.—Wheras we ar informed that Robert Adair of Kinhilt hath past in the Parliament at this tyme a ratificatioun of the patronage of the kirk of Kirkcadzow, in Galloway, and tythis therof, wherby both we and the kirk of Portpatrik to which thes kirks ar annexed, contrair to the generall course of laik patronages and other things mentional in our decrie, vpon the submission of surrenders and contrarie to a ratificatioun made lykwayes at this tyme in our owin favours confirmeing ws patron of the kirk of Kirkcadzow : Our pleasur is, that yow stay the said ratificatioun made in favours of the said Robert till our further pleasur be knowen heirin.—Berwick, the 16 July 1633.

To the Advocat.

Trustie, &c.—Wheras by the act anent our Advocation made in our late Parliament diverse gifts of pensions formerlie granted by ws ar made voyd, some whairof notwithstanding out of our gratious favour we ar willing to renew, we have thoght good to send yow heirwith the names of a few whom we intend to favour in that kynd, and to the effect that we may be assured that the gifts which shalbe presented to be renewed and ratifeid by ws in ther behalflis, ar conforme to the first gifts without any new addition : Our pleasur is, that haveing called for ther first grants yow conferre the new with them, and finding them answerable one to the other, that then yow docatt them that they may be readie for our hand.—Whythall, 2 August 1633.

To the Marqueis of Hamilton.

Right, &c.—Wheras we have constituted yow Collectour of the taxations granted vnto ws at our last Parliament dureing the space of six yeres, as lykwyse of the tno ont of everie hundreth merkis of annuellis, payable termelie, granted at the same tyme : Though we have gevin vnto yow power to transact, compone, and remitt and agree for the said tuo of the hundredth by yourself or your deputies, yit considering that yourself will ather be altogidder or for the most part absent so that others must be entrusted by yow with that charge : It is our pleasur that yow or your depnteis by whome the said composition for tuo of the hundreth out of the annells shalbe made, doe acquant our Thesaurer or Thesaurer deputie therwith from tyme to tyme as they ar made, what is receaved or compounded for, that the same may be certifeid vnto ws ; ffor doeing whairof, &c.—Grenwitch, 2 August 1633.

To the Clerk Register Sir Wm Hay.

Trustie, &c.—Haveing pervsed the Letter which yow sent vnto ws, and considering how necessar it is that we should confer with yourselff: It is our pleasur that so soone as convenientlie yow can yow repair vnto ws, and that yow bring with yow all the writts concerneing that bussines, which yow gave ws accompt of in your said letter: And lykwyse yow bring prepared with yow what is further requisit to be done therin : Expecting your comeing, we, &c.—Denmarkhouse, 3 August 1633.

To the Counsell.

Right, &c.—Wheras we have bene humblie petitioned by one Thomas Gordoun that he may have libertie to returne to his native cuntrie for setling of his estate and provydeing for his wyff and children, we have sene the Act of Counsell wherby he hath bene hithertills sequestrat from his cuntrie, and doe approve the course takin therin as being conforme to the custome and ordour establisched in the lyk caices : But yit being informed of the great prejudice the petitioner is lyklie to suffer if he shall not have libertie to returne home, and withall sieing (as we ar lykwayes informed) he hath ever bene frie from any particular and publict offence other than he is not conforme to the professed religion ther, we ar the rather gratiouslie pleased to signifie our pleasur vnto yow that he may be permitted to stay at home for setling of his said affaires so long as yow shall think fitt, or dureing such tyme as formerlie hath bene granted to others in that kynd, he alwayes behaveing himsellf soberlie and civilie without geving any publict scandell to hurt or derogate from the estate of the present professed religion for the which yow shall tak him bund : And for your so doeing.—Oatlandis, 9 August 1633.

To the Erle of Traquair.

Right, &c.—Being informed that the Countess of Airth intendeth at this tyme to repair to our Court, and we being vnwilling that sche tak any such journey without our speciall direction : Our pleasur is, that yow in our name desyre [her] to forbear to repair hither, vnless our further pleasur be signifeid to that purpois; for doeing whairof, &c.—Oatlands, 15 August 1633.

To the Bischop of Winchester.

Reverend father in God.—Wheras our trustie and weilbeloved Sir Thomas Dischingtoun, kny^t, genthman of our Privie Chalmer, had a Lease granted vnto his Authours of the great Park of Ferwham, and we vpoun consideratioun of his good service done to our late dear father and ws, haveing since the expyreing of that Lease and of the Vacancie of that See, whairof yow have now the charge, caused continew his possession of that Park at that tyme of his being abroad in our service in Germanie, we ar heirby pleased speciallie to recommend vnto yow to renew a lease to him of that Park according as we have intended, and to caus allow yeirlie a sufficient quantitie of hay for keiping of the deere therin : The doeing whairof we will tak weall at your handis : We bid, &c.—Oatlands, 19 August 1633.

To the Counsell.

Right, &c.—Vpon humble sute made vnto ws in behalff of Wm Bannatyne of Corhous, that we might be gratiouslie pleased to grant vnto him a protection for a yeir, therby the better to enable him (as he affirmeth) to tak the more safe and speedie way to give his creditours satisfaction we did thervpon signe the enclosed protection, bot withall thoght litt to refer it to your consideratioun, willing yow to tak such course therin as may best tend to the securing of the Creditours, and the better enabling of the pairtie for it, which is onlie our royall intention in this, and hath bene in all bussines of the lyk nature.—Denmark-house, 30 August 1633.

To the Counsell.

Right, &c.—Wheras we wer humblie petitioned at our being ther by a number of the Nobilitie and gentrie of that our kingdome that some course might be taken for repressing the insolenceis and thifts of certane disorderlie persones in diverse parts therof, we intended then to have had the matter debaited befor ws in Counsell ther, that by your advyses some good course concerneing it might have bene establisched; yit in regard of the schortnes of our stay and the multiplicitie of affaires, it took not then effect, bot considering how much in justice it doeth concerne ws to represse all oppression, and in honour to manteane the peace and rights of our good subjects, and with all that the speedines of the remedie may prevent the effects, which by delay may prove otherwayes more prejudiciall to the petitioners and dis-gracefull to the governement ther, we have thoght good to send yow heirwith the enclosed Petition, and it is our spetiall pleasur that, haveing considered thairof and called for such of the petitioners as yow shall think expedient for receaveing the more ample information in the particulars, yow tak such present ordour as they may be fred from all just fearis in tyme cuming, the offenders be severelie punisched for what is past by all possible meanes, and the peace of the cuntrie establisched : Wherin expecting ane exact accompt of your spedie endeavours, as yow wilbe answerable vnto ws.—Whythall, 4 Septr 1633.

To the Erle of Lawderdaill.

Right, &c.—Wheras we ar informed yow have a sone latlie borne vnto yow, we being willing to putt a mark of favour vpon yow, ar willing to give him our name, and to that effect have made choyse of our right, &c. the Erle of Winton, which we thought good to signifie vnto yow by these presents : And so we bid, &c.—Bagshot, 4 Sept. 1633.

To the Erle of Winton.

Right, &c.—Wheras we ar informed that our right, &c. the Erle of Lauderdaill hath a sone latelie borne vnto him, and we being willing to testifie our respect vnto him, have thoght good to mak choyse of yow in our behalff, to give him our name, and doe signifie vnto yow our pleasur heirby to the effect that yow may be present, and be witnes for ws at the Christeneing of the said Chyld, wherin yow shall doe ws acceptable service.—Bagschot, 4 Sept. 1633.

Charles, by the grace of God king, &c., defender of the fayth, &c.—To all Majors, Shirrellis, Justices of Peace, Vice-Admiralls, bailleis, constables, customers, comptrollers, searchers, and others, our officers quhom it may concerne, and to everie of them, Greeting—Wheras Andro Gray, sone to the Lord Gray, is to travell into France vpon some necessarie occasions him neirlie concerneing : These ar to will and command yow and everie of yow to suffer him to embark himself with his tuo servandis and ther neces-sarie provisions at any of our ports, for which, &c : Gevin, &c.—[No date.]

To the Exchequer.

Right, &c.—Wheras we have writtin at diverse tymes to our Colledge of Justice and Advocat, tuitching the reduceing of a grant gevin to Mr Wm Forbes, late of Cragievar, of the superioriteis of certane Landis and others thingis mentionat therin, which wer holdin of the Abbacie of Lindores, and tuitching the groundis and reasones whervpon we gave ordour for insisting in that reduction according to Law: Being informed that now of late a signature contening some of these Landis was presented befor yow to have bene exped vnder our sealls vpon resignatioun of Sir Wm Forbes of Cragievar, his sone, which vpon consideratioun of our right and interest was stayed by yow: Our pleasur is, that yow continew the lyk course whensoever any signature of these Landis shall heirefter be presented to be past vpon the resignation of the said Sir William, till we shalbe pleased to signifie vnto yow our further pleasur tuitching the same, for which these presents shalbe a sufficient warrant.—Theobalds, 18 Septr 1633.

To the Earle of Argyll.

Right, &c.—Wheras vpon certificat of the Cheiff Justice of the Kingis Bench tuitching diverse scandelous speeches and abuses committed by ane Ann, your naturall daughter, we wer pleased to authorize yow by our warrant to apprehend and send hir out of the kingdome, haveing heirby declared that if sche returned without our licence sche should be punished according to the Lawis and custome in the lyk caices, vnderstanding sche hath returned in contempt of our command, Our pleasur is, and we doe heirby will and requyre yow to caus diligentlie search and apprehend hir to be by yow sent vnto Scotland, from whence our further pleasur is that sche did not returne without our licence, and if sche did transgress therin, we ar heirby pleased to declair that vpon dew notice gevin thairof schoe should be punished as hir offences should be fund to deserve by the lawis and customes of this our kingdome: And for the better and more speedie executeing of this our command, we heirby will and require all Mayors, Shirreffis, Justices of peace, bailleis, constablis, searchers, governours, and keipers of our ports and harbours, and all masters and commanders of schips within our dominions, and all others our officers and subjects whom it dooth or may concerne, to be ayding and assisting vnto yow, your servant or servandis in the searching, apprehending, and transporting of the said Ann, to the kingdome of Scotland.—Theobaldis, 18 Sept. 1633.

To the Counsell and Commissioners appoynted or to be appoynted for passing the Patentes of Knyght Barronets and Infeftments of Lands in New Scotland.

A Letter concerneing New Scotland was passed 27 Sept. 1633 verbatim, lyk vnto that which was past 24 Aprill 1633.

To the Exchequer.

Right, &c.—Vnderstanding perfeetlie the sufficiencie of our Right, &c. the Erle of Southesk, and of his affection to our service, we ar moved in regard therof, and for the said Erle his further encouragment and enabling him for our service, to advance and promove him to be one of the Commissioners of our Exchecker in that our kingdome: It is therfoir our will and pleasur, and we doe heirby will and requyre yow, that haveing administred vnto him the oath accustomed in the lyk caices, yow admitt him to be one of the Commissioners of our Exchequer, receaveing him in that place as one of your number; for doeing quherof, &c.—Whythall, first Octo^r 1633.

Vpon the first Octo^r 1633 his Matie signed a Letter for admitting the Erle of Lawderdaill vpon the Excheker.

Serenissimo Principi Domino Vladislao Jv° Dei gratia Regi Poloniæ magno duci Litharnæ Russiæ Prussiæ Muscoviæ Samogitiæ Livoniæque Necnon Suecorum Gothorum Vandalorumque hereditario Regi Electo magno duci Moscoviæ fratri &c. Consanguineo nostro Charissimo.

Carolus Dei gratia magnæ Britanniæ Franciæ et Hiberniæ Rex fideique defensor Serenissimo principi Domino Vladislao Jv° eadem gratia Regi Poloniæ &c. nostro charissimo Salutem et prosperitatis incrementum Serenissimo Princeps frater consanguineo charissimo Præsens lator David Alexander natione Scotus jam ante variis expeditionibus bellicis multa sua in fortificationibus castrametationibus et machinationibus scientiæ et experientiæ nobis præbuit argumenta Nunc cum illis   nobis ac vestræ serenitatis multo vsui sese esse posse existimet et earum exercendarum voluntate et vestræ serenitati inserviendi cupiditate ductus humillimo nostras ad eam petiit literas Hisce igitur hunc virum qui sub vestris auspiciis regiis mereatur et cupidum et dignum vestræ serenitati commendare volumus fraterne rogantes vt cum hanc nostram benevolentiam cum probum boni viri studium æqui bonique consulere eumque suæ militiæ adhibere velit vestra serenitas Cui omnia fraterni amoris officia vicissim offerentes vt Deus eam quam diutissimo sospites et prosperet ex animo precamur.—Datum e nostro palatio Westministerii 3 Octo^ris Anno Christi M.DC.xxxiii. Regmique nostri sx°.

Vestra Serenitatis,   C. R.

Charles, be the grace of God king, &c., defender of the fayth, To all Mayors, Schirreffis, Justices of Peace, Vice-Admiralls, Bailleis, Constables, Customers, Serchers, and all others our officers whom it may concerne, and to everie ane of them, greting.—Wheras our trustie and weillbeloved Sir George Fletcher, kny^t, our servand, is to travell into France vpon some necessarie occasions him nearlie concerneing: These ar to will and command yow, and everie of yow, to suffer him to imbark himself, with his tuo servants, at any of our ports which shalbe most convenient for his passage; ffor which these, &c.—Whythall, Octo^r 1633.

To the Archbischop of St Androis.

Right reverend, &c.—We have occasion, vpon our late being in Scotland, observed some things which we think fitt to putt in better ordour, which we shall doe as we find caus; bot noe one thing appears to ws more necessarlie then the weill setling of our Vniversitie of St Androis, both for the service of God and good education of youth ther; now, as we wer then gevin to vnderstand, the whole companie of that Vniversitie, alsweill the doctours, as governours of Colledges, as the younger men, vse to goe to the ordinarie paroche churche to service and sermons, and ther sitt promiscuouslie with the rest of the auditours, which loses much of the honour and dignitie of the Vniversitie, and is quyt contrarie to the course he Him in other weill governed places of lyk nature, and is in diverse other respects verie inconvenient: Our expres will and pleasur therfor is, that all the students in that our Vniversitie, alsweill the governours of Colledges as they that live vnder them, shall at all tymes, alsweill terme as vacation, everie Sonday and everie holiday (that the church observes), repair at the hours both of morning and evening prayer to the Chappell of the Old Colledge in St Androis, commonlie called St Salvator's Colledge, and shall ther religiouslie continew all the tyme of divyne service and sermon; nather will we have any scoller, of what rank and degrie whatsoever, at the tymes aforsaid, goe to common paroche churches, nor any of the Inhabitants of the toun leave the paroche churche and mix thenselffis with the Vniversitie; The service ther red shalbe the English

II2 L

liturgie, vnto such tyme as another be made and publishscd by authoritie in that church, and they shall have a communion efter that forme, and kneling, vpon the first Sonday of everie moneth : And as for the sermons everie Sonday, bothe morneing and efternoone, and everie holie day in the morning, Our pleasur is, that they shalbe performed (ant per se ant per alium), by all and everie of the divynes liveing in that Vniversitie, beginning with the Junior that is [in] holy ordours and ascending to the senior, and in course, provyded that the governours of Colledges, being divynes, doe lykwayes preach by turnes, begining also at the junior of them, vpon the first Sonday morning in everie terme, and by reasone of ther governement shall not be putt to any other turne, vnless they pleas voluntarily to tak it : And further, in regard that this Colledge Chapell is thus to be made as a publict Vniversitie church, we think fitt that it be decentlie repaired, both within and without, so far as convenientlie it may, and that everie scoller in the Vniversitie doe contribut according to ther meanes and devotion : And last of all, we doe expreslie heirby command and requyre yow, as chancellour of that our Vniversitie, that yow doe reallie and strictlie putt these our commands in execution, and sie them kept, and that the scollers repair to the chappell or church aforsaid in decent gownes, according to ther severall degrees in schoolis respective ; and we will that these sermones begin at the church vpon the first Sonday of Januar nixt efter the date heirof, and so continew, and that yow give ws ane accompt by letter when this course is begun, and efterwards once a yeir at leist how it continewis vt supra.

　　　　Traquair.

To the Counsell.

Right, &c.—Forasmukle as George Lawder of Bass, and Issobell Hepburne, Lady Bass, his mother, as we ar certanelie informed, ar denunced rebells and putt to the horne at the instance of diverse of our subjects, and speciallie at the instance of James Levingstoun, our servitour, for not payment of great sowmes of money, and for not delyverie to the said James Levingstoun of the evidents of the Lands and baronie of Beill, sauld to him by them, and for not fulfilling vnto him the remanent heads of the Contract past betuixt them theranent, and that they remane most obstinatelie vnder the said proces of horning as our rebells, to the great contempt of our authoritie, and for maenteneing them in the said rebellion have retired themselffis to the Yle of the Bass, wherin they have remaned thir many yeres bygane, and intends still to duell securelie therin, not permitting access of any persone to them from whom they fear any executioun of Law : And sieing this tendis to the fostering of rebellion, and is ane evill and bad preparative, speciallie in parts so neir the place of Justice ; Therfoir it is our will and pleasur that yow direct letters at the instance of the Creditours forsaidis, and speciallie at the instance of the said James Levingstoun, charging them to compeir befoir yow to delyver the keyis of the said Yle of Bass to our Shirreff of Hadinton and his deputeis, and to devoyd and red themselffs therof, with certificatioun to them, if they failzie, our others Letters shalbe direct to charge them to doe the same, vnder pane of Treasone, and tak all other legall course which by Law may force them to satisfie ther said creditours, and speciallie the said James Levingstoun, our servand.—Whythall, 4 Octor 1633.

To the Session.

Vnderstanding that ane extraordinarie place of Session, befor discharged by the E. of Airth, doeth now vaik in our handis by removeing him from that charge, we have thoght fitt to present thervnto the reverend the bischop of Ross, requyreing yow to admitt and receave him therin according to the maner accustumed to be discharged and possest by him, with all honours, priviledges, immuniteis, and preroga- tives therto belonging, and also frielie in all respects as any extraordinarie Senatour in the said Colledge hath discharged and possessed thair place therin at any tyme preceiding ; ffor which, &c.—Whythall, 4 Octor 1633.

To the Vniversitie of Sᵗ Androis.

Trustie and weilbeloved, &c.—We ar informed at our late being in Scotland, that our Vniversitie of Sᵗ Androis did not keip and observe, ather in the habits or otherwayes, such decent ordour as befitts men that lives in such a societie, whois good exemple should not onlie be a direction to the younger sort that live amongst them, bot the whole bodie of that kingdome: And becaus our princelie care cannot extend itsellf better to any ane work then to the reformeing of this, we have directed our letters to our right, &c. the Archbischop of Sᵗ Androis, Chancellour of that our Vniversitie, for the setling of some good ordours ther, both tuitching the service of God and otherwyse; and we expect that all and everie of yow of what Colledge, degrie, or place soever yow be, shall reddelie and willinglie yeild your conformitie and obedience to them, as we doubt not bot yow will, both to give ws the better satisfaction, and to contribute your endeavours to the weill ordoring, and so to the honor of that Vniversitie, for we purpois to cum oursellf in persone at our nixt comeing to that our kingdome to visite that place, and it will be a great dale of joy to find it, as we hope we shall, full of ordour and conformitie to rules of governement; we are verie confident that yow wilbe so readie to yeild obedience to ws in thoes things, which so much tend to your owin good, that as vpon the hearing of them yow will outrun our commandements according as our royall progenitours and oursellf have ever fund yow vpon all other occasions.—Whythall, 6 Octoᵣ 1633.

To the Archbischops and Bischops.

Right, reverend, &c.—We observed many things at our late being in Scotland, whairof we conceave wer not so full in ordour and decencie for the service of God in that Church as we hartelie wish and desyre; And we doe conceave that our loveing and loyall people ther, being weill and verie religiouslie affected, would easelie be brought to embrace all good ordour if yow would goe befor them in a good exemple, and yow cannot goe better nor more befitting your calling then in the way of prayer: Our express will and pleasur therfoir is, that everie of yow, the archbischopis and bischops, carie your sellfis with the gravitie and devotion that beseames your place and calling; and particularlie that yow have in your severall dwelling housses prayers twyse everie day for your fameleis, and be present your sellfis, vnless it be at such tymes as indisposition of bodie, or necessarie bussines caus your absence; and we think it verie requisite vntill such tyme as yow will consider of and agrie vpon a fitt and full liturgie and forme of divine service for that church, that everie of yow respectivelie doe vse in your severall oratours the liturgy of the Church of England, by vse of which, as yow shall performe due service to God, so shall yow also come to be better acquanted with the formes of that Church, which will in tyme produce good effects for our service in both kingdomes: One thing more, we think fitt to requyre that whensoever yow shall appear at Edinburgh, vpon any occasion to mak stay, that yow vse your gownes and Typpetts, and appear with that gravitie which beseames yow in that and the lyk publict places, and particularlie in your places of residence and abroad: Bot especiallie we doe expresslie command all and everie of yow that ar of our privie Counsell of that kingdome, that yow cum not to the counsell table in cloaks bot in gownes and Tippetts, as beseemes yow to doe, in which, if any tak libertie to breck this our command, the persone so offending shall not onlie receave check by ordour of Counsall, but shall further fall into our displeasur, which we presume yow wilbe verie carfull not to doe; for other particulars, we doubt not bot yow will of your owin accord mak them answerable to these which will give ws a great daill of contentment, in a schort tyme bring much honour to that church and your sellfis, which we hartlie desyre.—Dat. vt supra.

ARTICLES.

1. Our expres will and pleasur is, that the deane of our Chappell royall that now is, and his successours salbe assistant to the right reverend father in God the Archbischop of St Androis at the Coronation so oft as it shallhappin.

2. That the book of the forme of our Coronatioun latelie vsed be putt in a litle box, and layed into a standard, and committed to the care of the deane of the Chappell successivelie.

3. That ther be prayers tuyse a day with the quyre alsweill in our absence as other wayes according to the English Liturgie, till some course be takin for making ane that may fitt the constitutions and customes of that church.

4. That the deane of the Chappell look carefullie that all that receave the blessed sacrament ther receave it kneeling, and that ther be a communion held in that our Chappell the first day of everie moneth.

5. That the deane of our Chappell that now is, and so successivelie, come corduelie thither to prayers vpon Sondayes and such holy dayes as that Church observe, in his whyts, and preach so when ever he preacheth, and that he be not absente from thence, bot vpon necessarie occasion of his dyocie or otherwyse, according to the course of his preferment.

6. That these ordours shalbe at our warrant to the deane of our Chappell, That the Lordis of the Privie Counsall, the Lordis of the Session, the Advocat's Clerks, Writters to the Signet, and members of our Colledge of Justice, be commanded to receave the holy communion once everie yeir at leist in that our Chapell royall, kneling for exempls saik to the kingdome, and we lykwyse command the deane aforsaid to mak report yeirlie to ws how we ar obeyed heirin, and by whom, as also if any man shall refuis in what maner he doeth so.

7. That the coupis which ar confiscated to our vse be delyvered to the deane to be keipit by inventarie by him, and in a standard provyded for that purpois, to be vsed at the celebration of the sacrament in our Chapell royall.

To these ordours we shall heirefter add others if we find any more necessarie for the regulating of the service of God ther.

To the Bischop of Dumblane.

Reverend, &c.—We have thoght good for the better ordoring of divyne service to be performed in our Chapell royall ther, to sett doun some Articles vnder our owin hand to be observed heirin, which we send yow heir enclosed, and it is our special pleasur that yow carefullie sie everie thing performed according as we have directed by these our enclosed Articles, and lykwayes that yow certifie to the Lordis of our Privie Counsall if any of these appoynted by our former letters to them to communicat in our Chapell royall shall not accordinglie performe the same to the effect such ordour may be takin by our Counsall therin, as by our saidis former letters to them we did appoynt ; wherin expecting your diligence and care, we bid, &c.

To the Chancellour.

Right, &c.—Wheras vpon the Commission by tryell of some treasonable speeches spokin by the Erle of Airth, we fund sufficient prooff to beleive the same, and in regard lykwayes he by his owin acknowledgment confessed in effect as much, togider with the great fault he committed in his service to the Erldome of Stratherne, and is conteyned vnder his hand in his late submission, we therfor find that he is not worthie to enjoy the charges which he hath formerlie borne in the State by our gift and appoyntment, nor the pension allowed to be payed vnto him out of our Exchequer, wherfor we have thoght good heirby to signifie the same vnto yow: And it is our pleasur that yow requyre the said Erle in our name to surrender vp to our handis these his charges of Presidentschip of the Counsell, Justice Generall, and place in Session, to be disposed of as we shalbe pleased to appoynt, as lykwyes the gift of his said pension, and that in the meane tyme yow confyne him to his owin houses and boundis belonging thervnto, which ar not neir to Halyrudhous, wher the publict meittingis of our State ar keiped.—Dat. vt supra.

To the Tuo Archbischops of S̱t Androis, Glasgow.

Right reverend, &c.—Wheras we intended in so far as may stand with the Lawis in that our king-dome to have the right of patronage of all Churches of erection, and of other Churches not apperteneing to bischoprikis, wherof the patronage did belong to our late dear father, of worthie memorie, to be establisched in our persone, it is our pleasur that yow or ather of yow conven your suffragan bischops, and efter good advyse and deliberatioun had with them, that yow sett doun some solide course wherby a List may be made of all patronages of Churches within everie presbyterie of the kingdome which apperteyned to our said late dear father, and which ar enjoyed or acclamed by any of our subjects, and that with all convenient diligence yow delyver the said list vnder your suffragant bischops handis to our thesaurers principall and deputie or ather of them, to the effect that they may give ordour to our Advocat to quhom we have writtin tuitching that purpois to intend summondis of reduction against these who pretend right thertо; which recommending to your care, we bid, &c.—Dat. vt supra.

To the Thesaurers, Principalls, and Deputie.

Right, &c.—Wheras we intend to have the rents and other things which belong to our Chappell royall restored to the full integritie, and to have all such patronages and Churches establisched in our persone, which by the Lawis of that our kingdome appertened to our late dear father and now appertene vnto ws by our late revocation and the general Lawis of that our kingdome, to which purpois we have gevin ordour of the tuo Archbischopis to give a list vnto yow vnder ther and ther suffragan bischops hands of the saidis patronages, Our pleasur is, that yow call and convene befor yow all persones pretending right to the landis, Churches, or tythis apperteneing to our said Chapell royall as the same shalbe gevin in list vnto yow by the reverend father in God, Adam, bischop of Dumblane, deane of the said Chapell, as lykwyse that yow call for the list of the saidis patronages vnder the saidis Archbischops and bischops handis, and that in both these particulars yow give ordour to our Advocat for intenting and following furth summondis of reduction and improbatioun therof, in so far as can be done by the Lawis of that our kingdome.—Dat. vt supra.

To the Advocat.

Trustie, &c.—Wheras we intend to have all such patronages of Kirkis establisched in our persone, which by the Lawis of that our kingdome appertened to our late dear father, and now appertene by our late revocatioun, and the generall lawis of that our kingdome, to which purpois we have gevin ordour to the tuo Archbischops to give to our Thesaurer and Deputie Thesaurer a list vnder ther and ther suffragan bischops handis of the saidis patronages: And wheras we have gevin ordour to our Thesaurer and deputie to call and convene befor them all persones perteneing right to the landis, churches, or tythis apperteneing to our Chappell royall as the same shalbe gevin in List to them by the Right, &c., the bischop of Dumblane, deane of the said Chapell, to the effect the rents and other thingis belonging therto may be restored to the full integritie : Our pleasur is, that in both these particulars yow proceid according to the advyse and direction of our said Thesaurer and deputie Thesaurer, and that accordinglie yow intend summondis of reduction and improbatioun aganst all such persones as pretend right to the said patronages, and to the landis, tythis, rents or other thingis belonging to our said Chapell royall.—Dat. vt supra.

To the Advocat.

Trustie, &c.—Wheras humble sute hath bene made vnto ws in behalff of the reverend, &c., John, bischop of Ross, that in all actions of Law that shall cum befor our Colledge of Justice for recoverie of the patronages and rents belonging to the bischoprick of Ross, he can have all the lawfull favour can be affoorded vnto him, Our pleasur is, that ather in our name or in name of the said bischop, or in both, as it sall seame most expedient vnto yow, yow compeir and give your best assistance in all actions of Law intended or to be intended by him before our said Colledge for the effect forsaid, wherin as yow shall doe ws acceptable service, so we will tak particular notice therof.—Whythall, 6 Octor 1633.

To the Chancelloun.

Right, &c.—Whems we have bene informed concerneing the abuse of forrane coyne current ther, and great scarcitie of our owin, we ar exceidinglie desyrrous that a speedie remedie may be fund for the same : Therfoir it is our pleasur that togidder with our right trustie consens and counsellours the Erles of Morton and Traquair, our principall and deputie Thesaurers, yow call vnto yow such others of our privie Counsell as yow shall think fittin to the effect that haveing carefullie informed yourselllis of the forsaids abuses in the matter of Coyne, yow may with all consider by what meanes the same may best and most speedelie be reformed, and that with all diligence yow certifie ws of your opinions theranent, that thairefter we may give such further ordour as in our princelie judgment shall be fund most expedient for the weill of that our ancient kingdome ; which recommending earnestlie to your care, we bid, &c.—Whythall, 6 Octor 1633.

To the Session.

Right, &c.—Wheras we ar informed that it will conduce to the good of our service that in all matters that heirefter shall cum befor yow, wherin we have a speciall interest as persewer or defender, or wherin yow shall find ws to have a special and particular interest by any other maner of way that our Thesaurer and deputie Thesaurer be present, Our pleasur is, that befoir yow proceed in any such action, yow hear our saidis officers for our interest ; flor which, &c.—Whythall, 6 Octor 1633.

To the Commissioners of Surranders.

Right, &c.—Wheras we intend to have the few maills of the superioriteis of erections bought to our vse from such persones as did subscryve the generall surrander, conforme to the tenour of our generall determinatioun, and becaus ther hath bene some scrupall moved heirtofoir (as we ar informed) anent what salbe accompted superioritie, which in our judgment is cleir and evident, That all most be compted superioritie to which the titularis of erections had not lawfull right of propertie befor ther erections, or whairof they have not acquyred rights of propertie, and by vertew of these rights have bene in possession thairof befor the generall surrander : Therfoir it is our pleasur that yow proceid in the course for buying vnto ws of the few maills of the saids erections, notwithstanding any doubt or scruple that may be made by the occasion forsaid.—Dat. vt supra.

To the Exchequer.

Right, &c.—Forsmuch as the superioritie of all erections pertenceing to ws by the late act of parliament made in our favours, reserveing to such titularis of erection who subseryved the generall surrander ther few maillis till they be satisfeit therfoir, Conform to our generall determinatioun ; and for as much as diverse of the vassalls of erections (as we ar informed) ar willing to advance the money for buying the few maillis for such yeres efter ther advanceing of the moneyis as in reasone and equitie may compense the money to be advanced by them ; and sieing we approve this course, and ar willing that these who advance have retention of ther few maillis for such space of yeres as yow shall think reasonable : Therfoir it is our pleasur, that yow cans mak publict intimatioun heirof to all our leidges, who have interest, be oppin proclamatioun at the mercat croce of Edinburgh, to the effect such of the vassalls of the Erections as ar or shalbe willing, may cum in befoir yow, and agrie with our Thesaurer and deputie-thesaurer for advanceing of these moneyis, and receave warrant and securitie by act of Exchequer for reduction of the saidis few maillis and few fermes for the space to be agried vpon ; and becaus ther hath bene heirtofoir some scruple made what shalbe compted superioritie, wheranent we signifed our royall pleasur by two severall letters registrat in the bookes of Commission : Therfor we have thought good to acquant yow heirwith, and with the equitie of our proceidingis therin, which is, that in justice all is to be accompted superioritie to which the titulars of erection had not lawfull right of propertie befor ther erections, or wherof they have not acquyred rights of propertie, and by vertew of these rights, have bene in possession therof befor the generall surrander ; and we will yow to proceid according to this rule : And in the meane tyme it is our speciall pleasur, that yow pass no signature of any kirk land perteneing to erection in favour of the saidis Lordis of erection, or in favours of any other, vpon ther resignation, bot of that which was ther propertie, in maner forsaid, to be holdin lykwyse of ws in few ferme, according to our late act of parliament made thereanent ; and becaus we ar informed that some Titulars of erection intend to ingrosse agane to them ther superioriteis, in whole or in part, by procureing resignatiouns from the vassalls in ther favours, whervpon they intend to pass new infeftments, and than to give subalterne rights and few to these who have resigned : It is our will that no such signaturs be exped of the saidis superioriteis in our prejudice ; to which recommending to your care, we bid. &c.—Whythall, 6 Octo^r 1633.

To the Bischop of St Androis.

Wheras we, vpon your remonstrance, have disvnited from the bischoprik of St Androis the landis and kirkis lyeing vpon the south syd of the watter of Forth, haveing erected the same in a severall bischoprik, as by the patent of erection may appear : Our pleasur is, that with all diligence yow assemble the Archbischop of Glasgow, and all the bischops of that our kingdome, representing to them the just reasones moveing yow to petition, and ws to condescend vnto the same, with the great charges and expensses we had vndergone, to provyd a compitent meanes for the honorabill mantenance of that Seat, all which we have done for the good peace and quyetnes of the Church of that kingdome, whairof we did and ever have bene verie cairefull : And that yow caus mak a generall act, with ther vniforme consent, allowing the said disvnion and erection of the said bischoprik vnder ther handis and sealls, which yow shall caus delyver to our Clerk of Register, to be keipit amongst the recordis of that kingdome, to which purpois we have written to them, wherof the letter we have sent yow heirwith, for causeing reid the same in your assemblie ; which recommending vnto your care and diligent performance, we bid, &c.

To the Toun of Edinburgh.

Wheras, of our princelie motive and zeall for the advancement and governement of the Church of that our kingdome, we have, by the advyse of the cheifest of our Clergy thairof, erected at our charges a bischoprik of new, to be called the Bischoprik of Edinburgh, wherby none of your priviledges nor liberteis ar anywayes to be infringed, bot rather preserved and increasced ; and wheras to that purpois it is verie expedient that St Geills churche, designed by ws to be the Cathedrall church of that bischoprik, be ordored as is decent and litt for a church of that eminencie, and according to the first intention of the Erectors and founders thairof, which was to be keiped conforme to the Largnes and conspicuitie of the foundatioun and fabrik, and not to be indecentlie parcelled and disjoyned by walls and partitions, as now it is, without any warrand from any of our Royall predicessours ; Our pleasur is, that with all diligence yow caus raise to the ground the east wall in the said church, and that lykwayes yow cause raise the west wall therin, between this Lambes ensueing, at or befor which tyme we requyre yow to caus finish the new tolbuith, to the effect it may be for the vse of our Excheker, and other Judicatoreis and Commissions, as the tyme and occasion shall requyre.—Dat. vt supra.

To the Commissioners of Tythis.

As we have heirtofoir writtin vnto yow at diverse tymes to proceid with all diligence in the valuatioun of tythis, as a purpois much conduceing to the good of our service, and speciallie the publiet good of that our kingdome : So we ar heirby pleased at this tyme to schaw yow which way it is our pleasur yow proceid in the same, and therfor we command that yow proceid in the valuation of tythes of all the kirkis of erections befor any vther valuation whatsumever, and that, for the quicker expeiding of the said valuation, and other particulars committed to your charge mentionat in your commission, yow appoynt another day of the weik for sitting then Wednsdays and Frydays : All which we speciallie recommend vnto your care.—Whythall, dat. supra.

To the Earles of Mortoun and Traquair, Clerk Register and Advocat.

Wheras it is expedient for the good of our service that a speciall care be had for the preservation of these submissions made vnto ws by the erectours and others persones mentionat in our decrie, tuitching Tythis and surranders, to which purpois we have heirby thoght fitt to requyre yow to consider if by a legall and convenient course the same can be registrat, and if it may be that yow give warrant to our Advocat to delyver them to our Clerk of Register to that effect ; and if by a dew and legall forme they cannot be registrat, that yow caus lykwayes delyver them to our said Clerk of Register to be saiflie keipit amongst the recordis of that kingdome : and for your soe doeing, &c.—Dat. vt supra.

To the Counsell.

Wheras ther was a petition prefered by the toun of Edinburgh to the late Parliament holdin by ws in that our kingdome tuitching the Ministers' stipends in setling therof, wherby it was desyred that the imposing of the same might be layed rateablie vpon the Inhabitants, as they wer fund able, the consideration and determyneing of which petition was remitted vnto yow, sieing the establisching and provydeing of the Church of that toun is a purpois wherof we doe verie much approve : Our pleasur is, that yow consider of the said Petition, and if yow find that the course propounded by them cannot convenientlie tak effect, that the said imposition may be rateablie layed and takin vp according to the proportion of the maill of the said burgh, appoynting therby to everie minister a competent stipend and a commodious duelling-hous, according to ther degree.—Dat. vt supra.

To the Advocat.

Haveing now fullie concluded what we intended at our late being ther for erection of a bischoprik, to be called the bischoprik of Edinburgh, the furtherance of which designe we did then recommend to your care, we have thought good, out of our acknowledgment of your carefull endeavour thairin, whairof we have fund the effects, to give yow harty thanks; and as hitherto we have alwyse fund the lyk care in anything might concerne our service, so we doubt not bot yow will still continew, being the more encouraged by this our particular taking notice of your bypast diligence and affection, which we shalbe readie further to acknowledge when any good occasion shall offer to that purpois: So speciallie recommending vnto your care to ayd and assist from tyme to tyme the bischop of Edinburgh, appoynted by ws, in all things that may concerne the setling and advancement of the bischoprik, we bid, &c.—Dat. vt supra.

To the Commissioners of Surrenders.

Wheras we have directed a bischoprik of new, to be called the bischoprik of Edinburgh, haveing for mantenance thairof appoynted thervnto certane kirks, tythis, and others benefices, as by the patent of erection may appear, to the end the Tythis, personage and viccarage, of the said bischoprik (which is our owin royall wark) may be in the same case and as frie as the tythis of any other bischoprik whatsumever within that our kingdome: Our pleasur is, that yow proceid no otherwayes therin then in the saidis tythis, personage and viccarage, of other bischopriks, and that yow remitt the provisions of the patrimoniall Churches of the said bischoprik to the modificatioun of the bischop and his successours, and that yow certifie the vnjust valuations of any tythis belonging thervnto whensoever the bischop shall intend proces to that effect.—Dat. vt supra.

To the Counsell.

Wheras it is expedient that the blanks in the Commission of the Lawis tuitching the number of persones to mak a session, the Quorum the tyme of endurance, and prorogation be filled vp: It is our will that sevin mak a session: That our Chancellour, the Erles of Mortoun and Traquair, President of the session for the tyme, be of the quorum, and that they, all or any of them, be alwayes present: The tyme of endurance of the said Commissioun to be betuixt this and Witsonday 1635 yeires, and to be prorogat dureing our pleasur: to which purpois we requyre yow to give warrand to our Clerk Register by ane Act of our Privie Counsall for filling vp of the said Commission accordinglie; ffor which, &c.—Dat. vt supra.

To the Toun of Edinburgh.

Wheras for the good of that toun we have establisched our Colledge of Justice, and have now ordeaned our Counsall and Exchecker still to sitt within the same, and wheras it is verie expedient that the recordis and publict registers of that kingdome be keiped and made vse of for our service and good of our subjects neir vnto our saidis Judicatoreis, and the rather becaus the Chartour-hous in our Castell of Edinburgh is not of sufficient capacitie to receave and conteyne all the recordis tuitching our Croun and others concerneing the publict esteat: Our pleasur is, that yow cause provyde a fair and large hous, with tua-thrie rownes, for keiping of the said register and recordis within that toun, which shalbe most vsefull for our service and commodious for our leidges: This faill not to doe with all expedition, as ye tender the good of our service and the good of our toun: We bid, &c.—Dat. vt supra.

II   2 м

To the Erle of Traquair.

Wheras our service is much hindred in the Commission of Tythis, in regard of not admission of ane clerk to the same : It is our will and pleasur, lykas we heirby give vnto yow full power and commission, to call befor yow Mr Wm Hay, Clerk to the said Commission, and admitt him thervnto, receave his oath de fideli administratione, that he may give furth summondis ather at our Advocat or leidges instance, for which these shalbe vnto yow and him a sufficient warrant.—8 Octo^r 1633.

To the Lord Naper.

Right, &c.—Wheras by reasone of the present wants in our Exchequer, and of some of our particular commandements laid at this tyme vpon our Thesaurers, principall and deputie, for imploying moneyis for our present and speciall service, it may fall out that these sowmes of money for which they ar bund vnto yow cannot be so convenientlie payed vnto yow as they intended and yow expect, in which caice we have heirby thoght good to desyre yow not to vrge our saidis officers or ther cautioners with extremitie of Law for payment of your moneyis, vntill the necessitie of our present vrgent affaires may convenientlie permitt them to give yow satisfaction, which we will not tak weill at your handis, and if yow shall find it neidfull thereftter, we will not be wanting in what we can lawfullie and convenientlie doe, for your more speedie satisfaction of these moneyis dew vnto yow : We bid, &c.—Whythall, 8 Octo^r 1633.

The lyk of this precedent letter was writtin to the Lard of Thornetoun, kny^t.—Whythall, 8 Octo^r 1633.

To the Chancellour.

Right, &c.—Wheras ther hath bene ane course taken for reduction of the Erle of Airth his service to the Erldome of Stratherne: It is our pleasur that, haveing conferred with our right, &c. the Erle of Traquair, togidder with him yow call vnto yow our Advocat, and such other advocatts as yow shall think fitting, and that by ther advyse yow informe yourself carefullie in all thingis concerneing the said reduction, to the effect yow may certifie ws of your opinion, not onlie how to annihilat the said service if ther be yitt anything wanting thervnto, bot also if ther be anything extant that may in any kynd give occasion to the lyk errour heirefter, bot such a course be taken as may abolish the memorie of the errour past in this service, and hinder such mistakings in tyme to cum ; ffor doeing whairof in what kynd soever yow shall find most expedient for the good of our service, we doe authorize yow by these presents.—Whythall, 8 Octo^r 1633.

To the Counsell.

Right, &c.—Wheras our late Royall father by severall Acts of Parliament ordeaned that thrugh all the schirrefdomes of that number a selected number of Justices of Peace should be choysen in each schyre for the more quyet and peacable government thairof, setting doun ther Instructions in the Parliament holdin in anno 1617 ; and wheras the same was ratifeid in our late Parliament holdin in Junij last, and commission gevin to yow for granting vnto them such further instructions as the necessitie of the service sall requyre : It is our pleasur that yow furth mak choyse out of each shirrefdome of a compitent number of the best and ablest gentlmen inhabiteing the same ; and that Commissions be issued furth of the Chancerie be the directour thairof to whome the same apperteneth, to be exped vnder the great scall, granting vnto yow and the saidis Justices of Peace in each shirrefdome such power and authoritie for keiping our peace as by the Lawis of that kingdome is due, and what further yow shall think fitt for the quyet and good governement thairof, and that yow cause them be receaved and admitted conforme to the ordour accustomed, and so that they keip the bench at the ordinarie tymes and all other occasions as the necessitie of the charge doeth requyre, appoynting the quorum and Custos Rotulorum : Which recommending to your care, &c.—Whythall, 8 Octo' 1633.

To the Counsell.

Right, &c.—Wheras we vnderstand that the Clerk of Register himselff and his deputies ar and ought to be the sole clerks to the Parliament and all commissions issueing from the same, the decreits to be gevin by the Judges by vertew of these commissions haveing the force of Acts of Parliament, which non can subscryve, nor can be valide without they be subscryved be the Clerk of Register and his deputts : Therfor it is our pleasur that yow receave nor admitt non to be clerkis to the saidis commissions bot such as shalbe presented by our present Clerk of Register : And wheras the keiping of all the publict registers of that kingdome ought and doeth appertene to our said Clerk of Register, and to such as he shall depute to that purpois, It is our will and pleasur that yow caus the havears and keipers of these registers delyver the same to the said Clerk of register, that he may saillie conserve the same for the vse of ws and our leidges.—Whythall, 8 Octo' 1633.

To the Commissioners of Surranders.

Right, &c.—Wheras we vnderstand that the Clerk of Register by himselff and his deputeis ar and ought to be sole clerks to Parliaments and to all commissions issweing from the same, and all decreits gevin by vertew of these commissions have the force of acts of Parliament, and therfor cannot be subscryved bot be him and them : And wheras our trustie and weilbelovit Counsellour Sir Johne Hay of Baro, kny', our present Clerk of Register, hath by his gift presented M' W'' Hay, his sone, to be Clerk to the Commission of Tythis, which present occasione we have of late ratifeid : It is our pleasur and will that yow receave and admitt the said M' W'' Hay to the said office of Clerk to the Commission of Tythes and surrenders, taking his oath de fideli administratione ; and that from tyme to tyme yow receave to be Clerks thervnto such persones and non others as shalbe presented by our said Clerk Register, in caice the said office of Clerkschip to the said Commission shall happin at any tyme to be voyd.—Whythall, 8 Octo' 1633.

To Sir William Seaton, Master and Comptroller generall of his Ma'''' Posts in Scotland.

It is our pleasur that by vertew of your office yow have of ws as master and Comptroller generall of our posts in Scotland yow authorize and requyre for the good of our service all the posts in the road from Edinburgh to Berwick to answer and send to and from our Court all such pacquetts and letters which they shall receave vnder the subscription of our trustie and weilbelovit Counsellour Sir John Hay. Whythall, 8 Octo' 1633.

To the Exchequer.

Right, &c.—Wheras we vnderstand from our right, &c. the E. of Mar that he and his sone, the Lord Erskene, had, for releiff of ther debts lying vpon the house of Mar, agried to sell to some of ther tennents in few-forme some Landis of theris which hold ward of ws, and had gevin satisfaction for the same from some of them, bot ar stopped in proceiding in the lyk course with the rest by reasone of ane act of our late Parliament prohibiteing any wardlands holdin of ws to be fewed by our vassalls without our consent : In regard of the good services done to our late royall father and ws by the said erle, and to the effect his hous by meanes arysing vpoun his owin revennes may subsist, Our pleasur is, that yow allow them to proceid in that course which they have alreadie begun for fewing of the Landis following, viz.—Ther Landis of the brae of Mar, Strathdee, Kildrumie, and Migvie in Cromar, and that yow give way to ane warrant necessarie to that effect.—Whythall, 11 Octo^r 1633.

L. Buchan.

A Letter was direct to the Counsell for admitting the bischop of Ross to be Privie Counsellour, as lykwayes to the bischop of Murray.—11 Octo^r 1633.

To the Archbischop of Glasgow.

Right, &c.—Haveing bene petitioned by the Lo^d Semple humblie schawing ws that the late Archbischop of Glasgow, your predicessour, intendit to proceid aganst him with the censures of the Church, and being loath to losse ane of his qualitie so long as ther remaneth hope to reclame him by fair meanes : Our pleasur is, that yow grant him yit some further delay vntill we may be particularlie informed by yow of his cariage and the reasones of the proceidings vsed against him, And that in the meane tyme yow suspend all further censure till our pleasur shalbe knowen efter your report to ws heirvpon.—Whythall, 12 Octo^r 1633.

To the Vice President of York.

Trustie, &c. and weilbeloved. Wheras we ar informed that ane Andro Ainstey, our subject in Scotland, is a sutter to yow to have justice administred according to the Lawis of this our kingdome vpon a band of moneyis payed by him to one Somervell ther, as suretie for ane Robsone, duelling in Northumberland, and that it is questioned (in regard the band is made according to the Scotts forme) if yow can be competent judge in that sute : Vnderstanding that our subjects heir have the benefite of the lawis of Scotland, and the executiouns vpon landis made according to the forme of this kingdome, and being willing that a reciprocall course of justice be observed heir vpon landis made according to the forme of that kingdome, we ar heirby pleased effectuallie to recommend vnto yow to proceid according to equitie in causeing dew and tymelie execution of justice be vsed vpon the said band, as if it wer made according to the forme of this our kingdome, and that heirefter the lyk course be observed when any such occasion shall occure befor yow : wherin not doubting of your conformitie to this our pleasur, we bid yow farewell.—Whythall, 15 Octo^r 1633.

To the Advocat.

Trustie, &c.—Being willing that the reverend father in God the bischop of Dumblane, deane of our Chappell, and his successours, deanes thairof, be freed from hence furth of all taxationes and impositions whatsoever in so far as may concerne ther owin personall esteats and goodis, and as for the rents payable to them belonging to the said Chappell, we ar lykwayes willing that they have what favour may be convenientlie affurded vnto them without prejudice of the course established for the levyeing of our

Taxations : Our pleasur is, that haveing to this purpois conferred with our right, &c. the Erles of Morton and Traquair, our Thesaurers principall and deputie, our Clerk of Register, and the said bischop, yow draw vp such a warrand to be signed by ws, and to pass our seallis as shalbe sufficient for frieing of him and them of the premisses, or what further they and yow in your opinions think we may convenientlie doe ; and that yow send the same docat by yow for our hand to be returned and exped accordinglie. Whythall, 15 Octo^r 1633.

Carolus Dei gratia Scotiæ Angliæ Franciæ et Hiberniæ rex fideique defensor dilectis nobis in Christo decano et capitulo ecclesiæ Cathedralis Insularum Salutem Ex parte vestra nobis humiliter et supplicatum vt cum ecclesia predicta per transportationem Reverendi patris in Christo Joannis vltimi ejus Episcopi, jam vacet et pastoris solatio sit destituta, alium vobis eligendi episcopum et pastorem licentiam nostram concedere dignaremur, Nos precibus vestris in hac parte favorabiliter inclinantes, alium vobis duximus concedendum rogantes ac in fide et dilectione quibus nobis tenemini precipientes quod talem vobis eligatis in Episcopum et pastorem qui Deo devotus nobisque et regno nostro vtilis et fidelis existat : In cujus rei testimonium has nostras literas fidei facimus patentes.—Teste meipso Apud, &c.

To the Deane and Chaptour of the Yles.

Trustie, &c.—Wheras the Bischoprik of the Yles is voyd by transportatioun of the reverend father in God Johne, late Bischop thairof, we latt yow wit that calling to mynd the vertew, learneing, and other good qualiteis of our trustie Mr Neill Campbell, Minister at Kilmichaell in Glasrie, sone lawfull of vmquhill Mr Neill Campbell, late bishope of Argyll, We have thoght good by these our letters to name and recommend him vnto yow, to be electit and choysen to the said bischoprik of the Yles, whervnto the Abacie of Icolmekill and pryorie of Ardchattan ar annexed : Therfoir we pray and requyre yow vpon recept heirof to proceid to your election, and according to the Lawis of that realme, and our Conge d'eslire sent heirwith, and the same election to be so made to certifie ws therof vnder your common seall.—Gevin 17th Octo^r 1633.

Carolus Dei gratia, &c. Dilectis nobis in Christo Decano et capitulo ecclesiæ Cathedralis Edinburgi Salutem : Quum novum Episcopatum ereximus Episcopatum Edinburgi nuncupandum, nobisque ex parte vestra humiliter sit supplicatum, vt cum Ecclesia predicta pastoris solatio sit destituta, Episcopum vobis eligendi et pastorem licentiam nostram concedere dignaremur ; Nos animum ad supplicationem istam favorabiliter inclinantes, Episcopum vobis concedendum duximus. Rogantes ac in fide et dilectione quibus nobis tenemini precipientes, quod talem vobis eligatis Episcopum et pastorem qui Deo devotus nobisque et regno vtilis fidelis existat : In cujus rei testimonium has nostras literas fidei facimus patentes.—Teste meipso Apud Whythall, 17 Octo^r 1633.

To the Deane and Chaptour of Edinburgh.

Trustie, &c.—Wheras we have erected a bischoprik of new, to be called the bischoprik of Edinburgh, we latt yow wit that calling to our remembrance the vertew, learning, and other good qualiteis of our trustie and weilbeloved Doctor Wm Forbes, preacher at Aberdene, we have thoght good by these our letters to name and recommend him to yow to be electit and choysen to the said bischoprik of Edinburgh :

Therfor we pray and requyre yow that vpon the recept heirof yow proceid to your election according to the Lawis of that our realme and our Conge d'eslire sent vnto yow heirwith, and the same election so made to certifie ws thairof vnder your common seall.—Gevin, &c.

To the Archbischop of Sᵗ Androis.

Right, &c.—Wheras we have bene pleased to have erected a new bishoprik, to be called the bishoprik of Edinburgh, and have named and recommended our trustie Docter William Forbes, preacher at Aberdene, vnto the deane and chaptour thairof, to be elected and choysen by them to the said bishoprik, according to the Lawis of that our kingdome and conge d'eslire sent to them for that effect : These ar to requyre yow that with all possible diligence yow cans call and convene the said deane and chaptour for his admission, that furthwith he may be fullie establisched in that See, for the more speedie enabling of him for our service in that charge.—Whythall, 17 Octor 1633.

Commission.

Wheras our right, &c. the Erle of Seafort hath submitted himselff to be disposed of by ws tuitching our right to the Lewis, and what we shall think fitt to determyne tuitching his clame and interest therin : To the effect that we may be the better informed concerneing the premisses and the particulars efter mentionat, Our pleasur is, and we doe heirby give full power and commission to yow, whois names are particularlie under expressed, to meitt and convene at such tymes and places as yow shall find meit and necessarie, and ther to advyse and consider of our said right to the said Iland, and of the said Erle his clayme and interest therin, the rentall therof, the arreiris of the few-dewteis of the same payable vnto ws, what portion of Land therin yow think fitt that we reserve for our owin particular vse, to be disposed of as we shall think fitt, the commoditeis and lyeing thairof most necessarie for our good and service, and what part thairof is equitable for ws to give and confirme vnto him ; the tenour, maner, and conditions to be mentioned in the disposition most necessarie for our service ; and to report the same, sealled vnto ws vnder your handis, betnixt this and the fyft day of Aprill ensueing, that, efter dew consideratioun had therin by ws, we may give such further ordour tuitching the same as we shall find caus.—Gevin at Whythall, the 17 Octor 1633.

To . . . the Erles of Kynnoull, Morton, and Traquair, Sir John Hay of Baro, and Mr Th. Hope.

To the Session.

Right, &c.—It being our cheiff care that Justice may be dewlie administred, and vnderstanding that the President's place amongst yow is voyd by the death of Sir James Skene, out of the desyre we have that a man fitt for the same be provydit thervnto, as our late dear father and ourselllis wer wont to doe in the lyk cases, we have thoght meitt heirby to recommend vnto yow Sir Robert Spottiswood as a persone for his sufficiencie and experience able to bear that charge : So not doubting bot his owin abiliteis, weill knowen to yow all, being accompanied with our owin recommendatioun, will preuiall, and requyreing yow all to have a speriall care to discharge yourselllis faythfullie in that charge wherwith yow ar entrusted by ws : Which, &c.—[No date.]

To the Archbishop of St Androis.

Right, &c.—Wheras we ar informed that vmquhil Mr John Rutherfurd, preacher, did, by ordour of our late dear father, manteyne le publict disputts the question of our authoritie in church affaires, proveing the same by the judgment of the Doctours of the Church, primitive and moderne, and that our royall father intendit for that caus to have recompensed him : To which purpois Mr John Rutherfurd, his sone, hath bene ane humble sutter that we wold so far tak notice of his father's good service therin as to present him to the first vacand church at our gift, and the rather becaus his abilitie for such a charge is proved by testimoneis of the presbiters of St Androis and Dundie, and by one vnder your owin hand : These considerations being inducements to ws to hearken to his demand, we ar heirby pleased effectuallie to recommend him vnto yow that he be preferred to the first vacand church within your dyocie on the north syd of the Forth which is at our gift; And to that effect that yow send a presentation vnder your hand when any church shall vaik : Which recommending to your care, &c.—Whythall, 17 Octor 1632.

To Sir Johne Hay.

Trustie, &c.—We haveing allowed and approven the signature of erection of the bischoprik of Edinburgh, and mortification of the particulars and all the liberteis and clausses therin mentioned, Our pleasur is, that with all diligence yow exped throw the Exchequer and Sealls the signature of Mortification, and that yow lay vp one thairof in the Chartour-house in our Castell of Edinburgh, and delyver ane vther to the bischop of Edinburgh, who shalbe made choyse for that bischoprik : For doeing, &c.—Whythall, 17th Octor 1633.

Our pleasur is, and we doe heirby will and requyre yow to call for and receave from our Advocat the submissions made vnto ws by the erectours and other persones mentioned in our decrie concerneing tythis and surrenders, and that yow putt the same in our Charter-house in the Castell of Edinburgh, to be saitlie keiped amongst the recordis of that our kingdome, and that registrat or vnregistrat as it shalbe condescended on by these to whome we have given warrand tuitching that purpois.—Whythall, 17 Octor 1633.

To Sir Johne Hay.

Our pleasur is, and we doe heirby will and requyre yow, that yow convene the vassalls of the Abbaceis of Halyrudhous and New Abay, and by ther consent, conforme to the Act of Parliament, yow caus mak ane extant roll for payment of his Mateis extents and releiff of the bischoprik of Edinburgh.—Whythall, 17 Octor 1633.

To Sir Wm Hay.

Our pleasur is, and we do heirby will and requyre yow to intromett with and receave the few maills, dewteis, and other rents of the Abbaceis of Halyrudhous and Newabey from the Vassalls and others adebtit in payment therof till ther be a bischop of Edinburgh establisched by ws to whome we will yow to mak accompt, reckonyng, and payment thairof ; ffor doeing whairof these presents shalbe vnto yow for receaving of the saidis dewteis, and to the saidis Vassalls and others for delyverie of the same to yow ane sufficient warrand and discharge.—Whythall, 17 Octo^r 1633.

To the Exchequer.

Right, &c.—Wheras diverse good and proffitable acts and statuts wer made in our favours in our late Parliament holdin in the moneth of Junij last, and speciallie anent the superioriteis of erectiones, regaliteis of erectiones, changeing of holdingis from ward in blensch or Taxt wards, annulling of Infeftments of our annexed propertie disponed by ane vther holding nor in few ferme, prohibition to our vassalls to dispone ward Lands without our consent ; And ane act that all the kirk lands perteneing in propertie to Lordis of erection shall hold of ws in few ferme for payment of the old few ferme dewteis : Therfoir it is our speciall pleasur that no signature be past nor exped in Exchequer which may derogate to the saidis acts and statutis made in our favours except we be speciallie consulted theranent, and that yow have our particular warrant to that effect : And wheras it hath bene enacted in Exchequer that no allowance should be gevin efter the date of the said Act to any Compter of no sowme or sowmes payed to whatsumever persones, bot onlie of the sowmes reallie payed in Exchequer to the Lo$^{\cdot}$ Thesaurer, and receavers of our rents, till it should be otherwayes ordeaned by yow, We doe approve the said act, and it is our pleasur that it continew so till our further pleasur be signifeid, or yow shall find speciall reasone to the contrarie. —Whythall, 17 Octo^r 1633.

These conteyne ane Infeftment granted to Sir Archibald Achiesone of the salt panes, the girnelhous, and salthous, with the ludgeing and yaird thairto belonging, lyand in Prestonpanes, and of the Lands of Broomehills and Leeterclough, lyand within the baronie of Prestongrange, All which was apprysed be him from vmquhill Mark Achiesone of Broomhills in his owin lyftyme, to be now holdin by the said Sir Ar^d Achiesone and his aires in few ferme.—Whythall, 18 Octo^r 1633.

To the Session.

Right, &c.—We vnderstand that the toun of Edinburgh haveing intended ane action befor yow tuitching the office of high Constabularie of that our kingdome, for tryeing wherof we wer pleased not long agoe to grant a commission, sieing it is a purpois which in honour doeth verie much concerne the estate of that our antient kingdome, we ar resolved, if ther be any just matter of complaynt against the proceidings alreadie vsit therein by our Counsall, to tak the same to our serious consideration, and therefter to give such further ordour therein as we shall find caus : Therfoir our pleasur is, and we doe heirby will and requyre yow not to proceed nor medle in that action vnless yow shalbe particuliarlie warranted by ws ; We bid, &c.—Whythall, 18 Octo^r 1633.

It is our pleasur that yow examyne what part of the moneys due by ws vnto our right, &c. the Erle of Stirling hath bene payed vnto him, and the accompt of the copper coyn being dewlie made, that yow certifie what is lyklie extend vnto for his vse, that ane vther course may be takin for his payment, wher it may not by that meanes be dew ; and if he cannot be convenientlie payed at this time, nor particular assignement be made vnto him for the same, lest his creditours at this time, mistrusting our intention to pay him, may persew him or your freindis, whom we vnderstand to be bund as sureteis for him : It is our pleasur, to the effect he may not suffer for so much as is due by ws, yow certifie ws what course ye think best for the tyme, ather for payment of the principall to his creditours, or of some part therof ; and that yow tak such course as yow shall think best to satisfie them for ther forbearing the same, that they may not charge him till we appoynt his payment some other way, which we warrand yow heirby to allow out of the benefite arrysing out of the copper coyne, that he may reap the benefite we intend for him, according to our warrand ; for doeing whairof, &c.—Whythall, 18 Octo^r 1633.

To Sir John Hay.

Trustie, &c.—Wheras it was declared by ane act of our late parliament that what ordour soever we should be pleased to appoynt for the apperrell of churchmen, and should send it in writt to our Clerk Register, should be a sufficient warrand for inserting the same in the bookis of parliament, to have the strenth of ane act therof ; we have now determined the same according to the warrand heirin enclosed, signed both above and vnderneath with our owin hand : And it is our pleasur, that accordinglie yow insert this our enclosed ordour concerneing ther habits in the bookis of parliament to have the strenth of ane act therof in all tyme comeing : For doeing quherof, &c.—Whythall, 18th Octo^r 1833.

The Ordour appoynted by his Maties for the Apperrell of Churchmen of Scotland, to be insert in the Books of Parliament, conforme to the Act of the late Parliament made theranent.

It is our pleasur that all the Lordis, Archbishops, and Bischops within that our kingdome of Scotland shall in all publict places wear goones with standing cappis (such as they vsed at our late being ther) and cassoks, and the inferiour Clergy, especiallie efter they have takin the degrie of doctours and batchellours in divinitie, or be preachers in any toun, shall wear the same for a fascheon, bot for worthie, according to ther meanes, and no typpettis, vnless they be doctours : And farder, our pleasur is, that the Archbischops and bischops shall, in all churches wher they shall cum in tyme of divyne service or sermones, be in whytts, that is, in a rockel or sleives, as they did wear it at the tyme of our Coronatioun, and especiallie whensoever they administer the holy communioun or preach, and they shall lykwyse provyde themselftis a Climer (that is a sattin or taffetie gowne without lyneing or sleives) to be worne over ther whytts, and the tyme of ther consecration : And we will that all Archbischops and bischops aforsaid, that ar of our privie counsell or of our session, shall cum and sitt ther in ther whytts, and manteane the gravitie of ther places : And for all inferiour clergiemen, we will they preach in ther blak gownes, bot when the reid divyne service, christen, burie, or administer the sacraments of the Lordis supper, they shall wear ther surplis, and if they be doctours, ther tippettis over them ; and as weill Archbischops and bischops as other ministers when they administer the holie communion in our chappell royall, or any cathedrall church within that our kingdome, shall wear copes ; and not onlie they bot all inferiour priests shall, at tymes and places befoir mentioned, vse ther square coppes, especiallie in all our Vniversiteis.—Whythall, 18 Octo^r 1633.

To the Counsell.

Right, &c.—Wheras we ar informed that ane John Meldrum, being convict as guiltie of the burneing of the tour of Frendraught, hath suffered death for the same, in regard it is thoght verie vnliklie that such ane odious and barbarous fact could be committed by one persone without complices therin, which the said Meldrum would not confess (as we ar informed), we think it verie expedient, according as we have bene pleased to signifie at diverse tymes heirtofoir, that all further care and diligence be vsed for trycing of that bussines ; to which purpois our pleasur is that, ather by yourselfis or by such a number as yow shall think fitt to select amongst yow, yow try and examyne all such persones as shalbe gevin vp to yow by our right, &c. the Marqueis of Huntlie or any other in this behalff aganst whom yow shall find that ther be presumptions or guiltines of the said fact : For which. &c.—Whythall, 28 Octo⟨r⟩ 1633.

To the Advocat.

Trustie, &c.—Wheras humble sute hath bene made vnto ws in behalff of the right reverend, &c. Archbischop of Glasgow for ratiefieing of tuo severall pensions granted vnto him, which we ar willing to doe if that which is desyred be conforme to the originall : Our pleasur is, that yow consider therof, and finding the same to be agrieable to what was formerlie granted, yow draw vp such ratifications therof to pas vnder our royall signature as may secure the said Archbischop of the premisses, and send the same vnto ws ducat by yow ; for which these presents, &c.—Whythall, 28 October 1633.

To the Counsell.

Right, &c.—At onr being of late in that our kingdome we wer pleased to grant to M⟨r⟩ W⟨m⟩ Wischart, minister at Leith, a gift of Preceptorie of S⟨t⟩ Antones for the benefite of the hospitall of Leith and ther kirk session, for the vse quherof some rents of that Preceptorie (as we ar informed) ar still accustomed to be payed, and that the remanent of that benefice hath bene of a long tyme suppressed, being disposed of to some persone by our late royall father hearing that the said M⟨r⟩ Williame hath passed the gift in his owin name, wherby not onlie that part of the said benefice dedicated to the hospitall and kirk session may by tyme be wrested to a particular from the intended publict vse, but that lykwyse our right, &c. the Erle of Dumfermeling wilbe prejudged in his right and possessioun of certane landis now holdin of ws, which ancientlie belonged to that Preceptorie, and wer acquyred (as we ar informed) by his late father vpon valuable consideration : Our pleasur is, that haveing called the pairties interested befor yow, yow deall with them to submitt the differences heirin vnto yourselfis or such of your owin number as yow shall appoynt for taking a fair course to setle the same, so that no prejudice may ensue by the said gift to the said hospitall, kirk session, or to the said Erle ; bot if the said M⟨r⟩ W⟨m⟩ will not condescend thervnto, adverteis ws therof, and with your opinions concerneing the same, and in the meane tyme that yow give ordour to stop any proceidings tuitching the same in any of our Judicatoreis, till our further pleasur be signifeid therin.—Whythall, 28 Octo⟨r⟩ 1633.

To the Counsell.

Right, &c.—Wheras we vnderstand that our late royall father did wryt to his Privie Counsall signifieing that though he gave warrant for ane Act to pass in Parliament in favouris of Phisitiannes, for restrayneing the practeis of ignorant and vnskilfull persones, yit it was not his meaneing that they should prejudge the Chyrurgianes in ther ancient and lawfull priviledges, To which purpois a complaynt hath bene made to ws in behalff of the Chyrurgians, that they may not be wronged as is intended by the Phisitianes ; we being willing to tak the lyk course that our late father did, and that none of them doe trench vpon others by making vse of the mistereis and skill peculiar to ther severall arts, Our pleasur is, that yow call the cheiff of both within Edinburgh and the Cannogait befoir yow, and so compose and ordour the differences amongst them as they may not wroug ane another, vpon pane of such penelteis as yow shall think fitt to preseryve ; and wheras the Chyrurgianes have petitioned that we would be pleased to recommend to yow to caus setle and ratifie some overturis amongst themselllis and ther apprentice for the better dischargeing of ther trade and good of our subjects, according to the enclosed note of ther demandis, Our pleasur is, that yow consider therof, recommending vnto yow to caus such of them be setled and ordered as yow vpon hearing them shall condescend vpon ; which recommending, &c.— Whythall, 28 Octo' 1633.

To the Advocat.

Trustie, &c.—Wheras we vnderstand by our right, &c. the Erle of Roxbrugh that he hath conferred with yow concerneing the Abbacie of Kelso, which he was allowed by ws to doe, It is our pleasur that yow consider of the propositions made by him, and therefter certifie ws what in your opinion is fitt for ws to doe therin for our good, wher it may be done without our prejudice ; so expecting, &c.—Whythall, 28 Octo' 1633.

To the Erle of Traquair and Sir John Hay.

Right, &c.—As we wer formerlie pleased to requyre yow to deall with the Provest, Bailleis, and Counsell of Edinburgh for taking from ws that bargane concerneing the baronie of Broughton, so now it is our pleasur that yow finallie conclude with them tuitching ther resolution in that purpois, receaveing ther answer vnder ther handis, to the end that if they doe refuis to accept of the same, we may tak such notice therof by disposing of it otherwayes as may be most expedient for our relieff and the good of our service.—Whythall, 28 Octo' 1633.

To the Archbishop of Glasgow.

Right reverend, &c.—Being informed by our right, &c. the Erle of Roxburght that Francis Stewart is adverteised that ane M' Thomas Abernethie, preacher, hath maliciouslie and vntruelie reported wordis of the said Erle for movving of words of forder differences between them, which we have bene pleased to reconceill with so much panes : It is our pleasur that, haveing considered the informatioun of these wordis to be govin yow by the said Erle, yow call the said M' Thomas befoir yow, and efter due examination, if yow find him guiltie of that which is alledged against him, that yow give ordour for punisching of him, in so far as the lawis or ordours of the Churche will allow, and as is compitent for yow to doe ; And if any further warrand be requyred or requisit from ws heirin, it shalbe granted vpon your adverteisment that is necessarie to terrifie all sedetiouslie disposed persones that would brew discord amongst others : Which recommending to your care, we bid, &c.—Whythall, 28 Octo' 1633.

To the Archbishop of S' Androis.

Right reverend, &c.—Haveing sene the copie of a Petition which was sent by yow to our trustie and weilbelovit servant Patrik Maull, one of our bedchalmer, that it might be shawin by him vnto ws, we sie therby how sedetiouslie such persones ar disposed that dar presume to have any such thing com into our sight : As we thank yow verie hartelie for the care yow have had to acquant ws therwith, so it is our pleasur that yow informe yourselff as far as yow can further to learne what doeth concerne the same in tryeing who hath bene the authour therof, or who ar accessorie thervnto, that vpon due tryell ther may be a course accordinglie taken with them.—[No date.]

To the Bischop of the Iles.

Reverend father in God—Haveing presented yow to the Bischoprik of the Iles, wherby our right, &c. the Marqueis of Hamiltoun will have occasion, by himselff, his freindis or tennents, to mak vse of your freindschip in diverse particulars falling out within the boundis of our bischoprik, we ar herby pleased effectuallie to recommend vnto yow that, what may concerne him or them, yow will befreind them therin in what yow can doe, so it be with the preservation of the Episcopall estate and proffite, which we will tak as acceptable service done vnto ws.—Whythall, first No^r 1633.

Our Soverane Lord, now efter his generall revocation made in the last Parliament holdin at Edinburgh in the moneth of Junij last bygane, considering the good, true, faythfull, and diligent service done to his Matie by his weilbeloved servitour Mr Alex^r Hay, ane of the ordiner Clerks of session within the kingdome of Scotland: And to give him the better encouragment to continew in the lyk ductifull service in tyme comeing, with advyse and consent of his highnes' right, &c. the Erle of Morton, Johne, Erle of Traquair, and with the advyse of the remanent, &c., Ordeanes a letter to be made vnder his Ma^{teis} privie seall to the said Mr Alex^r Hay, Ratificand, approveand, and confirmeand, Lykas by the tenour heirof our said soverane Lord, with advyse and consent forsaid, ratifeis and approves the fie of 40^{lib} sterling granted by his Matie to the said Mr Alex^r dureing all the dayes of his lyftyme for serveing his Matie as sole Clerk in sessioun to all his Ma^{teis} affaires occurring in that Judicatorie, incident and belonging to the place of ane Clerk ther, conforme to his Ma^{teis} gift granted to the said Mr Alex^r thervpon of the date at Whythall the 19 of Feb^r 1632, Ratificand and approveand the said gift in all poynts, and admittand this present ratificatioun to be als sufficient as if the samyne wer heir ingrossed: And sicklyk our said Soveragne Lord, with advyse and consent forsaid for the caus above writtin, hath of new gevin and granted, and by the tenour heirof gives and grants, to the said Mr Alex^r the said fie of 40^{lib} money forsaid, to be bruiked and possest by him dureing all the dayes of his lyftyme, to be payed furth of the readiest of whatsumever his Ma^{teis} rents and casualiteis within the kingdome, at tua termes of the yeir, Witsonday and Mertimes, be equall portiones, begineand the first termes payment at the feist and terme of Witsonday last bypast, and so furth yeirlie and termelie to continew dureing all the dayes of his said lyftyme; With power to the said Mr Alex^r to ask, crave, and receave the same, yeirlie and termelie, as said is: Commanding the Lordis, Auditours, and Commissioners of his highnes' Exchequer present, or who shalhappin to be for the tyme, to thankfullie allow the payment so to be made to the said Mr Alex^r of the said fie, for the whilk his discharge vpon the recept thairof, togidder with his Ma^{teis} letter of gift, to be produced and registrat in the books of Exeheker, shalbe ane sufficient warrand, and that the said Letter be extendit with all clauses neidfull.—Whythall, 12 No^r 1633.

> These ratifie to Mr Alex^r Hay, ane of the ordiner Clerks of Session, the fie of 40^{lib} sterling for serveing your Matie as sole Clerk in session to all your Ma^{teis} affaires occurring in that Judicatorie, incident and belonging to the Office of ane clerk ther, conforme to your Ma^{teis} gift formerlie granted thervpoun.

Our Soverane Lord, efter all his hynes' revocatioun, generall and speciall and namelie efter his highnes' revocatioun made and declaret in his highnes' last Parliament holdin at Edinburgh in the moneth of Junij last bygane, remembring the good, true, and thankfull service done to his Matie by vnquhill

Captane Archibald Dowglas, Orleanes, with advyse and consent of his highnes the right, &c. the Erle of Morton, Johne, Erle of Traquair, and the remanent Lordis and others Commissioners of Excheker, a Letter to be made vnder the privie seall in dew forme, Ratifieand agane and approveand, and for his M^tie and successours perpetuallie confirmeand the assignement formerlie ratifeid by his Matie made by the said vmquhill Ar^d Dowglas to his lawfull sister Elizabeth, of his pension of two thowsand merkis scottis yeirlie dureing his lyftyme following the feist and terme of Witsonday in anno 1633, togidder with the arreares of the said pension dew to him at the date of the Letter of Assignement made thervpon, to be receaved and vplifted by his factours and others in his name, haveing hir power to that effect, yeirlie and termelie, at the feist of Witsonday and Mertimes, be equall portionis, as the Letter of the said vmquhill Captane Ar^d Dowglas' gift at more lenth beires, and that furth of the first and readiest of the rents and casualiteis of the thesaurie and comptrollerie of the said kingdome from the said Thesaurer and Comptroller thairof present and being for the tyme : And moreover our said Soveragne Lord, with advyse and consent forsaid, wills and grants, and for his heyres and successours decernes and ordanes, that the said Assignement and this Ratification of his Matie agane thairof is and shalbe a sufficient right and securitie for the said Elizabeth Dowglas for bruiking and vptaking of the said pension for the space of the saidis two yeires allanerlie, and the arreares thairof as is above writtin, Notwithstanding of his highnes' revocatioun, generall and speciall, made in the said Parliament or otherwayes, with command in the said Letter to the saidis thesaurers, Principall and deputie, and others his Maties receavers of the said kingdome, to answer, obey, and mak thankfull payment to the said Elizabeth Dowglas or hir forsaidis of the said pension for two yeires, and arreares thairof, conforme to the assignement made to the said Elizabeth by hir said vmquhill brother, and that vpoun hir owin or hir assigneyis acquittances and discherges, whilk his Matie heirby onleanes the Auditours of Excheqer ther to allow, and the said Letter to be extendit in the best forme, with supplement of all clausses neidfull.—Whythall, 12 No^r 1633.

> Your Matie doe heirby Ratifie agane ane assignement formerlie
> ratifeid by your Matie made by vmquhill Archibald Dowglas
> to his sister Elizabeth Dowglas of his pension of 2000 merks
> Scotts, for the space of two yeirs allanerlie nixt and immediatlie
> following the feist and terme of Witsonday anno 1631 yeires,
> togidder with all the arreares of the same due to him at the
> making of the said assignement.

These conteyne ane Ratification of the Letter of Pension granted by your Matie to Sir William Murray and Dame Margaret Alexander, his spous, dureing ather of ther lyftymes, of ane yeirlie pension of 1200^lib scotts money, with ane other gift of the said pension, In respect it is in recompense of the true and faythfull service of his two vncles, Johne and Patrik Schawis, who wer shayne and killed in the service of your Ma^ies dearest father, by vmquhill Francis, sometyme Erle of Bothwell.

These ratifie to Mr Johne Oliphant, who was agent and solister to your Ma^ies late royall father, and now to your Ma^ies self, Your Ma^ies gift vnto him of that office, and a former ratificatioun thervpoun, with the fie of 500 merkes scotts.—Whythall, 12 No^r 1633.

Your Matie doe heirby ratifie a pension of 1200^lib Scotts to Sir James Stewart, brother to the late Erle of Orkney.—Whythall, 12 No^r 1633.

These in lieu of a locall assignement of a pension of 727^lib. 10^s scotts, and 24 bolls oatts granted by your Ma^teis father Sir Johne Prestoun of Pennycuik, kny^t and baronet, and latelie ratifeid by your Ma^teis grant vnto him a pension of 727 : 10s. Scotts, equivalent to the former, to be payed out of the Excheker at Witsondey and Mertimes, according to the maner approved ; The first termes payment at Witsondey 1633.

To the Session.

Right, &c.—Being informed that the action intendit befor yow in our name for reduction of the Infeftments of the heretable Isherie of our Exchequer, procured to tak away our right of placeing of ane immediate officer of ours in that charge, hath for a long tyme depended befor yow, and as yit doth remane vndecydit, to the prejudice of our right and of the persone whom of late we have appoynted to discharge that office : Therfor we have thoght good by these presents to recommend the said action to your speciall care that Justice may be administred therein, with all lawfull and convenient disposition, that no advantage be gottin by delay, in so far as lawfullie can be avoyded, that our right may be re-establisched in setling our servant in that charge.—Whythall, 12 No^r 1633.

To the Thesaurer and Deputie.

Right, &c.—Wheras Sir Wm Seaton of Kylsmure, kny^t, hath bene a faythfull and antient servand of our late deir father, did in his tyme tak speciall notice of the services done vnto him by the said Sir William, haveing bestowed vpon him and his tuo sones, W^m and John Setones, some pensions which we have bene pleased at this time to ratifie : Our pleasur is, that yow examyne what arrearis of these pensions ar due vnto them, and that yow pay the same with as much diligence as may be, togidder with the saids pensions yeirlie thereftar, according to our said father's gifts or ouris ; ffor which these presents shalbe vnto yow or ather of yow a sufficient warrand and discherge.—Whythall, 12 No^r 1633.

To the Session.

Right, &c.—The enclosed petition sent by ws to be considered vpon by yow, requyreing nothing but a speedie decision according to Justice, and therfor semeing vnto ws equitable, we ar heirby pleased to recommend vnto yow that caus in a serious maner, that cutting off all vnnecessarie delays, Justice, without respect of persones, may be administred with expedition : Which recommending, &c.—Whythall.

To the Thesaurer.

Right, &c.—Wheras we ar informed that it pleased our late royall father to grant to vmquhill Mr James Duncansone, a precept of 2500^lib. Scotts for good service done by him as ane of his ordinarie preichers, and that we, vpon sight of that precept, comiserating the estate of the petitioner, did requyre to be certified of the most convenient way for hir satisfaction, schoe haveing now represented vnto ws by petition, which we have sent yow to consider, that schoe, being a poore widow, haveing the charge of ten children, cannot longer subsist without some course be taken for . . .

To the Advocat.

Trustie, &c.—Being willing to secure Sir George Fletcher, kny^t, receaver of our rents in that our kinglome, of the pension latelie granted by ws, our pleasur is, that yow draw vp a Ratification thairof, a grieving in substance with our gift, and send the same, doeated by yow, to be signed by ws, and if at any tyme heireftor any of our subjects shall desyre yow to doeat any ratificatiouns of ther pension, our further pleasur is, that befoir yow doe the same yow acquant our secretarie therwith, to be imparted vnto ws at our best conveniencie, wherypon, if we shall find caus to approve therof, our plesur therfor therein signifeid by him vnto yow shalbe sufficient warrand for your doeateing and returneing the same thither to be exped by ws.—Whythall, 12 No⁺ 1633.

Your Matie doeth heirby dispone to Patrik Blak, your Chalmerlane of Fyff, his aires and assigneyis, the office thairof, with the accustomed fee of 200^lib Scotts, and four chalders wheat and bear, redimable to your Ma^teis vse vpon payment to him or them of 9000 merks Scotts.

These in place of a locall pension granted by your Ma^teis royall father to Archibald Hay, assigneing him to certane moneys, victuall, and other commoditeis of your Ma^teis propper rents, viz.—1000^lib Scotts, 2 Chalders oats, and eight scoir pair coneyis; change the same in a pension of 1200^lib Scotts money, equivalent in value to the saids moneyis, victuall and other commoditeis, to be vplifted yeirlie out of your Ma^teis Excheker to the ordinar and approved forme.—Whythall, 14 No⁺ 1633.

To the Session.

Right, &c.—Wheras in the late parliament holdin by ws in our citie of Edinburgh in Junij last it was ordeaned by a speciall act of the same that out of Ten payed yeirlie for ilk hundreth of annuell Two should be payed by the burrowis to ws for the space therin contenit, without defalcation, and by and attour what was formerlie granted to ws, notwithstanding whairof, being sufficientlie informed that some persones, against the dewtie of good subjects and to mak the grant of our estates voyd, intend to sue defalcation of what is due by allowance of the sowmes adebted by them, contrarie to the trew meaneing of the said act: Our pleasur therfor is, that yow grant no suspension of any charges directed by vertew of the said act to any persoun without consignatioun of two of ten for ilk hundreth of the whole sowmes dewlie adebtit by the borroweris in the handis of the Clerk of our Esteats, to be gevin vp by him to our Collectour-generall of the same extent, without any defalcatioun; and that yow caus the said act to be keiped in all poynts conforme to the tenour therof: Which recommending to your care, &c.—Whythall, 20 No⁺ 1633.

To the Threasurer and Threasurer Deputie.

Right, &c.—Wheras we ar informed that some of our subjects, to mak voyd the grants of the Estats of Parliament of that our kingdome, offered to ws in our late Parliament of two of Ten of the Annuell of ilk hundreth payable by the borroweris, intend to mak purches of the wodset of Landis, and vplift the rents of the same in retribution of ther annells; which being done onlie to frustrat ws of the said gratuitie offered to ws by our saidis Estatis, and they otherwayes to reap the benefite of the late acts, It is our pleasur that when any such signature is or shalbe presented vnto yow to be exped, that befor the same pass your handis in Exchequer, yow, besydis the Ordinarie Compositiouns accustomed in the lyk caices, add to the same what sowmes might accress to ws, and might be payed by the borroweris by the late Act of Parliament in caice these moneyis had bene lent for ten of the hundreth, and that for the whole space of thrie yeires, and cause them pay the same togidder befor the passing of the said signatures, for it is no reasone that ther fraud shall prejudge ws, or we contribute our favour to so ill deserving subjects: Which recommending, &c.—Whythall, 20 No⁺ 1633.

His Matie was pleased to grant a protection to Johne Geddes, and his cautioners interested and that stude suretie for him in levyeing moneyis for bringing 400 scheip from Scotland to England, according to his Ma^teis direction, for his Ma^teis vse, wherof he was and is as yit vnpayed; and the same protection to endure for ane yeir for them.

To the Thesaurer and Deputie.

Right, &c.—Haveing vnderstude that our late right trustie, &c. the Erle of Balcleuch is now departed this lyff, It is our pleasur that yow grant or rather caus expeid the waird of his sone's mariage, and his nixt air to him, and ther nonentrie, and what else doeth vaik in our handis by reasoue of his death, To our right, &c. the Erle of Stirling, he paying the ordinarie composition vsuall in that kynd; and that yow signifie this our pleasur, if neid be, to the remanent Lordis of our Exchequer ther: So we bid, &c.—Whythall, 22 No^r 1633.

To the Counsell.

Right, &c.—Wheras in our late Parliament holdin within that our kingdome the office of Muster Master-Generall was ratifeid as a purpois verie necessarie for the good and honour therof: The consideratioun of the fie for dischargeing that service, and the meanes for levyeing thairof, being by ane act of that court remitted vnto yow, and recommended by ws in a speciall maner, Our pleasur is, that yow proceid according to the said act, haveing alwayes a speciall care that both the said charge be putt in executioun in the most convenient way for the good of that kingdome; and lykwyse that the nobleman to whois care the overseieing of it is entrusted by ws may be encouraged to it by for a good and compitent allowance, to be levyed in such kynd as yow shall think most fitting.—Whythall, 22 No^r 1633.

To the Erles of Morton & Traquair.

Wheras, by warrant vnder our royall signature and cachet at Beaulie, 17 August 1633, we gave ordour to Johne Geddes, our servant, to bring from Scotland about Michelmes ensueing the lyk number of muttons for our vse as was accustomed to be bought for the vse of our late royall father, or for our owin, requyreing him to continew that service yeirlie till we should be pleased to discharge it: And wheras we vnderstand that the said Johne did bring hither at that tyme four hundreth scheip, for which he hath received no payment for his disbursments in buying therof, nor any allowance for bringing them hither, Our pleasur is, and we doe heirby will and requyre yow, that furthwith yow pay or caus to be payed vnto him such fie and allowance of the 400 sheip as gevin in the tyme of our said late father, and that out of the readiest rents, casualiteis, annuiteis, or dewteis whatsumever, payable vnto ws in that our kingdome, or which heirefter shalhappin to accrews vnto ws within the same by whatsumever maner of way: And our pleasur is, that heirefter this service shalbe discontinewed vnles yow shalbe particularlie warranted by ws to continew the same, which, if we doe, we ar willing that the said Sir John, for his former good service, be preferred to any other; for which thes presents shalbe vnto yow a sufficient warrant.—Whythall, 22 No^r 1633.

Our Soverane Lord ordeanes a Letter to be made vnder the privie scall in due forme to his highnes, &c. his aires and assigneyis, ane or mae, of the gift of ward and nonentress, maills, fermes, caynes, customes, casualiteis, proffeits, mylnes, fischings, annexis, connexis, outsets, parts, pendicles, tenents, tenandreis, service of frie tenents of the same, and all ther pertinents, with the Advocatioun, donation, and right of patronage of kirks, chaplanreis, and others benefices, whenever the same lye within this realme, which perteaned of befoir to wmquhill, &c., haldin by him immediatlie of his Ma'tie, by service of ward and releiff or otherwayes, and now perteneing to our said Soverane lord, fallin and becum in his highnes' hands, and at his gift and dispositioun by and throw the deceis of the said vmquhill, &c. or any others his predicessours, and that of all yeires and termes bygane, that the samyne hes bene in his highnes' or his predicessours handis as superiours thairof be reasone of ward and nonentress since the death of the said vmquhill, &c. or any other his predicessours last lawfull and immediat heretabill tennents to his Ma'tie and his predicessours of the samyne ; And lykwyse of all yeires and termes to cum, ay and while the lawfull entrie of the righteous air or aires therto being of perfyte aige with the releiff thairof when it shallhappin ; Togidder with the mariage of, &c., now Lord, &c., sone and appearand air to the said vmquhill, &c., and failzeing of him by deceis vnmaried, the mariage of any other air or aires male or female that shall happin to succeed to him in his lands, lordship, and liveing above specifeit, and all proffeits and commoditeis of the said Mariage, With power to the said, &c., his aires and assigneyis forsaidis, to intromett with and vptak the forsaid ward and nonentress, with the haill maills, fermes, caynes, customes, casualiteis, proffeits, and dewteis of all and sindrie the saids lands, lordships, baroneis, castells, touris, fortalices, maner places, woods, mylnes, fischings, and others above mentionat, with ther pertinents, alsweill of all yeirs and termes bygane as yeirlie and termlie in tyme cuming, dureing the whole tyme of the forsaid ward and nonentress thairof, and therypon with the releiff thairof, and vpon the forsaid mariage, whole proffeits and commoditeis of the samyne, to dispone at ther pleasur, and if neid beis to call, follow, and persew therfoir as accordis of the law, and to occupy the saids lands, lordships, baroneis, castells, tours, fortalices, wards, mylnes, fischings, and others respective above rehersed, with ther owin propper goodis, or to sett the same to tennents, remove, outputt, imputt, alter, and change them therintill as they shall think most expedient, and to give and confer the saids kirks and others benefices whenever and as oft as the samyne shall happin to vaik dureing the space above specifeit, with Court, plaint, herezeld, bloodwitt, &c., and with all other and sindrie fredomes, commoditeis, frielie, quyetlie, &c., but revocation, &c.: And that the said Letter be extended in most ample forme, with all clausses neidfull.—Gevin at Whythall, 24 No' 1633.

To the Session.

Right, &c.— Wheras it hath bene humblie represented vnto ws in behalff of Sir Alex' Gordoun of Cluny that by his absence from thence in our service heir he is lyklie to suffer in ane action in Law depending befor yow tuiteling the estate of Sir Johne Leslie of Wardess, as yow will perceave by the enclosed petitioun, which we remitt to your consideratioun and to setle the bussines so far as can be, &c. — 28 No' 1633.

To the Advocat.

Trustie, &c.—We wer pleased not long agoe to grant to M' W'm Drummond of Hathornden the mariage of W'm Scott of Ardross, and the few of the Newton of Biress, being at our disposall and gift by diminution of the rentall, which caus being now depending the Senatours of our Colledge of Justice, we have thoght fitt to will and require yow to concure in our name with the said M' William ; and in regard our croun hath sustened much prejudice by renewing many other securiteis of the lyk nature, that yow adverte diligentlie thervnto, leist we by the neglect of this proces, which will mak the first precedent of that kynd, should be prejudged in our lawfull recoverie against others heirefter ; wherin therfor not doubting of your care and diligence, &c.—Whythall, 29 No' 1633.

н 2 u

Our Soverane Lord vnderstanding perfectlie the good affection caryed to his Ma^{tis} service, and haveing takin in his royall consideration the panes and travells alreadie bestowed therin in tymes bypast by his, &c, Sir Robert Spottiswood, President of the Colledge of Justice within the kingdome of Scotland, for his better encouragment and enabling of him to continew in the same dewtifull obedience and service heirefter, his Matie, with advyse, &c., ordanes ane letter to be made vnder his highnes' privie seall of the said kingdome, Giveing, granting, and disponeing, lykas his Matie, with advyse and consent forsaid, gives, grants, and dispones to the said Sir Robert Spottiswood, dureing all the dayes of his lyftyme, Ane yeirlie pension of two hundreth and fyftie pundis Sterling money, to be payed to the said Sir Robert, his factours and servitours in his name, furth of the first and readiest, &c. stilo ordinario.—Whythall, last No^r 1633.

Mr Johne Lyndsay had a presentation past for him to be admitted minister at the Church of Carlouk, vacand in his Ma^{tis} handis by the deceise of Mr Johne Lyndsay, father to the said Mr Johne now preferred therto.—Whythall, last No^r 1633.

To the Session.

Right, &c.—Wheras it hath bene humblie represented vnto ws on behalff of Sir Alex^r Gordon of Cluny, kny^t baronet, that by his absence from thence in our service heir at this tyme he is lyklie to suffer in ane action in Law depending befor yow tuitching the estate of Sir Johne Leslie of Wardess, to whois creditours (as we ar informed) hath of a long tyme stood bund as cautioner, wherby he is lyklie to be much prejudged, as yow will perceave by the enclosed petition, which we remitt to your consideratioun, that if yow find the demandis therin to be agreeable to Justice and equitie, yow proceid accordinglie in administratioun of Justice, and setling the differences in so far as convenientlie can be done.—Whythall, last No^r 1633.

To the Advocat.

Trustie, &c.—Wheras the decay of Trade doeth much impoverish the estate of that kingdome, wher the incress and advancement of the same would much import the good therof and increase of our customes by exporting native commoditeis, which otherwayes for a great part of them prove vnprofitable, or at leist not much vsefull to our subjects, and by importing commoditeis both necessar and of great value, and wheras to the lyk end diverse associatiouns and companeis of this our kingdome, and of some flourisching kingdomes and stats abroad, for sieing what might lead to the advancement of ther publict good, have found that the tradeing in some remote parts (from whence ther be grounds of greatest benefite), and the setling of steplis and coloneis, ther ar inseperable wayes not onlie for matter of great benefite bot for incress of schipping and breeding of marineris : To which purpois our right trustie the Erle of Stirling, our Secretarie for Scotland, Sir Johne Hay, our Clerk Register, Patrik Maull and James Maxwell, of our bedchalmer, and . . . being to adventure and drawin societeis diverse of our good subjects, we have thoght fitt for ther better encouragement that a warrant be granted vnto them vnder our great seall of that kingdome, wherby they, ther aires, partiners, and assotiats, shall have a sole power dureing the space of . . . to joyne into Associatiouns and companeis all such our subjects that will vndertake any new traffique in America, Asia, Africa, and Muscovia not formerlie vsed in that kingdome : Therfor our pleasur is, that yow receave and consider thir overturis tuitching such privileges and liberteis as ar fitt and lawfull to be granted for encourageing our subjects to assotiat and adventure to trade in these parts, and haveing conceaved some such warrant or severall warrants as may best and most lawfullie conduce to that purpois, yow draw the same vp docated by yow for our royall signature, for which these presents, &c.— Whythall, last of No^r 1633.

To the Vice Depitie of York.

Trustie, &c.—Wheras we wer pleased of late to wryt vnto yow that one Ainslie, merchand, ane of our subjects of our kingdome of Scotland, might have justice for recoverie of certane moneyis dew to him by one Robiesone, dwelling in Northumberland, bot being since informed that notwithstanding the said Robesone did pay the moneyis to a factour of the said Ainstie, which he offeris himselff to prove, which maks the caus considerable in equitie: Iff yow find this trew which is alledgit, our pleasur is, that if at the sight of indifferent persones the matter cannot be composed betuixt themselffis yow suspend any proceiding vpon our former Letter, and remitt it to the ordinarie course of Justice into Courts whervnto caices of the lyk nature doe properlie belong: And for, &c.—Whythall, last No^r 1633.

To Sir Francis Windiebanks.

Trustie, &c.—Haveing formerlie gevin ordour for consideratiouns knowen to ws to our right, &c. the Erle of Argyll, by a warrant vnder our hand, to caus transport ane Anna Campbell, calling hirselff his naturall daughter, to our kingdome of Scotland, to be furnished for hir mantenance ther, which ordours of ouris sche hath not obeyed, and being informed that sche is entring ane endytment befoir the Justices of Peace, wherby to putt him to trouble and vnnecessarie charges: It is our pleasur that ye in our name caus discharge any proceiding therin till we shalbe acquanted with the esteat therof, and give such further ordour as we shall think fitt; for doeing, &c.—Theobald's, 1 Decr 1633.

To the Session.

Right, &c.—Wheras we wer formerlie pleased to requyre our Counsell to give ordour, by publict proclamatioun or otherwayes, as they should think fitting, that all the Lords of our Counsell, Colledge of Justice, and Members therof may communicat once everie yeir in our Chapell of Halyrudhous: bot now being willing for good consideratiouns that the communion should be oftner celebrat ther, and to nominat such tymes as we thoght good for that purpois, It is our pleasur that everie Sonday nixt ensueing your doun sitting in the winter and Sommer sessions, yow prepair and address yourselffis, with your Advocats, Clerkis, writters, and all others members of that Judicatorie, to whome yow shall caus intimat this our pleasur, to our said Chapell to the participatioun of the holie sacrament, that others by your good example may learne to observe the ordour in that caice preservyed: Which recommending, &c.—Whythall, 4 Decr 1633.

Vpon this day ther past a Protectione for the Erle of Lythgow and his Cautioners vnder his Ma^teis hand, dureing the space of ane whole yeir efter the passing thairof vnder the great seall of Scotland.— Theobald's, 5 of De^r 1633.

These doe conteyne a Ratification of the Letter of Pension granted by your Matie to Sir Archibald Achiesone dureing his lyftyme of a yeirlie pension of 200^lib sterling money, with a new gift of the said pension for his better encouragement to continew in his Maties service.—Theobald's, 5 De^r 1633.

To the Curatours of the Erle of Balcleuch.

Right, &c.—Wheras we have bene petitioned at diverse tymes by the Lady Jeane Stewart and hir husband tuitching the recoverie of certane Lands which wer in the possession of the late Erle of Balcleuche, who not long befor his death intended to have takin a course for ther speedie satisfaction at our sights which we requyre may be done with all expedition in regard of ther long sufferings by want of the benefite of these Landis: Our pleasur is, and we doe heirby will and requyre yow, that haveing seriouslie considered of the estat of that bussiness, yow tak a course for ther satisfaction, otherwyse that yow certifie ws of what expedient yow shall think fitt to that purpois, to the effect we may give such furtherance therin as we shall find just cause.

To the Thesaurer and Deputie.

Right, &c.—Wheras our trustie and weillbelovit servant Sir James Leslie, kny^t, hath a pension of ws dureing his lyftyme of the few maills and dewteis payed out of the Abbay of Lundoris, becaus we ar not willing to grant a locall assignement, nor yit that the said Sir James should want the benefite that was intendit for him, bot that he be payed out of the Exchequer in the ordinarie way as other persones ar: It is our pleasur that, haveing considered of his former gift, yow condescend vpon a reasonable rate for the victuallis yeirlie payed vnto him, and joyneing that in ane sowme with the silver rent he had, that yow give ordour vnto our Advocat for drawing vp a new gift for this effect docated by him for our hand.— Whythall, 5 De^r 1633.

To the Commissioners for Valvationis of Tythis of Erections.

Right, &c.—Wheras in your answer to that Letter which we did wryt vnto yow for discussing the valuation of tythis of Erections befor all other sort of tythis whatsumever, yow alledge that that being observed your commission will ly ydle, We sie no reasone bot that yow haveing power to warne all these that have tythis of Erections to cum in, yow may without loss of tyme proceide to the expediing of them befor any other, according to our former letter; and as for appoynting ane other day in everie weik, Though it is said that ther is no other day to be made vse of saife onlie Monday, which by our late royall father was allowed to be frie from bussines ; yit we think that for a bussines of this nature, tending to the generall good of all the kingdome, yow may mak vse of the same and of any such committeis as yow shall think expedient, which for the perfecting of this work wilbe verie acceptable vnto ws; and therfor not doubting of your best diligence, we bid, &c.—Whythall, 10 De^r 1633.

To the Session.

Right, &c.—We wer pleased some moneth is since, in consideratioun of our Cousen the Erle of Murray his being heir to requyre yow to stay the proceiding of that process intended against him by the reverend father the bischop of Murray ; bot now that caus ceissing, and perceaveing that the saids bischop is much prejudged by the said delay, we have thoght fitt therfor to will and requyre yow agane to proceid therin, and give that caus ane end according to Justice with expedition ; wherin not doubting of your care, we bid, &c.—Westminster, the 11 De^r 1633.

In regard of diverse good and acceptable services done vnto ws by our trustie and weilbelovet Counsellour the bischop of Dumblane, deane of our Chappell royall ther, speciallie at the tyme of our Coronatioun, and lykwayes in regard of the feyis dew vnto him for his attendance ther, We have frielie remitted and gevin frie to him the whole four yeires' taxatiouns of his bischoprik of Dumblane, Abaceis of

Crocragnall and Dundranan, and Pryorie of Monymusk annexed thereto, which was granted to ws by the convention of our estats in anno 1630 : These ar therfor to will and command yow not to charge nor suite him for these four yeires' taxations forsaidis, wherunent these presents shalbe your sufficient warrant, and heirby ordeanes the Auditours of your compts to defais and allow the same vnto yow, these being once schawin vnto them by yow for ther warrand.—Whythall, 11 De^r 1633.

To the Erle of Kynnoull, our Chancellour Collectour-generall of the Taxations granted anno 1630.

To the Lord Gordoun.

Right, &c.—Haveing heard of a proposition of yours by one directed from yow, we give yow hartie thanks for your care and affection to our service, both in that particular concerneing your companie and otherwayes, whairof we will consider at more lenth and lett yow know our pleasur therin at our best conveniencie, willing yow to goe on as yow have begun in that charge yow have ther abroad, according as we have bene pleased to signifie vnto your servant, and be confident we wilbe myndfull to give ordour at some litt occasion for satisfieing yow for such moneyis as ar dew vnto yow from ws, and in the meanetyme will not be wanting in any thing wherin we can convenientlie expres our further pleasure vnto yow : We bid yow, &c.—From Whythall, 12 De^r 1633.

To the Exchequer.

Right, &c.—Hearing that of late yow did grant presentations to churches at our gift, which befor being ordinarlie accustomed to be subscryved by the bischop of the dyocie wher the church did vaik, as a testimonie of the persones sufficiencie to whom they wer granted, wer thervpon signed by ws or our royall predicessours, which course, as we ar informed, hath bene long and vpon good considerations observed, spetiallie in the tyme of our late royall father; and therfor being willing that no Innovation be made therin, Our pleasur is, that from hencefurth yow grant no such presentations in Exchequer, bot that yow remitt the suitters for the same to the former accustomed way; for which these presents shalbe your warrand.—Whythall, 12 De^r 1633.

To the Thesaurer and Deputie.

Right, &c.—Being informed that ther ar diverse persones who, pretending right to the Landis of Salton, doe intend to tak new infeftments thairof, and that to the great prejudice of the now Lord Salton, we, out of our princelie favour and commiseratioun of the distressed estate of that antient familie, and being willing to schaw all the lawfull favour we can tending to the good therof, ar herby pleased to requyre yow not to permitt any infeftment or signature of these Lands or any part therof pass in our Exchequer to any person whatsumever, till we shalbe pleased to signifie vnto yow our further pleasur tuitching the same.—Whythall, 12 De^r 1633.

To the Session.

Right, &c.—Wheras a petition hath bene exhibited vnto ws be the Lo/ Saltoun, wherby remonstrance being made of his distressed estate and absence from thence, we ar gratiouslie pleased to recommend vnto yow what may lawfullie concerne him, being incident to that Judicatorie, and rather becaus our late royall father had a respect to the standing of that ancient house, which had of a long tyme deserved weill of him and other our royall progenitours : Our pleasur is, that haveing seriouslie considered of the said Petition, yow administer Justice vnto him in actiones intented or to be intended by him tuitching the Landis of Salton, and wherin we have any interest we ar willing to schaw him all the lawfull favour we can for his advantage, which recommending vnto your speciall care, we bid, &c.—Whythall, 12 De^r 1633.

To the Advocat.

Trustie, &c.—Haveing vnderstude that the gift of our right, &c. the Erle of Baleleuch his ward, which we signed in favours of our right, &c. the Erle of Stirling, was past and deposited in the handis of our right, &c. the Erle of Morton, our principall Thesaurer ther, till our further pleasur should be knowen ; and that in regard it was pretendit by the pairtie that the ward was taxed, we ar desyreous befor we proceid further to know the trew esteat of it, and how far legallie we may have title to it : Therfoir it is our pleasur, that haveing conferred with our trustie and weilbeloved counsellour Sir John Hay of Baro, kny^t, our Clerk Register, yow carefullie informe yourselff of the holdings of the said Erles landis, and lykwayes certifie ws with diligence what right we have vnto the said Ward, or may have by the Lawis of that kingdome, or by the benefite of our revocatioun or Interruptions, or the ratifications thervpon : wherin expecting your care, as yow wilbe answerable vnto ws in your charge, we bid, &c.—Whythall, 12 De^r 1633.

To the Thesaurer Principall.

Right, &c.—Haveing vnderstude that the gift of our right, &c. the Erle of Buccleuch his ward, which was signed in favouris of our right, &c. the Erle of Stirling, was past in Exchequer and deposited in your handis till our further pleasur should be knowen ; and that in regard it is pretendit by the pairtie that the ward is taxed, we approve of the course that is taken ; and befoir we proceid farther we have determined to know how far legallie we have interest to the said ward by the Lawis of the said kingdome, and have for that purpois writtin to our Counsellouris Sir John Hay and Sir Thomas Hope, kny^t baronet, our Advocat ther for serching of the registers, and giveing ws advyse concerneing it, which we thoght good heir to acquant yow with : So we bid, &c.—Whythall, 12 De^r 1633.

To the Erle of Baleleuch.

Right, &c.—Wheras we have bene petitioned diverse tymes by Lady Jeane Stewart and hir husband tuitching ther recoverie of certane landis which wer in the possession of the Erle of Buccleuch, who not long agoe befor his death intended to have taken a course for ther speedie satisfaction at our sight, which we requyre may be done with all expedition, in regard of the long sufferings by want of the benefite of these landis : our pleasur is, and we heirby will and requyre yow, that haveing seriouslie considered of the esteate of that bussines, yow tak a course for ther satisfaction ; vtherwayes that yow certifie ws of what expedient yow shall think fitt for that purpois, to the effect we may give such further ordour therein as yow shall find just cause.—Whythall, 12 De^r 1633.

We have, vpon good considerations and reasones knawen to ws, bestowed vpoun our trustie and weil-beloved counsellour Sir James Galloway, our Master of requests, the sowme of 2000^{lib} sterline, to be vplifted out of the first and readiest of all fynes and forfaults arysing be the transgression or breach of all or any of the acts of Parliament or counsall made against vnlawfull vsurie, transporting of gold and silver futh of the kingdome, and whisting or selling of it within the kingdome at higher rates than ar by Law allowed : Our pleasur therfor is, and we doe heirby authorise, will, and declair yow, that from tyme to tyme as the saidis forfeytis and fynes sall fall due vnto ws, caus the same be delyvered to our M^r of requeists, or his assigneyis, ay and whill the said sowme of 2000^lib st. be compleitlie made vp and payed vnto him ; and for his better securitie thereanent, that these presents, togidder with your ordour or act thervpon, be registrat in the books of Excheker ; for doing whairof, &c.—Whythall, 12 De^r 1633.

To the Masters of Work.

Trustie, &c.—Sieing the Abbay Church of Halyrudhous that had bene so dark befoir was by the course takin by yow becum so lightsome that it gave ws a great deall of contentment at our being ther : To the effect that it may continew so still, it is our pleasur that yow have a speciall care that no seatts nor lofts be built therin vnless it be such places as may rather impair the beawtie nor light of the said church, and this yow shall signifie to any whom this may concerne from ws ; and if any doe presume to doe the contrar heirof, that yow certifie the same to ws, that we may caus tak ordour with them ; for doeing quhairof, &c.—Whythall, 12 De^r 1633.

To the Exchequer.

Right, &c.—In regard of the good service done vnto ws by our M^rs of Works within that our kingdome, especiallie befoir our last comeing thither, that they may be encouraged to continew in the lyk course, and be carefull in manteaneing of our housses as yow have agried with them, It is our pleasur that, haveing informed your sellis what reward was bestowed by our late dear father at the tyme of his being ther vpon the Master of wark, or was efterwardis allowed vnto him for his service ther, performed in any maner of way, besydis his ordinarie feyis and allowances, that yow give the lyk vnto the saidis M^rs of works at this tyme, out of the readiest of our rents and casualiteis within our said kingdome ; for the which, and inserting heirof in the books of our Exchequer for ther further securitie, these presents shalbe vnto yow a sufficient warrant.—Whythall, 12 De^r 1633.

To the Session.

Right, &c.—Wheras, by the interruption made, as we ar informed, in bringing away of that tymber condescended vpon by contract betwene the Lard of Grant and Captan Maissone, our service, tuitching the repairing of some of our schips and other works belonging to ws, for which caus that bargane was cheiffie made, is lyk to be much hindred, and our subjects heir interested therin to be verie much damnifeid in ther particulars : Our pleasur is, that, haveing considered the wrong done vnto them, yow administer speedie justice in any action depending or which shall come befor yow at the instance of the said Captane Masson and his partiners tuitching this purpois, and that yow provyde heirefter, in so far lawfullie can be done, that they be not further wronged in that bargane, nor in any vther tymber for which they have barganes ; which we will tak as verie acceptable service done vnto ws.—Whythall, 16 De^r 1633.

Our Soverane Lord ordeanes a protection to be made vnder his highnes' great seall of the kingdome of Scotland To his highnes lovit Sir James Stewart, brother-german to the late Erle of Orkney, and Robert

Stewart, his eldest sone, makand mention that wheras his Matie is crediblie informed that the said Sir James Stewart and his said sone standis indebtit to ther creditours in diverse soumes of money, which they ar most willing and able to pay vnto them if some compitent tyme war allowed them, by making vse to that purpois of ther goodis, geir, and possessionis, and speciallie of such pensions and debts as ar due vnto them by his Matie, wher if the saids Creditours should tak a violent and rigorous course aganst them or oney of them it would both vndoe him, and consequentlie misable them to pay the saids debts, to the great hurt both of them and ther creditours, wherin his Matie, respecting the well of both, of his authoritie royall, kingly power, grace, mercie, and clemencie, hath accepted, and by the tenour heirof acceptis, the said Sir James Stewart and Robert Stewart, his said sone, vnder his highnes' protection, safeguard, mantenance, and defence from being in anywayes troubled, molested, or persewed by ther saids creditours or any of them for any debt due vnto them by the said Sir James and his said sone, or any of them, as principalls or cautioners: And gives and grants to the said Sir James and his said sone during the space of ane yeir, beginning from the passing of thir presents vnder the said great seall, licence, power, and libertie to peaceablie and safelie dwell, stay, and remayne within any part of the said kingdome without molestatioun, trouble, challenge, persuite, or danger of apprehending or warding of ther or any of ther persones for any contracted by them, as principalls or cautioners; discharging expreslie by thir presents all his Maties Shirrellis, Stewarts, Provests, bailleis, Constables, Justices of Peace, all Justices, Judges, officeris, and ministers of his highnes' lawis, both in burgh and land, ther deputeis, servandis, and all others whome it efferis within the said kingdome, that they nor nane of them presume, attempt, tak in hand, directlie or indirectlie, by day or night, to seik, tak, or apprehend the said Sir James and his said sone, or any of them, for any debt aforsaid, or mak any disturbance, interruption, or violation of his Maties protection, vnder pane of incurring his highnes' utter wraith and high displeasur, notwithstanding of any letters of horning, captions, warrants, commissions, charges, or commandis alreadie gevin or to be gevin by his Matie himsellf, the Lords of Session, or any of his Maties Judges, officers, or others persones whatsoever within the said kingdome in favours of the saids creditours, or any of them, for apprehending and warding of the said Sir James and his said sone, or any of them, for any debt whatsumever, wheranent his Matie of his highnes' royall and princelie power by thir present dispensses in that part during the said space of ane yeir: And to the effect the said Sir James and his said sone may be the more able to satisfie and pay to ther creditours the debt owing by them, and in the meanetyme recover payment of the moneyis due to them by ther debtours, his Matie, of his authoritie royall, princelie power, and prerogative, doeth heirby speciallie authorize the said Sir James and his said sone to stand in judgment, or persew or defend all actions intented or to be intented, as well at ther owin instance aganst ther debtours as at ther creditours' instance aganst them, notwithstanding of whatsumever procces of horning vsed or to be vsed aganst them, wheranent his Matie hath dispensed and be thir presents dispensses dureing the said space, Ordeaneing publication heirof to be made and intimat to the schyre wher they duell; Commanding heirby the Lords of Sessioun to grant and direct Letters of publicatioun heirvpoun for that effect; and ordeaneing lykwyse thir presents to be a sufficient warrand to the writter to the great seall and keiper thairof for wryting of thir presents thairto, and appending the said great seall to the same without passing any other seals or registers, wheranent thir presents shalbe vnto them a sufficient warrand.—Whythall, 18 De^r 1633.

TO THE SESSION.

Right, &c.—Vnderstanding that the extraordinarie place of Session discherged by our trustie and weilbeloved Counsellour Sir John Hay of Baro, kny^t, our Clerk Register, by his remove to ane ordinarie place therin, doeth vaik at our gift and disposition, and knowing the abiliteis and affection to our service of the right the Lord Lorne, we have thought fitt by these presents to recommend him vnto yow as a persone able for that charge, requyreing yow to receave and admitt him thervnto, according to the custome in the lyk caices.—Whythall, 23 De^r 1633.

To the Session.

Right, &c.—Wheras for distinguisching the tuo Judicatoreis of our Counsall and Session, we have gevin ordour that no nobleman being a pryme Counsellour should be admitted to be a judge in the Session, which course we will have still to continew, bot concerneing that the placeing vpon that Judicatorie some of our officers of estate who ar no noblemen is not derogation to and distinguisching of the tuo Judicatoreis, bot will be steidable to our service, who to that purpois have made choyse of our trustie Sir John Hay, kny^t, our Clerk Register, to supplie the rowme of Sir Robert Spottiswood, vacant be his admission to be President: And therfor our pleasur is, that yow receave and admitt the said Sir Johne to the said Ordinarie place in Session, with all honours, priviledges, and benefites belonging thervnto, lett him have vote amongst yow, and mak him participant of your contributiouns, and tak his oath as vse is, as yow will that justice proceid, and will doe ws acceptable pleasur.—Whythall, 23 De^r 1633.

To the Session.

Right, &c.—Wheras Interruption is made, as we ar informed, in bringing away that tymber condescended vpon by contract betuixt the Lard of Grant and Captan Masson, our servitour, tuitching the repairing of some of our ships and other works of ours, for which cans that bargane was cheiflie made, is much hindered, and our subjects heir interested therin verie much damnifeid, which course (if no sufficient reasone can be gevin to the contrarie) we hold not fitt to be suffered within the kingdome, or to goe any longer vnpunisched: And therfor our pleasur is, that, vpon evidence to be gevin befor yow by the said Captan of the guiltines of the offenders, yow tak a speedie course for punisching of them, that others may be terrifeid for attempting heirefter the lyk insolence and irregular way of proceiding: And in the meano tyme, that our servand be no farder neglected, our pleasur is that yow call the Lard of Grant befor yow, and caus him find sufficient securitie vnder sic penaltie as shalbe fund necessarie for securoing our saidis subjects heir, that no further hurt or interruption be made to him, his name, freindis, vassalls, or tennents, in taking away and in barking the said tymber, which we will tak as acceptable service done vnto ws.—Whythall, 23 De^r 1633.

To the Chancellour.

Right, &c.—We haveing taken great panes and bene at great charges in setling of the bischoprik of Edinburgh, as yow may perceave by the course taken by ws therin; and knowing that (as ordinarlie in all such new beginnings) ther may fall out occasions to hinder or delay the course of these our pious proceidings in the full and absolute setling of the persone made choyce of to be bischop therof, We have heirby thoght fitt to recomend vnto yow in a special maner, that not onlie in all thingis concerneing the absolute establisching of the said bischoprik, bot lykwyse in the particular encourageing and countenanceing of the persone made choyse of, yow will vse your best endevours, and sie our pleasur therin to tak the intendit effect, which we will compt as acceptable service done vnto ws, wherof we will not be vnmyndfull.—Whythall, 24 De^r 1633.

To the Archbischop of Sᵗ Androis.

Right, &c.—Haveing sene the testimoniall of the Election of Mʳ Wᵐ Forbes to the bischoprik of Edinburgh, vnder the handis of the deane and chaptour therof; and being willing that he be fullie settled therin according to our former directions tuitching the same, Our pleasur is, that to that purpois yow proceid with all possible diligence to the absolute setling and consecration of the said bischop according to the ordours of that Church accustomed in the lyk caices, for which these presents shalbe your warrand.—Whythall, 24 Deʳ 1633.

To the Archbischop of Sᵗ Androis and Bischop of Edinburgh.

Being informed of the Learning and good conversation of Mʳ Johne Home, bacheler in divinitie, who is desyreous to setle himsellf in that our kingdome, which desyre of his we ar willing to cherise, conceaveing it to be verie convenient for the vse of the church that such men, who both by the qualification, conformitie to the canons and ordours of the Church, and by ther laudable cariage may schaw good exemple to others, should be placed in our said kingdome: Our pleasur is, that whensoever any church shall vaik at our gift fitt for ane of his abilitie, or such as he shalbe willing to intrate, yow tak care that he may have it, and to that effect that yow send vnto ws a presentationn vnder your hand to be signed by ws; and for your so doeing, &c.—Whythall, last Deʳ 1633.

To the Advocat.

Trustie, &c.—Haveing writtin to yow of late in the behalff of the right reverend father in God, our trustie and weilbeloved Counsellour, the bischop of Ross, that in all actions of Law that sall cum befoir our Colledge of Justice for recoverie of the rents and patronages belonging to his bischoprik yow compeir and give your best assistance to him befoir our said Colledge; And being crediblilie informed that the Abacie of Ferne is annexed to the said bischoprik, and that the rent therof is detened from him by ane other, wherof we ar desyreous he should reap the benefite as being due vnto him; Therfoir it is our pleasur that, haveing carefullie informed yoursellf of the estate of the Abacie, and how it is annexed vnto that bischoprik, therefter, ather in our name or in name of the said bischope, or in both, as it shall seme most expedient vnto him, yow compeir befoir our said Colledge, and be aydand vnto him, that he may enjoy the benefite therof, as in all actions intended or to be intended by him for the effect forsaid; ffor which these presents, &c.—Whythall, last Deʳ 1633.

To the Thesaurer and Deputie.

Right, &c.—Being humblie petitioned by the reverend father in God the Bischop of Brechin that, in regard he hath not receaved payment of his pension, formerlie granted to him vpon good considerations, these diverse yeires bypast, contrarie to our royall intention, we would be pleased to grant him an assigne ment to what is due to ws out of his bischoprik by vertew of our taxatiouns; and we not being willing that any such course should be takin, if otherwayes yow would have a care to sie him satisfeit of what now is fund dew vnto him, and therefter according to his gift of pension, Our pleasur is, that efter dew tryell of how much he is behind of his said pension, that with all convenient and speedie diligence yow caus pay to him or his assigneyis the arreiris therof with the samyn yeirlie and termelie, conforme to his gift granted thervpoun; otherwayes, if he have recourse vnto ws agane, we most give ordour of new for the same: Which recommending, &c.—Whythall, last Deʳ 1633.

To the Archbischop of St Androis.

Right, &c.—Considering how by the priviledge we have in this our kingdome in preferring a successour to the vacant place of any who hath bene removed from the same by ws to be a bischop, we have the better opportunitie of the supplieing of ther places agane with one of approved sufficiencie, and that, notwithstanding of the title of any other thervnto, by being patron or otherwayes for that tyme when the present incumbent is preferred in such a maner by ws; Though it doe seme verie necessarie vnto ws that the lyk course should be keiped within that our kingdome, yit we will not proceid further therin till we should be first informed by yow by what right and in what maner it may best be done; And therfor these ar speciallie to requyre yow that, haveing informed yourself of the same, yow certifie your opinion therof vnto ws; And in the meanetyme, becaus the place in Aberdene vacand by preferring Doctour Wm Forbes to be bischop of Edinburgh, being a considerable place, would be supplyed by some man of good sufficiencie, we desyre yow lykwayes to have a speciall care how the same may be done, whether the donation therof be in ws, in yow, or any other; which speciallie recommending vnto your care, We bid, &c.—Whythall, 2 Jar 1634.

To the Commissioners of Surrenders.

Right, &c.—Being willing vpoun some good considerations knowen vnto ws to tak into your further consideration the extent of the tythis of the Pryorie of St Androis befor yow proceid in the valuation therof, Our pleasur is, that yow doe not insist therin till yow hear our further direction to that purpois, bot that yow goe on the valuation of other tythis according to our former warrants and your commission ; and for your so doeing, &c.—Whythall, 2 Jar 1634.

To the Advocat.

Trustie, &c.—Being willing to renew to our right, &c. the Erle of Kynneull the patent of Glasswork within that kingdome, conditionall that a work be sett vp to that purpois within the same, and kept goeing for the publict good, Our pleasur is, that yow draw vp a patent for our royall signature to him, his aires and assigneyis of these Glassworks, according to the former patent, to continew efter the expiration of the former the lyk number of yeres, with speciall provision for setting vp and manteneing the said work dureing the continuance of the said patent ; for doeing whairof these presents shalbe your warrand.— Whythall, 8 Jar 1634.

These conteyne a Ratification of the former gifts granted by your Maties father of royall memorie, and by your Matis self in favours of your Matis servitour Sir James Murray and Anthony Alexander, of generall surveyors and Masters of Works within your Matis kingdom of Scotland, granting them yeirlie for discheargeing the said office a yeirlie fie of 1200lib Scotts, with power allanerlie to them for presenting, exerceing, outputting, and imputting of all sort of workmen, as carpenters, maissones, &c., at ther pleasur, that shalbe or ar imployed at the repairing of whatsumever his Matis houses or castells,—Whythall, 9 Jar 1634.

Decanatus Ecclesie Cathedralis Sti Egidii pro Magistro Thoma Sydserff.

Carolus Dei gratia magnae Britanniae Franciae et Hyberniae Rex fideique defensor Reverendo in Christo patri domino Willielmo Episcopo Edinburgeno Salutem Sciatis quod nos ex gratia nostra speciali et nostro favore damus et concedimus dilecto nostro Magistro Thomæ Sydserff presbitero seniori Ecclesiæ Collegiatæ Edinburgenæ decanatum Ecclesiæ Cathedralis Sancti Egidii infra dictam civitatem et diocesim Episcopatus Edinburgeni vacantem et ad nostram donationem et presentationem pleno jure spectantem per mortem quondam Magistri Willielmi Struthers vltimi decani ejusdem Tenendum et habendum dictum decanatum predicto Magistro Thomæ Sydserff durante ejus vita naturali cum omnibus suis juribus et privilegiis vniversis Volentes et requirentes quatenus predictum Magistrum Thomam ad dictum decanatum admittere ipsumque decanum dictæ Ecclesiæ cum suis juribus et privilegiis vniversis rite et legittime institui et induci facere ceteraque peragere et perimplere que vestro in hac parte incumbunt officio pasturati digno cum favore In cujus rei testimonium sigillum nostrum privatum presentibus appendi fecimus.—Apud, &c.

TO THE ARCHBISCHOP OF S' ANDROIS.

Right reverend father in God, our trustie and weilbeloved Counsellour—Vnderstanding by your letter that M' Peter Hay of Naughton, from whom yow had that petition whairof yow sent a copie to ws, hath said vnto yow that he will discover the persone from whom he had it, if he be requyred to doe the same by ws : Thervpoun we have writtin a letter to him to that effect, which we send yow heirwith, and it is our pleasur yow send for him, and haveing gottin the name of the persone from him, that yow acquant ws presentlie therwith, not imparting to any other till yow shall hear further from ws.—Whythall, 16 Ja' 1634.

TO PETER HAY OF NAUGHTON.

Trustie, &c.—We have vnderstude that the copie of a petition sent vnto ws by the richt reverend father in God the Archbischop of S' Androis was gottin from yow : It is our pleasur, and we doe heirby requyre yow, to acquant the said reverend father with the name of the persone from whom yow had the said petition, which faill not to doe as yow wilbe answerable vnto ws.—Whythall, 10 Ja' 1634.

TO THE ERLE OF TRAQUAIR.

Right, &c.—Haveing occasion at this tyme to confer with yow tuitching some thingis concerneing our service, we requyre yow, with all convenient diligence, to repair to our Court, wher our further pleasur shall be made knowen vnto yow.—Whythall, 10 Ja' 1634.

TO THE ARCHBISCHOP OF GLASGOW.

Right reverend, &c.—Haveing sene a certificat of the deane and Chaptour of the See of Gla. Iles of the admission and election of our trustie and weilbelovit M' Neill Campbell to the bischoprik of the Yles, according to our warrant for that purpois, Our pleasur is, that with all convenient diligence yow give ordour for his translation to the said bischoprik, and for his enstalment therin in such readie and fitt maner as in the lyk caices is accustomed ; ffor which, &c.—Whythall, 14 Ja' 1634.

Our Soverane Lord being crediblie informed that diverse masters, merchandis, and owners of schipps, Skippers, mariners, and other persones doe secreitlie or vnder cullour of lawfull merchandice send away and transport furth of the kingdome of Scotland into diverse forran cuntreyis all sorts of vnlawfull and prohibited goodis without any licence, yea disconforme to ther licences, and without the knowledge of any customers, sercheris, or others his Ma^{teis} officers, to the great prejudice of his Ma^{teis} customes and good subjects, and in manifest contempt of his highnes' authoritie and lawis: Therfor his Matie, with advyse and consent of his highnes' right, &c. the Erle of Morton, principall Thesaurer of the said kingdome, and of Johne, Erle of Traquair, thesaurer depute ther, and remanent Commissioners of Excheker, Ordeanes a Letter to be made and past vnder the privie seall in dew forme, making, constituteing, and ordeaneing, lykas his Matie, with advyse and consent forsaid, doeth heirby mak, constitute, and ordeane Wm Barclay . . . . . and his assigneyis dureing his Ma^{teis} pleasur receavers of all sorts and quantiteis of vnlawfull and forbidden goodis and merchandice, to be caryed and transported from tyme to tyme dureing his Ma^{teis} said pleasur furth of any part of the said kingdome or ylis thairof, into any other kingdome, state, cuntrey, or place whatsoever belonging to strangers, by whatsoever persone or persones, nations or strangers, contrair to the acts of parliament made theranent, or more in quantitie or of other spaces or qualitie, or to any other place or at any other tyme ther is or shalbe speciallie or particularlie exprest in the severall warrandis or licences granted or to be granted for the same, ather without sufficient licence from his Matie or his highnes' successours, or from the Commissioners of Excheker in forme and maner specifeit in the severall Actis of Parliament, or other acts, lawis, statutis, or constitutions of the said kingdome or in defraud thairof: And lykwyse receaveris of all and sindrie the senders, havears, caryers, and transporters of the saids goods and merchandice, ather without or disconforme to the licence in any poynt whatsoever, giveing and granting lykas his Matie for his highnes and his successours, with advyse and consent forsaid, Gives and grants to the said William Barclay and his assigneyis dureing his Ma^{teis} said pleasur the office of receaver forsaid, with all fieis, priviledges, casualiteis, proffeits, and dewteis therto belonging, with full power to him and his foirsaids, dureing his Ma^{teis} said pleasur, to substitute deputeis and vnder receavers, ane or mae, in all and whatsumever tounes, ports, and places convenient within England, Irland, France, Spayne, Germanie, Sweden, Denmark, Norway, Polland, and others places, yls, and cuntreyis whatsumever (excepting alwayes the boundis conteynit in the conservatours' commissioun) into which any such vnlawfull or prohibited goodis and merchandice shall happin to be transported furth of the said kingdome or ylis thairof without licence, or disconforme therto, for whom the saids vnder receavers and everie of them the said William and his successours shalbe holden to answer, and with full power to the said William Barclay and his forsaids, ther deputeis and vnder receivers, and everie of them, dureing his Ma^{teis} pleasur, To search, seik, try, and enquyre efter all sorts and quantitie of vnlawfull and prohibited goodis and merchandice that shalbe sent and transported furth of the kingdome or ylis therof into any other kingdome, state, yle, or place whatsoever (excepting as is befor excepted), ather without sufficient licence, or disconforme thairto, vnto his Ma^{teis} said Thesaurer, principall, and deputie, or ather of them, or ather of ther deputeis present and for the tyme being, that all such fynes, penalteis, and escheits as ar respective and speciallie sett doun in the saids Acts of Parliament and others acts and statuts made against such trangressours may be duelie inflicted, imposed, levyed, takin vp, and exacted from them and everie of them, conforme to the tenour of the saids acts in all poynts: And for the said William Barclay and his forsaidis subsistence in the said office in the dew and fayfhull administratioun thairof, and for mantenance of the saids deputeis and vnder receavers, Our soverane Lord, for his highnes' and highnes' successours, with advyse and consent forsaid, hath gevin, granted, and disponed, and by these presents gives, grants, and frielie dispones to the said William Barclay and his forsaids, or deputeis, or ather of them dureing his Ma^{teis} said pleasur, ther heyres and executours, the just and equall haliff of all such escheits, fynes, and penalteis as shalbe inflicted and imposed, levyed, takin vp, and exacted from the transgressours of the saids acts whom the said William, or his forsaids, or t'er saids deputeis, or any of them, dureing his Ma^{teis} said pleasur, shall reveale and delate in maner forsaid, to be vsed and disponed vpon by them as ther owin propper goodis and geir at ther pleasur in all tyme cuming : And for that effect commanding and ordeancing his highnes' saids Thesaurers and ther deputeis, joyntlie and severallie, present and for the tyme being, To readelie and thankfullie pay and delyver, or cause to be payed and delyvered, vnto the said Wm Barclay, and his assigneyis, ther aires and executours, the forsaid one halff of all and sindrie the said escheits, fynes, and pecuniall mults respective above named, to be vsed and enjoyed by them for ever without any accompt thairof to be made in Exchequer ; And with command also to the auditours of Exchequer, present and to cum, to defease and allow the said halff of the saidis escheit, fynes, and penalteis vnto the saidis Thesaurers and ther deputeis respective, from tyme to tyme in all tyme cuming, in ther severall accompts to be made yeirlie of the premisses in Exchequer : Wherauent the said Letter, being once schawin and registrat in Exchequer as effeires, shalbe ther and everie of ther sufficient warrant and discharge in that behalff, and that the said letter be farder extendit with all clausses neidfull.—Whythall, 18 Ja^r 1634.

May it pleas your most Excellent Matie To prevent the abuse of transporting of vnlawfull goodis from Scotland. These appoynt Wm Barclay and his assiguayes, dureing your Ma^{teis} pleasur, to be revcallers thairof, and to that effect to setle substituts in forrayne parts. They ar to have from your Ma^{teis} Thesaurie the halff of the saidis goodis they shall reveall vnto them. The other halff is for your Ma^{teis} use.

To the Toun of Edinburgh.

Trustie and weilbeloved, &c.—Hearing of the death of Mr Wm Struthers, and being desyreous that Mr Thomas Sydserff, deane of the Chaptour of Edinburgh, be preferred to the first minister's place therin, as being fitt for his charge, bot speciallie in regard of his abiliteis and sufficiencie, wherof we ar crediblie informed ; we doe therfoir speciallie recommend vnto yow that, haveing conferred with your bischop herauent, yow would mak choyce of the said Mr Thomas to supplie the said place, wherin yow shall doe ws verie acceptable service.—Whythall, 18 Ja^r 1634.

Similar Letter to the Bishop of Edinburgh.

To the Bischop of Edinburgh.

Reverend father in God, &c.—Wheras the parochiners of the North syd of Leith hath recommended vnto ws a qualifeid persone (as we ar informed by them), that we might be pleased to present him to ther church, which is vnprovydit of a minister, whervnto if we shall condescend they offer to setle a compitent and constant stipend for the mantenance of him and the ministrie ther in tyme cuming, and to leave the right of the patronage thairof vnto ws heirefter, which offers, if the said persone be sufficientlie qualifeid and conforme to the ordours and discipline of the Church, would some verie fair ; yit being loath to signifie our pleasur heirin vnto them till yow had first considered of the same, Our pleasur is, that, haveing conferred to this purpois with the right reverend father the Archbischop of St Andrais, yow send vp vnto ws a presentation vnder your hand to be signed by ws for the said persone, if he shalbe fund fitt for such a charge ; otherwayes certifie ws with all diligence of your opinions what course is left to be takin in this case.—Whythall, 18 Ja^r 1634.

To the Thesaurer and Depute.

Right, &c.—Wheras humble sute hath bene made vnto ws in behalff of the musitians of our Chappell Royall, that the arreiris of the yeirlie allowance for ther mantenance may be payed, and a setled course taken heirefter, that by want thairof our service in that kynd be not neglected, haveing to this purpois writtin at severall tymes : And it being our spetiall pleasur that a course may be speedilie taken for ther satisfaction accordinglie, as we have formerlie signifeid, we doe heirby requyre that yow examyne what hath bene done heirin, and that, efter what yow find them to be behind of ther arreiris, it be furthwith payed without further trouble vnto ws ; and, till ane other course be takin for ther mantenance, that they be dewlie payed of the said allowance at ther tymes mentioned in the gifts ; which recommending, &c.—Whytall, 18 Jar 1634.

To the Counsell.

Right, &c.—Being informed of the sufficiencie of our trustie and weilbeloved William, Bischop of Edinburgh, and of his affection to our service, we ar moved in regard therof, and for his better encouragement and enabling for our said service, to advance and promove him to be one of our Privie Counsell of that our kingdome : Therfor our pleasur is, and we doe heirby requyre yow, that, haveing aluinistred vnto him the oath accustomed in the lyk caices, yow admitt him to be one of your number : And for, &c.—Whythall, 18 Jar 1634.

Margaret Stewart, his Maties Nurse, pension was ratified for hir and and hir sone's, Francis Russall's, lyftyme, and the langest leiver of them. The pension is 200^{lib} sterling, to be payed yeirlie to them or ther assigneyis according to ther gift.—Whythall, 20 Jar 1634.

To the Counsell.

Right, &c.—Wheras, out of our princelie commiseratioun of the distressed estate of the petitioner and hir children, we wer pleased, at our last being in that our kingdome, to referr vnto yow a petition delyvered vnto ws then by hir, wherof shoe hath had no answer : Therfoir, the lyk consideratioun moveing ws to compassioun at this tyme, we have heirby thoght fitt to recommend hir caus vnto yow, by considering of the inclosed petition and calling the creditours befor yow, and deall with them effectuallie, to grant vnto hir what ease they can convenientlie affoord hir, both tuitching hir owin and her husband's releiff, that we be not more troubled therwith, wherin we will accompt your panes as good service done vnto ws : We bid, &c.—Whythall, 24 Jar 1634.

To the Counsell.

Right, &c.—Wheras humble sute hath bene made vnto ws in behalff of Alexr Levingstoun of Greneyards, that we might be gratiouslie pleased to grant vnto him a Protection for ane yeir, thereby the better to enable him (as he affirmeth) to tak the more suife and speedie course to give his creditours satisfaction : if yow find that his grounds heirin may tend to the securing of the saidis creditours of what shalbe fund dew vnto them, and enabling him for doeing therof, Our pleasur is, that yow grant him a Protection for a yeir to this purpois, or for some such competent tyme as yow shall think fitt ; and for your soe doeing, &c. Whythall, 24 Jar 1634.

To the Session.

Right, &c.—Wheras we ar informed that by reasone of the great aige, seiknes, and inhabilitie of Alex[r] Keith of Benham, he cannot give that attendance for following some actions in Law concerncing him, depending or to cum befoir yow, as the estate thairof doeth necessarlie require, wherin, his caus deserveing our princelie commiseratioun, we heirby thoght fitt to recommend vnto yow that speedie justice be administred vnto him in these actions as by the Lawis and custome of that cuntrie can be affoorded vnto him : Which recommending vnto your care, we bid, &c.—Whythall, 24 Ja[r] 1634.

To the Thesaurer and Deputie Thesaurer.

Right, &c.—Wheras vpon consideration of the dangerous abuses tending to the great hurt and dishonour of that our kingdome by breach of the Acts of Parliament and Counsall made anent exhorbitant vsurie, transporting of gold and silver furth of the kingdome, and changeing and selling therof at heyer rates then by Law ar allowed, we ar pleased that the delinquents be furthwith censured and punisched, to restrayne the practeises and pernitious consequences thairof heirefter ; And becaus, without exacting the rigour of our Lawis, we may justlie and doe expect no small benefite by ther forfeytis, we have thoght fitt, and we will and requyre yow, to treat with our Advocat and others of our Counsall and Exchequer of the most convenient meanes to that purpois, ather by carving of generall compositions and discharges thervpoun, and so resolveing vpoun a certane proportion to be takin of everie sowme lent, changed, or transported contrarie to the Law, or any other course that yow shall find better, and thervpoun give ordour to our Advocat to prosecute the delinquents in our name, according to the course of Law, and the way that shalbe condescended vpoun amongst yow, for our best and readiest benefite, requyreing and authorizing yow, our Thesaurer principall and deputie, that from tyme to tyme, as the fynes thoght fitt to be exacted shall happin to cum in, yow cause pay the same to our trustie and weilbeloved Counsellour Sir James Galloway, kny[t], our M[r] of requests, or his assigneyis, till the sowme of 2000[lib] stg. be compleitlie payed vnto him, conforme to our precept thervpoun, causeing ane Act of Exchequer to be made vpoun this ; For which, &c.—Whythall, 24 Ja[r] 1634.

To the Archbischop of S[t] Androis.

Right, &c.—We have heard of some complaynts maide in behalff of our right, &c. the Marqueis of Huntlie and his Lady, that they have bene hardlie vsed tuitching ther religion beyond the boundis of discretion, they haveing gevin no caus of publict scandell to the religion professed, ther qualitie and great aige pleading for more than ordinarie convenience, according to the course that our late dear father did (as we ar informed) observe in ther behalff ; we have therby thought fitt that yow tak the proceidingis vsit aganst them into your consideratioun, and so mitigat and ordour the bussienes heirefter that nather any publict scandell be gevin to the Churche, nor they have any further occasion of complaint of such hard proceidingis aganst them as they affirme to have bene : For performeing whairof we trust to your long experience and approved judgment.—Whythall, 24 Ja[r] 1634.

To the Thesaurer and Deputie.

Right, &c.—Wheras humble sute hath bene made vnto ws in behalff of Margaret Stewart, who nursed ws, that in regard schee is far behind in hir pension, and therby reduced to great wants, the arreiris thairof, being the onlie meanes schoe hath, might be the more speedelie payed vnto hir for hir releiff, and that therefter schoe might have no such occasion to importune ws ; we, respecting hir former good service, and with all commiserating hir distressed estate now in her aige, have bene pleased to ratifie hir pensioun, which we will yow to caus expeid with diligence ; And haveing examined how much schoe is behind therof, yow mak hir speedie payment of hir arreiris, that schoe may have no further occasion of complaynt ; and for your soe doeing, &c.—Whythall, 24 Jar 1634.

To THE SESSION.

Right, &c.—Vnderstanding from our right, &c. the Marqueis of Hamilton the great care yow have had in the speedie administratioun of Justice with integritie in that service of ouris, (uitching tuo of ten for each hundreth of annalrent money, we give yow hartie thanks for the same, and doe recommend vnto yow in speciall maner that when any motion shall cum in befoir yow in that kynd, yow administer speedie justice therin according to our Lawis as yow have formerlie done : And be confident, as we have heard from our said Cousen, of such persones amongst yow as both justlie and affectionatlie hath bene a meanes at this tyme to advance our said service, so we will both distinguishe our respect to them from others who hath not bene so forward therin, and tak such particular notice of ther service as we will not be vnmyndfull thairof when any occasion shall offer for ther advantage and further preferment.—Whythall, 26 Jar 1634.

To THE SESSION.

Right, &c.—Wheras we ar informed, in behalff of our burgh of Dumbarton, that notwithstanding ther priviledges have both bene antientlie and of late yeres granted vnto them vpon verie considerable causses, yit they ar questioned now of late by particular persones, and spetiallie for privat respects drawing them to vnnecessarie charges in Law, who cannot without hazarding of ther poore privat meanes (ther common good not being of any important value) vndergoe any long proces in Law: Though we inclyne much to the conservation of the priviledges of our ancient burghes, yit being ever willing that Justice be administered indifferentlie according to our Lawis to all our subjects without respect of persones, we ar pleased so far to tak notice of ther cause, as speciallie to recommend vnto yow that Justice be speedelie administred in any action in Law which may concerne them, which we will tak as verie acceptable service done vnto ws.—Whythall, first Febr 1634.

To THE EXCHEQUER.

Right, &c.—Wheras we ar informed that a signature for erecting the village of Greenok in a burgh of baronie is ather alreadie past or to be exped vnder our seaills, wherby our burghes of Glasgow and Dumbarton wilbe prejudged in ther antient priviledges, granted be our royall progenitours vpoun verie considerable causses, the passing wherof (as they affirme) being contrarie to our lawis made in favours of our royall frie burghes ; and ther humble sute being so moderat as to be heard befoir what is intended by the said signature be putt to executioun to ther prejudice, we ar heirby pleased to requyre yow not to expeid the said signature (if it be not past alreadie) till ther reasones for staying therof be heard : bot if it be alreadie exped, that yow tak such course for ther satisfaction as may be most agreiable to equitie and the lawis of that our kingdome.—Whythall, first Febr 1634.

II 2 Q

To the Advocat.

Trustie, &c.—Haveing heard that it hath bene objected aganst yow that yow could not plead in favours of our right, &c. James, Lord Doun, in the action depending befoir our Colledge of Justice, betuixt him and James Home of Coldinknowis, concerneing the Erldome of Home : In regard it is alledgit that the said James Home, if he prevaill, will prove our ward, and consequentlie yow, being our Advocat, cannot be aganst him, yit till the treuth of that doeth appear, whether he is to be our ward or not, we allow yow to plead for him as yow doe for your other ordinarie clyents, till we be fullie informed of the estate of that bussines, signifie vnto yow our further pleasure heirin ; and for your soe doing, &c.— Whythall, first Feb* 1634.

To the Session.

Right, &c.—Wheras we ar informed that notwithstanding our right trustie and weilbeloved the Lord Ogilvie did punctuallie fulfill vnto his late mother and James Ogilvie, his brother, a decreit gevin by yow tuitching the setling of some differences amongst them, yit the said James, by instigatioun of some persones, intendeth to trouble the said Lord, his brother, by a further sute in Law ; we, being desyreous to be certifeid of the trew estate of your proceidingis in this bussines, ar heirby pleased to refer vnto yow the consideratioun of the inclosed petition, and with all to requyre yow to send vnto ws with all convenient expedition the trew estate therof, that we may thervpoun determyne to give such farder ordour therin as we in our judgment shall find caus ; we bid, &c.—Whythall, 1 Feb* 1634.

To the Chancellour.

Right, &c.—Wheras we have bene moved in behalff of our right weilbeloved the Lord Kirkcudbryght that we would cause our Colledge of Justice ther dismisse ane action in Law depending befoir them at the instance of our right, &c. the Erle of Annandale aganst him, tuitching a title to some Landis in Irland, becaus we could hardlie give trust bot that everie of our Judicatoreis should know the dew motions properlie belonging vnto them, we thoght fit onlie to wryt to yow for informeing your self if any such suitt have bene moved and insisted in befor them, which we cannot beleive ; and if ther be any such mistak, lett the sute be furthwith dismissed, that the pairteis may have recourse vnto Irland, wher it is onlie proper to be determined ; wherof not doubting of the speedie performance.—Whythall, 2 Feb* 1634.

To the Advocat.

Trustie, &c.—The proposition heirin enclosed haveing bene made vnto ws of late vpon a precedent of the lyk course taken by our late dear father and our self in this our kingdome, which we think lykwayes convenient to be established in that kingdome for reformation of abuses and incress of our revenewis, Our pleasur is, that yow tak it into your serious consideratioun, and that with all convenient diligence yow certifie ws of your opinion of the fittest legall way for the setling thairof : Which recommending to your care, &c.

To the Chancellour.

Right, &c.—The enclosed petition haveing been exhibite vnto ws in behalff of ane Humphray Norton, a tradesman, and native within this our kingdome, wherby he humblie represents that out of his love and too much trust in ane Adam Gordon, sone of John Gordon of Ardlogie, he is lyklie to lose a great part of his meane estate, besyde the hazarding of the remanent, by being forced to repair thither to seik Justice, for recoverie of what the said Adam did borrow of him, we ar pleased so far to tak notice of his case, and to comiserat the same, as seriouslie to recommend vnto yow the consideratioun of the petitioun, willing yow to sie justice administred vnto him with all possible and convenient expedition : We bid, &c.— Whythall, 17 Feb 1634.

To the Archbischop of Glasgow.

Right, &c.—Wheras, vpon hearing of the abiliteis and affection to our service of our trustie and weil-beloved Johne Boyll, Commissar of Glasgow, we wer pleased to mak choyse of him to be vpon our Commission for Tythes and surrenders, which, as we ar informed, he hath carefullie attended to his charge and paines ; and wheras in equitie he oght not suffer vthers to be discouraged in the following of our service of such consequence, we most ather releese him from attending the same (to which we ar vnwilling), or that yow dispense with his not residence at Glasgow : And becaus (as we ar lykwyse informed) his place is supplied by one sufficient man deputed for that purpois, we have thoght fitt to desyre yow that he be not troubled or anywayes questioned for his not residing to discharge his place dureing the continuance of the Commission.—Whythall, 7 Feb 1634.

To the Exchequer.

Right, &c.—Wheras our right, &c. the Erle of Ancrum is to pass a signature, wherby in tuo deidis he hath made over his landis, particularlie mentioned therin, to his eldest sone, the Erle of Lothian, reserveing his owin lyf, and that in caise he hath no aires-male the Landis to returne to his other sone's aires whatsumever, this being no new gift nor incress of rent to our servant, but a privat deid of his, to be confirmed by ws ; therfoir, and in regaird of the neirnes and qualitie of his service about ws, Our pleasur is, that yow pas and caus expeid these gifts at a verie small composition, and with as much diligence as can be vsed, for which these shalbe your sufficient warrand.—Whythall, 7 Feb 1634.

Commission for hearing the Thesaurer's Accompts.

Our Soverane Lord ordeanes a Commission to be made vnder the testimoniall of his highnes' great seall of his Ma^{tis} kingdome of Scotland in due forme, makand, constitutand, and ordeandand, lykas by thir presents maks, constituts, and ordeanes his right, &c. George Erle of Kynnoull, Lord Chancellour of Scotland ; and right reverend Johne Archbischop of St Androis ; his right, &c. Thomas Erle of Hadintoun, keiper of his Ma^{tis} privic seal ; the right reverend Patrik, Archbischop of Glasgow ; his right, &c. cousen, &c. Erle of Stirling, the Marqueis of Hamiltoun, George Erle of Winton, Alex^r Erle of Linlithgow, Johne Erle of Perth, Robert Erle of Roxburgh, Johne Erle of Lauderdaill, David Erle of Carnegie, Erle of Traquair ; the reverend fathers John Bischop of Ross, Adam Bischop of Dumblane ; his trustie Johne Lord Yester, Johne Lord Balmerino, Robert Lord Melvill, Alex^r M^r of Elphingstoun ; Sir John Scott, Sir James Baillie, and Sir Alex^r Strauchan, or any fyftene, ellevin, or nyne of them conjunctlie, Auditours of his Ma^{tis} Exchequer named in the former Commission, of which number they being alwayes six, or at the least four of the Commissioners of the Excheker present named in the said former Commission ; Geving vnto them, or any fyftene, ellevin, or nyne of them, as said is, his highness' full power and commission, at whatsumever tyme or place convenient, to hear, examyne, consider, admitt, subscryve, and end the compts and recepts of his Ma^{tis} right, &c. of George Erle of Kynnoull, Collectour of his Ma^{tis} taxatiouns granted in anno 1630, as the same accompts shalbe made and produced, and subscryve the same so reed, heard, examined, as said is ; And generallie all and sindrie other things to doe, vse, and exerce which in the premisses or theranent shalbe anywayes necessarie or requisit. firme and stable holding all and whatsumever the saidis Auditours of his Matie Excheker, or any 15, 11, or 9 of them, conjunctlie as said is, shall think rightlie to be done ; And that the said Commission be farder extendit with all clausses neidfull. —Gevin at Whythall, 9 Feb^r 1634.

COMMISSION FOR HEARING THE CHANCELLOUR'S COMPTS OF TAXATIOUNS.

(The Narrative or former part of this Commission is lyk vnto the precedent, saiff that the Chancellour's name must be left out in the beginning of the Commission, sieing it is for hearing of his Intromissions with his Ma^{tis} taxatiouns.) Or any 15, 11, or 9 of them conjunctlie, auditours of his Matie Exchequer named in the former Commission, of which number ther being alwayes 6, or at the least 4 of the Commissioners of Excheker present named in the said former commission : Giveand and grantand vnto them, or any 15, 11, or 9 of them conjunctlie, as said is, his highnes' full power and commission, at whatsumever tyme and place convenient, to hear, examyne, consider, admitt, subscryve, and end the compts and recepts of his Matie, &c. W^m, Erle of Morton, his Matie Principall Thesaurer, and of Johne, Erle of Traquair, his Ma^{tis} deputie theasurer in the saidis offices, of the whole rents of his highnes' patrimonie, casualiteis, and dewteis perteneing to the said offices, or any of them, as the same accompts shalbe made and produced, and to admitt and subscryve the same so red, heard, and examined as said is ; And generallie all and sindrie others things to dow and exerce which in the premisses or theranent shalbe anywayes necessarie or requisit, firme and stable, holding and for to hold all and whatsoever the saids Auditours of his Ma^{tis} Exchequer, or any 15, 11, or 9 of them conjunctlie, as said is, &c.—Whythall, 9 Feb^r 1634.

This conteyne ane Ratificatioun of ane gift of pension granted by your Matie father, of eternall memorie, to Patrik, then Bischop of Ross, now Archbischop of Glasgow, dureing his lyftyme, of eight chalders bear and fourtie four pundis money out of the few ferme maill of your Ma^{tis} landis of Pettindreich, with ane new gift of the samyne dureing his lyftyme.—Whythall, 7 Febrij 1634.

TO THE SESSION.

Right, &c.—Being informed by the enclosed Petition that ther is ane action in Law depending befoir yow betuixt some pairteis mentioned in the said petition anent some landis in Irland, whervpon landis past amongst them with conditiones respective indorsat thervpon ; and being lykwyse informed that the Landis which ar the subject of the contraversie betuixt them be in Irland, and the landis mentioned in the said petition wer made and to be performed ther, which yow doe find to be trew, as by the petition is affirmed : Our pleasur is, that furthwith yow dismisse that sute, that the pairteis may have recourse vnto Irland, wher it is onlie propper to be determined ; wherof not doubting of your speedie performance, &c.— Whythall, 11 Feb^r 1634.

TO THE COUNSELL.

Right, &c.—Haveing bene pleased to tak great panes vpon ws for setling the differences betuixt the E. Roxbrugh and Buccleuch and Francis Stewart, sone to the late Erle Bothwell, And being most willing efter so long a tyme that all possible meanes be vsed to putt them to a finall determinatioun, we doe heirby requyre yow to call befoir yow the tutours and curators to whome the late Erle of Buccleuchis children and ther estate ar entrusted, requyreing them in our name to draw vp a procuratorie or factorie in ther names, geving power to such of ther owin number as they shall think fitt who may stay heir, and who ar best acquanted with the estate of that bussines, to setle and finallie compose in our presens the saids differences betwen the Erle of Buccleuchis children and the said Francis, that the same being legallie and perfectlie done, be delyvered to the Erle of Roxbrugh, that at his cuming hither these matters may be fullie concludit: Which speciallie recommending vnto your care, we bid, &c.—Whythall, 11 Feb^r 1634.

These appoynt Johne Dowglas, sone to James Dowglas, ordiner Maiser of the privie Counsall, excheker and Commissioners, ane serjant at Armes, to supplie and discharge these services in his father's absence, and vpon occasion of seiknes, aige, or other inavoydable impediments, and efter his death to succeid to these charges and vplift the feyis and casualiteis thervnto belonging dureing his lyftyme.—Whythall, 16 Febrij 1634.

To the Counsell.

Right, &c.—In regard of the great prejudice lyklie to ensew by diminution of rent raised to ws vpon Coall transported from this our kingdome, if ther be not some reasonable imposition laid vpon Coall transported from in lyk maner, that ther be no such disparitie of pryces betwixt them when they ar sold in forraine parts as they ar for the present, everie chalder that goeth from thence paying to ws tuelff schilling 4^d st., which notwithstanding is no impediment to the transporting of them, bot by tyme breeding a great scarcitie at home may mak manie to suffer wher now onlie a few ar benefited by venting of them abroad, yit we ar willing that ther be a difference of the imposition ther from what is takin heir in respect of considerationns that necessarlie concerne the esteat of the severall kingdomes: Therfor, being content that the one halff onlie of that impositioun be takin ther, Our pleasur is, that six schillings sterline money be imposed to our vse vpon everie such quantitie of all coall which soever transported from thence vnto any part beyond the seas, not being of our dominions, as wilbe answerable in proportion to the watter measur of the chalder of sea coall vsed at New Castle vpon Tyne; and that yow give ordour to our Advocat to draw vp for our signature such warrant and ordour for layeing and levyeing of that imposition to the vse of ws and our successours at all tymes heirefter as yow to that purpois shall think most fitt, and therefter lett it be furthwith sent to ws docated by our Advocat, for which these shalbe vnto yow and him a sufficient warrant.—Whythall, 7 Feb^r 1634.

Right, &c.—Wheras we ar willing vpon verie good considerationns that the halff of the Imposition vpon Coalls transported out of this our kingdome to forrayne parts be laid vpon Coall transported from thence, as by our letter to our Counsell yow will perceive, in regard of the trust and charge yow have from ws, we have heirby thoght fitt particularlie to recommend that bussines to your charge, willing yow to give ws ane accompt therof ather at your comeing to our Court (if yow repair hither schortlie), or that ye send the same vnto [ws] with convenient diligence: We bid yow, &c.—Whythall, 17 Feb^r 1634.

Manu Regis.

I assure yow that is not for any courteous benefite, bot merelie for balanceing of trade and augmentation of my revenew.   Sub^r,   C. R.

These conteyne ane gift of the Abacie of Inchefray, whole teyndis and spiritualitie thairof, to Patrik Murray, sone to vmquhill Mr Patrik Murray, last Commendatour of the said Abbacie, indureing his lyftyme, with ane factorie of the few maills and temporalitie of the said Abbacie, and that according to the provision in ane patent made by your Matie to the said vmquhill Mr Patrik, whereby your Matie promises to provyde efter his deceis, his aires or others to be nominat by him to the said Abbacie, ay and whill they wer payed, of twelff hundreth pundis sterling, with expensses; Provision, That the said Patrik being satisfeit of the said sowme of twelff hundreth pundis sterling, he shall renunce all right he may pretend to the said abacie, spiritualitie, and temporalitie thairof in your Ma^tis favours, according to the tenour of the said patent made to his said vmquhill father.—Whythall, 18 Feb^r.

To the Session.

Right, &c.—Having receaved diverse letters from our Advocat representing the estate of the cause of Home depending befoir yow, with the difficulteis whervnto he was brought in respect of our interest, as was alledgit by the persewer James Home, and his duetie to his clyent, we wer gratiouslie pleased to permitt him to plead for the Lord Downe till the treuth of that our interest should more planelie appear, and to that effect signifeid our pleasur by a letter direct to himsellf, bearing date the first of Feb^r, since which tyme we have receaved the whole proceidings in that bussines vnder the Clerk Register's hand, by which it doeth appear to ws that the offeris made by the procuratours of the Lord Doun, confirmed efterward by himsellf and the Lord Maitland, doeth mak them lyable to the equivalent worth of the ward and mariage and other casualiteis due to ws by the said James if he should prevaill; And therfoir we, in our royall justice, will not permitt our name to be vsed to the prejudice of any wher we have no interest, so that if any haveing our name made ws seme to be partiall in either syd, we vtterly disclame the same, our officers haveing no warrant from ws to medle in it, bot so far as our particular interest was thought to be: Nevertheles, without partialitie to ather partie, this we have thoght fitt to expres, not out of any misdoubt, bot that our officers have done ws as becom them, bot merlie to showe love to justice, and to hinder ydle rumors: Therfoir we declair vnto yow the sinceritie of our intention to justice by the permitting of our Advocat to plead for his clyent since we have no interest in particular: So remitting the caus to your decision, and willing yow nather to regard any of the pairteis befoir the other, nor anything else, bot that justice be equallie administred by yow according to the Lawis and custemes of that kingdome, &c.—Whythall, 20 Feb^r 1634.

To the Thesaurer and Deputie Thesaurer.

Right, &c.—Wheras we ar informed that it is ordored by the generall decree vpon the Surrenders that no satisfaction be gevin by ws for the blensch dewteis conteynit in the infeftments of the erectiouns made to any of them or ther authours, bot that they shall frielie accress to ws and our successours in all tyme cuming ; And that it is lykwayes ordored by the said decree that we should have a proportion of the pryce or yeirlie dewtie payable for tythis of erections at the sight of the Commissioners of Surranders for the tyme, we being willing to schaw all favour to all such our deserveing subjects as ar intrested that way, ar heirby gratiouslie pleased to dispense with any part or portion of these tythes of erection reserved to ws to all such persones as shalbe willing to secure ws and our successours of the payment of the said blensch dewteis conteint in ther said Infeftments or erection, or shalbe allowit vnto ws proportionallie of the few dewteis of the vassalls, without any composition or satisfaction for the same.

To the Counsell.

Right, &c.—Wheras we ar informed that the quantitie of Copper money last ordeaned to be coyned ther is now fullie vented, and that notwithstanding the necessiteis of the cuntrie is not therby as yit sufficientlie supplied, It is therfor our pleasur that yow give present ordour for the coynage of the lyk quantitie as by our former warrants was last ordeaned, for which these presents shalbe your warrant.

To the Chancellour, Thesaurer Principall and Deputie, Clerk Register, Advocat.

Right, &c.—Though we ar crediblie informed of our vndoubted right to the Yle of the Lewes, and that ther wilbe a great many of the few dewteis bygane payable vnto ws for the same resting vnpayed, wherby we have great advantage in Law and otherwayes against our right trustie and weilbelovit the Erle of Seafort, who for the present hath the possession therof, yit being willing to schaw him favour herin, we ar gratiouslie pleased to content our selffis with such a proportion of the said Iland and others places fitting therin as shalbe by yow [thought] necessarie and convenient for the assotiation of the fischings of Great Britane and Irland, provyded alwayes that the said Erle tak a new gift right of ws of the rest of that Yle for payment of the old few dewtie, to which purpois we ar heirby pleased that yow so proceid for ordoreing and setling of that bussines as may best conduce to the vse of our service, for which these shalbe your warrand.

To the Commissioners for the Chancellour's Accompts.

Right, &c.—Wheras we have gevin Commission to yow for examining and fitting of the accompts of the taxations whairof our right, &c. the Erle of Kynnoull, our Chancellour, hath bene our Collectour generall : And wheras it appeareth by the Commission that the clearing of the said Erle of Kynnoull his intromission with the taxations granted in anno 1625 doeth necessarlie depend and hath relation vnto the former accompts of these who had the collection of the rest of that taxatioun, We doe therfor requyr yow that yow seriouslie consider of the accompts which hath bene made of the said Taxatioun, and if yow find any difficultie or matter considerable therin till to be imparted to ws, that yow acquant ws therwith immediatlie ; which recommending vnto your speciall care, we bid, &c.—Whythall, 26 Feb^r 1631.

To the Advocat.

Trustie, &c.—Haveing at lenth imparted our mynd vnto our right, &c. the Erle of Traquair tuitching diverse thingis importing the good and advancement of our service wherin we will have occasion to vse your assistance, Our pleasur is, vpon his signifieing vnto yow our intention therin, yow give him your best advyse for furthering what may tend to the good of our service, and accordinglie vse your best endeavours to sie the same performed ; and vpon his report to ws of your care therin, we will acknowledge the same as verie good service done vnto ws : So we bid, &c.—Whythall, 26 Feb^r 1631.

Another to the Clerk Register, verbatim.

To the Session.

Right, &c.—Wheras by our former warrant we recommended to your care that no action be pleaded befoir yow wherin our Theasaurer principall, deputie Thesaurer, and our Advocat ar pairteis, aither for our propper or generall interest, till our saidis Officers wer heard for ws : and wheras yow wer willing to give obedience to our said direction in all matters wherin we have propper interest, bot made some scruple in some actionis wherin our officers and advocat wer persoweris or defenders for our generall interest, as in escheits, nonentresse, improbationis, and such of that nature, Though in all such actionis it is the custome and practeis of that hous, as we ar informed, that our advocat is and most be persewer for our interest, and sieing, as we ar lykwyse informed, the proces most goe on ther at our advocal's instance for our generall interest, we sie no reasone why he should not also plead the same, and we think it nowayes agrieble to good ordour that privat advocats should tak vpon them to dispute such causses without assistance of our said Advocat : Therfor our pleasur is, that yow give ordour that all causses concerneing ws, ather in our propper or generall interest, wherin ther shalbe any dispute and ressoneing, be pleaded and disputed by our Advocat, and that no privat Advocats tak vpon them to dispute the samyne without his judicial assistance and concurse, and that yow caus thir presents be insert in your books of Sederunt, causeing intimate the same publicthe to the advocats, and sie the same observed in all tyme cuming : And for your so doeing, &c.—Whythall, 26 Feb^r 1634.

To the Archbischop of St Androis.

Right Reverend father, &c.—Being willing for considerable causses to know the estate and worth of the rent of the pryorie of St Androis, and what doeth properlie belong thervnto, we ar heirby pleased to requyre that with all convenient diligence yow consider of the rentall thairof, as it shalbe exhibited vnto yow by our right, &c. the Erle of Traquair, and therefter that by him yow certifie ws what yow find concerneing the value thairof, togidder with your opinion tuitching the same : Which recommending vnto your speciall care, we bid yow farewell.—Whythall, 26 Feb^r 1634.

Your Matie by a late Act of parliament being to tak in consideratioun how to dispose of the annuitie of Tythis, doeth heirby, for releiveing these your subjects by whome it is payable of ane heretable burden, give Commission vnto your Thesaurers principall and deputie to deall with such of them as shall, within tyme limited, desyre to enjoy the annuitie of ther Landis of all yeres bygane and to cum, tuitching the pryces to be gevin for the same, with power to the Commissioners, with advyse and consent of the persones abovenamed, or any of them, to resigne and sell the said annuitie of all the saids yeres to the persones disposed to buy it ; with power to them in maner forsaid to frie by renunciatioun vther securitie requisite the buyers of all obleidgments for payment of the annuitie, which being vnder the handis of the saids commissioners, and conteyning a clause to be registrat in the said register, with ane Act of Exchequer to pas thervpon, shalbe as valide a right to the receavers as if it passed vnder the sealls and registers wheranent your Maties dispensses : The Commission to indure till it be prorogat at your Maties pleasur.—Whythall, 28 Feb^r 1634.

To the Counsell.

Right, &c.—Wheras, for the better governement and preservation of our peace within all the parts of that our antient kingdome according to our Lawis, or wes to the effect our poore subjects may not vnnecessarlie be put to charges by haveing recourse for justice to our counsell in everie severall greevance that may be incident, Justices of peace wer established in severall parts of that kingdome wher it was thought necessarie, we have further thought fitt to that purpois to requyre yow, according to the landable custome of governement vsed in this our kingdome, to caus establisch in such maner as is requisit in that kingdome everie Bischop to be a Justice of peace within his own dyocie, and with all that yow requyre them to give vnto yow a list of the most able and sufficient ministers within ther dyoccis, wher it is most necessarie that a Justice of peace be establisched, and that accordinglie yow caus settle such of them as yow shall think fitting to that purpois : Which recommending to your speciall care, we bid, &c.—Newmerket, 2 March 1634.

To the Advocat.

Trustie, &c.—These ar to signifie our pleasur vnto yow that in all maner of writts that shall pas your hand, wherin yow may have occasion to vse the word presbiterie, that designatioun heirefter shall not be vsed, bot in place thairof yow shall vse ministers or preachers as a maner of expression which we conceave to be fitter : For your doeing wherof thir presentis shalbe your warrand.—Newmerket, 2 March 1634.

To the Thesaurer and Thesaurer Deput.

Wheras we wer pleased by our gift vnder the privie seall of the date the 4 Junij 1630 to bestow vpon our trustie Sir Thomas Hope of Craighall, kny^t, our Advocat, 2000^{lib} sterling money, to have bene payed at Witsondey 1631, furth of the first and readliest of our rents, propertie, and casualiteis therof, and furth of our ryneing taxatiouns for the tyme, togidder with the interest so long as the same should remane vnpayed efter the said terme of Witsondey ; and becaus our said servant hath not receaved payment of the said sowme of 2000^{lib}, therfor it is our pleasur yow mak payment vnto him, his aires and assigneyis, of the sowme of 2000^{lib} st^g at Witsondey nixt, and that of the first and readliest of these moneyis of our taxatiouns last granted vnto ws in that our kingdome, with the interest therof so long as the same remanes vnpayed, and that yow accept of this our warrant, testifieing to the said Sir Thomas vnder your hand your acceptatioun thairof, and that therefter yow sie ws discharged of that debt so owing by ws vnto him : And for your soe doeing these presents shalbe your warrand and discharge.—Newmerket, 2 March 1634.

To the Archbischop of S$_t$ Androis and Bischop of Edinburgh.

Right reverend and reverend fathers in God, our trustie and weilbeloved Counsellours, Right trustie and weilbeloved conseues and counsellours, and trustie and weilbeloved, &c.—Haveing sene the copie of a petition which hath bene in the hands of Mr Peter Hay of Naughton, and he being requyred by ws to declair from whome he had the said petition, hath done the same by nameing one Dunmure, a notter duelling in Dundie : It is our pleasur that yow call them befor yow, and haveing receaved the said Mr Peter Hay his information, and examined the said Dynmure concerneing the authour of that petition, and who may be any wayes accessorie to it, yow informe yourselff so far as yow can in all things concerneing it, and certifie ws what yow find thereanent, that we may caus tak such farder ordour, with these that shalbe fund to have had hand therein, as we shall think fitting : And for your soe doeing these presents shalbe your warrant.—Newmerket, 3 March 1634.

To the Session.

Right, &c.—Haveing vnderstude that in the action concerneing the Erldome of Home depending befor yow it was alledged that in regard of ane argument vsed concerneing our prerogative, any further proceiding in the cause ought to have bene delayed till we had bene acquanted therwith, and that notwithstanding ther was no delay granted, we conceave that ther most neidis have bene some great reasone for your denying of it, sieing wher our prerogative is named, vpon what groundis soever, we doubt not but that yow will alwyse advert to it with such tender care that is requisit : It is therfor our pleasur that yow certifie ws with all convenient diligence what was the reasones of your proceiding befor we wer made acquanted with what was alledged in such a case, requyreing yow in the meane tyme to delay any further proceiding in that cause till we signifie our further pleasur, efter we have receaved your answer : The speedie returneing therof will prevent any delay that may be prejudiciall to the pairteis, for in this we have respect to nather pairtie, bot onlie to that which was alledgit to concerne our prerogative ; wherin expecting your care, we bid, &c.—Newmerkit, 4 March 1634.

May it pleas your most Excellent Matie—
These give vnto Thomas Cadwell a gift of the escheit and lyfrent of Doctour Beaton for being denunced rebell, and lyeing vnder protest of horning vnrelaxed.—Newmerket, 7 March 1634.

To the Lord Lorne.

Right, &c.—Being informed that within some boundis wherin yow have interest ther ar some mangrell haulks, wherof we so much affect the kynd, and ar desyreous to mak tryell of some of them for our sport, These ar to recommend to yow that a falcon and tersell therof be sent vnto ws with as much convenient diligence may be, and that ye be ernest with such persones as ar otherwayes interested in these boundis, to sie that the aires of these haulks be carefullie preserved ; wherin yow will doe ws acceptable service.—Newmerkit, 18 March 1634.

To Sir Lauchlane N^cCleane.

Trustie, &c. and weilbeloved, we greet yow weill, &c.—We ar informed that ther ar some mangrell haulks within the bounds belonging to yow, wherof, sieing we doe verie much affect the kynd, we have bene pleased to wryt to our trustie, &c. the Lord of Lorne tuitching the preservation thairof, and particularlie to recommend to yow that the ayrie within your bounds be carefullie keepit, in caice that heirefter we shall think good to mak vse of some of them for our sport ; And in the meane tyme that a falcon and tersell of that kynd be sent vnto ws by the bearer so soone as they can be fund of grouth and strenth to be transported hither ; which we will tak as good service done to ws : We bid, &c.—Newmerket, 18 March 1634.

Precept to the Thesaurer and Depytie.

It is our pleasur that with all diligence yow caus pay vnto the bearer, James Quarriour, one of our falconers, the accustomed yeirlie allowance for bringing of some haulks vnto ws from the northerne pairts of that our kingdome, and that yow give vnto him your best furtherance for that effect ; for doeing whairof these presents shalbe your warrand and discharge.—Newmerket, 18 March 1634.

To Sir Filibert Warnat.

Trustie, &c.—Wheras we ar informed by our right trustie the Erle of Stirling, our Principall Secretarie for Scotland, that yow ar goeing in a course with him towards the advancement of the work of the plantatioun of New Scotland, the good whairof we exceedinglie tender, we cannot bot approve of your affection in this as in your other former publict vndertakings for the good of our service ; and as we ar willing to naturalise yow in that our kingdome of Scotland, and to conferre vpon yow the lyk honors and priviledges as other knyght baronettis vndertakeris in the forsaid plantation doe enjoy, so we shalbe ever readie to encourage yow and all others that shall tak the lyk courses with further testimonie of our gratious favour as occasion shall offer.—Newmerket, 18 March 1634.

To the Chancellour, Thesaurer, Privie seill, Thesaurer depot, Clerk Register.

Right, &c.—Wheras we vnderstand that ther wer some differences betwoene our right, &c. the Erle of Abercorne and the late Lord Rosse concerneing the right of the Landis of Inglistoun, the Lord Rosse alledgeing that he holdis the same in few, and the said Erle denying that he hath any few at all of any of them, who for the clearing of it did intend summondis of Improbatioun against the said Lord Rosse befoir our Colledge of Justice, The which course hath hithertills bene stayed in regard of the interest we wer conceaved to have in it : Therfor we, being desyrous to be informed of the trew estate of it without putting the pairteis to a publict and vnnecessarie trouble of a sute in Law, have thoght fitt to signifie our pleasur vnto yow that yow call the said Erle of Abercorne befoir yow and the La/ Rosse that now is, or such as ar intrusted with his estate dureing his minoritie, And that yow call for such of ther writts and evidents on both sydis as may concerne this particular, that efter yow have informed yourself sufficientlie thereanent, yow may certifie ws what yow find, to the effect we may give such further ordour as we shall think expedient concerneing it : And in the meane tyme that a care be had that nothing pass in Exchequer that may be prejudiciall to ather pairtie ; which recommending, &c.—Newmerket, 18 March 1634.

To the Session.

Right, &c.—Not willing to stay this our President of Session any longer, we cannot at this tyme give a full answer to your letter, onlie we think fitt to tell yow that since we sie that our prerogative was not so fullie clamed by our Advocat as we thoght it had bene, we doe not blame yow for not vseing the delay by him requyred, the rather sieing yow had our former commandis to eschew delayes in this pley as much as might be, so permitting proces to proceid till yow know our further pleasur, we bid, &c.—Newmerket, 19 March 1634.

Our Soverane Lord Ordeanes a protection to be made and exped vnder the great seall of the kingdome of Scotland to his highnes' lovit Patrik Dunbar, sone to Patrik Dunbar of Westertoun, Serjand-Major to his highnes' vncle the King of Denmark, making mention that the said Patrik hath bene a long tyme abroad from his Ma[teis] kingdome of Scotland, dureing which tyme he hath done to his Ma[tie] diverse good and faythfull services, in testimonie whairof his Ma[teis] said vncle the King of Denmark did not onlie tak speciall notice of the said Patrik his good and faythfull service, bot was lykwyse pleased by his letters effectuallie to recommend him vnto his highnes : And his Ma[tie] being in lyk maner crediblie informed that the said Patrik Dunbar intendeth now efter so long a tyme of his service abroad to setle himself in that his Ma[teis] ancient kingdome : And therfor his Ma[tie], of his princelie dispositioun for cherisching the good services of all such his Ma[teis] deserveing subjects, being carefull that he be not vnseasonablie troubled by any persone to whome he becam bund ather as principall or cautioner, And the rather becaus his Ma[tie] doeth conceave that his alledgments in that kynd wer done in his young yeres, And with all his Ma[tie] vnderstanding that the said Patrik doeth not intend any course to defraud his Creditours, bot rather, be setling himself and his fortouns ther, to give vnto them a further assurance to be satisfeit of what he is justlie owing to them : Therfoir his Matie, respecting the weill both of the said Creditours and debtours, of his authoritie royall, kinglie power, grace, mercie, and clemencie, hath accepted, and by the tenour heirof accepts, the said Patrik Dumbar vnder his highnes' protectioun, safeguard, maintenance, and defence, from being anywayes troubled, molested, and persewed by his saidis Creditours, or any of them, for any debt or debts due vnto them by the said Patrik, as Principall and cautioner, and gives and grants vnto the said Patrik dureing the space of one yeir, begining, &c. Cetera stylo ordinario.—Whythall, 28 March 1634.

TO THE COUNSELL.

Right, &c.—Wheras, for the better establisching of good ordour in the Middleschyres, and to the end the Commissioners for the same may the more readilie execute our Commissionis in each severall kingdome as they shalbe warranted therby, we have gevin ordour that a Commission be exped vnder the great scall oi this our kingdome, bearing the names of such persones of both kingdomes (thought most fitt and [able] to doe ws service ther) as ar particularlie sett doun in the enclosed list ; we, being willing that a reciprocall course be taken ther, are pleased that yow give ordour to our Advocat to draw a Commission for the midleschyris, conteneing all the names for both natioues as they ar particularlie sett doun in the said list, geving such power as hath bene granted to any former Commission of that kynd, and what further yow shall think fitt (efter dew advyse) to do for the better strenthning of them in executeing that service ior the good and quyet of these our kingdomes, and particularlie of these boundis, and therefter caus the said Commission to be furthwith exped vnder the great scall of that our kingdome in such maner as is requisit ; for which these shalbe sufficient warrant to yow and others our officers in particular whome it doeth concere : We bid, &c.—Whythall, 3 Aprill 1634.

TO THE ADVOCAT.

Trustie, &c.—Wheras Sir Alex^r Gordoun, kny^t and baronet, gentleman of our Privie Chalmer, hath caused represent to ws the great abuses daylie committed in that our kingdome by diverse persones in killing of reid and fallow deir, rae, and all sorts of wyld foull and haynes, by such vnlawfull wayes as ar expreslie prohibited by many lawlable lawis made by our royall predicessours, and particularlie by our late dear father, of worthie memorie : To which purpois our said servant being ane humble suitter to ws to have a Commission for putting these lawis in executioun, and we being verie willing that our service heirin be followed in a warrantable and legall maner, have hereby thoght fitt to requyre yow to peruse the inclosed informatioun, and thervpon draw vp to our said servand, his deputeis and officers, such a commission for the same of sevin yeires as may be warrantable in Law for the absolute authorizeing of them to pull these lawes in executioun throughout the said kingdome, and for the levyeing of the fynes of the said delinquents, wherof the one-halff to be payed by them for our vse vnto our Exchequer, and the other halff to be deteyned by them for the panes and charges to be vndergone and expended in the prosecutionn of that service ; and for avoydeing of trouble and charge to our said servant, we ar heirby pleased to requyre that the said Commission be immediatlie exped vnder our cachot and great seall ther with all expedition ; for doeing therof these presents shalbe to our Chancellour, and our other officers quhom it may concerne, and vnto yourselff, a sufficient warrant : We bid, &c.—Whythall, 3 Aprill 1634.

TO THE CHANCELLOUR.

Right, &c.—Being informed that the Bischop of Brechin, being to be cited in your name befor our Colledge of Justice for omitting in his Inventoris of some part of the extraordinarie taxatiounn vnpayed by him, is verie vnwilling that his name and respect due to his charge should be publictlie tuitchel in such a purpois, or that he should be forced to tak his oath therein; we have therfor thoght fitt to recommend to yow to tak the hearing of that caus to yourselff onlie, that it may be caryed in a privat maner, becaus we respect his charge, and have taken notice of the revenues belonging therto, which ar none of the greatest, and that otherwyse yow schaw him all the lawfull favour yow can; and if yow find any omission of his in this kynd concerning these taxatiouns, wherof yow have or had the charge, that yow accept and tak from him what can be justlie proved by any evidence other then his oath to be vnpayed by him of the said taxatioun, and that yow give him a discharge therof of all penelteis and forfeyts he hath incurred therby, for which these shalbe your warrand and discharge.—Whythall, 3 Aprill 1634.

To Nicolas Briot.

Wheras we have gevin ordour for coynceing the lyk quantitie of copper coyne and in the same kynds as was last coyned by yow vpon our former warrand, and being pleased to mak choyse of yow at this tyme lykwayes for the said work, these ar therfor to requyre and authorize yow with all convenient diligence to prepare yourselff for the performance of it, and that yow provyd yourselff sufficientlie of copper, plated and prepared in such sort as yow shall think most fitting for the expedition of the work, that it may be transported into Scotland, to be printed ther according to the ordour to be establisched theranent; and that yow hasten your owin repair thither to putt'n begining to it, haveing prepared all thingis necessar thervnto; ffor doeing whairof, &c.—Whythall, 3 Aprill 1634.

To the Thesaurer and Depctie, or any of them.

Right, &c.—Wheras humble sute hath bene made to ws in behalff of Nicolas Bryot, our servant, that by reasones of the charges and paynes susteined by himselff at first in establisching the work and fabrik of the coynage of that proportion of copper appoynted by ws and our Counsell to be coyned in that our kingdome, he might be preferred at this tyme to any other persone in the coynage of this proportion appoynted to be coyned of late, for the reasones mentionat in the inclosed petition, we, conceaveing his demand to be reasonable, ar pleased to grant the same vnto him, requyreing yow to sie him proceid in the said service as formerlie, and at the lyk former rates and conditions, wherin yow shall doe ws good service. —Wythall, 3 Aprill 1634.

Our Soverane Lord ordeanes a Letter to be made vnder the great seall of Scotland, makand mentioun that wheras the extraordinarie transportatioun of Coall to forrayne parts hath bene by diverse acts of Parliament prohibited, notwithstanding vpon some good considerationns the transportation of Coall is tolerated for payment to his Ma'tie of a certane custome: And his Ma'tie being sufficientlie informed that, for diverse considerationns importing the good of his Ma'tes service, it is requisit that ther be a further imposition of custome, and that it may be takin without prejudice of the trade or of the owners of the Coall potts, to whome his Ma'tie will give no just reasone of encouragment: Therfoir his Ma'tie, with advyse and consent of his Ma'tes Privie Counsell of Scotland, hath ordeaned, and by the tenour hairof ordeanes, that the Custome formerlie raised vpon Coall be doubled, by addition of just so much thervnto as hath bene formerlie payed, and that this new addition, with the said former custome, be imposed and levyed vpon and of the chalder of Scotts measur of Coall transported or to be transported from Scotland to any part beyond the seas, and being of his Ma'tes dominions, and that for and towards satisfaction to his Ma'tie and successours of all customes and impositions whatsoever to be levyed and takin of the said Coall so to be transported; and his Ma'tie ordeanes and commandis his Ma^tris officers to whois charge it apperteneth to have a speciall charge and regard that this impost and custome so raised vpoun the Coall be trewlie vplifted and payed to his Ma^tris vse in the samyne maner as the former impost was levyed befoir, and that the Lordis of his Ma^tris Excheker grant letters heirvpoun for payment of the new addition of custome with that which was formerlie paid, in forme as effeirs : And his Matie, with advyse and consent forsaid, ordeanes publicatioun to be made heirof be oppin proclamatioun at the mercat croces of the head burghes of the said kingdome, and others places neidfull, that none may pretend ignorance of the same; and that thir presents be a sufficient warrand to the Directour of the Chancerie for wryting of the samyne to the great seall, and to the Lord Chancellour for appending the great seall thervnto, without any farder precepts to be direct heirvpon.—Gevin at Whythall, 28 March 1631.

These bear that the custome formerlie raised vpon Coall be doubled,
   by addition of just so much therto to be raised for your Ma^tis
   vse vpoun the chalder of Scotts measur therof transported from
   Scotland beyond seas, not being of your Ma^tis dominions.

Our Soverane Lord ordeanes ane Letter to be made vnder his highnes' privie seall in due forme, ratificand, approveand, and for his M^tie and his highnes' successours confirmeand, lykas his Matie by thir presents ratifeis, approves, and for his Matie and his highnes' successours confirmes the Letter and gift of pension made by his Ma^tris vmquhill deirrest father, King James the Sext, of eternall memorie, to his highnes' servitour Mungo Murray, one of his Ma^tris Cupbearers, dureing all the dayes of his lyftyme, of ane yeirlie pension of the sowme of Tuo hundreth markis sterling money, to be vplifted and paid to him yeirlie at tua termes in the yeir, Witsondey and Mertimes in winter, be equall portiones, furth of the first and readiest of his Ma^tris customes of his highnes' kingdome of Scotland, by his Ma^tris theasurer principall and comptroller of the said kingdome, thesaurer and comptroller deputeis thairof, and by his Ma^tris receavers of his highnes' rents and customes within the said kingdome then present and to cum, and in the said letter and gift of pension, gevin vnder the privie seall of the dait at Whythall, the 28 of De^r 1621 yeres, at more lenth is conteynit in the haill heads, clausses, articles, and circumstances thairof whatsumever : And his Matie wills and grants, and for him, his highnes and successours, decernes and ordeanes that this present confirmation is and shalbe of alse great avail, force, strenth, and effect to the said Mungo Murray as if the said Letter and gift of pension wer word be word insert heirin : Anent the which, and with all inconvenients that may follow thairvpoun, and alse with all other objections and imperfections, if any be, which may be opponit or alledgit aganst the validitie of the samyne, or of this present confirmatioun thairof, Our said Soverane Lord, for his highnes and successours, hath dispensed, and be thir presents dispensses : Attour his Matie, for the good, true, and thankfull service and due attendance done to his Matie and highnes' said vmquhill father by the said Mungo Murray in tymes bypast, Therfor his Matie, of certane knowledge and propper motive, now, efter all his highnes' revocatiouns, hath of new gevin, granted, and disponed, and by these presents of new gives grants, and dispones, to the said Mungo Murray, dureing all the dayes of his lyftyme, All and haill the forsaid yeirlie pension of Tuo hundreth merkis sterling money forsaid, to be vplifted and payed to him at the termes above speciefeit, furth of the readiest of his Ma^tris said customes of Scotland, by his Ma^tris said Thesaurer principall and comptroller of the said kingdome, thesaurer and comptroller depute thesaurer thairof, and by his Ma^tris receavers of his highnes' rents and customes thairof, now present and to cum ; with power to the said Mungo Murray, his factours and servands in his name, to crave, receave, intromet with, and vptak the forsaid yeirlie pension restand awand of all yeres and termes bygane since the date forsaid of his gift thairof above written, and sicklyk yeirlie in tyme and maner and at the termes abone specifeit dureing his lyftyme as said is, and to vse and dispone thervpoun at his pleasur acquittances and discharges thairof, in whole or in part, to mak, give, subscryve, and delyver, which shalbe sufficient to the receavers of his Maties rents and customes of the said kingdome, present and to cum; and that the said Letter be extendit in the best forme with all clausses neidfull; with command therin to the said Thesaurer and comptroller deputeis, receavers of his Ma^{tis} rents, customes, casualiteis, now present and to cum, to readelie answer, intend, obey, and mak thankfull payment to the said Mungo Murray, his factours and servitours in his name, of the yeirlie pension above writtin yeirlie of the termes above specifeit, dureing all the dayes of his lyftyme, yeirlie and termlie, in tyme cuming, which shalbe thankfullie allowed to them in ther accompts be the Lords Auditours of his highnes' Exchecker, whome his Matie commands and ordeanes to allow the same, this letter heirvpon to be raisit being once schawin and produced vpon compt, and registrat as efferes.—Whythall, 10 Aprill 1634.

Pleas your Matie—

> These ratifie and give of new to Mungo Murray, dureing his
> lyftyme, a pension of 200 Merks sterling, granted by your
> Ma^{tis} royall father. It is payable out of the customes of
> Scotland by your Ma^{tis} Thesaurer, and others officers whom
> it concernethh.

Our Soverane Lord ordanes a protection to be made vnder his highnes' great seall of the kingdome of Scotland to his highnes' trustie and weilbeloved Colonell Robert Monro of Contalick, making mention that his Matie perfectlie vnderstanding how that the said Colonell Robert Monro haveing for the space of four yeres togidder done verie good and acceptable service to his highnes' vncle the King of Denmark in his late Warrs aganst the Emperour, has since for the lyk tyme (out of his generous and vertuous disposition) not onlie acquyrit great reputation and credit abroad in the late Swedish warrs of Germanie vnder the King of Sueden, of late and famous memorie, by verie notable services and exployts therin, wherby he hath gevin sufficient prooff and testimonie of his curage and realie judgment, and whairof his Matie hath both formerlie and now of late takin particular notice; Bot also the said Colonell (who intendeth to continew that course in these warrs for the advanceing of the common cause in so far as in him lyeth) is lyklie by his vertew and industrie otherwayes to mak vp a fortune and estate within the said kingdome, if his Creditours doe not at his returne hither vnseasonablie trouble him, and therby divert him from that purpois: And his Matie considering how that by his taking of that course to setle ane estate ther, his creditours, to whom he standis engadged onlie as cautioner, and that in his younger yeres, will rather be secured of ther principall sowmes and annual rents then endangered to lose the same: Therfor his Matie, of his princelie care, for setling within his said kingdome of [so] worthie and deserveing a persone, and for the good lykwyse of the saidis Creditours, hath of his authoritie royall, kinglie power, grace, mercie, and clemencie, accepted, and by the tenour heirof accepts, the said Colonell Robert Monro as cautioner, vnder his highnes' protection, safeguard, mantenance, and defence, from being anywayes troubled, molested, or persewed by the saidis Creditours, or any of them, for any debt dew to them by the said Colonell Robert Monro as cautioner aforsaid, and gives and grants vnto him dureing the space of ane yeir, beginning, &c.— Cetera stylo ordinario.

Our Soveraigne Lord Ordeanes a Protection to be made vnder his highnes' great seall of the kingdome of Scotland to his highnes' trustie and weilbeloved Hectour Monro of Foulls, makand mention that wher his Matie is crediblie informed that his vmquhill brother Robert Monro of Foulls (who, haveing the charge both of a horse and foot regiment, was killed in his charge in the feillis in the late Swedish warres of Germanie), did diverse yeres befor his death contract such great debts as have almost turned the estate of that antient familie; And that his Matie lykwyse is crediblie informed that the said Colonell Hectour Monro, now of Foulls, forsieing the danger of the ruyn of that house, did follow these warres, and is now verie lyklie by acquyreing charge and reputation therin to recover that estate, if so be his Creditours now at his returne will permit him, without being vnseasonablie troubled, to setle and ordour his affaires ther; and his Matie considering that by his recoverie of that Estate it will rather secure than anywayes endanger his Creditours of ther principall sowmes or annuel rents: Thairfoir his Matie, of his princelie and tender respect to the good of both the saids creditours and debtour, doeth of his authoritie royall, kinglie power, grace, mercie, and clemencie, accept, and by the tenour heirof accepts, the said Colonell Hectour Monro vnder his protection, safeguard, mantenance, and defence from being anywyse troubled, molested, or persewed by the saids Creditours, or any of them, for any debt due vnto them by the said Colonell Hectour Monro, as principall or cautioner, and gives and grants to the said Colonell dureing the space of ane yeir, begining, &c.—Cetero stylo Ordinario.—Whythall, 10 Aprill 1634.

To the Counsell.

Right, &c.—Wheras we intended to have imposed six schillingis sterline vpon everie chalder Scotts coall, Newcastell measur, transported from Scotland to forrane partis: That vpon humble remonstrance made to ws by our trustie, &c. Mr Ro^t Bruce, in behalff of the Coal Masters of that kingdome, of the estate of the coall trade ther, we have bene pleased to signe a signature onlie for doubling of the former impost raised vpon coall, which we requyre may be exped vnder our great seall, with diligence; for which, &c.—Whythall, 10 Aprill 1634.

To the Session.

Right, &c.—Wheras we ar informed that ther is ane actiou in Law depending or to be intended befoir yow betuixt our trustie and weilbelovit Generall Ruthven and Sir James Lundie, his brother-in-Law, becaus of the said Generall his importante and necessarie imployments abroad in the service of our freindis and confederats, he cannot convenientlie attend to sollicite the issue of that caus as is requisit in the lyk caiees, and becaus of the notice that otherwayes we have takin of his worth and cariage, these ar effectuallie to recommend him vnto yow, to the end that not onlie in that particular action betwene him and his said brother, bot in all other causes that may concerne him comeing befor yow, he may have speedie justice according to our Lawis administred therin, which we will tak as acceptable service done vnto ws.—Whythall, 10 Aprill 1634.

To the Lordis Chancellour and Privie Seall.

Right, &c.—We ar informed from the M^r of Forbes that, besydis his many misfortunes abroad, some of his freindis at home, to whome he entrusted the manageing of his estate for releiff of his creditours, hath, out of a fals surmeis of his death or continuall detention in prisone, converted his trust into ther owin propper vse, and frustrat his creditours of ther releiff, to his great loss and prejudice, in so much that he, being now both willing and able to satisfie a great part of his debts, cannot, without great hazard of his libertie and in this vacatioun of Justice, without assistance of our authoritie, goe about or performe that his intention: we therfore have thoght fitt to grant vnto him our royall protection, and that it may be the more vsefull to him, farder to will and requyre yow to give him your assistance against the vnjust deteners of his esteat and the vnseasoneablenes of his creditours, so far as yow in equitie and justice shall think fitt; wherin not doubting of your care, &c.—Whythall, 15 Aprill 1634.

To the Commissioners of Surranders.

Right, &c.—Wheras we ar informed in behalff of Mr James Blair, minister at Portpatrik, that he is vnprovydit of a necessarie and competent meanes for serveing the cure at the said kirk, humblie craveing that we would be gratiouslie pleased to recommend to yow the consideratioun of his charge and meanes of his provision, being far schort, as he informeth ws, of what is ordinarlie allowed to any other in such a charge : Our pleasur is, that according to any other former course takin by yow in the lyk kynd, in sua far as yow ar warranted by our commission, yow setle such a competent meanes as is requisite for such a charge and eminent place, being the ordinarie port of that our kingdome to and from whence our subjects of all our dominions haveing the occasion doe ordinarlie repair to and from Irland ; for which these shalbe your warrant : We bid, &c.—Whythall, 19 Aprill 1634.

To the Counsell.

Right, &c.—Haveing bene pleased to tak peculiar notice of the enclosed petition exhibited to ws by our faythfull servand Patrik Young in behalff of his Nephew Charles Young, In regard he is minor and now absent in France, and the estate left to him by his father, Sir James Young, our late servand, is lyklie (if tymelie remeid be not vsed) to be vndone, and in regard of the long and faythfull service done to our vnquhill dear father by Sir Peter Young, both at home and abroad, in diverse embassages, and of diverse of his sones to our selff, our pleasur is, that haveing considered of the petition, yow appoynt some auditors of your number, with power to call befoir them Sir Johne Carnagie of Athie, knyt, who hath comprysed the Landis of the minor, willing them to examyne particularlie according to the heads of the petition what is justlie owing to the said Sir John or to any other creditour vpon his disbursments, and what the trew yeirlie value of these Landis and estateis, or might have bene since the death of the said Sir James, and therefter to compose the differences according to the desyre in the petition ; otherwayes to certifie ws of the trew estate thairof, that we may give such farther ordour therin as we shall find just caus, till such tyme we will yow to recommend to the session that there be no proceidingis befor them for further troubling the estate of the minor.—Whythall, 19 Aprill 1634.

To the Thesaurer and Deputie.

Wheras by our former precept to our Exchequer 17 March, and by our letter to them of the 8 of Der following, we did requyre them to pay to Sir Hew Wallace of Craigie 20,000lib Scotts, which precept and letter ar registrat in Exchequer books : In regard the granting of these moneyis was for selling to ws and our Croun of the heretable offices of the bailliarie of Kyle and regalitie of Newtoun, and that besydis we wer pleased to tak notice of the good service long since done by William Wallace, whois discent was from the said Sir Hew his house, and whois memorie is left as a worthie record to the posteritie ; And withall, haveing a tender comiseration of the estate of that antient familie, the standing wherof doeth at this tyme (as we ar crediblie informed) depend vpon the readie payment vnto him of these moneyis : Our pleasur is, that yow readelie pay the said Sir Hew, his aires and assigneyis, the said sowme of 20,000lib scotts money, at the terme of Witsonday nixt ensueing the date heirof, and that out of the first and readiest of these taxations last granted to ws, with the interest therof from the terme of Witsonday last bypast, 1633, till the nixt ensueing terme of Witsonday 1634, with interest yeirlie and termelie therefter, so long as the said principall sowme, or any part thairof proportionallie, shall rest

H   2 s

vnpaid to the said Sir Hew or his forsaids, and that yow accept of this our warrant, testifie vnto him vnder your handis your acceptatioun heirof, and that therefter yow sie ws discharged of that debt so owing be ws vnto him ; And for your soe doing these presents shalbe your warrant.—Grenewitch, 2 May 1634.

To the Advocat.

Trustie, &c.—Haveing for some respects moveing ws, mentionat in our letter at this tyme to our Colledge of Justice, signifeid our pleasur vnto them for prorogating the reversion of the estate of the Erle of Airth, as by the enclosed copie therof yow will perceave, we ar heirby pleased to will and command yow to sie that prorogatioun legallie and surelie done as may secure that estate from being evicted or troubled by his cautioners, or any haveing power from them dureing the tyme that shalbe condescended vpon, and that yow assist and concurre with his procuratours for all legall helps which may be affoorded vnto him for preserving him from the rigour of his cautioners, and in all other things that may concerne his esteat theranent.

To the Session.

Right, &c.—Wheras we ar informed that the reversion of the whole estate of the Erle of Airth is to determyne at the nixt terme of Mertimes, wherby it will fall to his cautioners without hope of recoverie, notwithstanding that it far exceideth the just sowmes of money dew to his creditours ; yit sieing some course is to be taken for his releiff, which is to be done by the greatest conveniencie that may be : and in regard the cautioners ar sufficientlie secured of the moneyis dew vnto them, and that ordour wille taken for payment of ther annuell dureing the not redemptioun : Our pleasur is, that yow deall with them for prorogating the reversion for so many yeires, as by mutuall consent of the said Erle and his cautioners and procuratours shalbe agreid vpon ; and in caice of the cautioners' refuisall and obstinacie in pressing for the extremitie of Law aganst the said Erle, it is our further pleasur that yow grant vnto him all lawfull means which may be affoorded for avoydeing the forfeyt of his esteat, sieing out of our grace and favour we intend with all conveniencie to caus minister some meanes for releiff of his burdenis.—Grenwitch, 2 May 1634.

To the Chancellour.

Right, &c.—Wheras at the tyme of our goeing to that our kingdome we wer pleased to signe some writts of honour, intending therby to sett a mark of our favour vpon some deserveing, calling now to mynd that some of these signaturis wer then vpon good considerations restrayned by ws from being exped vnder our sealls, as particularlie these of the Lordis Lyndsay and Lowdoun from being Earles : It is our pleasur that yow call to the saidis Lordis commanding them to render these signaturis bak vnto yow, and that yow tak the lyk course with any other who had any signature of honour at that tyme which was not therefter exped vnder our great seall, to be disposed of as we shall think fitt ; bot if they or any of them vpoun your demand refuis to give vp these signatures, adverteise ws with diligence of the same, and in the meanetyme give ordour by advyse of our Advocat by ane act or declaratioun that any signature refuised to be delyvered vp vnto yow be declaret ineffectuall.—Vt supra data.

To the Advocat.

Trustie, &c.—Wheras the copie of ane outragious Lybell which was fund in the handis of ane Dinmure, wherof we have govin a coppie to our right, &c. the Erle of Traquair, doeth so much express ill disposition in some of our subjects as we have resolved to have the same exactlie tryed, and the authours thairof censured according as they shalbe fund to deserve, To which purpois we have signed a commission to some whom we speciallie trust, whairof yow ar one ; Therfoir it is our pleasur that yow carefullie attend the said commission and vse your best endeavours for discovering and examyneing of any persones thoght guiltie or accessorie thervnto as yow yourself shalhappin to cum to the knowledge thairof, or as yow shalbe informed by any other of the Commissioneris or otherwayes howsoever ; Which we will tak as acceptable service done vnto ws.— Dat, vt supra,

Wheras of late ther is a seditious bill, first fund in the handis of one Dynmure, dispersed throughout that our kingdome vnder the name of a supplicatioun, tending to the disturbance of our peace, and impairing of our royall honour and authoritie, the copie whairof we have delyvered vnto our right, &c. the Erle of Traquair ; These ar to authorize and give yow full power and commission vnto yow, in maner vnder writtin, to convene at Ed^r the first of Junij nixt, and at other convenient dayes thereftir ; and haveing called befor yow the authors and others whom yow hear or find to be accessorie into the same, that yow examyne them tuitching that purpois vpon oath or production of witnesses, putting ther depositions in writt vnder ther and your handis ; and thereftir, if yow find them guiltie or anywayes accessorie to so high ane offence, to committ them to close prissone, and to acquant ws from tyme to tyme with your proceidingis heirin, till the whole authours and others haveing hand in the same be cleirlie knowen : So willing and requyreing yow expreslie, as yow will answer vnto ws vpon your perrell, to omitt no diligence in discherg of your dewteis heirin, and approveing your selffis our faythfull subjects and counsellours ; ffor which these shalbe vnto [yow] ane sufficient warrant.—Grenwitch, 5 May 1634.

Names of the Commissioneris.

John, Archbishop St Androis,	John, Bischop of Rosse.
William, Erle of Morton.	David, Bischop of Brechin.
William, Erle of Stirling.	Sir John Hay, kny^t.
John, Erle of Traquair.	Sir Thomas Hop.
Robert, Erle of Roxbrught.	

Or to oney 7 of them, the Archbischop of St Androis being one, or in his absence the said bischop of Ross or Brechin, or any of them.

Wheras we have conferred with sindrie of our Excheker concerneing the affaires thairof, and thervpon did find it necessarie, for the good of our service and of our subjects of that kingdome, that sindrie abuses in the vnnecessarie burdings of Excheker, with great errors and dissorders creipt therein, be dewlie and speedelie reformed : To which purpois we have thoght fitt to select yow to represent vnto ws the trew estate and remedeis therof ; and therfor we doe heirby authorize and give full power and commission vnto yow, or oney sevin of yow, the Chancellour, Archbischop, or Thesaurer principall being of the number, to convene at Edinburgh, at the sitting of the accompts of our Extents bypast, and Thesaurer's accompts, and ther to tak into your consideratioun the whole burdenes of our Excheker, and what therof ye think necessarie, or vpoun just grounds and reasones may be cutt of, how the errors and abuises therin may best be reformed ; and that yow consider of all other things which may lawfullie tend to the raising and increase of our rents and the good of our service heirin, and efter mature deliberatioun, what shalbe fund by yow all joyntlie, or most voyces, to sett the same doun in writt vnder your hand, and send the same with all diligence vnto ws, that thereftir we may setle such a solid course as may be most agrieable to our servandis and our subjects : and this Commission to indure to the first of August, and longer dureing his Ma^{teis} pleasur : ffor which, &c.—Grenwitch, 5 May 1634.

Chancellour.	E. Roxbrught.
Arch. St Androis.	John, Erle Traquair.
Thesaurer Principall.	Bp. Ross.
Privie Seall.	Sir John Hay.
Marqueis Hamilton.	Sir Th. Hope.
E. Stirling.	

To the Counsell.

Right, &c.—Wheras Colonell Ro^t Munro hath caused represent to ws That diverse of our poore subjects who hath done good service in the warres abroad doe ordinarlie ather becum old or lame, wherby they ar vnprofitable for further service, and consequentlie burdenable to strangers, and no credit to our other subjects ther : ffor remedie and help of such persones, he hath proposed that diverse of these whom it hath pleased God to blisse with preferment and meanes in these warres ar willing to give a voluntarie contribution for erecting of ane hospitall within that our kingdome for ther vse, and dedicating some yeirlie allowance thervnto. besydis what will accress vnto them by the bountie of the prince in whois service they wer imployed or by ther paction with him otherwayes, according as may more fullie appear by the inclosed information : To which purpois the said Colonell, being willing to vndergoe great panes for settling of that bussines, vpon conditions expressed in the Information (which seame to be fair and reasonable) hath bene a sutter vnto ws (for his more warrantable proceiding therin) to be authorized by our letters patents vnder our great seall, wherin, his intention being verie commendable and the purpois worthie of due respect and consideratioun, we have heirby thoght fitt to recommend to yow seriouslie to consider of the information, and of the most convenient way for authorizeing him by letters patents, or what commission or warrant yow think fitt or necessarie, or as may agrie with his demandis in the Informatioun ; and for that effect that yow give ordour to our Advocat for drawing vp therof, which we requyre may be furthwith exped vnder our cachett and great seall ther, that the gentlemen, of whois good cariage and service abroad we have been pleased to tak particular notice, be not putt to further trouble or charge tuitching the passing thairof ; ffor which these presents shalbe vnto yow, and our officers whom it doeth particularlie concerne, a sufficient warrand.—Grenewitch, 5 May 1634.

To the Session.

Right, &c.—Wheras humble remonstrance hath bene made vnto ws that diverse noblemen and others our subjects of east Lothian have most injustlie intruded themsellis vpon our communtie at Dunbar, to our great prejudice, wherin we have takin notice of ther bold proceidingis in what doeth so particularlie concerne ws in our right ; ffor remedie whairof, and preventing the lyk heirefter, we doe speciallie will and requyre that vpon summonndis and proces to be intendit and prosecute at our instance by our Advocat, to whom we have writtin tuitching this purpois, yow try and cognosce of ther rights and infeftments therof, and if yow find them insufficient, that yow administer Justice with all expedition for reduction therof, according to our Law for establisching our right.

To the Advocat.

Trustie, &c.—Haveing writtin to our Colledge of Justice for considering the validitie of the Infeftments of such persones as have intruded vpoun our Communtie at Dunbar, to our great prejudice, as by the copie of the enclosed letter vnto them yow will perceave : Our pleasur is, and we command yow, that yow consider of ther rights, and in our name and for our interest insist aganst such persones as have injustlie intruded thervpon, by intenting and prosecuteing summondis and proces in our name for reduction of these Infeftments, in so far as yow shall find agrieable to justice and the lawis of that our kingdome ; for which, &c.—Grenwitch, 5 May 1634.

To the Exchequer.

Right, &c.—We being willing to vse all lawfull and fit meanes to disburdome our Exchequer of the debts wherwith at this tyme it is charged, and to mak the best vse we can of the rents and casualiteis of our Croun of that kingdome at all tymes heirefter ; Our pleasur is, and we doe heirby will and requyre yow, to exped no signature in Exchequer of any landis whatsoever, or to any persone of what qualitie or condition whatsoever, without first a dew consideratioun be had of the worth and yeirlie rent of these landis, and that accordinglie yow putt Compositions of the same to be furthwith levyed for our vse ; for doeing wherof, &c.

To the Erls of Southesk and Traquair, and Sir John Hay.

Right, &c.—Wheras yow wer appoynted to revise the accompts of the extents in anno 1625, befor they be presented vnto the whole Commissioners nominated for hearing therof, and that the saidis accompts have relation to Sir James Baillie his accompts of ane part of the saidis extents, and that therfor it is necessarie that the same be also revised : These ar to will and command yow to review the saidis accompts, and if yow find any thing worthie our knowledge or to be considered by ws, it is our pleasur that yow adverteis ws with all diligence, that yow may know our further pleasur theranent befor the tyme appoynted for the fitting of the others accompts ; wheranent these presents shalbe your warrant.

To the Session.

Right, &c.—Wheras we ar informed that our right dearlie beloved cousen the Countess dowager of Westmerland hath ane action of Law depending befor yow at hir instance, as executrix to hir daughter the Countess of Home, deceissed, for so much of the late Erle Home's personall estent in that our kingdome as by the Lawis therof did fall dew to hir daughter, wherin hir saite appeareth to be more equitable, becaus of the great portion that was gevin with hir said daughter : In regard therof, and that our said cousen is altogidder vnacquanted with the forme and lawis of that our kingdome, wherby a long and tedious sute wilbe verie inconvenient to hir being resident heir, we ar heirby pleased effectuallie to recommend to yow that speedie justice, without respect of persones, be administred in that action, cutting off all vnnecessarie delayes that shalbe sought by hir adversareis for protracting of tyme to hinder the due and speedie course thairof ; whairof not doubting of your care, &c.—Grenewitch, 5 May 1634.

To the Exchequer.

Right, &c.—Wheras we ar informed that ther was a signatur presented vnto yow by our late Parliament, holdin in that our kingdome by our trustie and weilbeloved William Gray, merchand of Edr, for ratifieing vnto him ane infeftment of the baronie of Saltoun, holdin by him few of his superiour, who holdeth the same of ws by ward and releiff, which signature was then continewed (as we ar informed) becaus at the tyme of our first incomeing to that kingdome the Commissioners of Exchequer, who war to attend vpon our service vtherwayes, could not meitt agane befor the Parliament to dispatch any bussines of Exchequer ; We being vnwilling that he should suffer prejudice by the first continewing therof, ar heirby pleased to will and requyre yow to expede the said ratification and signature made thervpon, with this provision alwyse, that if in caice the said W^m shall procure ane discharge of the reversion granted to his said superiour, that then he shalbe obleidged to tak that baronie holdin of ws in the same maner as his superiour, who holdis the same of ws now, &c.

To the Exchequer.

Right, &c.– Wheras vpon consideratioun that Patrik Blak, our servant, had in the tyme of our late royall father payed nyne thowsand merkis scotts for the heretable Chalmerlaurie of Fyff, we wer so far furth pleased vpon his humble sute for securing of him therin to signe of late a gift therof vnto him, redimable alwyes vpon payment of the moneyis so debursit be him, and therefter to returne to our croun, wherin sieing the redemption (which is at all tymes in our power) doeth distinguisch that our gift from the nature of heretable offices, and in the meane tyme being willing that he be secured of what he hath payed of that office, which according to our princelie justice and equitie, our pleasur is, that yow forthwith expeid our said gift vnder our sealls according to the tenour thairof, and that he peaceablie discharge and enjoy that office till he be payed of these moneyis.—Dat. vt supra.

To the Exchequer.

Right, &c.—We have bene pleased, vpon considerations knowen to ws, to signe a Licence to one Johne Pilmure for making of Soap within that our kingdome, and to that purpois to mak therin or bring into the same all ingredients necessarie, paying custome as by the signature will appear : Our pleasur is, that with all diligence yow expeid the same vnder our great seall ; ffor which these salbe vnto yow and them sufficient warrand, &c.

Your Matie by ane late Act of Parliament being to tak in consideration how to dispose of the Annuitie of the Tythes, does heirby, for releiveing these your subjects by whome it is payable of our heretable burden, Give Commission to your Thesaurers principall and deputie, or any of them, to deall with such of them as shall within tyme limited desyre to enjoy the annuitie of ther landis of all yeres bygane and to cum, tuitching the pryces to be gevin for the same, with power to them or any of them, with advyse and consent of the persones above named, or any thrie of them, to renunce and sell the said annuitie of all the saids yeres to the persones disposed to buy it, with power to them in maner forsaid to frie by renunciation or other securitie requisite the buyers of all obleidgments for payment of the annuitie, which being vnder the hands of the saids Commissioners, and conteyneing a clause to be registrat in the books of Exchequer, with ane Act of Exchequer to pass thervpon, shalbe as valide a right to the receavers as if it had passed vnder the sealls and registers wherapent your Matie dispensses. This Commission to indure till the first of August 1635, and to be further prorogat at your Ma^{tis} pleasur.—Grenewitch, 6 May 1634.

To the Advocat.

Trustie, &c.— We have bene pleased at this tyme to give some direction to our right, &c. the Erle of Traquair, our Thesaurer deputie, and to our trustie Counsellour Sir John Hay, our Clerk Register, tuitching the Pryorie of St Androis: It is our pleasur that with all expedition yow draw vp such writts tuitching the Pryorie, whairof the groundis shalbe by them signifeid vnto yow; Ror which, &c.—Grenwitch, 6 May 1631.

To the Exchequer.

Right, &c.—Vnderstanding sufficientlie the habiliteis and affection to our service of Johne, bischop of Ross, and the better to enable him thervnto heirefter, being willing to promove him to be ane of the Commissioners of our Exchequer, Our pleasur is, and we doe heirby will and requyre yow, to receave him vpon that Commission as ane of your number, and that yow caus administer vnto him the oath accustomed in the lyk caices; Ror which, &c.—Grenwitch, 6 May 1631.

To the Exchequer.

Right, &c.—Wheras ane offer hath bene made vnto ws by our right, &c. the Erle of Abercorne that he will frielie quyt all the superioriteis and few dewteis of the great vassalls of his Abbacie of Paisley, who ar knowen to be worth of yeirlie rent above 500 merks Scotts money, and that without any composition at all to be gevin by ws for the same, wher by our decree it is appointed that payment be made by ws in all cases of the lyk nature, proyded that he may be suffered to retene his small vassalls in the former estate whois rents doe not exceid the yeirlie value offering; lykwayes to resigne vnto ws all the interest he hath in a verie antient regalitie of the said Abbacie, in so far as doeth concerne these vassalls of the better sort, Reserveing his right of that regalitie over the saids small vassalls: The lyk proposition not being as yit made by any other then himsellf, doeth seme so fair vnto ws that we intend to accept therof, bot doeth refer to give ordour for dispatch of the same till we have sene some further progres made concerneing erections: Bot in the meane tyme, leist the passing of any new signature of these small vassalls whom he demands to reserve might whollie dissapoynt this our purpois, Our pleasur is, that no signature of this nature of any of the said Erle his small vassalls be exped in Exchequer.—Grenewich, 6 May 1631.

To the Session.

Right, &c.—Efter receipt of your letter from the President of the Session, haveing had conference with him about that poynt of our prerogative which was conceaved to have bene clamed befor yow, we did by our letters directed with him signifie how we wer not displeased with your proceidings therin; and now we have thoght it fitt to signifie vnto yow that as we ar confident that if at any tyme our prerogative royall shalbe alledged befor [yow] by any of our officeris of state, that yow will consult ws befoir yow proceid any further in that caus, so be assured we shall tak care that none shall presume to prostitute it in a caus that shall not necessarlie requyre the same: The diligent adverting heirvnto we recommend vnto yow, and we will that thir presentis be registrat in your books of sederunt.—Grenwitch, 8 May 1631.

To the Chancellour, Mortoun, Traquair, Sir John Hay, Sir Th. Hope.

Right, &c.—Though we be crediblie informed of our vndoubtit right to the Yle of the Lewes, and that ther wilbe a great many of the few dewteis bygane payable vnto ws for the same resting vnpayed, wherby we have great advantage in Law and otherwayes against our right, &c. the Erle of Seafort, who for the present hath the possession thairof : yit being willing to schaw him favour heirin, we ar heirby graciouslie pleased to content our selfis with such a proportion of the said Yle and other places fitting therin, as by yow shalbe fund necessarie and convenient for the assotiation of the fisching of Great Britane and Irland, provyded alwayes that the said Erle tak a new right of ws of the rest of that yle for payment of the old few dewtie : To which purpois we ar heirby pleased that yow so proceid for ordoreing and selling of that bussines as may best conduce to the good of our service, ffor which these presents shalbe your sufficient warrant.—Grenwitch, 8 May 1631.

To the Advocat.

Trustie, &c.—We have imparted our pleasur to the Erle Traquair, our Thesaurer deput, and Sir Johne Hay, our Clerk Register, tuitching ane offer made to ws by the E. Roxbrugh concerneing the Abacie of Kelso, whervpoun a bargane being condescended vpon betwixt ws and him, Our pleasur is, that yow particularlie informe your self from them of the conditions mutuallie to be performed by ws and him, and that accordinglie yow draw vp such writts at the sight of his advocat as shall secure both ws and him of what by the said bargane is intended to be past and signed by ws both respectivelie : And for your soe doeing, &c.—Grenewitch, 8 May 1631.

Warrant.

Wheras by ane Act made in the 22 parliament of our late royall father, holdin in Junij 1617, a publict register is ordeaned wherin all reversions, seasines, and others writts therin specifeit should be registrat within 60 dayes efter the dait of these writts, vnder the restrictions mentionat in the said Act, and that these registers should belong to the Clerk of Register and his deputts for the tyme, to be annexat and incorporat to and with his office as a propper part and pendicle thairof, with power to appoynt such deputeis for ther lyffis or otherwayes as he should think expedient to be resident at the places, and to the effect specifeit in that act, they being alwayes of good fame, literature, conversation, appoynting the Registeris to be marked by him or his saids deputeis, with a note of the particular number of ther leiffis as in that act at more lenth is mentionat : Bot we being informed that some of the keipers of these registeris have be negligence or otherwayes omitted to caus the Clerk of Register for the tyme or his deputts mark these registers according to the said act, whairvpon great prejudice may aryse to our subjects, Our pleasur is, and we doe heirby will and command yow, to call befor yow the whole keipers of these registeris, and to tak speciall notice of ther dewteis in dischargeing of ther saidis offices, and to sie abuses therin rectifeit for the case and securitie of our subjects ; And if any of them have omitted to mark the saidis registeris which yow trewlie find to be trewlie writtin and filled, knowing the keiperis thairof to be reputed honest men, that yow mark, or caus your deputeis appoynted to that effect to mark them : And therafter we doe heirby ordeane the same to be as sufficient to all our subjects interested as if the same had been marked befor the wryting and filling, wheranent these presents shalbe a sufficient warrant.—Grenewitch, 8 May 1631.

To Sir Joⁿ Hay of Baro, knᵗ, Clerk Register.

To the Counsell.

Right, &c.—Wheras by our warrant we have requyred our Clerk Register to call befor him the whole keipers of these Registers in which by act of Parliament of our late royall father, all reversions, seasings, and others mentionat in that act ar appointed to be registrat, and to tak notice of ther dewteis in discharge of ther saidis offices, and particularlie to mark such of ther registeris as have by ther neglect or ignorance bene omitted to be marked befor the wryting and filling thairof, to the intent our subjects interested may not suffer by the putting of that act in tyme by executioun : Our pleasur is, and we doe heirby requyre yow, to ratifie and approve our said warrant by Act of Counsell, and to enact that the marking of the saidis buiks (if any be vnmarked) by the said Clerk Register present, or his deputts, shalbe as sufficient to all our subjects interested as if the same had bene marked befor the filling and wryting thairof ; for which these presents shalbe to yow sufficient warrant.—Grenewitch, 8 May 1634.

These ratifie to the Erle of Roxburgh his aires a chartour of the baronie of Brughtoun, comprehending the landis, burgh of Regalitie, tounes, mylnes, offices, priviledge of Regalitie, superioriteis, and others in the signatur at lenth specifeit, reserveing to your Matie and successours the accustomed rights and securiteis : Ordeaneing this confirmatioun to be as sufficient as if the infeftment vpon the chartour wer insert heirin, and speciallie reserved in the 14 act of the late parliament, and that the exception of that baronie mentionat in the 13 act of the said Parliament shalbe as valide dureing the not redemption as if the said exception had bene resumed in the 14 act.—Grenewitch, the 7 of May 1634.

To the Counsell.

Right, &c.—Wheras the inclosed informatioun hath bene exhibited to ws by some persones from Zetland in the names and behalff of sindrie the Inhabitants of these Yles, wherby ar represented diverse grevaneis and abuses, both in the church and government in these parts, for remedie quherof they have bene humlie sutters to ws, that some judicious and discreit persone might be directed thither for tryeing the estate therof, that vpon exact search and knowledge had therin the same might be rectifeid for the good of our service and of our subjects ther in such maner as shall be thoght fitt for ther releiff, and agrieable to our lawis : Our pleasur is, that haveing carefullie perused and considered the informatioun, and if yow shall find that hiertofoir it hath bene fund necessarie, or that now, vpon the considerations therin, or any of them, yow shall find it expedient to send to this purpose a commissioner at this tyme, yow sufficientlie authorise in our name, by commission or otherwayes as yow shall think fitt, our trustie and weilbelovit servand Sir Robert Gordoun, kny^t, baronet, vice-chalmerlane of Scotland, whom we have made choyse of to that purpois, and for such tyme as yow shall think fitt, with such instruction as yow shall find necessarie, requisit for tryeing and executeing such things as the informatioun thought fitt by yow to be tryed and performed, and with what other instructions yow shall think expedient for further rectifieing of these abuses and enabling of him to that service ; and to that purpois that yow particularlie authorize him to call befor him whatsoever persones, committers of these abuses, or accessorie thervnto, to examyne them vpon oath or witnesses, to censure, imprisone, and punisch them in such maner as yow shall think fitt to preseryve ; and wher yow sall find the caus fitt to be decydit befor your selffis, or to impart to ws that yow authorize him to try and mak report accordinglie, and to proceid in all other things that may tend to the publict good and increase of our revenews, and that yow tak ane accompt of him of his proceidingis at his returne : All which we speciallie doe recommend vnto your care, &c. : We bid, &c.—Grenwich, 7 May 1634.

To the Advocat.

Trustie, &c.—Wheras we find the estate of the church is much damnifeid by the dilapidation of the patronages of the churches antientlie apperteneing to the Archbischoppis and bischoppis of that our kingdome, and our intention is to restore them to all that formerlie did belong vnto them ; these ar therfor to

H   2 T

will and requyre yow that, as yow shalbe particularlie informed by them, yow intend proces aganst the deteyners of these patronages, and insist therin with all diligence till the finall decision, omitting nothing which may bring our princelie purpois to the desyred ends, and the church what did formerlie pertene vnto it, as yow will tender our service, and answer to the contrarie.—Grenwitch, 13 May 1634.

To the Commissioners for Tythis.

Right, &c.—Wheras by our Commission to yow we have reserved power in ourselflis to change such persones vpon that Commission as we should think fitt ; being now crediblie informed that the reverent father in God the bischop of Dunkeld is not able, in respect of his infirmitie and aige, to attend further vpon our service in that commission, It is therfor our pleasur, and we doe heirby will and requyre yow, to admitt in his place, in such maner as is requisit, the right reverend, &c. Thomas, bischop of Brechin, of whois abilitie and affection to our service we ar confident ; for which these presents shalbe your warrant.—Grenwitch, 13 May 1634.

To the Commissioners for Tythis.

Right, &c.—Wheras ther was presented vnto ws in Parliament be the Lord Torphechin, and by ws remitted to your consideratioun : These ar to will and requyre to tak tryell thairof without delay, and that yow report vnto ws your opinions therin befoir yow give any decrie vpon the same ; which recommending, &c.—Grenwitch, 13 May 1634.

To the Advocat.

Trustie, &c.—Wheras we have formerlie signifeid our pleasur vnto yow for delyverie vnto our trustie Sir John Hay, our Clerk Register, of all submissions of the Lordis of Erectioun and others our subjects concerneing Tythis which ar in your custodie, that the same may be putt vp in the chartour-hous in our Castell of Edinburgh, to remane amongst the recordis thairof : These ar therfor to will and requyre yow that vpon sight heirof ye doe not faill to delyver all these submissious to our said officer, to the effect forsaid ; ffor the which, &c.—Grenwitch, 13 May 1634.

To the Advocat.

Trustie, &c.—Wheras we have at lenth imparted our pleasur vnto our right, &c. the Erle of Traquair, our Thesaurer deput, and Sir Johne Hay, our Clerk Register, tuitching the excambing of the Erle of his house at Halyrudhous, for the vse of the bischop of Edr, with the hous belonging to the said bischop which is ther, and which we have appoynted for the vse of the deane of our Chapell royall and his successours ; provyded that in caice the said bischop shall at any tyme heirefter be provyded to the deanrie of our Chapell royall, then the said hous to be for any bischop to whome we shall think fitt to lend the same dureing that tyme, and no further ; and we have lykwyse condescended with our said Thesaurer deputie for his hous neir that ablay, with yards and parcell of land adjoyneing therto, for the vse of the principall Minister of the Abay Church of Halyrudhous, and his successours : To which purpois it is our pleasur that yow receave intention heirin from our said officers, and accordinglie draw vp such writts and securiteis as to that purpois yow shall find to be necessarie and legall ; ffor which these presents, &c.—Whythall, 13 May 1634.

To the Commissioners for Tythis.

Right, &c.—Wheras by your letter to ws yow ar desyreous to have our pleasur signifeid if (wher tythis ar alreadie valued) the common benefite granted by ws to our subjects in bnyiug ther owin tythis from taksmen of bischops or beneficed persones ; we ar heirby pleased to declair that the saidis heretours shall have the benefite of buying ther saidis tythis, commonn with others our subjects, without prejudice to the bischop or beneficed persone to enjoy the saids tythes as they have bene accustomed, and according to our pleasur declaired by our acts of Parliament ; and that if the said bischop or beneficed persone (to whome we will have granted the first prerogative in this place) will buy the same to the vse of the church, that he be preferred to any other ; bot in caice he doe refuis the same, that then the heretours shall have the said commoun benefite, as aforsaid, without any reservation ; which course will be observed in all tythis, alsweill valued as to be valued, of taksmen of all tythis of beneficed persones ; as also, anent heretours and taksmen of the tythis of laik patronages, it is our pleasur and will that the heretours may buy the taks, and that yow proceid accordinglie in the valuatioun therof to that effect and conforme to your commission, without prejudice to the laik patronages or Church efter the expyreing of these takis to enjoy the benefite of our Acts of Parliament made theranent ; wherin, approveing of your care to our service, and willing yow to proceid therin with as much diligence as may be, We, &c.—Grenwitch, 13 May 1634.

To the Session.

Right, &c.—Wheras we wer pleased to bestow vpon Mr Wm Drummond of Hauthornden the few of the Newtoun of Rires, falling at our gift by diminution of the rentall with the mariage of William Scott, eldest lawfull sone of vmquhill Sir William Scott of Elie, to whome these landis did formerlie belong, tuitching which the said Mr Wm hath long since (as we ar informed) intended action of Law befor yow : In respect our granting therof was both vpon consideratiouns of his good service and that it doeth neirlie concerne ws to prevent that we be not defrauded of what our vassalls ar bound to pay vnto ws by the infeftments, leist both in this particular and by the consequent it will prejudge ws and our Croun hereifter, we ar pleased seriouslie to recommend vnto yow to administer speedie justice in that action, without vnnecessarie protracting of tyme, which, as we ar informed, is occasioned by the Advocatts of the partie who standeth out against our right, wherin yow shall doe ws acceptable service.—Grenwitch, 13 May 1634.

To the Archbischop of Sᵗ Androis.

Right reverend father in God, &c.—Wheras we have recommended the Election of the reverend fathers the bischop of Edr and Brechin, as by our letters to that purpois ye will perceave, Our pleasur is, that furthwith vpon the electioun yow proceid to ther consecratioun in setling of them in ther severall bischopriks efter the custome and solemnitie requisit in such caces, and as yow shall think further necessarie to this purpois, which we will tak as acceptable service done vnto ws.—Grenwitch, 13 May 1634.

To the Counsell.

Right, &c.—Wheras we wer pleased not long since that yow should repair to our chappell at Halyrudhous for receaveing the holie communion ther, vpon everie Sonday immediatlie ensueing the doun sitting of the session in the winter and sommer sessions yeirlie, bot haveing now, vpon good considerations knowen vnto ws, resolved to alter the same, we ar heirby pleased to declair that it is our speciall will and pleasur that yow receave the same yeirlie vpoun the first Sondayes of July and December, which we will have to be inviolablie keiped, and to that purpois that yow not onlie proceid to encourage all others by your good and hartie exemple, bot wher occasion shall offer, and so far as yow can lawfullie and convenientlie doe, that yow proceid with authoritie for sieing this our royall and pious intention dewlie performed, which we will tak as good and faythfull service done vnto ws ; so willing yow to caus insert these letters in your books of Counsell, &c.—Grenwitch, 13 May 1634.

To the Counsell.

Right, &c.—Wheras it hath bene humblie represented vnto ws in behalff of the Clergie of that our kingdome the great hurt arysing to the estate and patrimonie of the church by wanting of publict registeris, wherin all evidents and writts disponed by beneficed persones ought to be registrat, and consequentlie made knowen to such as affect the standing therof, To which purpois we have thoght necessarie to establisch such publict registers, and incorporat them with the office of our Clerk of Register, and with persones fittest and readiest to tak ane accompt of that charge, wheryon we have granted a signature to our present Clerk of Register; And therfor it is our pleasur that yow mak ane act of Counsall theryon, causeing it to be exped vnder our great seall, with all diligence, and that yow cause publicatioun to be made heirof to all our leidges as it effeires; ffor doeing, &c.—Grenvitch, 13 May 1634.

To the Counsell.

Right, &c.—Wheras we did wryt formerlie vnto yow for establisching of Justices of Peace throughout the whole schyres of that kingdome, conforme to the lawdable custome of these our other realmes, bot speciallie conforme to diverse acts of Parliament made thernnent, which as we ar informed is not yit fullie done: These ar therfor to will and requyr yow to proceid therin with all expedition, according to our former warrants to that purpois; which recommending, &c.—Grenwitch, the 13 of May 1634.

To the Counsell.

Right, &c.—Wheras the estaits of our late Parliament gave commission for surveigheing the acts therof, and other constitutions of that our kingdome fitt to have the force of Law, to certane selected persones of each esteal who did accept therof vpon them; These are therfor to will and requyre yow to caus them convene and prosecute the said commission according to the tenour therof, as they wilbe answerable vnto ws.—Grenwitch, 13 May 1634.

To the Thesaurer and Deputie Thesaurer.

Right, &c.—Wheras we have pleased to tak into our princelie consideration the esteal of our royall frie burghs at this tyme, and speciallie of our citie of Edinburgh, who for many good respects to our service and otherwayes haveing vndergone a great charge and trouble of late; these ar therfor to will and requyre yow to forbear to putt in executioun against them the acts made tuitching the transporting of moneyis till our further pleasur be signifeid, ffor the which these presents, &c.—Grenvitch, 13 May 1634.

To the Session.

Right, &c.—Wheras we wer formerlie pleased to requyre the Lordis of our privie Counsell to give ordour by publict proclamation, or vther ways as they shall think fitt, that they and yow of our Colledge of Justice, and members therof, should communicat twyse everie yeir in our Chappell of Halyrudhous, bot now, being willing for good considerations that the communion be oftener celebrated ther, and to nominat such tymes as we have thoght good for that purpois, It is our pleasur that everie first Sonday of the monethis of July and December yeirlie yow prepare and adress your selffis, with our Advocatts, clerkis, writters, and all vthers members of that Judicatorie, to whom yow shall caus intimat this our pleasur, to our said chappell, to participat of that holie sacrament, that others by your exemple may learne to observe the laudable ordour in that caice preseryved ; whairin faill not, as yow tender our princelie respect and pleasur, and as yow will answer to the contrarie, for we will not suffer yow, who should proceid others by your good exemple to be leaders of other subjects, to contemne and dissobey the ordours of the Church : So requyreing yow to cause these our letters to be registrat in your books of Sederunt.—Grenwitch, 13 May 1634.

To the Chancellour.

Right, &c.—Wheras we wer informed that ther was a Lybell exhibited befor our Colledge of Justice by Mr Robert Craig, Advocat, against our trustie, &c. Sir Thomas Hope, our Advocat, which was taken vp by yow, and whairof yow have refused to give our said servand the copie or sight therof ; These are to will and requyre yow to delyver vnto him ane authentik copie of the same, that, being therwith advysed, and accordinglie as he shall find himsellf therby wronged, he may have recourse to Justice against the said Mr Robert, for vindicating himsellf from any injust imputation or scandell ; for which, &c.—Grenwitch, 13 May 1634.

To the New Colledge of St Androis.

Trustie, &c.—Wheras we have sene some acts and statuts made by yow tuitching these students, who ar to be promoved vnto degrees, and ar informed that yow have concluded to keip act and commencement yeirlie for supplie of the want of graduats, wherin we doe verie much approve of your proceidingis, and ar graciouslie pleased that yow continue as yow have begun ; with reservation also of power vnto ws to add to these acts and reforme them in such maner and at what time we in our princelie julgment shall think fitt, requyreing yow to send vnto ws yeirlie ane note or list of the names of all the graduats that shalhappin to be made heirefter in your Vniversiteis, that we may tak such notice of them as we in our princelie judgment shall think fitt : All which we recommend vnto your speciall care, as purposes which we doe verie much respect.—Dat. vt supra.

To the Bischop of Aberdene.

Reverend, &c.—We have vpon occasion of our late being in Scotland observed some thingis which we think to putt in better ordour, which we shall doe as we find caus, but as we have writtin to the right reverend, &c. the archbischop of St Androis, no one thing appeareth vnto ws more necessarie then the weill setling of our vniversiteis, both for the service of God, and good education of youth ther : Now, as we wer then gevin to vnderstand, the whole companie of Vniversiteis, both in the old and new tounes, alsweill the Doctours and Governours of colleges as the younger men, vse to goe to the paroche churches to service and sermons, and ther sitt promiscuouslie with the rest of the auditorie, which losseth much of the honour and dignitie of the Vniversiteis, being quyt contrarie to the course held in other weill governed places of the lyk nature, and is in diverse respects verie inconvenient : And wheras to this purpois, by our letters to provest and bailleis of both tounes, we have willed and requyred them to provyde fitt and convenient places within the queyeris of the severall churches of these tounes as ar most eminent, and whither the saids doctours and others doe ordinarlie repair for hearing of divyne service : Our speciall pleasur is, that alsweill these students of these vniversiteis as the governours, doctours, and others who live therin shall at all times, everie Sonday and holieday (that that church observes), repair thither at the hours both of morning and evening prayeris and sermones, and that togidder and in decent maner, with ther gounes, according to ther severall degrees in schooles respectivelie, and that they doo vse the said habite of gownes according to ther degrees in schooles, vniversiteis, and streits, and that yow give ws ane accompt by letter when this course is begun, and efterward once a yeir at leist how it doeth continew: Which recommending, &c.—Grenwitch, 13 May 1634.

To the Bischop of Murray.

Reverend father in God, &c.—Wheras we wer pleased, out of a respect of the age and qualitie of the Marqueis of Huntlie his Lady, to recommend to yow to have a tender hand over them for matters of ther religion, being then confident that they would otherwayes cause the familie, and such as doe depend vpon them, keip and observe the ordours of the Church, and conforme themselffis to the religion and good ordour presentlie professed, and as is agriable to our Lawes ther, without geving any offence or scandell thervnto: Bot being informed that our princelie clemencie and tender care over the said Marqueis and his Lady ar made a pretext by ther servants, followers, and such as schelter themselffis vnder them, to contemne these ordours, we ar heirby pleased to declair, and our speciall pleasur is, that yow proceid against ther saidis servandis and dependers according to our Lawes for reduceing them to conformitie, wherin we will yow to vse all convenient diligence that may be; and haveing writtin to the said Marqueis that, by your speciall advyse, a pedagogue be choysen for breeding such of the Lord Gordoun his children as ar with him in letters and grounds of the professed religion, we are pleased that yow sie the same accordinglie done: All which recommending vnto your care, &c.—Grenwitch, 13 May 1634.

To the Bischop of Edinburgh.

Reverend father in God, &c.—Haveing requyred our Citie of Edinburgh to consent to the removeing of Mr Alexr Thomesone, second minister at St Geill's, to be the Principall at the Colledge Church of that our citie, we are heirby pleased to requyre yow to sie the said transplantatioun speedelie and ordourlie done, according to the custome in the lyk caices, and as yow shall think requisite to that purpois, which we will tak as acceptable service done vnto ws.—Grenewich, 13 May 1634.

To the Exchequer.

Right, &c.—Wheras the Resignatiouns made by the Inheritouris of ward Lands in favours of the children being Minors, and passing signatouris thervpoun, ar verie prejudiciall vnto ws, by defrauding of ws of these casualiteis due to our Croun: These ar therfor to will and requyre yow to accept of no such resignatiouns in tyme comeing, nor pass any signatures of the same, without our speciall warrant vnder our hand.—Grenwitch, 13 May 1634.

To the Archbischop of St Androis.

Right, &c.—Wheras we have gevin speciall directioun to our trustie Sir John Hay of Baro, knyt, our Clerk Register, to impart diverse particulars vnto yow tuitching the advancement of our service: To which purpois it being requisite that the bischops of that our kingdome be present, to whome we have writtin tuitching the same, It is our pleasur, efter yow have conferred with our said Officer and perused the copie of ther letter, that yow warne them to meitt vpon the 3 of July, at St Androis or Edinburgh, as yow by his advyse shall think fitt, and efter the delyverie of ther letter, and perusing thairof, yow impart vnto them our further pleasur as shalbe communicated vnto yow by our said Officer; which recommending, &c. —Grenwitch, 13 May 1633.

To the Bischop of Galloway.

Reverend, &c.—Wheras by your aige and infirmitie, wherwith it hath pleased God to visite yow, our service doeth much suffer in your dyocie, and ministers ther left to ther owin libertie, wherin we have signifeid our pleasur to the right reverend, &c. the Archbischop of Glasgow : Sieing that we have therby intended is, with respect to yow and in such caices, usuall in the church, we expect that yow will humbly submitt yourselff to our directioun, and conforme yourselff to the said Archbischop his ordour, and assist him of whome he shall mak choyse to be your coadjutor with your best advyse in all things tending to the good of the churche, whairof faill not.—Grenwitch, 13 May 1634.

To the Archbischop of Glasgow.

Right, &c.—We, taking into our princelie consideratioun the estate of the dyocie of Galloway, and how these many yeres bypast, by the seiknes, aige, blindnes, and weaknes of the father in God Andro, bischop thairof, it hath bene destitute of that comfort and help which is necessarie for good ordour within the same : and therfor, being willing to prevent disordours which may creip therin, we think litt that a coadjutor be joyned to him for the better governeing of the affaires of that dyocie in the spirituall and temporall estate thairof : To which purpois, we being sufficientlie informed of the qualificatioun of Mr Henrie Pollok, minister of the Colledge kirk of Edinburgh, and of his abilitie to serve in the churche, wherof we ar willing to mak tryell, and of his forwardnes therin, doe therfor recommend him vnto yow to be choysen coadjutor to the said bischop; willing yow to call the deane and chaptour of that bischoprik togidder, and with ther consent to elect and choyse the said Mr Henrie Pollok to be the coadjutour to the said bischop within the said dyocie, geving him power to exercise all spirituall jurisdiction in the absence of the said bischop, enjoyneing him to doe nothing in temporall things without the consent of the said Mr Henrie ; ffor which these presents, &c.—Grenwitch, 13 May 1634.

To the Archbischop of Glasgow.

Right, &c.—We have, vpon occasion of our late being in Scotland, observed some thingis which we think litt to putt in better ordour, which we shall doe as we find caus ; bot as we have have writtin to the right, &c. the Archbischop of St Androis no one thing appeareth to ws more necessarie then the weill setling of our Vniversiteis, both for the service of God and good education of youth ther, now, as we wer then govin to vnderstand, the whole companeis of that vniversitie, alsweill the doctours and governours of the Colledge as the younger men, vse to goe to the church to service and sermon, and ther sitt promiscuonslie with the rest of the auditorie, which losses much of the honour and dignitie of the Vniversitie, being quyt contrarie to the course held in other weill governed places of the lyk nature, and is in others diverse respects verie [in]convenient, and wheras to this purpois, by our letter to the provest and bailleis of that citie, we have willed and requyred them to provyde fitt and convenient places within the Cathedrall church of that citie for hearing of divyne service : Our speciall pleasur is, that alsweill the students of that vniversitie, as the governours, doctours, and others who live therin, shall at all tymes, everie Sonday and holiday that that church observes, repair thither at the hours both of morning and eveneing prayer and sermones, and that togidder and in decent maner with ther gownes, according to ther severall degreis in schooles respective, and that they doe vse the said habite of gounes according to ther degreis in the scooles, vniversiteis, and streits, and that yow give ws ane accompt by letter when this course is begun, and efterwards once a yeir at least how it doeth continew : Which recommending to your speciall care, we bid, &c.—Grenewitche, the 13 May 1634.

To the Exchequer.

Right, &c.—Whems we have thoght fitt for the good of our service that the rolls of all former extents, alsweill of the spiritualitie as temporalitie, granted to ws and our predicessours befor this our last Parliament, in whois handis soever they be delyvered to our Clerk of Register, to be keipit amongst other our recordis : Our pleasur is, that furthwith yow call befor yow the Clerk of our last Extent, and all others havears of the rolls of all former extents, and caus delyver the same to our said Clerk of Register, to be keipit by him and his successours in that charge amongst our recordis ; and becaus the first terme of the ordinarie extent, granted to ws in our late Parliament, begineth at Mertimes nixt, and that it is fitt the rolls be renewed, and if any other errour or defect be in the samyne it be amended, It is therfor our will and pleasur that yow tak the same to your consideratioun, and caus review the whole rolls of the pound Land of the severall schirreffdomes, stewartreis, and bailliareis, and all others spirituall landis of that our kingdome, and mak ane perfyte inventar of the same, subscryved with your hand, which yow sall delyver to our said officer to be keipit amongst our recordis, whairof he shall delyver ane authentik extract vnder his hand and subscription to the Clerk of Extents, whilk shalbe a sufficient warrant to him for directing the charges theranent ; and it is our further pleasur in all tyme cuming the Clerk of Extents shall delyver to our Clerk of Register the authentik coppie of the rolls of spiritualitie, and that thervpon yow mak ane act : Which recommending to your care as yow tender our service, we bid, &c.—Daitit Grenwich, 13 May 1634.

To the Bischop of Ross.

Right, &c.—Wheras we ar informed that yow have entred in agriement with the Lord of Innesse tuitching the patronages of nyntene churches within your bischoprik which ar in his possessioun, and that by the advyse of the right reverend in God, &c. Archbischop of St Androis and bischop of Murray, yow have agreit with him for restoreing sextene therof to your bischoprik, he being secured of the remanent which ly in his owin Landis, wherin we doe verie much approve of your care and panes in advanceing the estate of that bischoprik, willing yow to continew as yow have begun, as from tyme to tyme yow shall find the occasion, and be confident that we will not be wanting or vnmyndfull of your good service heirin, bot will from tyme to tyme contribute to that purpois in what we can convenientlie and lawfullie doe : So we bid, &c.—Grenwitch, 13 May 1634.

To the Marqueis of Huntlie.

Right, &c.—Wheras we have alwayes out of a tender respect to yow and your Lady bene cairfull that yow might not be troubled for your religion, in so far as might concerne yourselffis, by which our princelie clemencie cheiflie extended toward yow, we expected that yow would have bene the more carefull that none of your familie or vnder your command would have gevin any offence or contempt to the ordoures of the church and religion professed therin, which, as we ar informed, hath bene committed of late by some of your houshold or followers, to which purpois we have writtin to the reverend father the B. of Murray to tak such a course against them being fund guiltie heirin as shalbe agrieable to our said Lawis, and we [ar] heirby pleased to requyre yow to concurre with him to that purpois aganst such of your servandis or dependers as have offended in this kynd, that no occasioun heirefter be gevin vnto ws to suspect that our princelie clemencie and tender respect towards yow be a meanes to schelter others aganst our lawes : And in the meane tyme our further pleasur is, that by the advyse of the said bischope such of the children of our right, &c. the Lord Gordon your sone, as ar with yow, be carefullie bred in the professed religion, and to that purpois that by the speciall advyse of the said bischop a pedagogue be choysen for attending and breeding of them in letters and groundis in the said religion : Which speciallie recommending to your care, we bid, &c.—Grenewitch, 13 May 1634.

To the Counsell.

Right, &c.—Vnderstanding perfytelie the sufficiencie and abilitie of the reverend father in God, the bischop of Edinburgh, and his affection to our service, we ar heirby pleased, for his further encouragment and enabling thereto, to promove him to be ane of our privie counsell of that kingdome : Therfoir it is our pleasur, and we doe heirby will and requyre yow, to receave him as ane of your number vpon our said counsell, and that yow tak his oath as is accustomed in the lyk caices; for which these presents shalbe your sufficient warrand.—Grenwitch, 13 May 1634.

To the Toun of Edinburgh.

Trustie, &c.—Wheras we have writtin to the reverend father, the bischop of Edinburgh, that it is our pleasur that alsweill the doctours and governours of the Colledge of that citie as the younger men and students therof, shall repair to the cathedrall church of the same to hear divyne service, without sitting promiscuouslie with the rest of auditorie, to which purpois it being necessarie that a place wher they may sitt togidder in a decent maner be provydit, we ar heirby pleased to requyre yow to sette such a fitt and commodious place within the said cathedrall church as yow to that effect, and by the bischopes advyse, shall find to be most decent and commodious, wherin our royall intention being for establisching of good and decent ordours amongst them, it cannot bot redound to the good and credite of the citie, wherof we will alwayes have a speciall care, when occasion shall offer, to doe yow good : We bid, &c.—Grenwitch, 13 May 1634.

To the Toun of Edinburgh.

Trustie, &c.—Wheras the deanrie of Edinburgh is a place of dignitie within the Church, to which a speciall care belongeth of all things tending to the good governement of your churches within that citie, and thairfoir ought to have a competent maintenance, conforme to the eminencie and charge thairof, and with a lodging accordinglie : These ar therfor to will and requyre yow to have a speciall care both of the ane and the vther, as yow will doe acceptable service.—Grenwitch, 13 May 1634.

To the Toun of Edinburgh.

Trustie, &c.—Wheras vpon verie good considerations of the habilitie and sufficiencie of our trusty and weilbelovit Mr James Hannay, minister at Halyruidhous, we have recommended to be deane of that our citie of Edinburgh, wherin our zeall and princelie care being for the service of God and for provydeing of yow with qualifeid ministeris, we have heirby thoght fitt to recommend to yow in spetiall manner that yow present him to the reverend father in God the bischop of Edinburgh, to be elected to the place of principall minister at St Geillis, vaiking by the removeing and promotion of Mr Thomas Sydserff to the bischoprik of Brechin ; which we will tak as acceptable service done vnto ws.—Grenvitch, 13 May 1634.

To the Toun of Edinburgh.

Trustie, &c.—Wheras we have often recommended vnto yow the setling of your ministers with compitent stipends able to manteane them according to ther charge, haveing contribute to yow to effectuat your desyres to this purpois ; and now, haveing appoynted Commissioners to meitt with yow to this end, These ar to will and requyre yow with all convenient diligence to meitt with our saidis commissioners, and be ane vniforme consent sett doun the same and secure them and ther successours of what shalbe mutuallie agried vpoun, as yow tender our service and will expect our favour in what yow will have ws to contribute to your good ; wherin expecting your conformitie, we bid, &c.—Grenvitch, the 13 of May 1634.

To the Bischop of Dumblane.

Reverend, &c.—Wheras by our letter to yow we signifeid our pleasur that yow should prepare for administratioun of the communioun in our chappell at Halyrudhous to our Counsell, Colledge of Justice, and others therin expressed, everie Sonday immediatlie ensueing the doun-sitting of the session in the winter and sommer seasones, but now finding that these dayes ar not so fitt, in respect that it may fall out that many of that number be absent, and thairfor have thoght fitt to alter the same, and ar heirby pleased more particularlie to express vnto yow that it is our pleasur that yow prepare and administer the communioun yeirlie vpon the first Sonday of the monethis of July and December, which we will have inviolablie to be keiped ; and to that purpois that yow give them dewlie and tymelie advertisment, if yow shall find it neidfull, and that by all other meanes to advance our pious and princelie intention heirin, in so far as yow can possiblie doe : We bid, &c.—Grenvitch, 13 May 1634.

Commission.

Wheras, out of our princelie zeall, we have alwayes had a speciall care that the churches of that our kingdome, and speciallie that of our cheiff citie of Edinburgh, be provydit with able and sufficient ministers, so being lykwayes carefull that they be provydit with compitent meanes titt for ther charge in so eminent a place of that our kingdome, we have thoght fitt, and doe heirby authorize the persones, and in maner vnderservyed, with power to convene at such dayes and places as they shall think necessarie, and ther, by advyse and consent of the provest and bailleis of that citie, to consider of ther present stipends and mantinence, and therefter to moditie unto them what further meanes they shall find to be fitt and necessarie, whervpon if they do not mutuallie condescend, let ws be certifeid with all diligence of the differences vnder ther handis for which these our letters shalbe sufficient warrant, &c.—Grenvitch, 13 May 1634.

Names of the Commissioners.

Johne, Archbischop S[t] Androis.

E. Traquair.

B. Edinburgh.

B. Rosse.

Sir Johne Hay ; or to aney thrie of them.

To the Colledge of S[t] Androis.

Trustie and weilbelovit—Wheras we ar informed that, by the procurement and informatioun of ane Doctour Seaton, yow have sent the degree of Doctorat to one M[r] Bostock, resideing in this our kingdome of England, who was not present : which mauer of promotion, as it is ill by the exemple and disgracefull, especiallie to that part from whence it was conferred, so it tendeth to our disparagement to all these who have or shall receave heirefter any such degree ther, without a remedie titt to purge such a fault be speedelie vsed : Our pleasur therfor is, that yow proceid both aganst the said Bostock and the said Doctour Seaton, by degraduating of them in such maner as hath bene accustomed in the lyk cairces, or as yow shall find necessarie to that purpois, making such intimationn therof as yow shall find to be titt and convenient, causeing ane act to be made that no such maner of promotion be made heirefter, as yow will tender our royall pleasur : We bid, &c.—Grenwitch, 13 May 1634.

To the Bischop of Edinburgh.

Reverend, &c.—Wheras we have gevin ordour to our Citie of Edinburgh for building of tuo churches ther, and decoreing St Geill's, by dimolisching of the wester wall and the walls of the yles therof, the goldsmyth chopes and song schooll, with the walls of the vesterie, wher it is disjoyned from the church, and restoreing the vesterie thervnto, and otherwayes repaijring and decoreing therof as is titt for such a church : These ar to will and and command yow to tak notice heirof and sie them diligentlie proceid in that work, wherin we have willed our trustie and weilbelovit counsellour Sir John Hay of Baro, kny^t, our Clerk Register, to assist yow ; which recommending vnto your care, we bid, &c.—Grenwitch, 13 May 1634.

Wheras we have at sindrie tymes signifeit our royall intentioun and pleasur that a dew consideratioun might be had of such lands and rents to have bene antientlie doted to the vse of our Chapell Royall, and for establisching therof vpon the same : To which purpois we have thoght it necessarie, for the more speedie furthering of this our royall purpois, to select such persones, and in maner vnder seryved, to convene at such dayes and places as they shall think titt to that purpois, with power to tak exact tryell of all these rents which by any maner of way have belonged and doe belong to the said Chapell, how they have bene taken away or keiped bak from the intendit vse, by whom they ar deteyned, and vpon what grounds and how they may be recovered or reduced to the first foundation, and therefter to certifie ws with all diligence of their proceidings heirin, and with ther opinions joyntlie tuitching the same ; ffor doeing whairof, &c.—Grenwitch, 13 May 1634.

To the right reverend father in God The Archbischop of St Androis,
Primat and metropolitane of all Scotland, The Erles of Morton
and Traquair, our Thesaurers, Principall and deputie, The
Bischops of Edinburgh, Rosse, and Dumblane, Sir Johne Hay,
Sir Thomas Hope, or any fyve of them.

To the Citie of St Androis.

Trustie, &c.—Wheras we intend to have the paroch church of that citie, being the metropolitane of that our kingdome, ordored in such decent and conspicuous maner as we have alreadie caused begin at St Geill's Church, in our citie of Edinburgh, to the end the fabrik may, according to the first lawdable intention of the founder, appear in the trew forme and proportion thairof, without being any wayes parcelled or pestred within in the beautie of the walls or lights obscured without : To which purpois our speciall pleasur is, and we doe heirby command, that with all diligence yow caus dimolisch that little house builded within the eist end, and that yow be carefull to doe and performe all things elso that may tend to the further decoreing of that church, by the advyse of the right reverend the Archbischop of S⟨t⟩ Androis; which we do the rather requyre in regard that Citie is not onlie the seat of the cheiff Metropolitan Archbischop of that our kingdome, bot lykwayes of the cheiff vniversiteis therof ; so willing yow to proceid accordinglie, as yow will respect our princelie will and pleasur.—Grenewitch, 13 May 1634.

COMMISSION.

Wheras we have bene pleased, out of our zeall and princelie care of what may tend to the service of God in planting of the Church in that our kingdome with able and qualifeid persones, To mak choyse of our trustie and weilbeloved M⟨r⟩ Henrie Pollok to be coadjutor to the reverend, &c. the bischop of Galloway in the governement of that bischoprik peculiar to that charge, in regard of the said bischop his infirmitie, blindnes, and aige; we ar heirby pleased to authorize yow, the persones and in maner vnder subscryved, to inritt and consider of a proportionable rent out of that bischoprik for the mantenance of the said M⟨r⟩ Henrie dureing the lyftyme of the present bischope, and that yow prescryve a sure way, and fullie establisch the same, for securing and setling of him therin, which, if neid be, we will approve after what maner yow shall find necessarie.—Grenwitch, 13 May 1634.

To the Archbischop of Glasgow, Bischops of Argyll and Iles.

To the BISCHOPE of EDINBURGH.

Reverend, &c.—We have vpoun occasion of late being in Scotland observed some things which we think fitt to putt in better ordour, which we shall doe as we find caus, bot, as we have writtin to the right reverend the Archbischop of S⟨t⟩ Androis, no one thing appeareth to ws more necessarie then the weill setling of our Vniversiteis both for the service of God and good education of youth ther now, as we wer then gevin to vnderstand the whole companeis of that vniversitie of that citie, alsweill the doctours as governours of the Colledge, as the younger men, vse to goe to the paroch churches to service and sermon, and ther sitt promiscuouslie with the rest of the auditorie, whiche losses much of the honour and dignitie of the Vniversitie, being quyt contrarie to the course held in other weill governed places of the lyk nature, and is in diverse other respects verie inconvenient ; and wheras to this purpois, by our letters to the provest and bailleis of that citie, we have willed and requyred them to provyde a fitt and convenient place within the cathedrall church of that citie for hearing of divyne service : Our pleasur is, that alsweill the students of that vniversitie as the governours, doctours, and others who live therin shall at all tymes, everie Sunday and holyday, that that church observes, repair thither at the hours both of morning and eveneing prayer and sermones, and that togidder and in decent maner with ther gownes, according to ther severall degreis in schoolis respectivelie, and that they doe vse the said habite of gounes according to ther degrees in the schoolis, vniversiteis, and streits, and that yow give ws ane accompt by letter when this course is begun, and afterwards once a yeir at least how it doeth continew ; which recommending, &c.—Grenwitch, 13 May 1634.

To the WHOLE BISCHOPS.

Right reverend, &c.—We tendring the good and peace of that Church by haveing good and decent ordours and discipline observed therin, wherby religion and God's worschipe may encrease, and considering that ther is nothing more defective in that church then the want of a book of common prayer and vniforme service, to be keipit in all the churches therof, and the want of canonis for the vniformitie of the same : We ar heirby pleased to authorize yow, as the representative bodie of that church, and doe heirby will and requyre yow, to condescend vpon a forme of church service to be vsed therin, and to sett doun canonis for the vniformitie of the discipline therof, to be kept alsweill in the colledges, vniversities, and ther awin privat famileis as in the whole churches throughout that kingdome ; wherin expecting your great care and diligence as yow will tender the good of that church and our service.—Grenwitch, 13 May 1634.

To the Thesaurer and Deputie.

Right, &c.—Wheras the granting of the ward and mariage of all noblemen's children requyreth our owin consideration, and doeth much concerne ws to be tender thairof, as importing both our honour and service : It is our pleasur that yow pass none of them till we be first adverteised both of the particular and esteat therof, and give our further warrand therin as yow tender the good of our service.

To the Thesaurer and Deputie.

Right, &c.—Wheras we doe find many patronages of churches vnjustlie takin and deteyned from ws and from the Church, and that it is fitt that befor any new few be granted of aldlay, manses, or precincts thairof, or bailliareis of erection, that we should be acquainted therwith, and that the rentalls wer cleared : These ar to will and requyre yow that yow pass no signature of the same till we be first acquainted therwith, and that the same pas vnder our owin hand as yow tender our service ; and for which these presents shalbe, &c.—Grenwitch, 13 May 1634.

To Mr Henrie Pollok.

Trustie, &c.—We ar pleased, vpon information of your sufficiencie in the calling of the ministrie, and of your affection to our service, to conjoyne yow with the reverend father in God the bischop of Galloway in the charge of that bischoprik, becaus of his infirmitie, blindnes, and aige ; and being confident that yow will not be wanting in what is propper for so eminent a charge, nor in that which heirefter we shalbe pleased to recommend vnto yow tending to God's service in the decent and lawdable governement of the church, or which yow yourself shall from tyme to tyme think may best conduce to that purpois and our royall pleasur, so often signifeid tuitching the same, and accordinglie as we find yow painefull and fordward, we will tak your further preferment into our princelie care, and not otherwayes.—Grenwitch, 13 May 1634.

To the Citie of Edinburgh.

Trustie, &c.—Wheras yow by your Commissioners have presented vnto ws the necessiteis pressing yow to build the Churches for the vse of your Inhabitants, we ar weill pleased with your pious resolution therin, and if our vrgent affaires at this tyme would permitt, we would presentlie satistie your desires tuitching the same : but sieing we cannot convenientlie at this present tyme, these ar onlie to will and requyre yow that with all convenient diligence yow build one of these Churches for ease of that parochin which is now destitute of a church, and for the other we ar resolved to think vpon some meanes wherby this good work may be effected. In the meane tyme, being satisfeit with your service in that kynd, we bid, &c.—Grenewitch, 14 May 1634.

To the Counsell.

Right, &c.- We pitieing the distressed estate of James Arnot, elder, who, efter due tryell takin by our Colledge of Justice, was fund to have bestowed all the meanes he had (which then as we ar informed was of good worth) for payment of his cautionreis, and that otherwayes he was deceived in the trust he reposed on others, haveing never wronged his creditours, so that he left no thing to himsellf, bot is manteaned vpon the Charitie of his freindis, vpon which reasones ther was a protection granted vnto him from the violence and the extremitie of his creditours, which protection is now expyred : We finding still the same reasones to protect him from that rigour, doe heirby requyre yow to grant him a protection dureing the space of sevin yeres efter the dait heirof, [which] we will yow to caus immediatlie exped vnto him vnder our great Seall without any further warrant from ws.—Grenwitch, 14 May 1634.

To the Counsell.

Right, &c.— Wheras yow have writin to ws that yow have continewred the proceiding tuitching the article presented to ws and our late parliament, concerneing the Lord Spynie, his patent, till the fourt day of Junij nixt, Our pleasur is, that in that purpois yow proceid in such maner as may best conduce to the good of our service and the weill of our subjects, which recommending to your care, we bid, &c.— Grenwitch, 14 May 1634.

To the Counsell.

Right, &c.—Wheras ther ar divers particulars presented to ws and our estats at our late parliament ther by our royall frie burghes requyreing due consideratioun speciallie tuitching the fraud vsed by sellers of playding in presenting therof to the mercat in hard rolls, wherby vnder trust they deceave the buyeris, Our pleasur is, that yow tak these particulars into your serious consideratioun, spetiallie that tuitching the playding, causeing ane ordour, speedelie takin and punctuallie keiped, that the saids commoditeis be sold at all tymes heirefter in oppin folds, exposeing to the full view of the buyer ; so expecting all possible expedition heirin for dispatch of these Commissioners of our burrowis that shall attend the same.—Grenewitch, 14 May 1634.

To the Citie of Edinburgh.

Trustie, &c.—Wheras we have bene petitioned by your Commissioners to signe a patent for distributing your Inhabitants in severall companeis, and haveing takin the same into our royall consideratioun, we have thoght fitt, befoir we proceid farther tuitching that purpois, to requyre yow to erect within your citie such severall companeis as yow intend, and so to fitt the way therof that it may appear that our intentions ar reall, and certiefie ws thairof vnder your handis, and by ane act of your Counsell vnder the subscription of your clerk and seall of your citie, wherupon be confident that yow shall find ws readie to advance your just and lawfull designes by endoweing these companeis with such liberteis and privileges as shalbe thoght fitt for your good, and so shall protect them by our authoritie, and otherwayes that it shall appear that nothing shalbe wanting in ws which may tend to the advancement thairof, wherin expecting your diligence, we bid, &c.—Grenwitch, 14 May 1634.

To the Bischop of the Yles.

Reverend, &c.—Haveing taken the association of the fischingis of Great Britane and Irland into our protection in a peculiar maner, and intending to caus setle a solid course tuitching all impositions and dewteis whatsoever to be raised vpon these fischings : Our pleasur is, that yow doe not trouble them by exacting tythis or tythe dewteis from them till yow know our further pleasur, wherin if yow shall suffer we shall tak it to our consideration, and tak such a course as yow shalbe no lousser.—Grenwitch, 14 May 1631.

To the Exchequer.

Right, &c.—We have formerlie writtin to yow for passing a signature in favours of our citie of Edinburgh, tuitching the liberteis and privilidges, and being informed by ther Commissioners that by reason of your and ther owin vrgent affaires it is not expeid ; These ar therfor to will yow to consider the said signatur, and if yow find the same agrieable to the infeftment lawfullie granted to them by our royall predicessours, that yow expeid the same with diligence, otherwayes to acquant ws with your reasones to the contrarie, wherin expecting your performance, we bid, &c.—Grenwitch, 14 May 1634.

To the Counsell.

Right, &c.—Haveing considered of your letter of the differences betwixt our right, &c. the Erle of Erroll, our high Constable of that our kingdome, and the citie of Edinburgh, and of the suspension raised by them of the tuo decreits obtenit by the said Erle befoir yow, and finding that the question now doeth aryse which should be the convenient judicatorie befoir whom the cause should be decydit, whither befoir yow or befoir our Session, in regard of the nature of ther right they pretend to have, we have thoght fitt heirby to requyre yow that if yow shall find your selfis compitent judges in this difference according to the Lawes and customes of our said antient kingdome yow proceid therin, bot if yow shall find that it properlie belongeth to our Session, remitt it vnto them bot withal that no dilatoreis or tedious formes of Law be vsed, and that, befoir which of yow this shal happin to be heard, we command that yow defer sentence yntill ye acquant ws with the particulars of the proces.—Grenwitch, 14 May 1631.

[Similar Letter to the Session.]

To the Exchequer.

Right, &c.—Wheras diverse complaintis have bene made vnto ws by our frie royall burghes of that our kingdome aganst ane patent granted to the Lord Erskene tuitching tanceing of Leather and impositions vpon the same, to the prejudice of our subjects, and that the said patent is neir expyred : These ar to requyre yow to pass no grant of the same of new efter the expyreing of the former, bot that all tanneris of Leather within the same be frie as they wer befor the granting of that patent : Which recommending, &c.—Grenewitch, 14 May 1634.

To the Counsell.

Right, &c.—Wheras diverse complants have bene made vnto ws by sindrie of our subjects, speciallie by our royall frie burghes, of the great prejudice they susteane by the too frequent granting of protections, passing over the acts of Parliament tuitching that purpois, we have thoght fitt to recommend vnto yow that none pass heireftter bot vpon verie just and considerable causses, with speciall provision that the annualrents be payed to the creditours, and that yow caus the acts made tuitching the same be keipit, that no occasion of grevance be gevin to our good subjects by breach therof; which recommending, &c.— Grenewitch, 14 May 1634.

To the Frie Burghes.

Trustie, &c.—Wheras we have bene petitioned by your Commissioneis for granting freedome to erect within your burghes severall Companeis of all sort of tradeing, ather within or without the kingdome, and to endow each companie with severall liberteis and priviledges which shalbe onlie dew and peculiar to the generall assotiations respectivelie ; we being pleased with your demand heirin, as conceaveing it to be a readie way to encrease trade amongst yow, and for avoyding of that confusion which the lake of vnitie and governement in such trades doe ordinarlie begett, have heirby thought fitt to encourage yow to proceid in the destribution of your Inhabitants in companeis and assotiations, To which purpois we are pleased that yow represent vnto ws or our Counsell ther what shall be fund fitt in each citie and brugh according to the proportions thairof, and draw the same vp in generall patents, assureing yow that we shalbe readie both by our authoritie to protect and endow them with all liberteis and priviledges fitt for such Incorporations, and with what may increase ther trade : So willing yow to be also fordward in advanceing of so worthie a purpois, tending cheiflie to your owin good, as yow shall find ws at all tymes readie to protect and second your endeavours thairin.—Grenewitch, 14 May 1634.

To the Session.

Right, &c.—Wheras we ar informed that ther is ane action in Law depending befor yow at the instance of certane persones agenst some of our royall frie citeis and brughes for tythes of fisches taken in our Yles, sieing that vpon verie important considerations we have establisched ane assotiatioun for the fischingis of Great Britane and Irland, whairof we have in peculiar maner taken vpon ws the protection, and wherby diverse conditions and restrictions ar provyded for advanceing that great work tending to the generall good of all our dominions, and especiallie of that our ancient kingdome : These ar therfoir to will and requyre yow not to proceid any further therament, and tuitching all impositions which for the generall good of our subjects shalbe fund necessarie to be payed by the members of that Association.—Grenewitch, 14 May 1634.

To the Commissioners for the Burrowis.

Trustie, &c.—Wheras the improveing of the native commoditeis of that our kingdome by erecting manufactoreis is a work much tending to the advancement of trade, and setting many ydle people to work, besydes many other benefits that may redound therby to your good and benefite, we have therfor thought fitt to recommend the same to your serious consideratioun, assureing yow that we will grant to the vndertakers who shall erect any Manufactorie for improveing of any native commoditie whatsumever, all such liberteis, priviledges, and immuniteis as in such caces ar accustomed and necessarie, and shall omitt nothing that may testifie our favourable acceptance of ther endeavours : So being confident that yow will give ws a tryell of your willingnes heirin, and of all other things redounding to the publict good and your owin privat benefite, least we be forced to mak vse of strangeris to that purpois, which we will be loath to doe.—Grenewitch, 14 May 1634.

To the Counsell.

Right, &c.—Wheras we have formerlie signifeid our pleasur vnto yow that the taking of Pearle within that our kingdome in the rivers therof, should not be reserved for any one's privat persone, bot communicated to all our subjects, speciallie to the merchands of our frie royall brughs, to whom we did formerlie bestow the gift of that trade : It is our pleasur that yow pass ane act of Counsell dischargeing all former patents or acts made for the ingrossing therof in the persone of ony ane of our subjects, granting libertie to our leidges, speciallie our frie brughes, to fisch pearle in all the rivers of that kingdome without let, and that yow cause mak publication heirof, that none pretend ignorance of our royall intention and pleasur heirin.—Grenewitch, 14 May 1634.

To the Archbischop and Bischopes.

Right reverend and Reverend fathers in God, &c.—Wheras the translatioun of the Psalmes of David done by our late royall father is now fullie renewed, approved, and fitted for the Presse, as we wer formerlie pleased to writt vnto yow tuitching that purpois, being desyreous that his intentioun, besydis the goodnes of the work, may remane a monument of his pious disposition, which is of all others best knowen vnto yow : Our pleasur is, that yow condescend vpon a way how it may be receaved and sung vniversallie in the churches of that our kingdome, to the effect ordour be gevin for such number of books as shalbe fund fitt and necessarie, To which purpois we will yow to confer with our Clerk of Register, who will impart to yow our further pleasur heirin ; which recommending to your speciall care, we, &c.—Grenwitch, 15 May 1634.

To the Counsell.

Right, &c.—We ar informed from Johne Lundie of that ilk that his vncle Sir James haveing these many yeres bene in possession of that estate, bot vnder trust, and to the behalff of his nephewis, hath notwithstanding, by taking advantage of the weaknes and incapacitie of the eldest and the absence of the second furth of the cuntrie, converted the whole or most part of the benefite therof to his owin vse, and still intendeth by indirect pretexts to keip the petitioner, his third nephew, from enjoying the possession of his just and lawfull heretage, contrair to all justice and equitie, as may appear more at large by the enclosed information ; we therfor have thought fitt to will and requyre yow to tak the premisses into your serious tryell and consideration, and according as yow find caus to tak such ordour thairin as nather the fraud, if it be such as is informed, scape vnpunished, nor the petitioner be longer keipit from his right, bot that he receave such present redress as yow in reasone and equitie shall think fitt ; wherin not doubting of your care, we bid, &c.—Grenwitch, 16 May 1634.

To the Exchequer.

Right, &c.—Being gratiouslie pleased that no advantage be takin aganst Margaret Stewart, daughter of umquhill Hercules Stewart, brother of the late Erle Bothwell, by the forfaltour of the late Erle of Bothwell, Our pleasur is, that with all diligence yow expeid vnder our great seall a signature of rehabilitation granted in favours of hir aires and successours, for which these presents shalbe sufficient warrant, otherwayes, if yow have any reasone to the contrarie, that yow adverteis ws therof.—Grenwitch, 18 May 1634.

II   2 x

To the Counsell.

Right, &c.—Being informed by some of our Officers that our trustie and weilbelovit Wm Dick, merchand burges of Ed^r, hath advanced great sowmes of money for our speciall service, whairof we have takin particular notice. Our pleasur is, that no protection be granted heirefter, or expel vnder our sealls, ather heir or by yow, to his prejudice in favours of any persone whatsumever, by which he can mak it appear befoir yow that he in his owin particular interest will suffer, and to that effect that yow caus give him dew warning of any protection that shall happin to be granted; and for, &c.—Grenewitch, the 18 May 1634.

To the Counsell.

Right, &c.—Whems by our direction Sir Johne and Sir William Scotts, tuo of the Erle of Buccleuch's tutors, have repaired to our Court to know our pleasur tuitching the particulars of our decreit-Arbitrall and exposition therof, with whom we have conferred therin; and sieing formerlie we gave ordour to our Advocat to draw vp a mynut for a contract betuixt the Erle Buccleuch and Francis Stewart for setling of them conforme to our decreit, which mynut was not then subscryved be the pairteis, Therfor it is now our pleasur that the said mynut be extendit in forme by advyse of ther mutuall Advocatts, if they be present, and by advyse of our Advocat, whom we doe heirby will yow appoynt to sie the same formallie done according to the intent of the inclosed mynut in all poynts; and our pleasur is, that the said Francis be entred to the vplifting of the fermes and dewteis of the landis dew to him since the dait of our decreit, and in tyme cuming, and being secured in these landis formerlie possessed by the late Erle and his father, and whairof they or oney of them wer in vse to vplift the maills and dewteis, that he renunce all title to the rest of the saidis Landis, tithes, and superioriteis in favours of Francis, now Erle of Buccleuch, except such landis and tythies as wer not valued by the said late Erle, and also cam not vnder our decree, nor wer by him, the said Erle, recomend in your presens, at leist any right thairof which he had thervnto by the forfeyt of the late Erle of Bothwell, whervnto we formerlie did and now doe declair that we will enable the said Francis pro tanto that he may plead ather for the vnvalued or renunced lands and tythis as said is, to the end he may recover the same to the lawes of the kingdome if he hath right thervnto, and that ordour may be gevin to draw a signature or gift of forfaultour therof to the said Francis, conforme to the intention of our decreit-arbitrall and acts of counsall made thervnent of befoir; And the contract being so exped, it is our pleasur that both the saids pairteis subscryve the same in your presens or some of your number appoynted by yow, and which, if ather of the pairteis refuis, we will that our Advocatt concurre with the other pairtie and vrge the fulfilling of the said decreit-arbitrall and our exposition therof by ordour of Law, wherunent this shalbe his warrant; All which seriouslie recommending to your care, we bid, &c.—Grenwitch, May 1634.

To the Chancellour, Archbischop of St Androis, Thesaurer, Privie Seill, Marqueis of Traquair, Clerk Register, Advocat.

Right, &c.—Haveing at lenth conferred with our right, &c. the Erle of Roxbrught in a proposition made by him to ws testiefieing his willingnes to putt in our hands his right of all such churches and tythis as doe belong to the Abacie of Kelso, and that ar vndisponed by him, others then these churches and tythis which lyes within Teviotdaill and the Forrest, and doe concerne his owin landis and some of his particular freindis, with whome he hath alreadie agried for the right of ther tythis, according to the ordinance that we did sett doun that everie man should have his owin tythis: And considering that this overture made by our said right, &c. to ws may much contribute to these lawfull and just endis, and to the good of our service, we have thoght it expedient to remitt the further consideration of the particulars to your conference with our said right, &c., earnestlie desyreing yow that the most convenient course may be taken for establisching of his right of these churches and tythis in our persone, satisfaction being gevin him as we acknowledge reasone and equitie doeth allow; and sieing the bussines will requyre tyme and leasure befoir it can be weill digested, and we adverteised of that course which shalbe fund fittest and best to be taken, Our will and pleasur is, that yow tak such course as that ther be no further proceiding concerneing these churches and tythis, bot that all may be conteued and stand in the same caice they now ar in, till our farther pleasur be signifyid theranent; which recommending, &c., we bid, &c.—Greinwitch, 21 May 1634.

To Mʳ James Home.

Trustie, &c.—Haveing bene moved by the Erles of Murray and Lawderdale to admitt of ane appeall to ws in this proces depending concerneing the Erldome of Home; bot considering the troubles and inconveniences which may ensue if we should bot hearken to the said Appeall, we have thoght rather fitt that both of yow condescend vpon a submission vpon equall termes to tuo or thrie weill affected on ather part for setling all bussines amicablie betwene yow, and one to be oversman, cutt schort and end all differences that may fall out (ourselff not being vnwilling to vndergoe the said trouble of oversman, both pairteis requeisting ws thervnto); concerneing which motion of ours, haveing the willing consent and approbation of the Erles of Murray and Lauderdale, in name of ther sones and daughters in Law, we doe heirby demand and expect of yow the lyk; wherof being verie confident, we bid, &c.—Grenewitch, 24 May 1634.

To the Session.

Right, &c.—Wheras we have signifeid our royall pleasur to our right, &c. the Erles of Murray and Lawderdaill, in name of ther sone and daughters in Law, and to our, &c. James Home of Coldinknowis, for submitting of all questions amongst them anent the succession to the estate and liveing of Home to the amicable decision of freinds: It is our will that yow not onlie forbear any further proceiding in any processe depending theranent befor yow, bot lykwayes that yow stay all proces intended or to be intended, ather at the instance of any of the saidis tuo pairteis aganst others, or at the instance of any other aganst them or any of them, as aires or successours to vmquhill James, Erle of Home, till yow shall vnderstand our further pleasur.—[No date.]

To the Advocat.

Trustie, &c.—Haveing fund it more expedient that all questions anent the succession and right to the estate and liveing of Home be decydit amicablie [rather] than be Law, we have acquanted the Erles of Murray and Lawderdale with our will heiranent; and finding them, in the names of ther sones and daughters in Law, willing to obey, we have by this other letter (which yow shall delyver) demanded the lyk of the other pairtie, James Home of Coldinknowis: It is therfor our pleasur that yow draw vp a full submission, conceaved vpon equall termes, wharby all matters questionable amongst them may be absolutelie referred to freinds; and least in the meane tyme ather pairtie receave prejudice, we have gevin warrant to the Senatours of our Colledge of Justice to stay all proces by this letter direct to them, which yow shall delyver at the first sitting: Which recommending, &c.—Dat. vt supra.

To the Session.

Right, &c.—Wheras the distressed esteat of Sir Wm Keith of Ludwharne hath bene humblie represented vnto ws, as being vnable any longer to attend the issue of ane action of Law depending befor yow
betweene him and Johne Gordon of Haddo; in which cace we, taking into our princelie consideration the
hard estate of such persones, ar heirby gratiouslie pleased to recommend vnto yow that speedie justice be
administred in the said action, admitting of no dilatours that convenientlie can be avoyded to putt him in
further charge or delay.—Dat. vt supra.

To the Session.

Right, &c.—Wheras we ar informed of ane action in Law depending befor yow betuixt the now
bischop of the Yles and the bischop of Rapho, late of Yles, tuitching a yere's fruit of that bischoprik;
becaus the one's ordinarie residence is in Irland and the other in remote parts of that our kingdome, from
that our seat of Justice, and that his charge requyreth more then ordinarie panes and vigilancie in persones
of the lyk function, we ar heirby pleased seriouslie to recommend vnto yow that speedie Justice be administrat, not onlie in that action, bot in all others that shall cum in befor yow concerneing the said bischop of
Yles, which we shall tak as acceptable service done vnto ws.—Grenwitch, 24 May 1634.

In regard your subjects of Scotland had never any continewed trade in Affrick, wherby to benefite
themselffis or your Custome, These give power for 31 yeres to the persones above written to trade with all
native and forrayne commoditeis to and from Scotland, in and to the bounds begining at the river Senega,
lyeing in the 16½ degree of northerlie latitude, and southerlie to Cap de Bon esperance in the 34½ degrie of
southerlie latitude. They ar to pay to your Matie dues and customes for outward and inward commoditeis.
Others of that kingdome ar discharged vpon pane of confiscation of thair schipis and goodis, whairof your
Matie is to have one-half and the Patentees the other. Your Matie promeises to give no power of that
tenour to any others dureing that tyme without ther consent. They may assigne ther interests to other
persones who ar to have the lyk power. They may sett to sea so many schipps furnished with Ordinance
as they shall think necessar to incress and secure ther trade. No access to be made of ther schipis and
mariners bot for saftie of the kingdome. Thay ar to have what Commissions shalbe further requisit for
the more safe trading. Your Matie is to assist them in procureing right if they be wronged by any forraigne
Prince or state. They may adjoyne to them such competent number of Dutch merchands and other
strangers as they shall think fitt to be denizens, and to have the lyk friedome in that trade. They may
convene and establisch such ordours as shalbe fitt for regulating their trade which your Matie requyres to be
keiped if not repugnant to your lawes. All your Officers whom it concerneth ar to assist them when
occasion requyris. The names of the persones to whom this signatur was granted went home in blank.—
Grenwich, 26 May 1634.

Mynute.

Francis Stewart is to have all the Lands in Lothian which belonged formerlie to his father, paying
bak to the Aires of Buccleuch for the superplus which shalbe fund above eight thousand fyve hundreth
merks of yeirlie rent, being ane thousand punds for everie hundreth merks, which was estimated befoir his
Matie to extend to thretie-tua thowsand pundis Scotts money or therabout, and that in full satisfaction of
the whole thrid part of all the estate which the Erle of Buccleuch did value and mak subject to his Matie
decree as belonging vnto him by vertew of the Erle Bothwell's forfeyture.

And whatsoever landis or rents the said Erle did renunce, or wer not valued and made subject to his Ma[teis] decree, as lykwayes whatsoever tythes or patronages of churches out of which the said Erle had any rent, they being renunced or not valued and made subject to his Ma[teis] decree, the said Francis is to be enabled pro tanto to plead for them by Law, and to recover them to his owin vse, they taking them to ther other rights and quyting Bothwell's forfaltour in that.

Everie of them is to delyver to the other all the evidents that they have of the proportions of Lands that is disposed to the other, renunceing all right they can pretend thervnto, and giveing warrandice fra ther owin deidis. Non of them is to hold any stok, tythis, or superioriteis of ane other whatsumever, but immediatlie of his Ma[tie] if they wer holdin so formerlie, or otherwayes as they wer holdin of old.

As for the patronages that shallhappin to be questioned betweene them, it is his Ma[teis] pleasur that his Advocat consider of his right thervnto. If any question shall aryse vpon new grounds betweene the pairteis further than is explayned, his Ma[tie] is to be acquanted therwith that he may declair his further pleasur theranent.—Grenwitch, 26 May 1634.

Wheras by our former precept we appoynted 3000[lib] sterling to have bene payed to Sir Alex[r] Strauchan of Thorntoun, kny[t] baronet, vpon consideration he had friclie dimitted our commission to him tuitching omissions and conceilments, wherby for the panes and charges he was at it was fitt he should have receaved recompence; To the end that both we who ar so engadged by our precept, and yow who ar particularlie bund for paying these moneyls vnto him may be tymelie disengadged, and he by that meanes releived of debts contracted by him for his charge in that our service, Our pleasur is, that yow pay vnto him, his aires and assigneyis, the said sowme of 3000[lib] sterling with all convenient diligence, and that out of the first and readiest of these taxatiouns last granted to ws, with interest for such tyme heirefter as the said sowme shallhappin to be vnpayed to him or his forsaids, and that ye accept of this our warrant, testifieing vnto him vnder your hands your acceptatioun heirof, and therefter that yow sie ws discharged of that debt and yourselflis releived; for which, &c.—Grenewitch, 26 May 1634.

To the Erles of Morton and Traquair, Thesaurers principall
and depute.

TO THE EXCHEQUER.

Right, &c.—Wheras our royall father, of happie memorie, wyselie considering how much it did import the good of that our kingdome, that the administration of criminall justice should not be communicat to ilk subject, bot that the same should be committed to such judges as should be able and qualifeid persones for exerceing the same, and befor whome pairteis may plead for themselflis, and have these ordinar helpes which ar allowed by the lawis of that kingdome, to the which ther wer no greatter lett then the liberteis and priviledges granted by our predicessours by infeftments to ther weill deserveing subjects, which as we doe nowayes intend to abrogat nor infringe, so we doe not see it agrieable to reasone that they may mak saill of these Liberteis, nor transact the same to whome they pleas, nor that ther new erections of barroneis should be granted in that kynd: Our pleasur is, that yow grant no new infeftments to any subject of Lands, with power to hang, head, imprisson, putt to death, scourge, or anywayes priviledge in that kynd, nor that yow accept resignations of the same priviledges, bot onlie of the Lands and such other priviledges as ar inherent to them, without any new grant of these royall priviledges inherent to the croun, which we cannot think transmissable nor fitt to be exposed to seall; wherin expecting yow will be cairefull, we bid, &c.—Grenewitch, 26 May 1634.

To the Counsell.

Right, &c.—Wheras it is not vnknowen vnto yow with what care we have intendit the good of the Assotiation of the fischings within these our kingdomes for the vse of our subjects, and that we wilbe provident to protect them from the exactions of the heretours in the Yles, who, as we are informed, without a warrant exact sindrie dewteis from them, to ther great prejudice, bringing in strangeris and loading ther vessells with fisches and other native commoditeis, contrair to our lawis : Our pleasur is, that yow call befor yow the Landislordis of these Yles wher the fisching is, and take accompt of them by knowing vpon what warrant they tak these dewteis, and that yow discherge what yow think not dew in that kynd vpon verie good grounds, sending vnto ws a note of all that is exacted ; and that yow tak ordour with strangeris who resort and trade ther, contrarie to our Lawis and the course intendit by the patent of Assotiation : So, expecting that no such demeanour be committed in tyme cuming, &c.—Grenwitch, 26 May 1634.

To the Counsell.

Right, &c.—Wheras, in our late parliament holdin within that our kingdom, ther was complaynt made of diverse insolenceis and oppressions made in the hielands of that our kingdome, the caus of which complant is not as yit removed, we being willing to represse the same, and to establisch such solide ordour wherby our peace may be manteaned, and these rebellious and dissobedient subjects reduced to the obedience of our lawes, or punisched accordinglie : It is our pleasur that yow caus putt in executioun the acts of Parliament made the 7 parliament holdin by our dearest father, of happie memorie, cap. 93, 94, 95, 96, 97, aganst the induellars in the hielands and borders, or vther places wher these rebells resort or duell, as lykwyse the act of our late parliament made anent the Clangregour ; And that yow tak such further course for quyeting in these and vther parts in that our kingdome, as in your judgments shalbe thoght fittest for intertening of our peace and protecting our good subjects from all violence and oppressions, and that from tyme to tyme yow mak ws accompt of your diligence heirin : bot wher yow find any lett or stay we will, vpoun your signiefieing thairof vnto ws, and our opinions tuitching the same by our further authoritie to remove the same : Which recommending, &c.—Grenewitch, 26 May 1634.

These conteyne a grant to John Tinynghame, and his aires or assigneyes of the coall win and to be win in the lands of the burrow mure of Craill, the acres of land lyand betuixt the baronie of Barnes and the said Mure, and within halff myle eistward and northeistward from that baronie, with power to brek ground, they satisfieing the heretours or persones interested : They ar to pay to your Matie and successours at ther making vse of this gift, 20 merks Scotts yeirlie in name of few-dewtie, doubling the same at the entrie of the air.—Grenwitch, 29 May 1634.

A presentatioun for Mr Patrik Lyndsay to the church of Maxtoun, vacand by the death of vmquhill John Smyth, last minister ther.—29 May 1634.

To the Counsell.

Right, &c.—Wheras for reformation and prevention of the abuses and inconveniences heirtofoir occasioned throw the vngouerned sale and immoderat vse of Tobacco, we have resolved for to ordour the sale of that commoditie throughout our dominions, that non bot such as vpon examination shalbe fund to be fitt may be permitted to sell or use the same by small or retaill, and these to be licenced by authoritie from ws, putting in at the receaveing of the licence sufficient band alsoweill for selling wholsome and uncorrupt tobacco as for keiping good ordour and rule in ther severall housses and shops : The prosecution and ordereing of which service within that our kingdome we have bene pleased to committ (dureing the space of sevin yeires) to our trustie Sir James Leslie, knyᵗ, and Thomas Dalmahoy, as by our gift, daited at Whythall the 19 Aprill 1631 yeres, may appear : Our pleasur is, that, according to this our royall intention, yow tak ordour that efter the 15 of Sept. nixt ensueing, no persone whatsoever presume to sell or utter tobacco in small or by retaill within that our kingdome bot such and so many as shalbe therunto licenced by our saids commisssoners, under pane of our high displeasur and such a penaltie as yow shall think fitt to impose, on such as shalhappin to transgres, the one half to belong to the informer and the other half to the saids Commissioners ; and that yow mak this our pleasur knowen to all our loveing subjects by letters of publication therof, direct by yow in dew forme ; ffor doeing wherof, as also to yow of Exchequer for expeiding the said grants, these presents shalbe a sufficient warrand.—Grenewitch, 29 May 1634.

To the Exchequer.

Right, &c.—Wheras we had formerlie writtin unto yow concerning ane petition exhibited unto ws by our trustie Sir Alexʳ Setone, knyᵗ, one of the Senatours of our Colledge of Justice, for some moneyis dew unto him for imbringing to our use of the concealment of our taxations, which he alledged to be payable unto him by the Erle of Mar as being then Collectour of Taxations, and now finding by your letter that according as we had requyred yow yow have convened both pairteis, and that efter dew tryell yow have fund the said Erle to be frie of the same, and the sowme of 6077 merks of that our kingdome resting justlie dew unto the said Sir Alexʳ, and besyds being certifeid by yow of the extraordinarie panes and charges he hath bene at in the said service, Our pleasur is, that out of any of the saids concealments ungevin out, or which he shalhappin discover himself heirefter yow pay unto him his aires and assigneyis the said sowme of 6077 lib., or otherwayes that yow tak oney such trew course for his speedie satisfaction as yow shall think fitter, ffor the which, &c.—Grenewitch, 29 May 1634.

To the Session.

Right, &c.—Wheras we understand that Wᵐ Scott of Ardross, whois mariage we bestowed upon our trustie and weilbeloved Mʳ William Drummond of Hathornden, is verie schortlie to marie ather without consent of him who is the donatour, or of his owin curatours, contrarie both to Law and his dewtie, and wherby he intendeth to defraud ws and the donatour of the double availl of the mariage, Our pleasur therfor is, that if the donatour efter the solemnization of the said intendit mariage shalhappin to intend action in Law befoir yow for the double availl thairof, that without delay ye administer unto him speedie justice according to our Lawis, without unnecessarie protraction of tyme, which we doe the rather requyre to be the more speedelie putt to a poynt, in respect it wilbe a preparative important for ws in diverse causes of the lyk nature, wherin we find our selflis prejudged ; we bid, &c.—Grenewitch, 29 May 1634.

To the Commissioners for Tythes.

Right, &c.—Wheras by ane Act of our late parliament holdin in that kingdome dischargeing all leading of Tythes, ther is a provision conceaved in favours of Churchmen possessing thairof, haveing relation to ther submission and the meaneing of our decree gevin thairvpon, not intending to extend the benefite thairof to any laick persones who by themselffis or authours have procured taks of the tythis of other men's Lauds from any bischop or beneficed persone : Our pleasur is, that so long as these tythes doeth remane in the persones of laymen, yow tak such present order for the heretors leading and intro-metting thairwith vpoun sufficient suretie to pay according to the valuatioun as yow doe in the tythis of erections, and whems we intend so to meassur our favour to all our subjects as we may enjoy the same without hurt and detriment of ane other : To which purpois being informed of the prejudice susteuit by these who doeth not receave payment for ther tythis till the finisching of ther valuatious which by our former letters ar delayed till all the tythes of erections be first valued, we ar heirby pleased to remitt to your consideration some propositions for remedie of this prejudice seameing fair to ws, which yow may hear from our servand and Sir James Lockhart : So recommending to your care the approveing thairof, or finding some better expedient to that purpois.—Grenewitch, 29 May 1634.

To the Counsell of Scotland.

Right, &c.—Haveing understude by a letter from our President of York that one Ralff Fetherston-halgh being sentenced in a caus befor them to frustrat the effect of Justice in contempt of our Authoritie hath fled to that our kingdome, and being nowayes willing that any of our kingdomes shonld be a saiff refuige to shelter them that retire thervnto, being censured as malefactours in ane other bok, that our Justice should reach them wherever they ar in any of our dominions : It is our pleasur that if the said Ralff be within that our kingdome, yow caus apprehend him with diligence, and send him with a saiff convoy to our toun of Berwick to be delivered to the Mayor therof, to the end he may send him to be convoyed from Shirreff to Shirreff to our Citie of York to be answerable to Justice : For doeing quherof, &c.—Grenewitch, 29 May 1634.

To Sir James Balfour.

Trustie, &c.—Wherin at our late being within that our kingdome, we wer pleased to conferre vpon our right Robert, Viscount of Belheaven, that title as a degree of honour which we have estemed due vnto his merite, to the end ther be nothing wanting (vsuall in this kynd), wherby this our favour and the remembrance of his good and fayfthfull service dew vnto ws may be preserved, we requyre yow according to the dewtie of your place to insert and register in your books his coat of armes sent heirwith vnto yow according to the custome, and as is fitt, provyded it wrong no other ; for doeing whairof, &c.—Grenwitch, penult May 1634.

To the Counsell.

Right, &c.—Wheras we ar informed that about the begining of our Reigne the petitioner Alex[r] Blair was, by act of Counsell, made to abandon that kingdome, which we ar confident yow caused doe vpoun verie good consideratiouns, bot being now humblie petitioned by him that in regard of the death of his brother to whom he doeth succeeid in his right to certane Lands in that kingdome, he may repair thither for recoverie thairof, Our pleasur is, that yow grant him such a tyme for that purpois as yow shall think necessarie, that he may seik for his right according to Justice and the Lawis of that our kingdome ; for doeing, &c.—Grenewitch, penult May 1634.

Our Soveraigne Lord ordeanes a commission to be made vnder his Ma[teis] great seall of the kingdom of Scotland, making mention that his highnes, being crediblie informed that a great part of his Ma[teis] houshold stuff and plenisching, as plate hangings, &c., within the said kingdome wer vnder the charge and custodie of Sir Johne Auchmowtie, knyᵗ, Master of his Maᵗⁱˢ Wardrope, conforme to a book bearing his charge of the said plenisching and houshold stuff subscryved by the late Clerk Register and him, lyeing in his Maᵗⁱˢ register, be vertew of his highnes' commission vnder the great seall of the date at Whythall, 13 Aprill 1626, till a few yeres befoir his Maᵗⁱˢ late comeing to Scotland : The said Sir Johne was commanded by a warrand direct from his Maᵗⁱˢ Privie Counsall of the said kingdome to delyver out of his said office to such persones as had charge from the Lords thairof, and the grencloth, all such silver-plate, naprie, vessells, fyrework, and others plenischings as wer in his charge, which for obedience' to ther command he did accordinglie performe : But in regarde ther may be some loss or spoyle of some of these particulars wherwith the said Sir Johne cannot be convenientlie charged without a new commission, wherby his charge may be renewed and the plenisching redelyvered vnto him vpon a new accompt : Therfor, and to the effect the said Wardrob may be visited of new and putt in good ordour, his Maᵗⁱᵉ hath made, constitute, and ordeaned, lyk as his Maᵗⁱᵉ by the tenour heirof maks constituts and ordeanes, Chancellour, Sᵗ Androis, Thesaurer, Privie Seall, Marqueis of Hamilton, E. Roxburgh, E. Stirling, E. Lawderdale, E. Southesk, E. Traquair, B. Ross, Clerk Register, Advocat, and such of his Maᵗⁱˢ officers who shalbe in these places for the tyme, or any thrie of them, his Maᵗⁱˢ commissioners conjunctlie, with power to visite all and sindrie his highnes' said plenisching and wardrob stuff whatsoever within the custodie of the said Sir Johne, and to call for the said book and whole particulars therin, to try in whois custodie they ar, and to bring them bak and repose them in his charge, and thervpon to tak ane Inventure of new of all the plenisching which yow shall find in his custodiie and as shalbe reposed in his charge agane by vertew of this commission, and delyver it to the Clerk of Register to be keipt amongst his Maᵗⁱˢ records, and that he be no further charged than according to the said new Inventar, vnless a farther supplie of plenisching be made by his Maᵗⁱᵉ or his highnes' royall successours firme and stable holding, and for to hold whatsomever the saids Commissioners shall doe and ordeyne to be done in the premisses, and that the said commission be further extendit with all clausses needfull.

PRESENTATIONS.

The Church of Forgund of the Mearnes to Mᵣ Pa. M'Gill, The Church of Barrie to Mᵣ Olipher Howstoun, The Church of Balmerino to Mᵣ Arthour Granger.

TO THE COUNSELL.

Right, &c.—Wheras we ar informed that it is enacted by our frie burghes that everie thrie yeir the ordiner taxt roll for raising the ordinarie taxatioun payable by them should be renewed for the better knowing of the present estate of our said burghis, which, as we ar informed, lykwyes hath bene neglected these many yeires bypast, to the prejudice of the brught of Dundie, whairof the trade and commerce, as is affirmed by them, is much decayed of late, as may appear by our customers' books, which course semeing to be verie equitable and fitt to be observed, Our pleasur is, that yow signifie to your Commissioners that it is our will that at the meitting in July nixt they mak choyse of some of ther number, with some of the fernoeris of our great customes, in renewing of the stent roll of our brught of Dundie, and if yow shall find just caus of such other brughis as desyre the lyk care to be takin, that according to the trade and commerce which they now have they may be stented : We bid, &c.—Grenwitch, 5 Junij 1634.

To the Exchequer.

Right, &c.—We have bene humblie petitioned in behalff of our frie burgh of Dundie for ratifieing ther priviledges granted by our predicessours, wherin ther demand semeing to ws to be reasonable, by granting of what is fit to encourage them to our service, and to farther trade and commerce, it being without prejudice or [hurt] of the liberteis of other subjects: Our pleasur therfor is, that yow consider the signature of ther liberteis and priviledges, and if yow find the same agrieable to ther infeftments lawfullie grante1 to them by our royall predicessours, and not derogatorie to any act of Counsall tuitching them, that yow exped the same with diligence, otherwayes acquant ws with your reasones to the contrarie ; wherin expecting your performance of this our pleasur, &c.—Grenwitch, 5 Junij 1631.

To the Counsell.

Right, &c.—Wheras we have bene humblie petitioned in behalff of the brugh of Dundie for granting to them the office of schirrefschip within the same, and liberteis thairof as other burghes have, wherin ther demand being for the preservatioun of our peace therin : Our pleasur is, that with convenient diligence yow caus expeid vnder our great seall what chartour or surtie shalbe necessar for establisching heirefter that office of schirrefschip vpon them within ther brugh and liberteis, in such absolute and beneficial maner as other our frie brughis doeth enjoy : Provyded alwayes that the said office be by ws and our successours recallable at what tyme and maner we or they shall think fitt, to be disposed of at our or ther pleasurs : Which recommending, &c.—Grenvitch, 5 Junij 1631.

To Mr John Forbes.

Trustie and weilbelovit, &c.—Haveing at your late being befor ws willed yow to repair vnto Scotland vpon some considerations which we thoght fitt to impart vnto yow, bot vnderstanding that yow ar not as yit gone from hence, Our pleasur is, that vpon sight heirof yow repair with all diligence to our said kingdome, and we will have a care of your preferment ther; not doubting of your deserveing heirof, we bid, &c.—Grenvitch, 5 Junij 1631.

To the Clerk Register.

Trustie, &c.—Becaus we ar desyreous that a course should be takin with our right trustie counsellour the Lord Napar for his satisfaction of these moneyis which ar due vnto him as soon as it can be convenientlie done for that effect, it is our pleasur that yow deall with the said Lord and with them that ar bund vnto him for the saidis moneyis dew, that yow may bring them to condescend vpon some certane course wherby he may be payed, or otherwayes, that yow certifie ws in whois default it is that they doe not agrie, wherof not doubting bot yow will have a certane care to give ws ane accompt.—Grenwitch, 9 Junij 1631.

To the Justice Deputeis.

Trustie, &c.—Wheras, for the better tryell of the burneing of the house of Frendraught, we did formerlie writt vnto yow that ane Toschooch, who hath alreadie bene tuyse tortured, should be putt to the tryell of ane assyse, which semeth vpon considerations to have bene hitherto delayed ; and being desyreous that that bussines should be putt to ane poynt, Our pleasur is, that whensoever the pairtie shall persew nim, yow proceid according to our said former letter, and that these who ar to goe on his assyse be fairlie and lawfullie choysen, as is vsed in the lyk caices, that ther may be no just cause of complaynt ; and that in aney exception which shalbe proponed by the said Toschcoch in his defence yow tak the advyse of our privie counsell as in all things which may tend to the clearing of that bussines.—Grenwich, 10 of Junij 1634.

To the Advocat.

Trustie, &c.—Wheras, for the better tryell of the burneing of the house of Frendraught, we have gevin ordour to our Justice deputeis to putt ane Toschcoch (who hath bene alreadie tuyse tortured) to the tryell of ane assyse, as we had formerlie writtin vnto them : Our pleasur is, that haveing informed your self of these proceidingis, yow persew him befoir our said Justice deputeis, and till the bussines be fullie cleared, according to Justice and the Lawes of that our kingdome ; and for your so doeing, &c.—Grene-witch, 10 of Junij 1634.

To the Counsell.

Right, &c.—Wheras, for the better tryell of the burneing of the house of Frendraught, we have writtin to our Justice deputeis to putt ane Toschcoch (who hath alreadie bene tuyse tortured) to the tryell of ane assyse, according to our former pleasur signifeid vnto them for that effect : Our pleasur is, that wherin our saidis deputeis shall have neid of your advyse or concurrance, yow assist them with the same, in so far as shalbe requisit : Which recommending to your care.—Grenewitch, 10 Junij 1634.

To the Counsell.

Right, &c.—Wheras we have at diverse tymes signifeid our pleasur vnto yow for restraynt of frequent granting protections, especiallie by tuo letters of late, the one in favours of our frie royall brughes, the other in favours of Wm Dick, merchand, wherof we ar not vnmyndfull, yit we, having formerlie, vpon most just considerations, granted vnto our trustie and weilbeloved servand Sir Alexr Home, knyt, a pro-tection, for some tyme now expyred, which for the same reasones, and in regard that his caice in a singular maner deserveth our consideratioun, especiallie he being our owin domestick servand, we have now thoght fitt to renew and prorogat to him for the space of ane yeir : Our pleasur is, that immediatlie yow caus exped the same vnder our great seall, notwithstanding any of these letters befoir mentionat, or oney vther direction to the contrarie ; for which these presents salbe your warrand.—Grenwitch, 10 Junij 1634.

Archbischop St Androis, Erlis Morton, Stirling, Roxbrugh, Traquair, Bischops of Ross and Edinburgh, Sir John Hay, Sir Thomas Hope, or any seven of them, the Archbischop being ane, or, in his absence, the saids Bischops or any of them.

Right, &c.—Wheras we wer pleased to give a commission vnto yow for trying the authours and such as could be fund anywayes accessorie to the seditious lybell fund in the handis of ane Dymmure, wherin it may fall out that the qualitie of ther persones and nature of ther faults and evidents tuitching the same, as being less or more suspect or guiltie, will requyre a distinction in the places of ther committement (our castells of that kingdome and tolbuith of Edr being the accustomed parts for that purpois), we ar heirby pleased to express our further pleasur that, as in the said poynts yow shall find the case to differ, yow accordinglie have a speciall regard of ther confyneing and imprissonement, as to be commanded to ther ludgeingis to the custodie of bischops to the Clerk of our Counsell, and to such our castells and prisones as yow shall find caus : So, being confident that yow will omitt no diligence for examining that bussines, according to our commission, and to proceid according to our pleasur heirby signifeid, We bid, &c.— Grenwitch, 14 Junij 1634.

CHANCELLOUR, ARCHBISCHOP Sᵗ ANDROIS, MORTON, HADINGTON, MARQUEIS HAMILTON, STIRLING, ROXBURGH, TRAQUAIR, B. ROSS, SIR JOHNE HAY, Mᵣ THOS. HOPE.

Right, &c.—Wheras we thoght fitt to authorize yow of late by our commission to represent to ws the trew estate of some abuses in the vnnecessarie burdens of our Exchequer, with the errors and disordrs exeipt therin, wherin, for your better enabling to proceid with the greater expedition, we have heirby thoght fitt farder to authorize yow, vpon remonstrance made befor to yow of these abuses by our Thesaurer principall and deputie, and our Clerk of Register, as persones best acquanted with the estate of our Exchequer, To call for such records, registers, and others bookis of our Exchequer, as may best con-duce to that purpois, And generallie to doe in everie thing tending to the advancement of that service, ather as yow are formerlie warranted by our commission, or vtherways as yow shall find to be requisit to this end ; ffor which these presents shalbe vnto yow, and all others quhom it may concerne, a sufficient warrant.—Dated vt supra.

To THE ADVOCAT.

Trustie, &c.—Wheras, vpon verie considerable causes, our Right, &c. the Marqueis of Hamilton is to be secured by ws of moneyis raised and to be expended by him for our service, and by our speciall command, as was signifeid to our Thesaurers principall and deputie, wherin we will not that he in any wayes should suffer for his affection in his vndertakingis therin ; Our pleasur therfor is, and we doe heirby will and requyre yow, that vpon his relation of his burdings vndergone and to be vndertakin, to which we remitt the particulars, yow draw vp such legall and sufficient warrants for these moneyis, and in such maner as he shall find needfull for his securitie ; and for your so doeing.—Grenwitch, 14 Junij 1634.

To SIR JOHNE HEPBURNE, KNYᵗ AND COLONELL.

Trustie, &c.—Vnderstanding that our right trustie the Lord Leveingstoun hath the charge vnder yow of a foot companie, and that he hath bene detened from that employment beyond his desire and expecta-tioun by his father's occasions, in attending some erection tuitching our service, we have heirby thoght fitt to recommend vnto yow that he receave no prejudice by his absence in that charge, bot that at his repairing vnto yow schortlie, if any neglect or inconvenient hath bene occasioned by his absence, yow will the rather for this one recommendatioun pass over anything that may reflect vpon that cause ; which we will tak kyndlie at your handis.—Grenewitch, 14 Junij 1634.

To THE EXCHEQUER.

Right, &c.—We ar informed that ane Monteith, late preicher at Dudingstoun, whois foull fact of adulterie is a scandell to the church in the highest degrie, and therfoir deserveth exemplarie punischment, is about to procure a pardon for his cryme : Our pleasur is, that none be granted vnto him vpon any con-dition whatsoever, without a speciall warrant from ws.—Grenwitch, 14 Junij 1634.

To the Commissioners.

Right, &c.—We have writtin to yow a litle befoir the recept of your letter vnto ws tuitching the scandalous and seditious lybell, to proceid with all diligence, according to your commission, in the tryell of the authours, and others fund anywayes accessorie thereto ; and now haveing thereby perceaved your diligence and care therein, we give yow hartie thanks for the same, willing yow, in regard the exact tryell therby doeth so highlie concerne ws in our honour, to insist by all possible diligence to find out, not onlie the authours, bot lykwayes all such who, in any maner of way whatsumever, have had any hand at being accessorie or conceavers therof ; and in the meane tyme we wilbe carefull that all possible and secreit diligence be vsed for apprehending of William Hay, and returneing of him for his tryell befor yow, which we doubt not, if he shall chance to be apprehendit, yow will verie carefullie and exactlie performe, becaus much may depend thervpoun for cleiring the treuth of that bussines, and becaus that possiblie he may escape by retireing into that our kingdome or midlschyres, we will yow to have a watchfull ey over those parts in such close maner as may best conduce for his quick apprehending ; and if yow sall find it necessarie that our further authoritie be vsed in that particular, that yow acquant ws therwith, that accordinglie we may give such further ordour as we shall think fitt : All which recommending to yow, &c.—Grenwitch, 22 Junij 1634.

To the Erle of Traquair.

Right, &c.—We receaved your letter, wherby we perceave your cair in these particularis concerneing our service entrusted to yow of late as the tryeing of the authours of that scandulous and seditious lybell, for which we give yow hartie thanks; we have heirwith writtin at lenth vnto our Commissioners, as by our letter (which we will yow to delyver with all diligence) yow will perceave ; and thairfoir we have heirfoit thoght fit to recommend vnto yow in a particular maner to proceid accordinglie with the greatest care and diligence that can be vsed by yow, which we will tak weill at your handis, as also the expediting of all the accompts ; which recommending, &c.—Grenewitch, 22 Junij 1634.

To the Erlis of Morton and Traquair.

Wheras by a certificat vnder your hand tuitching the accompts of Nicolas Briot, cheiff graver of our mynt heir, yow have declared that vpon the sight of our warrand for his payment yow will give present ordour : It is our pleasur that according to that which shalbe fund dew vnto him vpon his said accompts yow pay the same to him with diligence out of the first and readiest of whatsumever benefite shall accruss or belong to ws by silver or gold in our cunzie hous ; ffor your so, &c.—Grenwitch, 22 Junij 1634.

To the Bischop of Caithnes.

Reverend father in God, &c.—Being informed of a good and lawdable act made by yow in the synodall assemblie in your dyocie, wherby the first fruits of all entring ministers ar assigned heirefter to the repairing and vpholding of the Cathedrall Church thairof : Our pleasur is, that by the advyse of the right reverend, &c. Bischop of St Androis, yow strenthen and putt that act in executioun by all the lawfull meanes yow can, being willing that all succeiding bischopis ratifie that act at ther entrie to that bischoprick ; and haveing now recommended to the most eminent persones within the dyocie the helping to raise such a contribution for building the bodie of that church as shalbe fund necessarie [and] requisit, as by a copie of our letter vnto them yow will perceave, we will expect at your handis your best encourageing of them and others of that dyocie with your best assistance, otherwayes and in such maner as may best conduce to the effecting of that our work so requyreing to be adverteised from yow, of the bountie of such persones as shall stand best affected to the bussines, and desyreing that thir presents be insert in your synodall books of Caithnes for testimonie of our consent to the said act; we will, &c.—Grenwitch, 22 Junij 1634.

Similar Letter to the Archbischop of S*t* Androis.

To the Erle of Caithnes and his sone the Lord Berridaill.

Right, &c.—Wheras we as informed that a begining was made of late in repairing of the Cathedrall Church of the dyocie of Caithnes, wherin we do commend the endeavours of such as did contribute to that purpois, bot hearing that the bodie of that Church is not as yet sett vp, which will reqnyre the assistance of the most eminent and able persones of that dyocie, we have thoght fitt heirby speciallie to recommend vnto yow to assist so pious a work by vseing the advyse and direction heirin of the reverend the bischop of Caithnes, and by helping to mak vp such a generall contribution amongst all the inhabitants of that dyocie as wilbe sufficient to finisch that work; wherin, as yow shall schow a zeall to Godis service, so we will tak it weill of your handis.—Grenwitch, 22 Junij 1634.

Letters to the Erle Sutherland, Lord Rae, Lards Assint, &c. wer writtin verbatim, conforme to the tenour of the former letter, dat. vt supra.

To the Erle of Traquair.

Right, &c.—We receaved your letter and ar weill satisfeit with the services therin exprest. Our letter writtin of late to the Commissioners for the lybell will answer ther letter writtin to ws at this tyme. We have signed the Contract betwixt ws and our right, &c. the Marqueis of Hamiltoun, with the warrant sent by yow for hearing the accompts. As tuitching our Colledge of Justice, we ar lykwayes weill satisfeit with ther proceidings tuitching our prerogative, and as for other our affaires entrusted to yow, we remitt yow to that which we have writtin to the Marqueis; Wherin not doubting of your care and affection, we bid, &c.—Wanstead, first July 1634.

To the Counsell.

Right, &c.—Vnderstanding the abiliteis and affection to our service of our servant Sir Robert Gordoun, vice-chalmerlane of that our kingdome, we ar pleased in regard thairof, and for his better encouragment and enabling for our service, to advance and promove him to be ane of our privie counsell of that our kingdome: Therfoir it is our pleasure that, haveing administred to him the oath accustomed in the lyk caices, yow admitt him to be one of your number of our privie Counsell ther; ffor doeing wherof, &c.—Wanstead, 4 July 1634.

To the Counsell.

Right, &c.—We being humblie petitioned in behalff of Johne M'intosch that we would be graciouslie pleased to grant to him a protection for a yeir, in regard, as we ar informed, he is both willing and able to satisfie his creditours, if they would allow him some small tyme to dispose of a part of his estate to that purpois : Our pleasur is, to refer the consideratioun of his demand vnto yow, willing yow, if yow shall find it fitt to be granted, to caus expeid vnto him vnder our cachet and great seall a protection for the space desyred, ffor which these presents shalbe vnto yow and our officers, whom it concerneth in particular, sufficient warrant, provyded alwayes he pay to them the annual rent dew at that tyme at such a day as shall be condescended vpoun by yow.—Wanstead, vt supra.

To the Session.

Right, &c.—We have bene petitioned in behalff of Johne Stewart of Coldinghame, that by the act Salvo jure cujuslibet made in our late Parliament, his esteat is lyklie to be evickt from him by the partie who standeth out against his right, notwithstanding the same (as we ar informed) was established on him by ane act of Parliament 1621, wherin the one act seameing to cross the other in that poynt, we desyre to vnderstand your opinions tuitching the same befor yow give out your last determinatioun thervpoun, and that with as much convenient diligence as may be, &c.—Theobald's, 8 July 1631.

To the Advocat.

Trustie, &c.—We wer pleased of late to signifie to our Colledge of Justice and yow our royall intention that all questions anent the right and succession to the Estate of the late Erle of Home might rather be decydit in amicable maner then by law, To which purpois we now requyre yow in our name to vrge a conclusion according to that arbitrarie course intended by ws for good of both pairteis, and if any difference shalhappin to aryse amongst them, or a way be fund in aney of them which yow shalhappin conceave may justlie seame to breid any stop in setling these bussines and differences, Our pleasur is, that both pairteis acquant ws therwith by paquet, bot not cum to count till we give further ordour tuitching the same as we shall find caus : We bid yow farewell.—Theobald's, 10 July 1631.

To Sir John Hay.

Trustie, &c.—Haveing occasion at this tyme to confer with yow tuitching some things concerneing our service, we requyre yow, so soone as the accompts of your taxations and other things concerneing our service which ar now in hand ar at a poynt, to repair to our Court, wher our further pleasur shalbe imparted vnto yow ; and for your, &c.—Notinghame, 10 July 1631.

To Sir John and Sir Wm Scotts.

Trustie, &c.—We have now sent doun Robert Ellot and his wyff, the Lady Jeane Stewart, with assurance that as yow promised to ws at your being heir yow will speik with the rest of the Erle of Buccleuch's curatours, and amongst yow tak such a course to give them satisfaction, that we be not troubled with it any more, wherby yow will doe ws good service ; and this recommending it earnestlie to your care and discretion, we bid, &c.—Theobald's, 7 Julij 1631.

To the Counsell.

Right, &c.—Haveing bene pleased to remitt to the Lord Gray and Patrik Maull, our servitour, a signature of our soap works for consideratiouns mentionat therin, Our pleasur is, that yow pass the same with all diligence ; and if it be fund that Nathaniell Edward, who hath a former grant of these works, hath not forfaulted the same in that caice, we will that his lease be continewed ; bot otherwayes, if it shalbe fund to be voyd, we requyre that it be furthwith discharged, and the other pairteis authorized and enjoy the benefite of our grant to them.—Theobald's, 11 July 1634.

To the Advocat.

Trustie, &c.—Being informed that yow have at this tyme vsed your best endeavours by concurring with the Erle of Airth for prorogating the reversion of his esteat, we give yow hartie thanks for the same, and doe heirby recommend vnto yow that from tyme to tyme as he shall have occasion tuitching that purpois yow will continew as yow have begun ; which we will tak as good service done vnto ws.—Dat. vt supra.

To the Session.

Right, &c.—Wheras we wer pleased by our former letter vnto yow that the reversion of the Erle of Airthis esteat might be prorogat, which we did vpon consideratioun that his creditours wer sufficientlie secured of his Landis for his moneyis dew vnto them, and that we had bestowed vpon him the sowme of sex scoir tuelff thowsand merks Scotts for giveing them satisfaction, with a consideratioun for the forbear-ance of so much of the sowme as should not then be payed : The lyk considerations moveing ws at this tyme, and that we have heirwith writtin to our thesaurers for making speedie payment vnto him of these moneyis, it is our pleasur that yow stay all further proces at the instance of his creditouns, or any of them, against him, and the executioun of any decreit ; which we will tak as acceptable service done vnto ws.—Dat. vt supra.

To the Thesaurers.

Right, &c.—Haveing by our former precepts requyred that sex scoir tuelff thowsand merks Scotts might be payed to the Erle of Airth towards the releiff of his debts, togidder with fyve hundreth pundis sterling yeirlie dureing the not payment of that sowme, or most part thairof, Our pleasur is, that yow pay vnto him the saidis moneyis according to the said precept ; bot if the estate of our Coffers be such that the said sowme cannot be convenientlie payed vnto him at this tyme, we requyre yow to caus present payment be made vnto him of the consideratioun for the forbearance : And wheras we ar informed that he hath alreadie resigned in our favours his hous neir Halyrudhous, and that the surrender of his Ladeis pension of 500^{lb} st. is made, and redie to be delyvered for our vse, wherin he hath performed his part of the said bargane, which we will yow to accept vpon his offer thairof. It is our further pleasur that vpon recept of these surrenders yow pay vnto him the sowmes condescended vpon, conforme to the former precept, viz.— for his hous 18,000 merks Scotts, and for his pension 30,000 merks Scotts lyk money : Of all which we will expect the performance at your handis, that the noblemanes estate be not longer endangered or we further troubled heirin ; flor which these presents shalbe your warrant and discherge.—Theobald's, 11 July 1634.

To the Lord Gordoun.

Right, &c.—We have receaved your letter, and, as we have assured your Lady accordinglie, we shalbe carefull that the payment of these moneyis dew vnto yow, alsweill for the schirrefschippes as for the pension, be not long delayed, that your esteat may not any wayes suffer by want of the same ; which we will be the more cairefull to performe in regard of the care yow have had in the religious breiding of your sones thair, whairof we have takin speciall notice, and desyre that yow may continew, assureing yow that when any occasion shall offer we will not be vnmyndfull of, &c.—Abthorp, 20 July 1634.

To the Advocat.

Trustie and weilbeloved, &c.—Being pleased, according to our former intention to this purpois, that our servant Michaell Elphingstoun prosecute that our service for inbringing the benefite aryseing by such concealld ward's mariages and nonentresse whatsoever as shalbe reveiled by his meanes and informatioun, according to the Commission gevin by our Thesaurer : It is our pleasur that yow, in our name and for our interest, intent proces aganst all such our vassalls of the royaltie and principalitie to be reveiled by him as held ward or few of ws, who have not had lawfull gifts vnder our scalls, or have not accompted for the same in Exchequer befoir the tyme mentioned in the said Commission, and that from tyme to tyme yow effectuallie assist and concurre with him for performeing of that service according to the Commission ; ffor which, &c.—Beaver Castell, 24 July 1634.

To the Counsell.

Right, &c.—Wheras by our former letter tuitching the ordoring of the sale of Tobacco was signifeid our royall pleasur vnto yow for establlisching ane effectuall ordour that none within our kingdome should presume to sell or vtter the same by small and retaill bot such as shalbe thervnto licenced by our Commissioners appoynted for that purpois, vnder payne of our high displeasur, and such penaltie as yow shall think fitt to impose vpon the transgressours : To the effect that all matter of cavill may be takin away, and that the delinquents may know what danger they ar to incurre by ther contempt, Our pleasur is, that in the letters of publication heirof yow caus express alsweill what is menit by small and retaill—to witt, the vnce, pund, or other proportion vnder the stone weght—as the liquidat sume that he shall think oght condignelie to be inflicted toties quoties by [way] of penaltie vpon the conteaners of our royall will and pleasur heirin, the one halff therof to belong to the informer, the other halff to our Commissioners; wherin expecting your care, we bid, &c.—Beaver Castell, 24 July 1634.

To the Advocat.

Trustie, &c.—Being desyreous to be informed in what way the honour and title of Earle was by our late dear father granted to the late Erle of Dumbar in that Erldome, Our pleasur is, that yow tak inspection ather of the said Erle his principall patent, or of the copie therof in the register of our great scall, and certifie ws whether the same be conceaved with particular restrictioun to the aires-maill of his bodie, or generallie to his aires-maills, or to his aires whatsoever, and who it is that to whom that title of honour (if it be not extinguisched) ought now legallie to belong; so we bid, &c.—Beaver Castell, 24 July 1634.

To the Commissioners appoynted for Tryell of the Scandalous Lybell.

Right, &c.—Haveing considered your last letter, with the depositiouns which yow sent ws, and conceaveing it not to be necessarie at this tyme that yow call any of the rest of the Lords befor yow, sieing the clearing of that bissines dependeth much vpon the apprehending of Haig, who is as yet fugitive, we ar pleised heirby to signifie the same vnto yow: And sieing yow have bene alreadie so long vpon this bussines without performeing any thing, we ar desyreous that the Lord Balmerino come to his tryell, that so everie ane may sie the great reasone we have to prosecute this bussines: Therfor it is our pleasur that yow proceid to putt him to a tryell, bot that yow superseid the executeing of any sentence against him vntill such tyme as yow shall know our further pleasur, which we ar to keip verie secreit till sentence be gevin: So we bid, &c.—Beavor Castell, 21 July 1634.

To the Advocat.

Right, &c.—Considering that our Croun of that kingdome doe suffer by many wardes of cheiff housses, which being now taxt can never vaik in our hands, and if not all, at leist many of them may be dew course be reduced to the esteat wherin they wer: It is our pleasur that from tyme to tyme yow vse your best endeavours for reduceing of taxt wards wher yow find any just ground in Law to that purpois: And now haveing bestowed the ward of the Erle of Buccleuch vpon our right, &c. the Erle of Stirling, which, as we ar informed, is taxt for the present, we have expreslie commanded him to enter in action for reduction thairof, and therfor faill not to give him your best concurrance and help for effectuating of the same, wherin yow shall doe ws verie acceptable service; and for which these presents shalbe your sufficient warrant.

To the Thesaurer and Deputie.

Right, &c.—Being informed befor the death of Sir George Elphingstoun, knyt, late Justice Clerk of that our kingdome, ther wer some arreires of his pensioun due vnto him, and vnderstanding since of the distressed esteat of George Elphingstoun, his sone, by reasone of the great burdens contracted by his father, which he wilbe vnable to discharge, except we shalbe pleased to extend our favour vnto him in the payment of these moneyis, and being vnwilling (in regard of the good services done vnto ws by the said Sir George) that his sone should anywayes suffer in his esteat by want of these moneyis: It is our pleasur that what arreires yow shall find to be dew justlie resting of the said pension yow caus pay the same (the said George being as yit minor) vnto James Elphingstoun, his vncle, that by that meanes he may doe his best for the satisfaction of the creditours and saftie of his esteat: And for your soe doeing, &c.— Bagschot, 4 Sept. 1634.

To the Provest and Baillies of Edinburgh.

Trustie and weilbelovit, &c.—Wheras our late dear father and other our royal predicessours wer accustomed vpon occasioun of ther services to give ordour for electing such persones to be magistrats of that our citie as they in ther judgments thoght most fitt and able for the publict good: We lykwayes, for the good of our service, tending to the benefite and advancement of that citie, being willing that able and discreit persones be made choyse of to bear publict charge heirin, have heirby thoght fitt to requyre that at your nixt ensueing election yow present vpon the lyte of your provest, David Aikinhead, and vpon the lytes of your bailleis, Alexr Speir, And. Tod, Edward Edzer, and Alexr Dennestoun, Vpon the lyts of deane of gild Johne Sinclair, and vpon the lyts of your thesaurer, David M'Call, and that accordinglie yow mak election of the said David Aikinhead to be your provest, the said Alexr Speir, And. Tod, Edward Edzer, Alexr Dennestoun to be bailleis, Johne Sinclair to be deane of gild, and David M'Call, thesaurer for this yeir, as yow tender the good of our service, which notwithstanding we declair shalbe without prejudice of your liberteis and priviledges: We bid, &c.—Dat. vt supra.

To the Lord Privie Seall.

Right, &c.—Yow will perceave by the copie of our enclosed letter to the provest and bailleis of our citie of Edinburgh our purpois for making of choyse of able and sufficient persones for bearing publict charge within that citie : To which end we will yow delyver our letter with all diligence to the magistrats and Counsell thairof, recommending to them a readie obedience to our desyre heirin, and that presentlie efter the election, incaise the persones elected refuis to accept your cause, direct letters of horning for charging them to accept, and that yow advertiss ws with all diligence of the obedience heirvnto : Which recommending, &c.—Theobaldis, 16 Sept' 1634.

To the Thesaurer and Deputie Thesaurer.

Right, &c.—Wheras, in consideratioun of a precept of 6000 Lib. st. granted be our late dear father to our right trustie and weilbeloved Cousen and Counsellour the Erle of Stirling, our principall Secretarie for Scotland, for good and faythfull service done by him, and of a warrant of ten thowsand punds granted by ws vnto him vpon verie good considerations, as may appear by the same, we wer pleased to grant vnto him the benefite arysing by the coynage of the copper money within that our kingdome for the space of nyne yeres, and further, till he should be compleitlie payed of all sowmes whatsumever due by ws vnto him ; now, to the effect our said servant may have the more assurance to mak bargane with others anent the said benefite for his releiff, and that ther may be a certane tyme appoynted for his payment and for our haveing the benefite of the said coyne to returne vnto ws, we doo heirby ratifie vnto him his grant of the whole benefite arysing dew vnto ws of that copper coynage during the tyme yit to rin of that his patent ; And it is our speciall pleasur that yow grant a warrant such as shalbe requisite of Coynadge of sex thowsand stane weght of copper, without intromission, immediatlie efter the ending of the coynadge of 1500 stane weght presentlie in hand, and for continewing of the coynadge efter the full perfyteing of the said 6000 stone from yeir to yeir for the accustomed quantitie as we coyned these tuo yeres past, and that during the whole tyme yit to rin of his patent, if ther sall any of it remane efter the full perfyteing of the coynadge of the 6000 stane, and that yow give ordour to our Advocat for drawing vp a sufficient discharge of the saids tuo precepts to be signed by our said servant, with a discharge to him from ws of his intromission, with any benefite arysing with the coynadge during the tyme past or to cum of his patent (of the which we doe lykwayes heirby discharge him), and that without any accompt to be made vnto ws or any in our name for the same in regard of his discharge of his saids tuo precepts, and caus registrat this our letter, and mak such order in counsell and exchequer as may be most expedient for the farder securitie and satisfaction of our said servant of such as he shall have occasion to treat or bargane with for making the best advantage of this our gratious intention towards him ; for doeing whairof thir presents shalbe vnto yow ane sufficient warrant.—Theobald's, 18 Sep' 1631.

Au Roy Tres Chretien.

Treshaut tresexcellent et trepuissant prince, nostre trescher et tresame bon frere beau frere cousin et auncien allie, Complant nous a este farte per nos subjects Escossois qu' aprez avoir jouy en France paisibliement et sans aucun distrubler ou interruption par plusieurs siecles de divers priviledges immuniteis et libertateis, et a cause d'un tresauncienne alliance renouvele et ratifie de temps entemps, et d'reason de beaucoup de bons offices passes entre l'une et le autre nation, ilz sen trouvoient neautmoins de puiz quelques moix encore trubles et deprives a leur grand prejudice et au detriment du commerce mutuall qui est (comme vous scaves) le moyen le plus ordinare d'entretiner l'amitie et bonne voisinance entre les subjects de part et d'autre, Nous supplicans de vouloir moyenner leur redresse : cest pourquoy nous vous avons bien voulu prier tresaffectieusement par celleey et par l'instance de nos agents de leur vouleur continuer maintenir et confirmer les priviledges et franchises que vous mesmes avez ey devant ratifies, et de mire ordre et charge a vous ministres et officiers de voz ports, havres, et la ou il sera necessair, de tenir la main a ce que noz diets subjects Escossois en puissent (comme ilz on faiet ey devant) jouy pleinement et paisiblement, et que ceux que ey voudroit opposer ou contre viendront soyent puniz selons vos lois, et ainsy que la reason et equitie requeirant ce que nous promettcints de nostre Justice et toute nous serons tousjours presls en pareill occasion de fair le mesuire en vostre endroit, ainsi que nos diets agents vous enformeront plus amplement, aux quelles nous remittants : nous prierons Dieu treshaut, tresexcellent nostre trescher et tresame bon frere beau frere cousin et auntien allie, que vous ait tousiours en sa sancte et digne gard : A nostre palace de Theobald's, le 19 Sepr 1634.

To the King's Agents at Paris.

We have bene pleased to wrytt to our good brother the French king on the behalff of our subjects and merchandis of Scotland for restoreing the ancient priviledges they injoyed in France, which of late (as we ar informed) have bene infringed to ther prejudice, as by the enclosed coppie of our letter and the present bearer his further instructions yow will vnderstand : Our pleasur is, efter yow have fullie informed yourselff of the estait of the bussines, and knowen how far and wherin they ar prejudged and hindred, contrair to the said former liberteis, yow doe delyver our saids letters, and efterward carefullie sollicite the cause with our said brother, and others his ministers and officers whom it doeth concerne, that a speedie course may be taken for giveing our saids subjects satisfaction, and for preventing the lyk abuses hereefter by causing the infringers and delinquents to be punisched according to the Lawes and customs of that kingdome : Heirin not doubting of your readines and endeavours, we will expect ane accompt from yow, and tak it as acceptable service at your hands.—Theobald's, 19 Sepr 1634.

To the Archbischop of St Androis, and Dunie Sessioner.

Right, &c.—Being informed that ane Mr Johne Pape, Advocat, is desyreous to have a book writtin by him (intitulat De Jure regum apud Scotos) fullie reveewd by such as we should appoynt, we have thoght fitt to mak choyse of yow to that purpois, that, haveing carefullie pervsed that book, yow certifie ws of your opinions tuitching the same, that therefter we may give such farder ordour for publisching or suppressing thairof as we shall find just caus : Which seriouslie recommending to your care, we bid, &c. —Theobald's, 19 Septr 1634.

To the Exchequer.

Right, &c.—Wheras we wer pleased to give licence ynto ane Young, a native in this our kingdome, for printing in our citie of Edinburgh, which was done in consideratioun of the publict good of that kingdome by hindring of moneyis from being transported in bringing in of books, bot hearing that now efter his charge in transporting thither and setting vp his works ther, with the buying of yrnes and others provisions necessar for such a work, he is questioned befor yow by some persones who would infringe his priviledges : Our pleasur is that he enjoy the benefite of that our licence or grant, conforme to the tenour thairof in all poynts, and to that effect that yow doe not suffer him to be any further questioned or troubled from executeing his charge in that service for the publict good ; for which these presents shalbe your warrand.—Theobald's, 19 Sept. 1634.

To the Session.

Right, &c.—We have sent vnto yow the enclosed petition and information of the Lady Jeane Stewart and Robert Elliot, hir husband, tuitching the differences betweene the Erle of Buccleugh and them, wherin we ourselffes wer formerlie pleased to tak panes, and had composed that bussines, as we have done the differences betweene him and Francis Stewart, hir brother, if the death of the late Erle, his father, had not hitherto prevented our royall intention: And now, sieing the said Lady and hir husband ar to tak them to the ordinarie course of Justice, we have thoght fitt that yow seriouslie consider of the said informatioun and petition, and of ther distressed esteat and long sufferings, recommending vnto yow that speedie justice be administred in any action of thers comeing befor yow, and that they may have what benefite in being reponed to pleid for ther right that lawfullie can be granted, or hath bene accustomed in the lyk caice and of the lyk nature; Which speciallie recommending, &c.—Theobald's, 19 Septr 1634.

To the Exchequer.

Right, &c.—Haveing bene pleased vpon good considerations to signe vnto our servant Patrik Maule tuo signatours, the ane of the baronie of Brechin, the other of Balmakellie, which we have sent yow heirwith, Our pleasur is, that yow pas the saids signaturis without a composition, and thairefter caus expeid them vnder our great seall according to the tenour thairof, and that with as much diligence as can be vsed; ffor which these presents, &c.—Theobald's, 19 Sept. 1634.

To the Thesaurer, Clerk Register, Advocat.

Right, &c.—Wheras David Prestoun of Whythill, being suretie for his vncle the late Erle of Desmond for great sowmes of money, had recourse to ws, efter his vncle's death, to be relieved by some parts of the benefite arysing by the ward of his daughter, whervpoun we appoynted some of our Counsell to tak notice of the burdenes, who found them to be as he affirmed, and that he had no assurance for his releiff bot ane assignement fra his vncle to a small pension for 19 yeres of some silver dewteis and mailles of the lordschip of Dingwall; Bot no furder course being takin at that tyme for his releiff then the clearing of his burdens, he hath now offered to surrender vnto ws the whole right of that Lordschip which he was forced since to compryse for that debt: In regard of the premisses, and that his offer is onlie to have, in lieu of his right to that Lot, the moneyis for which he comprysed the same, with the continewing of his pension (though schort of the annualrent of his principall sowmes) till he be payed thairof, And in regard he affirmeth the worth of that Lordschip doeth far exceid the value of his moneyis, and that the benefite thairof will daylie improve, it being setled vpon the Croun, becaus it consisteth much in superioriteis and few-dewteis, and that the estats of many of these vassalls ly in nonentrie; Our pleasur is, that yow seriouslie consider of his offer, and, finding it fitt to be accepted by ws, that yow agrie with him for the same, and that yow give him good assurance of enjoying his pension till the moneyis condescended vpon can convenientlie be payed vnto him, and to that effect that yow give ordour to our Advocat to sie the same legallie done, and to expeid his infeftment of that Lordschip, and to tak his surrender; ffor all these shalbe vnto yow and him a sufficient warrant.—Theobald's, 19 Sept. 1634.

To the Thesaurers and Deputie.

Right, &c.—Wheras Sir James Stewart, brother-german to the late Erle of Orknay, hath bene an humble sutter vnto ws at severall tymes that a consideratioun might be had of his distressed estate, and the rather becaus that he alledgeth the absolute right of that Erldome was devolved vpon him by his said brother long befor his forfeyture : Our pleasur is, that yow not onlie consider of his clame, bot lykwayes of what in your opinion can lawfullie be pretendit by any of the other brothers who hath bene humble sutters vnto ws tuitching that purpois, and therefter certifie ws of your opinions tuitching the same, that we may give such farder ordour theranent as we shall think fitt.—Theobald's, 19 Septr 1634.

To the Chancellour.

Right, &c.—Being crediblie informed that some yeres agoe our right, &c. the Erle of Galloway haveing by ordour of Law apprehendit ane James Kennedie for a debt of 22,000 merks Scotts, which the said Erle had payed as suretie for him, the Erle of Cassillis did in a violent maner, without warrant, bring the said Kennedie out of the Erle of Gallowaye's ludging in Edinburgh, and that therefter, vpon ther reconceilment and the said Erle of Galloway not insisting aganst the other for that ryot and wrong done to him, it was mutuallie condescendit that the said Erle of Galloway should be releived of the said cautionrie, which notwithstanding is not done : Our pleasur is, that yow call the said Erle of Cassillis befor yow, and requyre him to performe what was so conditioned by taking a present course to releive the said Erle of Galloway of that debt, and in caice of the others being refractorie thairunto, by refuising or delay, that yow certifie ws thairof with diligence, that we in our princelie judgment may sie some course taken for Gallowayes releiff, that by exemple thairof the lyk ryotts may be repressed heirefter : Which recommending, &c.—Hampton Court, 29 Sept. 1634.

To the Commissioners for Surrenders.

Right, &c.—We being certanelie informed that the Pryorie of Whithorne is annexed to the bischoprik of Galloway, and that our right, &c. the Erle of Galloway is taksman of sindrie tythes belonging to that pryorie, and haveing taken the estate of that bischoprik to your consideratioun, Our pleasur is, that yow medle noe farder with the tythes belonging to our said consen till our further pleasur be farder heard theranent ; for which these shalbe to yow sufficient warrant, Provyded alwayes that no prejudice doe heirby ensue in the vplifting of the annuitie dew to ws.—Hampton Court, 29 Sepr 1634.

To Mr Maule.

Haveing occasion at this tyme to mak vse of your service in your charge about ws till we shall think fitt to spare yow some other tyme for dispatch of our affaires ther, Our pleasur is, that with diligence yow repair to our Court.—Hampton Court, Last Septr 1634.

Haus et puissants Seignewres Nos bons amis voysines et allies : requeste nous a este treshumilment faicte par nostre Consen le Comte de Baleleuch dont le pere et les ayeulx depuitz longs temps ont porte des charges militaires soubs vous de vous vouloir racomander ses affaires esquells a raison des domages et pertes soustinues en vostre service il alloct grandement suffrix sans la redresse quill attendoit de vos mains par le payment des arrerages tant de pensions lesquelles pour quelques debtes vous avez octroye, que de tout ce qui peut estre encore deu a few son pere pour tout le temps de son service, quoy que quelques fois a cause de nostre employ par deca ainsi que Lors nos lettres vous fient entendre il ait este forse de sen absenter au bien que nous soyons assures et de la satisfaction que vous estes accustumes de donner a ceux qui fidelment vous servent, et de la bien vueillance que vous portes mesment a la memorie de ceux qui vous ont servi tellement, que nous jugeons estre chose superflue de vous en importuner si est ce Neantmoins que la cognoisance que nous avons de sa necessite, et a sa tresinstante requeste nous avons bien voulu faire ceste intercession pour luy et vous prier tres affectueusement de donner ordeur que promptement il soit satisfait de tout ce qui se trouvera luy rester deu en vos provinces Ce ne sera pas seulement un acte de nostre equite et faveur pour en acquerir et confirmer les devotions des autres a vous servir, mais aussi un tesmoignage de vos affections en nostre endroit qui nous invitera a vous en respondre pareillement et toute occasion nous monstrer que reellement nous sommes Hauts et puissants Seigneurs vos amis Voysins et allies.—Hampton Court, last Septr 1634.

Vostre bien bon amy.   C. R<small>E</small>.

AU PRINCE D'ORANGE.

Mon Cousin Le Comte de Bucclugh dont le pere et ancestres ont longuement servi en ces guerres la se trouve tellement incommode que sans le prompt payment de tout ce que luy reste deu par les Estates et Pais bas il craint grandement de souffrir Cest pour quoy ayants (a sa requeste) fait intercession envers les dits estats nous vous avons bien aussi voulu recommander ses affaires vous priants tres effectuensement selon l'authorite et pouvoir que vous avez de vouloir mojenner et tenir la main affinque satisfaction entiere luy soit donne sans plus delay de tout ce qui sy trouvera rester deu a feu son pere, nonobstant que pour nostre service nous le ayons quelques fois retenu et force de s'absenter de sa charge, et nous vous asseurons que par ceste faveur vous ne vos obligerez pas seulement de plus en plus la noblesse estrengere mais aussy que nous mesmes vous en serons redevables et quand l'occasion se presentera nous revaucherons voluntiers estants tous jours Mon Cousin.

Vostre tresaffectionne Cousin,   C. R<small>E</small>.

A nostre Palace de Hampton Court le 30 de Septr 1634.

TO HIS MA^{tris} LEGAT IN HOLLAND.

Trustie, &c.—As we wer pleased heirtofoir to signifie our pleasur vnto yow for solliciting the estats generall for payment of such arreirs of pensions and vthers rests dew by them vnto the late Erle of Bucclugh, so the lyk consideratioun moveing ws at this tyme in behalf of our right trustie and weilbeloved Cousen the Erle of Bucclugh his sone, who is minor, and whois estate (as we ar informed) will be much impaired by his father's engadgments in raising of money for the service if a speedie course be not takin for his releiff, Our pleasur is, that yow tak particular informatioun from his kinsman, the bearer, of such moneyis as ar dew vnto him, and of such evidences as he can produce for cleating the debt, and that accordinglie yow carefullie sollicite the Estates and Prince of Orange (to whome we have writtin tuitching this purpois) for speedie recoverie of these moneyis, which we will tak as acceptable service done vnto ws.—Hamptoun Court, 30 Sept. 1634.

Wheras we ar crediblie informed that diverse ordours, priviledges of jurisdiction, immuniteis, and exemptions wer institut and granted to the Vniversitie of Aberdene by our royall progenitour, James the Fourt, founder thairof, and since ratifeid and enlarged by diverse others our royall predicessours, which ar now infringed to the great hurt of that vniversitie and members thairof, in the exerceis of ther studeis and severall faculteis, and to the great disparagement of our Vniversitie : To the end these priviledges and others aforsaid be re-established according to the laudable intention of the founder, and that such further ordours, priviledges, and immuniteis may be added of new thervnto as ar enjoyed by others famous vniversiteis, whervnto ther antient records have relation, and as may best conduce to the good of that vniversitie, and stand with the estate of that kingdome, Our pleasur is, and we doe heirby requyre and authorize yow, our Commissioners, or ony two of yow, to pervse the antient writts and records of that vniversitie, and to call befoir yow our Advocat, that haveing by his advyse in poynt of Law dewlie considered thairof, and of what other testimonie can be fund to give further light tuitching these ordours and priviledges, that with all convenient diligence yow certifie ws what yow find therin, with your opinions vnder your handis what is fitt to be done by ws tuitching the same, that a Chartour and new gift may be thervpon exped vnto them vnder our great seall, and in the meane tyme, that by advyse and concurrence of the reverend father in God the bischop of Aberdene, Chancellour of that Vniversitie, yow visite the same, and represse such abuses and setle such good ordour thairin as yow can lawfullie and convenientlie doe ; ffor all which these presents shalbe to yow and others, quhom it may concerne, sufficient warrant.—Dat. vt supra.

To the Archbischops of St Androis and Glasgow, The Bischops of
    Aberdene, Murray, and Rosse.

To the Session.

Right, &c.—Wheras humble remonstrance hath bene made vnto ws, in behalff of the Vniversitie of Old Aberdene, that diverse landis, housses, tythis, annuiteis, and others things dedicated thervnto ar ather vnjustlie withholdin from them or they defraudit in not receaveing the dew and tymelie benefite thairof, wherby they doe not onlie suffer by want of what is justlie dew vnto them, bot that (if tymelie remeid be not provydit) the said Vniversitie will wholie decay : For the recoverie of which things in a legall maner they ar to intent action of Law befoir yow, to the end they be not distracted from ther studeis and exerceis of ther severall functions by attending vpon your Judicatorie, which is far distant from them, and that our royall intention may tak effect in seing that and all other seminareis of learneing within that our kingdome to floorisch, we ar heirby pleased to recommend vnto yow in a serious and effectuall maner that from tyme to tyme, as any such action of thers shall cum befor yow, Justice be administered thairin with as much diligence and convenience vnto them as can be affoorded by the Lawis of that our kingdome which as we will tak good and acceptable service done vnto ws : We bid, &c.—Hampton Court, last Septr 1634.

To the Advocat.

Trustie, &c.—We haveing vpon verie good considerations writtin to our Session that speedie justice be administred in any action that sall cum in befoir them tuitching the reduceing of such lands, rents, tythis, housses, and annuiteis as ar vnjustlie withholdin from the Vniversitie of Old Aberdene, or of such rents and dewteis as ar not dewlie and tymelie payed vnto them, as by the enclosed coppie of our letter yow will perceave : Our pleasur is, and we doe heirby will and requyre yow to compeir and concurre with them in all such actions of theris as may tend to the advancement and flourisching of that Vniversitie, and to that effect that yow vse your best endeavours that all ther laufull causes may be caryed for the best advantage and with the least delay, trouble, or charge that may be, that no occasion be govin of distracting them from ther studeis and exerceise of ther severall functions which we will tak as verie acceptable service done vnto ws, for which these presents, &c.—From our honour of Hampton Court, last Septr 1634.

To the Counsell.

Right, &c.—Wheras by this enclosed petition as yow will perceave there ar some things desyred by the petitioners for advancement of our service committed to ther trust : Our pleasur is, that yow give them your best assistance according to our desyres so far as justice may permitt, and that no tolleratioun be granted to the sellers of Tobacco derogatorie to the proclamations alreadie past ; so not doubting, &c.— Vt supra.

Vnderstanding the sufficient qualificatioun and good affectioun to our service of Doctour W[m] Guild, doctour of Divinitie and minister of our brugh of Aberdene, within our kingdome of Scotland, we of our speciall royall favour and grace have accepted, and doe heirby accept and admitt, the said Doctour William to be one of our ordinar chaplanes, and to attend our service therin as we shall think expedient, ordeaneing his oath of fidelitie to be taken to ws as our speciall servand and chaplane, to be taken therament by our right reverend father in God, and right trustie and weilbeloved Counsellour the Archbischop of S[t] Androis. —Gevin at Hampton Court, 7 Octo[r] 1634.

To the Counsell.

Right, &c.—Being crediblie informed that the lyk abuse of counterfyteing of copper money is lyk to creip in that our kingdome as it was of late in this, wherby great disorders and hurt did ensue to our subjects heir, for tymelie preventing quhairof in the begining, befoir it cum to a further light of prejudice to the publict, it is our pleasur that by proclamatioun at all places requisite yow strictlie prohibite all such vnlawfull coyneing of copper money, vnder such panes of censure and punischment as is fitt to be inflicted vpon delinquents in the lyk caces, intimating that it is our further pleasur that the halff of the benefite aryseing by fynes by transgressours shalbe allowed to the discoverers for ther panes, and the other halff to the persones who by our warrant ar at the charges of coyneing such a proportion of that coyne as is designed for the publict good, and that towards the loss to be sustened by them, and that yow vse what farther lawfull meanes yow shall think fitt for the tymelie repressing of that abuse.—Hampton Court, 7 Octo[r] 1634.

To the Thesaurers Principall and Deputie.

Right, &c.—Wheras we have bene pleased to signe tuo patents for our subjects of Scotland to trade in Affrick and East Indies, though yow forbear to sett your handis heir to any bussines propper to be dispatched at our Exchequer table of that kingdome which we approve, yit sieing yow ar both heir, and that the seasone (as is affirmed) doeth neir approach for the adventurers putting out to these parts, ther being a necessitie that ther patents be first exped vnder our great seall of Scotland, whither they ar to returne with diligence for that purpois : Our pleasur is that yow signe them heir, that such a competent number of others our Commissioners of Excheker as is requisite may the more warrantablie doe the lyk ; for which these shalbe to yow and them sufficient warrant.—Gevin at our Honour of Hampton Court, 13 Octo[r] 1634.

To the Counsell.

Right, &c.—Being informed that ther ar some who have presumed of late to vent within that kingdome not onlie the farthings of this kingdome formerlie (as we ar certanelie informed) discharged by

u 3 a

act of Counsell ther and proclamatiouns following thairvpon to have vent in that cuntrey, yea and as is probable such farthings as for ther insufficiencie ar not permitted to have course heir, bot also false and counterfyted turnours, to the high contempt of our authoritie royall: Therfor, for preventing of the incress of this abuse and the punischment of such as ar or shalbe fund guiltie for the same, Our pleasur is, that wherever any of the coyneris of the saids counterfitted turnours or of the English farthings shalbe fund, or any of the inbringers or first venters or disperseris of them amongst the people, they be strictlie and exemplarlie punisched according to the nature of ther fault, and that the one-half of the benefite to aryse ather by thir confiscations or fynes shalbe for the vse of the discoverer, and the other for our owin, as we shalbe pleased to dispose of it; inserting lykwayes in the saids proclamations such clausses and strict commandis as may cause the vse of these vnlawfull and publict abuses instantlie to ceise amongst the people, with certificatioun of such punischment or fynes vpon the contraveners as yow shall think expedient for the strict observation of what yow shall think fitting to ordeane for the reformatioun of the said abuse. All which recommending to your best and speedie care, we bid, &c.—Date vt supra.

To the Exchequer.

Right, &c.—Wheras we gave a commission to a select number of our Exchequer to consider of the estent thairof, and to represent to ws such remedeis as they thoght most fitt and agreable to the Lawis of that our kingdome for releiving the burdens thairof and incress of our rents, who haveing humblie represented vnto ws ther advyse in severall articles subscryved by them, which we have approved and taken as acceptable service done vnto ws: It is our pleasur that by ane act of Exchequer yow ordeane the said Commission, togidder with the said advyse of the Commissioners, and our approbation of the same, to be registrat in the bookis of Exchequer, making such particular Acts of Exchequer heirvpon as from tyme to tyme shalbe fund necessar, and that yow give your best advyse, assistance, and concurrance for the good of our said service so often as yow shalbe requyred therto; wherof not doubting of your readie performance, we bid yow farewell.—Hampton Court, 13 Octo^r 1634.

To the Thesaurers.

Right, &c.—Wheras it is fund that ther is no necessitie both of Ishearis and Maissers in Exchequer, nor of Chalmerlanes, for ingathring of our rents of Rosse, Dunfermeling, and others places of that our kingdome; bot in respect that some have standing rights and patents therof, our pleasur is that yow tak the speediest course yow can ather for annulling or making them surrender the same.—Dat. vt supra.

To the Thesaurers.

Right, &c.—Wheras we have bene pleased to signe two Patents for our subjects of Scotland to trade to Africk and Eist Indeis, though yow forbear to sett your hands heir to any bussines propper to be despatched at our Excheker table of that our kingdome.—Dat. vt supra.

To the Exchequer.

Right, &c.—Wheras vpon verie important consideratiouns we establisched ane assotiation for the fisching of Great Britane and Irland, wherof we have in particular maner taken vpon ws the protection, and wherby diverse conditions and restrictions ar provyded for advanceing that great work, tending to the generall good of all our dominions, and speciallie to that our antient kingdome; we being vnwilling that any of our subjects be discouraged in ther lawfull prosecution of the fisching trade, by being troubled for the exeyse of any herrings taken by them in the places designed for the vse of the said Assotiation till our Counsell thairof setle a constant course both tuitching the tythis and excyse, Our pleasur is, that in the meane tyme no action nor proces be granted aganst our burrowis, or any of them, for the forsaid Excyse of herring till the said course be takin; for doeing whairof these shalbe your warrant.—Dat. vt supra.

To the Counsell.

Right, &c.—Vnderstanding the abiliteis and affection to our service of our trustie and weilbeloved Sir James Carmichaell of that ilk, knyᵗ, our Justice Clerk of that our kingdome, and one of our Sueris, and being willing, for his better enabling and encouragement to our said service, to promove and advance him to be one of our privie counsell thairof, Our pleasur is, that, haveing administred vnto him the oath accustomed in the lyk caices, yow admitt him vnto our said Privie Counsell; For which, &c.—Hampton Court, 13 Octoᵣ 1634.

To the Counsell.

Right, &c.—Wheras it hath bene humblie compleyned vnto ws in behalff of our trustie and weilbeloved William Gray, merchant in Edᵣ, that efter he hath, to his great charge and loss of tyme, brought the soapworks to that perfection wherby forrayne soap is made vnvsefull, and the cuntrey servit with better soap and at easier rates then heirtofoir, he is lyk to be depryved of the benefite of his travells by Mᵣ Nathaniell Vdward, contrair to all equitie, as by the enclosed petition which we have sent yow heirwith will at more length appear: Our pleasur is, haveing called both pairteis befoir yow, and haveing considered of the said information and petition, and of what farther can be alledged by any of the pairteis, that by yourselffis, or by a Committie to be appoynted by yow of your own number, yow so order the differences between them as yow sall find to be most agrieable to equitie, and as may best encourage all such introducers of vertew, by whom our subjects ar bettered and supplied with all or the lyk necessarie commoditeis. Dat. vt supra.

To the Commissioners of Tythes.

Right, &c.—We being willing, for good causses and considerations tending to the good of our service, that yow doe not valuo the personage of Dundie, or any tythis whatsoever belonging thervnto, Our pleasur is, that yow proceid not in any maner of way in the valuation therof till our further pleasur shalbe signifeid to that purpois; For which, &c.—Hampton Court, 13 Octoᵣ 1634.

To the Erle of Seafort.

Right, &c.—Wheras yow did heirtofoir signifie that yow wer willing to submitt to ws your right to the yle of the Lewes, and to acquiesce with our royall determination in what maner we thoght most fitt for the good of our service: To which purpois we, being willing to deall favourablie with yow, have appoynted Commissioners to tak tryell of your right, and accordinglie to transact with yow which hitherto hath bene neglected, and therfor have appoynted some Commissioners of new for taking ordour therunent: Our pleasur is, that vpon ther adverteisment yow come instructed for tryell of your rights, that vpon report of our Commissioners we may tak such course tuitching that purpois as we shall find to be most fit for our service, and just and equitable.—Hampton Court, 13 October 1634.

To the Toun of Edinburgh.

Trustie, &c.—Haveing bene petitioned in your behalff for such moneyis as ar fund dew to vmquhill George Heriot, and wer doted by him to the vse of his Hospitall, for payment whairof we have alreadie gevin ordour to our Thesaurer heir, and wille carefull to sie the samyne done according to the authour his pious intention so soone as with conveniencie may be : It is our pleasur that yow proceid in that work for finisching the buildings intended by yow with all diligence, and not to neglect what may conduce to that purpois ; which we will tak weill at your hands.—Hampton Court, 13 Octo^r 1634.

To the Exchequer.

Right, &c.—Haveing for the good of our service erected ane assotiation for the fischings of Great Britan and Irland, whairof we have taken vpon ws the protection, and intending (for ther incouragments) to frie them from all vnjust and vnlawfull exactions and impositions wherwith (as it is compleaned to ws) the heretours of the Yles doe trouble them : Our pleasur is, that yow call befor yow all these heretours wher the saids fischings ar or may be, and caus them produce ther rentalls of such impositions, with ther warrants or rights wherby they exact the same, dischargeing them from any such further exactions hoirefter further than yow shall find tham lawfullie warranted, and that yow tak a speciall note of all customes or assyse levyed, ather to our vse or to the vse of any of our subjects within that kingdome, of the fischings ; and that yow adverteis ws therof, that we may setle such a course therunent as may both encourage the said assotiation and may best conduce to the good of our service.—Hampton Court, 13 Octo^r 1634.

Wheras our right, &c. the Erle of Seafort hath submitted himselff to be disposed of by ws tuitching our right to the Lewes, and what we shall think fitt to determyne tuitching his clame and interest therin, to the effect we may be the better informed concerneing the premisses and the particulars efter mentionat : Our pleasur is, and we doe heirby give full power and commission vnto yow, whois names ar particularlie vnder expressed, to meitt and convene at such tymes and places as yow shall think meitt and necessarie, and ther to advyse and consider of our said right to the said yland, and to the said Erle his clame and interest therin, the rentall therof, the arreiris of the few dewteis of the same payable vnto ws, what portion of land therin yow think fitt that we reserve for our owin particular vse, to be disposed of as we shall think fitt, the commoditeis and lyeing therof most necessarie for our good and service, and what part therof is equitable for ws to give and confirme to him, the tenour, maner, and conditions to be mentioned in the disposition most necessarie for our service, and to report the same sealled vnto ws vnder your hand betuixt this and the first day of May nixt, that efter dew consideration had therin by ws, we may give such further ordour tuitching the same as we shall find caus, and discharges all former Commissiones heirunent, &c.—Vt supra.

     To Erles of Morton, Sterling, Traquair, Sir Johne Hay, Sir Thomas
         Hope or oney thrie of them.

Our Soveraigne Lord Ordeanes a protection to be made vnder his hignes' great seall of the kingdome of Scotland to his hignes' lovit William Gordoun of Kirkconnell, John Fullerton of Carleton, Johne Gordoun of Carlones, Hew Gordon of Grange, Alex^r Gordon of Erlstoun, and Niniau Herron of Culquha, making mention that whems the saids persones being cautioners for the late Viscount of Kenmure for diverse sowmes of money, willbe all uterlie vndone if at this tyme they should be vnseasonablie pressed by their creditours, befoir they can possiblie dispose of ther owin estats to mak vp sowmes of money for ther releiff, which is verie difficult to be so quicklie done as is requisit ; And that for diverse considerations or to gett releiff out of the meanes and esteat of the said Viscont, he being bot so latelie deid, leaveing no aires-male of his bodie to succeid to his estate, his lady, who is with chyld, being neir the tyme of hir delyverie, his Matie, considering the intricat estate of these affaires, occasioned by the verie late and vnexpected death of the said nobleman, but withall cheiflie considering that the estats of the saids principall and cautiouners ar of far greater worth then the moneyes so owing by them, and that they are both willing and able to give satisfaction to the saids creditours, if any competent tyme wer allowed vnto them for that purpois, wher if they wer vnseasonablie troubled it would be a meanes both to disable them and to dissapoynt the creditours : Reliqua stilo ordinario.—Hampton Court, 14 Octo^r 1634.

Our Soveraigne Lord having sufficient prooff and tryell of the good, thankfull, and fayfull service done vnto his Matie by his highnes' trustie and weilbelovit Sir James Carmichaell of that ilk, kny^t, gentleman suer to his Matie in ordinarie ; And vnderstanding his abilites, literature, and qualification for vseing and executeing of the place and office of his Ma^teis Justice Clerk of the kingdome of Scotland, and of the place and office of the M^r of the Ceremoneis of the said kingdome, both which places and offices doe now vaik in his Ma^teis handis, and ar at his highnes' gift and disposition by the death of vmquhill Sir George Elphingstoun of Blythiswood, kny^t, late Justice Clerk and M^r of the Ceremoneis : Therfoir his Matie ordeanes a Letter to be made vnder his hignes' great seall of the said kingdom, making, constituteing, and ordeaneing the said Sir James Carmichaell, kny^t, Lykas by the tenour heirof maks, constitutes, and ordeanes the said Sir James Carmichaell his Ma^teis Justice Clerk and M^r of the Ceremoneis of the said kingdome, with full and absolute power vnto him, the said Sir James, to choyse and appoynt deputeis, ane or more, in the saids offices, as oft as he shall think fitt, and from tyme to tyme to vse, bruik, posses, and enjoy all and whatsumever feyis, rents, proffeits, precheminences, priviledges, immuniteis, casualiteis, digniteis, and emoluments, appertencing and belonging to the saids severall offices of Justice Clerk and M^r of Ceremoneis, and ather of them, by whatsumever maner of way, with power to him, for his more absolute obteneing and enjoying thairof, to call, persew, and recover them by due course of Law, and everie way and in all respects whatsoever, as frielie to exerce, vse, bruik, and enjoy the saidis offices, and everie of them, with all the benefites, priviledges, and digniteis thairof, as the said vmquhill Sir George Elphingstoun, or any vther his predicessours in the saids offices, or any of them, have bruiked and enjoyed the same at any tyme preceiding : Ordaneing the said Letter to be writtin to the said great seall, and exped vnder the same, without passing any vther sealls or registeris, and that no farther nor greater feyis or moneyis whatsoever be taken or exacted for wryting and expediing heirof vnder the said seall than if aney ane of the abovenamed severall offices wer heirin onlie expressed or comprehendit, and to be exped at the ordinarie rate accustomed in the lyk caices ; ffor which these presents shalbe your sufficient warrand, both to the keiper of the said great seall and writter thairof.—Gevin at, &c.

To the Thesaurers.

Right, &c.—Haveing bene pleased, in consideration of the long service done to our late royall father, he, James Dowglas, the late Secretareis depute, and as we ar informed of his necessiteis, aige, and great infirmiteis to ratifie his pension of 200^lib st. payable out of our Exchequer : Our pleasur is, that yow not onlie exped the ratificatioun with diligence vnder our sealls, bot lykwayes that yew mak good and readie payment vnto him of the said pension yeirlie and termelie heirefter, and that yow tak a present accompt of the arreiris dew vnto him, and furthwith mak payment thairof in respect of his saids necessiteis and debts; ffor which, &c.—Hampton Court, 14 Octo^r 1634.

To the Erle of Traquair and Clerk Register.

Right, &c.—Wheras it is represented vnto ws that it is necessarie that a constant charge be made of our rents, wherby our Thesaurers may be charged in tyme cuming, it is our pleasur that with all diligence yow mak a perfyte charge of all our rents, alsweill propertie as principalitie, and of all casualiteis and particulars wherwith they may or oght to be charged, and that yow sett donn a forme to be observed heirefter for making the charge of the accompts, and heirefter that yow present the same to the remanent Commissioners of Exchequer to be pervsed and allowed by them.—Hampton Court, 14 Octo^r 1634.

To the Citie of Edinburgh.

Trustie, &c.—Wheras we did formerlie wryt vnto yow to modifie and provyde your Ministers with sufficient stipends fitt for ther places and qualitie, haveing accordinglie gevin commission to certane of our Counsell to treat with yow and sie the same done, which (as we ar informed) yow have continewed till No^r nixt: Our pleasur is, that yow appoynt Commissioners to meit with these whom we have so authorized, and setle that bussines by mutuall consent without further pley, that by your forwardnes in obeying our princelie and so just desyres, we may be the rather induced to extend our gratious favour vnto yow, when yow shall have recourse to ws for that purpois: We bid, &c.—Hampton Court, 14 Octo^r 1634.

To the Citie of Edinburgh.

Trustie, &c.—Haveing fund your readie obedience to our desyre concerneing the election of the Magistrats at this tyme, we thank yow hartelie for the same, and as our predicessours did not tak the lyk course bot vpon a verie speciall consideration, both in regard of what is past and we intend heirefter, it is our pleasur that yow readelie obey and assist them who have authoritie amongst yow in all things that may tend to the good governement of that citie and advancement of our service, that they may cheirfullie proceid to execute ther charges, assureing yow that we will not onlie protect yow, bot will contribute what is further necessarie to that effect for confirmeing of your present liberteis, and increaseing of them heirefter as reasone shall requyre; so being confident of your best endeavours for geving ws satisfaction heirin, we remitt all particulars to be imparted vnto yow from ws by our trustie and weilbeloved Counsellour Sir John Hay of Baro, kny^t, our Clerk Register.—Dat. vt supra.

To the Bischop of Edinburgh.

Right reverend, &c.—We haveing thoght it fitt for the good of our Church of that citie that in each paroch ther be a principall and second minister, sieing paritie in such caces doeth vsuallie breed confusion and disordour; and being sufficientlie informed of the qualification of Mr David Fletcher, minister, These ar to will yow to confer with him, and efter yow have informed your self of his abiliteis and conformitie, that yow tak such a course as is most fitt for his admission to the vaikand place to the south-eist paroch of that citie, willing to tak to your consideration the abiliteis and conformitie of Mr James Reid, Minister at St Cuthbert's, and according as yow shall find him fitt to prefer him to the first vacant place in your dyocie: Which recommending to your care, &c.—Hampton Court, 14 Octo^r 1634.

To the Advocat.

Trustie, &c.—Whereas we have often signifeid our pleasur vnto yow to delyver vnto our trustie and weilbeloved Counsellour Sir Johne Hay of Bara, knyt, our Clerk of Register, all submissions of the Lords of Erections and others our subjects concerneing tythes which ar in your custodie, that the samyne may be putt vp in the Chartour hous of the Castell of Edinburgh, to remane amongst the rolls thairof: These ar therfor to will and requyre yow that vpon sight heirof yow doe not faill to delyver them to our said Officer; for which, &c.—Dat. vt supra.

To the Archbischop of St Androis and remanent Commissioners for the Rents of the Chapell Royall.

Right, &c.—We being gratiouslie pleased, according to our pleasur heirtofoir expressed, signifeid to this purpois, that the rents properlie belonging vnto our Chapell to be visited and ordored for the good therof, conforme to the Commission granted be ws to that effect: Our pleasur is, that haveing taken dew consideration of the Contents of our said Commission, yow proceid accordinglie with all dilligence, and that yow gave ws ane accompt of your proceidingis tuitching the same.—Hampton Court, 14 Octor 1634.

To the Commissioners for Tythes.

Right, &c.—Whereas we ar crediblie informed that by the valuatioun of the tythes of parcells of parochines, without adverting that the whole Tythes of each parochine may be valued, we ar prejudged in our annuitie, the ministers' stipends not weill payed, and wherby some others pious vsses cannot be so convenientlie done as is requisit: Our pleasur therfor is, that yow have a speciall care that the valuatioun of all the tythis of each parochin be wholie exped, and that yow may so proceid as yow may witnes to ws your care and diligence in the trust committed by ws to yow by the dew and exact execution of your Commission for performeing of good and pious works, planting of the Church, and provydeing ministers with compitent stipends, and for the good of our service entrusted to yow: All which recommending to your care, we bid, &c.—Hampton Court, 15 Octor 1634.

To the Counsell.

Right, &c.—Whereas we vnderstand, according to our pleasur signifeid to yow of late, yow have establisched Justices of peace throughout the kingdome, which we doe approve, and therfor ar willing, for the better preservation of our peace therin, that yow requyre them to putt our Lawis in execution with all care and diligence in so far as they ar warranted, that nather any complant be made vnto ws, nor that table of our Counsall so often pestered (as we ar informed it is) with ryotts vnfitt for the gravitie of such a place, and that yow authorize the saids Justices if neid beis, with what further power and authoritie yow shall find necessarie and speciallie in such parts of the kingdome wher yow shall find the greatest necessitie to requyre the same, taking such ordour for the peace and quyeting of the hielands as we by our former letter to yow for this purpois did preseryve, and that with all convenient diligence as yow shall find the necessiteis and present disordours of these parts: And as tuitching the Ylanders, that yow caus keip the ordour anent ther yeirlie compeirance befoir yow, to the effect that if any disordour should aryse from thence, the same may be the more easelie repressed, and our peace keipit with greater assurance: We bid, &c.—Hampton Court, 15 Octor 1634.

To the Counsell.

Right, &c.—Wheras we ar sufficientlie informed of the prejudice ensueing to our subjects be not registratioun of processes and decreits of apprysingis led and deducit at the instance of creditours aganst ther debtours, for remedie whairof we have thoght fitt and necessarie to establisch ane publict register for registration thairof, and to incorporat the same with the office of our Clerk Register, as persones to whom the same belongeth, and fittest to tak charge thairof, we have granted a signature to our present Clerk of Register: And therfor it is our pleasur that yow mak ane act of Counsall thervpon, and caus exped the said signature vnder our great seall, with all diligence, causeing publicatioun to be made thairof to all our subjects, that non pretend ignorance of the same; For which these presents, &c.—Vt supra.

To the Commissioners for Tythes.

Right, &c.—Wheras we doe conceave that a proportionable part of the pryce of all tythes of Erections or payable rent of the same, valued or sold, doeth belong vnto ws, notwithstanding sindrie persones have valued and approved befoir yow ther valuations of tythes of Erections without considering our interest or modifieing to ws any proportionable part of the pryce or valued bolls of the same: Our pleasur is, that yow call befor yow all such persones as have alreadie exped ther valuations of the saids tythes, and haveing heard and considered of our interest that yow modifie vnto ws such a proportionable part thairof as yow shall find to belong vnto ws, and heirefter that no valuations of tythes of erection be approven by yow vntill such tyme as our Thesaurer and Thesaurer deput be heard for our interest, and that a proportionable part thairof be modifeit vnto ws according to the tenour of our decreit: We bid, &c.—Hampton Court, 15 Octor 1631.

To the Commissioners, Thesaurer, Archbischof of St Androis and Glasgow, Secretar, Thesaurer Deput, Bischop of Edinburgh, Bischop of Ross, President of Session, Clerk Register, Advocat, or oney fyve of them, the saidis Thesaurer Principall and Deput, and ane of the saidis Archbischops making alwayes tuo.

Right, &c.—Wheras we have bene pleased to command our Thesaurers principall and deputie to vse all possible diligence in bringing in of the bygane annuitie of tythes, alsweill vnvalued as valued; and being gratiouslie pleased to give all ease and favour to our weill deserveing subjects, we by these presents doe will and allow yow to sell the heretable right of the said annuitie, and give a discherge of all byganes dew vnto ws for the same, for fyftene yere's purches, to all such persones as shall pay the said sowme for the saidis byganes, and heretable right of the same, within such competent tyme, as shalbe thoght fitt by yow: And becaus we conceave that these who postpone and delay to buy the same deserve not the lyk favour, our pleasur is, that yow proceid aganst them with all diligence for payment of the byganes, and if at any tyme heirefter they be desyreous to buy, yow mak them to pay for the same at the ordinar rates or custome in buying and selling of inheritance.—Dat. vt supra.

To the Session.

Right, &c.—Wheras we wer formerlie pleased to wryt vnto yow that, in regard of the submission intended betuix the pairteis claimeing interest to the erldome of Home, that no action concerneing the same should be insisted in befor yow for a time till the said submission war by a decree determined, or some other course taken for setling therof: And now, haveing heard that ther is ane action begun or to begin concerneing the Landis of Coldincknowis, which formerlie belonged to James Home; and least our meaneing in our former letter should be misconceaved as comprehending the saids lands within the said esteat of Home, we have thoght good to explane our selffes heirby, that it is our pleasur that whensoever any action or aney right or title whatsumever of the saids landis of Coldinknowis, which we vnderstand doe not belong to our right, &c. the Erle of Hadinton, Lord Privie Seill, shall cum to be persewed befoir yow, that yow administer Justice therin with diligence, according to the course of our Lawes, and in all other things that yow schaw him as much favour as lawfullie yow can: Which specially recommending to your care, we bid, &c.—Hampton Court, 15 Octo^r 1634.

TO THE ADVOCAT.

Trustie, &c.—Wheras we have agried with our Consen the Duik of Lennox for his right to the pryorie of St Androis, vpon the Articles which ar to be schawin vnto yow by our right, &c. the Erle of Traquair: Our pleasur is, that haveing sene and considered of these Articles, yow draw vp with all convenient diligence the rights and securiteis of the said Pryorie, and a mortificatioun thairof, with all other writts which by these Articles yow shall find requisite, both tuitching our right and our said cousene's ; and having prepared the same, that yow delyver them vnto the said Erle, to the effect that such persones as our said Consen doeth trust in that kynd, haveing sene and approved such of them as concerne him, yow may therefter send them to ws docated vnder your hand.—Hampton Court, 15 Octo^r 1634.

TO THE DEANE AND CHAPTER OF EDINBURGH.

Trustie, &c.—Wheras we ar informed that the widow of the late bischop of Edinburgh hath bene at great charge during the tyme of hir stay at Halyrudhous, she and hir children haveing had litle benefite of the rents of that bischoprik, occasioned by the small tyme of hir late husband's enjoying thairof, wherby sche is disabled to pay vnto yow, the members of that bischoprik, these moneyis dew vnto yow for the cropt 1633: Therfor we doe recommend vnto yow to quyt these moneyis vnto hir, extending, as we ar informed, to 100^{lib} sterling, and so gratifie hir with the lyk favour for the cropt 1634 ; which, as it will be ane meanes to help hir and hir children to returne to the part of ther former residence, so we will tak it as ane acceptable service done vnto ws.—Hampton Court, 15 Octo^r 1634.

Haveing signifeid our pleasur in sindrie particularis concerneing our service to our Thesaurer and deputie Thesaurer, wherin as we ar verie confident of your best concurrence and assistance whensoever any of the particulars shall cum befoir yow wherin we have any interest, ather as persewer or defender, that yow will acquant them therwith befor yow proceid therin ; which we will tak as acceptable service done vnto ws.—Hampton Court, 16 Octo^r 1634.

To the Erle of Kynmouth, Chancellour, Sir Robt Spottiswood,
President, and remanent Lords and Senatours of the Colledge
of Justice in that our kingdome of Scotland.

TO THE ADVOCAT.

Trustie, &c.—Wheras the place of Justice Generall of that our kingdeme doeth now vaik in our hands, and that the necessitie of our present service for the tryell of the Lord Balmerino, alledged authour of that scandalous lybell fund in the hands of John Dynmure, or accessorie thervnto, requyreth that some persone of qualitie and sufficiencie be putt in that charge : Our pleasur is, that yow draw vp a Commission with all clausses neidfull to W^m, Erle of Arroll, high Constable of Scotland, for being Cheif Justice for the tryell of the said Lord till the finall decision of that procos, and that with all possible diligence yow send it hither vnto ws docated by yow, that it may pas our owin royall hand and be returned with the lyk diligence ; for which, &c.—Dat. vt supra.

To the Commissioners of Lybell.

Right, &c.—We have vnderstude by your letter of your proceidings tuitching the tryell of that bussines of the scandelous lybell fund in the handis of Johne Dinmure, and of the care and panes takin by yow thairin, wherof we doe approve, so we give yow hartie thanks for the same, being now resolved that the Lord Balmerino be putt to the tryell of ane assyse, and with all desyreing that all possible meanes be first vsed that the trew estate and treuth of that caus be brought to light for our Advocat's better informatioun how to insist therin, it is our pleasur that yow carefullie and punctuallie examine the said Lord, and that yow vse all other lawfull wayes and meanes yow shall think fitt and necessar to bring that bussines to the vttermost tryell, in so far as any evidences or presumptions can mak way thervnto; which we will tak as acceptable done vnto ws.—Hampton Court, 15 Octo^r 1634.

To the Exchequer.

Right, &c.—Haveing resolved vpon good and important causes to tak into our owin princelie consideratioun the estate of the particulars efter specifeit, whairof offer of resignatioun shalhappin to be propounded befor yow for passing of new gifts thairvpon; Our pleasur is, that yow doe not exped in Exchequer any signature bearing infeftments of Abbayes, and pryors' housses, monasteris, nunreis, preceptoreis, collegiat churches, precincts of the same, nor lands thervnto belonging, not formerlie fewed, nor accept of any resignatioun of heretable offices in Excheker, vnless the gifts therof be signed vnder our owin hand or without a speciall warrant from ws to that purpois; for which these presents shalbe your warrant : So willing yow to mak ane act of ane Excheker heirvpon, we bid yow farewell.—Hampton Court, 15 Octo^r 1634.

To the Counsell.

Right, &c.—Wheras we wer pleased not long since to expres our royall pleasur tuitching the new imposition putt vpon Coall transported from that kingdome, and haveing at this tyme, amongst other things that may improve our rents thairof, gevin speciall charge to our officers to advert to our customes that we be not prejudged therin : And withall being informed how that by the great disproportion of Coal meassuris (some being bigger, some lesser in severall parts of the kingdome, no one certane syse or measur being kept) we ar prejudged in our customes, and our subjects troubled and hurt in ther lawfull trade, It is our pleasur that yow call befor yow the Coalmasters and others cheiflie interested in the said trade of Coall, and that yow sie them condescend vpon a certane syse and coall measur to be onlie vsed throughout the whole kingdome for venting ther Coalls abroad, and therefter that yow prescryve such penalties to be inflicted vpon the delinquents as yow shall think fitt ; wherin yow shall doe ws acceptable service, and for which these presents shalbe a sufficient warrant.—Hampton Court, 15 Octo^r 1634.

To the Exchequer.

Right, &c.—Haveing by our letter requyred our right, &c. the Erle of Mar to mak accompt to yow of his intromission with the concealments of the taxatioun 1621, Our pleasur is, that yow bear of his accompts thairof to the end such moneyis as shalbe fund to be restand awand to ws, ather of these concealments or otherwayes, may furthwith be receaved by our Thesaurers Principall and deputie for our vse ; for doeing quherof, &c.—Hampton Court, 15 Octor 1634.

To the Exchequer.

Right, &c.—Whems, for the increase of Manufactours in that our kingdome, and speciallie for provision of schipping, we gave a Patent to David Jonkine and Patrik Wood, merchants of Edinburgh, for bringing workmen fra forrayne parts for making of Cable and Taklen within that our kingdome ; and in regard that work is both necessarie and will conduce verie much to our service and the publict good of our subjects ther, by furnisching convenientlie at all occassions the schipping of that our kingdome with sufficient provision, which now they ar forced to bring from forrayne parts, wher they ar often destroyed in the exportation therof, to the great domage of our schipping : Sieing this work (as we ar certanelie informed) cannot be vndertakin without   and payues to the patentes and ther associatts, It is our pleasur that furthwith yow expeid the said Patent vnder your hands, and, for ther better encouragement to prosecute the said work, yow grant vnto them such immunitie of custome for the materialls imported by them for that work, and for what Cables and Taklene made by them shalbe exported to forrayne parts, and that for so maney yeires as yow in your judgment shall think fitt, wherby they may be the more willing and readie to vndergoe the said work ; For doeing quherof, &c.—Hampton Court, 19 Octor 1634.

To the Bischop of Edinburgh.

Being willing that our trustie and weillbeloved Mr James Hannay, Deane of Edr, reside at Halyrudhous till he hath performed some service ther to ws, which we ar the rather confident he will the more readelie doe in regard of the good and long prooff he hath alreadie gevin by his great care and affection to our service, Our pleasur therfor is, that he be not removed from thence till our further direction be gevin to that purpois, willing yow to continew the election of the principall Minister of St Geills' kirk of Edr till we give ordour theranent ; and in the meane tyme that yow deall earnestlie with the Magistrats of the citie for provydeing of ther ministers with sufficient stipends, according to ther severall charges, to which purpois we have signifieid our pleasur to our Clerk of Register, to be imparted vnto yow : And wheras we have provyded a sufficient Mansion for yow and your successours in our charge from ws, our further pleasur is that yow give him possession of the house that was the old mansion of the Lord Halyrudhous, with such a compitent proportion of the yard belonging thervnto as the Archbischop of St Androis, the Erle of Traquair, the Bischop of Rosse, and Clerk of Register, or any thrie of them, shall think fitt ; For doeing, &c.—Dat. vt supra.

To the Toun of Edinburgh.

Wheras we did formerlie wryt vnto yow that in modifieing the stipends of your ministers yow would have a speciall care of the Principall Minister of St Geills', as of ane appoynted for the most eminent charge of the church of that citie, wherin by your letter yow promised to give ws satisfaction, and to provyde compitent stipends for the rest of your ministers : It is pleasur that yow have a care to performe the same accordinglie, as yow will respect our service ; wherin, haveing more particularlie imparted our will to our Clerk of Register, to whom we remitt the same to be signifeid vnto yow, we remitt the same to be signifeid vnto yow, we bid yow farewell.—Hamptou Court, 19 Octo^r 1634.

To the Advocat.

Trustie, &c.—Wheras the reverend father in God, our right trustie and weilbeloved Counsellour, Johne, bischop of Rosse, hath reported vnto ws your great care and diligence in concurring with him in his action of reduction of the Abbacie of Ferne, and of your opinion and encouragement to him that it may be lawfullie reduced, for which we give yow hartie thanks ; in regard it is for the good of our service, and for the said bischop and his successours' better enabling in that charge to propagat and mantene religione in these remote parts, we doe heirby effectuallie will and requyre yow to continew as yow have begun in reduction of that Abbacie, till it be brought to a finall end ; and in other things that may concerne the said bischop his affaires, wherin he shall requyre your advyce and help, that yow give vnto him your readiest concurrence, which we will tak as speciall good service done vnto ws, whairof we will not be vnmyndfull.—Hamptou Court, 19 Octo^r 1634.

To the Counsell.

Right, &c.—Wheras we have resolved to putt the Lord Balmerino to the tryell of ane assyse, to which purpois we have made choyse of W^m, Erle of Erroll, high Constable of Scotland, to be Cheiff Justice for that tryell, whome we will yow to assist in all such things wherin he shall requyre your help and furtherance in the dew executioun of his charge : And it is our pleasur, for the more exact and better proceiding in that tryell, that therof the senatours of our Colledge of Justice, whom the bodie of that Judicatorie shall think most able to mak choyse of to that purpois, be appoynted for assisting of the said Justice at all tymes and occasiones vsed for that tryell ; wherin both yow and they shall doe ws acceptable service, and for which these presents shalbe vnto yow and them a sufficient warrant.—Hamptou Court, 20 Octo^r 1634.

To the Erle of Erroll.

Right, &c.—Wheras ther is a scandelous lybell fund in the handis of ane Johne Dynnuure, wherof the Lord Balmerino is alledged to be the author or accessorie thervnto, in regard of the speedie and exact tryell heirof doe speciallie concerne ws in honour and the estate of that our antient kingdome, and that the office of Justice Generall thairof is now vakand at our gift, and that it is necessarie that one be establisched to this purpois, we ar pleased by our Commission vnto yow, for which we have gevin ordour, to mak joyse of yow, of whois abiliteis and affection to our service we ar confident, willing yow to accept thairof, and accordinglie to proceid as the case in Justice salbe fund to requyre.—Dat. vt supra.

To the Advocat.

Trustie, &c.—Efter dew consideratioun haveing resolved to caus the Lo/ Balmerino be putt to the tryell of ane assyse, and to this purpois it being necessarie that yow informe yourself of such particulars as concerne your charge in the legall prosecutioun of that bussines, it is our pleasur that with all convenient diligence yow insist thairin by produceing ane Indytment fitt for that purpois, and that yow carefullie goe on in everie other thing tuitching the prosecution thairof, as yow will answer to ws vpon your trust, and that by the advyse of the Cheiff Justice yow prefix a day for the same.

To the Erle of Mar.

Right, &c.—Haveing resolved, for our better informatioun and knowledge of the Estate of our Exchequer, that all Comptis and intromissiones with our rents, casualiteis, or taxations, or any part thairof, be cleared, compted for, and payed to our Exchequer, and being certanlie informed that at the fitting of the accompt of your intromission 1621, ther is allowed vnto yow 12,000ᵘᵇˢ for which yow ar to be comptable in the subsequent accompt of the contentments of the said taxatiouns, and that as yit yow have not made accompt of your intromission with these concealments : Our pleasur is, that yow mak ane accompt heirof to the Commissiouners of our Exchequer, whom we have appoynted to receave the same, to the end that what shalbe fund restand awand by yow, yow furthwith mak payment thairof to our Thesaurers principall and deputie, the readie performance whairof we expect from yow, &c.—Hampton Court, 20 Octoʳ 1634.

To the Chancellour.

Right, &c.—Haveing sene and considered of what was done by the Commissioners appoynted for hearing of your accompts and intromissions with our Taxatiounis, we ar pleased therwith, and doe allow of the same, and our pleasur is that these moneyis that ar fund resting in your hands, or for which yow ar obledged to give in hornings or payment, that yow delyver and pay the same to our thesaurers principall or deputie, or otherwayes give in the horning lawfullie and dewlie execute agaynst such as have not made payment of what is dew by them, and that at this nixt terme of Mertimes 1634, and as for that which is not accompted thairof, that yow mak course and payment of the same to our officers betuixt this and Candlemes nixt ensueing ; The readie performance quhairof we will expect at your hands : So we bid, &c.—Hampton Court, 20 Octoʳ 1634.

To the Commissioners for the Lawes.

Right, &c.—We haveing vpon good and important considerations gevin Commission to yow to surveigh our Lawis which wer ratifeit in our late parliament, it is our pleasur that, haveing condescended vpon certane dayes of meitting, yow goe on according to your Commission, and that with as much care and diligence as convenientlie can be vsed, and that yow certifie ws from tyme to tyme of your proceidings therin, by which yow will doe vnto ws acceptable service.—Hampton Court, 20 Octoʳ 1634.

To the Commissioners Chappell Royall Rents.

Right, &c.—We being graciouslie pleased, according to our pleasur heirtofoir signifeid to this purpois, that the rents properlie belonging to our Chapell Royall be visited and ordered for the good thairof, conforme to the Commission granted by ws to that effect : Our pleasur is, that haveing taken dew consideration of the contentes of our said Commission, yow proceid accordinglie with all diligence, and that yow give ws ane accompt of your proceidings tuitching the same.—Hampton Court, 20 Octoʳ 1634.

To the Dᵖ of Sᵗ Androis and remanent Commissioners for visiting
the rents of the Chappell royall.

To the Arch Bischop of Glasgow.

Right, &c.—Wheras these diverse yeres past we suffered the bischop of Caithnes to reside at Jedburgh, it being now fitt that he returne to his dyocie for supplieing his charge, and in the meane tyme being willing that the Church of Jedburgh may be supplied with ane able and qualifeid persone, we have to that purpois thoght fitt to nominat and present vnto yow M. James Burnett, persone of Lawder, of whois sufficiencie and abiliteis in the function of the ministerie we ar sufficientlie informed, and therfoir do heirby will and require yow to authorize him in the said charge of Ministrie at Jedburgh, goving vnto him letters of collation and admission as in the lyk caces is requisit.—Dat. vt supra.

To the Advocat.

Trustie, &c.—Being informed that the taks of our customes ar sett for mae yeires then is vsuall, and at lower rates and pryces than otherwayes we can have for the same : It is our pleasur that yow tak the estate heirof into your consideratioun, and that yow vse your best endeavours to reduce the saids taks by Law, otherwayes to move the takers to surrender the same, wherin we will yow to proceid from tyme to tyme as yow shall receave forther directions from our Thesaurers, or oney of them, for the furthring of our service heirin : So not doubting of your care and diligence in what may tend to the advancement of our service, we bid, &c.—Hampton Court, 20 Octo^r 1634.

To Sir John Auchmoutie.

Trustie, &c.—Haveing vpon good consideratious gevin Commission for surveighing of all our wardrop stuff, plate, and furnisching belonging to ws, as by the Commission yow may perceave, it is our pleasur, and we doe heirby will and requyre yow, to produce and delyver vnto them the said plaitt stuff, hangingis, and furnisching wherof yow have or hes had the charge at any tyme preceiding, that the same may be disposed of by the Commissioners as they ar warranted by our said Commission.—Dat. vt supra.

Wardrop Stuff Commissioners.

Erle Morton.	Erle Southesk.
Erle Hadinton.	B^p Edinburgh.
Erle Traquair.	Sir John Hay.
Erle Murray.	Sir Th. Hope.
Erle Winton.	

To the Thesaurers.

Right, &c.—Haveing considered of the humble advyse and opinion of these our Counsall and Exchequer to whome we pleased to give Commission for considering the Estate of our Exchequer, and the wayes how to releive the burdenes thairof, and to remedie the abuses latelie crept therin, We ar weill pleised therwith ; and therfoir our pleasur is that yow prosecute everie particular thairof in so far as concernes your office, and as for such particulars as we have entrusted to be performed by Commission, that yow in lyk maner have a speciall care to sie the same prosecuted accordinglie with all convenient diligence, suffering nothing to be done contrarie to the trew meaneing heirof ; ffor which these presents shalbe your warrant.—Dat. vt supra.

To the Exchequer.

Right, &c.—Wheras by advyse of some of our Commissioners of Excheker, vnto whom we have intrusted the consideratioun of the burdenis therof and remedeis of the same, we ar to mak the best vse of our rents and casualiteis within that our kingdome : Our pleasur is, heirefter yow pass no gifts of any nonentresse, wardis, eschcits, or of any other casualiteis, bot with a dew consideratioun of the benefite arysing therby, and speciallie of these that ar denuncit our rebells for not payment of any part of our rents or taxations, for which these presents shalbe your warrant.—Hampton Court, 20 Octo^r 1634.

To the Commission.

Wheras by our letter to the Commissioners of Tythes we have willed them to modifie to ws a proportionable part of the pryce and rents of all tythes of erection, ather valued or vnvalued, conforme to the tenour of our decreit, notwithstanding, being willing to tak such ane fair course with our subjects as may give them ease with the least prejudice to our service that may be, We have heirby gevin and granted, lykas be the tenour heirof we give and grant, full power and commission to yow, the persones in maner vndermentional, to treat and agrie with the Lords of Erections and others persones whatsoever haveing any part of the saids erections or tythis belonging thairto, for making retribution vnto ws for our said part of the saids tythes, ather by surrander of the whole, or of a proportionable part of the few maills of erections or otherwayes, as yow shall think most convenient for our service, and the rights and securiteis to be made by yow to them, being registrat in our Thesaurer's books and books of Exchcker, shalbe vnto them sufficient warrant.—Hampton Court, 20 Octo^r 1634.

Tythes.

Archb. St Androis.	B. Rosse.
Morton.	Sir Johne Hay.
Stirling.	Sir Th. Hope.
Traquair.	Or to any 5 of them, Thesaurer or
B. Ed^r.	deputie being one.

To the Exchequer.

Right, &c.—Haveing made choyse of yow to be Commissioners of our Exchequer for judgeing of all such cases shall occure befor the said judicatorie, and for assisting of our thesaurers principall and deputie in the manageing and ruleing of our rents and casualiteis of that our kingdome, it is our pleasur that yow furthwith accept heirof, and carefullie and diligentlie carie your selffis in the discharge of that trust we have bene pleased to pult vpon yow : and becaus we intend to have the same kept as a solemne and formall judicatorie in all tyme cuming, Our further pleasur is, that at your first meitting yow tak such a course that no persones except your clerks and necessarie members of Exchequer be admitted to stay amongst yow, and that yow mak and establisch such other acts and statutes for regulating the ordour and forme to be keipit in that Judicatorie as yow efter dew deliberatioun shall think fitt.—Hampton Court, 20 Octo^r 1634.

To the Commissioneris of Surrenders.

Right, &c.—Wheras we ar informed that vpon our letter to yow in May last, signifieing our pleasur that if any bischop or beneficed persone had a desyre to buy for the vse of the church any tythes which did formerlie belong thervnto, they should be preferred to any other persone, yow have assigned the first of Januarie nixt to the right, &c. of St Androis for buying in of some tythes of that pryorie for the vse aforsaid, bot in regard of the schortnes of that tyme, he cannot convenientlie tak that speedie course for buying these tythes that is requisite, and which we desyre may be takin for the good of the Church : It is therfor our pleasur that yow assigne vnto him a longer tyme, and that we may be made acquanted with it befor it doe expyre, that we may give such furder ordour theranent as we shall find just caus.— Dat. vt supra.

To the Exchequer.

Right, &c.—We receaved your letter and doe approve your opinion concerneing the same, being willing that Mr Nathaniell Edward enjoy the full benefite of his patent till the expiration of the yeres therof, efter which tyme he cannot in reasone expect farther: haveing now resolved for the good of our service and furthering of the work of the soap bussines intended for the publict good by the continewing thairof in the persone of some one, speciallie of so antient and weill deserveing a servant to our late dear father and ws, we have to that purpois signed a grant vnto him, as yow will perceave by the same; and thairfoir it is our pleasur that yow caus exped the said grant vnder our great seall with all possible diligence, that the patentee and his partiners may enjoy the benefite thairof efter the expiration of the said former grant.— Hampton Court, 20 Octor 1634.

To the Archbischop of St Androis.

Right, &c.—Wheras we have condescended with our Consen the Duik of Lennox for surrendering the Pryorie of St Androis, as by the Articles sent by our right trustie, &c. the Erle of Traquair; to which purpois, haveing requyred our Advocat to draw vp the said surrander and a mortification of that priorie for the intended vse, It is our pleasur that with all possible diligence yow repair vnto our citie of Edinburgh and sie the saids writts legallie drawin vp, which we will accompt as verie acceptable service for ws : And for which these, &c.—Hampton Court, 20 Octor 1634.

To the Archbischop of Glasgow.

Right reverend, &c.—Wheras our royall predicessours have bene carefull for advancement of learning to endow the Colledge of Glasgow with the tythes of some churches for the better intertenement of some professours and schollers ther, being now informed that some ar about to tak advantage of them by some small defects in the maner and forme of ther rights, to the prejudice and vndoeing of that so antient and famous a seminarie of the church and commonwell : It is our express pleasur and will that, if any persone shall purches from ws a presentatioun to any church or benefice belonging to the said Colledge, yow nowayes give collation to any such persone or persones presented by ws till he give sufficient suretie to yow and the said Colledge that he nor they shall not disturb, by Law or otherwayes, the right or profession of the said Colledge; wherin as we ar confident yow will give to the masters and others of that Colledge your best assistance, so yow may be confident that we will accompt it good and acceptable service done vnto ws.—Hampton Court, 20 Octor 1634.

To the Archbischop of St Androis.

Right Reverend, &c.—We ar weill pleased and accompt it acceptable service that yow ar so carefull according to our command to have a book of common prayer and a book of Canons establisched in the church of that our ancient and native kingdome, the one being a necessarie meanes to advance God's worschip, the other ane soverane help to avoyd confusion, As we give yow hartie thanks for this care, so we ar heirby pleased to encourage yow to the continuance and perfyteing of both; and for the book of common prayer, It is our expres will and pleasur that yow caus fram it with all convenient diligence, and that as neir as can be to this of England, and till yow have framed your owin, that, as befoir we commanded, yow doe tuyse a day service in your owin privat familie according to this of England; And that yow caus the same be done in your Cathedrall Churches in all holydayes, and in all publict assemblies, and that in our name yow command all our bischops and colleges within your provinces to doe the same; and if they dissobey, that yow certifie ws, as ye wilbe answerable for the same, in all which we expect your loyall obedience for advancement of God's glorie, the good of our service, and honour of that church, as yow may be confident of our princelie care to advance all your pious and good designes.—Hampton Court, 20 Octo^r 1634.

Similar letter to the Archbishop of Glasgow, of same date.

To the Commissioners for Tythis.

Right, &c.—Wheras we have heirtofoir signifeid our pleasure vnto yow that in the valuation of tythis that yow proceid first with the churches of erectioun, and till these valuations be exped, that yow goe with no other, haveing lykwayes ordeaned that in other churches which ar not of erectiouns heretours may convene befor yow the taksmen of ther tythis, to the end they may denude them selfis of their rights in favours of the heretours, and withall have expressed our pleasur that churchmen shalbe preferred to buy ther taks and leases first : Therfor we will that if any churchmen pleas to tak the benefite of that our Commission by buying of the rights of taksmen, according to the course taken by yow in favours of the heretours, though the heretours themselfils doe not change, the churchmen may conven the taksmen for denudeing themselfils in favours of the church : And it is our further pleasur to have a caire to provyde the Ministrie with good and compitent meanes, proportionable to the valuations, and not to mak 800 merks of 8 chalders of victuall the highest proportion of competencie, nor wher the ministrie ar alreadie in possession of ther viccarages, yow value these viccarages that so yow may mak the less proportioun of ther augmentatioun, bot that the proportion of augmentatioun be conforme to the valuatioun of the tythis of the parochin.—Hampton Court, 20 Octo^r 1634.

To the Provest and Baillers of Edinburgh.

Trustie, &c.—We ar informed that though yow find a great inconvenient by our seat within the paroch kirk of that citie, built for the vse of our late royall father, in regard it doeth stop the cisterne light and window of that churche, yit yow have heirtofoir foirborne to medle therwith without direction, which we tak weill at your handis : And being now trewlie informed that it is verie necessarie to be helped, it is our pleasur that with all diligence yow cause remove the said seat, and place it in some more convenient part ; for which these presents shalbe your warrant.—Hampton Court, 20 October 1634.

To the Session.

Right, &c.—Vnderstanding that the reverend father in God the Bischop of Rosse hath intented action of Reduction and Improbation befor yow of the Alueie of Ferne, wherin, sieing his endeavours ar

u   3 c

for the right and good of the church, and for the better enabling of him and his successors in such a charge, and in so remote a place, for the propagating and manteneing of religion in these parts, we ar heirby pleased to recommend vnto yow in a most effectuall maner that speedie justice be administred in the said action : And that in all things else comeing befor yow concerneing him yow schow him all the lawfull favour and justice yow can ; which we will tak as done vnto our sellfis, and wherof we will not be vnmyndfull.—Hampton Court, 20 Octor 1634.

To the Counsell.

Right, &c.—Haveing gevin ordour to our Archbischops and bischops of that our kingdome that the high Commission shall sitt constantlie in Ed{r} dureing the tyme of the Session everie Thursday betweene ten and twelff hours in the foirnoone, without stop or hinderance alwayes that it may sitt anywher else and at any vther tyme, vpon ane vrgent and necessar occasion : It is our will and pleasur that yow cause proclamation to be made at all places neidfull, that our subjects may have dew notice heirof.—Hampton Court, 20 Octr 1634.

To the Commissioners of Tythes.

Right, &c.—Whems we ar informed that by the delay in approveing the valuatioun of the Tythes of Crawfurd Lyndsay, made by the sub-commissioners of Lanerk at the instance of John, Lord Halyrudhous, the reverend father in God the bischop of Edinburgh, and the relict and children of his predicessour, the late bischop therof, ar verie much prejudged, in regard these tythes ar a part of the Patrimonie of that bischoprik, for setling wherof we have had so great a care, and that our royall intention is rather to add thervnto some furder meanes of new than that any part of that patrimonie should ather be astricted or made vnusefull ; We ar heirby pleased that yow seriouslie consider of ther severall rights and claymes to these tythes, and of ther sufferings by want therof, in regard of the one's charge and troubling in setling himselff ther of late, and of the otheris poore estate, being a widow, and left with a charge of children ; and therefter it is our further pleasur that with all expedition yow proceid to the allowing of the said valuatioun, that vpon speedie execution, according to your decreit thervpon, they may receave and enjoy these tythis, great and small, according to ther severall rights and claymes, and as shalbe fund agrieable to the tyme, intent, and meaneing of our generall determinatioun vpon the submission of the Clergie : Wherof remitting to the said bischop the further informatioun, we bid, &c.—Hampton Court, 20 Octor 1634.

Wheras we ar pleased, by our gift vnder the privie scall in that our kingdome of Scotland, to bestow vpoun the right reverend father in God the Archbischop of Glasgow the sowme of 5000{lib} sterling money, to have bene payed vnto him at the termes mentionat in the said gift ; and becaus the said Archbischop hes not as yet receaved payment of the same, Therfoir it is our pleasur that yow furthwith mak payment vnto him, his aires and assigneyis, of the said sowme of 5000{lib} st., and that out of the first and readiest of our rents, propertie, and casualiteis therof, or out of the first and readiest of our taxatiouns last granted vnto ws of that our kingdome, with the interest therof, if any shalbe fund dew, so long as the samyne remanes vnpayed, and that yow accept of this our warrant, testifieing vnder your hand to the said Archbischop your acceptatioun therof, and that therefter yow sie ws discharged of that debt so owing be ws vnto him : And for your soe doeing.—Hampton Court, 20 Octor 1634.

To our Thesaurers, the Erles of Mortoun and Traquair
　　Principall and deputie.

To the Counsell.

Right, &c.--We have bene informed of a great abuse that hath prevailed within these late yeires in that our kingdome by the disordourlie behavour of some dissobedient people, who, leaveing ther owin paroche churches, ran to seik the Communion at the handis of such ministers as they know to be disconforme to good ordour, which is the meanes of ther dissobedience to our lawes, and to manteyne a schisme in the churche, the repressing whairof being onlie in our power: It is our expres pleasur that by oppin proclamatioun yow discharge all such wandrings of our people from ther owin teachers, vnder the pane of our high displeasur; with certificatioun that whosoever sall not communicat in ther owin paroche churches once at leist ane yeir, shalbe called and punished as none communicants, according to the act of Parliament made theranent: Wherin expecting your diligence, and for which these presents shalbe your warrand, we bid, &c.—Hampton Court, 20 Octor 1634.

To the Commissioners of Tythes.

Right, &c.—Wheras we ar informed that the tythscheaves of the Lands of Pilrig, and sindrie others tythes within St Cuthbert's paroche, apperteneing to the patrimonie of the bischop of Edinburgh, wer valued befor that Commission far vnder the trew worth, and that the valuatioun was vnlawfull and informallie deduced, without any probatioun : Our pleasur is, that yow tak such a course for revalueing of these tythes by rateing thairof to the trew worth, that the reverend, &c. bischop of Edr suffer no prejudice, or have just occasion of complaynt heirefter, bot may enjoy, as other our subjects doe in the lyk caces, the trew value of these tythes; wherin yow shall do ws acceptable service, and for which these presents shalbe your warrant.—Hampton Court, 20 Octor 1634.

To the Lord Lorne.

Right, &c.—We ar informed that ther is a question moved by yow to the reverend father the bischop of Argyll vpon some right of yours pretendit to the Commissariot of that dyocie, which being an ecclesiasticall jurisdiction cannot convenientlie be exercised by any other then a spirituall persone, the power whairof being to flow from the ordinarie of the boundis : Therfor we have thoght fitt to recommend vnto yow to forbear the moveing of any such contraversie, suffering the said bischop and his successours in that charge to enjoy that commissariot and priviledges thairof as ther predicessours have vsed in former tymes, which we expect of yow as of one that is weill disposed in all things concerneing a readie obedience to our princelie and just desyres, assureing yow that when occasion shall offer we shall not be vnmyndfull heirof.—Hampton Court, 20 Octor 1634.

To the Advocat.

Trustie, &c.—Haveing writtin to our Commissioners for Surrenders to rectifie the valuatioun of the Tythes of Pilrig, belonging to the Bischop of Edinburgh, alledged to have bene valued far vnder the worth therof, and for allowing of the valuatioun of the tythis of the parish of Crawfurd Lyndsay, made by the sub-commissioners of Lanerk, as yow will perceave by the copeis of our letters writtin to them : Our pleasur is, that yow concurre and assist the reverend father the bischop of Edr for revalueing of these tythes of Pilrig, and for the obteining of ther approbatioun of the saids tythes of Crawfurd Lyndsay, and that yow vse your best endeavours to mak these tythes to be payed to the said bischop, and to the widow of his predicessour, the late bischop of Edr, according to ther severall claymes and rights, and for the cropis 1633 and 1634, and yerlie therefter, and that in all other things that may tend to the advancement of the said bischop his just and lawfull desyres, yow give your best and readiest ayde and concurrence, in so far as concernes your charge, which we will tak as verie acceptable service done vnto ws, and for which these presents shalbe your warrant.—Hampton Court, 20 Octor 1634.

To the Session.

Wheras by a former letter we willed yow not to proceid in any action in Law at the instance of any persone aganst our frie burghs tuitching the tythes of the Yles fischings, for the reasones therin contenit: And wheras we ar now informed that ane Mr Alexr Guthrie of Gegay did purches a lease of these Tythes from one who (as it is pretended) had a lawfull right therof from the late bischop Knox, sometyme bischop of the Yles: To which purpois, being humblie moved in behalff of the said Mr Alexr Guthrie that a dew consideratioun might be had that he procured that Lease vpon valuable conditions, both his owin and his authour's right being sufficient and just, and that therfor he might have the benefite of our Lawes, We have thoght fitt to recommend vnto yow the consideratioun heirof, that if yow find considerable grounds for his right, he may have justice administred vnto him in his cause, without interruptione: So we bid yow farewell.—Dat. vt supra.

To the Bischop of Edinburgh.

Wheras we have gevin ordour to the Archbischops and bischops of that our kingdome that they use the common Book of Prayer, used in this our kingdome, not onlie in ther owin privat famileis twyse a day, bot also in the Cathedralls; and considering how much the exemple of Edr may ather advance or hinder this work, and being confident of your abiliteis and good affection to our service and to so pious a work, doe heirby will and requyre yow that with discretion and forwardnes yow endeavour to obey our just and pious commandments heirin, and that yow have a speciall care that none enter the service of the Ministrie of Edr bot such persones as ar most able and conforme, and of a peaceable and quyet cariage, or such as we shall recommend vnto yow, sieing vpon the peace and good governement of that churche depends the quyet of the whole churche of that our kingdome: As we ar confident of your care and obedience heirin, so we will compt it as acceptable service done to ws, and be confident we will strenthen yow with our royall countenance and protection, and shall give yow our best encouragements for these and all other good services of the church of that kingdome; so we bid yow farewell.—Dat. vt supra.

Commission.

Wheras vpon good consideration [we have] gevin yow ordour for examing the Lord Balmerino, and considering by the Commission granted vnto yow the 5 of May last ther must be at the least 7 of yow necessarlie present, we conceave that so great a number may perhaps hardlie at all occasions be fund readie to meitt, many of the Commissioners being otherwayes severallie and particularlie imployed in matters concerneing our service: Therfor, least by the want of that full number ther may be delayes aryse in the tryell of that bussienes which we desyre may with all possible diligence be cleired, it is our pleasur and we doe heirby authorize yow, or ony fyve or four of yow, geving yow full power and commission to meitt and examyne the said Lord Balmerino, and to performe all other things whervnto yow war warranted by our said former Commission or letter, which we declaire heirby shalbe as sufficient as if the full number had mett : And if yow shall think fitt it is our pleasur lykwayes that yow requyre our Cheiff Justice to assist yow at the said re-examination wheranent thir presents shalbe a sufficient warrand.—Hampton Court, 20 Octo^r 1634.

The Names of the Commissioners which wer in the last Commission of the 5 May 1634 ar to be heir insert, 4 or 5 being the quorum, and the rest as it is in that other Commission.

To the Exchequer.

Right, &c.—Wheras for the increase of our manufactoreis within that our kingdome, and speciallie for provision of schipping, we gave ane patent to Davide Jonkene and Patrik Wood, merchandis of Ed^r, for bringing in of workmen from forrane parts, for making of Cabell and Takell within our said kingdome ; And in regard that work is both necessarie, and will conduce much to our service and the publict good of our subjects, therby furnisching convenientlie at all occasions the schipping of that our kingdome with sufficient provision, which now they ar forced to bring from forrane parts, from whence they ar often restrayned in the exportation therof, to the great damage of our schipping, sieing this work as we ar certanlie informed cannot be vndertakin without great charges and panes to the patentels and ther assotiats . It is our pleasur that furthwith yow exped the said patent vnder your handis, and for the better encouragement to prosecute the said work, yow grant vnto them such immunitie of custome for the materialls imported to them for that work, and for what cables and takline made by them shalbe exported to forrane parts, and that for so many yeires as yow in your judgment shall think fitt, wherby they may be the more readie and willing to vndergoe the said work.—Dat. vt supra.

To the Deputie of Irland.

We wer pleased tuo yeires since to requyre our Vice Thesaurer of that our kingdome to pay vnto Wm Hay, esquyre, the sowme of 500 Lib. stg., furth of the fynes and doubled rents of our province of Vlster, wherof accordinglie the payment being commenced, ther followed a generall restraynt of all moneyis till such tyme as that kingdome wer able to bear ther owin charge ; whervpon the said William, searching efter some extraordinarie casualitie, hopeing out of it to be payed, and haveing fund, as he affirmes, at his owin charge and industrie certane concealed moneyis dew vnto ws, he now requeists that out of the first that hath or salbe receaved therof, he may retene 250 Lib. for being a moytie and residue vnpayed of his first warrand : We therfor, calling to mynd the speciall occasion of our service wherupon that money was by Sir Alex^r Hayes and him disbursed, and withall allowing the equitie of his requeist, have therfor thoght fitt to recommend vnto your care his speedie payment furth ather of these conceilled moneyis by him brought in, or any other casualitie which yow in your judgm^{nt} and convenience of our affaires ther shall think fitt : Wherin not doubting of your conformitie to this our pleasur, we bid, &c.—Hampton Court, 20 Octo^r 1634.

Writtin be Sir James Galloway at his Ma^{teis} command.

To the Session.

Right, &c.—Wheras the deanrie of the Cathedrall Church of St Geills in that our citie of Edinburgh not being confirmed in Parliament, and as (for the better establisching of the samyne in the priviledge and benefite therto belonging) we intend at the nixt ensueing Parliament in that our kingdome : These ar seriouslie to recommend vnto yow that if any action or caus in Law shallhappin to cum befor yow in behalff of our trustie Mʳ James Hannay, present deane, or any of the prebenders, befor the confirmation, that yow grant vnto him or them all lawfull and speedie favour yow can in recoverie of what shalbe fund dew vnto that deanrie and prebends or in defence of ther lawfull rights; and in the meane tyme, for ther better securitie, Our pleasur is, that yow mak ane act in your books of sederunt heirvpon, in the most sure and favorable termes yow can conceive, for securing the right of the said deanrie and prebends in ther rents and benefice belonging vnto them, which we will tak as acceptable service done vnto ws,—Hampton Court, 20 Octoʳ 1634.

To the Thesaurers.

Wheras we ar crediblie informed that our trustie Mʳ James Hannay, deane of Edⁱ, hath, as we requyred him, interteyned at his owin charge the service of the organe since our returne from that our kingdome ; and being vnwilling that he be a loser for so good service, or that that service should desert in tyme cuming by want of maintenance, Our pleasur is, that yow repay vnto him what vpon just accompt he hath debursed therin, and that the persones neidfull for that service be heirefter honestlie provydit according as we spok vnto yow ; and being informed that the said Deane hath not as yit receaved full payment of the moneyis disbursed be him at our speciall direction for repairing the Church of Halyrudhous, it is our further pleasur that yow repay the same vnto him, with the Interest thairof, at mertimes ensueing.—Hampton Court, 20 Octoʳ 1634.

To the Session.

Right, &c.—Wheras ane ordinarie place in the Session doeth vaik at our gift and dispositioun by the death of Sir Andro Hamiltoun of Reidhous, vnderstanding the qualificatioun of Wⁿ Elphingstoun, we have made choyse of him to succeid in that place : Therfor it is our pleasur that yow receave and admitt him in the ordinarie place of Session, and tak his oath as is accustomed, and to be pertaker of all your contributions.—Hamptoun Court, 20 Octoʳ 1634.

To the Archbischop of Sᵗ Androis and Edinburgh.

Right, &c.—Wheras vpon approved informatioun of the learning, good conversation, and conformitie of Mʳ John Home, batchler in divinitie, who is desyreous to setle himsellf in that kingdome, we did, by our letter in the tyme of the late bischop of Edinburgh, signifie our pleasur that vpon the first vacancie of any church at our gift within ather of your dyoc*eis, fitt for ane of his abiliteis, or such as he should be willing to embrace, a signed presentatioun thairof might be sent vnto ws to be granted to him, the doeing whairof hath hitherto been deferred : Now, to the end he be not longer frustrat of our gratious intention towards him, we ar heirby pleased again effectuallie to recommend vnto yow that whenever vacancie of any church at our gift within ather of your dyocⁱs, yow tak care to give him notice of the first, that he shalbe willing to accept, that yow signe and send to ws with diligence a presentatioun to be returned for his vse : Whairof not doubting, &c.—Hampton Court, 28 Octoʳ 1634.

To the Session.

Right, &c.—Being informed that our late dear father, of worthie memorie, did grant vnto ane Andro Sinclair a gift of some part of the church revenues, to the end it might be recovered for the vse of our chapell royall, and that the said gift is lyklie to be made vnvsefull by our late gift therof procured by the burgh of Elgin, wherby our said father's pious intentioun therin is lyk to prove ineffectuall for remedie, whairfor we ar heirby pleased to recommend to yow that vpon dew consideratioun had of any processe and action intented or to be intented befor yow by the said Sinclair, or any other in behalff of that chapell, for reduceing the said last gift, yow not onlie proceid in your administrating speedie justice therin, bot in all other causses that shalhappin to com befor yow concerneing that chapell, which we will tak as acceptable service done vnto ws.—Hampton Court, 29 Octo^r 1631.

To the Exchequer.

Right, &c.—Being informed that the burgh of Elgin is about to exped a new gift vnder our sealls of some church revenues formerlie granted by our late royall father to ane Andro Sinclair for the vse of our Chapell royall. It is our pleasur that, if the said new gift be not alreadie exped, yow stop the passing thairof, and that yow vse your best endeavours for settling of these revenues according to our royall father his gift granted thervpoun, wherin yow will doo ws acceptable service ; for which these presents shalbe your warrant.—Dat. vt supra.

To the Archbischop of Glasgow.

Right, &c.—Wheras we ar informed that our right, &c. the E. of Annandale is not as yet setled with the ministers of such churches as ar within the boundis belonging to him, and lykwayes that the said Erle is readie to performe all that in reasone can be expected from him vnto them, We have thoght good, out of our particular respect of the said Erle, and in regard of the willingnes he expresseth to submitt himselff to your arbitriment in any thing that salbe requisit for him to performe heirin, to recommend him and the setling of the matters between him and the saids ministeris vnto your care and favour, which we expect with such convenieneie as may be : We bid, &c.—Whythall, 3 No^r 1634.

To the Session.

Right, &c.—We wer formerlie pleased by our letter the 2 of May last to recommend to your care the mediating with the Erle of Airth his creditours and cautioners for a prorogatioun of the reversioun of his estate, and that in regard that, as we ar informed, the pairteis wer sufficientlie secured of his estate and the annualrents dewlie satisfeit, and efterwards hearing that the said pairteis wer proceiding in rigour against him for the strict advantage of the Law, we gave ordour for present payment to him of a sowme of money out of our Exchequer, by which we intended the better to enable him for ther satisfaction, and withall leist in the meanetyme he might have suffered irrevocablie if the preceis poynt of the Law had decyded against him befor the present help we intended for him had taken effect, akweill for ther satisfaction as for his releiff, we wer pleased to desyre by our letter 14 July a stay of the processe ; bot being now informed that the saids cautioners and his creditours, haveing convened befor yow, war and yit ar content to give obedience to the desyre of our said first letter, and to prorogat the reversion, the ground and conditions thairof being performed to them by the said Erle, it is our pleasur that yow proceid, without any further delay, to administer justice vnto them in any action or caus whatsoever depending or to be intended at ther instance against the said Erle, to the end they may recover payment of ther just debts and releiff of ther distresses, according to ther rights and the lawes of that our kingdome : Yit in regard we have presentlie renewed our warrandis for the said Erle his speedie payment of what we have bene pleased to allow for his help, and that we desyre the standing of that house and estate in so far as it may consist without the prejudice and losse of these to whom it stands presentlie engadged, we cannot bot earnestlie recommend vnto your care that the reversion of the said Erle his estate may be prorogated, according to the desyre and conditions of our said first letter, for such tyme as yow shall think reasonable efter tryell taken by yow of the rentall and worth of his Landis : We bid, &c.—Whythall, 5 No^r 1634.

To the Counsell.

Right, &c.—Vnderstanding the abiliteis and affection to our service of our right trustie, &c. William, Lord Alexander, and being willing, for his better encouragement and enabling for our service heirefter, to promove him to be ane of our privie counsell of that our kingdome : It is our pleasur that, haveing administred to him the oath accustomed in the lyk caices yow admitt him vpon our said Counsell as one of your number ; ffor which, &c.—Hampton Court, 5 No^r 1634.

Our Soveraigne Lord, with speciall advyse, &c., Ordeanes a Letter to be made vnder the privie seall of the said kingdome of Scotland to Robert Walker, serjant to his Ma^{teis} Buckhounds, ratifieing and approveing, and for his highnes' and successours perpetuallie confirmeing, lykas his Matie, with advyse and consent forsaid, and now, efter his highnes' revocatioun made in the late parliament holdin be his Matie in persone within the said kingdome in the moneth of Junij 1633, does heirby ratifie and approve, and for his highnes and successours, with advyse and consent forsaid, confirme a gift of a locall assignement granted to the said Robert by his Ma^{teis} late dear father, of worthie memorie, to certane victuall and other things, viz.— Fourtie bolls of Oatts to be vplifted of the best and readiest ducties payed to his Matie for the Ketle, in Fyff, Thrie darg of hay, thrie darg of peitts, a buck in the seasone, and a doe in winter out of the Park of Falkland, with the pasturage and gressing of tuo horsses in the said Park, as the said gift, being of the dait at Hampton Court the 26 of Septr 1614 yeres, is particularlie expressed : And now his Matie, for the said Robert his better securitie and readie payment of the said yeirlie rent and others aforsaid, without distracting of him in performeing his Ma^{teis} service in his charge, and in regard of his long and faythfull service done to his Ma^{teis} said late father long befoir his first vpcomeing to the Croun of this his Ma^{teis} kingdome of England, and of his long and faythfull service done ever since both to his Matie said royall father and to himself, and for his better encouragement and enabling to continew in the lyk good service heirefter : Therfoir his Matie, with speciall advyse and consent forsaid, Gives, grants, and dispones of new to the said Robert Walker, all the dayes of his lyftyme, the saids Fourtie bolls of Oatts, to be vplifted and receaved by him yeirlie out of the best and readiest of his Ma^{teis} rents, dewteis, and fermes of the Kettell, in Fyff, thrie darg of hay, thrie dairg of peitts, a buck in the seasone, and a doe in winter out of the Park of Falkland, with licence to the said Robert to have tuo horsses pastured and gressed therin, the saids oatts, hay, peitts, and venisone to be vplifted and the saids horsses grassed as said is yeirlie and each yeir, wherof the first to be and begin . . . and so furth yeirlie dureing all the dayes of his lyftyme : Commanding heirby his said Ma^{teis} Thesaurer, and others officers for the tyme being whom it doeth concerne, to caus thankfullie payment to be made to the said Robert dureing his said lyftyme of the saids dewteis and others aforsaid, which shalbe thankfullie allowed in ther compts, commanding lykwyse the Lords of counsall and session to grant his Ma^{teis} other letters in forme as efferes, to charge whatsoever persone or persones whom it concernes for payment of the saids dewteis, and his enjoying of the others particulars above expressed, And that the said Letter be extendit with all clausses neidfull.—Gevin at his Ma^{teis} Court at Whythall, the 7 No^r 1634.

To the Thesaurer Deputie.

Right, &c.—Vpon petition from the tennents of late Mr Wm Kellie concerneing Eistbarnes, parcell of our Lordship of Dunbar, now in ther possession, we have, with advyse of our Thesaurer and Chalmerlane of that Lordship, condescended to give vnto any of them that will tak presentlie the benefite of our offer, for ilk chalder of bear or wheat promiscuouslie, so it be mercatt mett, 2000 merks, and that ather in readie money or sufficient securitie befor they ather surrander ther right or relinquish the possession: These ar therfor to requyre and authorize yow to transact accordinglie with all of them that ar willing, bot furthwith John Ramsay and Cornelaus Inglis, who for ther owin shares have agreid heir to this proportion, and for so doeing these shalbe your sufficient warrant; so not doubting of your care and diligence.—Whythall, 10 No^r 1634.

Presentatioun for Mr George Johnstoun to the church of Linton.
Presentatioun for Mr John Hamilton to the church of Eskdaill.—Whythall, ij. No^r 1634.

To James Home.

Trustie, &c.—Wherns we wer formerlie pleased to signifie to yow, that considering the trouble and inconveniences that might ensue if we should hearken to ane appeal (as we have bene desyred to doe by the Erles of Murray and Lawderdale in that proces depending concerning the Erldome of Home), we had rather thoght fitt that both pairteis should condescend vpon a submission to tuo or thrie weill affected on ather syd, and ane to be oversman (our self not being vnwilling to vndergoe the said trouble of oversman, both pairteis requeisting ws to it), whervnto we had the willing consent and approbatioun of the saidis Erles, in name of ther sones and daughters, demanding and expecting the lyk of yow, we ar still of the same mynd, and out of our earnest desyre to have that bussines fairlie composed, finding still that amicable course to be the best, we have thoght good to send vnto yow this submission, which we have sene and approve the conditions therof, that yow may subscryve the same, and therby taking away the ground of demanding ane appeall vnto ws, assureing yow that we shalbe verie carefull that the bussines be so fairelie caryed that nather pairtie may have just occasion to repent themsellis of following so freindlie a course: And expecting your performance heirof, we bid, &c.—Whythall, ij. No^r 1634.

To the Session.

Right, &c.—Humble remonstrance haveing bene made to ws by our trustie and weilbelovit Archibald Hay, gentlman vsher to our dear Consort the Quene, that he is vnjustlie sued befor yow by one Wm Tailzeour, who (as we ar informed) taketh the advantage of his absence pressing a spedie determinatioun in his action to cutt off that tyme which necessarlie our said servant should vse for haveing of witnesses and produceing of good evidences for clearing the treuth of that clause, as by the enclosed petition yow will perceave: We are heirby pleased to recommend vnto yow the consideratioun therof, granting to our said servand for the saids respects till the tyme of the nixt summer session for his compeirance: and in the meane tyme that yow examyne the said W^m and such witnesses as shalbe produced befor yow, receaveing ther depositions and answeris vpon oath to such severall interrogatoreis as shalbe demanded of them, to the end that against that tyme the cause may be made the more clear, and prepared for a full hearing and determinatioun, According as it shalbe fund in equitie to requyre.—Whythall, 11 No^r 1634.

H   3 D

To the Thesaurer.

Right, &c.—Wheras we have gevin ordour to our trustie and weilbeloved Counsellour Sir Thomas Hope, our Advocat, to draw vp a surrender of the erected pryorie of St Androis to be made by our right, &c. James, Duik of Lennox, inheritour of the said erected pryorie in our favours ; and wheras our said Advocat (as we ar informed) did acquyre from Lodovick, late Duik of Lennox, the right of the Lands and Tythes of the baronie of Kynmonth and tythes of Ardrydie in 1619, whervpon (as we ar lykwayes informed) our said Advocat was infeft in these lands and tythes by our vmquhill dear father, which is ratifeid in our late parliament holdin by ws within that our kingdome : Therfoir it is our speciall pleasur that the saids lands and tythes perteneing to our said Advocat be omitted furth of the said surrender or exceptit from it in such maner as shalbe fund requisit.—Vt supra.

To the Archbischop of St Androis.

Right reverend father, &c.—Wheras we have gevin ordour to our trustie and weilbeloved counsellour Sir Thomas Hope, our Advocat, to draw vp a surrender of the erected pryorie of St Androis to be made by our right, &c. James, Duik of Lennox, inheretour of the said erected pryorie in our favours : And wheras our said Advocat (as we ar informed) did acquyre from Lodovick, late Duik of Lennox, the right of the Landis and tythes of the baronie of Kynmonth and tythes of Ardryde in anno 1619, whervpon (as we ar lykwayes informed) our said Advocat was infeft in these landis and tythes by our vmquhill dear father, which is ratifeid in our late parliament holdin by ws in that kingdome ; and intending our said Advocat should have also much favour as aney have had in that kynd, and not be prejudged of aney thing which is due vnto him, we have sent yow heirwith ane enclosed warrant, direct to our, &c. the Erle of Traquair, that in caice yow find the premisses to be trew, as we ar informed, yow sie these Lands and tythes perteneing to our said Advocat accordinglie omitted or excepted from the said surrender : Which recommending, &c.—Whythall, ij. No^r 1634.

To the Session.

Right, &c.—Though we have often and diverse yeires agoe signifeid vnto yow to putt a finall determinatioun, acording to Justice, to that action of reduction of Cragievar's infeftment, alledged to have bene surreptitiouslie procured from ws in the begining of our Regne : In regard we wer therby much prejudged in diverse particulars which wer principall subjects of our royall intention in our late revocatioun, as the case of the vassalls, reduceing of laik patronages to our Croun, and the lyk, notwithstanding the same is not as yit determined nor account made to ws of the caus of the delay, we have therfor thoght fitt heirby to requyre yow of new that with all diligence the said action be putt to a finall determinatioun, according to justice and our Lawes, or to report to ws a reasone of the stay thairof : To which purpois, haveing Commanded our Advocat to insist for our entress, we will expect in yow readie obedience to our princelie desyre heirin : We bid yow farewell.—Whythall, the 11 No^r 1634.

To the Advocat.

Trustie, &c.—Wheras we have writtin of new to James Home of Coldinknowis, haveing sent the submission drawn vp by yow enclosed in our letter vnto him to be subscryved by him, for the better setling of the things questioned tuitching the estat of the Erldome of Home, least the bussines should miscarie or be delayed ; We, out of the trust we repois vpon your diligence and affection to our service, ar heirby pleased to entrust to your care the speedie delyverie of the said letter conteneing the said submission vnto the said James Home, willing yow to returne with diligence his answer vnto ws tuitching his resolutioun and the course he shalhappin tak heirin : For which these presents, &c.—Theobald's, 13 No^r 1634.

To the Advocat.

Trustie, &c.—Wheras we ar informed that great misdemeanours and offences ar of late committed in the midlschyres of these our kingdomes, the malefactours of the ane scheltring them selfils in the other, so that ther hopes of impunitie begett in them a boldnes of offending, for punisching whairof and better preventing the lyk heirefter we have, according to the lyk lawdable custome of our late royall father, gevin commission to certane of our trustie and weildisposed subjects of both kingdomes, as yow will perceave by the enclosed list of ther names, for sieing our peace preserved and justice executed in these parts : To which purpois it is our pleasur that yow draw vp a Commission of the Midleschyres, inserting these names within it, and that according to any precedent in the lyk kynd, or as yow by advyse of our Privie Counsall shall find necessarie for repressing these present disordours, and preventing the lyk in tyme cuming, and therefter that yow ather immediatlie exped it vnder our cachet and great seall, for which these shalbe vnto yow and all others whom it doeth concerne a sufficient warrant ; otherwayes, if yow find a necessitie, that yow send it to ws with all diligence, that we may signe and returne it bak for passing our said seall : And to the end yow may the better perceav our royall intention tuitching the taking of the lyk course heir, we have directed that a just coppie of the Commission to be exped heir to be sent vnto yow : All which we recommend to your care, and bid yow farewell.—Whythall, 17 No^r 1634.

To the Counsell.

Right, &c.—Wheras we ar informed that Alex^r Hamilton, younger of Lawfeild, being deiplie engadged in debt for his father, of whois estate he had never any benefite, and being forced for dangers of arreists to keip himself privat, is therby disabled from taking aney course ather for his owin releiff or satisfaction of the Creditours, wherby they ar lyk to suffer prejudice, and his estate lyklie altogidder to perisch : We, pitieing the distressed estate of the gentlman, ar heirby pleased to recommend him vnto yow that he may have libertie for one yeir to cum in publict for setling his affaires, provydeing he pay the annuells of all such debts as ar particularlie his owin, and not originallie contracted by his father : We bid, &c.—Whythall, 20 No^r.

To the Counsell.

Right, &c.—Wheras by the inclosed petition, as yow will perceave, we ar informed of diverse sinistrous practeises tending to the hinderance and secludeing of our Ordinances tuitching the sale of tabacco in that our kingdome : Our pleasur is, that not onlie in the poynts of that petition, bot generallie in all thingis which our Commissioners shall from tyme to tyme reasonablie desyre, yow give them your readie assistance for advancement of that our service, and punischment of all such as directlie or indirectlie shalbe fund to transgresse, that we may nather be disappoynted of the benefite to aryse therby vnto ws nor our loveing subjects of the good of the intended reformatioun ; wherin expecting your serious care, as yow will doo ws acceptable service, &c.—Whythall, 20 No^r 1634.

To the Archbischop of S$_t$ Androis.

Right, &c.—Haveing bene humblie petitioned by Sir George Gordoun of Gicht, kny^t, that in regard his not being capable to persew or defend any of his lawfull actions in that our kingdome, by reasone of the censure he lyeth vnder, as he sayeth, for his not conformitie in religion, we would be pleased to extend our royall favour towards him by enabling him for that effect; To which purpois (as we ar informed) our late dear father did wryt ather to yourself or to the bischop of the dyocie wher he lived, wherby dureing the lyff of our said dear father he was out of that danger vnder which he is now; and being lykwyse informed that he giveth no publict scandell, nor practizeth to prevent any others, we ar the more willing to desyre your advyse which way we may best grant him the favour he desyreth in the estate he now standeth, and that without making it a preparative to others : Expecting your answer heirin, we bid yow farewell.—Whythall, 20 No^r 1634.

Mr Maull procured this letter.

It is our pleasur that, by vertew of your office yow have of ws as M^r and Comptroller generall of our posts of England, yow authorize and requyre for the good of our service all the posts in the roade from London to Berwick to answer and send to our Court all such packetts and letters as they shall receave vnder the subscription of James Prymrois, Clerk of our Counsell of Scotland : For which, &c.—Whythall, 20 No^r 1634.

To Charles, Lord Stanehop, Master and Comptroller generall of all
our Posts of England.

To the Erle of Erroll.

Right, &c.—We perceave by your letter vnto ws your affection to our service in your readie embraceing the charge we have bene pleased to committ vnto yow in the tryell of the Lord Balmerino, in the prosecution wherof as we doubt not bot yow will carie your self fairlie and justlie according to the lawis of that our kingdome, so we ar confident yow will advert carefullie to any thing that may tend to the clearing of that bussines which doeth so neirlie concerne ws : Which recommending vnto your care, &c.—Whythall, 20 No^r 1634.

To the Advocat.

Trustie, &c.—We have sene the effects of your judicious care in the dittay yow have formed concerneing the late seditious lybell, for the which we give yow hartie thanks : And sieing now the tryell of the Lord Balmerino is immediatlie to goe on, we have thoght good heirby seriouslie to recommend vnto your care the continuance of the prosecution of that bussines that doeth so neirlie concerne ws in that kynd as may best tend till the full clearing of it, which we will tak as acceptable service done vnto ws : We bid, &c.—Whythall, 20 No^r 1634.

To Sir Johne Hay.

Trustie, &c.—Haveing signed latelie a Commission to the Erle of Erroll for judgeing in the case of the Lo$_r$ Balmerino, and the tyme appoynted for it being now so neir at hand, we have thoght good heirby to recommend vnto yow the continuance of your accustomed diligence in adverting to everie occasion may occure in a thing so neirlie concerneing ws, which we will tak as acceptable service done vnto ws : We bid, &c.—Whythall, 20 Noʳ 1634.

To the Erle of Traquair.

Right, &c.—According to your last desyre, we did presentlie signe the Commission sent vnto ws, and we give yow hartie thanks for the continewance of your diligent care, which we have approved from the beginning, in that particular which so neir concernes ws, the serious prosecution wherof we doe still earnestlie recommend vnto your care, in all yow can conceave may conduce to the cleiring of it, expecting a speedie account of your accustomed diligence heirin ; we bid, &c.—Whythall, 20 Noʳ 1634.

To the Toun of Edinburgh.

Trustie, &c.—Hearing of a great inconveniencie to the lights of your Church of Sᵗ Geills by meanes of our seat therin, it being interposed betwixt the window and the pulpitt, it is our pleasur that yow furthwith caus remove the same, that it be no more impediment in that kynd, for which these shalbe your warrand.—Whythall, 20 Noʳ 1634.

To the Shirreff of Aberdene.

Trustie, &c.—Wheras we have directed the enclosed letter (wherof yow shall heirwith receave a copie) to our bailleis and Counsall of Aberdene, These ar to will yow to mak speedie delyverie therof, and accordinglie that yow report vnto ws or to our Clerk of Register the performance of the same, that we may accordinglie tak such course as is most fitt for our service : Which recommending, &c.—Whythall, 20 Noʳ 1634.

To the Counsell.

Right, &c.—Wheras at the tyme of our late parliament holdin in that kingdome we wer pleased to remitt to yow a petition then exhibited tuitching some insolenceis bursting out of the hiclands, and some of the northerne parts thairof, to which purpois we have since writtin vnto yow at severall tymes, and now being crediblie informed that such insolenceis and troubles ar cum to a greater hight, to the great hurt of our good and peaciable subjects, and to the great contempt of our authoritie and lawis, we ar heirby pleased agane to seriouslie recommend vnto your care to sie our acts of parliament tuitching the repressing of such disorders putt in dew and tymelie executioun, and to omitt nothing that may curb the same, ather by meanes of the executioun of these acts, or as yow shall think most fitt to conduce to that purpois, wherby our peace may be preserved and all our good subjects fred of greater troubles and farder feares in that kynd, assureing that from tyme to tyme vpon your adverteisment we wilbe ayding and assisting vnto yow in what may concerne that purpois.—Whythall, 20 Noʳ 1634.

To the Thesaurers.

Wheras we have at sindrie tymes signifeid our pleasur that Sir Hugh Wallace of Cragie, knyᵗ, be payed of these moneyis condescended vpon for the heretable offices which some yeires agoe he did surrender vnto our Croun : To which purpois haveing by our letter vnto yow in May last signifeid our pleasur at lenth, and whervpon yow and others of our Exchequer did returne a Letter vnto ws of the necessitie and equitie that he should be satisfeit without furder delay, it is our pleasur that, according to the said letter in May last, yow pay all these moneyis so dew vnto him, that we be not farder troubled in that purpois, and for, &c.—Whythall, 20 No^r 1634.

These ratifie to the Lady Ragamore a pension of 400 merks Scotts, to indure your Ma^{teis} pleasur.—Whythall, 23 No^r 1634.

To the Archbischops of S_t Androis and Glasgow.

Right reverend, &c.—Wheras we did formerlie wryt vnto our right, &c. the Lord Lorne to forbear the moveing of any contraversie in Law aganst the reverend, &c. bischop of Argyll to the Commissariot thairof, in regard it was ane ecclesiasticall jurisdiction, and could not convenientlie be exercised be ancy other then a spirituall persone, or such as had his power : Whervpon the said Lord haveing at this tyme humblie remitted vnto our consideratioun to tak what course therin we should think fitt, it is our pleasur that yow call both parteis befor yow, and examyne what right is pretendit by them to the said Commissariot, and therefter to certifie ws therof, togidder with your opinions tuitching the same, that we may give such further ordour therin as we shall find just caus.—Whythall, 2 De^r 1634.

To the Advocat.

Trustie, &c.—Wheras we wer informed that the office of the keiper of the table of Actions intended befoir the Colledge of Justice of that our kingdome is now vacand in our handis by the death of ane Bannatyne, who had the same by the gift of our late dear father, and we now intend to bestow it vpon a servant of ours, and his deputeis, Our pleasur is, that yow accordinglie draw vp and send vp with all diligence vnto our secretarie a blank signature thairof in dew forme, with all rights, priviledges, and casualiteis that hath bene at any tyme heirtofoir enjoyed ather by the said Bannatyne or ancy of his predicessours in that office ; and for your soe doeing, &c.—Whythall, 2 Decr 1634.

To the Exchequer.

Right, &c.—Wheras it hath bene latelie complaynned of vnto ws by the Erle of Mar that the Castell of Stirling is lyklie to prove ruinous for lake of reparatioun, haveing heard the lyk also of our other housses ther, and in regard (as we ar informed) the keipers of our Castells and palaces ther ar bund for the performance of some things towards the mantenance of them, which would exoner ws of some measur of that charge which we ar at yeirlie by Covenant with the M^{rs} of our Works ther, who (as we ar lykwayes informed) ar dissabled from the performance of ther dewtie by wanting a long tyme the meanes allowed by ws vnto them for that effect : Therfor, and for preventing the ruyn of our saids housses, Our pleasur is, that haveing called for the rights of the keipers of our housses for ther keiping of them, yow give such ordour vnto them as yow shall find expedient for the performance of what they ar bund vnto, and accordinglie abate such a proportionable share out of the yeirlie allowance which the Masters of our Works ar to have as shalbe fund dew to be performed by the saids keipers of our houses, or that yow alter or annulle the said bargane with our M^{rs} of Works in tyme cuming, as yow shall find just occasion, geving them first satisfaction for what is alredie dew vnto them, bot above all ye have a speciall care that these our housses be preserved in that maner as is fitting for the state of that our ancient kingdome; which speciallie recommending vnto your care, and expecting a speedie and exact account heirof from yow, we bid yow farewell.—Whythall, 2 Der 1634.

To the Earles of Murray and Lawderdale.

Right, &c.—Wheras for diverse wechtie considerations we have thoght fitt to have the differences tuitching the succession of Home submitted to the decision of tuo or thrie freindis to be choysen of ather syde, and in caice of ther variance, to be determinat by ane indifferent oversman that shalbe agred vpon by both pairteis: To which purpois we have sent to James Home, and willed him to subscryve, a forme of submission drawin vp by our Advocat, and sene and approvin by ws: Now, becaus (if it sould so fall out that the Arbiteris cannot setle it without ane oversman, which we forsie may be layed vpon ws, haveing govin way thervnto in caice of necessitie) we hold it fitt that the bussines be alse fullie debated and prepared as may be by the Arbiters befor it cum into the hands of aney oversman, We have thoght good therfor heirby to give yow notice of our pleasur that all pairteis subscryve that submission drawin vp by our Advocat, leaveing blank for the oversman, to schaw (hat we desyre (if it be possible) that it might be endit without him, bot at leist that things be drawin to such a neirues between yow, that the oversman's part may be the easier: Which trouble of oversman we our self will not be vnwilling then to vndergoe, according as in former letters we have declared, assureing yow that our care shalbe to sie things so fardie and impartiallie caryed for the good of both parteis as nather shall have just caus to repent ther obedience to this our desyre.—Whythall, 2 Der 1634.

To the President of the Session.

Trustie, &c.—Wheras we, vpoun informatioun latelie made to ws by the Creditours of the Erle of Airth, wer pleased to give ordour to our Colledge of Justice for proceiding in the processes and actions intented or to be intended aganst the said Erle at the instance of the saids Creditours, in respect that, as we ar informed, they ar willing to give obedience to our first letters writtin theranent, anent the prorogating of the reversioun, the grounds of our said letter being fulfilled vnto them by the said Erle; and sieing we remember weill that the meaneing of our first letter was that if the Creditours wer fullie secured in the lands and estate perteneing to the said Erle, and receaved payment of ther annual-rents, that the estate of the said Erle should be fred of the rigour intended by the Creditours to selle and distribute the samyne amongst themselfis, heretablie and irredimablie; and seing the said Erle hath affirmed vnto ws, upon his honour and credit, that his creditours standis fullie infeft and seased in his estate, and that he is willing and readie to lay doun to them ther annual-rents; Lykas we have govin ordour to our Thesaurer to pay to the said Erle for the vse of his creditours the sowme of Ten thousand punds sterling, togidder with fyve hundreth punds sterling yeirlie dureing the non-payment therof; we conceave that these things being performed vpon the part of the said Erle, that all actions which ar rigorouslie vrged by the saids creditours aganst the said Erle, which ar ather for selling or division of his Lands without redemption, or for dispossessing of him therfor, as long as he payeth the annual-rents, should surcease for some reasonable time: And therfor we have thoght good heirby to clear the trew meaneing of these our former letters, to the effect that if any doubt shall aryse theranent, that yow may have a care according to the intention of our former letters, if it be fund that the creditours standis lawfullie infeft in the whole lands and the estate perteneing to the said Erle; and if the said Erle performe his offer in making payment to his creditours of the annual-rents of the sowmes justlie awand vnto them, efter tryell to be takin by yow and the remanent Lordis of our Session of the just sowmes owing by him to them, that then ther be a stay and surcease made of the proces at the instance of the saids creditours aganst the said Erle, or his tennents, for selling or division of landis, or dispossessing him of the same for some reasonable tyme.—Dat. vt supra.

To the Bischop of Edinburgh.

Reverend, &c.—Haveing receaved a letter from the Archbischop of St Androis, your selff, and some others of the Clergie and our officers, tuitching the right of the patronage to the Church of Dunbar, and finding therby that our right, &c. the Erle of Roxbrugh standeth cled with a better right then is ordinarie in such cases, and being vnwilling to dispossess him or to hinder his possessioun till by dew course of Law his right be evicted : It is our pleasur that therefter yow admitt of his presentatioun to that church, and (in regard the charge thairof doeth now vaik) if yow find the persone to be presented by him able and qualifeid for such a place, that yow give him collatioun vpon the said Erle's presentatioun : Which speciallie recommending vnto your care, &c.—Whythall, 10 De^r 1634.

To the Toun of Aberdene.

Trustie, &c.—Wheras we ar informed of some seditious Convocatiouns practeised amongst yow, comeing, as we hear, especiallie from the election yow have latelie made of ane Patrik Leslie for your Provest, whom we wer informed to have wronged your trust in his cariage at our late parliament, and therfor to have deserved no such charge : And in regard we have alwayes formerlie found yow forward for our service, and accordinglie have dispensed our favours to yow in what might concerne your liberteis and privedges, now, being carefull of that which may concerne our service and the peace and weall of that our citie, in redressing of the abuses past, and preventing the lyk inconvenientis, it is our pleasur for that effect that yow remove the said Patrik Leslie from being your provest, and in his place we wish yow to mak choyse of Sir Paull Menzeis, who was formerlie in that charge : So not doubting of the performance of this our pleasur, we bid, &c.—Whythall, 10 De^r 1634.

To the Exchequer.

Right, &c.—Wheras we ar informed that ther is some question to aryse between the Erle of Annandale and the Lord Napeir tuitching halff a yeires dewtie of the 7000 merks scotts which at first wer deteyned from ws by the said Erle's meanes added to our revennes of Orknay, whervpon we bestowed the same vpon him for some tyme ; And wheras the said Erle affirmeth that the said dewtie doeth by our grant justlie belong vnto him, and that some yeres agoe he was desyred by the said Lord to accept thairof, which he than refuised by direction of some of our officers for the tyme, for cleiring of which question and preventing aney trouble to the said Erle tuitching that purpois yow (as we ar informed) ar the fittest persones and best vnderstanding the estate of our rents : Therfoir it is our pleasur, that yow examyne the premisses with the first tyme of our grant to the said Erle, and if ye find the dewtie so questioned to be comprehended within that tyme, and consequentlie to belong vnto him, that in our name yow recommend to the Session not to admitt of aney proces or sute in Law against him, or oney others in that behalff, or to dismisse the same if it be alreadie begun ; and as for aney preceiding dewteis of this kynd as yit vnpayed to ws by the said Lord, wherwith the lyk course ought to be taken for our satisfaction for the tymes preceiding as since our said grant, we will yow to examyne what is due vnto ws, that therefter we may give such farder ordour theranent as we shall think fitt.—Whythall, 10 De^r 1634.

To the Counsell.

Right, &c.—Wheras we ar crediblie informed that at the tyme ane Ritchart Fullerton, Collectour of our late taxationis of the shirrefdome of Aberdene, was imployed in that our service, he was violentlie assaulted, and to the hazard of his lyff beaten to the ground and wounded by ane Nicolsone, baillie of Aberdene for the tyme, and his complices : Though such a barbarous act had not bene directlie committed against ane particularlie authorized in our service, it had justlie moved ws to tak notice thairof by causeing inflict dew punischment vpon the offenders : Therfor it is our speciall pleasur that yow tak particular information of the proces or complaynt of the said Fullerton tuitching this purpois, and efter dew and speedie tryell, which we speciallie recommend vnto yow, if yow find the offence to be such as is affirmed, that yow so punish the offenders that others may be terrifeid from attempting the lyk heirefter : We bid, &c.—Whythall, the 10 of Dec̅ 1634.

To James Phymbois.

Trustie, &c.—Haveing at the humble requeist made vnto ws by our right, &c. the Erle of Stirling, our Secretarie, authorized yow with power to direct letters and packetts vnto our court for the more readie dispatch of the affaires of our Privie Counsell of that our kingdome, it is our pleasur, and we doe heirby will and requyre yow, that weiklie from hence furth, at each session of our said Counsell, yow give vnto our said Secretarie dew notice of all affaires treated of and dispatched therin, to the effect that at our conveniencie he may give ws trew accompt therof : We bid, &c.—Whythall, 10 Dec̅ 1634.

To the Bischop of Rapho.

Reverend, &c.—Wheras humble remonstrance hath bene made vnto ws in behalff of diverse persones in your leases in that bischoprik, that yow ar about to mak voyd ther leases, schawing withall that in regard they did expoise ther lyffis and meanes to hazard in being the first British planters who setled them selffis in these remote and then barbarous parts, being thervnto encouraged by letters patents of our late dear father for letting these lands vpon easie conditions, ther case should be more considerable then wher ther hath not bene the lyk hazard and trouble ; we ar so far furth pleased to tak notice of ther desyres as heirby to recommend vnto yow to be kynd vnto them, and heirin to vse such a moderat course as yow sall think fitt in a case of such consideratioun, which we will tak weill at your handis.—Whythall, 12 Dec̅ 1634.

To the Excheqver.

Right, &c.—Haveing receaved from such as wer appoynted Commissioners by ws for surveighing the estate of our Exchequer in August last ane accompt of all the debtis dew by ws in that our kingdome ; And intending to satisfie what is justlie owing as soone as the estate of our affaires will convenientlie permitt, as we have alreadie vnderstude our burdens, so we desyre lykwayes to know what will rest dew vnto ws, wherby we may defray the same, or at leist so much thairof as may convenientlie be payed : And therfor it is our pleasur that yow informe your selffis, with all diligence, what yow find or is lyklie to be fund resting, to be payed vnto ws, not assigned or disposed of alreadie, ather by taxatiouns, annuiteis out of tythes, yeirlie rent, or any other way ; and haveing condescended thervpoun, that yow presentlie therefter send ws vp ane accompt thairof, that haveing conferred that which is cum in vnto ws with that which we ar to give out as due by ws vnto others, we may give such ordour therefter as we shall think most fitt for our service.—Dat. vt supra.

The lynes following ar writtin with his Ma^{tein} owin hand in the principall letter, and vnder subscryved by his Matie :—

I must have ane exact accompt, that I may know both how weill I have bene served in the well managers of these last taxatiouns, and sic trewlie in whate state my revenew ther is, or is lyklie to be in heirefter.

C. Rex.

To the Excuequer.

Right, &c.—Though we have refuised to confirme the right of anie heretable keepers of our housses within that our kingdome, yit it is noway our purpois to mak them leave ther charge therof till it be done in a legall way, nor that any meanes be abstracted from them which was by our noble progenitours or our selffes allowed for that purpois; it is our pleasur that they still enjoy the rents, which ar allowed to them for keiping of our housses whairof they have the charge, as they formerlie did, so long as it is not evicted from them by course of Law, they alwayes performeing that which they ar bund to doe ather for keiping or for mantening of the saidis housses, for we have a speciall care that all our housses be keiped in good ordour and not suffered to decay.—Whythall, 12 De^r 1634.

To the Excuequer.

Wheras we ar informed of a bargane betweene our right trustie and weilbelovit cousen the Erle of Antrim and the Lord Kintyre tuitching the said Erle his purches of the lands of Kintyre; and being humblie sued vnto in behalff of the said Erle and the Lord Danluce, his sone, that a clause in the said Lord of Kintyre his securiteis of these lands, wherby it is provydit that they be not sold to aney of the Clandonald, may be noe hinderance to them to goe on in that bargane, We ar heirby pleased to declare that we doe dispense with that clause, provyded we be not heirby putt in worse caice tuitching aney thing concerneing these Landis then we wer befor the said bargane was made; and this signification of our pleasur shalbe a sufficient warrant tuitching this purpois to all whom it may concerne : We bid, &c.—Whythall, 13 De^r 1634

Charles, by the grace of God King of England, Scotland, France, and Irland, defender of the'fayth, &c., To all Mayors, Shirreffis, Justices of Peace, Vice-Admirallis, Searcheris, and all others our officeris whom it may concerne, and everie of them, Greeting—Wheras Mr Lodovick Alexander, sone of our right, &c. the Erle of Stirling, our Secretarie of Scotland, is to repair vnto France : These ar to will and command yow, and everie of yow, to suffer him to embark himsellf, with his tuo servandis and other necessarie provisions, at aney of our ports which shalbe convenient for his passage and journey, and no further; for which these presents, &c.—Whythall, 15 De^r 1634.

To the Counsell.

Right, &c.—Haveing bene latelie informed of the great disordours and ryotts committed in the northern parts, which insolent beginnings we would have to be repressed in tyme, and the offenders to be severlie punisched, as the course of Justise requyreth in the lyk caices; for which purpois we hear yow have alreadie charged the Landlords and cheiff of Clanes, and, amongst others, the Marqueis of Huntlie, for the name of Gordoun, of whome some, as we ar informed, have bene cheiff actours of these outrages, to compeir befoir yow, that ordour may be taken concerneing the same; and though we beleive that, as the said Marqueis professeth, he is not accessorie to the violence committed by diverse of his name, yit in regard it is presumed by some that if he is not guiltie of acting of it, at leist he might ather have prevented it at first or have taken a course for redressing of it in some meassur efterwards : Our pleasur is, that yow putt our Lawes in executioun aganst the saidis Landlords, cheiff of Clanes, and Marqueis of Huntlie, and all others whom yow have for that purpois cited, or shall think fitt to cite heirefter, according to the generall Law, or to aney ordour that our Lawes doe allow for that effect, whairof we will yow to be carefull, as yow wilbe answerable vnto ws for your diligence in a thing so neirlie concerneing ws in honour and justice and the generall good of that our kingdome.—Whythall, 16 De' 1634.

To the Session.

Right, &c.—It being fitt and necessarie for the good of our service that the extraordinarie place in our Session appoynted for our right, &c. the Erle of Stirling, our Secretarie for that our kingdome (who necessarlie must attend our service about our persone), be suppleid in his absence, and vnderstanding the abiliteis and affection to our service of our right trustie and weilbeloved counsellour the Lord Alexander, whom we hold fitt to supplie that place and charge ; It is our pleasur that, haveing administred vnto him the oath accustomed in the lyk caices, yow admit him to the said extraordinarie place in session, and that he enjoy all the priviledges and liberteis belonging thervnto ; for which these presents shalbe your warrant.—Hampton Court, 20 De' 1634.

To the Counsell.

Right, &c.—Wheras, by severall warrants to the Clergie of these our kingdomes, ther hath bene a carefull survey had of that Translatioun of the Psalmes whairof our late dear father, of happie memorie, was authour ; We now, being fullie resolved of the exactnes thairof, have determined no longer to delay the publict vse of them for the benefite of the Churche ; and to the end the first begining may be made in that our ancient kingdome, wher our said dear father, the Authour, was borne, according to our pleasur signifeid to that purpois to some of our Clergie ther, It is our pleasur (sieing we have alreadie gevin ordour for ane Impression of that Translatioun) that yow give present ordour in such maner as is requisit, that no other Psalmes of aney edition whatsoever be ather printed heirefter within that our kingdome or imported thither, ather bund by themsellfs or otherwayes, from aney forrayne port ; And that yow vse your best endeavours by all possible and lawfull meanes from tyme to tyme to assist our Clergie, and to sie these Psalmes receaved and sung in all the Churches of that kingdome.—[No date.]

To the Archbischop of S' Androis.

Right reverend, &c.—Wheras, by our severall warrants to the Clergie of both kingdomes, ther hath bene a carefull surveigh had of that Translatioun of the Psalmes whairof our late deare father, of happie memorie, was Authour ; And being now fullie certifeid of the exactnes of the same, we have determined no longer to delay the publict vse of them for the benefite of the church ; And to the end the first begining may be made in that our ancient kingdome, wher our said deare father, the Authour, was borne, It is our pleasur that, by the advyse of the remanent Clergie ther, or such as yow can convenientlie mak choyse of for the tyme, yow tak such course as the said new Translatioun may be practized in the Churches of that kingdome with such diligence as possible, and that in the meane tyme yow signifie our pleasur to all Printers, or others within that kingdome whome it may concerne, that no Psalmes books in meeter of the old translatioun be printed or brought in to be sold heirefter within the same, vnder pane of confiscatioun of ther books and punischment of ther persones; and if it neid be, that yow requyre such further warrant from ws or our Privie Counsall to that purpois as yow shall find expedient, &c.—Whythall, &c.— [No date.]

Sir James Carmichaell was appoynted to be admitted vpoun the Commission for Surrenders stylo ordinario.—Whythall, 23 Der 1634.

To the Archbischop of St Androis.

Right, &c.—Wheras humble sute hath bene made vnto ws in behalff of our right, &c. the Erle of Morton, that none be admitted to be preacher at the Church of Aberlour (which is now at our gift by the death of Mr Wm Paton, late minister ther) bot such a persone whois sufficiencie by your approbation may merite the said Erle his consent; sieing we ar crediblie informed that the said Erle's intention heirin is onlie to have ane able and sufficient preacher ther, it is our pleasur that by the advyse of the said Erle yow mak choyse of such a persone as yow and he shall best condescend vpon, he being by yow fund qualifeit for the same, and conforme to the Canons and ordours of the Church: And for your soe doing, &c.— Whythall, 22 Der 1634.

To the Counsell.

Right, &c.—Vnderstanding of the sufficiencie, long experience, and long affection to our service of the right reverend father in God our right trustie and weillbeloved Counsellour the Archbischop of St Androis, it is our pleasur that he succeid in the place of the late Erle of Kynnoull to be our high Chancellour; And that yow caus delyver vnto him the great seall of that our kingdome, to be keipit by him as our Chancellour, with all the benefites, priviledges, and immuniteis that hath belonged to that place heirtofoir, whervpon we will our Advocat to draw vp a gift of the same to be sent vnto ws.—Whythall, 23 Der 1632.

Our Soveraigne Lord, vpoun good consideratiouns of the sufficiencie and abiliteis of his Matie trustie and weilbeloved Sir Patrik Abercrombie, knyt, ane of his Matis gentlmen pensioners, to exercise and discharge the office of tabulating all summondis raised and to be raised in actions to be persewed befor the Lordis of Counsall and session, now vacand in his highnes' hands, by and throw the deceis of Mr Nicoll Bannatyne of Standandflatt, last tabuler and exercer and vser of the said office, haveing for the good of his service and his owin frie princelie knowledge and propper motive made choyse of him to supplie and discharge the same, ordanes a Letter to be made and exped vnder the privie seall of Scotland, making, constituteing, and ordeaneing, lykas his Matie by thir presents maks, constituts, and ordeanes the said Sir Patrik Abercrombie, dureing all the dayes of his naturall lyff, Tabuler of all summondis raised and to be raised in actions to be persewed befor the Lordis of Counsall and session, and grants vnto him the office thairof, with all feyis, casualiteis, dewteis, and priviledges belonging therto, with full and absolute power to him to mak, constitute, and creat deputts and substituts vnder him in the said office at his pleasur, for whome he shalbe hoblin to answer, and to vse and exerce the said office be himselff, his deputts, and substituts, with all feyis, dewteis, casualiteis, inmuniteis, and priviledges pertenceing thairto, sicklyk and als friclie in all respects as the said vmquhill Mr Nicoll Bannatyne or any of his predicessours in that office bruiked, joysed, vsed, or possesst the same at any tyme preceiding, and with all such feyis, dewteis, priviledges, and casualiteis whatsoever which hath bene anywayes knowen heirtofoir, or heirefter shalbe fund justlie to belong thervnto, and with all and sindrie others commoditeis, friedomes, frielie, quyetlie, weill, and in peace, but any revocation, or agane calling whatsoever; dischergeing and annulling, lykas his Matie by these presents discherges and annulls, all former gifts of the said office, or any power or libertie (if any be) granted to any persone whatsoever for vseing and exerceing the said office; Ordeaneing the saids Letters by these presents to be exped vnder the privie seall, without passing of any other sealls whatsomever, and with all clausses neidfull : Gevin, &c. vt supra, &c.—Quhythall, 21 Der 1634.

To the Commissioners for Tythes.

Right, &c.—Wheras we have bene petitioned by Mr Thomas Forrester, Minister at Melros, that we would be pleased to recommend vnto yow that he might have the benefite of ane act made befor yow concerneing his entrie to the augmentatioun of his stipend of that parochin, which augmentatioun is allowed vnto him (as he affirmeth) by a decreit arbitrall of the right reverend the Archbischope of Glasgow and our trustie the Erle of Hadinton, to whom the Modification of the Augmentation was submitted by mutuall consent of him and his parochiners: Our pleasur is, that yow consider of the inclosed petition, recommending vnto yow to grant vnto him the benefite of the said act according to the custome in the lyk caices.—Whythall, 30 Der 1634.

To the Exchequer.

Right, &c.—Wheras we ar pleased to grant a gift of the Abbacie of Inchefftray, tythes and superiorteis thairof, to vmquhill Charles Murray, sone of vmquhill Mr Patrik Murray, late Commendatour of that abbacie, and to his aires and assigneyis, redimable alwayes vpoun the sowme of twelff hundreth punds sterling, the respects of the father's long and faythfull service done vnto ws, and the present estaite of Patrik Murray, the brother and heyr of the said Charles (who hath no other meanes wherby to subsist, bot that grant from ws), moveing ws out of our accustomed princelie comiseration not to alter what we have formerlie granted in that behalff, speciallie since the redemption therof to our Croun is at all tymes in our power: It is our pleasur that yow caus exped vnder our cachet sealls to the said Patrik the lyk grant to his said brother, and accordinglie that he enjoy the benefite intended therby without oney innovation to be made tuitching the same from the said former gift; For which these presents salbe vnto yow, and others our officers whom it may concerne, a sufficient warrant.—Whythall, 30 Der 1634.

Our Soveraigne Lord ordeanes a protection to be made vnder his highnes' great seall of the kingdome of Scotland to his highnes' lovit Johne Kennedie, some tyme of Babquhan, making mention that wheras his Matie is crediblie informed that the said Johne Kennedie standeth engadged to diverse persones, his creditours, in diverse sowmes of money, which he would be able to pay vnto them with ther annual-rents, if so be that by ther leaveing of to prosecute him by Law and casting of him in prissone, if he wer permitted for some small tyme to follow his owin affaires, wherby to obtene the moneyis due vnto him, for the better enabling to give them speedie satisfaction, wherin his Matie, respecting the weill both of the creditours and debtours, of his authoritie royall, &c., stilo ordinario.—Whythall, last Der 1634.

To the Exchequer.

Right, &c.—Haveing vpon good considerationns determined not to have our Chancellour vpon the Exchequer, least it might be a hinderance to him to attend that charge, which may import our service in a greater measur, and haveing now made choyse of the right reverend father in God the Archbischop of St Androis for the said charge, and being fullie resolved to continew our resolution heirin, we ar heirby pleased that the place which he had in Exchequer shall heirefter ceise, till such tyme as we shalbe pleased to appoynt such a one for the same as we shall think most fitt.—Whythall, last Decr 1634.

To the Archbischop of St Androis.

Right, &c.—Haveing determined, as is knowen to yow, not to have our Chancellour vpon ane Exchequer, to the end it may be no hinderauce to him to attend that charge which doeth so much import our service, and haveing now made choyse of yow for the same, we ar heirby pleased to have your place in Exchequer to ceise, that yow may have no occasion to withdraw yow from attending the said charge, and that yow may the more narrowlie look to such things as from tyme to tyme shall cum to be passed vnder our great seall, to the effect we may be acquanted with aney thing which yow shall find necessarlie worthie of our consideratioun.—Whythall, last De^r 1634.

To the Counsell.

Right, &c.—Wheras we did formerlie wryit vnto yow that yow should tak into your consideratioun the fraud vsed by the sellers of playding in presenting thairof to the mercat in hard rolls, wherby vnder trust they deceave the buyers; and now vnderstanding that vpon good considerations yow have delayed our Commissioners of our frie brughs who did prosecute the rectifieing of the same befor yow vntill Ja^r nixt, it is our pleasur that at the said tyme, efter a trew tryell of the said abuse, yow caus such ane ordour be speedelie taken and punctuallie keipit that the said commoditie be sold at all tymes heirefter in oppin foldis, exposeing it to the full view of the buyer: so expecting all possible expedition heirin for the speedie dispatch of these Commissioners of our burrowis who shall attend the same, we bid, &c.—Whythall, last De^r 1634.

To Sir Ferdinando George, Kny^t.

Trustie, &c.—Haveing fund it of late necessarie that some good course be establisched for right prosecution of the work of the Plautation of New Scotland in such kynd as may be most for the advancement thairof and the encouragement of such as vndertak therin, And haveing (in regard of your affection and long endevours therin) bene pleased to mak choyse of yow for vndertaking the cheiff charge in manageing of such things as shalbe for the good of that cuntrie, and the governement to be establisched therin, we have thoglt good at this tyme to requyre yow, so soone as yow can convenientlie, to repair to our Court, that we may have your opinion, and yow receave our direction in such things we shalbe pleased to requyre and appoynt tuitching this bussines.—Whythall, 5 Ja^r 1635, stylo Anglicano.

To the Advocat.

Trustie, &c.—Humble sute hath bene made vnto ws in behalff of our Officers of the Coyne-house of that our kingdome, that we would be pleased to signe a ratification of ther priviledges and immuniteis granted vnto them by our royall progenitours: wherin, being willing to grant ther demand if nothing be added by ws of new bot what hath bene formerlie granted and confirmed vnto them, It is our pleasur that yow examyne the signatur sent vnto ws and ther former rights, and if yow find no materiall difference betweene them, that yow docat and returne it with all convenient diligence to be signed by ws ; otherwayes (if yow find it may be convenientlie done), that yow caus expeid it immediatlie vnder our cachat and scalls ; ffor which these presents salbe to yow, and our other officers whom it may concerne, sufficient warrant.— Dat. vi supra.

To the Commissioners for Tythes.

Right, &c.—Being informed by our right, &c. the Erle of Stirling, our secretarie for that kingdome, that he is desyreous to have the parische of Tullibodie disunited from the parische of Alloway (as formerlie it was), to the effect ther may be a new minister agane established ther, wher it hath bene a long tyme silenced ; desyreing lykwyse that, for the convenieneie of a greater mantenance for that purpois, the Landis of Menstrie and Gogar may be vnited to the paroch of Tullibodie, being all adjacent with it, and belonging to himselff, we cannot bot approve of his intention, and, for the encouragement of others to the lyk, grant him our favourable assistance for effectuating of it : And therfor we doe heirby speciallie recommend to your care that, haveing considered of his demands, yow grant all possible speedie furtherance for so good a work in the vniteing of these severall Lands for the re-establisching of that ministrie of Tullibodie, and that out of ther severall tythes yow allow such convenient mantenance as yow shall think fitting ; wherin expecting your diligent care, we bid yow fareweill.—Whythall, 5 Jar 1635.

A protection was granted to John Erskene, indueller in Monross, for the space of ane yeir, he paying alwayes to his creditours ther annual-rents.—Whythall, 7 Jar 1635.

A protection was granted to the Erle of Lythgow for the space of ane yeir efter the maner accustomed.—Whythall, 7 Jar 1635.

Our Soveraigne Lord, with speciall advyse and consent of his right trustie and right, &c. the Erle of Morton, and of John, Lord Traquair, his Matis Thesaurer principall and deputie of Scotland, and of the remanent Lordis and others of his Matis privie Counsall and Excheker of the said kingdome, Ordeanes a Letter to be made vnder the great seall, making mention that wheras his Matie is crediblie informed of the sufficiencie, great skill, and industrie of his Matis trustie and weilbelovit James Colquhoun, citizen of Glasgow, in working, casting, moulding, and frameing of all sorts of works of Lead, till not onlie for theiking, covering, strenthning, and decoreing of all sorts of housse work and structurs thervnto belonging, as weill for vse or ornament and decencie, as also of all conduit pypis for conducting and raising of watters raised for many necessarie vses, wherin his Matie is lykwyse informed that these many yeres the said James Colquhoun hath gevin such sufficient and approved testimonie of his skill within the said kingdome as few artificers in that kynd have done more exquisite and curious peices of work in any part of Europ : And wheras his Matie is lykwyse crediblie informed that the said James Colquhoun, by his long experience in searching out the secrets of that trad, hath fund out a peculiar way, never heirtofoir practized within the said kingdome, wherby he will mak a scheit of lead weying twelff stane weght to be more vsefull, of longer continuance, and to abyd greater extremiteis of wind and weather, nor aney scheit of lead vsed weyand heirtofoir weyand sextene stane weicht, in regard of his artifice of making thairof more solide, less poric, and consequentlie more voyd of all craks, holls, or popill, and speciallie in the exact squaring and proportioneing of the evennesse to the thiknes of the saidis scheits : Thairfoir, and that everie ane of his Matis subjects may be encouraged to invent and putt in practeis what is good for the comonweall not formerlie vsed or practized for the benefite therof, according to the laudable course observed by his Matis dear father, which was that everie ane of his Matis guid subjects might have the benefite of his owin inventioun, his Matie, with advyse forsaid, has gevin and granted, and by the tenour heirof, for him, his aires, and successours, gives and grants to the said James, his aires and assigneyis, and ther and ather of ther pertiners and deputeis whatsumever, full and absolute licence and power, dureing the space of 21 yeres nixt and immediatlie following the date of the passing of thir presents vnder the said seall, To cast, frame, and caus to be made framed and wrought all such scheits of Lead whairof ane weying tuelff stane wecht more vsefull and of longer continuance then a scheit weying sixtene weght, and so proportionable, and that for the vses aforsaid, with full and absolute power to the said James Colquhoun and his forsaids to work, frame, cast, and putt in practeis the works of his said Inventioun of the scheits of Lead so to be vsed by him, and to apply the benefite aryseing therof to ther owin propper vses as they shall think fit, without trouble, lett, or molestation whatsoever, and the kingdome being all served with that commoditie at such reasonable rates as they can afford, To sell, exchange, and vent the same in all forrayne parts being in league and freindschip with his Matie: And his highnes perfectlie vnderstanding how hurtfull it might prove to the said James and his foirsaids, if efter so long tyme, travells, charges, and panes vndergone by him in searching out of the said way in making of the said commoditie more good and vsefull for the common good then heirtofoir it hath bene, aney other persone or persones than he or his forsaids should intent or cast, frame, mak vse of, dispose, or sell the commoditie, his Matie doeth therfoir expreslie prohibite and discherge all and whatsumever persones within the said kingdome, dureing the said space of 21 yeires, to cast, frame, work, or practeis the said Inventioun, or aneywayes to dispose, sell, exchange, or vent any work made therof by them, without the said James or his forsaids speciall warrand, licence, and power first had and obtenit therto; with power to the said James and his deputeis, partiners, servands, and others in ther names, to search, find out, apprehend, and sease vpoun the said Inventiouns, ther toolis, structuris, and modells made for that vse, and to tak the same from the saidis persone or persones not authorized as aforsaid, or from aney others in whois custodie they ar knowen to be, to be vsed and disponed vpon at the pleasur of the said James and his forsaids; and with expres command to the Lordis of his Ma^teis privie Counsall and Exchcker now for the tyme to cause punish and censure the saidis transgressours by imprissonement, fyneing, and otherwayes as they shall think fitt, wherby the said James and his forsaids may enjoy the full benefite of his Inventioun dureing the space foirsaid according to his Ma^teis gratious intentioun heirby expressed: And his Matie doeth heirby also will and requyre the saidis Lordis of privie Counsall and Exchcker, and the Lordis of Session, to direct letters of horning to charge all schirrellis, provests, bailleis of burghs, and others his Ma^teis officers whatsumever, to ayde and assist the said James and his forsaids in searching, seasing vpon, and confiscating of the saidis works, inventiouns, toolis, instruments, modells made for the same, the one-halff of the benefite aryseing by the vse or sale thairof to be applyed to his Ma^teis vse, and the other halff to the vse of the said Sir James and his forsaids: And with speciall command to the saidis officers, and everie of them, to search and apprehend and punish the saidis transgressours as the saidis Lordis of Counsell shalbe pleased to appoynt, as the saidis officers and everie of them will answer the contrarie at ther highest perrellis: And it is heirby speciallie provydit, that if within the space of thrie yeires nixt and immediatlie following the date heirof the said James nor his forsaids, nor nane of them, shall not putt in practeis the said inventioun for the publict good, then thir presents to be voyd and of non effect: Onlaneing the said Letter to be writtin to the great seall, and exped vnder the same without passing any other seall or register, for which these presents shalbe a sufficient warrand to the keeper thairof and writen therto.—Gevin at his Ma^teis Court at Whythall, the 7 Ja^r 1635.

May it pleas your most Excellent Matie—

    These licence James Colquhune, his partiners, &c., for 21 yeires to mak vse for the publict good of a New Inventioun of his, wherby scheits of Lead and conduit pypes, heirtofoir mould and cast for publict au t privat vsses, may be reduced to a lesser proportion of weght and made more vsefull and of longer continuance : Others ar discharged, vnder pane of confiscatioun of ther works and tools, wherof the one half of the forfalture is to cum to your Matie, the other to them : The transgressours to be censured as the Counsall shall think fitt : The cuntrie being served with that commoditie at reasonable rates, the patentees may sell it abroad : If the Inventioun be not practized for the publict good within thrie yeres efter this date these presents to be voyd.—STERLINE.

The Conjunct Commission of the borders of Scotland and England drawin vp by your Ma^tris warrand, to endur ay and whill your Matie declare your pleasur vnder the privie seall or great seall of Scotland in the contrair, and signed by your Matie.—Whythall, 7 Ja^r 1635.

May it pleas your Matie—

Your Thesaurer principall doe heirby lett for fyve yeires to William Dick, his aires and assigneyis, of no higher degrie nor himselff, the Customes of all goods (the Imposts of wyne and customes of Orkney and Zetland excepted) imported and exported from Scotland, with the Custome of the vnlawfull and prohibited goodis imported or exported, or fund wrongfullie entred or not entred : They ar to pay the one half to your Matie, the vther for ther owin vse.

For which thay ar, vpoun certane provisions and penalties, to pay yeirlie to your Matie 60,000^lib. Scotts, at four termes in the yeir abovementionat, with 20,000 merkis Scotts as grassum.

Thay ar not to allow of any oversight in the transporting of vncustomed goodis so prohibited to be imported or exported, and to confiscat them, the half to your Matie, the other for themseltlis : In cace dureing the prohibition any licence shalbe granted for importing or exporting aney goodis so to be prohibited, they shalbe comptable in Exchequer for the customes therof.

They ar yeirlie to give vp true accompt of all Inglish beir imported and sold at dear rates ther, 18 penneyis Scotts the pynt, that the fynes may be levied to your Matie : If licence be granted dispensing with the importation, they shalbe comptable for the customes thairof, your saids officers allowing them such feyis as hath bene payed in the lyk cases.

They ar to be accomptable to the officers and masters of the Mynt in ther names for bullion payable for goodis transported : In cace that by plague or civill warre they be hindred of the proffeit of the customes, they may renunce this tak.

If the said William be ordeaned by the Thesaurer to answer precepts he and his forsaids shall accept therof, and the same shalbe allowed vnto them on the first end of ther quarter payment, and if your Thesaurer shall desyre the advancement of ane yeir, half or quarter yeirs' dewtie of the customes, and if thervpon they shalbe content vpon payment of ther annuall-rents to advance the same, your officeris ar to defease it in what they ar bund to pay of the said tak-dewtie.—Whythall, 7 Ja^r 1635.

To the Session.

Trustie, &c.—Wheras we ar crediblie informed that Sir Samwell Johnstoun of Elphingstoun, kny^t, refuiseth to mak payment of the value of his tythes of his Lands of Elphingstoun to the relict of the late bischop of Ed^r of the cropt 1633, and the reverend father in God David, now present bischop of Ed^r, the cropt 1634, bought by ws from our trest cousen Johne, Lord Halyrudhous, then possessour of the samyne, to be ane part of the patrimonie of the said bischoprik, alledging that the Minister of Trauent, haveing recovered ane sentence of augmentation befor the Commissioners appoynted by ws for surrenders and tythis of thrie chalders of victuall to be adebtit to his former stipend, to be payed furth of the valued

II   3 F

teynd bolls within the said paroche, hath arreisted the samyne in his handis, and by our letters of horning hath caused Charge the said Sir Samwell to mak payment of the said augmentatioun, omitting other the tythes within the paroch, wheras the said minister should have insisted aganst the remanent heretours within the said paroch, each ane of them for ther proportionall part of the said augmentatioun, conforme to the value of ther tythes whairof they ar present taksmen, and sieing ther ar sufficiencie of tythes within the said paroche whervpon the said minister his augmentatioun may be locallie imposed, the rate thairof amounting to thrie Chalders: And to the end that this our royall work, and the rent thairof appropriated by our patent of Erection, may be conserved and manteyned, Our pleasur is, that yow tak such course that the said relict have full satisfaction from the said Sir Samwell for the value of the personage tythes of the saids lands of Elphingstoun the said crop 1633, and the said reverend father in God for the said crop 1634, and his successours to the bischoprik, yeirlie in tyme cuming, and that the saidis tythscheaves, as ane part of the revenue of the said bischoprik, whairof the said Lord Halyrudhous was in possession the tyme of the surrender made to ws, may be conserved for the vse that was appoynted by ws, and that the minister present and his successours be answered and obeyed of the said augmentatioun of thrie Chalders victuall furth of the readiest of the remanent tythes within the said paroch disponed and sett in tak by the said Lord Halyrudhous and his predicessours to the saidis heretours and ther authours, ther being competencie of tythes by and attour the saids tythes of Elphingstoun; Ifor doeing whairof these presents shalbe your warrand.—Whythall, 9 Ja^r 1635.

To the Commissioners for Surrenders.

His Matie was pleased, by a Letter of his hynes to his Commissioneris for surrenders vpon the 9 Ja^r 1635, to requyre them to admitt the Lord Alexander to be ane of ther number.

A. B.

To the Arch-Bischop of St Androis.

Right reverend, &c.—Hearing by a presentatioun that latelie past vnder our hand for admitting of ane to the ministrie of Long Forgun, Mr Wm Ogstoun, now Chaplane of that our kingdome, is dissapoynted, haveing formerlie presented him to that charge as ane whois sufficiencie for the function of the ministrie and affection to our service was speciallie recommended vnto ws: It is our pleasur, if the said other persone be not as yet fullie setled at that church, that our said servand, whom we had first designed for it, be preferred and placed thairwith, otherwayes that yow provyd him to the first vacant church within your province fitt for ane of his sufficiencie, and mark of that respect which we have bene pleased at this tyme to putt vpon him; which speciallie recommending to your care.—Whythall, 9 Ja^r 1635.

To the Commissioners of Excheker.

His Matie was pleased the 9 of Ja^r 1635 to requyre the commissioners of his Exchequer of Scotland to admitt the Bischop of Brechin to be one of ther number for supplying the Archbischop of St Androis place vaikand by his preferment to be Chancellour.

To the Counsell.

Right, &c.—Wheras of late we did wryt to yow at severall tymes for taking ordour with the abuses and outrages committed in the North, and vnderstanding since of the great care and panes yow have takin in the same by vseing all lawfull meanes for rectificing therof, we give yow hartie thanks, and doe desyre yow earnestlie to continew as yow have begun, it being a bussines which we have so much taken to hart as importing in so high a measur the good of our service, and the generall peace and quyet of that our kingdome : In regard thairof, and that it is so presumptuous and extraordinarie a cryme, we will yow to pull in executioun aney law or precedent whatsumever which hath bene vsed at aney tyme heirtofoir in the lyk caices ; ffor doeing whairof, &c.—Whythall, 9 Jaʳ 1635.

To the Chancellour.

Right reverend, &c.—Haveing heard of the great disorders that proceidit by the inordinat concurse of people at the severall tymes of the sitting latelie vpon the tryell of the Lord Balmerino, and being desyreous that some course be taken for preventing the lyk now at the tyme of his goeing to the tryell of ane assyse, we have gevin our particular directions concerneing the same to our right, &c. the Erle of Traquair : And it is our pleasur that, haveing conferred with him heiranent, yow tak accordinglie such course by your self or by ordour of the counsell as shalbe fund requisit for repressing of lyk disorders in the proceiding of his tryell ; which recommending to your speciall care, we bid, &c.—Whythall, 9 Jaʳ 1635.

To the Erle of Errolt.

Right, &c.—Haveing bene informed of your good cariage in the Charge to which we wer pleased to prefer yow of late, and of your great care and panes taken in the same, we give yow hartie thanks, and assure yow that we shalbe readie to testifie the same when occasion shall offer ; and we will yow to continew therin as yow have begun, till the work shalbe brought to ane end, according to the information yow shall receave from our right, &c. the Erle of Traquair, to whom we have geven directions tuitching that purpois. —Whythall, 9 Jaʳ 1635.

To the Advocat.

Trustie, &c.—Haveing bene informed of the great panes and care yow have taken in the tryell of the Lord Balmerino, for the which we give yow hartie thanks, and whairof assure yow we shall not be vnmyndfull when occasion shall offer : And sieing ane end is not as yet putt to the samyne, we have thoght good heirby agane seriouslie to recommend vnto your care the continuance of the prosecution of that bussines which doeth so neirlie concerne ws, till it be fullie finisched, according to the information yow shall receave from our right, &c. the Erle of Traquair, to whome we have gevin directions tuitching this purpois.—Whythall, 9 Jaʳ 1635.

To the Clerk Register.

Trustie, &c.—Haveing taken speciall notice of your great panes and care in our service wherin we doe employ yow of late, we give yow hartie thanks for the same, and doe seriouslie recommend vnto yow the continuance of your accustomed diligence in that bussines which doeth so neirlie concerne ws till it be fullie finisched, and lykwayes to consider of the informations which our right, &c. the Erle of Traquair hath receaved from ws at this tyme, wherwith he will acquant yow, that yow may concurre with him for the good of our said service.—Whythall, 9 Jaʳ 1635.

To the Commissioners for the Garderobe.

Right, &c.—Wheras we wer pleased to give a commission vnto yow for surveyghing all the garderobe stuff, plaite, hangingis, and furnischings belonging thairto, to ws within that our kingdome, and for disponeing and changeing so much thairof as in the reservations conteynit in the said commission shalbe by yow thought necessarie, to which purpois we think it expedient that, haveing called for our trustie and weilbeloved Sir John Auchmowtie, M^r of our Garderobe, yow mak the said surveigh befor him, and dewlie consider thairof with him, and therefter, with all convenient diligence, yow with him acquant ws with your opinions thairin ; and being informed that the said Sir John is comptable to ws for his intromission thairwith, according to a book subscryved by a number of our Counsell and him, one wherof is keipt in our Register and the other by himsellf, and that at our being ther, by command of our counsell, diverse of the goods entrusted to his charge and for which he is answerable wer gevin out to sindrie persones, wherof as yet he hath not receaved a full accompt, it is our pleasur that yow caus the havears of the saids goods redelyver them vnto him, that the said book may be renewed and subscryved as formerlie it hath bene [one copy], whairof to be delyvered to our Clerk Register to be kept amongst our rolls, and the other to himsellf his warrant.—Whythall, 9 Ja^r 1635.

To the Session.

Right, &c.—Wheras we ar informed of the great hurt that our trustie and weilbeloved Sir Alex^r Home may sustene in his absence by the issue of some differences now in agitation befor yow for obteneing declaratour vpon severall gifts of his father's escheits and lyfrent, which, sieing the rights therof ar deryved from ws, we ar vnwilling should tend to our servand's prejudice : Our pleasur is therfor in the meane whyle, till we vpon farther informatioun shall mak knowen our pleasur vnto yow, that yow mak stay of all proceidings in any action tuitching his said father's escheit and lyfrent intended or to be intended befor yow, and suspend the giveing out and executioun of decreits, if any be, thervpon ; wherin not doubting of your performance.—Whythall, 15 Ja^r 1635.

To the Session.

Right, &c.—Wheras we ar informed that in the action intended at the instance of Mr Wm Drummond against William Scott of Ardross (latelie recommended by ws vnto yow) for reduceing his fewes of Newton Rires, and for the double availl of his mariage, nothing as yit is done, wherby we ar prejudged in our right, and the said Mr William, to whom vpon good considerations we have granted the gift thairof, is putt to vnnecessar charges and delayes in following that our service : In regard that we ar lykwyse crediblie informed that the said casualitie of our Croun, these lands being holdin few, with the mariage, hath bene obscured and detened from ws and our predicessours these hundredth yeires bypast, and that it doe neirlie concerne ws in the estate of our revenues to reduce what is unjustlie abstracted from ws, speciallie wher we and our predicessours have bene so long and fraudfullie keipit bak from our right, It is our pleasur that yow carefullie advert to that action, and putt it to a finall end, that our donatour be not putt to any furder trouble or vnnecessar delayes tuitching the determining of that caus, wherin, sieing it doeth so particularlie concerne ws, we will expect from yow a readie care to performe our just and princelie desyre heirin : We bid, &c.—Whythall, the 15 Ja^r 1635.

To the Bischop of Brechin.

Reverend father in God—Being informed that Robert Maull, our servant, is the cheiff man of the parochin of Monekie, and being confident that he will present a sufficient and qualifeit persone for discharging the function of the Ministrie at that Church whensoever it shallhappin to vaik, it is our pleasur, quhomsoever he sall name vnto yow at that tyme, yow admitt him to the said churche, as yow will doe ws acceptable service.—Whythall, 13 Ja^r 1635.

To the Session.

Right, &c.—Being willing to prevent any question or trouble that may enseu heirefter tuitching the vplifting and disposing of the rents of the estate of the late erldome of Home till by arbitrall decision of frendis all questiones betuein the pairteis be amicablie composed and setled, Our pleasur is, that till the tyme of that decision the rents of that estate be not intromettted with by any of the pairteis, bot that yow tak such course therin as the rents thairof may be sequestred or sufficientlie secured in the hands of such as may be responsible for the same, to be made furthcomand to the vse of the pairteis who shalbe fund to have best right thervnto.—Whythall, 16 Jar 1635.

To the Exchequer.

Right, &c.—Wheras we vnderstand how that according to our pleasur, signifeid of late for improveing our customes, yow had legallie evicted the former cess therof, haveing in a fair and publict way made offer of the fermeing of the same to such as would give most for them, wherin we approve of the course taken by yow, and though that thervpon yow had condescendit with Wm Dick and sent to ws a Lease of these customes, wherby our fermes ar approved respecting what was formerly payed for the same, and which we (till we hear further from yow) conceave to be the saifest and most constant way in respect of the Leases, sufficiencie, and assurance offered vnto ws, yit one Robert Bar, seeming by the enclosed proposition to mak a further offer for improveing our rent of these customes : Our pleasur is, that haveing called befor yow the said Robert, yow consider of his proposition, and report to ws your opinions tuitching the same, that we may give such further ordour therin as we shall think fitt, and in the meanetyme we recommend vnto yow that a speciall care be had for the tyme and exact vplifting of these customes as they shalbe fund to grow dew vnto ws.—Whythall, 16 Jar 1635.

Robert Bar his Propositions tuitching the Customes of Scotland.

Robert Bar and his partiners took a Lease of your Maties Customes in Scotland for 15 yeires, and gave ellevin hundreth pundis sterling a yeir more then formerlie was made of them.

Ther Lease is now takin from them by my Lord Traquair, and granted to some other man, without any improvement to your Matie, bot onlie ellevin hundreth pund fyne.

Robert Bar now humblie offers to give your Matie this ellevin hundreth pund fyne, togidder with ane Increase of 300lb a yeir rent, and to give verie good securitie for performance of the same.

Bot if from first to last your Matie shall not think this good service, let my Lord Traquair mak a better offer for improvement of your hynes' revenue, and your petitioner shalbe weill content.

To the Erle of Traquair.

Right, &c.—Wheras we wer pleased of late to signifie our pleasur for dispenseing with a clause of the infeftment of the Lord Kintyre, quherby it is provydit that the Landis thairof be not sold to any of the Clandonald; bot haveing now received some information requyreing our further consideratioun tuitching that purpois, It is our pleasur that, haveing signifeid our intention heirin to the remanent of our Exchequer, yow stay the passing of any signature of these lands till we shalbe pleased to give further ordour heiranent ; ffor which these presents, &c.—Whythall, 16 Jar 1635.

To the Advocat.

Trustie, &c.—Wheras we ar informed that our late royall father, for the better intertenement of the professours and schollers of the Colledge of Glasgow, did endow the same with the Tythes of the Churches of Given, Kilbryd, and Renfrew, wherof the rights being (as we ar lykwayes informed) to be questioned in Law by some privat persones and for privat endis, we being desyrous that the said pious act of our father's may accordinglie tak effect in so far as may be agrieable to justice and our lawes, they performeing such conditions as wer condescendit vpon tuitching the mantenance of divyne service at these churches, and performeing the places of the Chaptour of Glasgow, ar heirby pleased to requyre that yow in our name compear and plead in defence of the rights and priviledges of these tythes befor whatsumever judge or Judicatorie within that our kingdome.—Whythall, 16 Jar 1635.

To the Erles of Murray and Lawderdaill.

Right, &c.—Wheras we have taken to our consideratioun that the submission desyred be ws tuitching the Erldome and Estate of Home can hardlie tak effect vnless the Arbiters to be choysen of ather syd may have sicht of the writts and evidents concerneing the same, wherby they may the better know the severall clames of the pairteis, and consequentlie compose all differences tuitching that purpois, wherin baveing writtin at this tyme to the Colledge of Justice, we have therby thought good lykwayes to signifie our pleasur vnto yow, that immediatlie efter James Home hath subscryved the said submission, all writts and evidents whatsumever concerneing the said Erldome or estate may be delyvered vnto the saids arbiters at the sight of the senatours of our College of Justice; wherin not doubting of your care and readie endeavours, we bid, &c.—Whythall, 16 Jar 1635.

To the Session.

Right, &c.—Wheras, for the more speedie conclusion in the submission desyred by ws tuitching the Erldome and Estate of Home, we have signifeid our pleasur to the Earles of Murray and Lawderdale that all writts and evidents whatsoever concerneing the said Erldome or estate be delyvered to the arbiters, wherby they may the better know the severall claymes of the pairteis, and consequentlie compoise all differences concerneing that purpois: Our pleasur is, that immediatlie efter the said James Home his subscryveing of the said submission yow call befor yow, vpon his information, all such persones as yow thervpon shall find requisit, or therby suppois to have in ther custodie, or to have abstracted or conceilled any of these writts and evidents, and that yow tak a summar course to have so many of them as by examinatioun vpon oath can be fund exhibited vpon inventar, and delyvered to the Arbiteris vpon both sydis, and to be returned bak when they have made vse of them.—Whythall, 17 Jar 1635.

To the Bischop of Dunkell.

Reverend, &c.—As we wer pleased of late to signe a presentatioun to Mr Walter Stewart for his admission to the kirk of Aberdour, to which purpois we have signifeid our pleasur at this tyme to the right reverend father the Archbischop of St Androis, our Chancellour; So it is still our pleasur, and we doe heirby will and requyre, that none be receaved in that charge bot the said Mr Walter, he being fund qualifeid and conforme to the canons and ordour of the Church, and to that effect we will yow to sie our pleasur heirin accordinglie performed, wherin yow shall doe ws acceptable service.—Whythall, 22 Jar 1635.

Similar Letter to the Archbischop of St Androis.

To the Session.

Right, &c.—Wheras we have at sindrie tymes signifeid our pleasur how desyreous we wer that the Erle of Airth should have a reasonable tyme to frie his estate, having at this tyme gevin expres onlour to our thesaurers for making tymelie payment of ten thowsand punds sterling for the releiff of his burdenis ; and wheras we ar now crediblie informed that he hath made severall reall and legall offers to the Lords Lowdoun and Foster in behalff of themselffis and rest of the creditours of ther whole bygane annual rents, wherof they refuised to accept, notwithstanding they have infeftment of his Lands confirmed by ws, which is sufficient suirtie ; and being withall that therefter he offered to the rest of the creditours a part (who ar lykwayes secured of his Estate for what is dew to them) ther annual rents, whairof they would willinglie have accepted, bot that the Lord Lowdoun had them bund not to admitt of any such offer, we could doe no less (out of our princelie compassion of that noblemanis sufferings heirin) than so far as to tak notice of such rigorous proceidings as heirby speciallie to recommend the consideratioun therof to yow, and to requyre yow to tak any course that possiblie may stand with our Lawis, wherby everie ane of his creditours from whom at first he did borrow moneyis or wer engadged as sureteis for him may onlie have recourse to himselff for debts dew to them according to ther first severall suirteis, or (if he and they shall find it requisite) according to such new suirtie as they shall mutuallie consider vpon, for we conceave it to be more hard and prejudiciall to him to pay all his debts (which ar now amassed to one or tuo sowmes) at one tyme than in many severall parcells as he did at first receave them, wher some ease (both in respect of tyme and otherwayes) may be gevin him by these with whom he did bargane at first : And in the meane tyme that our further pleasur is, till we be further acquainted heirin, that no proces goe on for dispossesseing him or his tennents of any lands or housses belonging to him : Which speciallie recommending to yow, we bid, &c.—Whythall, 23 Jar 1635.

To the Erle of Traquair.

Right, &c.—Wheras we have writtin at this tyme to our Colledge of Justice concerneing the action depending befor them betweene the Erle of Airth and his Creditours, wherby yow will perceave our loyall intention tuitching that purpois, and wherin we will yow to give your best furtherance and assistance yow can, to the end his estate (which is now enlangred) may be the more quicklie relieved, and we fred of further trouble heirin, which consists in the speedie payment of these moneyis which we have designed for him : Our pleasur is, that yow tak a present course for payment of such moneys as yow and he hath condescended at this tyme, and as for the remainder, that yow certifie ws of any expedient way yow shall find the same may be best done (becaus we doe verie much tender the preservatioun of his houts), and we will give ordour accordinglie : For all which these presents salbe vnto yow a sufficient warrant.— Whythall, 23 Jar 1635.

To the Counsell.

Right reverend, &c.—We receaved your letter, wherby we perceave yow have gevin ordour to stop all proceidings in the bargane concerneing the sale of Kintyre to the Erle of Antrim or the Lord Dunluce, his sone, for which we give yow harty thanks, acknowledgeing the same to be good service done vnto ws, tuitching which purpois we had of late by our letter signifeid our pleasur to the Erle of Traquair, to be imparted to our Exchequer, which apparentlie cam not to his hands at the wryting your letter to ws ; we ar heirby pleased, for the considerations mentioned therin, whairof we have bene pleased to tak particular notice, speciallie to recommend vnto yow that if the Lord Kintyre hath alreadie done any thing contrair to our royall intention heirin, that yow vse your best endevours to mak it ineffectuall, and that yow lykwyse prevent any interest or possession the said Erle, his sone, or any of that name, may have in these landis, by whatsumever maner of way, and to that effect that yow give such ordour as yow to that purpois shall think fitt to preservye, and in the meane tyme that yow signifie our pleasur heirin to our Exchequer, that they give way to nothing contrair to this our intention, vnless we shalbe pleased to give further ordour theranent ; for which, &c.—Whythall, 28 Jar 1635.

To the Thesaurers and Advocat.

Right, &c.—Being crediblie informed that notwithstanding of our pleasur signifeid for stopping all procedings concerneing the sale of Kintyre to the Erle of Antrim or the Lord Dunluce, his sone, the Lord Kintyre hath insisted in that bargane, in giveing infeftment to the said Erle of these Lands, we, in consideratioun of our owin particular interest therin, haveing resolved that no such bargane shalbe concluded at this tyme ; and withall taking into our princelie consideratioun how far the disposeing of that estate may concerne ws and the estate of that our kingdome, which hath bene represented to ws by our Counsell, we ar heirby pleased that in our name yow intent proces and action of reduction of these lands to our Croun, and that yow insist therin by all the legall wayes that can be vsed ; ffor which, &c.—Whythall, 28 Jar 1635.

To the Exchequer.

Right, &c.—Wheras we have expressed our pleasur at severall tymes that in regard Patrik Blak, our servand, had in the tyme of our royall father payed 9000 merks Scotts for the heretable Chalmerlanrie of Fyff, he should be secured of that office by haveing a gift thairof, redemable alwayes vpon payment of these moneyis, and therefter to returne to our Croun, wherin (as we did formerlie wryt) sieing the redemption which at all tymes is in our power doeth distinguish that our gift from the nature of heretable offices, and that it is nowayes our royall intentioun to tak that office from him without satisfaction, it is our pleasur that vpon his surrander thairof to our Croun, or if the surrander be alreadie legallie made, that yow exped vnder our scalls the signature sent by ws vnto yow concerneing that purpois, or that yow exped vnder our Cachet or scalls any other which will secure him for bruiking that office till he be payed of the saidis moneyis debursed by him, that therefter it may returne to our Croun ; ffor which, &c.—Whythall, 28 Jar 1635.

To the Exchequer.

Right, &c.—Humble complaint haveing bene made vnto ws by Doctour David . Beaton, our phisitian in ordinarie, that now of late our gift of pension vnto him and his wyff (ratifeid in our late parliament ther), and acquyred by them vpon valuable considerations, is questioned, to ther great hurt : Our pleasur is, that they and the tennents be not further troubled nor questioned dureing the tyme of ther grant, bot at the expiratioun thairof we will have that pension to returne to our Croun without any further locall assignement to be made thairof, wherin this our pleasur signifeid at this tyme shalbe sufficient to stop any such grant heirefter : We bid, &c.—Whythall, 28 Jar 1635.

To the Archbischops.

Right, &c.—Wheras our late royall father and our selffes have bene alwayes accustomed to caus frie from payment of our taxations such of the ministrie as wer knowen vnable to pay any part thairof : Though we do beleive that ther is no such great caus at this tyme for exempting them in this kynd, we haveing bene so carefull to sie them more compitentlie provydit than they wer heirtofoir, yet, least any should suffer who ar poore, and have not as yit had the benefite of our pious intention for augmenting ther stipendis, it is our pleasur that yow consider the estate of such as ar within your provinces, causeing the lyk course be taken by the remanent bischops throughout ther severall dyoceis, and vpon list to be gevin vp to yow of ther names, and exact tryell of ther estate, yow delyver the same vnder your hands to our collectour-generall of our taxations, or to his deputeis and collectours, that they be not troubled for any ordinarie taxations dew by them, and no otherwyse : For doeing wherof, &c.—Whythall, 28 Jar 1635.

To the Advocat.

Trustie, &c.—Wheras some yeires ago we did condescend with the Erle of Airth for his hous at Halyrudhous, for the vse of the bischops of Edinburgh, to which purpois it being requisite that the present bischop be secured by ws, to the end he may setle himselff therat ; it is our pleasur that yow draw vp securiteis fitt and necessarie to be exped by ws, as yow shall find to be requisite for his and his successoirs in that charge ther right thervnto at all tymes heirefter ; And that yow insert a speciall provision therin that the said bischop and his aires, and each of his successours in that charge, and ther aires successivelie, shalbe band, vnder such a penaltie as our treasurer and yow shall condiscend vpon, to leave that house in no worse esteat then it is at this tyme ; ffor which, &c.—Whythall, 28 Jar 1635.

To the Session.

Right, &c.—Being informed that the action in Law tuitching the reduction of the infeftments of the heretable Isherie of our Exccheker ther, which hath so maynie yeires depended befoir yow, to the prejudice of our right, and of the persone whom we appoynted to discharge that office, doeth remane as yit vndecyded, notwithstanding of diverse of our letters to yow and our Advocat, for insisting and putting it to a finall end : And in regard, as we ar lykwyse crediblie informed by some of our cheiff officers, that we have now ane vndoubtit right to the said office ; It is our pleasur that with all diligence, as yow tender the good of our service, yow give out your decrie in the said action, that (if it be as our saids officers have informed ws) our right from which we and our predicessours hath bene so long keiped bak may without further delay be restablished, and our servand whom we appoynted to discharge that office setled therin ; wherin, sieing it doeth so particularlie concerne ws, we will expect from yow a readie care to performe our just and princelie desyre herein : We bid yow farewell.—Whythall, 28 Jar 1635.

To Sir James Balfour.

Trustie, &c.—Wheras we did formerlie signifie our pleasur vnto yow that our right trustie, &c. the Erle of Stirling, our secretarie for Scotland, should have the Armes of New Scotland in ane Inscutcheon with his owin paternall coat, and that other coat (which we lykwayes allow him to bear for reasones signifeid at that tyme vnto yow, as by our letter may particularlie appear) ; now, considering that he hath in particular and singular maner deserved the said augmentatioun of the Armes of New Scotland, and to the effect he may bear it in a way propper vnto him selff, and different to all others who are authorized for bearing of it, we ar pleased to allow it vnto him, to be quartered in the first quarter with his other coats; and thairfor it is our pleasur that yow draw such further warrant for this purpois as shalbe expedient; and withall that yow register this our letter in your books of office, to remane therin, according to the custome in the lyk kynd, to the effect no other may tak vpon them to bear the said augmentatioun in this maner, to the prejudice of the gracious favour which we doe heirin intend to him alone: ffor the which these presents, &c.—Whythall, 28 Ja' 1635.

To the Deputie of Irland.

Right, &c.—Wheras, by our letters bearing date at Beaulieu the 15 of August, in the 8 yeir of our Reigne, directed to the then Lords Justices of Irland, we requyred them to cause proclamation to be made in that our kingdome that none of our subjects of any of our dominions should pay ather more or other customes or dewteis than such as the natives of the place wher the custome is taken ought to pay; which proclamation we then sent, togidder with our saids letters, in such maner as the same had bene befoir publisched in our realmes of England and Scotland: And for as much as we ar informed by our frie burrowis of our kingdome of Scotland that the said Proclamatioun hath not bene yit publisched in that our realme of Irland, be reason whairof our subjects hath not receaved the benefite of our gracious intentions towards them, we doe therfor heirwith send yow the Proclamatioun, requyreing yow furthwith to caus the same to be publisched in that our kingdome in such sort that all our subjects may tak notice of our pleasur heirin, and to tak care that the same be dewlie observed accordinglie; And this shalbe your sufficient warrant and discharge in this behalff.—Gevin vnder our signet at Whythall, the 5 of Feb' 1635.

To Thomas, Viscount Wentworth, our Deputie of our realme of
Irland and President of our Counsell established in the
Northerne parts of England.   Sub', Fran. Windibank.

Our Soveraigne Lord now, efter his Ma^{tis} full and perfyt aige of tuentie fyve yeires compleit, and efter his highnes' revocations, generall and speciall, made in parliament or outwith, haveing remembred the good tyme and thankfull services done to his Matie, and his highnes' vnquhill father, of happie memorie, by his highnes' trustie and weilbeloved James Fenton, keeper deputie of his highnes' palace of Halyrudhous, and garden within the same, was gratiouslie pleased, by his highnes' letters of gift vnder the Privie Seall of Scotland of the date at Whythall the 5 of May 1626, not onlie to ratifie and approve the said James his former gift thairof, bot also to constitute him of new Ordiner keeper deputie of the said Palace, and gardene within the same, Granting him the office therof for all the dayes of his lyftyme, with all fevis, casualiteis, priviledges, immuniteis, proffeits, and dewteis therof perteneing and belonging therto; And in speciall to have assigned to the said James Fenton, in name of fie, Tuentie schillings Scotts money, to be vplifted furth of the readiest of the maills, fermes, and dewteis of his highnes' rents and propertie, to be payed to the said James daylie ilk day for all the dayes of his lyftyme, Togidder with a Chalder of Bear yeirlie, to be payed out of the readiest fermes and dewteis of the Landis of Ballincreiff, at the termes vsed and wount, begining the first dayes payment of the said money at the day and date of the said gift, and the first yeires payment of the said Victuall to be made for the said cropt and yeir of God 1626, and so furth daylie and yeirlie therefter respective dureing the said space, as in the saids Letters at mair lenth proports: And his Matie being now most willing to corroborat and strenthen the said former gift granted vnto the said James, for his better encouragment to continew in the said service, dooth, with the speciall advyse and consent of his Ma^{tris} right, &c. William, Erle of Morton, his Ma^{teis} principall Thesaurer of the said kingdome, of Johne, Erle of Traquair, his Ma^teis deputie Thesaurer therof, and of the remanent Commissioners of Exchequer, Ordeanes a Letter of new to be made and exped vnder his Ma^teis privie seall in due forme, ratifieing and approveing, and for his highnes and his successours perpetuallie confirmeing, lykas by the tenour heirof his Matie, with advyse and consent forsaid, ratifeis, approves, and for his highnes and successours perpetuallie confirmes the said Letter of gift, of the date at Whythall the 5 of May 1626, as aforsaid, in the haill heads, clausses, articles, and conditionis therin conteynit, and efter the forme and tenour therof in all poynts, save onlie wher the said James assigned by the said former gift immediatlie to receave the said Chalder of bear out of the lands of Ballincreiff yeirlie from the handis of persones adebtit to pay them, or from any others haveing power to receave the same, he is heirby appoynted to have the pryces thairof yeirlie, as the Lords of the Excheker, or any of them appoynted by the bodie of the Table, shall find the same to be conforme to the fiars of the pryces of the lyk victuall in these parts ilk yeir, and that out of his Ma^teis Excheker, rents and casualiteis whatsoever : And his Matie, with advyse and consent forsaid, hath made and constitute the said James Fenton of new deputie Keeper of the said palace, and garden within the same, granting to him the office thairof for his lyftyme, with all feyis, casualiteis, priviledges, immuniteis, proffeits, and dewteis perteneing and belonging thairto ; And in speciall hath gevin and granted, and by the tenour heirof gives, grants, and dispones of new to the said James Fentoun dureing his lyftyme, All and haill the said fiall of Tuentie schillings Scotts money daylie dureing all the dayes of his said lyftyme, Togidder with the said pryce of a chalder [of] bear yeirlie out of Ballincreiff, as they shall happin to be fund by the saids Lords of Exchequer to be answerable to the fiers of ilk yeir, to be receaved out of the Excheker yeirlie in maner forsaid, the first payment of the said tuentie schillings daylie to be and begin at the day and date of thir presents, and so furth daylie dureing all the dayes of his lyftyme, and the first payment of the pryces of the said bear to be and begin at the terme of   , and so furth yeirlie at the said terme dureing all the dayes of his lyftyme ; with command in the said letter to the Commissioners to sie the same exped with all clausses neidfull.—Whythall, 6 Feb^ry 1635.

A signatur was past his Ma^teis hand in favours of Doctour Craig, one of his Ma^teis doctours in ordinarie, ratifieing vnto him a pension of 100^lib sterling per annum dureing his lyftyme.—Whythall, 6 Feb^ry 1635.

To the Session.

Right, &c.—Wheras by our former letter we requyred yow to mak stay (till yow should know our further pleasur) of all proceidings in any action intended or to be intendit befor yow tuitching Sir George Home of Manderstoun his escheit and lyfrent, we now, haveing taken into our princelie consideratioun that non hath so just reasone to demand the same as Sir Alex^r Home his sone, as weill in regard of the great prejudice he hath sustened by engadgments for his father as that he is a neir servant to ws, from whom the right of that casualitie is to be deryved : In respect whairof, and the other gifts (declaratours not being past thervpon) have not yit taken effect, we have gevin ordour to expeid a new grant to our said servant of his father's escheit and lyfrent, which, that it may be effectuall vnto him by obteneing declaratours thervpon, it is our pleasur that yow grant him process for insisting therin, and that no other may tak advantage against him vpon pretence of prioritie of tyme ; wherin not doubting of your care, we bid yow farewell.—Whythall, 6 Feb^r 1635.

To the Exchequer.

Right, &c.—Wheras we ar informed that yow have (according to the usuall practeis) for compositions payed for our vse passed diverse gifts of Sir George Home of Manderstoun his escheit and lyfrent to severall persones, which none hath so just reasone to demand as Sir Alex^r Home his sone, in regard of the great prejudice which (as we ar crediblie informed) he hath susteyned by engadgments for his father : In respect whairof, and that he is a neir servant to ws, from whom the right of that casualitie is to be deryved, and that the other gifts (declaratours not being obteynit thervpoun) have not yit taken effect, Our pleasur is, that for the lyk compositions that any of the others have payed, yow pass a gift also vnto him of his said father's escheit and lyfrent, and if our said servant his owin escheit and lyfrent be fallin into our handis (which in that caice will includ the other). let it be frielie past to his owin vse to Mr Alex^r Home of St Leonard's ; ffor which these presents, &c.—Whythall, 6 Feb^r 1635.

To the Exchequer.

Right, &c.—Humble sute hath bene made to ws in behalff of Mr Robert Murray, Commissar of Stirling, for continewing the pension he had of our late royall father, in regard it was granted to him for his dimitting diverse churches within his commissariot for augmenting the patrimonie of the bischoprik of Glasgow : Though the grounds of his demand be considerable, yit we ar altogidder vnwilling to ratifie oney pension which hath bene locallie assigned, as we ar informed this is : Therfor it is our pleasur that, haveing considered the nature and value thairof, yow condescend with him for being payed heirefter out of our Exchequer, according to the approved maner, and to that effect that yow aither cause draw vp a signature to pass immediatlie vnder our cachet and privie seall ther, or that yow send ane vnto ws for our signet, to be returned for his vse, for aither of which these presents shalbe sufficient warrant; and in the meanetyme that yow from hencefurth caus that locall pension be made vse of for our best advantage, and payed in yeirlie to our Exchequer : We bid, &c.—Whythall, 6 Feb^r 1635.

To the Chancellour.

Right, &c.—Wheras we wer formerlie pleased that these patentes of honour intended for the Lords Lyndsay and Lowdon at our late entrie to that our kingdome, which wer not exped our great seall, should be recalled, to which purpois we gave ordour to the late Chancellour, and wherof we had takin accompt of him at his late being at our Court, if his death had not prevented the same : It is our pleasur that yow call for these signaturs, and returne them saiflie to ws, wherin expecting that all possible diligence be vsed, and ane exact account thairof made vnto ws, &c.—Whythall, 6 Feb^r 1635.

To the Session.

Right, &c.—Being informed that ther is ane action in Law alreadie intended or to cum befor yow at the instance of Sir Alex^r Falconer of Halkerton, kny^t, which, in respect of his aige, he is vnable to follow with that diligence and care that is requisite, we ar heirby graciouslie pleased to recommend the said action vnto yow, that justice may be administred therin with as much expedition as can be possible affourded by the lawis and custome of that our kingdome, wherin yow shall doe ws good and acceptable service.—Whythall, 8 Feb^r 1635.

His Ma^{teis} warrant was directed to the Lo^r Stanehop to authorize and requyre the posts on the road from London to Berwick to send to court all packetts receaved by them vnder the subscription of the Archbischop of St Androis, Chancellour of Scotland.

To the Advocat.

Trustie, &c.—Haveing taken notice of tho good affection to our service of our burgh of Aberden, speciallie at this tyme by the readie obedience to our pleasur for receaveing of Sir Paull Meinzeis to be ther provest, we have bene now pleased by our letters to them to acknowledge ther good service heirin, and to give them thankis for the same : And wheras humble sute hath bene made to ws in ther behalff to ratifie ther priviledges and liberteis, as our royall progenitours wer accustomed to doe, to which purpois they have sent vnto ws a confirmatioun to pass our signature heir : We ar heirby pleased to will and requyre yow to confer the same with the ratificatioun of our late royall father last granted to them ; and if yow find nothing materiallie disconforme therin, or if that any things be added of new wherby we nor none of our good subjects ar prejudged, that yow furthwith signifie vnto our Exchequer that it is our pleasur that it be expcd vnder our cachet and sealls ther, or send it docated by yow vnto ws that it may be returned vnder our royall signature for passing our saidis sealls ; ffor which these presents shalbe vnto all our officers whom it may concerne sufficient warrant.—Whythall, 12 Febr 1635.

To the Citie of Aberdene.

Trustie, &c.—Vnderstanding of your willing and readie obedience to our letter in removeing your late Provost and accepting Sir Paull Meinzeis, knyt, in that charge, we doe therin acknowledge your good affection to our service, and gave yow hartie thanks for the same, assureing yow that heirefter we wilbe spareing to give any such further ordour vnless ther be some speciall occasion moveing ws thervnto : As for your signature sent vnto ws for ratifieing your liberteis, we have at this tyme returned the same to our Advocat to be conferred with the last ratificatioun of our late royall father, and if nothing be materiallie disconforme, or if anythings be added by yow of new wherby we nor none of our good subjects ar prejudged, that he furth caus expeid the same vnder our cachet and sealls, otherwayes returned docated by him vnto ws that it may pass our signature heir, and be returned bak for that purpois : We bid, &c.— Whythall, 12 Febr 1635.

To the Counsell.

Right, &c.—Wheras it hath bene humblie represented to ws in behalff of John Leslie, younger of Piteaple, that in regard of the great scarsitie of moneyis in the northerne parts of that our kingdome, or by vnwillingnes of such as have them to lend the same, he cannot possiblie raise moneyis at this tyme for his creditours' satisfaction, bot is most willing to secure them sufficientlie, both of ther principall sowmes and annual-rents, by giveing them surtie of his Landis, and otherwayes to dispose vnto them heretablie such part therof as shalbe proportionable in worth to his debts, wher if they should insist with rigour by troubling his persone, it would both prejudge them and whollie dissable him to tak any course for ther satisfaction ; whervpon, though we have bene pleased to signe the inclosed protection, yit we have thoght withall litt that yow call befor yow his creditours for accepting such reasonable offers, bot if they shall obstinatlie ; Our pleasur is, that yow caus expeid the protection vnder our great seall, that therby he may have some tyme to mak the best vse he can of his estate for payment of his debts.—Whythall, 18 Feb. 1635.

To the Session.

Right, &c.—We ar informed that one Johne Robertsone, heretable proprietar of the halff mylne of Innernesse, which is of our propertie, hath raised summondis befor yow aganst ane James Cuthbert of

Drakeis, from whom he bought his right to that mylne, for abstracting the multuris of the Cornes of his Landis alwyse thirled thervnto, wherin, as we ar lykwayes informed. sieing we ar prejudged in our right, and our tennent fraudulentlie abused in his purches. by the others selling vnto him at ane dear rate what he intended to mak vnprofitable, we have heirby thought fitt to recommend the consideratioun of the cause vnto yow that speedie justice be administred therin. in so far as yow shall find agrieable to equitie and our Lawes: We bid yow farewell from our Court at Whythall, the 18 Feb' 1635.

To the Advocat.

Trustie, &c.—Haveing bene pleased to recommend to our Colledge of Justice that speedie justice be administred in ane action of ane Johne Robertsone, hereitable proprietar of the half mylne of Innernesse, against ane James Cuthbert of Drakeis, in regard the mylne is of our propertie, and that the wrong alledged to be done to Robertsone doeth lykwayes prejudge ws, we ar heirby pleased to will and requyre yow to informe your self of the trew estate of the caus, and particularlie of our Interest; and therefter that yow concure with the said Robertsone for sieing our right preserved, in so far as the equitie therof and our lawis will permitt, and for putting it to a speedie end. according to justice; wherin not doubting of your care and diligence, we bid, &c.—Whythall, 18 Feb' 1635.

Our Soveraigne Lord ordeanes a protection to be made vnder the great scall of Scotland to his highnes' lovitts, Johne Leslie, elder of Pitcaple, Johne Leslie, younger of Pitcaple, his sone, and James Leslie, his brother, making mention that wheras his Ma'ie is crediblie informed that now in regard of the great scarcitie of moneyis within the northerne parts of the said kingdome (wher ther esteats doe ly), or otherwyse of the small trust which ordinarlie at this tyme any gentlman haveing estate of landis can have of such persones as have moneyis, in regard of ther ends and respects for making benefite thairof otherwayes, the said Johne Lesleis, elder and younger, and the said James Leslie, cannot possiblie raise sowmes of money for ther Creditours' present satisfaction, vnless they would tak such proportions of land belonging vnto them as might be equivalent in value to the moneyis due to the saidis creditours: And wheras his Ma'ie is lykwyse crediblie informed that if the saids Creditours should tak any rigorous course at this tyme aganst the persones of ther saids debtours (who ar both most willing and able to give them satisfaction if some compitent tyme wer allowed for that purpois), it would be a meanes to dissable them to tak way which is necessarie and convenient for all ther good; wherin his Ma'ie, respecting the weill of both the creditours and debtours, &c. Cetera stylo ordinario.—Whythall, 21 Feb' 1635.

Att his Ma'tis Court of Whythall, the 23 of Feb'y 1635, stilo Scotico, the King his most Excellent Ma'tie, taking to his princelie consideration the great panes and travells takin by his Ma'tis servand the present Conservitour of the Low Cuntreys in ministring of Justice to his subjects ther, keeping them in decent ordour amongst themsellfis and strangers, protecting them from all wrongs, and sueing for reparation of all injureis done to aney of them in the sevintene provinces; And that it is fitt for the credit of the kingdome of Scotland that he live in good and honourabill fashon befitting his place, which he cannot possiblie doe vpon the feyis of the said office in regard of ther smalnes: And vnderstanding that the factours, his Ma'tis subjects, resideing at the staple port, altho they receave no less benefite by the said Conservatour his labours than the merchands doe, yit they contribute nothing to his mantenance in the said place: Therfor his Ma'tie gives and grants to the present Conservatour, dureing his lyftyme, as much of everie seck of goudis, to be payed by the factour who receaves the same, as the saids factours doe now

pay of everie seck, ather by vertew of any acts of burrowis, or by ther voluntar grant, for making vp of the
minister's stipend ; Commanding and ordaneing all the saids factours which at the said staple, present and
to cum, to mak thankfull and readie payment of to the said Conservatour and his Collectours in his name
dureing his lyftyme of the lyk quantitie of dues of everie seck of goodis wherto they ar imployed factours,
which they now pay for the vse of the minister and payment of his stipend by any maner of way
whatsoever, With power to the said Conservatour or his Creditours of the forsaids dues to depryve them
of the office of factorie and all liberteis of that kingdome : And his Matie vnderstanding that Fleymings
and other strangers doe for ther benefite repair to the said kingdome, and sayll from thence with coalls and
other merchandice, as thogh they wer his subjects, who nevertheles refuis to mak payment to the said
Conservatour of the dewis of ther coalls and other merchandice and wares, pretending immunitie becaus
they are strangers, althogh they not onlie enjoy all the same liberteis which his Ma^teis^ naturall subjects
doe, bot lykwyse doe hinder his Ma^teis^ owin subjects much in ther trade : Therfor his Matie ordeanes the
saids Flemings resideing in Scotland or tradeing to the Low Cuntreyis, and his Ma^teis^ subjects, and
particularlie Cais Mais, sumetyme of Roterdame, and now of Burrowstounnes, to mak good and thankfull
payment to the present Conservatour or his Collectours of all such dues as ar payed or oght to be payed
vnto him by his Ma^teis^ natives of the said kingdome, or oney of them, in all and everie respect whatsoever,
and that for all tymes bypast and to cum, as these dewteis shall happin to accress at any tyme heirefter
throughout the whole bounds of the saids sevintene provinces, and all parts therof, and that of all coalls
and other sort of goods and waris whatsoever transported to the said bounds, or any part thairof, out of
the said kingdome ; With power to him to arreist and poynd and distraine for not payment of the saids
dues, for all tymes bypast and to cum, when and whersoever he can apprehend the persones or goodis of
the infringers of this present act within any of his Ma^teis^ dominions : And in caice the said Cais Mais refuis
to mak thankfull payment to the said Conservatour or his Collectours of all bygane dues, and for the tyme
to cum, we doe heirby declair the said Cais Mais nor no stranger whatsoever to have no benefite or libertie
within the said kingdome of Scotland, or without the same within the saidis 17 provinces, or oney of them,
by reasone of any warrant, certificat, power, exemption, or writt whatsoever from his Ma^teis^ Admirall of
the said kingdome, or any vnder or from him, or from any other officeris or persones whatsoever, ordaneing
the said Admirall to draw bak from the said Cais Mais any such warrand, certificat, or writt whatsoever
which is alreadie gevin, and that he give nane such to any stranger in tyme cuming, vnles they obleidge
themsellfis by good sufficient bandis that they shall pay to the Conservatour and his Collectours readelie
and trulie the fall dues of all coalls and others goods which they shall transport at any tyme out of the
said kingdome, or any toun or haven within any of the saids 17 provinces of the Low Cuntreyis, And
shall vndergoe such burdens and fulfill these dewteis which the natives of the said kingdome doe :
Which Acts and Ordinances above specifeit his Matie ordeanes to be acted and registrat in the books of the
privie Counsall of the said kingdome ad futuram rei memoriam, and the samyne being registrat, his Matie
lykwyse ordenes his highnes' great signet to be appendit thervnto ; for which these presents shalbe
sufficient warrand to all whom it may concerne.

To the Burrowes.

Trustie, &c.—Wheras we ar informed that notwithstanding of your Acts, wherby the inhabitants of
these brughes tradeing in the Low Cuntreyis ar ordeaned to pay to our trustie and weilbeloved servand
the present conservatour the dewteis for his charge and intertenement, yit some of them have defrauded
him thairof, to his great prejudice and dissabling of him in that charge, as we have appoynted him to
procure the good and benefite of all our subjects of that kingdome tradeing in any of the sevintene
provinces ; so we hold it to be just and necessarie that, according to your acts, these dewes (which ar the

meanes allotted him for his maintenance) be generallie and indifferentlie vplifted by him of all goodis belonging to any of our saidis subjects arryveing within these 17 provinces, or any pairt thairof, the consideratioun whairof, and of the good and panefull services hitherto performed by him in that charge, wherof (as we ar informed) he did of late give an extraordinarie prooff by procuring a speedie redresse of a wrong done to some of your nighbours, hath justlie moved ws to recommend vnto yow in a speciall maner to sie a speedie course taken for paying such dewteis as ar resting vnpayed to him, and that they be punctuallie payed heirefter to him, as they shal happin to grow dew: And wheras he hath informed ws how willing yow ar to augment his dewes, in regard of the bie rates and pryces of all necessareis in these tymes, respecting what formerlie they wer, we give yow hartie thanks for the same, and doe heirby speciallie recommend vnto yow, to sie him so weill and compleitlie provydit, as both may best befitt his his charge and your credit, and may be a meanes to him, and by his readie endeavours heirefter to testifie his further care and affection for advanceing your trade in those parts.—Whythall, 23 Feb^r 1635.

To the Session.

Right, &c.—Wheras it hath bene humblie schawin vnto ws that our trustie and weilbeloved David Murehead, mereland, of London, haveing about thrie yeires since lent some moneyis to the late Erle of Home, he cannot be repayed thairof becaus of a letter from ws prohibiteing the vplifting of any dewteis of that estate till the differences betweene the pairteis interested in the title of succession thervnto wer determined, wherin our intention was onlie to seclude ather of these pairteis from medling with these rents, bot did not therby meane to dissapoynt the trew creditours to seik what is justlie dew vnto them, least by want of ther moneyis beyond the time condescended vpoun they be prejudged, and possiblie, by the inhabilitie of the tennents or others interested for the tyme, they be putt to vnnecessar trouble and charge to recover the same by Law, which is nowayes our royall meaneing : Therfoir we have heirby thought fitt to recommend vnto yow that, in so far as can be agreeable to equitie, yow preservve a way wherby the said David may be speedilie repayed of the rents of the Lands resting in the tennents' handis, or which shall accress heirefter, till he be satisfeid of what shalbe justlie dew vnto him, that (being payed) the handis may be withdrawin, and by yow reserved as discherges of that debt to the pairtie interested, to whom this course cannot be prejudiciall, bot rather in vantage, by being exonered from payment of vnnecessarie interest heirefter, and consequentlie fred of so just a debt.—Whythall, 23 Feb^r 1635.

To the Session.

Right, &c.—Wheras we ar informed that in ane action depending befor yow between William Seaton of Meldrum and George Chalmers of Balbithan, tuitching a trust reposed in the said William by the other of his lands of Balbithan in the tyme of his absence, yow had gevin out your decrie in favours of the said George tuitching the inheritance, and that the poynt now left disputable doeth onlie concerne the said William's accompts or disbursments for the other, and that the rents of his Lands received, or which he might have received ; wherin, sieing his cariage may prove such as in the preceiding case of trust which he did disclame, in hope to gane the propertie of these landis to himsellf, and that he now endeavoureth, as lykwayes we ar informed, to protract tyme by delayes, becaus of the others aige and occasion of some necessarie bussines in this our kingdome : We ar pleased, in consideratioun thairof, and of the interest that our trustie servant Doctour Chalmers, his brother-german, hath at this tyme acquyred in that estate, who cannot convenientlie follow that action himsellf, according to the vsuall course in the lyk caces, becaus of his attendance in our service heir, to recommend to yow that speedie justice be administred tuitching the clearing of these accompts and debursments, according to the course of our Lawes; And in all other causes which may concerne our said servant his interest in the said Estate, and hurt done thervnto in absence of his said brother, in so far as is competent to your Judicatorie, that he be not diverted from attending his charge heir.—Whythall, 23 Feb' 1635.

To the Bischop of Edinburgh.

Reverend father in God, Vnderstanding the good abiliteis of M' Johne M'Math, minister at Symprene, hath to serve ws and the Church, and that hitherto he hath lived conformable and conscionable in his charge : It is our pleasur that, sicing he may elsewher doe ws and the Church better service than wher he presentlie serves, that whensoever any good occasion shall offer wherby he may be preferred within your dyocie, to aney charge wherof we or yow ar patron, that he may be preferred and presented, not onlie for his better encouragment, bot that others, sicing our and your care of such, they may be encouraged to keip ane constant course in our church service ; wherin expecting your obedience.—Whythall, vt supra.

To the Session.

Vpon the 18 Aprill 1635 ther passed a letter his Matie hand directed to the Session in favours of M' Samwell Johnstoun, for recoverie of some moneyis lent by him to the Erle of Home about 3 yeires befor the daite heirof, verbatim lyk vnto the other writtin in favours of David Murcheid.—Vide in precedentibus foliis apud Whythall, 23 Feb' 1635.

To the Archbischop of St Androis.

Right, &c.—Wheras out of our princelie respect of the good education to our Nobilitie of that our kingdome as ar of younger yeires, speciallie of these who ar our wardis, we have bene pleased at this tyme to have a care of the good and religious breiding of our right trustie and weilbeloved cousen the Erle of Buccleuch in letters and what else is fitt and necessarie for ane in his place and qualitie : To which purpois we have heirby thoght fitt to recommend vnto yow that by the advyse of our right trustie and our right weilbeloved Cousen and Counsellour the Erle of Stirling (to whome we have granted the gift of his ward and mariage), and of aney tuo of such of his most speciall freinds and kinsmen as yow shall think fitt to mak choyse of, yow sie a course taken with him and setled accordinglie, which we will tak as acceptable service done vnto ws.—Whythall, 27 Feb' 1635.

To the Exchequer.

Right, &c.—Haveing heard that yow have stopped the passing of that gift which we wer latelie pleased to grant vnto our right trustie and weilbeloved Sir Anthonie Alexander, kny^t, M^r of our Works, of our kingdome of Scotland, by reasone of some objections made by Sir Wm Sinclar of Roslin, kny^t, pretending ane heretable Charge over the maissones of our said kingdome : Though we have never gevin warrant for strenthning of aney heretable right, yitt we intend not to wrong aney man who is sufficientlie secured therin, bot to recover it by dew course of Law : Therfoir it is our pleasur that yow caus the said Sir Wm Sinclar mak it appear vnto yow and to our Advocat what right and title he hath wherby the passing of the said signature should be stayed, and if yow find that ther be just caus in his part why the said signature should be stayed, and that it contoyne any new clause more to his prejudice than other Masteris of Works formerlie had, we desyte that our Advocat may certifie ws of the trew estate therof,

ii   3 u

and if ther be no just caus of stay, sieing we will that the present M^r of Work have as much priviledge as aney of his predicessours in that place have ever had, it is our pleasur that immediatlie yow cause pass the same throw our sealls, and we will lykwayes for the better clearing of the said bussines that yow examyne the massones of that our kingdome, and that not by paperis whervnto ather of the pairteis may have procured ther handis in a privat way, bot that yow give ordour to the magistrats of everie toun, and to the scherreffis of everie schyre, or to aney other officers whom yow shall think fitt, that so they, haveing called befor them and heard the saids massones, may report vnto yow what they shall find in the same.—Whythall, 27 Feb^r 1635.

To the Chancellour.

Right reverend, &c.—We expected befor this tyme the Lord Balmerino should have submitted himsellf to our mercie in a satisfactorie maner by some publict expression, or that otherwayes with all diligence he should have bene present to his tryell, as we had signifeid our pleasur to the Erle of Traquair, who we doubt not did communicat the same with yow and such others as we wryt vnto, that yow might have joyned your endeavours for the advancement of that service, and though it had some stay by prorogating the day in regard of the absence of the Cheiff Justice, who could hardlie repair thither becaus of the stormie weather, it is our pleasur, that advyseing with the said Erle of Traquair, to whome we formerlie imparted our pleasur therin, and such others as ar entrusted from ws by Commission from that bussines, that in caice he did not submitt yow proceid with all diligence to his tryell according to the course of Justice, and that yow certifie ws bak as soone as possiblie yow can what is done or resolved to be done heirin.—Whythall, 2 March 1635.

To the Exchequer.

Right, &c.—Haveing bene pleased vpon good considerations to signe a gift of the escheit and lyfrent of George Buchanan of that ilk to Robert Drummond of Medhope, Our pleasur is, that with diligence yow pas it, suffering no former gift therof (if aney be alreadie granted by yow) to tak place, and if aney declaratour be gevin thervpon, we requyre that the said Robert be secured in such legall maner as he can devyse of the benefite of the bakland gevin to our Thesaurer, becaus that as heirby we intend not to defraud aney creditour of what he hath disbursed, or of what at first he was engadged for the said George, without amassing of other men's moneyis adebtit to them, and to the which they have taken assignations, so that our royall meaneing is that his estate should not be takin from him without verie just and equitable consideratiouns flowing from the Creditours ther owin simple disbursaments : To which purpois it is our further pleasur that (if neid be) yow signifie our will heirin to the Lords of Session for preventing what may be done to the contrarie, and to proceid in justice for granting a declaratour vpon that our request, stopping all others of this kynd ; for which these presents shalbe vnto yow and them a sufficient warrant.

To the Lord Kintyre.

Wheras we ar fullie resolved vpon speciall considerations knowen vnto ws that the bargane tuitching the Lord of Dunluce his purches from yow of the Lands of Kintyre shall ceise, haveing to that purpois gevin ordour to the Erle of Stirling, our Secretarie, to sie a renunciatioun signed by him for relinquisching his interest therin, Least such bandis or moneyis as hath bene gevin to yow by his father the Erle of Antrim or himsellf be a hinderance to this purpois, it is our pleasur, and we doe heirby will and requyre yow furthwith, to pay and delyver bak vnto the said Lord Dunluce all such moneyis and bandis as yow have receaved tuitching that bargane.—Whythall, 3 March 1635.

The gift of the escheit and lyfrent of George Buchanan of that ilk was granted by his Matie to Ro^t Drummond of Medhope, which did fall and was at his Ma^{teis} dispositioun by vertew of the said George his being putt to the horne and declared rebell at the instance of Agnes Barclay, relict of vmquhill Mr James Haig : Stilo ordinario.—Whythall, 4 March 1635.

To the Erle of Arrell, Cheiff Justice.

Right, &c.—Being adverteised of the delay of the tyme appoynted for Balmerinois tryell in Februar last by reasone of the extraordinarie tempest of weather, and that the same is protogat to the ellevint of March instant, we have thoght fitt heirby to requyre yow to caus the said tyme be kept, and to remitt the bussines to the tryell of ane assyse, for as we desyre nothing bot right to be done, so we will not have tyme lost by the discourse and disput of Advocatts : Therfor, as at the first yow did well to give them tyme aneuch for oppugneing the relevancie of the lybell, yow will advert now when the interloculour is pronunced to have no more dayes spent into that in that sort, bot that yow cause the Jurie to be sworne and to give out ther verdict, which, whatsoever it be, yow shall immediatlie adverteise ws of, and haveing pronunced the sentence in caice he be convicted, yow shall continew the executioun therof till our pleasur be knowen ; and otherwyse, if he be absolved, yow shall remitt him bak to his prissone till yow have signifeid the same vnto ws and hear from ws bak agane : In all this we expect your carefulnes according to the trust we have in yow.—Whythall, 5 March 1635.

Wheras we did latelie signifie to the right, &c. the Archbischop of St Androis, Chancellour of that our kingdome, that albeit befor we did appoynt him President of our Exchequer, yit haveing promoved him to the dignitie and place of Chancellour, we thoght it not fitt and propper for him to bruik the said place of President in Exchequer, and sicing our thesaurers principall and deputie ar our cheiff officers in the Excheker, it is most fitt for our service that our said Thesaurer principall, and in his absence the Thesaurer depute, should preside : Therfor it is our speciall pleasur that this ordour be keped in Exchequer in all tyme cuming, and that thir presents be registrat in our books of Exchequer to be a sufficient warrant for that effect.—Whythall, 5 March 1635.

To the Erles of Morton and Traquair, and remanent
of the Exchequer.

To the Chancellour.

Right, &c.—Haveing bene pleased of late to signifie our pleasur vnto our right, &c. the Erle of Erroll, our Justice Generall deputed by ws for the tyme, that the Lord Balmerino should be putt to the tryell of ane assyse, according as it is mentionat in our letter to that purpois, and haveing fullie resolved, in caice of the absence of our said Justice Generall by seiknesse, indisposition of bodie, or otherwayes, that the tryell of that bussines shall not be further delayed, we ar heirby pleased to requyre yow to caus our Justice deputeis and the assessours appoynted by ws to goe on in that tryell with all diligence, and to that effect that yow signifie vnto them that such is our pleasur, and for which these presents shalbe to them a sufficient warrant.—Whythall, 10 March 1635.

To the Lord Deputie of Irland.

Right, &c.—Wheras we ar informed that the late primate of Ardmach had the fynes of recusants of that realme by letters patents of our late dear father, which wer broght bak for our vse, wherin the bearer Johne Butler, Esquyre, had takin great panes by improveing that casualtie, and wheras our late father had (for the better prosecution of that bussines) geviu ordour for granting commissions to him to collect these fynes for our vse, with power to nominat a receaver and auditour, according to articles condescended vpon betwcen our said royall father and him latelie befor his death : To which purpois the said Johne Butler hath now made humble sute vnto ws to have our letters patentes for 31 yeires of the moytie or halff part of these fynes that shall accrew over and above the 20,000lib alredie payed to ws, with all commissions and writts requisit for collecting therof, though his panes therin by improveing our revenews doe appear by these articles and other circumstances; yit being loath to proceid in such a purpois without dew advyse, we have heirby thought fitt to remitt the consideratioun of the bussines vnto yow, that if yow find it to be beneficiall to ws, and that the prosecution therof will tend to the good of our service mentional in these articles, or to other writts tuitching that purpois, yow grant vnto him letters patents for 31 yeires of the moytie or halff part of all these fynes which shall accrue over and above the 20,000lib, with all com-missions and warrants necessarie to him and his assigneyis, togidder [with] the nameing of a receaver and auditour ; for which these presents shalbe vnto yow a sufficient warrant.—Whythall, 10 March 1635.

To the Exchequer.

Right, &c.—Haveing bene pleased to signe vnto yow a commission for hearing of the accompts of the taxations, ordinarie and extraordinarie, the accompt whairof hath not bene as yit gevin vp vnto ws by our late Chancellour, Collectour of the same, and of our Treasurie, Collectorie, and treasurie of our new augmen-tations befor the entrie of our new treasureris, as by the said Commission yow will perceave, it is our pleasur that yow accept of the said Commission, and proceid carefullie therin according to the trust we have committed vnto yow ; and efter yow have finished the said accompts, yow advertise ws what yow have done therin.—Whythall, 12 March 1635.

To Sir Lauchlane McCleane.

Trustie, &c.—Wheras we wer informed that of late yow and your vmquhill brother Hectour McCleane did without ordour or any right violentlie intrude yourselff in the possession of the Yle of Icolmekill, which belongeth to the Bischop of the Yles for the tyme, whairof they have bene in peaciable possession these many yeres bypast, and that yow still doe deteyne the same from the present bischop therof ; We holding such a violent and indirect a course as a contempt done vnto the Church, and consequentlie vnto ws, and withall taking to our princelie consideratioun the detriment therby arrysing to the patrimonie of that bishoprik, wherof we doe rather desyre the incress than anywayes to sie it impaired, It is our pleasur, and we doe will and command, that furthwith yow restore vnto the said bischope the absolute possession of the said Yland without further hearing or delay.—Whythall, 14 March 1635.

To the Session.

Right reverend father in God, and trustie and weilbeloved—Wheras we ar crediblie informed that, vpon letter in favours of the late Bischop of Yles, now of Rapho, the taksmen of the tyth-fieshes of the Yles did dimitt ther taks in his favouris, tho right and possession whairof he suffered to be assigned to a laick persone, who now enjoyis the same, it being the cheifest benefice of that bischoprik; whervnto, sieing it was, and still is, our royall intention that these tythes should be inseperablie conjoyned, we doe seriouslie recommend to yow that, haveing takin into your consideration the loss the present bischop of the Yles hath suffered by the want thairof, and the other's benefite by his bypast possession, yow sie the said reverend father in God receave the lyk benefit and favour his saidis predicessours had in the lyk kynd, and that yow administer speedie justice in all other causses concerneing him, whensoever they shall cum befor yow ; Which we ar rather pleased the more carefullie to recommend to yow becaus of the remotnes of his See off that our seat of Justice, the meannesse of his benefice, and greatnes of his charge, To which purpois it did pleas our royall father and ourselff so often to wryt vnto yow and others Judicatoreis in that our kingdome. — Whythall, 14 March 1635.

To THE BISCHOP OF RAPHO.

Reverend father in God—We ar informed that Andro, late bischop of Rapho, at his transportatioun from the bischoprik of Yles, did, without just caus or aney warrant from our late royall father or ws, carie with him tuo of the principall bells that wer in Icolmekill, and place them in some of the Churches of Rapho, To which purpois we doe remember that at the tyme, your being bischop of Yles, yow wer a sutter to ws for effectuating that thing at your predicessour the bischop of Raphoes hands which we now requyre of yow : Therfor, and in regaird we have gevin ordour to the present bischop of Yles for repairing the Cathedrall Church of that bischoprik, and that it is titt that such things as doe properlie belong thervnto be restored, it is our pleasur that yow caus delyver vnto the said bischop these tuo bells for the vse of the said Cathedrall Church with such tymlie conveniencie as may be, which we will acknowledge as acceptable service done vnto ws.—Whythall, 14 March 1635.

To THE ERLE OF TRAQUAIR.

Right, &c.—Haveing by our warrant required Nicolas Briott, our servand, to buy and prepair within this our kingdome a certane proportion of copper plate for the fabrication of copper money within that our kingdome, condescended vpon as necessarie to be coyned ther, for which impost, custome, and all other dewteis wer payed heir, and that, being transplanted thither, it is stopt, as we ar informed, for further custome and impost, which is contrarie to reasone, it being for our and the cuntreis service, and not merchinable commoditie : Therfoir it is our pleasur that yow furthwith command our Customeris, and others interested, that they mak no further stop of that commoditie, to be disposed of for the vse forsaid, nor tak aney impost or custome for the same, or for aney other necessarie provision for the said fabrication, ather inward or outward, not exceiding the quantitie ordeaned by ws for the said coyne, causeing them mak restitution to our said servant of all such moneyis taken by them for custome of the said plaite since November last ; ffor which, &c.—Whythall, 14 March 1635.

To THE COUNSELL.

Reverend father in God, and trustie and weilbeloved, &c.—Wheras we ar informed that Patrik Maull, indueller in St Androis, being of late mutilat and dangerouslie wounded to the great hazard of his lytf by Patrik Lyndsay of Wolmerstoun, his tuo sones and sone-in-law, that cautioun and assurance is not taken as yit of them for being lyable to Justice that is requisit in such caces, we have taken speciall notice of the foulnes of the fact ; and being willing that the doers be exemplarlie punisched in so far as lawfullie can be done, it is our pleasur that yow tak sufficient cautioun and assurance of them, as justice be nather prevented or delayed for aney respect whatsoever, in so far as can be agricable to our lawes.—Whythall, 16 March 1635.

To the Exchequer.

Right, &c.—Wheras the reverend father in God the bischope of Yles is by our direction to repair the Cathedrall Church of Icolmkill, the doeing whairof in such maner as is requisite will requyre (as we ar credible informed) great panes and charges, which he cannot possiblie vndergoe without our assistance and help : Therfoir, and in regard it is a work which we affect, we have thoght fitt to allow vnto him and his assigneyis the sowme of four hundreth pundis sterling, ffor the more readie payment whairof we doe heirby requyre and authorize yow to assigne him and them to all the few-dewteis payable vnto ws by Sir Lauchlane McCleane, till the said sowme be compleitlie payed, the first termes payment whairof to be at Mertimes nixt 1635 ; and, in the meane tyme, that yow be carefull he goe on with the said reparation, authorizeing him with full power to requyre service of all such persones in these parts as doe ow the same vnto ws, and that for caryeing and transporting of commoditeis vnto that work ; ffor doeing of all which these presents shalbe vnto yow and everie ane of yow a sufficient warrant.—Whythall, 24 March 1635.

To the Lord Lorne.

Right, &c.—These ar to recommend vnto yow to send vnto ws by the bearer ane of the Mangrell haulkes that ar in some of the boundis wherin yow have interest, tuitching which purpois we did formerlie wryt vnto [yow], and that with as much convenient diligence as may be ; and that yow be carefull according to our former pleasur to sie the ayreis of these haulks carefullie preserved, wherin yow shall doe ws acceptable pleasur.

There past a gift of pension to Sir James Leslie, knyᵗ, dureing his lyftyme of ane yeirlie duetie of 1000ˡⁱᵇ Scotts, to be payed furth of whatsoever your Maⁱᵉⁱˢ rents and casualiteis, which is doeated by speciall direction of the Erle of Morton, your Maⁱᵉⁱˢ principall Thesaurer, as haveing your Maⁱᵉⁱˢ warrant for that effect.—Whythall, 25th March 1635.

Subᵣ,   Sir Th. Hope.

To the Counsell.

Right, &c.—Haveing vpon your advertcisment vnderstude the inconvenients lyklie to aryse by the sale of Kintyre to the Lord Dunluce, we wer thervpon pleased furthwith to caus stay the bargane, wherin we doe acknowledge your care and give yow hartie thanks for the same : We being now willing that the said bargane be made so ineffectuall (notwithstanding of any proceidings whatsumever betweene the pairteis) as the said Lord, his aires or successours, cannot therby at any tyme heirefter pretend any interest or clayme to these landis : It is our pleasur that yow tak such a course as yow shall find best conduce to this purpois ; and that besydis yow give ordour to our Advocat for drawing a renunciation in a sure and legall maner, which we will to be sent with all diligence vnto our Secretarie for that kingdome, for sieing the same subscryved be the Lord Dunluce, that it may be returned registrat and keipit amongst the records thairof ; for doeing whairof these presents shalbe sufficient warrant : We bid yow farewell.—Whythall, 25 March 1635.

It is our pleasur that with all diligence yow caus pay vnto the bearer George Haliburton, ane of our fa coners, the accustomed yeirlie allowance for bringing some haulks vnto ws from the northern parts of that our kingdome, and that yow give vnto him your best furtherance for that effect; ffor doeing whairof these presents, &c.—Whythall, 25 March 1635.

To the Erles of Morton and Traquair, Thesaurers principall and
Deputie of Scotland.

TO THE THESAURERS AND ADVOCAT.

Right, &c.—Wheras we ar informed that at our granting of the lyfrent escheit of ane Gawin Blair of Heby to Johne Boyll of Kelburne, yow receaved (according to your custome) his bakband, restrayneing his making further vse of that gift than the payment of the just debts owing to him at that tyme, declareing the benefite of the said gift to accress therefter to such persones as shalbe warranted by yow to receave the same : And being informed that since the begining of that bakband the said Johne hath, for the others vse in helping of his right to the commontie of the Larggs, advanced further sowmes of money, Our pleasur is, that he enjoy the benefite of the said lyfrent escheit till he be payed of that and all such moneyis as at this tyme shall appear vpon just accompt to be dew vnto him ; and withall, being informed that our servant Sir James Lockhart hath compyrysed the said Gawin his Landis for moneyis dew to him, and being willing to prevent the prejudice he may suffer if that lyfrent right should be disposed otherwayes, it is our further pleasur that yow declare the benefite of the said bakband in favours of our said servant, that what benefite may flow from ws in this particular may whollie accress to him, till he be compleitlie payed of what is dew to him : ffor which these presents shalbe your warrant.—Whythall, 25 March 1635.

TO THE CHANCELLOUR.

Right, &c.—Haveing vnderstude from yow that the Marqueis of Huntlie hath vndertaken the suppressing of the rebells in the North, and that he hath gevin caution for the same, and vnderstanding lykwyse that for performeing therof he desyreth libertie to returne thither, that he may be the more able (being ther himsellf in persone) to look vnto the quyeting of the cuntrie and preserveing of the peace in these pairts heirefter, we conceave, since he was cited ther by warrant from our Counsell for geving vnto them ane accompt of such things, as they wer to charge him with, that the prosecution of the whole bussines doeth lykwyse belong vnto them, trusting vnto ther judgments that they will doe therin as they will find most advantageous for our service in the establisching of peace and restrayneing of such rebellions heirefter; and if they shall licence him to returne, which we remitt wholie vnto yow and them, that they will doe it vpon such conditions as yow shalbe answerable vnto ws to be sufficient, which we will yow to signifie vnto them from ws, expecting lykwayes that yow will have a speciall care of the same, according to the trust we repose in yow : We bid yow farewell.—From our Court at Whythall, 2 Aprill 1635.

TO THE EXCHEQUER.

Right, &c.—Haveing bene informed of the long and faythfull service done vnto our late dear father for many yeres togidder by his and our old servand Mr William Broun, in his charge of presenting the signatures and making the Counsell dispatches, we wer pleased in regard therof, and of the abiliteis and sufficiencie of Mr Patrik Broun, his sone, for dischergeing that office, to confer the same vpon him ; whairof, being willing that he enjoy such priviledges as dœ propertie belong thervnto, our pleasur is that yow suffer none to encroach vpon the same, or to trouble him in anything concerneing the dischargeing of that service, vnless by his owin misbehaviour and insufficiencie, to be examined and tryed befor yow, and to be reported vnto ws, yow find him vnworthie of that charge.—Whythall, 2 Aprill 1635.

Ther past a Protection for one James Chambers, sometyme Maisser to the Lords of Session, who did both long and faythfullie serve his Maᵗⁱᵉ and his Maᵗⁱˢ late royall father, of blissed memorie, and the subjects in that kingdome in that charge, Making mention that wheras his Maᵗⁱᵉ is informed that the said James Chambers doeth stand indebted to some Creditours in some sowmes of money, which he is most willing to pay if some compitent tyme wer granted vnto him to vse his best endevours to that purpois: Cetera stilo ordinario.—Whythall, 10 Aprill 1635.

Our Soveraigne Lord now, efter his speciall and generall revocatiouns made in Parliament holdin at Edinburgh Junij 1633, and outwith, doeth, withs peciall consideratioun of the good and faythfull service done vnto his Maᵗⁱˢ late dear father, of worthie memorie, by vmquhill Johne Mylward, doctour in divinitie, who was speciallie employed by his Maᵗⁱˢ said father to preach the gospell within Scotland, and whom it pleased God to call out of this mortall lyff befor his returne to England, wher he was borne, and with speciall advyse and consent of his Maᵗⁱˢ right, &c. the Earles of Morton and Traquair, his Maᵗⁱˢ Thesaurer Principall and deputie of the said kingdome of Scotland, and of the remanent noblmen and others, his Maᵗⁱˢ Commissioners of Exchequer ther, Ordeanes a letter to be made and exped vnder the privie seall in due forme, ratifieing, approveing, and confirmeing, lykas his Maᵗⁱᵉ by the tenour heirof, and with speciall advyse and consent forsaid, ratifeis, approves, and confirmes a gift of pension of ane thowsand tuo hundreth pundis lawfull money of Scotland, granted by his Maᵗⁱˢ father vnder the great seall thairof vnto Ann Mylward, the widow of the said Doctour Mylward, and to James Mylward, ther sone, and to the longest leiver of them two, which is of the date at Whythall the 9 of Noʳ 1609, Togidder with a former ratification of the said pension made by his Maᵗⁱᵉ himsellf vnder his privie seall, of the daite at Theobald's the 17 of July 1627, in the whole heads, clausses, articles, and conditions therof; Declareing this present ratification to be as valide, effectuall, and sufficient to the said Ann Mylward, now called by the name of Agnes Bell, the wyff of Johne Bell of Pertenhall, in the countie of Bedford, dureing all the dayes of hir lyftyme, as if the said originall leitter of gift and ratification following thervpon war word ingrost and exprest heirin, wheranent, and with all objections whatsoever which anywayes can be proponed aganst the validitie thairof, or of this present confirmation, his Maᵗⁱᵉ hath dispenssed, and by thir presents dispensses for ever: Mairover, our said Soveraigne Lord, for good and considerable causses abovesaid, dœ, of new give, grant, and dispone, lykas by these presents his Maᵗⁱᵉ, with advyse and consent forsaid, gives, grants, and dispones of new vnto the said Agnes Bell dureing hir lyftyme the whole aforsaid yeirlie pension of 1200 pundis Scottis money, to be yeirlie vplifted by the said Agnes, hir assigneyis, factours, or others haveing hir power to receave the same, furth of the first and readiest of his Maᵗⁱˢ rents and casualteis whatsoever of the said kingdome, from his Maᵗⁱˢ Thesaurer Principall and deputie, or any of them, or any other his Maᵗⁱˢ officers who shall happin to have charge of his Maᵗⁱˢ rents or casualiteis, or ather of them for the time; Commanding the said Erls of Morton and Traquair, and ather of them, and all others his Maᵗⁱˢ Thesaurers, receavers, and officers for the tyme, to mak good, thankfull, and readie payment of the said pension of 1200ᵗʰ Scotts to the said Agnes Bell or hir forsaids, or any of them, yeirlie, at the termes prescryved in the said gift and ratification following therom, dureing all the dayes of hir lyftyme, and that of the readiest moneyis in his Maᵗⁱˢ Exchoker, and of his Maᵗⁱˢ rents and casualiteis whatsoever; And with speciall command and direction vnto the said Erlis of Morton and Traquair, and ather of them, to mak readie and present payment vnto the said Agnes or hir forsaidis of the whole arrears of the said pension, according to a trew and just accompt of what sche is behind, ffor which these presents shalbe to them sufficient warrand; Commanding lykwyse the Auditours of the said Officers' accompts, and each of them, to defease and allow the said yeirlie pension and arreires in ther first accompts, thir presents being registrat as effeires.—Gevin at Whythall, 10 Aprill 1635.

These conteyne a gift of the baronie of Craighall, and peice of Land therof called Thornydyks, baronie of Tasses, the baronie of Kynmouth, and the tythis therof, and the lands of Wester Granton, to Sir Thomas Hop, your Matie Advocat, vpoun his owin resignatioun, with a new gift of the same, and of the burgh of baronie of Seres, mercatts and faires therof, and also in few to him of the haill mettalls and mineralls within the said lands and baroneis, and within his other lands of the kirk landis of Seres, Arnydie, Hiltarvyt, and Dallasse, holdin by him of other superiours nor your Matie, and that with consent of the Erle of Stirline, your Matie Secretarie, Master of the Mynes and mineralls; With ane vnion of all iu ane baronie, to be called the baronie of Craighall, to be holdin by your Matie in blench ferme, Taxtward, and few ferme respective, in maner particularlie above specifeit.—Whythall, the 10 Aprill 1635.

To the Counsell.

Right, &c.—Being humblie sued vnto in behalff of the Lady of our right trustie, &c. the Lord Almond, that we wilbe pleased to give ordour that sche might not lose that place which sche had as the wyff of hir late husband, the Erle of Dumfermeling, sum tyme our Chancellour of that our kingdome; We, for some good respects moveing ws, ar heirby pleased that sche have place as Countesse of Dumfermeling, and to that effect that yow give such ordour as yow shall think fitt to preseryve.—Whythall, 10 Aprill 1635.

To the Thesaurers, Principall and Deputie.

Right, &c.—Haveing taken speciall notice of the grounds whervpoun the pension of the widow of vmquhill Johne Milward, Doctour of Diviuitie, was granted by our late dear father, and of his care in causeing hir be dewlie payed dureing his lyftyme; We have bene pleased to ratifie his gift therof of new, which we will yow to caus expeid vnder our sealls with diligence, and to mak such readie payment of the pension heirefter as sche may have no occasion to importun ws for the same, or putt hir sellf to further vnnecessarie Charges and trouble in seiking thairof: And whairas we ar informed of her sufferings by want of the same these diverse yeires bypast, wherby sche hath engadged hir sellf in debt, we doe heirby lykwyse requyre yow to mak speedie payment vnto hir and hir assigneyis of the whole arreires of the said pension, wherby the intention of our dear father towards hir may be dewlie performed; for such is our royall pleasur.—Whythall, 10 Aprill 1635.

To the Advocat.

Trustie, &c.—Haveing bene pleased to wryt agane vnto our Colledge of Justice for putting to a speedie end according to Justice that action in Law depending befor them tuitching our Commontie of Dunbar, as yow will perceave by the enclosed copie of our letter vnto them: It is our pleasur that yow goe on accordinglie with all diligence, that our right, &c. the Viscount of Belheaven, who for causeing that our service be the more speedelie followed is to repair thither, be not hindred to returne with all possible diligence ; and if yow shall mak it appear befoir them that it is necessarie for the good of our service that perambulation be made for the better distinguisching of that our Commontie from other Lands, we will yow lykwayes carefullie to insist by your best endeavours and panes to sie it rightlie and speedelie done ; flor doeing whairof, &c.—Whythall, 18 Aprill 1635.

To the Session.

Right, &c.—Wheras we wer pleased by our letters in May 1634 to requyre that vpon summondis and proces to be intended by our Advocat at our instance for tryeing the right of such persones as have intruded vpon our commontie of Dumbar, speedie justice might be administred therin according to our Lawes, in regard that action (now depending befor yow) doeth so neirlie concerne ws in the right of our propertie, and therin our right, &c. the Viscount of Belheaven hath speciall interest as our Chalmerlane of the Lordschip of Dumbar, who is to repair vnto that kingdome for causeing it be putt to a speedie poynt according to our lawis, and whom we will to returne hither with possible diligence : We ar heirby pleased againe seriouslie to requyre yow to administer such speedie justice therin as possiblie and lawfullie can be vsed, and in the mean tyme if our Advocat (to whome we have lykwyse writtin tuitching this purpois) mak it appear befor yow, and if your sellfis shall find it expedient that a perambulation be made to distinguisch that our Commontie from others Landis, It is our further pleasur that to that purpois yow give ordour to such persones for doeing thairof as yow shall think fitt, and that with the greatest expedition may be that it be no difference to the Clearing of that action : So not doubting of your speciall care heirin as a purpois so neirlie concerneing ws.—Whythall, 18 Aprill 1635.

To the Advocat.

Trustie, &c.—Wheras it hath bene humblie represented vnto ws in behalff of Mr Alexr Bisset, minister at Brechin, desyreing that in regard he hath obtened a Decrie befor the Colledge of Justice tuitching the priviledges of the Mairschip of the schirefdome of Aberdene, he might accordinglie discharge that office, and enjoy the priviledges and benefite belonging thervnto : Though we be vnacquanted with the nature of that office, yit being will that a dew consideration be had of a caus wherin ther hath bene so judiciall a proceiding : Our pleasur is, that haveing called the said Mr Alexr befor yow, and haveing examined the grounds of his right, yow acquant our Thesaurers principall and deputie, or ather of them, therwith, and with your Opinion in Law tuitching that purpois, that they may certifie vnto ws what they think fitt and necessarie to be done tuitching the same ; whervpon we will declair our further pleasur.—Whythall, 18 April 1635.

To the Session.

Right, &c.—As we wer pleased by our letters in September last to recommend vnto yow that action of the Lady Jeane Stewart and Robert Ellot, hir husband, so now the consideratioun of ther distressed Estate, and of the panes alreadie taken both by ws and yow to have ane end putt to that cause, hath moved ws againe at ther humble sute seriouslie to recommend vnto yow that speedie justice be administred in any action concerneing them, ather depending or which shall happin to cum befor yow, and the rather becaus ther present estate doeth requyre our princelie Commiseration, and from yow what present benefite our Lawes can affurd vnto them.—Whythall, 18 Aprill.

To the Chancellour.

Right, &c.—The differences tuitching the schip called the . . . which was questioned by Thomas Lyndsay as lawfull pryse, being debaited by the pairteis interested, who have condescended vpon the dismissing thairof, and gevin suretie each to other to be answerable to the Lawes tuitching these differences : It is our pleasur that yow furthwith give ordour for enlargeing the said Thomas Lyndsay from prissone ; for which these presents salbe your warrand.—Whythall, 18 Aprill 1635.

To the Exchequer.

Right, &c.—This signature of the baronie of Craighall contencing nothing bot what vpon good consideratiouns we wer pleased formerlie to grant vnto our trustie and weilbeloved Counsellour Sir Thomas Hope of Craighall, kynt and barouet, our Advocat, save onlie a gift in few of the mettalls and mineralls fund in his owin Landis : It is our pleasur that with diligence yow caus expeid the said signature according to the tenour thairof, and without any composition ; ffor which these presents, &c.—18 Aprill 1635.

To the Counsell.

Right, &c.—Wheras it hath bene humblie represented vnto ws that in the tryell befor yow tuitching the wounding of Patrik Maull, indueller of St Androis, yow had for that fact caused imprissone John Lyndsay, sone to Mr Patrik Lyndsay of Wormestoun, referring to further tryell in Law the action tuitching the mutilation of the said Patrik Maull, In respect of the barbaritie and foulnes of the fact, and of the place wher it was committed, and the better to prevent any further inconvenient that may therby ensue for brecking onr peace, it is our pleasur that the said Johne be not released from prissone till ather he be tryed according to our Lawes provydit in the lyk caces for the said mutilation, or otherwayes that he give such satisfaction to the pairtie wronged as he shalbe willing to accept.—Whythall, 20 Aprill 1635.

To the Session.

Right, &c.—Wheras we wer pleased, for reasones mentionat in our letter in May 1634, to signifie our pleasur vnto yow for staying all processes intented or to be intended at the instance of any of the persones clameing interest in the Estate of Home aganst others, at the instance of any other aganst them, as aires or successonrs to the late Erle of Home, till yow should receave our further directions therannent, and now humble sute hath bene made vnto ws in behalff of our right, &c. the Countess of Home, that sche might not therby be impeidit to have recourse by Law for the rent of these Lands of Bergum, Lithin, and Kellie, for securing of hir, in caice John Stewart of Coldinghame should, in default of aires-male of his bodie, recover fra hir the tythes of Fals Castell and Auld Cambesse, wherin her caus being much differed from the caice or others, and for diverse good consideratiouns requyreing more then ordinarie respect : It is our pleasur that sche have frie libertie to insist by Law and have speedie justice for acquyreing what shalbe fund justlie dew vnto hir in that particular, which we will tak as acceptable service done vnto ws ; and for which these presents shalbe vnto yow a warrant.—Whythall, 5 May 1635.

Our Soveraigne Lord ordeanes a Letter of naturalization to be made and exped vnder the great seall of the kingdome of Scotland, Making mention That whetas . . . lawfull sone of Lord Duderhellie, late ambassadour to his Matie from the Quen of Sueden, hath bene ane humble sutter to his highnes for being made a naturalized persone of the said kingdome of Scotland, in respect that his descent in blood on the mother syd is from thence ; And that he intendis ane action of Law for recoverie of certane Landis which (as is affirmed) did belong vnto his guidsyr vnquhill James Neave : Therfor, and for diverse other good consideratiouns moveing his Matie, his highnes hath declared, and for him and his successours does declair, the sad . . . to be naturalized as a native subject borne within the said kingdome in all tyme cuming, and to be capable of whatsumever digniteis, offices, and benefites within the same, and to have full libertie and power not onlie to insist by law for recoverie of what is justlie due vnto him, bot to purches and acquyre within the said kingdome whatsoever landis, heretages, annualrents, and others goods and geir, moveable and immoveable, and the same to posses and enjoy by whatsumever title, as weill by way of successioun as by donation, acquisition, or otherwayes : And that the aires to the said . . . shall have right and power to succeid to whatsumever lands or heretages to be acquyred to them within the said kingdome, and shall have libertie to dispose of by ther testaments and latter wills vpon whatsoever goodis and geir which shallhappin to appertene vnto them within the said kingdome, and to nominat executours in ther testaments, and to leave and dispone thervpon by legacie to whatsumever persone or persones, and also to nominat tutours, ane or mae, to ther children, male and female, procreated or to be procreated of ther bodeis, and to bruik, posses, and enjoy all other priviledges, immuniteis, faculteis, and liberteis whatsoever which ar compitent or may be compitent to any native borne subject within the said kingdome : And his Matie wills and commands that thir presents shalbe ane sufficient warrand to the writter to the great seall and keeper thairof for writting heirof to the said seall, and appending the great seall thervnto without passing any other seall or register.—Grenwich, the 9th of May 1635.

To the Session.

Right, &c.—We have Vnderstude by a letter from our allie and dear freind the Quen of Sweden, how that it pleased our late father, of worthie memorie, to writt vnto Johne the 3 King of Sweden that libertie might have bene granted to vnquhile James Neave, a native of that our kingdome (then employed in his warres), to returne for taking possession of some Landis affirmed to belong to him within the same, and that his comeing was prevented by death ; and wheras it hath bene represented vnto ws that by the act of prescription the Lord Duderhell, present ambassadour vnto ws from our said allie the Quen of Sweden, who maried the daughter and air of the said James Neave, and ther children, ar lyk to be defrauded of these Lands ; We being willing, for diverse good respects and considerable circumstances heirin, that all the possible furtherance of Justice be granted that the Lawes can affoord to the said Nobleman, ar heirby pleased seriouslie to recommend vnto yow to tak the reasones to be propounded in his behalf into your serious consideratioun, and thervpon to administer such speedie justice as possiblie and lawfullie can be granted in all actions of Law to be intended by him, or any haveing his power, or ony right deryved from him and his Lady or ather of them for recoverie of what doeth justlie belong vnto them.— Grenwitch, 9 May 1635.

To the Erle of Traquair.

Right, &c.—Being willing to prevent any vnnecessarie charge that may aryse to the persones interested in the Copper moneyis which for the publict good ar appoynted to be coyned in that our kingdome by building or hyreing of housses fitt for such a work, it is our pleasur that yow give speedie ordour to the generall and master of our mynt for accommodating them with all rownies and places within our Coyn- hous, fit for fabrication and keiping of that coyne, and for fixing and setting vp of such works, presses, and Instruments within the same as they shall find requisit ; For which these presents shalbe, &c.—Grenwitch, 9 May 1635.

To the Advocat.

Trustie, &c.—Hav-ing bene humblie petitioned to pass the ratificatioun of the priviledges of the Mynt in that our kingdome, we did forbear to doe the same, not questioning any act or lawfull thing that had bene done in ther favouris by any of our royall progenitours, bot to be assured that nothing wer added of new that might prejudge ws or oney of our good subjects: It is therfoir our pleasur that yow confer the ratificatioun sent heirwith, with ther originall chartour, or any other ther authentik evidents, and if yow find nothing materiallie disagriee[n]g between them, or added of new to prejudge ws or our said subjects, that yow furthwith sie that ratificatioun, or ony other they shall draw vp to this purpois, exped immediatlie vnder our Cachet and sealls ther, without further trouble to ws or them; ffor which these presents shalbe vnto yow, and all others our officers whom it doeth or may concerne, sufficient warrand.—Whythall, 9 May 1635.

To the Advocat.

Trustie, &c.—Wheras it hath bene humblie represented vnto ws by the enclosed petition that diverse oppressions have bene made and ar daylie vsed against the petitione-is by the Lard of Innes, vnder cullour of ane heretable office called the Mairdome of Rosse: Though we have resolved to vse our owin royall discretion and tyme tuitching the reductioun of such heretable offices as ar not as yit brought bak vnto our croun, yit this being one against which the complent of oppression hath come to our eares befoir the nature or necessitie of the office hath bene made knowen vnto ws, it is our pleasur that, haveing carefullie considered of the petition and examined the nature of the office, yow insist with all diligence, in our name and for our interest, to reduce the same in a legall maner, and in the meane tyme that yow vse your best endeavours to stop all proceidings that may further trouble these our poore subjects tuitching this purpois, that they, being fred of such oppressions, it may be in our power to suppress or continew the said office, as we shall find caus.—Whythall, 9 May 1635.

Right, &c.—Hearing that some question in Law is lyklie to aryse betwixt the reverend father in God the bischop of Brechin and our servant Patrik Maull, of our bedchalmer, tuitching the power of election of one of the tuo bailleis of Brechin, which for diverse good respects we desyre be composed in a freindlie maner, without vnnecessarie charge or trouble to any of them, and to that purpois haveing made choyse of yow to examyne and setle these differences by mutuall consent of them, both according as yow shall find it most just and lawfull; it is our pleasur that with diligence yow or any six of yow proceid heirin accordinglie, bot if they doe not mutuallie condescend to this course, we will yow to certifie ws thairof, with your opinion in Law to which of them yow think the said priviledge doeth justlie belong.—Whythall, 9 May 1635.

Carolus dei gratia Magnæ Britanniæ Galliæ et Hyberniæ Rex fideique defensor Serenissimæ principi ac dominæ Christianæ Dei gratia Suecorum Gothorum Vandalorumque Reginæ designatæ Magnæ Principi Finlandiæ ducissæ Esthoniæ et Careliæ Ingriæque dominæ Salutem et omnis felicitatis incrementum Serenissima Princeps consanguinea et amica clare constat serenitati vestræ nobilissimisque Tutoribus et Senatui Sueticæ quam bono cum animo et inequo successu Dominus Jacobus Spensius liber baro de Orholin inservierit coronæ vestræ non solum diebus parentis vestræ (semper divæ memoria) verum etiam tempore Caroli noni avi vestri placuit Deo optimo maximo nunc ex hac vita cum sibi ipsi vocare antequam debita in Anglia contracta legatione ejus vltima fuerant persoluta Ita vt nunc subditi nostri Robertus Hamilton a Strueth et Dominus Carolus Howard eques auratus summis quibusdam pecuniæ pro eo persolutis maximo eorum damno ab heredibus ejus vorentur qua propter quoniam omni cum equitate constat divina et humana vt justa debita creditoribus persolvantur (si alia via magis commoda inveniri non poterit) per presentis S^m V^m R^m M^m obnixe rogamus pro licentia Liberis predicti Domini Spencei concedenda vt possessiones in regnis vostris plenissimo quo poterint pretio divendant Et ita Creditoribus hisce persolutis quæ supersunt in vtilitatem viduæ ejus et liberorum convertantur presertim vt licentia vestra cum consensu S^æ R^æ V^æ Majestatis Tutorum concedatur Gulielmo Spencio filio predicti domini natu maximo qui pro presenti nobiscum in Anglia versatur gratissimoque animo parentis debita et persolvere est paratus si modo licentiam istam et commodum mercatorem obtinere poterit hoc sicut equissimum et amicitiæque nostra consonum sic non dubitare possumus quin hoc quasi novo vinculo vobis obstricti et obligati erimus Ideoque obnixe rogamus vt non solum hac in re verum etiam in omnibus ejus honestis negotiis gratificetis manum salutarem porrigatis Deus optimus maximus S^m V^m diutissime salvam et incolumen præservet.—Dabantur Grenovicæ, 12 May 1635.

Vestræ Serenitatis bonus frater et consanguineus.   C. Rex.

Ther past a Conge d'eslire vnder his Ma^tie^s hand, direct to the deane and Chapter of the Cathedrall Church of Aberden, for choysing of a new bischop to that bischoprik, sieing it was vacand by the death of the last bischop who supplied that place.   Stilo ordinario.—Att Grenwitch, the   of May 1635.

Ther past a letter vnder his Ma^tie^s hand, direct to the deane and Chapter of Aberdene, for admitting the Bischop of Dumblane to the bischoprik of Aberdene, which was then vacand by the death of the last bischop who supplied that place.   Stilo Ordinario.—At Grenwich, the   of May 1635

Ther past a Conge d'eslire vnder his Ma^tie^s hand, direct to the deane and chapter of the Cathedrall Church of Brechin, for choysing and admitting of ane to the Bischop of Brechin, sieing that bischoprik was vacand by the transportation of Thomas, then bischop therat.   Stilo Ordinario.—Grenwich, the   of May 1635.

Ther past a letter vnder his Ma^tie^s hand, direct to the deane and chapter of Brechin, for admitting Mr Walter Whytfurd to that bischoprik, sieing it was vacand than by the transportatioun of the last incumbent, Mr Thomas Sydserff.   Stilo ordinario.—Grenwich,   of May 1635.

Ther past a Conge d'eslire vnder his Ma^tie^s hand, direct to the deane and chaptour of the Cathedrall Church of Galloway, for choysing and admitting of ane to be bischop ther, sieing that bischoprik was vacand by the death of the last bischop who supplied that place, viz., Lamb.   Stilo ordinario.—Grenwich, of May 1635.

Ther past a letter vnder his Ma^tie^s hand, direct to the deane and chaptour of Galloway, for admitting the bischop of Brechin to the bischoprik of Galloway, which was than vacand by the death of the last incumbent.   Stilo ordinario.—Grenwich,   of May 1635.

Ther past a Conge d'eslire vnder his Ma^{teis} hand, direct to the deane and chapter of Dumblane, for admitting of ane Doctour James Wedderburne to the bischoprik of Dumblane, vacand by the transportatioun of the last bischop of Dumblane to the bischoprik of Galloway, which was than vacand by the death of the last incumbent therat. Stilo ordinario.—Grenwich,   of May 1635.

Ther past a letter vnder his Ma^{teis} hand, direct to the deane and Chapter of Dumblane, for admitting of ane James Wedderburne, doctour of divinitie, to that bischoprik, than vacand by the transportatioun of he last bischop therof to the bischoprik of Galloway. Stilo ordinario.—Grenwich,   of May 1635.

For admitting of Mr Walter Whytfurd to the bischoprik of Galloway ther went a letter from his Matie, in caice the Bischop of Brechin should refuis the same. Stilo ordinario.—Grenwich,   of May 1635.

To the Session.

Right, &c.—Hearing that ther be some differences in Law between the reverend father in God the bischop of Yles and Sir Lauchlane McCleane of Dowert, concerneing the possession and right to the propertie of certane Lands of the Yle of Icolmekill, tuitching which if any action shalhappin to cum befor yow at the said bischop instance for removeing of the said Sir Lauchlane from the possession therof, we doe heirby recommend vnto yow to administer such speedie justice therin as possiblie can be vsed by the lawis of that our kingdome, which we will tak as acceptable service done vnto ws.—Whythall, 15 May 1635.

To the Commissioners of Tythes.

Right, &c.—Being informed that John McNaucht, citizen and merchand of Edinburgh, is so infirme of bodie and heavilie diseased that he is altogidder vnable to attend the Commission of Tythes, it is therfor our pleasur that he be fred therof, and that Williame Gray, merchand ther, be Commissioner in his place, and that yow receave his oath according to the custome in the lyk caices; for the which these presents, &c.—Whythall, 15 May 1635.

To the Counsell.

Right, &c.—Wheras it hath bene humblie represented vnto ws in behalff of . . . Gordoun of Rothemay and . . . Vrquhart of Leatheris, that being Minors, and ther Landis left vnto them with great burdens, they nor ther cautioners cannot possiblie at this tyme pay the principall sowmes dew to ther creditours, bot ar willing to secure them of the same and thankfullie, and dewlie to pay the annualrents; wherin, the minors' caice deserveing our princelie consideratioun, we have heirby thoght good to recommend vnto yow to call the creditours befor yow, and to tak some fair course with them, not to trouble the saidis minors nor ther sureteis for ther principall sowmes, the saids Creditours being always secured thairof, and dewlie payed of ther annualrents till the minors be of perfect aige, which we will tak as good service done vnto ws. We bid, &c.—Grenwich, 15 May 1635.

To the Counsell.

Right, &c.—Wheras the Lard of Raith, vpon a testamentarie declaration made by the late Lord Melvill, hath assumed vnto him, as we ar informed, the title of a Lord and barron of Parliament, without acquanting ws of the reasones thairof, the lyk whairof hath not bene practised heirtofoir : It is our pleasur that yow call the said Lard of Raith befor yow, and discherge him from vsurping any such title of a Lord heirofter, till he be further warranted by ws; for which these presents shalbe your warrand.—Grenwich, 15 May 1635.

To the Citie of Edinburgh.

Trustie, &c.—Haveing vnderstude how that in obedience of our pious and princelie desyre yow have of late modifeid a provision in favours of the ministrie of that our Citie, which we tak as acceptable service done vnto ws, and for which we give yow hartie thanks, we ar heirby pleased to ordeane your said modificatioun to stand as a constant stipend at all tymes heirofter to them and ther successours in ther charge.—Grenwich, 15 May 1635.

To the Counsell.

Right, &c.—Haveing vnderstude of your proceidings in so far as hitherto yow have gone on in quyeting the disordours of the hielands, and speciallie of your proceidingis with the Marqueis of Huntlie, we doe approve of your good service therin, and give yow hartie thanks for the same, being willing that, conforme to the Acts of Parliament and lawdable custome observed in the tymes of our royall predicessours, yow proceid with all diligence in quyeting of all the rebellious and disordourlie people ather in the hielands or vther parts of that kingdome, and from tyme to tyme to give ws accompt of your care and panes therin, assureing yow that by our authoritie (if neid be) we will not be wanting in any thing to strenthen all your proceidings tuitching this purpois in such maner as yow shall think necessarie.—Grenwich, 15 May 1635.

To the Commissioners of Tythes.

Right, &c.—Being informed that the Church of North Berwick is a principall Church, the parochin populous, and that out of the tythes thairof a liberall provision may be made for the vse of the ministers serveing the cure therat, which provision is at this tyme deficient in that maner, that it is scarselie compitent for such a Church in such a place, it is our pleasur that yow sie the said Church endowed with good and sufficient provision for the ministerie therat, according to the quantitie of the Tythes of the parochin, that they may live in the way befitting such a charge ; wherin yow shall doe ws acceptable service.—Grenwich, the 15 May 1635.

To the Clergie.

Right, &c.—Vnderstanding that the course which of late hath bene in custome amongst yow that succeiding bischopes doe pay to the executours of the deceissed ane Annat, with some vther satisfaction for ther charges in repairing or building of bischops' housses, is verie hurtfull vnto them, by dissabling of them through pouertie from our and the Churches service ; and vnderstanding that neither the said custome is warranted by any municipall Law of that kingdome, nor is practised in any vther part whatsoever, it is our expres will and pleasur that in all tyme cuming the vnwarranted custome be no more in vse, and that the executers have no more of that yeires rent and benefice wherin the late bischop does die than is dew in a just proportion to the tyme of his service therin : This we will have to be putt in practeis in the tuo bischopriks of Aberdene and Galloway, now voyd by the death of the late bischops thairof, and to be inviolablie kepit in all tyme cuming; for which these presents shalbe a sufficient warrant.—Grenwich, of May 1635.

To the Archbischops and Bischops.

Right, &c.—Wheras our Croun hath bene wronged much that the right of the patronages belonging thervnto hath bene vnjustlie conveyed away to other persones not haveing right to them ; And we being carefull to have them agane restored to our Croun, knowing that none can contribute more to it then yow that ar archbischops and bischops of that our kingdome, not onlie by informeing your selflis of such as trewlie belong to our Croun, and representing therof vnto ws, bot also by not giveing way to strenthen any in ther right contrarie to ws : It is our expres will and pleasur that all and everie one of yow, when any benefice is royd, the patronage wherof did belong to our Croun before the beginning of the Regne of our dear grandmother, Queen Marie, yow obtene ane presentatioun to ane conformable man, and that yow give collatioun, and doe what is more requisite in that kynd for confirmeing of our right, and that yow nowayes admitt of any presentatioun from any other persone whatsoever ; ffor doeing whairof thir presents shalbe your warrand; which service, if yow doe it carefullie and faythfullie, as we ar confident as we will accompt weill of it, so be assured that if any be negligent, or doe in the contrarie, we will not faill to tak notice and censure them according as they deserve; And to the effect this may be the better done, we doe recommend to the tuo archbischops, not onlie to be answerable for ther owin dyocesis, but vpon ther owin perrell not to faill to adverteis ws if any bischops within ther province to ther contrarie.—Grenwich, May 1635.

To the Session.

Right, &c.—Wheras we vnderstand that some tymes the Executors of deceissed bischops have intended action befoir yow, according to some custome not warranted by our Acts of Parliament, have gevin proces and sentence for Annatts and charges bestowed on building and repairing of housses, to the prejudice of intrants, we, for good and considerable reasones moveing ws, ar heirby pleased to discharge that there be no more proces granted in this kynd, bot that the executers of the deceissed have action onlie for [so] much of that yeires rent and benefite wherin the late bischope does die as in a just proportion is dew for the tyme of his service therin; ffor doeing whairof these presents shalbe your warrand : So, willing yow to caus the signification of our pleasur heirin be insert in your sederunt book ad futuram rei memoriam, for warrand of your lyk proceiding in such caces in all tyme cuming.—Grenewich, May 1635.

Right, &c.—We ar informed that the Lo/ Naper haveing bene by our direction some yeres agoe charged to pay the Witsonday termes dewtie 1629 of the augmented dewtie of Orkney, he offered to mak payment thairof in Exchequer, which then at the desyre of our thesaurer was delayed, bot not refuised to be accepted ; And wheras the said termes dewtie being since payed (as we ar informed) be Wᵐ Dick to our right trustie and weilbeloved, &c. the Erle of Annandale, to whom it did belong by our gift of that augmented dewtie, the said William is now questioned for the same, and thairvpon wilbe forced to have recourse to the said Erle for his releiff in regard of his band of warrandice gevin to the said William : In which case, it being equitable that both be fred of all trouble that may heirby ensue, and in regard of the said Lord his offer and payment made by the said William to the said Erle of that termes dewtie, it is our pleasur that for the considerations forsaid you in our name requyre the said Lord Nepar to discherge the said William Dick of that termes payment, and that yow cause the band of warrandice be furthwith rendered bak vnto the said Erle.—Grenewich,   May 1635.

II   3 K

To the Counsell.

Right, &c.—We ar verie weill perswaded of the care yow have had to proceid with decencie and ordour in all things which cam befor yow. yit we have thought fitt to recommend particularlie vnto yow concerneing this purpois, first, that no pairtie cited befor yow cum in accompanyed with any, except yow allow to them, when yow find it necessarie, ane Advocat, and tuo of ther speciall freinds, that none be present bot such as ar of Privie Counsall, whom we will to sitt them in ther owin places, and not to ryse and stand disordourlie at any tyme, and clerks which ar sworne for our service ther when yow have disputed any caus to the full, and resolved to putt the question stated to votts, be asked in this ordour following for the present. and at all tyme cuming, begining at the Lo.' Archbischop of S' Androis, nixt the Lo.' Chancellour, when any other salbe, then the Archbischop of Glasgow, our Theasurer principale, the Lord Privie Seall, Marqueisses, Erles, and Viscounts, according to ther ranks, and this ordour we will have to be inviolable keipit, not onlie at our Counsell table, bot in all Judicatoreis and other places of that our kingdome.—Grenwich,   May 1635.

To the Counsell.

Right, &c.—It haveing bene humbilie represented vnto ws by the inclosed petition, exhibited in behalff of Robert Fletcher of Benschaw, that he hath bene dangerouslie wounded and mutilat of one of his fingers by the Lord Spynie and his complices or followers, and that besydes he is lyklie to lose the vse of one of his hands ; It is our express pleasur that yow informe yourselflis of the trew estate heirof, and if yow find what is affirmed by the petition to be trew, that yow censure and caus punisch the said fact as yow shall find the same to deserve ; Bot if yow find the caus propper to be tryed befoir our Justice and his deputts, that yow give ordour vnto them to proceid therin, and that yow give vnto them, if neid be, your best assistance for sieing justice administred in so far as is agrieable to our Lawes and custome of the kingdome ; For which these presents, &c.—Grenwich,   of May 1635.

To the Counsell.

Right, &c.—We ar informed in behalff of Sir Andro Fletcher, one of the Senatours of our Colledge of Justice, that at the tyme of his attending our service as one of that number the Lord Spyneis men and tennents cam in his name, armed with swords and others weapons, and haveing violentlie stopped the said Sir Andro his tennents from leading of ther peitts out of the ground whairof he and his authours war in peaciable possession of casting and wyneing of that fewell past memorie of man, the said Lord his men did lead them away for his owin vse : All which being done (as is affirmed) without any ordour of Law and justice, or without any just occasion gevin by the said Sir Andro, whois just right we ought in a particular maner tak into our princelie protection in respect of his said charge in our service, It is our express pleasur that yow tak ane exact tryell of the trew estate heirof, and if yow shall find that ther hath bene any such violent oppression contrarie to justice and our Lawes, that according therto yow punisch the delinquents and such as was any wayes accessorie thervnto, that others by ther exemple may be terrifeid from attempting the lyk heirefter, wherin ye shall doe vnto ws verie acceptable service, and for which thir presents, &c.—Grenwich,   May 1635.

To the Justice Deputeis, or any of them.

Wheras we ar credibilie informed that ther is a criminall action in Law intended at the instance of Sir Robert Innes of Balveny, kny', aganst John, George, Patrik, and James Innesses, and ther complices, for invadeing the said Sir Robert and schooting at him with gunes and pistolls, to the great contempt of our authoritie and lawes, and to the great hazard of his lyff: We being willing that a legall tryell be takin with all the convenient diligence that may be, and that the offenders (if [they] be fund guiltie) be exemplarie punisched, according to the lawes provyded in the lyk caices, that all others may be terrifeid from attempting the lyk heirefter, it is our pleasur, and we doe heirby will and requyre yow, that with all diligence yow try the same in a legall maner, and according as yow find that yow proceid according to our Lawis and acts of Parliament provyded in these cases.—Grenwich,   May 1635.

To the Advocat.

Trustie, &c.—Haveing bene crediblie informed of a barbarous ryott committed by John, George, Patrik, and James Innesses aganst Sir Robert Innes of Balveny, kny^t, by assaulting to tak his lyff by gunes and pistollets, and being willing that the tryell thairof be exactlie prosecuted according to our Lawis, It is our pleasur, and [we] doe heirby will and command, that yow in our name carefullie insist in the said persute, according to the acts of Parliament provyded in the lyk caices, till it be brought to a full conclusion ; for which these presents, &c.—Grenwich,   May 1635.

To the Counsell.

Right, &c.—We did heirtofoir seriouslie recommend vnto your care that our Chapell royall should be kept in all good ordour, conforme to the custome and ordour keipit heir, wherof we ar confident that yow ar carefull ; and for the better advancement of that work, we have made choyce of Doctour James Wedderburne to be our Deane, one for that or any other ecclesiasticall imployment, that this good work may have the intended good effect ; We ar pleased to recommend to your care that yow mak choyse of tuelff or more of the most able and conformable preachers of that our kingdome to be our Chaplanes in Ordinarie ther, who may by ther turnes and course about doe all services dew, of whois travells and good services in this kynd we will not be vnmyndfull.—Grenewich,   May 1635.

To the Counsell.

Right, &c.—Wheras we, from our princelie and pious affection to God, and His worship, ar bund to advance by all meanes God's service in that our native and ancient kingdome, and certanelie vnderstanding that not in any thing more that Church is defective than in the want of a book of Common Prayer, a book of Canons Ecclesiasticall, a forme and maner of consecrating of bischops, presbyters, and deacones ; and haveing recommended the help of these defects to the Archbischops and bischops ther, We have now sene them amended, and whervnto we have gevin our royall assent and approbation, with a licence of printing of them, and with a command for the vse and practique therof : It is our expres will and pleasur, that what shalbe requyred by our Clergie ther from yow, wherby by the power yow have from ws yow may strenthen, authorize, and sett forward so good and pious a work, yow concurre with them by all possible meanes to that purpois, ffor which thir presents shalbe your warrand, and wherin yow will doe vnto ws acceptable service : And in regard the Psalmes done by our late dear father, of worthie memorie, ar approvin by the Clergie, to whome we have writtin for causeing them to be printed with the Liturgie, and receaved and vsed togidder in the Church of that our kingdome, it is our further pleasur that yow likwayes assist them to that purpois, both by the authoritie yow have from ws and by your owin good exemple, and in the meane tyme that yow discharge all other Psalmes in Meeter to be printed within the same ; ffor doeing wherof these presents shall lykwayes be your sufficient warrant.—Grenwich,   May 1635.

To the Clergie.

Right, &c.—We have sene and approved of the Liturgie sent by yow to ws, with the Book of Canons, the forme and maner of making and consecrating of bischops, presbiteris, and deacones, with these corrections and instructions which we have signed and sent vnto yow : Therfoir, being verie desyreous that they be all printed, and with all convenient diligence receaved and practised in the Church of that our ancient kingdome, for God's service and the good and beawtie of that Church, we recommend that all be furthwith printed, and by thir presents gives power vnto all whom it doeth or may concerne for doeing of the same, whom we doe heirby authorise to that purpois; and our further will and command is, that immediatlie efter they ar printed yow mak them all to be vsed in the Church ; ffor doeing whairof these presents shalbe your warrand : Lykwayes sieing the Psalmes in meeter done by our dear father, of blessed memorie, ar now approvin by yow, it is our expres will and pleasur that yow caus lykwayes print them, and mak them to be generallie receaved and vsed, togidder with the said Liturgie, throughout the whole kingdome, and that in such volumes as yow shall think most fitt for the service of the Churche, for the better and more speedie effecting [of which] we have by our letters requyred our Privie Counsell to give vnto yow (if neid be) that strenth and authoritie yow shall find necessarie heirin.—Grenwich,   May 1635.

To the Advocat.

Trustie, &c.—Wheras by the accompt yow made vnto ws vnder your owin hand of such particulars concerneing our service wherwith we had entrusted yow, and by the information we have had from some of our officeris of your cariage and care to bring the Lo/ Balmerino his criminall proces to a good conclusion, we perceave your affection and diligence in our service, with which we ar well satisfeid, and for which we give yow hartie thanks; and as to these particulars wherin yow crave our resolution and direction, we have signifeid our pleasur fullie in everie particular to our Thesaurers principall and deputie, whom we have commanded to signifie the same vnto you, and, with yow, have commanded them to proceid in these particularis with that care and diligence the trust that we have putt vpon them and yow requyres, &c.—Grenwich, May 1635.

To the Commissioners of Tythes.

Right, &c.—Being informed that the Lands of Eister and Wester Weymes, perteneing to our right, &c. the Erle of Wemyes, ar valued vpon the 8 Septr and 15 No^r for the Sub-Commissioners with the schirrefdome of Fyff, and that he is delayed of the benefite of approbation of the same befor yow, wherby the same as yitt is ineffectuall [to] him : Our pleasur is that, notwithstanding of our command ordeneing yow to begin at the kirks of Erections, yow receave his valuatioun, and approve the same in a fair and legall way.—Grenwich,   May 1635.

To the Commissioners of Surrenders.

Right, &c.—We, being willing for some speciall considerations knowen to ws that the Tythes of the Churches of Lincluden, which did belong to our Chapell royall of that our kingdome, be not valued at this tyme. It is our pleasur that whensoever any tythis belonging to these Churches shall cum befoir yow to be valued, yow doe not anywayes medle or proceid therin till our further pleasur be signifeid tuitching this purpois ; For which, &c.—Grenwich,   May 1635.

Presentation Church of Crawmoud, for ane Mr Johne Clapperton, vacand by transportation of Mr William Selem.

Presentation Church of Coducie for ane Mr John Blyth, by transportation of Mr John Clapperton.—Grenwich, 18 May 1635.

These contene a gift to John Veitch of Dawick of the nonentrie of Certane Landis of Ester and Wester Dawicks.—Whythall, 22 May 1635.

NAMES OF THE COMMISSIONERS APPOYNTED FOR HEARING THE THESAURER'S ACCOMPTS.

Archbischop St Androis, Chancellour.	Bp. Dumblane.
E. Hadinton, Lord Privie Seall.	A blank was left for Lo/ Lorne and Alex^r.
Marqueis of Hamilton.	Sir Ro^t Spottiswood, president of Session.
Archbischop Glasgow.	Sir Johne Hay.
E. Roxburgh.	Sir Thomas Hope.
E. Dumfreis.	Sir James Lermonth of Balcoune.
E. Stirling.	Sir James McGill of Cranstouriddell.
E. Southesk.	Sir James Carmichaell, Justice Clerk.
Bp. Ross.	Sir William Elphingstoun.
Bp. Edinburgh.	Sir Alex^r Strauchan.

The Quorum was 15 or 9, whairof ther should be alwayes four of the Commissioners of Exchequer.

Right, &c.—Wheras we wer formerlie pleised to tak to our princelie consideration the humble advyse and opinion of these our Commissioners, whom, by our warrant from Grenwich, 7 May 1634, we appoynted to consider of the estate of our Exchequer burdenes and remedeis therof, and thervpon gave ordour that our said warrant, togidder with ther advyse, should be registrat in the books of Exchequer, that accordinglie yow might proceid in everie thing which did concerne our service in any of these particulars so represented to ws by them ; and considering now how much the dew execution thairof may conduce to our service, we have thought fitt heirby to requyre and command yow, and each of yow, punctuallie to proceid in everie thing that concernes our rents and revenewis ther, or which concernes any of these articles so represented to ws by them, according to ther opinion gevin to ws, and registrated in our books of Exchequer, and incaice vpon sinistrous information any warrant or deid be procured from ws to the contrarie heirof, our pleasur is, that yow stop the same vntill we be by yow further acquainted with the trew estate therof.—Grenewich, 22 May 1635.

COMMISSION FOR ORKNAY AND ZETLAND.

Commissioners' Names.

Bischop of Orknay, William Stewart of Maynes, Patrik Smyth of Braco, Th. Buchanan.

We have bene petitioned in name of the Inhabitants of Orknay and Zitland to tak vnto our princelie consideratiounn ther distressed estate, occasioned by a great famyne throughout these whole Yles these tuo yeres bygane, have resolved, efter a dew and exact tryell taken thairof, and of the rediest and fairest wayes for supplie of the same, to tak such a course as, according to ther necessiteis and calamiteis, they may find the effeots of our princelie care and compassion of them and ther estatis : To which purpois we have ordeaned, lykas by these presents we ordeane, the personnes vnderwrittin, viz. :—the reverend father in God the bischop of Orknay, &c., as aforsaid, commissioners, or any thrie of them, Wm Stewart being alwayes ane, to tak a survigh of these Yles, and exactlie try what hath bene the sufferings of each inhabitant, fewer, rentaller, or indweller these tuo yeres bypast, and what they [are] lyklie to suffer this present yeir, and whether the calamitie be such as that without our princelie help they be not able any more to labour and posses the ground ; and lykwyes to try what support cam to them by the voluntarie contributiouns latlie collected for ther vse, and what way the same wer disposed vpon ; and to mak report of all these particulars to our Privie Counsell of Scotland, that accordinglie therefter we may give such further ordour therin as we in our princelie judgment shall think expedient.—22 May 1635.

> To the reverend, &c. Bischop of Orknay, Wm Stewart of Maynes,
> Patrik Smyth of Braco, and Thomas Buchanane.

To the Session.

Right, &c.—Vnderstanding that it pleased our late dear father to rehabilitat John Stewart of Coldinghame by act of Parliament 1621, and that thervpon he obtenit decreit aganst diverse persones who have possest parts and portions of the Estate of Coldinghame, and hath possession of diverse tythes and other things belonging thervnto, till now of late, since the Par¹ 1633, diverse of them refuis to pay vnto him ther tythes, wherby he is putt to a new trouble in Law, his estate being whollie vndone if a speedie course be not putt to such actions as he hath or shall have tuitching that purpois : The consideratioun whairof, and of the paynes taken by our late father and our self to sie that estate setled vpoun him, conforme to the said act 1621, decreits, and interloquitours pronunced in his favours by vertew thairof, have moved ws seriouslie to recommend vnto yow to administer speedie justice in the actions depending or which shalhappin to be brought in befor yow heirefter tuitching him and the vassalls of Coldinghame, or others interested in oney part of that estate, conforme to the said act 1621, and interloquitours alredie pronunceit in his favour be vertew thairof, that be long and tedious attendance vpon the issue therof he be not reduced to further extremiteis and trouble.—Grenewich, 22 of May 1635.

> To the Archbischop of S¹ Androis ; Erles Morton, Hadinton, Stirling, Traquair, Southesk ;
> Bischops of Rosse and Edinburgh, Sir Johne Hay, Sir Thomas Hope.

Right, &c—Being informed of the great abuses latelie crept in within that our ancient kingdome by the allowance gevin to the passage of forrayne Coyne abone the trew worth, by which meanes our owin good money is exported, and our said kingdome filled with the laser sort of forrayne Coyne, to the great prejudice of all our good subjects, and to the vtter vndoing of our Mynthous : And considering withall that some good may be done heirin without tuitching vpon or medling with the Coyne of our owin stampt (wherin both our kingdomes hath equall interest), our pleasur is, that furthwith yow meitt and consider vpon the readiest wayes that may be for remedie heirof efter, by crying doun presentlie of the dollours to the trew value, or by crying them doun by degrees at such tymes as yow shall think fitting, or by tyeing the Inhabitants not to accept for ther inbred commoditeis of no peice of forrane money bot such as will mak bullion, or if ther be any other maner of way yow conceave fitting for remedie of this abuse, that yow represent the same vnto ws with possible diligence, and whatever be your resolution heirin, our further pleasur is that yow immediatlie certifie ws therof vnder your or most part of your hands.—Grenwich, May 1635.

To the Frie Burrowis.

Trustie, &c.—Wheras vpon the consideratioun of the good and benefite of the merchand trade of that our antient kingdome, the office of Conservatour was establisched in the 17 vnited provinces, which was procured to be ratifeid by diverse of our royall progenitours : To which purpois we wer lykwayes pleased to give charge to our trustie and weilbeloved Mr Patrik Drummond (present Conservatour) to have a speciall care in the dew and tymelie executioun of that office for the generall good of that kingdome, as he would be answerable vnto ws : It is our pleasur that the lyk dewis, which at any tyme preceiding have bene payed to any of his predicessours in that office, be punctuallie payed vnto him for all goodis and merchandice whatsoever imported within the 17 said provinces, or any part thairof, and that yow lykwayes pay vnto him such arreiris as he can mak appear ar justlie dew vnto him by any of our subjects in that kingdome : And wheras he hath informed ws how yow ar to augment his dewes in regard of the high rates and pryces of all necessareis in these tymes respecting what formerlie they wer, we give yow hartie thanks for the same, and doe heirby speciallie recommend vnto yow to sie him so weill and compleitlie provyded as both may best befitt his charge and your credit, and may be a meanes to him by his readie endeavours heirefter to testifie his further care and affection for advanceing your trade in these parts.—Grenwich, 22 May 1635.

To the Burrowis.

Trustie, &c.—Wheras we ar informed that it is enacted by yow that everie thrie yeires the ordinarie taxt roll for raising the ordinarie taxatioun payable by yow should be renewed for the better knoweing of the present estate of your Inhabitants, which (as we ar lykwayes informed) hath not bene these many yeires altered : Our pleasur is, and we doe heirby will and requyre, that at your nixt meitting in July ensuing yow proceid and tak a course for renewing the stent roll of all burghes conforme to our Acts of Parliament, vnless yow find some just reasones to the contrarie, whairof faill not to adverteis ws.— Grenwich, 22 May 1635.

To the Session.

Right, &c.—Wheras we now expect that the submission long desyred by ws tuitching the differences of the succesion of Home shall now come to a speedie end, in hopes whairof we have heirtofoir requyred yow to mak stay of all processes tuitching the same : Our pleasur is, that notwithstanding of any particular warrant whatsoever granted or to be granted to any persone whatsoever for insisting by Law against any of the pairteis pretending claime to that succession, yow stay all actions wherin any of the saids pairteis have interest to be defenders, as airis and successours to James, late Erle of Home, till such tyme as we shall think fitt to licence processes on all sydis ; and for doeing therof these presents shalbe your warrand.— Grenwich, 22 May 1635.

To the Advocat.

Trustie, &c.—Being informed that we ar prejudged in our annuitie, the church in plantation, the titulars and taksmen in ther particular interests be the valuation of the rents of the Lands within the parochin of Kilconquhar : It is our pleasur, and we doe heirby will and requyre yow, to concurre with the saids titulars and Taksmen of the tythes of the said parochin for rectificing of the said valuations ; ffor which, &c.—Grenwich, 23 May 1635.

To the Commissioners of Tythes.

Right, &c.—We ar informed that sindrie valuations ar led befoir sub-commissioners and approved by yow with diminution of a thrid part of the just rent presentlie payed wher we ar prejudged in our annuitie, the Church in plantation, the titulars and taksmen in ther particular interests, wherinto being willing that yow carefullie advert and speedelie help the abuse ; it is our pleasur, and we doe heirby will and requyre, that if yow shall find any such valuation deduced with the lyk diminution, howsoever it be proved by the parteis oathes and not by witnesses, and howsoever the givers of oathes be deid or alyve, yow rectifie the same by giveing way to our Advocat, the titulars, and others interested to deduce new and lawfull valuations.—Grenwich, 23 May 1635.

To the Chancellour.

Right, &c.—Haveing gevin satisfaction vnto our right, &c. the Marqueis of Hamilton for the Abacie of Aberbrothok, and being to be secured thairof by him in a legall way, we have writtin to our Advocat to draw vp the surrender by your advyse ; and therfor we ar willing that yow sie it carefullie and weill done, and that yow contribute to that purpois your best advyse and furtherance.—Grenwich, 23 May 1635.

To the Advocat.

Trustie, &c.—Haveing gevin satisfaction to our right, &c. the Marqueis of Hamiltoun for the Abacie of Aberbrothok, and yow, by advyse of his lawyer, being to draw vp a Contract of surrender, it is our pleasur, and we doe heirby will and requyre yow, to sie the surrender done in such legall way as may best secure ws of the said Abacie, wherin we will yow to vse the advyse and help of the right reverend father in God Johne, Archbischop of St Androis, our Chancellour, to whome we have lykwayes writtin tuitching this purpois.—Grenwich, 23 May 1635.

To the Chancellour, Thesaurer Depute, The Bischopes of Rosse and Edinburgh, and Clerk Register.

Right, &c.—Wheras we wer pleased to wryt vnto yow in May 1634 tuitching the expediencie of a proposition made vnto ws by, &c. the Erle of Roxbrugh, as by our letter may appear, wherin, as we ar informed, nothing hath bene hitherto done, tuitching which purpois a motion being made vnto ws of new, that in regard it doeth much conduce to our benefite, by advanceing of our just and lawfull ends in matters of that kynd, we would be pleased to give ordour for speedie effectuating thairof according to our former reall intentioun, Our will is, that yow tak our former pleasur heirin to your serious consideratioun, and haveing conferred with the said nobleman tuitching the same, yow proceid with diligence to value the rents of the Churches and tythes expressed in our said letter, that a convenient course may be taken for establisching of his right thervnto, vpon our satisfaction being gevin to him for the samyne, as we acknowledge equitie and reasone doe allow ; and in the meane tyme (according to our former directioun) that all proceidings befoir our Commissioners tuitching these Churches and tythes be continewed till our further pleasur ; for which these presents shalbe your warrant.—[No date.]

To the Session.

Right, &c.—Haveing vnderstood of that report of the Erle of Airth his Cautioners' and Creditours' fair and legall proceidings for recoverie of these moneyis which they have payed and vndertaken for him and releiff of his debts, we ar weill pleased therwith ; and haveing taken to our princelie consideratioun his distresse and ther sufferings, We have gevin ordour to our Officers to pay to him with all possible diligence these moneyis which we wer formerlie pleased to grant vnto him towardis the releiff of his burdenis, that therby his estate may be recovered, and his cautioners and creditours fred of ther reall disbursments and vnderlakinges for him; bot becaus we conceave that the convenience of our other just affaires will not allow all to be payed at one terme, Our pleasur is, that yow tak some fair course for secureing legallie his cautioners and creditours for ther principall sowmes, provydeing the same infer no present possession of his estate, or any part therof, for ther saidis sowmes, for the space of tuo yeires, or longer if yow shall think fitt, for payment thairof, and efter the expyreing of that tyme they have such ane irrelimable suirtie as may infer reall and actuall possession of his estate for ther principall sowmes, at leist for so much as shallhappin to be vnpayed at the tyme; And that he be not further obleidged for exhibition and delyverie of his writts than to exhibite such as may mak appear to yow and them that he is infeft in the Estate; and that he and his appearand aires cannot dispone thairof to the cautioners' and creditours' prejudice; and that dureing the forbearance of ther principall sowmes they may not suffer be want of ther due interest, Our further pleasur is, that furthwith yow sie them fullie secured of ther termelie payment thairof; and if the said interest be not termelie payed, that he omitt the benefite of the said forbearance, the legall performance of all which we recommend to your care, and bid yow farewell.—From our Manour at Grenwich, the day of May 1635.

COMMISSION.

Wheras we wer informed that the right of the Yle of Lewis did belong to ws, to which purpois we did intend to give ordour heirefter in such maner as we should think fitt for our service: Bot now our right trustie and weilbeloved Coussen the Erle of Seafort, haveing repaired thither to our Court, representing his vnwillingnes, ather in that purpois or in any other, to appear in Law against ws, being withall ane humble sutter that we would be gratiouslie pleased to caus informe our selffis of the trew estate thairof from such of our Officeris as we did cheiflie trust befor any legall proceiding should be made therin, to the effect we might the better give such ordour tuitching the same as we should find just caus, Our pleasur is, and we doe heirby authorize yow, or any four of yow, our Advocat being one, to informe your selffis of the best and spediest way yow can tuitching our right to that Yle, and therefter to declare to ws your opinion tuitching the same with all convenient diligence, that therefter we may tak such further course therin as we shall think fitt; for which these presents shalbe your warrand.—Grenwich, 26 May 1635.

Commissioners' Names.

Chancellour, 2 Thesaurers, Bischops of Rosse and Edinburgh, Clerk Register, Advocat, Balcomie, or any four of them, the Advocat being ane.

To the Exchequer.

Right, &c.—We wer pleased not long since to refer the petition of Mr William Chalmers, our Thesaurer Clerk, clameing the presentatioun of signatures as belonging to his place, to the consideration of the Commissioners of our Exchequer for the tyme, requyreing them ather to setle that difference betwixt him and his competitour, or to certifie ws of ther opinion thereanent: Bot the change of our Exchequer intervening, and therby the cognition being interrupted, we have thoght fitt of new to recommend to yow the tryell of that claime according to our former reference, notwithstanding of any thing intervened, since that may prejudge ather of the pairteis, requyreing yow furthwith to proceid in the tryell, and ather to compose by way of submission from both pairteis the said difference, otherwayes to certifie ws of your

II   3 L

opinion which of the saidis pairteis hes the best right, that accordinglie we may give such further ordour therin, as we in justice shall think necessarie and expedient for our service; wherin not doubting of your care and diligence, we bid yow farewell.—Grenwich, 26 May 1635.

To the Counsell.

Right, &c.—Wheras we ar informed that notwithstanding of your great care which we tak as acceptable service to setle the course directed by ws concerneing the sale of Tobacco within that our kingdome, our intention therin is still frustrat, partlie thrugh the perversnes of some refractorie persones, sellers of Tobacco, partlie thrugh slaknes of Magistrats in discovering and punisching the offenders : To the end therfor that all service heirin may be no longer deluded, our pleasur is, that yow tak effectuall ordour that all magistrats to brugh or land whatsoever, and all heretours within that our kingdome, may sie our proclamations tuitching the selling of Tobacco strictlie observed, and that they suffer no vnresponsall persones to remane within ther severall boundis and jurisdictions that shalbe fund to contravene the same ; wherin and in what also may tend to the better assistance of our Commissioners for advancement of this our service, expecting the continuance of your care, we bid, &c.—Theobald's, 29 May 1635.

To the Exchequer.

Right, &c.—We ar petitioned by David Simme, that for suppressing the continewed abuse of such as, in contempt of our Lawis and to the great prejudice of the Cuntrie, doe in buying of victuall, exact some quantitie over and above the established metts and measuris of the kingdome, we would be pleased to grant vnto him the halff of the foirfeytis who shal by him be discovered, which being so provyded in the statute, we have thoght fitt to will and requyre yow ather by Commission or otherwayes as yow in your judgments shall think most convenient, to authorize him for prosecuteing of the same : Wherin not doubting of your care, we bid, &c.—Grenewitch, the first Junij 1635.

To the Exchequer.

Right, &c.—Humble sute hath bene made vnto ws in behalff of George Sinclair of Rapnes to signe enclosed signature of the sevin penney Land of Rapnes and sex penney land of Claister, the tuo vres land of Rackwick, and sex penney Land of Kerhister, in regaird that he and his progenitours have possessed these landis past memorie of man as kyndlie and native tennentis thairof, we thoght fitt to returne it vnto yow vnsigned, referring it to your consideration : Therfoir, if yow shall find this to be a purpois that doeth not prejudge ws, bot may encourage our tennents to be the more industrious when they shall have some assurance not to be removed, It is our pleasur that yow rentall and receave the said George and his aires as our kyndlie and vnremoveable tennents and rentallers of the aforsaidis parcells of Land, to be possest by them till the tyme that the whole Landis belongeing to ws within the erldome of Orkney be fewed, in which cace we ar heirby pleased to declair that he shall have the Lands possest by him sett in few to him and his aires vpon such termes and conditions as other Lands, and to that effect that yow tak such course for secureing of him as yow shall think necessarie ; ffor which these presents, &c.—Grenwich, 5 Junij 1635.

To the Counsell.

Right, &c.—The writts and securiteis made and granted by the Lord of Kintyre to the Lord of Dunluce of the Lands of Kintyre and others mentioned in these securiteis being to be exhibited befoir yow, it is our pleasur that we doo heirby will and requyre yow to cancell the saids writts with the toynut of seasine which is in the keiping of James Prymrois, and that yow caus mak record of the cancelling thairof, ather in the Counsell books or exchequer rolls, as yow shall think most fitt, that our royall intention tuitching such a purpois may remane with the posteritie; wherunent thir presents shalbe vnto yow sufficient warrant.—Grenwich, 5 Junij 1635.

To the Advocat.

Trustie, &c.—Being informed that the prosecution in Law of that which is propounded in the enclosed information will conduce to the good of our service, it is our pleasur that yow tak it vnto your consideration, and if yow find anything materiall therin tending to that purpois, that yow putt it to a legall tryell; wherin expecting your care and diligence, and for which these presents shalbe your warrant, &c.—Grenwich, 5 Junij 1635.

To the Bischop of Argyll.

Reverend father in God, &c.—Wheras we have at that tyme gevin leave to the Erle of Argyll to repair to that our kingdome, though we ar confident that no important effect can flow from him by meanes of his religion to give any offence to that which is ther professed; yit being willing that the least circumstance that can be vsed in that kynd be prevented, And in the meane tyme that all possible and fair meanes be vsed for changeing his opinion tuitching the same, it is our pleasur that yow carefullie advert heirvnto within the boundis of your dyocie; and as for him that yow vse your best endeavours and panes to the purpois aforsaid, in so far as yow can convenientlie doe, wherin referring what further is fitt to be imparted vnto yow to our right trustie Counsellour the Lord of Lorne.—Grenwich, 5 Junij 1635.

To the Freinds of the House of Argyll.

Trustie, &c.—Wheras we bene informed of late by our right trustie Counsellour the Lord Lorne of your affection and readie concurring with him in keiping peace and good ordour within the bounds con-credited by ws vnto his charge: Though we expect no less both at his handis and yours, yit we ar heirby pleased to give yow hartie thanks for the same, and withall to requyre yow to continew the lyk dewtifull assisting of him in all such things as may concerne the advancement of your service and his good; which we will both expect and tak weill at your handis.—Grenwich, 5 Junij 1635.

To the Exchequer.

Right, &c.—Being informed that ther is a question depending befor yow betuixt the Lord of Lorne and some burghes ther, tuitching payment to be made to him of the Excyse dewtie of the fisching as our taksman therof in the bounds preseryved to him, it is our pleasur, since the bussines concerneth ws, and that he is onlie entrusted as our servand therin, that yow carefullie advert to our right in his persone, which we will tak as acceptable service done vnto ws.—Grenwich, 5 Junij 1635.

To the Advocat.

Trustie, &c.—Wheras we ar informed that our servand Sir Patrik Abercrombie haveing obtenit from ws vpon certane knowledge a grant of the office of tabular of summondis befoir our Colledge of Justice, is forced to ane action of reduction of ane other pretendit gift of the said office granted to ane Bannatyne, and we conceave it to be more fitt (if it is in our power to give) that our owin servand should enjoye it then any other to whome we never did intend it : To the effect thairfoir it may appear to whois donation the said office doeth of right belong, our pleasur is, which we will yow to signifie to all whom it may concerne that all such recordis and wrytings as may give light therin be produced befor them, and if yow find the right of donation to be ours, we will yow then to concure for our interest with our servant for mantenance of our said grant, and a legall reduction of the other ; wherin not doubting of your care, we bid, &c.—Grenwich, the 5 of Junij 1635.

To the Session.

Right, &c.—Wheras we have bene informed, as yow will perceave by the inclosed petition, of the hard measur and extremitie vsed by Johne Home of Renton to Sir George Home and his sone Sir Alex' Home, our servand, and of ther willingnes to give him all satisfaction that he in equitie can demand ; our pleasur is, that yow call the said Johne Home befoir yow and deall with him, that, according to the desyre of the petition, vpon payment to be made vnto him of such sowmes of money as yow, efter strict examination of the accompts, and deduction of his receipts, shall find remayneing justlie dew vnto him, he may transfer for the petitioner's vse all these rights of his father's estate, which if he refuis, we then requyre yow to certifie ws particularlie of the trew estate of the bussines, that we may tak such further ordour for our petitioner's releiff, as we in equitie shall think meitt, and in the meane tyme that yow give no way to the said Johne for acquyreing any further power over the estate, bot assist our petitioner in all such wayes as may tend to a legall recoverie thairof out of his hands ; which we will tak as acceptable service, &c.—Grenewich, 5 Junij 1635.

Wheras we have bene petitioned by our servand Sir Patrik Abercrombie (on whom by our grant 24 Dec' 1634 we conferred the office of tabulating of summondis in all actions intended befor our Colledge of Justice), that for the ease, benefite, and securitie of our loveing subjects, and for preventing diverse great inconveniences that many of them now suffer, we might be moved, not onlie to revive and restore the said office of the table for actions befor the Colledge of Justice, bot lykwayes to enlarge and extend it over that our kingdome to all other inferiour Judicatoreis (Toun-Counsells and Baron Courts excepted) ; and we being willing to gratifie our servand in any litt way, especiallie such as may withall tend to the good and conveniencie of our loveing subjects, we have therfor thought good to direct the petition to be considered of by yow, or any fyve or more of [yow], whairof our Chancellour, our Thesaurers, principall or deputie, or the President of our Colledge of Justice, to be alwayes ane, to the effect that if yow shall find the course propounded to be a thing beneficiall to our good subjects, yow may then consider what fie or gratification in the severall Judicatoreis respective may be litlie allowed to the officer for everie action so to be tabulat, toties quoties, in regard of his panes and of our subjects benefite therby to ensew, and that accordinglie, as yow or any such fyve or more of yow shall determyne, a certificat may be returned to ws vnder your hands, togidder with a signature, docated by our Advocat for our royall hand, of a new grant to the petitioner or his assigneyis and thair deputeis of the said office so enlarged and extended ; for which these presents shalbe your warrand.—Grenwich, 5 Junij 1635.

To the Counsell

Right, &c.—Wheras some yeires agoe the dangers at the entrie of the firth of Forth, and the frequent losse of our subjects' lyffes and goods, and of strangers adventureing ther, speciallie in the night tyme, wer represented vnto ws : And now the lyk humble sute haveing bene made to ws for giveing onlour to prevent the lyk heirefter ; and haveing sene a great many subscriptions of owners and masters of schipps and barks desyreing a course to be taken for ther saiftie, it is our pleasur that yow call befor yow such persones as yow shall find most interested therin and best affected to the publict good, and that yow consider of this bussines ; and if thervpon if yow shall find that it is necessarie for our subjects' good, that yow caus expeid a grant from ws immediatlie, vnder our cachet and sealls ther, in the most effectuall and sure maner that can be devysed, vnto Johne Cunynghame, younger of Barnes, and wherby they, dureing fourtene yeires, may have power to erect and keip ane Light vpon the most convenient place of the Yle of May (belonging to the said Johne Cunynghame), to be choysen by liable and experienced seamen, who best know the dangers ther ; and that by our said grant the patent have such a reasonable and constant dewtie vpon the True and last of all merchandice transported that way, as yow shall find necessarie ; ffor doeing of all which these presents shalbe vnto yow, and all others whom it may concerne, sufficient warrant.—Grenwich, 5 Junij 1635.

To the Counsell.

Right, &c.—Wheras vpon good considerations we have resolved to suffer no levyes of men to be raised in that our kingdome, or to be transported out of the same : These ar to will and requyre yow that, without speciall warrant to that purpois, yow permitt to leavie no be made ther heirefter in any sort whatsumever, as yow will answer to the contrarie.—Grenwich, 9 Junij 1635.

To the Thesaurers.

Right, &c.—Wheras the place of M^r of our Coynehous is now vaiking by the death of the late master thairof, and knowing how necessarie it is for our service that the place be supplied with ane able man, and being vnwilling to dispose till the course to be taken for regulating of our Coyne ther be brought to some perfection, we have in the meane tyme made Choyse of our servant Nicolas Briot for performance of such things as belong to that charge, and have sent him thither for that purpois, and to the effect he may be present to give his advyse and assistance in such things as yow shall direct him for the weill ordering of our Coyne ther : Therfoir it is our pleasur that yow give such ordour that he may be sufficientlie authorized for excercising of things belonging to that charge of M^r . . . of our Conzie house, and that he enjoy all the privileges and benefits of the place vntill our further pleasur be signifeid ; ffor which these presents shalbe yonr warrand.—Grenwich, 9 Junij 1635.

To the Advocat.

Trustie, &c.—Haveing caused renew our Commission for the Midleschyres vnder the great seall of this our kingdome, and haveing added of new to the number of our Commissioners tuo of our subjects heir verie vsefull for the good of that our service, authorizeing them to give notice to the nearest of our Scotts Commissioners of the occasion of holding of goale delivereis, and in caice of ther absence to sic of themselflis, and execute justice according to the Commission, as by the duplicat which we have sent by our servant Sir Ritchart Grhame, kny^t and baronet, yow will perceave, Our pleasur is, that yow draw vp a Commission of new agrieable to the lawis and custome of that kingdome, to be exped vnder our great seall with diligence, inserting the lyk clause of equall power to our Commissioners ther, as it is in the Commission for this our kingdome, and that yow ad to the number of the Commissioneris Johne, Lord

Herreis, appoynting in the quorum William, Marqueis of Dowglas, Robert, Erle of Nithisdale, William, Erle of Queinsberrie, Johne, Erle of Traquair, and the said Lord Herreis ; For doeing whairof, &c.—Grenewich, 18 Junij 1635.

Right, &c.—Haveing for the furtherance of our service in the Midleschyres gevin ordour to our Advocat to renew the Commission thairof, it is our pleasur that yow caus expeid it vnder our great seall with diligence, and haveing thervpon convened the Commissioners for that our kingdome togidder, that yow publisch our Commission and duplicat of that which is exped heir, whiche we have heirwith sent vnto yow, wherby yow will perceave the equall power yow have in these parts of this our kingdome, as the English have ther for executeing of Justice according to the Commission : And it is our further pleasur that yow appoynt certane tymes thryse a yeir for meitting with our English Commissioners, wherby they may confer and setle such things as will conduce to the good of our service and preservation of our peace ther ; wherin not doubting of your care and diligence, &c.—Grenewich, 18 Junij 1635.

To the Erle of Traquair.

Right, &c.—Wheras we ar informed that diverse grantis and signatures doe pass our register and sealls without the warrant and ordour which in such caces is requisit for the good of our service : It is our pleasur that no letter or signature whatsoever, though signed by our selffes, be exped thrugh our registers or sealls till first it be presented to our judicatoreis or officers to whois charge it doeth properlie belong, to the effect the nature thairof may be cleirlie knowen, and thervpon ordour gevin by them for passing or staying thairof ; and that yow signifie this our pleasur to all the keipers of our sealls and registers to whom these presents shalbe ane sufficient warrant : We bid, &c.—Grenwich, 24 of Junij 1635.

To the Erle of Traquair.

Right, &c.—Wheras we vnderstand by letter from yow to the Erle of Morton that yow have made stay of a signature of the Abbacie of Lundoris for Mr Andro Lermouth, wherin we approve your proceiding, and wills yow that nothing pass in Exchequer concerneing that purpois, vnless we shalbe pleased to signifie our further pleasur therin, and in the meane tyme that yow call for the signature and keip it in your custodie ; ffor which these presents shalbe your warrant : We bid yow farewell.—Grenwich, 24 Junij 1635.

To the Counsell.

Right, &c.—We wer formerlie pleased to give order that ther might be some speedie course takin for the reformation of the abuses of the gold and silver coyne within that our kingdome ; And now being informed that ther ar lykwyse diverse complants made anent the copper coyne, we have therfoir the rather ordeaned our servant Nicolas Briot, whois judgment in that kynd is approved vnto ws, to hasten his repair thither with all possible diligence : And it is our pleasur that at his comeing thither, haveing called him befoir yow, and heard him for our interest, with such others as ar interested in it from ws, togidder with these that ar the compleiners of the abuses of the same, that then yow acquant ws with ther reasones and answer on both sydis, that therefter we may give such ordour concerneing the same as we shall find expedient ; And that in the meane tyme the coynage of the said copper coyne may goe on, and that with all possible diligence yow proceid in the tryell of the abuses past concerneing the gold and silver coynes, and of the cheiff occasions of the said abuses, togidder with the best meanes of keiping gold and silver from being transported out of the cuntrie, and how they may be best drawin into the cuntrie, that vpon your report thairof we may give such ordour as the present evill may be redressed, and the lyk prevented in tyme coming; ffor doeing whairof these shalbe vnto yow sufficient warrant.—From our Court at Grenwich, the 24 of Junij 1635.

To the Commissioneris for Surrenderis.

Right, &c.—Being informed that our trustie and weilbeloved cousen the Viscount of Kenmure hath some Lands vnvalued which ar desyred to be valued, and considering that he is as yit ane Infant, we ar the rather gratiouslie pleased to recommend to your care that whiche may concerne him; And therfoir it is our pleasur that, with such speed as may be, ther be a course taken for valueing the saidis Landis according to the course vsed in the lyk caces; ffor which these, &c.—Grenwich, 24 of Junij 1635.

To the Chancellour.

Right reverend, &c.—Haveing bene humblie petitioned in behalff of the late Wyff of David Drummond, deceissed some tyme, ane of our late royall father's genthman pensioners, that haveing acquyred some meanes in his service heir, and haveing at his death appoynted (according to the lawis and custome of this kingdome, wher he died) ane Archibald Drummond ane of his executours, to distribute the same to his wyff and children, he will tak no course to performe what was entrusted vnto him, bot remaneth ther in Scotland, wher the Lawis heir can tak no hold of him; It is our pleasur that yow consider of the enclosed petition, and if yow find just evidences for what is affirmed, that in our name yow command the said Archibald ather to give satisfaction with convenient diligence to the pairtie entrusted according to the Lawes heir, otherwayes that he furthwith repair hither to answer vnto the same.—Dat. vt supra.

Signature of Sir William Alexander, Earl of Stirling

A. Alexander

INDEX.

II   3 M

www.ingramcontent.com/pod-product-compliance
Lightning Source LLC
Chambersburg PA
CBHW052340110726
47901CB00005B/1305